Twisted Together

By

PEPPER WINTERS

Twisted Together
Copyright © 2014 Pepper Winters
Published by Pepper Winters

All music lyrics used in this book are written by Pepper Winters.

Published: Pepper Winters 2014: pepperwinters@gmail.com
Publishing assisted by Black Firefly: http://www.blackfirefly.com/
(Shedding light on your self-publishing journey)

Editing: Jenny Sims from Editing For Indies
French Translation: Louise Pion
Cover Design: by Ari at Cover it! Designs:
http://salon.io/#coveritdesigns
Formatting by: http://www.blackfirefly.com/
Images in Manuscript from Canstock Photos:
http://www.tagxedo.com/

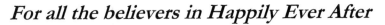

For all the believers in Happily Ever After

Prologue

The blackness tried to swallow us whole, kill us, ruin us, capture our soul

"**I**'m not marrying you for the pleasure of calling you my wife, *esclave*. I'm not marrying you because it's the evolution of a relationship. I'm marrying you so I have claim on you forever. Your soul will be mine for eternity. In sickness and in health, in life and in death, you will belong to me. And I will belong to you."

Q brought me closer, whispering his passion into my mouth. "Don't think this is a contract between two people in love. Don't think this legal document is something flimsy and insignificant. By marrying me, you're taking all of me. Everything that I am. All that I will be. You're accepting my lightness, my darkness, my fucking eternal spirit. By signing your name to mine you are no longer Tess Snow."

"What am I?" I murmured, accepting his feather-soft kiss.

"You're Tess Mercer. Now and for always. Forever and ever. It's done."

Chapter One

But our demons didn't play well with others, the beast broke free to make them suffer

"Do it, puta. Kill her."

"No! Stop this. I'm done. No more—"

"Yes, more. Every night, you're ours. Every time your pretty fucking eyes close, we're waiting. Every time you succumb to sleep, we're waiting to drag you into insanity."

It's not real. It's not real.

No matter how many times I screamed the truth, the dream would never free me. Leather Jacket somehow tricked my mind into leaving the sanctity of Q's presence, yanking me into the depths of despair.

"Please don't hurt me," Blonde Angel moaned.

I didn't want to. I never wanted to hurt another living thing again.

"Don't think about disobeying, puta. You know what happens." Leather Jacket flickered into two monstrosities: one moment the man I knew—the man who'd tortured, hit, and taunted me—then another moment, the drooling carnivorous Jackal who'd raped Blonde Angel only minutes before Q found me.

The smog, the fog, crept over my mind, swarming around me with sickly warmth. "No! Not that." I never wanted to be held hostage by chemicals again. Drugs made me forget. Drugs made me become them.

"Do it, precious. Otherwise I'll do something worse," Leather Jacket cooed.

My heart sank into the depths of my soul. Every night they visited. Every night they shattered my healing, throwing me back to a past I couldn't forget. Every night they reminded me that pain was atrocious. Pain was the devil. Pain was horrendous and terrible and cruel.

Pain.

My nemesis.

My burden.

I shook my head, standing over Blonde Angel. Our eyes met—just like hundreds of times before—and I wordlessly shouted my grief, my sadness, my lifetime of apologies.

But it made no difference.

Just like the drugs made me incapacitated in Rio, the dream had power over me in the present. I wouldn't be free until I gave into the inevitable. I wouldn't wake until I killed her.

A heavy crowbar rested in my sweat-slippery hands. I tried to scuttle backward but some ominous force pressed against my shoulders. The phantom pressure raised my arms against my will—stealing all motor control, leaving me screaming until my throat rivered with blood and rawness.

Mildew and reeking rubbish clouded my nostrils even though I knew it wasn't real. The only scent I should inhale was the comforting notes of citrus and sandalwood of my master sleeping beside me.

The master who swore to protect me from everything. The master who failed every night. How could a man fight nightmares? How could he slay men he'd already killed from taunting my mind in slumber?

Simple. He couldn't.

Every night was the same. Q fought to save me from demons he couldn't fight, and I fought to stop dreaming.

Once the nightmare claimed me, I couldn't get free until the horrible conclusion. It happened differently every time. Sometimes by bullet. Sometimes by axe or blade. But no matter how I did it, committing murder was the only way to hurtle me back to consciousness.

If I concentrated hard enough I could feel him. If I squeezed my eyes and searched for the tether to my mortal body, I knew I wasn't lying quietly and serene. My body was sweat-dewed and thrashing in tangled sheets; my cheek smarting from a stinging slap as Q tried to rouse me.

More pain.

Pain on top of pain.

It all had to stop, before I went mad.

"Little girl, I won't ask again," Leather Jacket sneered.

The crowbar was no longer heavy in my hands; the unseen malicious entity arched my back, swinging the weapon, high and deadly.

No. No, no, no. Not again.

Close your eyes. Don't look. Don't fill your mind with yet more killing.

Blonde Angel crawled backward, cradling her already broken wrist and knee. Her mouth twisted into pleas. "Don't. Please don't. Haven't you done enough? You killed her! You killed the other girl. Do you have no mercy?" Her eyes were wild, green and clear as cut glass. Her blonde hair no longer shone like gold but hung in bloody clumps.

"I'm sorry!"

My heart-filled apology only made her snarl. "No, you're not. You're one of them. You're lying to yourself, to him, to me. You loved killing the other blonde so much, you thirst to murder. You're a monster. A fucking demon spawn."

My lungs suffocated with her hatred, drowning in sorrow. The crowbar swung above my head, controlled by the puppeteer of this horrible dream.

"That's it, pretty girl. Do it. What's another life? You obeyed so brilliantly before. Every night you fucking murder. Every night you come back to us."

The man who'd owned me. Who'd drugged me, sold me, and ultimately broken me, appeared from dream-mist. White Man looked suave and immaculate in a white shiny suit. His feral touch landed on my chin, cupping my jaw, holding me prisoner. "You'll never be free of us. We took your mind back in Brazil. Your bastard of an owner might've slaughtered my men and whisked you away to safety, but you know the truth." His mouth descended on mine, his monstrous tongue diving past my lips, making me retch.

Breathing hard he pulled away. Manic anger glowed in his blue gaze.

"Tell me the truth."

The truth?

What truth? I didn't know what to believe anymore. Was my mind so twisted the truth was only visible in my sleep? Was I deceitful every moment I was awake—pretending to deplore pain and horror when really I craved it? Craved to inflict it. Craved to kill.

Questions and uncertainty sprouted like vile weeds, growing thick and fast, suffocating all reason and clarity.

Am I truly what they say? I'm no longer a protégé. I'm truly the devil.

I squeezed my eyes, blocking the dream, grasping with panicked fingers to latch onto the weak tethering of awareness.

Wake up, Tess.

Please.

"Tell. Me." White Man's breath fanned my eyelashes, smelling of candy floss. Why did the demon of my nightmares smell of innocence and sugar?

Shaking my head, I whimpered, "There's nothing to tell." My arms stayed raised above my head, holding the crowbar in an unnatural pose. I had no control. None.

"Oh, but there is." His white slacks whispered as he stepped to the side, dragging me forward.

Blonde Angel shook so much, my ears rang with the jangling of her bones. "Night after night you return to me. Night after night you kill for me. You're not free, pretty girl. And that's the fucking truth."

Leather Jacket moved to my other side, grinning like a psychopath. "Truth's a bitch and then she dies. You know how this ends, puta. Do it, *then we'll let you wake up."*

A gale whirled from nowhere, kicking up dust and mould from around the dungeon, howling in my ears: Do it. Do it. Do it.

"No! Not again. I can't do it again."

I'm crazy. I've lost it completely.

Blonde Angel stopped shaking and raised her head. Our eyes locked, understanding flowed. Mutual need to have this over with made her nod in heart-wrenching acceptance. In one fluid moment, she bowed forward. She didn't say a word—she didn't need to.

We could beg and cry and scream.

But ultimately, we had no power.

The truth burned my eyes, puncturing my heart.

I was a killer.

I am a killer.

I'm a monster.

The force holding my arms up suddenly released, and the weight of the bar came smashing down. Blonde Angel jerked and jolted. I blinked as the crunch of bone shattered beneath the weapon. Her arms splayed to the side as her body tipped over, succumbing to death.

I willed myself to wake up. Freedom normally came once I'd killed, but this black-laced dream was different.

Manic laughter filled the reeking dungeon. I dropped the crowbar and the clanging metal echoed in my ears. Something heavy morphed into my hands. Sinister and cold and deadly.

A gun.

The *gun. The gun I'd used to take a life—a* real *life. The gun I'd tried to find freedom with. We had history, that gun and I. An intimate past with a murderous object forever linking me to this—this…never ending cycle of dreams.*

"You tried to kill yourself last time, puta. *Care to try again?"*

I refused to look at Leather Jacket. His voice scurried like a thousand spiders over my skin. I craved the bland cushioning of the drugs. I wanted oblivion. Peace.

"Pull the trigger. Go on. You know you want to be free. This is your only way," Leather Jacket said, prowling around me.

My malnourished, bleeding hands shook as I looked at the dead woman with her vacant eyes. Her skull looked odd—cracked and concaved from the killing blow.

I did that.

Me.

God, what has become of me?

Q sacrificed so much to bring me back—it was sacrilege not to keep fighting—to be worthy of his gift. But I had no reserves—no more strength to live these nightmares and stop them from trickling into reality. My nerves were raw. My mind broken. My spirit ruined.

No more.

One bullet, lightning pain, then it could be all over.

Leather Jacket yelled, spitting in my face. "Do it. You belong to us. You do what we command!"

I didn't have the strength to fight back. I no longer wanted to exist in this world. Raising the gun, I opened my lips and guided the metallic chamber into my mouth. It tasted just like I remembered. The taste of finality. Closure. Squeezing my eyes, I tensed.

"That's a good girl. Send yourself to hell. We're waiting for you there."

I pulled the trigger.

The sulphur of gunpowder itched my nose.

The loud detonation of a bullet rang in my ears.

Disbelieving tears streaked from my eyes.

Desperation and utter grief crushed my heart.

The dream howled and gusted and I split into identical images of myself.

One Tess jerked in death-throws as the back of her head exploded in a horrible mess of tissue and red rain. Another Tess, an omniscient dreamer, silently screamed—unable to do anything but watch.

"No!" This couldn't be possible. I just killed myself.

I ended my own life.

I'm weak.

I'm a coward.

I'm worthless.

I screamed.

"Tess! Fuck, it's okay." Q caught me, just like he always did, as I shot upright and clung to his hard shoulders. I couldn't suck in a breath; I scrambled nearer, trying to get closer, trying to morph into him to steal his endless reservoir of strength. *Give it to me. Give me your sanity and warmth.* I couldn't let him see how rattled and ruined I'd become.

Q scooped me close, resting his chin on my head. "Goddammit, *esclave*. You're ice cold."

I shivered in his arms like a rapidly decaying leaf. "Sorry.

Sorry—I'm—"

His muscles bunched beneath smooth, naked skin as his arms wrapped tighter, giving me safe harbour. *"Arrête. Tout va bien."* Stop it. You're okay. His voice was level and full of unmistakable authority, but he couldn't hide his own trembling. His hard body quaked with silent flurries of tension. But Q didn't tremble from horror. Oh, no. My *maître* shook with undiluted rage. He bristled with ferocity. He smouldered with temper. His anger wasn't directed at me but at the ghosts haunting my mind.

"You have to stop fucking letting them in. You're safe. How many times do I need to tell you that?" His anger heated the ice in my blood, reminding me I was still alive and survived. If I could survive being forced to kill, having my finger snapped with pliers, drug overdoses, and rank living conditions, I could survive the residual memories. I *had* to survive. I owed Q my life. I wouldn't fail him—not after what he did to bring me back.

Maybe I need help.

The thought of talking to a therapist filled me with horror. I wouldn't be able to stomach their carefully blank faces as I confessed to killing a woman. I wouldn't be strong enough to look into their eyes while I spoke of being high on a cocktail of toxins all formulated to cripple my mind and make me their little toy to be sold and used.

And antidepressants? I would go completely mad if I ever took another mind-altering drug again.

You owe it to Q to put the past where it belongs. He believes you're healing. I hated lying. I hated that I *sucked* at lying because Q saw everything I tried to hide. Getting professional help might be the only thing left for me.

I looked up, sucking in a breath as I made eye contact with the most amazing, kind, fearful, *stunning* male in my life. His hair was slightly longer but still showed his regal widow's peak and perfect bone structure. His lips were twisted in anger, sending wings of gratitude and weakness through me.

After everything, he still cared for me. Still fought for me.

Q stared back, his pale jade gaze ripping me apart, seeing so far inside I had nowhere to hide. And that was what made it so damn hard to pretend.

Q had turned himself into a human punching bag for me to take out the seething anger inside. He let himself be the scapegoat of the bastards in Rio, so I had someone to direct my rage onto. He did so much. *Too* much. But it wasn't enough.

Love suffocated my heart, stitching me up until I felt mummified with confusion. Bandages upon bandages held me hostage with no way out of the horrible prison I was in.

"How many times must I wake to you screaming and crying? How many fucking times must I slap you, try and save you from whatever horrors you're reliving, only for it to do no good?" Q's French accent thickened as he sat higher, pummelling a pillow into comfortable submission behind him. Leaning back, his thumb caressed my hot and no doubt red cheek from his attempt at breaking my nightmare. "Contrary to what you think of me, hitting the woman I'm about to marry while she's unconscious is not one of my perversions."

A soft laugh escaped me. "God, Q. You have the strangest sense of humour."

The sickly tension existing in the room and the fearful anxiety still thrumming in my blood dissipated. He not only put up with my screams, but he knew just how to free me from the residue of such terror.

The stitching in my heart tore wide, spilling my chest with love so deep and eternal I knew I would do anything, absolutely *anything*, for this man. He was the reason I was alive. The only reason I wanted to *stay* alive.

His forehead furrowed. "What makes you think I'm joking?" His fingers dropped from my cheek as his eyes darkened with self-hatred. "I have many perversions, *esclave*. You think because I fell in love with you, they're miraculously cured?" He leaned closer, his nose an inch from mine. "You think you know me…" His voice trailed off as thoughts swooped him away from my arms and into the dark I'd hoped he'd left behind.

After I'd hurt him—made him bleed and escorted him to death's door with a whip in my hand—I feared I'd ruined him. He'd been shut off—remote. Not cold or cruel but protecting his inner thoughts. He'd always been private around me—guarding his inner secrets like a sentinel with a castle full of unspeakables—but it wasn't until yesterday when Q proposed and branded me that the crack in his façade finally gave me hope.

The burning on my neck amplified, taking over my senses with a dull throb. The scorched skin hurt—even the numbing balm Q rubbed into it yesterday hadn't halted the singeing, searing ache. But unlike all the other parts of me that'd been hurt over the past month, I welcomed it. It gave me something to focus on.

It gave me purpose.

It reminded me I was owned, and my sanity wasn't just my responsibility but a necessity. I'd made an oath to Q. I'd signed a contract the moment the 'Q' sigil scorched my neck. I was his as he was mine. Therefore, I had to be whole—not just for me but for him.

A chill scattered over my body. What was he thinking? What did he hide behind his tough outer-shell?

Wanting to dispel the darkness in his eyes, I murmured, "I know all I need to know. I know you're kind and generous; the best lover, protector, and master I could ever want."

Q clenched his teeth as a flash of ferocity etched his features. "Is that all I am?"

"You're all that and more."

"Are you forgetting the question I asked you yesterday? The one where you said yes?"

I smiled, ducking my eyes to trace the sweeping lines of his chest. "No, I haven't forgotten."

"I'll no longer just be your lover, *esclave*."

The swell of love hit me again like a squall of hot air. I

couldn't contain it. I didn't *want* to contain it. "You'll be an amazing husband, too."

Q tensed. "So amazing you didn't want to run away and get married yesterday. So amazing you said you were tired and wanted to stay here for a few more days."

My shoulders hunched. I knew he didn't take my reasoning well. When he'd gone to whisk me away only moments after proposing, I'd been hit by a brick wall of grief. Not just grief but guilt and sorrow and every complicated emotion left over from what happened. How could I explain I wanted to embrace our future and happiness with wide open arms—to throw myself into eternal bliss—but couldn't. Not while my entire soul was weighed down with the crimes and sins I'd committed. *I can't tell you my nightmares. I can't share my guilt or trauma.* I didn't want to burden him any more than I had.

Speak to Suzette. Maybe she could help me. Then again, it wouldn't be fair to talk about such darkness, not after everything she'd survived herself.

Suddenly, Q crushed me against him, dragging my head to rest against his chest. "So much has passed, yet it seems like just yesterday I had my first taste of you. I feel like I know everything about you—the fundamental parts of you. You're like me in so many ways, but really...I don't know you at all." He pressed a fierce kiss to the top of my head. "Not anymore. *Pas depuis qu'ils t'ont kidnappée*" Not after they stole you.

I'd never seen Q so melancholy, so withdrawn. He held me as if he expected me to drift away—like he was petrified all of this—us, our connection—was an illusion.

I didn't know how to bring him back. "All you need to know is that I adore you," I whispered. The nightmare took what energy I had, so I did the only thing I could—I snuggled closer, letting him bind his relentless arms around me until my body creaked and pain echoed in my spine.

Q didn't speak.

Closing my eyes, I let the *clug-clug* of his strong heart calm the flickering images of blood and murdered Blonde Angel.

Her broken skull, the white shards of bone. I'd lost count how many times I'd killed her in my sleep. But no matter how many times I stole her life, she was always there—reincarnated for my torment night after night.

Q was right. He knew nothing. *Because you haven't told him.*

I sighed. What could I tell him? He'd seen me snap and come undone when I beat him bloody. He knew whatever I lived with was too big, too hard to put into words. Only time could heal me. Only the tick-tock of life blotting out what I'd done stood a chance of making me whole again. There was no rushing the process, and that was why I didn't want to talk to a psychiatrist or anyone who would judge me.

I carried my sins deep—after all, I was a murderer. For someone who'd been unwanted all her existence, the act of taking a cherished life filled me with something transcendent of guilt.

It filled me with shame and inner hatred.

It filled me with filth.

Q sighed hard, stirring the air in the bedroom. Each thought and conclusion jerked his muscles, transmitting his anger through body-Morse code.

My stomach shrivelled with yet more guilt. Guilt for hurting him yet again. "I'm sorry, Q," I whispered. My lips sealed over the small bandage over the 'T' branded above his heart. The mark I'd seared into his skin.

I still couldn't understand how he'd forgiven me. He'd tried everything over the past month, all in the name of fixing me: being tender. Firm. Angry. Gentle. I pretended each day it was easier. I smiled and nodded and let him believe he was fixing me with every passing moment.

I'd become a better actress than I ever dreamed of, but it made no difference when he could strip me of my lies with one look. Some moments I even believed my pantomime. I swallowed my fibs and felt pure happiness at being better.

But then I remembered.

I wasn't better. I'd just learned how to bury it so the

horror became a part of me. The flashbacks, the recollections—they were a constant companion, and I fought so hard to keep my reactions free from my face.

I couldn't tell him the truth. It wasn't fair after everything he sacrificed. I lied when I told him I was strong enough. I spun tales every time I assured him I no longer thought of my tower or felt the urge to barricade myself behind its rotund walls.

I whispered, "I'll get better. I'm sorry you have to put up with the sleepless nights. I'll understand if you want me to move downstairs for a while."

Q squeezed me angrily. "Get that ridiculous thought out of your head. You're not moving from my fucking side. *Tu m'entends?*" Do you hear me?

Of course, I heard him. He was my master. Obeying him gave me a sanctuary I never knew I needed. It took away the pressure of thinking for myself when my mind was too jumbled with remorse.

I nodded.

Q swallowed his temper, softening his voice. "Do you want a bath?" His voice may be whisper-soft, but his body didn't relax. The vice of his arms cut off the blood supply to my fingertips, but I didn't care. He needed to hold me tightly. He needed to convince himself I was still there and no matter how bad the nightmares got, I would never leave him the way I had before.

I gave him a promise.

Pulling back, I shook my head. Yet another thing tarnished in my life. I used to love baths. Hot water never failed to wash away my worries and turn me into a puddle of contentedness. That was before Leather Jacket almost drowned me, then drugged me while I'd dozed in Q's tub in Paris.

I couldn't stomach the thought of submersing myself anymore. I didn't think I'd ever want a bath again. Not that I'd ever tell Q that. He didn't need to know the stupid things I feared. I would cease to be the strong woman he needed. And I refused to have him see me as one of his rehabilitated slaves who needed help, rather than an equal who deserved him.

The moment Q stopped seeing me as strong was the day our relationship was over.

Sucking in a breath, I pushed him away, smiling bravely. Locking away my fear and torment, I turned my worries onto the man who would kill for me. The man who *had* killed for me. The man who'd proposed. The man I was going to marry.

"No, I'm okay. Thank you, though."

Q frowned. The silver of the moon had given way to pink and purple bruises of dawn. The fading scars looked darker across his face in the gloom. He wore my mark in more ways than one.

I did that. I scarred his beautiful face. *I hurt him so much he almost died; all because I couldn't differentiate between real life and nightmares.* I knew Q had undergone a massive transformation when he allowed me to whip him. The fresh scars on his face and body highlighted just how much he surrendered.

How much does he expect in return?

I would gladly pay anything to show him my eternity of gratitude, but I couldn't deny I was different.

Q clenched his jaw; his five o'clock shadow was thick. The stress of the past few months decorated both our faces, and I feared we'd never go back to who we were.

"I told you not to lie to me. You can't fool a seasoned bastard like me. Do you think I can't smell your tales?" His voice rasped, bringing comfort and reprimand.

Dropping my eyes, I focused on the room rather than him. The huge bed cocooned us in a sea of black sheets, and if I looked up to the ceiling, the silver chains from where he'd secured and fucked me glinted in the new dawn.

The fireplace of hunted deer and the mirrored chest at the foot of the bed granted a strange blend of trepidation and homeliness. Both emotions plaited together, forever linked where Q was concerned.

My eyes fell on the chest holding Q's myriad of toys. Toys

he'd locked away. *Will I ever crave pain the same as before?*

The memory of forcing him to orgasm overwhelmed me. The carpet burn on my knees, the ache in my jaw as I sucked his cock, the salty taste of him as he exploded down my throat. I missed the passion. I missed the inhibitions between us. *I miss liking pain.*

"I'm not lying. I truly am better. I don't need a bath."

"Then what do you need?" He reached for my hand, planting it over his left pectoral. The heat of his skin set fire to my fingertips; I couldn't stop staring at the sparrows and barbwire on his chest.

"I need you," I whispered, wishing for the burn, the overwhelming sexual hunger. However, it was scarily absent. Either my libido hadn't woken up or that too was broken.

You know what's broken. You just don't want to acknowledge it.

I slapped the voice away, raising my eyes.

Q sat stonily, looking part-sculpture, part-monster. "Yet another lie. *Qu'est-ce que je vais faire de toi?*" What am I going to do with you? Leaning forward, his pale eyes searched mine, tearing through my defences, uncovering things I never wanted him to see.

"I told you to stop lying to me."

"And I don't."

He snorted, his mouth tightening.

I said, "There is such a thing as *too* much knowledge. Give me time, then I'll have no need to keep things from you."

"I gave you time before and look what happened. You built a fortress and blocked me out. You were so damn cold, so fucking untouchable. Forgive me if I don't trust you won't do it again." Q's hand flew up, his fingers latching around my throat.

I froze, battling two emotions: I knew Q wouldn't hurt me—not like Leather Jacket—I knew it was love driving him to anger. But I couldn't stop the panic bubbling in my veins or my wide eyes from giving away too many secrets. I was a victim, and Q didn't do well with brokenness.

His gaze darkened as my heart thrummed under his

thumb. "For God's sake, Tess. You can't even let me touch you. How ever did you let me fuck you yesterday?"

I bit my lip to keep from spilling my dirty lies. I let Q hit me yesterday as he needed to remember himself before it was too late. I gifted my pain and would gladly do it every night for the rest of my life to keep him happy. But I would have to fake it. Fake something that before was as much a part of me as inflicting pain was for Q. We'd been the perfect mirror image of each other, and now the image was dimmed, clouded.

When he took me yesterday, I forced the memories and horrible history away. When he hit me, the clenching of my insides wasn't from pleasure, but instead from panic. I allowed Q to believe it was lust.

I didn't want to hurt him. He didn't need to know my dreadful secret. It would break his heart and wedge a canyon between us. Time would heal me. Time would fix everything.

It would.

I had to believe that.

Keeping my voice as steady as possible, I said, "I love it when you touch me. And sleeping with you yesterday meant the world to me." I brought my arm up, breaking his contact around my throat. Flashing my diamond ring in his face, I added, "You proposed yesterday. You offered me your life, your fortune. Everything you've done for me, I'll never be able to repay. Let me try to find normalcy by loving you and accepting everything you need to give me."

Q scowled. "You're saying you would happily let me string you up and use the cat o' nine tails on you right now?" His gaze glinted. "You would grow wet for me and pant for my cock just like you did before?"

My heart galloped. Why did he have to ask such probing questions? *He knows.* I was stupid to think he didn't. Did he guess I no longer craved the delicious line of pain and pleasure? "Yes," I breathed. "I would give you everything. Just like you've given me."

Q grabbed my hand, twisting the filigree wings wrapping

around my wedding finger. The diamonds glittered even in the dawn, and my heart glowed knowing Q had imbedded a tracker in the gold so he would always know where I was. The comfort knowing he would hunt for me was tremendous. My monster would come. Just like he'd done before.

"You hide so much from me, but you forget I can smell fear." His eyes locked onto mine. "Do you regret saying yes? Have you had second thoughts about marrying me?"

"What? No!" A spike of horror pierced my heart. "Why on earth would you ask that?" Yanking my hand back, I glared. "Accepting you was the best thing that's ever happened to me. If I smell of fear, it's because I don't feel worthy of you."

"Worthy?" Q snarled. "You don't feel fucking *worthy* after everything you've lived through because of me?" Dragging hands through his hair, he glowered. "You still don't get it."

My pulse thudded. The memories I never allowed to surface bombarded me: the grisly bloody heart Q lay at my feet. The black raven wings he'd worn as my dark angel when I was drugged up and hallucinating. How could I feel worthy of someone so much *more* than me?

"No. *You* don't get it. I came to you as a gift. You tormented my mind, turned my body against me, and showed me things I never would've been strong enough to want before you. Not only did you send me away because you thought you would ruin me, but you massacred an entire trafficking ring to save me." My larynx snapped closed with emotion. I wished I could make him see how in awe I was. How much I loved him. Half of my soul throbbed with cosmically bright love while the other dripped in filth and ruin.

"You gave me not only your empire and love but also your greatest fear. Don't you think I know how hard it was for you to let me tie you up and abuse you? You let me be your master, Q. How can I ever repay that?"

I expected Q to scream. To list the ways I'd repaid him in his fucked-up rationality, but instead he propelled himself off the bed and stalked to the bathroom.

The door slammed shut; I waited in the centre of the bed for the shower to turn on or for something to smash as he took his violence out on the amenities.

Seconds after the door rattled in its hinges, Q stormed back out. "I'll tell you how you can fucking repay me. You can marry me. Today. I'm not waiting any longer." Q's melodic accent cut through the room, whipping me with urgency.

"Any longer? You proposed yesterday."

"Don't answer back, Tess. Not unless you want me to drag your delicious body down the bed and fuck you. Having you argue is the worst kind of aphrodisiac, and I know you don't want me." Pacing like a caged animal, he snarled, "The knowledge you'd still spread your legs for me is wreaking havoc with my barometer of right and wrong."

He took all choice away. He was right. I didn't want him. Not while anger poured off him in crimson waves. But I *did* want the connection. I wanted to be reminded I hadn't pushed him away even though I'd tried so damn hard. I wanted to apologise in more ways than words.

Q spun away and yanked open a dresser. Grabbing shirts and underwear, he snapped, "Get dressed. We're leaving."

I scooted off the bed, obeying instantly. "Where are we going?"

"Away from here. Away from memories."

Stopping at the end of the bed, I frowned. "You can't run from this. Only time will help us forget."

Q stalked toward me. His low-slung cotton trousers defined his hard erection, clinging to his powerful thighs. He bristled, towering over me with authority. "I'm not running *from*, esclave. I'm running *toward*. Our future is unwritten. I'm sick of living in the past. It's time to make you mine permanently. I'm taking you to a place where no one can find us."

"Tess. *Tu dors?*" Are you asleep?

My eyes shot wide, connecting instantly with Q's pale ones. Giving him a gentle smile, I shook my head. "Not asleep." If I could have my way, I would never sleep again. I wanted to quit reliving my nightmares and live in the present where I had so much to be thankful for.

Q scowled, but slowly a soft smile danced on his lips. "We're almost there. I didn't want you to miss it."

My heart hammered against my ribs, affirming I was still alive and the catastrophe of our past was over.

Looking out the oval plane window, I glimpsed glittering ocean and landmasses on the horizon. *I'm on my way to get married!* Ever since Q placed the ring on my finger, he'd seemed possessed. Rushing forward, dragging me faster and faster toward the moment where we said 'I do.' It was crazy to hurry, madness to marry so fast, but all I could do was hold on and not let go of this magical whirlwind.

"I won't miss a second." I forced my smile to beam; Q relaxed under my gaze. He looked so dashing, so understatedly powerful. The corner of the bandage over his brand peeked through the open buttons of his green shirt.

The plane's engines softened, nudging the nose toward earth. I'd grown so used to Q's wealth—his helicopter, mansion, and property empire—but I would never like this aircraft.

Too many bad memories existed in the cream leather and honey wood. First being sold to him and freaking out while Franco watched, grinning like the devil, then when Q sent me home to Brax after turning my world upside down.

"I fucking love it when you smile." Standing, he crossed the small aisle to kneel by my legs. My stomach twisted at seeing him bow before me. I'd never get used to the way he looked at me, or the sheer gratefulness glowing in his eyes.

Once, I'd believed life made me go through hell in order to deserve Q—to be worthy of the priceless gift of true love. Now, after Rio, my thoughts hadn't changed. If anything, it'd been confirmed. I'd lived through hell in order to be deserving of this precious connection.

I had to be purged by evil to know perfection.

"Do you feel it? Do you feel lighter? Freer? There's no better medicine for troubles than going somewhere new." Sitting on his knees, he leaned forward, coming within kissing distance. His tongue came out, licking his bottom lip, drawing my attention.

My stomach clenched; I sucked in a fluttering breath. "I do feel it. I feel...." *Scared and hopeful and frightened and happy and...*

Q's eyes dropped to my mouth; I couldn't breathe. "What do you feel, *esclave?*" Slowly, his large hands landed on my denim-clad knees. While he wore stylish black slacks and a light-green shirt, I wore designer jeans and a wraparound cardigan with matching white scarf. France hadn't been warm when Q rushed me out of the house and up the plane steps.

Q's hands trailed higher, branding me beneath the heavy cotton. The 'Q' he'd burned onto my neck flared with heat, willing him to kiss me there—to take possession.

"Tell me. What do you feel?" His voice turned gruff and gravelly while his chest rose and fell.

I couldn't sit upright. My bones melted—my entire body became hypnotized by his spell. I let myself drift, trying so hard to stay in the moment, chasing the slow burn of lust in my blood. "Your fingers. I feel your heat. I feel your breath on my face. I feel your lips achingly close to mine."

Q's fingers turned to talons on my upper thighs, pressing me into the plush leather. "Do you feel how much I need you? How much I want to take you. My way. All the fucking way." His eyes flashed, sending sparks through my heart. "I want you, Tess. So damn much."

Memories of him taking me in his helicopter clouded my mind. I'd wanted him past all sanity that day. I'd been wild at the thought of him spanking me, filling me...now all I felt was a hum of need—a dull light-bulb compared to the lightning bolt it used to be.

Add fuel. Coax it to grow.

Throwing myself into his control, I willed my need to build. I nodded. A small moan escaped my lips as his hands caressed upward. Gliding over my hips, he gripped my waist, holding me in place.

"Would you let me take you? Here? Now?" Q murmured, brushing his lips over mine in a teasing barely-there kiss.

"Yes," I breathed. "Take me. Here. Now. Anywhere. I want—" *I want to be me again. I want to be free.*

Deliberately keeping my thoughts from skipping, I cupped his face, thrilling at the rough-smoothness of his jaw. He'd shaved but not to bare skin. I loved how untamed he looked even while he wore expensive clothing.

"What do you want?" he murmured, his lips a fraction from mine.

"I want—" *I want to be able to love pain again.* But it was like wishing upon a useless star. I might never be able to find passion in pain again. Not after what they made me do.

"Say it, *esclave.*"

Say what? The dreadful truth that I'd ruined our marriage before it'd even begun, or perhaps he wanted to hear yet more lies about how I hadn't changed into a shadow of myself.

Q didn't move, waiting for me to speak.

My chest hurt as I sucked in courage. "I want you to kiss me. Make me forget everything but your tongue and taste and need."

Q didn't hesitate.

His lips crashed against mine, pinning the back of my head against the leather. I moaned as his tongue speared into my mouth with his trademark self-assurance and domination. He tasted of darkness and sin, making me want to follow him to the ends of the earth.

Tilting his head, he licked my tongue, encouraging me to kiss him back. Willingly, I kissed harder, shivering in his hold as he groaned. Intensity built between us, wrapping us in a tight web of heat and want. Needing more—to show him how indebted I was—I grabbed his hands, placing them on my breasts. The instant his large grip covered me, he lost control, kissing me brutally.

His lips bruised mine, heating, melting. It was soul-scorchingly deep as he devoured me into his world. Every sweep of his tongue helped bring me back to life. Every lick shed the greyness, granting colour once again.

His touch turned hard; I flinched as he twisted my nipples through the material. The threat of pain would've sent me skyrocketing before but now it dampened my lust. The needful bubbles and sexual frustration popped in my blood, leaving me cold and lifeless.

No. Stop.

I hated how frigid I'd become. How conditioned I was to run from all types of pain.

Q stiffened; his touch froze.

I couldn't let him guess how much I hated all forms of agony. It turned me from wet to dry. From willing to averse.

He can't know.

"Q—God, make me forget. Please make me forget," I panted into his mouth. *Please don't guess.*

Q didn't kiss me back, instead he pulled away, pinning me with his pale stare. Goosebumps broke out over my skin as I shuddered. Ominous foreshadowing prickled my spine. What if I never found that part of myself again? I couldn't let him marry me thinking I was his perfect other when I no longer wanted his belts or chains or whips.

Cupping his cheek I breathed hard, fighting against the prick of tears. "Kiss me. Do anything you want to me."

The pain in his eyes almost unravelled my despair. His face shut down to unreadable. Tenderly, he turned his head, pressing a kiss against my palm. "God, I want to. How I want to hurt you, kiss you, fuck you. " Hiding his emotions behind a careful mask, he smiled. "But I rather like denying myself. Looking at you, fantasising of all the things I want to do but not giving myself permission to do them."

My heart broke. Q just lied. He lied to give me space. He lied to keep me from going back to the one thing he hated and feared the most—my tower.

He leaned closer, bringing his intoxicating heat and smell of citrus. "Stop."

I didn't know what to stop. My black thoughts? My terror at fucking up the best thing that'd ever happened to me?

I threw my arms around his neck, dragging his mouth to mine. I blocked off my endless questions and pretended. I found solace in acting the part of unbroken Slave Fifty-eight who Quincy Mercer hadn't been able to send away. I gave him everything I could.

But it wasn't enough.

Q slammed the heel of his palm against my chest, holding me against the chair. "You can't lie with words, and you can't lie by actions. Stop. Stop making a fool out of me by thinking I buy your bullshit, Tess."

Smashing my lips together, I looked down. I hated myself. I hated this. I fucking hated Leather Jacket and White Man.

"I don't know how to stop," I whispered. There was no 'get well' help-book or guidelines on how to evict the slime from my soul. I entered into a relationship with Q never believing he would change or that he would find a balance between light and dark. I gave him my heart, all the while knowing I might only get a small sliver back in return.

But Q surprised me completely. He'd given his life freely to save mine. He let me murder his sense of self all in the name of bringing me back. And now I was asking for more. More— too much more.

Q seemed to follow my thoughts, my fears. His lips curled in frustration. "*Toujours en train de mentir*" Still lying.

I sucked in a breath as he jerked me forward; the thrill of his sharp teeth teased my ear lobe. His hot mouth made me tremble as he nibbled my skin. "It makes me so fucking hard for you, *esclave*, knowing you'll be mine. All mine. My wife. It gives me unbelievable power knowing I'll be responsible for your happiness."

My head fell back as Q trailed threatening kisses down my neck to my collarbone. "And I take my responsibilities very seriously. I'll make you happy again. I swear it."

Tears sprang to my eyes; all I wanted to do was sink. Sink into his promises. Sink into the safety of letting him fight my battles.

Q's body bristled, his hands dug into my thighs as his voice changed to a growl. "And when you're happy again, I'm going to take you so hard you'll scream. I'll show you just how fucking happy you've made me by saying yes." His teeth sank into my skin.

Pain.

"Kill her. If you don't, we'll cut off her fingers one by one." Leather Jacket's voice roared into my head.

I froze.

No. Stay. Don't remember.

Piercing panic bulldozed its way through my heart. Horror and repulsion doused me in sleet and ice.

"Hit her, puta. *Obey us otherwise we'll do it ten times worse."*

Pain—it wasn't a tool of love but a weapon of hate. It was heinous. It was barbaric.

Please...

I hated that I had no power to keep the badness from staining my life. I hated that I was so weak.

Squeezing my eyes, I focused on Q's hot breath, the predatory way his teeth clamped hard. He didn't break my skin, but the threat of pain was enough to make me lose it.

Blonde Hummingbird came alive behind my eyes. She'd been scratched and mutilated—by me. My stomach rolled. I wanted to throw up.

Stay with him. Stay in the present. Stay safe.

The cabin was too small. The air too stifling. The light tinged to soot while the scents of mould and sweat rose from the bowels of my nightmares.

"Tess. Tess!" Q reared back, grabbing my cheeks in both hands. "Goddammit, Tess." His harsh temper acted like a vacuum, sucking up the horror as fast as it consumed me.

Where there had been rottenness and rank recollections, all that remained was my hyperventilating and jittery nausea.

I opened my eyes. Q's gaze delved into mine, looking as if he'd reach in and tear my demons free if he could. I smiled as bright as possible. "Sorry. Airsickness."

Q growled, standing upright. "Lies. What did I just say?" His face twisted into a mask of hurt anger. "That's the last one I'll let you say. The next one I don't fucking care if you're terrified, I'll make you speak the truth." He stalked across the small aisle and sat stiffly in his chair.

Shit.

Breathing hard, I looked around the cabin, trying to think of some way to fix this—fix myself. Nothing about the luxury interior or cylindrical aircraft gave hints of how to clear my mind from fear and be free.

Unbuckling my seatbelt, I crossed the small distance between us. It was my turn to kneel, settling myself between Q's spread thighs. The sheer size of him, the air of ruthlessness, let me place all my trust in his belief—his belief that he could fix me.

"I wish I had something else to say. It seems as though all I do these days is apologise."

Q sighed and for a moment I worried he'd cross his arms and ignore me. But then he brushed a blonde curl off my forehead, his jaw tight. "I wish I could tear out your memories so they leave you in peace. I wish I could kill those fucking bastards all over again. I want to forget about being human and let my inner monster tear them limb from limb."

Q's entire body tensed, vibrating with rage. Once upon a time I would've been turned on, scared, and intrigued by Q's wrath. Now, after everything we'd been through, he no longer scared me. His anger filled me with happiness—he would do anything, be anyone, for me. To have such a wondrous gift made me ache with gratefulness.

I placed my hands on his knees. "I wish that, too." The smoothness of the material over the hardness of his body sent my heart skipping a beat.

"What else do you wish for?" he demanded, sensing everything I wasn't saying. Demanding to know the truth.

Sitting straighter, I confessed, "I need you to promise you won't hate me. If I know you'll be patient, I'll fix myself. I swear it."

Q shook his head sadly. "*That's* what you're afraid of? That I'll grow impatient and leave you because you're battling things you refuse to tell me?" Sitting tall, he glared into my eyes. "Have I given you any reason to doubt that I won't wait for you past death if I must? Have I given you any cause for insecurity?"

Shit, he had a gift at making me suffer guilt. How could I ask him to wait for me when secretly I believed he'd walk away long before I was repaired?

"No. I'm sorry." My shoulders slouched. Every part of me was heavy and cold. "You've been nothing but gentle and supportive."

"I may get angry and pissed off at everything they've done to you—that's my right as your future husband—but I give you my word: I take our relationship seriously. When I say the words 'til death do us part' I'll mean them. There's no escape once you sign that contract, Tess. Call me old fashioned or a possessive bastard, but you're mine. Forever."

My heart grew wings, and the fear that he'd throw me away dissolved. I believed him. No matter how long I took to come right, he would be there for me every step.

"I haven't been fair to you. *Je suis à toi*, Q." I'm yours.

His face lost the hardness; a flicker of adoration warmed his gaze. Pulling me upright, he placed me in the seat beside his. He pursed his lips as a thought flickered, then he shifted to reach into his back pocket. A crinkling sounded as he pulled something free. "I wasn't going to give this to you, but I think you need reminding how strongly I feel for you. Yes, you're mine, but I'm fucking yours through and through." Passing the tattered piece of paper to me, he twisted in his seat, scowling out the window.

The plane's engines whirred and purred as we descended faster from clouds to earth. The islands on the horizon were now spread below us, dotted with buildings and a slash of grey runway. My engagement ring flashed with expensive rainbows as I stroked the still-warm note.

I stared at the folded piece of paper as if it only had doom to tell me. I never expected Q to write a love letter. If he hadn't wanted me to read it, why had he given it to me?

"Read it, woman. It's not going to bite you," Q muttered, still staring out the window.

Sucking in a breath, I unfolded the crinkles and smoothed it out. The sight of Q's masculine cursive made me fall in love all over again. Everything he did was flawless.

Esclave...*Tess*

You won't see this—just like I won't tell you certain things about me no matter how long we're married.

Fuck me. Married.

Me? I never thought I'd experience what others took for granted—until you, of course. You landed on my doorstep and stole my fucking heart the moment you fought me over the pool table. I'd never been so turned on and so utterly confused.

I tried to keep you safe from me, but I never thought I'd have to keep you safe from the bastards in my sordid life. I failed you, and I don't think I'll ever get over how much you've suffered—all because of me.

You were tortured because of me.

I could promise you the world. I could cut out my heart and present it at your feet. I could write sonnets and poems and lyrics all designed to spill my fucking guilt and remorse, but nothing will make the ache go away.

You were so strong once and now you're stronger still. You think you're broken, but I see the truth. Not only did you cut me out and force me to face my worst nightmare, but I feel as if you'll disappear at any moment.

But you won't be able to leave once you've said 'I do.' The moment you've signed and become Tess Mercer, your soul belongs to me. You'll truly be mine, and I'll own you forever. Maybe then the fear will go away.

Fuck, I truly hope so, because every day I'm going mad. Going insane with the thought of you walking out the door and leaving.

Once you're truly mine, I might find the guts to show you a little of what I've hidden all my life. I want to welcome you into my world. I want to share everything that I am. I want to teach you everything that I know.

Fuck, Tess, you don't get it. Do you understand that I'm not the one with the power—it's you. You're the one in control, and it kills me to admit it.

Will you ever forgive me? Will you ever look at me the same? Will you ever stop thinking that if you had never met me, you'd never have been taken the second time? If only I fucking sent you home when I had the chance. If only I stopped the darkness from building. If only—hindsight is a fucking bitch.

But if I had sent you away, my life would've remained the same. Empty. Lonely. So then I can't regret falling for you even though my need for you almost killed you.

So you see? Vicious circle. Around and around. I'm the cause of your pain, yet I want more of it. I'm the reason you're shattered but I want to be the one to glue you back together.

I'm such a selfish bastard.

Forgive me. Forgive my sins and I'll split open my soul and let you in.

How ironic that you think I'll leave you. How pathetic that you think you don't deserve me. The truth is, I'm petrified you'll finally see me as a monster and despise me. I'm a fucking mess.

You think I'm invincible. But I'm not. I'm weak. Weak for you and everything I taste when I'm with you.

Say yes. Please fucking say yes.

If you do, then I'll be the best master and husband the world has ever seen. I'll give you a life full of experiences and passion.

We'll finally find peace in the dark—

There was no ending, almost as if Q couldn't bear to write another word. Not even a full-stop gave closure to such a brutally exposing letter.

I'd been living a lie. A lie where I thought I only loved Q. I didn't love him. I *adored* him. I worshipped him. I was alive because of him.

Light and colour and effervescent joy gave me the strength to slap away my guilt and embrace what Q just showed me.

Forgive him? There was nothing to forgive. We were both victims of cause and effect—pawns in a game of happiness and loss. We had each other—we won in the end despite everything we'd been through.

"I don't need to say any vows, Q. You own my soul already." I glanced at his frozen form. "I don't need to forgive you because there's nothing, *nothing*, that you're guilty of. No crimes. No sins." I waited for some acknowledgement that he was listening. He remained unyielding in the chair, only a twitch of his hand signalled he'd heard.

The airplane tyres slammed against tarmac as we went from flying to charging down the runway. My heart had been left in the clouds, dancing with the knowledge that a man so loyal and amazing as Q loved me.

I'd gone from unwanted to idolized. The shift in my world was so earth-shattering, I didn't know how I stood or followed Q down the steps after we'd taxied to the airport. I existed in a bubble of awe as Q guided me into a sleek black limousine, and we pulled out of the airport. We hadn't spoken, too flayed open to risk admitting that his letter had done what words could not. *It gave us hope.*

Safely seated in the back of the limo, Q turned to me, asking softly, "Now, do you understand?"

My eyes shot to his, holding his tortured gaze. "Now, I understand."

Chapter Two

We're altered, we're abnormal, our souls stained with each other's mark. Our souls are that of monsters born in the dark

Time was a fickle bitch.

It seemed only hours since I met Tess. Seconds since I touched her for the first time. Only moments since I hunted for her to take her home. All those blocks of twenty-four hours that built a wall from ever finding her had disintegrated, seeming to hurl me headlong into the future—the future I wanted so fucking bad.

My heart stopped as my mind filled with Rio. Seeing her like that—naked, tortured, bound—enraged me to the point of shedding all human fakery and turning savage. The metallic stench of death still coated my nostrils; the warmth of spilled blood steaming on my hands. Tess had looked like a corpse—a cracked out, mentally broken corpse. They'd infected her mind, her lungs, her very fucking soul, and I'd stolen her back only to lose her all over again.

It seemed only a minute ago when Tess walked away from

me, shutting herself off forever, inciting panic, causing me to free all my birds because I couldn't stomach the thought of ever caring for another life. It felt as if it were yesterday when I broke down and let her take my life—using me to spew all her internal blackness away.

I'd hoped it would be enough. I'd hoped I no longer needed to watch the hands of time, fearing Tess's state of mind.

But time liked to fuck with me.

Instead of Tess growing whole again and leaning on me to help, she lied.

Every lie she told whittled at my temper until I knew eventually I'd explode. I could only accept her tales for so long before I forced her to tell the truth.

For three weeks she healed. We spent time together as man and woman rather than master and slave. We became friends.

Friends who didn't tell each other anything.

I sat in the back of the limousine staring at the woman who owned my balls, body, and heart, but ultimately she was a ghost. An unknown riddle of human spirit who was too stubborn to burden me with any of it. Why couldn't I get her to accept me? Why didn't she trust me to help? She'd let me brand her. She wore my ring. I *knew* she was mine. But the knowledge meant jack-shit when she lied so blatantly.

Nothing would grant me peace because I knew *she* had no peace. It was elusive, evasive, and I was fucking tired.

Tess suddenly scooted across the seat, pressing against my side. Her blue-grey eyes connected with mine, looking so pure, so fucking ancient. Her soul was mangled and bruised and the light that'd always existed no longer glowed like the cosmos; now it flickered—spurting with blinding light only to be dimmed by sorrow. Sorrow she refused to talk about.

I'd tried to show her the depth of my feelings by sharing that ridiculous letter. I'd regretted giving it to her almost instantly—those were my chaotic thoughts, not for her to read. Scribbled in the dark while she thrashed with dreams.

But in a way, I was glad she'd glimpsed into my psyche. She owed me the same courtesy. I could force her to share hers—a trade.

Grabbing a handful of her silky blonde hair, I held her still. Threading my hands through the strands, I made my way till I cupped the back of her neck. Her cupid lips parted, sending a thrill through my stomach to my cock. I'd struggled the entire four hour journey with a massive hard-on. She'd kept her eyes closed most of the way, but I knew she wasn't asleep.

I knew because she wasn't drenched in sweat and screaming like the holocaust had come again.

"Let me fight them for you, *esclave.*" My fingers tightened around the delicate cord of muscles. She felt so breakable, so damageable. It was a lie. Her body may bleed, her bones may break, but her mind? That was a fucking fortress.

And I wanted in.

I wanted to ram the gates, cross her moat, and send an entire army of artillery to massacre her nightmares. I needed to know what swirled and swelled behind her eyes. I needed to know how to help her.

"Just by being you, you're fighting them for me." She bowed her head beneath my hold, giving me her weaknesses, her vulnerability.

My mouth went dry at the thought of threatening her. Squeezing her throat until she spilled her unspoken secrets. Maybe then I'd find the truth.

Forcing her to meet my eyes, I murmured, "I'll be by your side forever, but I won't allow you to push me away again." Brushing her nose with mine, I added, "And I sense it, Tess. Your reluctance to tell me. You're floundering on your own, and it's pissing me off that you're not leaning on me. So lean, otherwise, I can't promise I'll keep my temper."

The opaque screen between driver and car interior slid down. I glowered as Franco spun in his seat, cocking his head. "We planning on sitting on this runway all day, or do you have a destination?"

Tess spun in my hold; I let her go. Her perfectly white cheeks rushed with colour. "Franco. What? How…" She gawked at my head of security.

Tess and Franco had formed an unlikely alliance. He'd treated her roughly when she first came to me—feeding off my need, letting himself taunt a slave who wasn't broken. He'd chased her when she ran, he'd hunted her when she was stolen, he'd been beside me every step, and I knew he had a deep respect for Tess. Even though he took a while to forgive her for leaving me bloody and oozing a month ago.

Franco's green eyes connected with Tess as I relaxed into the seat. I would never admit it, but I liked watching them interact. I liked that Tess wasn't afraid of him. I liked that Franco had developed an older brother protectiveness toward her.

When Franco didn't reply to Tess's mismatch of questions, she shifted in the leather to face him. "How did you get here?"

"Who do you think flew the bloody plane?"

Her eyes flew to mine; I kept my face blank. I shrugged, holding back a smile as she whipped to look at Franco again. "You fly, too?" Her shoulders were tense, head cocked warily. A swell of pride filled me. She didn't believe him.

As she shouldn't. He was a bullshitter.

"He flew in the cockpit to give us privacy," I said, letting the small smile twist my lips.

Tess's eyes locked onto mine. The blue looked softer, warmer. She must've known I wanted privacy in the hopes of another membership into the mile-high club.

I still couldn't get the thought of her on her knees with her cheek pressed to the helicopter carpet out of my mind. My cock throbbed at the memory of driving into her from behind. She'd been so hot and wet. After denying her an orgasm and being pissed at her for making me come against my will, the tension between us was out of this fucking world.

I swallowed, remembering how wild she'd been when I

spanked her. How her back arched and she moaned that delicious fucking moan.

It had been the last time we'd been connected completely. Master and slave. Dominator and dominated. It linked us more than anything. It also made me realise I would do absolutely anything for this beautiful woman until the day I died.

It was also the day she disappeared.

Fuck. Even that memory was tainted by the bastard traffickers.

My hands curled on my thighs, wishing to all that was mighty to reincarnate Red Wolverine so I could rip open his chest, cut out his heart, and feed it to him while he choked for life.

Franco smiled, looking less civilized and more feral these days. Rio had changed both of us. "Privacy, huh? Doubt you'll get much of that with a wedding coming up. You're a lucky little lady, not having any in-laws to impress. Mercer, on the other hand, better be on his best behaviour."

Tess leaned back in her chair, fastening her seatbelt. "As far as I'm concerned, we're both on our own in this world. Just him and me." She flashed me a look full of shy promise and blatant loyalty.

Fuck me, I loved her. Overpowering awe grew day by day inside me. I'd sold my soul to her.

Her.

This woman who I would never take for granted.

I grabbed her hand, linking my fingers through hers. I didn't say a word. I didn't need to. Our souls did enough talking.

"Take us to the island, Franco. I need to take Tess somewhere completely private."

Her fingers twitched in mine. "Wait…what island?" Amazement widened her eyes. "Oh, my God, you own an island? We're getting *married* on an island that you *own*?"

Franco laughed. "Guess what it's called. Go on. You'll never guess."

Tess shook her head. "You own an island that you *named?*" Her fingers went loose as she looked at me like I was a stranger. "This is too much. Q—how..." Her question faded under the weight of wonderment.

I hated that. Hated the look of awe and confusion. Just like she looked at me when I showed her *Moineau* Holdings for the first time. She made me so fucking self-conscious of my wealth.

Yes, I own an island.

Yes, I'm fucking rich.

Yes, I'm happy I'm loaded because without it, I would never have found you.

Be fucking grateful rather than afraid.

My heart raced and I opened my mouth to yell, but Franco jumped in before I could upset her. "It's called *Volière.*"

My heart thudded at the word. At the time, it was perfect for the slice of paradise. Now, I wished I'd named it *esclave*. After her.

Tess whispered, "You named it Aviary?"

Everything inside me was hot, boiling, exploding. Did she have a problem with everything related to wealth, or was it shock making her look at me so intensely?

I scowled. "Yes, I own an island. Yes, I called it *Volière*. No, I don't feel guilty for owning it, and no, no-one else has been."

Franco chuckled. "Shit, boss. She was only asking." Grinning at Tess, he whispered, "You'll love it. Looks exactly like the owner." Spinning around, he slid the partition back into place, and the car rolled into motion.

What the fuck was that supposed to mean? Just like me? The entire island was overgrown and wild.

"I didn't mean to upset you, Q," Tess said, her eyes dancing worriedly over my face.

Shit, I couldn't do anything right. Not while I had so much bubbling inside. How could she know my anger was at her but *not* at her? It didn't even make sense. My frustration was at her nightmares not because she had them but because she didn't *share* them. My brain hurt.

"I know, *esclave*. I didn't mean to snap." Giving her a soft smile, I added, "I've owned it for a while. It was one of the first things I bought when I took over the family empire."

"Tell me?" Her hand shot to hold onto the door handle as Franco took a corner too fast. Her slim body slid on the shiny leather reminding me yet again she was so fucking tiny. She still had a few kilos to gain before getting back the stunning sexy curves she'd had before.

I frowned, letting my mind rewind to ten years ago. "I bought it off a floundering investor." I shrugged as if it was the most natural thing in the world to own a tiny haven. "He accepted a lowball offer, then I had to fork out three hundred thousand euros to have a water purifier installed."

I glanced at her, making sure she remained in the car and hadn't flown away from sheer fear. Fear of what? Money? I'd never met anyone so averse to wealth. Or not averse. Just overwhelmed.

A small burst of happiness soothed my annoyance. *At least you know she'd marry you if you were dirt poor.* She wasn't marrying me for my bank account or what I could give her.

She's marrying me because she loves me.

The knowledge sucker-punched me every fucking time.

"It's untamed. Uninhabited. Completely impracticable, but none of my associates knows I own it and no one will find us there." I'd protected Tess from a lot of things—things like the consequences of killing Red Wolverine and slaughtering his operation.

That sort of stuff had large ripple effects. Payback was coming. I was sure of it.

I didn't need to tell her why I had the sudden urge to hide her. If I didn't keep tabs on the need to shut the world out, I could easily become a recluse with sentries on my front door and drones flying overhead, ready to sniper anyone who came within fifty metres.

Might not be a bad idea.

Wolverine and his operation might be dead, but there were others. Way too many sick and twisted fucks in the world.

"And we're getting married there?" Tess asked. "How will that work if no one knows it exists?"

"Franco will source a justice of the peace or a celebrant—whoever you want to marry us—and he can be our witness."

Tess bit her lip, thoughts parading in her eyes.

I almost groaned or wrung her neck—either to get her to finally speak to me. "What are you thinking, *esclave*? You don't like this elopement idea?"

She smiled hurriedly, giving me reassurance I so stupidly needed. "No, I love it. I love the thought of our own private paradise. Just us. But…"

I swiped a hand over my face. "But…" *Goddammit, get to it so I can annihilate your concerns.*

"Well, not that I mind of course, but I don't have anything to wear."

"You don't need a white dress. That's just a gimmick."

She laughed. "I suppose so. I'm not a girly girl, so I don't mind not having the princess dress or the flowers or the food but…"

I sighed heavily. "Another but."

Her face flushed. "I want it to just be us, but… and I don't want my family there as they aren't part of my life anymore—" flashing me a shy smile, she rushed "—you're my new family. My chosen family."

Goddammit, she knew just how to cut me in half. Now I'd give her anything. What a clever woman. What a conniving, intelligent fucking woman. Did she know I would bow to her every command now—hearing her call me family. Shit, I'd hire out Disneyland if she wanted a princess wedding. I'd invite woodland animals and fairy godmothers if that's what she wanted.

You're my family.

I forced my heart to stop hammering and glowered. "You

stopped what you were going to say. Spill."

She sucked in a breath. "I would've liked Suzette to be there." Her eyes flickered away almost guiltily. "And…it doesn't matter."

"What doesn't matter?"

Taking another deep breath, she set her jaw. "Brax was the one who gave me any sense of self-worth. I never loved him more than a friend—not the way I love you, but he *is* a friend and the only one from my past who I would've liked to share you with." Ducking her head, she breathed, "I'm so proud of you. So amazed and stupefied and happy. I want to show you off. I want one moment where I'm on your arm. To show off how stupendously lucky I am to be worthy of loving you."

Fuck. Me.

My brain split her words into two categories—she loved me and wanted to show me off which made my heart chug harder with joy. But all I could focus on was one word: Brax.

The ex. The boy who spent years with her before me.

I couldn't look at her. My voice dropped to a deadly whisper, "No fucking chance in ever-living hell is that boy going to be at my goddamn wedding."

Tess froze.

My heart took on a life of its own, thundering like a bloody mess. I rubbed my temple, easing away the sudden headache. "You think I'd let your ex spend time with you? You want to show me off—throw me into his face and say what, Tess? That I'm the one in your bed now? That you didn't fuck him before I claimed you?" My voice was barely a whisper but icicles could've formed on the car windows it was so cold. "You want me to say the most important words of my life in front of a twerp who let you get kidnapped in Mexico?"

He may have let her be taken in Cancun, but she was stolen from your fucking office. You have things in common.

Fucking hell, that comparison had to die. And fast. I'd turn into a monster if I started comparing myself to a boy from Tess's past.

I needed out of this car. I needed to get away from her to calm my temper.

Tess's soft touch landed on the back of my hand. "I get it, Q. I'm sorry. I should've thought it through. I wouldn't want your ex-girlfriends there either. Can you forget I said anything?"

Breathing hard through my nose, I said, "You're forgetting I don't have any ex-girlfriends." *Only whores.* Shit, we both had baggage. I had no right to be so high and fucking mighty. Sighing, I forced my muscles to relax. "Sorry, *esclave*. That was out of line." Giving her a half-smile, I added, "Jealousy is a new demon I'm trying to understand."

The limousine went around a corner, sending Tess sliding over the leather. Her body nudged against me. The instant her shoulder touched mine, everything that'd been pulled tight snapped back into its rightful place inside. Who was I kidding? I'd give her anything. I *wanted* to give her everything. She *deserved* everything.

But that twat still wasn't coming.

"You have nothing to be jealous of." Tess smiled. "I was just thinking aloud. They aren't deal breakers."

"Deal breakers?" My eyes narrowed. "What you're saying is, you don't want to get married unless those conditions are met?" I couldn't believe this. My stomach twisted. It meant yet more time not having her as my wife. More time not having the commitment and piece of paper I needed.

Tess's lips parted. "What? No! I have no conditions, Q. None at all. Marrying you is already one dream come true. I don't need any others."

Then what did that make me? A heartless bastard who was rushing her into accepting me, all because this was how I wanted it? I wasn't being fair.

You won't change your mind, though.

Nope. I was so close to having her sign her soul to me. I ached to hear her say the vows. I bled to sink inside her hot body the night she became Mrs. Mercer. I may *want* to change my selfish ways, but I wouldn't.

"Good. Because I'm not stalling or changing." I couldn't manage anymore. I didn't want to admit if she asked right now to give her time, I'd buckle and give her anything. I needed this more than her. I was the weakest—wanting to marry her *my* fucking way.

Tess nodded; happiness painted her face with a healthy glow. A few minutes passed as she looked out the window, watching passing motorists, colourful buildings, and sunburned tourists. She turned to face me. "Where exactly are we?"

Forcing my body to shed the remaining jealousy, I said, "The Canary Islands."

Tess laughed quietly. "I can't believe before I met you I'd never travelled apart from one family holiday to Bali. Now the world is open to me. Not that I'm counting Mexico and Brazil as part of my travels."

The pain in my heart made me gasp. Goddamn, her flippancy. Her strength to make jokes would've made me fall to my knees if I wasn't sitting down.

"I'll take you wherever you want to go, *esclave*." I would spend the rest of my life creating new memories for her to suffocate the ones living inside her.

We fell silent as Franco drove us through congested streets of weathered locals and quaint shops. Buildings favoured plasterwork and pastel colours. The Spanish archipelago had never been a favourite destination of mine, but it'd proven to be a worthwhile investment with a few developments and one mid-size hotel.

It also had a low tolerance on sex slaves, unlike the rampant mess and disgusting trade done in Spain. In fact, I'd only accepted one girl from the Canary Islands in turn for a bribe on a condominium, which was nothing compared to the fifteen from Spain.

The sun beamed through the windows, making my skin prickle with heat. Tess unwrapped her scarf, and shrugged out of her cardigan, before settling back wearing a white singlet top.

She didn't do it coyly or to get my attention, her focus remained outside, but my eyes locked onto her chest. The contours of her lacy bra indenting the cotton made my mouth go dry.

I'd never get used to the need I had for her, or the joy at knowing she could withstand my unconventional needs. My fingertips ached to stroke her flawless skin; my cock throbbed at the thought of her touching me. I wanted her hot slick mouth between my legs.

I clenched my jaw. "You have no thought for my sanity do you, *esclave? J'ai tellement envie d'être à l'intérieur de toi.*" I need to be inside you so fucking bad.

Her head whipped around, blue eyes blazing with sudden lust. Her nipples hardened beneath the cotton, reacting to the desire in my voice, perfectly programmed to me.

Her mouth parted, but she didn't speak.

I didn't move. If I did, I'd end up stripping her and forcing her to sink down on my straining erection. Looking away, I muttered, "Next time I touch you, you won't freeze up on me. I'll guarantee it." I'd guarantee it because I'd make her so fucking wet she'd pant and gasp and *beg* for me to fill her. I'd bind her and stroke her and worship her in every way I knew how.

A second ticked past before she cleared her throat. The thick tension simmering between us sat heavy and unresolved. Her lips twisted, asking, "So, how big is this island?"

I chuckled as she raised her eyebrow in a lewd way, deliberately making an ass out of herself. The power she had over me was crushing. How could she make me laugh when all I wanted to do was shake her and tumble all her sadness away? How could she make me care so fucking much even while pissing me off?

Her gaze locked with mine, darkening with desire. I lashed out, grabbing her hand, giving her a hard smile. Ever so slowly, never taking my eyes from hers, I pinched her forefinger and slid it into my mouth. Inch by inch, I sucked, tasting her, cursing the fucking need in my blood.

Her eyes snapped closed, shuddering as I swirled my tongue around her finger. I intoxicated myself on her subtle feminine taste. A hint of orange remained from the fruit she had for breakfast on the plane.

Just as slowly, I withdrew her digit from my mouth, murmuring, "Big enough." I smiled, but there wasn't anything jovial in my face. I transmitted a warning—a message that the moment I had her alone, I was taking her. The monstrous craving in my blood was a ticking time-bomb ready to explode at any moment.

Awareness and intensity fogged the interior. I couldn't breathe without dragging her into my lungs. I couldn't think without her being centre place in my mind.

My eyes fell to the bandage on her neck—the tiny piece of protection hiding the brand from others eyes. I wanted people to know she was mine *now*, not when it was healed. I needed to see it, so the urge to bite and consume would stay dormant.

I released Tess's hand. Franco took another corner at hyper speed, and we jerked to a stop at our destination. Thank God we were there because another few minutes in the limo and I would've locked the doors and not cared if violent rocking gave us away.

Franco jumped out, coming to open the door for Tess. Bright island sunshine beamed into the shady car no longer inhibited by the tinted windows. The heat scorched my skin, making me wish I'd worn something cooler. Coming here had been impulsive. After Tess's nightmare, all I wanted to do was run. Run far away from evil, madness, and responsibilities.

I wanted to be happy, but I couldn't snap out of my mood. It wasn't just Brax being mentioned but a combination of things. And just like Tess wouldn't share things with me, I couldn't share my worries with her.

She's about to become mine for eternity. She loved me. So why did I sense something awful coming?

I hadn't been to *Volière* in years. The last time was when

my house was a convalescent home to five saved slaves all of who were mentally destroyed. I did what I could—hired what therapists were available but then had to leave. Hearing their screams down the corridors or their sobbing while trying to work proved too similar to listening to my father torture his harem in the east wing when I was a boy. I'd been a fucking pussy and run to *Volière* where I stayed until they were well enough to return home.

"Looking forward to seeing paradise?" Franco asked Tess. His muscular form was crisp and professional in his black suit and no doubt sweating his fucking balls off. I lost sight of them as they walked around the back of the car. The familiar burn of rage of another man touching the most precious thing in my life reminded me Tess might have issues to work through, but so did I. I trusted Franco with my life. I had no reason to be jealous. *Try telling that to your fists.*

Quickly exciting the car, I glowered at Franco until he dropped Tess's hand. He grinned. "Should I wait here, boss? Or do I get a ticket to utopia, too?"

"You're coming." Never again would I go without a man with reflexes like Franco's and a license to carry concealed weapons. Frederick, my business partner and the man I left in charge, was right. On our daily phone calls discussing property projections and what the future meant for *Moineau* Holdings, I knew I'd painted a bull's-eye on my back. More would come for me, and I had no intention of being unprepared.

A loud bang sounded from a piece of rigging along the pier. Such an everyday innocent noise but Tess fucking leapt like a gazelle. Her curls flurried as her head turned to the noise; her eyes round and terrified.

Goddammit.

I knew she struggled with loud noises or surprises. I watched her jump and freeze if Suzette dropped something in the kitchen or Franco slammed the front door too loudly.

"Tout va bien, personne ne peut te faire de mal ici" It's okay. Nothing can hurt you here. I stalked toward her, jerking her

close. Whispering in her ear, I said, "Stop letting it have power over you."

She pulled away, a slight flush on her cheeks. "Sorry. I'm just tired. My reactions are a little jumpy." She smiled, cupping my cheek. "Truly. I'm fine." Her eyes dropped, hiding her lies.

Lies had a scent. The stench of decay and terror. I hated when she told untruths—she undermined me every time.

"Tess, what did I—"

"Bloody hell, I'm hot," Franco said loudly. I looked up to snarl at him for interrupting, but his eyes pierced mine. They blatantly said *you're in public with a lot of people milling around. Let's get on the fucking plane where we're safer.*

As much as I wanted to brush off his warning, he was right.

Swallowing my frustration, I let the tension between Tess and I disperse. Stepping backward, I nonchalantly looked around. Everyone was a suspect. It was time to get somewhere less populated. Just in case.

"Wish I'd packed a pair of shorts," Franco grumbled. "I'm bloody steaming in this suit."

Tess chuckled. "I agree. Q dragged me out of bed so fast this morning, I have no idea what I packed. I'm hating these jeans with a passion. I'd give anything for a skirt."

My mind instantly thought of how convenient a skirt would be. A skirt would let me touch her, finger her, all while she remained hidden and dressed. It seemed I couldn't think about Tess without getting fucking hard. The incessant need to fill her built behind my eyes. The churning in my gut filled with darkness as my ears roared needing to hear her cries. My mouth watered at the thought of tasting her—all of her—her blood, her tears, her desires.

But then the need rushed to another part of my body.

My heart *throbbed* with tenderness plaiting with the ugliness of my soul. I wanted her symphony of screams, but not as much as I wanted the glittering sounds of her laughter. My body filled with terrifying softness and warmth.

She'd changed me.

Through hurting me and showing me compassion even while I was a bastard to her—she changed me. The chilly exterior I favoured melted with one look of her dove-grey eyes. Fuck. *I'm ruined.*

Needing to redeem my manhood, even if it was just to myself, I growled, "You're not putting a skirt on."

Tess's eyes flew to mine, confusion making them flare. "Did you just tell me what I can and can't wear?" The soft blue turned to steely grey. "I love you, but if you think you can dress me—like you did when I first arrived—you have another thought coming." Her temper rose from nowhere swirling around me like a blustery breeze.

The tenderness switched to lust once again, and I wanted to reach out, squeeze her neck, and kiss her fucking stupid. I was turned on by her meekness, but her temper turned me feral.

I needed to get away from her. We needed to leave.

"Fine." Stalking away, I called over my shoulder, "Bring the bags, Franco. I'll tell the pilot we're here."

The pier was the same as always. Tenerife was nectar to holiday-seeking newlyweds and families. The port acted as the gateway for island hopping, sightseeing, and was always manically busy. However, I had a long standing arrangement with the top seaplane pilot whenever I came. The gruff old ex-RAF commander knew when I visited not to accept any other jobs but remain on call for me. I paid him a shitload to be at my every whim.

So where the fuck was the plane?

I stomped down the pier, looking in the distance to moored vessels, trying to glimpse the white and black twin prop Otter somewhere on the turquoise water.

Nothing.

"Are you Mr. Mercer?" a youngish man asked. He had short black hair and a face that'd been tanned and weathered by the sun. My fingers twitched in preparation. I no longer trusted anyone—especially foreign strangers.

Scowling, I nodded. "Yes. Captain Morrow was supposed to be here. He's on call."

The man shook his head. "I'm Bill Castro. I've been assigned instead." His white uniform, with gleaming black buttons and a crest of an embroidered wave on the pocket, marked him as one of the many yacht crew in the port. "I'm afraid the captain is currently in hospital, sir. Triple bypass, unfortunately. I've been asked to escort you to where you want to go on one of the newest speedboats in our fleet."

Twisting his torso, he pointed at a sleek white and silver vessel that looked like a bullet on the water. Mahogany and cherry wood decorated the interior panels gleaming richly in the sun.

A boat? No fucking chance.

"I'm not sailing. I always fly." Flying was my thing. Flying was my one passion—the air was meant to be explored with the help of thrusters and powerful turbines. The ocean—that was meant to be avoided at all costs. I *hated* the water. I hated how innocent it looked at first glance, but beneath the depths it hid monsters, while the surface was home to waves eager to drown unsuspecting victims.

"We wouldn't sail, sir. It has a top speed of fifty-eight knots. You'll be holding on for dear life while tears stream from your eyes." The captain grinned.

I wanted to punch him. What if he'd been hired to take us out to sea and dispatch us on behalf of Emerald Dragon and his concubine hoard, or the Rattlesnake assholes in Australia with their harem of drugged-up slaves?

"Surely there's another pilot who can fly the Otter?"

"Q?" Tess appeared by my shoulder, flanked by Franco. Her eyes landed on the man who I wanted to throw off the pier.

"Everything okay, boss?" Franco asked, eyeing up the speedboat captain with a glint best described as wolf-like. Franco had embraced what we'd done in Rio, and I had no doubt he'd like to have a reason to do it again.

"Apparently our pilot is on his death bed, and our transportation now includes a flimsy dingy."

"Not a dingy, sir. It's a top-of-the-line vessel. And unfortunately it's your only option as the Otter is in for its regular maintenance and the other seaplane operators are fully booked this week with a Japanese tour group." Bill raised an eyebrow. "If you want to travel, I'm your only option."

"A boat doesn't sound so bad," Tess said, smiling at Bill. She may look unafraid and cool but no one knew her like I did. The nuances of the way she held herself hinted she didn't like being around strangers.

I glanced at the line of boats all bobbing like fucking corks in the water. So unreliable. So rudimentary. "How long will it take?"

"Depends on where you're going. I've been sworn to secrecy and was told you'd provide coordinates."

Shit, yet another bribe-able human who would know about *Volière*. Was there another way?

Bill seemed to hear my thoughts. "I'm your only choice, unless you want to swim."

I glanced at Tess. She seemed fairly relaxed—not too tense. I trusted her instincts and she wasn't throwing off alarm signals.

"Fine. It's 29.0580 North and 16.8796 West. How long?"

Bill's forehead furrowed, doing some quick math. "About thirty to forty minutes. That's at thirty-five knots. Can't have you falling overboard at top speed."

I glowered.

"If it's the only option, it's the only option," Franco said, stating the fucking obvious.

We'd only been away from home for five hours, and I already missed the security and sanctuary of my chateau.

"Fine," I muttered. "Let's go." Grabbing Tess's elbow, I guided her toward the sparkling white speedboat. State of the art instruments and glass radar screens refracted the sun, blinding me as I stopped. How the hell were we supposed to get on board?

Bill dashed past us, hurling himself onto the deck looking nimble and a regular seafarer. The creaking of the salt-drenched pier sounded haunted as he placed a small platform across the gap. In another second, he'd attached a handrail, beckoning us across.

"You go first." I motioned at Franco. He rolled his eyes but took our bags, striding over the plank. Bill took the duffels and placed them inside one of the mahogany bench seats.

Tess went to move forward, but I couldn't unwrap my fingers around her wrist. I hated the thought of letting go—even though I'd be able to touch her the moment we were on board. *Let go of her, you idiot.* My fingers released, and I cursed the burn deep inside me. I needed the 'Q' branded on her neck to be in full view. I needed everyone to see who her master was.

Flashing a fleeting smile, she crossed the gangway, following Franco's example. A lash of anger filled me when Bill's eyes lit up. He offered her his hand to jump the small distance into the boat.

Franco might have rights to touch my woman but no other male did. Never fucking again.

Ignoring the plank, I leapt over the side, narrowly missing an embarrassing plunge into the sea, and spun to offer my hand. The roll and buoyancy of the boat beneath my feet gave me instant seasickness. Give me planes, helicopters, even gliders and parachutes, and I was fine; put me on a boat, and I fucking hated every moment of it.

Tess looked between me and the captain, her lips pressed together. She knew what I was doing. She knew I wouldn't let him touch her, and she knew exactly what I would do if she took his hand over mine.

Lucky for her she didn't play games, otherwise I would've had to break the captain's legs.

With a soft smile, she reached for my palm. The moment

her fingers looped with mine, my cock thickened. I might be governed by my heart nowadays but having her delicate, very breakable touch in mine turned the man into a monster, and fuck I wanted her. I wanted her spread below me, bound before me. I wanted her gagged and chained, so I could worship her for hours.

Squeezing my eyes briefly, I kept a tight hold on my needs and very carefully grabbed her waist. Lifting her the small distance downward, I deliberately kept her body away from mine. I swallowed hard. *"Tu vas bien?"* You okay?

She nodded. Her lips parted, and the scent of mint and Tess's unique smell enveloped me. "Yes. I'm always okay when I'm with you."

I couldn't help asking why? Why did she trust me? Why had she forgiven me? She'd been stolen when she'd been with me. Taken when I'd promised to keep her safe. My chest concaved with a quarry of guilt.

I turned to face the man who had our lives in his hands while crossing an ocean. Hell, I hated boats. "I don't want to be on this piece of shit any longer than necessary. Let's go."

Bill jumped to action. Tess moved to sit on the back wraparound seat while Franco perched on one of the high seats by the control hub. His eyes were hidden behind dark sunglasses, and he'd taken off his black blazer, revealing the shoulder holster with his two guns.

Tess eyed the weapons but instead of looking distasteful, she looked relieved. I wanted to know what she thought. I wanted into her damn mind. If she didn't start talking soon I'd have to use drastic measures to get information out of her.

I sat beside Tess. She instantly slid closer, pressing her hip against mine. I wasn't one for public displays of affection but if she so much as touched me again, I would strip her in seconds and take her in full view.

Goddammit, the images in my head were thick and tempting. Her panting while I licked her pussy. Her tears streaming as I re-introduced her to pain and pleasure. My balls tightened in anticipation.

The captain unhooked the boat, coiled the rope, and headed to the instruments. The vessel started with a powerful purr and he nudged the acceleration lever so we coasted forward. A froth of bubbles were left in our wake, and we meandered our way around docked boats and impressive yachts.

The moment we hit open waters, he floored it.

"Crap!" Tess squealed as the boat went from sitting low in the water to almost hydro-planing. Okay, the piece of shit could go fast. I would still much rather be in the sky.

Waves crashed and shuddered with harsh slaps against the hull, faster and faster.

My heart thudded with a rush of queasiness. I was too hot. Too tense. Unbuttoning my shirt, I ripped it off, revealing the thin white t-shirt beneath. Tess's eyes went wide; she licked her lips. I looked down to what she focused on, noticing the ink from my tattoo shadowed beneath the material, giving hints at the hidden design.

Her hand landed on my torso, trailing her fingers over my abs.

Sucking in a breath, I lifted my arm, letting her snuggle into my body. I groaned softly as her fingers clutched my t-shirt. My arm locked around her shoulders, restraining her against me. Rubbing my nose in her hair, I whispered, "You keep doing that, and you'll be half-naked with my tongue between your legs in front of witnesses."

She froze. "You wouldn't."

I raised an eyebrow. "Keep your hands in one place and I might be able to hold on until we have privacy."

Tess gave me a look that shot my heart to pieces, then placed her hands in her lap demurely and rested her head against me.

The rest of the boat ride was fucking torture. The warm wind whipped Tess's curls into a mess of mayhem, filling my mouth and tickling my neck and face. All I wanted to do was grab a fist of it and use it to hold her delicious lips over my cock.

Even now. Even after everything she'd been through, I still wanted to use her like a whore—like a slave. I was still fucked up. Still my father's son.

I tried to focus on the expanse of ocean around us. Not one whitecap or wave in sight. The turquoise looked like glass reflecting the perfect sky I longed to be in. Islands popped up in the distance only to be passed in a whirl of salt spray.

Tess looked peaceful, resting against me. But the bags under her eyes and hollow cheeks spoke the truth. The moment she was on *Volière* I would make her happy again. I would spend my days feeding her delicious food to replace the curves she lost, and dedicate the nights reminding her how unbreakable she was. The ghosts in her mind wouldn't survive out here. Nothing dark could exist in this vivid sunshine.

Finally the boat slowed. We bumped gently against a decrepit jetty jutting out from a wild and rugged island.

Everything about it looked vicious and untamed. There was no helipad, no landing strip, nothing of great luxury. When I'd bought it, I toyed with the idea of chopping it down and destroying the thick jungle to make way for a hotel or other commercial development. But then I fell in love with it. With its exoticness, unruliness. It was perfect in its untouchedness.

"This is your island?" Tess asked, her eyelashes fluttering in the sunlight.

Franco jumped onto the jetty, helping Bill moor to the post. Old tyres were the only things stopping the sleek sides from being punctured by rusty nails and splintered wood.

"Yes. In all its natural glory." Standing, I bent down, wrapped my arms around Tess's back and legs, and picked her up.

"What are you doing?" she whispered.

"Te porter pour passer le seuil." Carrying you over the threshold. Cradling her in my arms, I made my way across the bobbing vessel and placed her ever so gently on the wooden

platform beside it.

Climbing up beside her, I took a large lungful of air. The nausea I'd been battling since we took off miraculously stopped the moment my feet touched firm ground. The jetty wasn't on buoys but anchored onto the sandy bottom of the atoll.

A large flock of local birds suddenly took flight from the thicket of trees, squawking and shrieking at us interrupting their wilderness. I instantly felt better. I didn't want to change a thing, but one thing was a must—an airstrip—so I never had to step foot in a boat again.

"I'll go make sure the house is still standing." Franco gave me a look as he strode off. He knew where the path was, hidden by foliage leading toward the large six bedroom dwelling the previous investor had built for his family. Franco had been here with me while I worked, and the original home was well built if not a little rustic. It would be spotlessly clean thanks to a regular maintenance crew who came once a month.

Tess spun around in awe. "This place…it's…"

I smiled; tension siphoned from my muscles. Blue ocean surrounded us, hemming us in like a wall-less cage. Intruders would have a hard time touching shore without the security cameras noticing them first. Tess would be perfectly safe. *I* would be untouchable for any bastard who wanted revenge.

"Q, I had no idea it would be like this. I visualized a tiny sandy island with one palm tree."

I chuckled. "It has a fair bit more than one." Moving closer, I ignored Bill and his hellish boat. "You don't find it underwhelming…more suited for a boy's fishing weekend rather than a wedding?" After all, from here it looked as if we'd need a machete and dynamite to make our way through the undergrowth. She didn't know the house in the centre had manicured gardens and metres of idyllic paradise.

She laughed. "No. It's perfect. More than perfect. Untamed. Animalistic. Completely untouched and unruined." Her eyes dropped; she whispered, "Just like you. It fits you perfectly."

I looked again at the thick palm trees, trying to see it through her eyes.

"Don't take this the wrong way, but it's the home of a beast."

I glared. "You think I'm a beast?" Fuck, what else did she think of me? What did she suspect I'd done while trying to get her back?

She came forward, taking my hand. "No. But you're unpredictable and dangerous and protect those you love fiercely. You should be proud. To me you're more than a knight in some stupid shiny armour. You're the monster who no one can tame but the woman he loves." She moved to leave, but I went with her, stomping a few metres away from the captain.

I grabbed her shoulders, turning her to face me. "You're right." Wanting to share a part of myself she didn't know, I murmured, "Do you know the moment I fell for you? The exact moment you tamed me?"

Her eyes grew heavy, glazing with overpowering love. "No."

I let my mind skip back to the night I knew I'd found the one. The woman I hated to want. "When you offered to massage my migraine away in the conservatory. You didn't have to do that—you should've hated me for what I'd done to you. But you offered to soothe me. You let me find peace under your fingers even while I was a fucking bastard."

She sighed, raising her hand to rest over my heart. Her fingers irritated my brand, making me wince. "That was the first moment I let myself give into the overwhelming confusion inside. I wanted you so much, Q. I wanted you even then. I'd hoped by showing I cared, you'd be kinder, gentler." Her eyes shadowed, remembering how the rest of the night played out. The police arriving. My drinking. The mind-blowing sex in my room.

"You've taught me so much. I've *grown* so much. I can't even recall the girl I was before I was sold to you."

I bristled. "Don't use that word. You weren't sold. Fate just brought us together a little unconventionally."

Linking my fingers with hers, I said, "Come on. Let me show you the island."

Tess stood on tiptoes and kissed my cheek. "I'd love that."

We traversed the small jetty, only for Tess to freeze as a loud *boom* echoed from the centre of the island. Birds flurried from trees while leaves cascaded into the sea.

Her fingers turned to pinpricks of ice in mine; her entire body went from supple to trembling.

The noise was a backfire on the generator. Franco must've turned it on while preparing the house for us.

Tess lost all colour. "No," she breathed.

I shook her, looking deep into her vacant eyes. "It's okay. *Juste le générateur.*" Just the generator.

She didn't respond. Her mouth opened in a silent scream as the ghosts she battled with every night swarmed her. Panic and fear glowed like black horror in her eyes.

Grabbing her cheeks, I snapped, "Tess. Stop!" Her panic attacks had to fucking end. This one was so similar. Almost identical to the way she looked in my office when she'd been taken.

The last time I'd slapped her to get her to return to me. This time, I kissed her. Smashing her lips with mine, I gathered her close, willing my energy and heat into her frozen form. I forced her to grab onto the present, dragging herself from her nightmares.

Her slack lips suddenly responded below mine, and she wobbled in my arms. I pulled away, never looking away from her. "Are you alright?"

She looked strung out and quivery but she nodded. "Yes." Tears welled in her eyes. "Q, I'm so sorry. I didn't mean to—"

The way she trembled pissed me off but worse, it made me remember. Remember why she'd had the panic attack in my office. Why she'd shut down. She'd sensed the fucking bastards who'd come to steal her—somehow she'd known. There was no way anyone could be on this island, so the only other conclusion was an overload—a complete bombardment of new locations and people.

Shit, I'm a grade-A asshole.

Tess pushed me away, moving on unsteady legs to get some air.

"Come here, Tess." I stormed toward her, capturing her shoulders again. "I didn't think. I'm a fucking idiot."

She blinked. "Think about what?"

I'd been so stupid. "Being here—in a completely new place. The last time that happened—" I couldn't finish. I wouldn't remind her. Not that she needed reminding—it lived in her mind, suffocated her lungs, itched her skin with memories.

"I shouldn't have brought you somewhere so far from where you're used to."

Tess shook her head, clasping my hands on her shoulders. "That's what you think? Q, it wasn't the office that upset me. It isn't a new place I'm afraid of. It was them. I *knew*. Somehow I knew."

"And now? Do you sense them here? Are you afraid?" I wanted to yell at her to never be afraid again—unless it was of me. But I kept my temper tightly controlled.

"This wasn't a full attack—just a memory."

I would've killed for her to admit exactly what memory haunted her. "So being somewhere new isn't filling you with fear?"

She pressed a finger against my lips, hushing me. "No. If anything, it's helping. My instincts knew evil was close by that day. I should've listened instead of brushing them off. That's twice I've ignored my sixth sense. And I promise on both our lives I will *never* ignore it again."

I glowered around the island, seeing threats where there were none, suspicious of the swaying palm trees, contemplating annihilating them just for existing. I didn't believe her—now I suspected everything and everyone.

Maybe it's the fucking captain. I glanced over my shoulder. At the end of the jetty, Bill had on a headset talking through the radio. He looked innocent enough. If he wasn't, I would break his neck in a second.

Yet more violence to protect the woman I'd dragged into the darkness to be with me. The guilt layered more rocks in my chest. I looked back at Tess. "That day in the office. I should never...I was an idiot to leave...I'll never be able to tell you how sor—"

Tess's residual fear morphed into hot temper. "Stop it. It wasn't your fault. You need to let go of your guilt, Q." Cupping my chin, she ran a thumb over a thicker cut that'd needed stitches. She lacerated my heart just like she lacerated my body.

I bowed my head, leaning into her touch. I felt like a wild animal letting himself be soothed. "I love you, *esclave*, but you're a hypocrite."

She cocked her head, squinting in the sunlight. "I don't know what you're talking about." Trying to change the subject, she said, "Can we go? I'm dying to see the island and explore." Her eyes sparkled with forced merriment.

My teeth clenched. She was a master at guiding subjects away from the ones she couldn't bear. My voice was a growl. "Don't try to hide what just happened." Leaning closer, I ran my nose gently over her ear and down her throat. She shivered as I gently peeled the bandage away from the red mark on her neck.

My stomach twisted at the sight of the angry 'Q' branded into her skin for life. Eventually it would heal to a delectable silver and everyone would know she belonged to me. "I refuse to be lied to for another fucking minute. I sense everything you're trying to mask. The mixed signals are giving me a headache, so stop it."

She winced as the air touched her sore neck. "Fine." The air grew static as her anger sprang from nowhere. Her temper fed mine.

"Fine," I snapped. "Oh, and this?" I rolled up the

bandage, shoving it in my pocket. "It stays off. I want to see the mark. I *need* to see the mark. You're not to cover it up again."

Tess huffed, crossing her arms. "Fine."

Why the hell was she pissed at me? What the hell had I done? "Good. Glad we understand each other."

She muttered, "Perfectly." She looked away, cutting me off from her thoughts. The familiar burn of anger rushed down my arm, causing my fingers to lash out and imprison her chin.

Guiding her eyes back to mine, I said, "You think I don't know what you're living with, but I'm living with the same demons. You're forgetting I have a front row seat to your unconsciousness in the form of your nightmares." My fingers tightened, making her flinch. "Something else is bothering you. Spill it."

Her eyes narrowed. "There's nothing else."

"Don't." I tutted under my breath. *"Dis moi la vérité!"* Tell the truth.

We glared, fighting a silent war. A minute ticked past, then another, until Tess finally weakened. "I'm slightly overwhelmed."

I held my breath. "Overwhelmed?"

She sighed, shifting her feet. "A little. This is happening so fast. It's a crazy whirlwind, and I need time to breathe."

I jerked away. "You're saying I'm *forcing* you?" For fuck's sake, was she marrying me only to keep me happy? All the promises I made in the limo of not changing my plans disintegrated. How could I rush her when I'd already put her through so much?

"No! Not at all. It's just a lot to take in. I mean, Q, I'm standing on your *island*. I'm marrying *you*. After a lifetime of loneliness, you're giving me the *world*. It's a lot to take in."

I frowned. Wasn't that reason to rush? To solidify perfection before it was stolen once again?

Her head tilted, eyes darting over my face. "Every time you move, your skin glitters with tiny scars. Scars that I put there." Her voice was barely audible. "If you're suffering with guilt, how do you think I feel living every day with evidence of what I did to you?"

Goddammit, she thought I *minded*? She thought I was so superficial to care about the small marks she'd laced my body with? I didn't. I fucking loved them. I loved that I wore my love for her. I loved that I was strong enough to face my terror.

Softening my voice, I murmured, "Every lash and wound you gave me brought you back to life. I never want you to think I begrudge them, because I don't."

She swallowed hard. "You always know what to say."

"You're forgetting I sense everything you feel." I didn't admit that was only a half-truth. Trying to figure out her lies had become harder and harder. Her skill at fibbing was adapting, which meant I had to break her habit fast. I refused to let her protect me by bottling everything inside.

Bill cleared his throat, his footsteps loud on the jetty behind us.

I let Tess go, spinning to face him. "What?"

His eyes flickered to Tess before saying, "I'll be on radio frequency 3139 when you're ready to leave. Give me an hour to get here, but I'll be on call for you for however long you need."

I nodded. "Fine. Thank you."

Bill dragged a hand through his hair, then turned to patrol back to the boat.

A rush of pride filled me. This was right. This was as it should be. No one else mattered in the world but Tess, and I didn't want to share the most special day with anyone else.

Tess suddenly planted a swift, chaste kiss on my lips, taking me by surprise.

I froze, fighting the swelling in my trousers. "What was that for?"

She smiled, bowling me over with how fucking beautiful she was. "For being you. For being perfect."

I chuckled, but it held pain and a slight web of confusion. "I'm not perfect, *esclave*. You're mistaking me for someone else."

She bit her lip, shaking her head. She threaded her fingers with mine. Her touch kept the darkness and snarling monsters locked inside. "You're perfect to me. Perfect *for* me."

My heart thudded, sending warmth through my veins. I didn't deserve her. I blinked, suddenly seeing the rush—the manic journey to an island in the middle of nowhere—as a desperate attempt at locking her to me forever.

What the fuck am I doing?

I was about to marry the one person I would love past all existence, and I'd forced her to marry me in private. She didn't deserve to be squirrelled away. She deserved to be in a gorgeous gown dripping with diamonds and placed on a pedestal where I could honour her for the rest of my life.

This might be what *I* wanted, but it wasn't fair to her.

I sighed, expelling the air in a rush. Raising my voice, I shouted after Bill. "Don't leave. Not yet. We're going back to the mainland."

Bill turned, acknowledging my request with a small wave before jumping back into the boat.

Tess flinched. "Why did you say that? We just got here."

This wasn't right. But I would *make* it right. I brushed a curl behind her ear. *"C'est une erreur."* This is a mistake.

She took a hasty step back. "Excuse me?"

My heart stuttered at the pain in her voice. The insecurity in her eyes, the terror in her body only confirmed my decision. I wanted her happy and strong. I wanted her joyous and walking with no burdens or heavy shackles when I made her mine. So much darkness layered our lives, overshadowing us from too many corners.

If we got married like this it would stain our entire lifetime together. And I wouldn't do it.

Not when I had the chance to fix it.

"I can't marry you. Not like this." I waved between us, indicating the distance, the ghosts separating us. "We haven't resolved what we went through. We've shoved it away, hoping to forget, but we'll *never* forget. What happened is a part of us, as much as we'd like to pretend otherwise."

My face twisted with ferocity. "I want to pretend you were never taken and hurt. I want to imagine you were never drugged and made to take another's life. And I want to forget the bone-crippling pain when I couldn't find you and thought I'd lost you forever."

Something shifted. The heaviness I'd been living with faded just a little as Tess met my eyes. "Q…"

The delicate agreement between us—the one that said we'd try to protect each other by not sharing—shredded. Gone was the need to pretend we were alright. Gone was the stupidity to act as if we were normal.

We weren't normal. And we needed to address our past before it swallowed us whole. Sincerity and hope broke through the clouds like sunshine in a storm.

Tess whispered, "I want to be a carefree again. Someone slightly naïve, a little gullible, and a lot in love. I want to believe in fantasies again, see the magic in the world, and not be terrified of shadows or going to sleep."

My arms fucking demanded to be wrapped around her. Finally. The truth. Just a little but it was more than before.

Then her eyes glossed with tears, and the storm swallowed us again. "But whatever we want, it isn't going to happen overnight. It'll take time."

I growled low in my throat, wanting to tear apart every clock and watch. Time had kept me from finding her. Time meant jack-shit to me. I wanted her to be happy *now*. I wanted to marry her *now*.

Time was my fucking enemy.

Tess mistook my silence as consideration. She continued, "What we lived through is part of our identity. We can never erase it. The only way to survive is by accepting—"

My hands balled. "I'm not accepting that this is our life." Motioning between us, I hissed, "This…distance. These…lies. I want more than that, *esclave*. And I know you do, too."

I looked toward the captain, glad he had his back to us and out of hearing distance. He would never understand the violence, the aggression, the all-consuming passion between us. He would never accept my overbearing temper or quick to flare anger.

But Tess did.

She understood me just like I understood her. I was hers just as much as she was mine.

My eyes drank in the island. I didn't want to leave. I liked this slice of paradise. Nothing could touch me here. An oasis in thousands of gallons of seawater. It would be a good place for Tess to heal. But not yet. I had work to do before I could bring her back.

"We're leaving. We can't do this."

"Can't do what?" The sun shone on her head, looking like melted gold on her shoulders.

"I'm not marrying you tomorrow, Tess."

Her face went white; I swore her heart plummeted into her feet. She looked away, locking her jaw. I loved she was distraught at the thought of no longer marrying me.

In some fucked-up way it gave me the assurance I needed. Time and secrets might wedge us apart but she'd sworn to love me and grow old by my side. That was enough for now.

Rejection wrapped around her, blanketing her in depression. "You've changed your mind?" she whispered. "I knew it was all too good to be true. After all, you deserve so much more." Her voice trailed off.

How many fucking times must I assure her?

"Every second you doubt my feelings for you, you kill another part of me," I growled. "Did my letter mean nothing? Did seeing my raw thoughts on paper not help you realize I would do anything for you?"

My heart stuttered at the thought of her reading my innermost thoughts. The rambling mess I'd jotted down.

The salt-laced air whipped her hair, blowing a few strands around her neck. She searched my face. "Then what are you doing?"

"I'm going to marry you, *esclave*. That's non-negotiable."

Her chest rose and fell with relief. "Okay…when?"

My mind raced, putting a haphazard plan into effect. "I don't know yet." I gave her a reassuring smile. "But we both know we can't get married like this." I had no idea how I would fix it. If it was even fixable. I wouldn't stop until I'd smashed through the clouds of madness we lived in. I didn't tell her I doubted it was possible to heal entirely or eradicate what we'd done.

I'll make it happen.

I would find a way. I would fix her. I would fix myself.

Holding my hand out, I vowed, "I'll find a way to free you. I'll find a way to make it right." Her fingers interlocked with mine, and I dragged her close. Breathing in her soft innocent scent, I murmured, "And when you're finally happy, I'll give you whatever you want.

"I promise."

Intertwined, tangled, knotted forever, our souls
will always be twisted together,
our demons, our monsters belong to the other,
Bow to me, I bow to thee, now we are free

"**W**ell that was the shortest wedding in bloody history," Franco muttered as I slid into the car and slammed the door. Sunshine gave way to shade, providing relief from the piercing glare. I breathed a sigh of relief.

Melting into the leather upholstery, I angled the vents to receive an artic blow from the air-conditioning. Being in the high-noon sun and dealing with the stress of being told I wasn't marriageable material had taken its toll.

Q slid into the limo, slamming the door just as loud as I had. We hadn't spoken a word on the way back; I didn't trust myself not to burst into tears. I'd make a fool of myself by showing how insecure and truly afraid I was.

I don't want you, Tess. How could I love you now you've become one of them? The voice from when I'd been drugged in Rio kept repeating in my mind. Q didn't know that while I hurt and maimed under the command of my captors, he'd visited me often. My phantom conjuring with his whispers of me no longer being pure or worthy.

I knew it was irrational to believe he didn't want me—not after his letter and everything he'd done—but I wasn't strong enough to stop the voices from undermining everything I knew to be real and replacing them with lies.

Damn lies.

Insecure filthy *lies*.

I sneaked a glance at Q. He glared out the window, his forehead furrowed, eyes dark with planning. He'd withdrawn once again, focusing inward on whatever idea he'd latched onto. The last time he'd been this intense, he'd ordered me to beat him practically to death.

My eyes refused to stop drinking him in. His white t-shirt clung to his body made from pure stone. His longer hair was wind-swept and messy. His five o' clock shadow hid some of the tension from his jaw but not enough.

He was so perfect. *Too* perfect. How could I ever compete, always feeling second best? My heart had leapt out of my throat and dived into the waves when he'd said he couldn't marry me. Every dark thought and worthless aspiration I secretly nursed came true in that one, horrifying minute.

I'd always known it was only a matter of time before he finally realized he was marrying a girl with sin in her soul and a woman's blood under her fingernails. And not just any woman. A *trafficked* woman—a bird he would've done anything to save.

He might suffer guilt for letting Leather Jacket take me. However, I suffered guilt for murder.

Franco lowered the barrier between us. "Couldn't wait to get to the honeymoon, huh?" He threw a look over his shoulder, his emerald eyes catching mine.

My stomach twisted. What would he say if he knew Q had postponed it? Would he nod as if it made perfect sense? Would he tell Q he was worthy of a woman who was pure and not a killer like me?

I looked away, unable to stare at the man who'd been beside Q for years. I was jealous. Jealous of his time with Q when I'd had so little.

Franco cleared his throat, catching my attention again. He raised his eyebrow, kindness softening his fierce features.

I smiled weakly, then froze when he winked. He *winked*.

Q muttered, "No honeymoon. Not yet."

Franco rearranged his face from kind and open to cool and professional. Ignoring me, he looked at Q. "Where to then?"

Take her back to Australia. I'm done. The snide cruel voice in my head answered on Q's behalf, filling me with damp iciness. Oh, God. I had to get the negativity under control. I had to find a way to clear my mind.

Q glanced my way, his mind elsewhere. Finally, he answered, "Just drive for a bit. I'm still thinking. I want something impersonal."

Impersonal? First he took me to an island that obviously meant a lot to him, then he wanted to take me somewhere that meant nothing. *Trust in him, Tess.* I had to keep my chin high and my heart believing.

"Sure thing." Franco nodded, putting the glass back up.

Q looked out the window without a sideways glance.

I wanted to go to him. I wanted his arms around me, so I could focus on what was real and not what was in my head. My mouth opened, spilling an unauthorized question. "Why couldn't we have stayed on *Volière*? Even if you don't want to get married, surely it was a good place to spend time together?"

Q didn't turn around. It took a moment for him to reply, as if sorting through the words to make sure he said nothing wrong. "I want the impersonality of somewhere we've never been. I want somewhere on neutral ground." He kept staring out the window, brooding. His hands curled on his thighs, saturating the atmosphere in the car with energy and frustration.

I ignored the splinters in my heart. "For what?" *He wants somewhere where no memories exist for either of us.* It made sense—I supposed.

"I don't know yet," Q muttered.

I couldn't help the quick intake of breath or the tickle of tears. Why the fuck was I so weak? I *hated* being weak. I wanted to be strong again—to understand why Q had done what he did. I wanted to have the strength to allow life to guide me without being terrified of what was around the corner.

Anger filled me; I smashed my stinging eyes. Twisting my body, I tried to see through the swimming tears, focusing on the passing view.

Rustling sounded as Q shifted. "I'm making this up as I go along, *esclave.* I'd forgotten how overgrown that hovel of an island is. Someone needs to go in with a chainsaw." His accented voice that normally radiated with honesty dulled with the lie.

I looked over. He smiled, softening the brutality of such a fib. "Please, Tess, let me do what I need to do."

The anger hadn't left my veins. I wanted to argue. I wanted to fight. I wanted to prove I still had the guts to stand up for something I desperately wanted. And I desperately wanted to be married to Q. If I hadn't let the memories take me hostage, I could've been Mrs. Mercer in a few short hours. Now, I might never wear his name.

"You said you liked it wild. You deliberately left it untouched." A thought came to me, I asked, "Why did you buy it in the first place? There must've been a reason." Images of him sending women to heal and recoup there filled my mind. Maybe he hadn't bought it for himself but for another.

As much as I wished I could read his secrets and unravel his past, I couldn't. Q was still an enigma. I wanted to pledge my life to his even while we fumbled in the dark.

I didn't think he'd answer, but quietly he replied, "I had a crazy notion I would retire there."

I sat taller, twisting my hands in my lap. "You wanted to retire on *Volière?*" I narrowed my eyes, trying to picture him bumbling around on an island as an old man all on his own. But he wouldn't be alone. He would've found someone worthy if I hadn't been sold to him. He would've fallen in love— eventually. A man like Q deserved to be loved unconditionally.

Still not looking at me, Q admitted, "A few years ago, I was dealing with a lot of shit. I had more slaves being rehabilitated than I could keep count of. The pressure of dealing half in the light and half in the fucking dark messed me up inside. All I wanted was peace. Serenity. Somewhere no one could find me. It seemed the perfect place."

I understood his need for a bolt-hole. Somewhere he wouldn't be judged or be a stranger in his own home. Keeping my voice low, so as not to shatter the gathering softness between us, I said, "That's a good reason."

Q looked over, his pale eyes delving into mine. "A good reason but no longer valid. I'll never retire there. Not now."

My heart beat harder at the thought of the future. I loved that I had the privilege of watching him age. I'd love every year as his dark hair turned to salt and pepper and the faint frown lines by his eyes became laugh lines instead. I didn't picture him hidden away on an island though—it just didn't fit.

I murmured, "No matter how hard I try I can't visualize you sequestered on some wild oasis. You have too many people relying on you. You love your birds too much. Your…vocation. You'd miss France."

Q's forehead furrowed. He gave the impression I'd guessed right on every account. He may be well travelled and crave silence and space occasionally, but he was a French man to the last drop of blood. He would miss the local cuisine, the language. He would miss the seasons, and the satisfaction of his unique charity.

I would miss all of that, too. His life was now mine, and it couldn't be more perfect. I couldn't wait to help others, or be by his side while playing a real life game of monopoly. My university degree would be put to use, and I'd finally earn my place.

He chuckled, shedding some of the stress in his eyes. "Stupid idea, right?" He picked a non-existent piece of lint off his trousers. "I thought it was the only place I would find what I was looking for. That I could stop lying to myself and running from a past I can't forget." He suddenly looked up, his gaze blazing with jade fire. "I've grown up since then. There *is* no running, only accepting. I found what I needed the moment you entered my life. And as much as I dislike that the chateau belonged to my father, I finally have the inclination to turn it from his to ours."

Ours.

Ours.

My lungs stuck together. "Ours?" I breathed.

Q twisted his body to face me. "Yes. Ours. Yours. Mine. *Ours.*" He gently took my hand, squeezing hard. "I no longer need *Volière*. Next time I speak to Frederick, I'll get him to draw up the papers to sell it."

I managed to suck in a reedy breath even as my eyes popped wide. "Just because you won't retire there doesn't mean you have to sell it." I looked to where our hands were joined and couldn't contain the sharp spasm of lust and love. "Keep it. I hate to think of that perfect wilderness being ruined."

Q chuckled. "You were there for a moment. You can't have grown attached." His gaze dropped from my eyes to my mouth, turning the faint awareness into something tangible and throbbing.

I licked my bottom lip, quickly becoming drunk on the thought of kissing him.

Q stiffened; his fingers clamped fiercely around mine. His eyes remained on my mouth. "If you want me to keep it, I will."

"Just like that."

"Juste comme ça." Just like that. His gaze flickered up, drawing fire and the beautiful wonderful feeling of want. I'd

missed the flush; worried I'd be destined to be cold and lifeless inside. Q ran the pad of his thumb over my knuckles, sending shivers arching over my skin.

My entire body grew heavy, lethargic, spreading with warm, scrumptious anticipation. What were we talking about? Ah, yes, *Volière*. "I'll never get used to your wealth."

Q unwound my fingers from his, moving his palm to my hip. I jolted at the fierce shock of him touching me. Every second that passed the car fogged with whatever built between us. It dewed on my eyelashes, spreading lazy fronds through my heart.

Q's hand drifted down my side where the seat-belt fastened. With his eyes locked on mine, he pressed the button and released me. The car continued to drift forward through traffic, shuttling us to who knew where in our own private world.

Tugging me forward, Q murmured, "Well, you better get used to it because it's all yours. No pre-nups, no stupid documents or lawyers. As far as I'm concerned, every euro is yours."

He didn't stop pulling until I slid into his lap. Every inch I travelled over his rock hard thighs, I struggled to catch my breath. I existed purely on the lust-filled cognizance budding between us. "I can't take it."

I couldn't take a penny from this man. Not after he'd given me so much. Even now he gave me so much in the form of remembrance—bringing my body back to life, filling me with liquid heat and joy.

Q's right. Getting married with the clouds hanging over our heads was a mistake. The clouds were building, thickening, filling with threatening thunder and lightning. The storm would ruin our fragile happiness in one strike. I didn't want to risk losing this. Losing *him.*

I'd already lost myself—still trying to wiggle through the bars of my captivity to grasp freedom. I would never be the fierce young woman I'd been. I had to find who I was *now,* before I could give Q everything.

Q captured my hand, spinning the new ring on my wedding finger. The diamonds danced and pranced, set perfectly in wing-shaped gold.

"Knowing there's a tracker in there—knowing I'll always have you close, is the only reason why my migraines have given me a reprieve." Q's voice barely rose above a whisper. "You've cured me in so many ways, *esclave*, but you've ruined me in so many others." He brought my hand to his mouth, kissing my knuckles with barely hidden reverence.

"How? How have I ruined you?" I tingled where our bodies touched. His arm rested around my back, holding me close while his chest and legs cushioned me like a living chair.

Q chuckled, bringing his head up to nuzzle my throat. "In so many fucking ways. You've proven I'm not untouchable." I shivered as the tip of his tongue licked me. "You've taught me how vulnerable I truly am."

My head fell back as he tugged on the ends of my hair, forcing me to arch in his arms. "You're not vulnerable, Q. Not ever."

His teeth grazed across my neck and for a millisecond my heart raced with fear instead of lust. The sharpness of his teeth sent my lungs suffocating for breath.

If only I needed pain like I used to. If only I could accept what he would give. There was no doubt Q would eventually want to hurt me. It was who he was. Who I loved.

And when that day came, I would whimper and fight and pretend I loved every moment of it. I would force myself to come for him. I would train my body to accept and hide the stark reality that I no longer lusted for pain. He would never know. He never needed to realize my sacrifice or gift.

The pinpricks of his teeth disappeared—soothed by a worshiping lick. "I am. Terribly."

I moaned as his large hand teased up my side, his thumb stroking me in ever widening circles.

"You're not. You're the strongest, bravest—" My brain

stopped working as his thumb found my nipple, whispering around it in perfect possession.

Q's breathing increased until hot puffs tickled my neck with temptation. The swirling of his touch scrambled my coherency and I let myself drift—let myself come undone by his control.

"Pour la première fois de ma vie je suis vulnérable, parce que je suis tombée amoureuse." For the first time in my life I'm vulnerable, all because I fell in love.

Mouth. Hands. Tongue.

Sounds ceased to exist. The hum of the tyres on the road faded; the stop and sway of the vehicle didn't enter our realm of superb synchronicity. Every second brought a heavy blanket around us, drawing tight, shutting out the world.

"They took you. Those motherfuckers took what I treasured the most." His lips pressed against my throat, then collarbone, then shoulder. "They tore my heart out. *You* tore my heart out by making me care so much." His voice wavered with a mixture of strength and weakness.

My heart broke for him. I'd lived my own hell but Q had his own nightmares to bear. "Tell me…talk to me."

Touch. Breath. Lick.

Q suddenly grabbed my knee, twisting me to straddle him. With my legs spread over his lap, he thrust upward, grinding his erection against the tight web of my jeans. The dark look in his eyes was possessed, consumed with the desire to be inside me—to join us while we were linked by this brittle connection.

"I'm not ready," he growled. "Not ready." His face contorted with barely restrained violence; his cock twitched, craving me just as I craved him.

He'd spoken the truth. The unwilling truth. *Will we ever be ready to rip ourselves open and bring our devils to light?*

Lips. Heat. Mouth.

I stiffened, trying to keep my thoughts from knotting into an incomprehensible ball. "Will you ever be?"

I moaned loudly as his hand fisted my hair, holding my

head tight and unmovable. His beautiful features flashed with rage so bright and vibrant, I sucked in a breath of pure terror.

Q glared, wrenching all my fear and ghosts to the surface. "I'll be ready when you are, *esclave*. A life for a life. A tale for a tale."

I didn't have time to breathe before his lips descended on mine and my brain died an ambrosial death. His taste shot right through my heart, body, and soul, entering every molecule. He touched the nucleus of who I was, smashing through the chains, bulldozing through the wreckage of my tower, and picking me up in his ever strong arms.

I found one piece of myself in that shattered wasteland of my psyche: I remembered the luscious taste of violence.

Pulling. Sucking. Licking.

Every slippery swirl of his tongue resonated and throbbed in my pussy.

Q groaned as I went from submissive and obeying to needing and demanding. My arms wrapped around his head, gluing his mouth to mine, making sure he would never get free. My core melted, sending pinwheels and sparklers igniting in my blood.

I bruised us. I tasted the almost foreign flavour of metallic from my teeth slicing my bottom lip. I kissed him harder than I'd ever kissed before.

Our breathing tangled, our hands became separate entities as we groped and stroked and pinched.

I'm ready, I wanted to say. *I'm ready to share my tale just so I can learn yours. I want to know you. Every part of you. I want to own you.*

Q forced my mouth wider, his tongue almost choking me he kissed so deep. I duelled him, waging a battle, trying to win the war on who would break and speak the loathsome truth first.

My jaw ached, my nipples screamed to have his mouth sucking. My pussy twinged and throbbed for him to fill—to turn me from empty to full.

I was ready. I was strong. I wanted to talk.

The indecision and unknowing had to stop. We'd cinched our lives together—it was time we started trusting and pulled the ends of our connection tight, stitching ourselves together forever.

I panted as Q broke the kiss. Crashing back to earth, I noticed how wild and enthralled we'd been—how transcended from mortal bodies the kiss had taken us. Q sucked up all the energy in the car, consuming me. All I could see was him. Not the wondrous view, or the quaint buildings streaming past the window. Just him. Always *him*.

My jeans were unbuttoned, Q's hand half in my knickers, trying to touch me. My own hand cupped his cock through his trousers; my fingers white from squeezing him so hard. Q's lips were red and wet while his hair stuck up in all directions.

He'd never looked so sexy or tempting.

Never breaking eye contact, Q reached behind me to the intercom button. With a smile dancing on his lips, he growled, "Take us to the closest hotel, Franco. I need to do something rather urgently."

I was hot then cold.

Excited then afraid.

Turned on then repulsed.

My heart went from thrumming with life to a lump of unmovable muscle.

The thrill of wanting, craving, *panting* for Q to deliver what he'd started in the limo wouldn't stay constant. Confusion doused me, hesitation chilled me.

Franco pulled the car to a halt outside some huge fancy hotel. All whitewashed and pristine, it glittered with mocking purity. I instantly hated it. I felt too dirty, too messed up to enter such an immaculate establishment. I missed *Volière*. It was chaotic and unkempt and forgiving. The polar opposite of this place.

Q hastily smoothed his trousers, running a hand through his hair to hide the obviousness of what we'd been doing.

We were here. We were about to go somewhere just the two of us. Q would take me in his way. He would hurt me.

I bit my lip, looking out the window. I couldn't let him see my desire swiftly becoming fear.

"Do you know why you're tied up?" Leather Jacket's voice hissed in my ear. *"It's so we can do what you did to those girls but ten times worse."*

Oxygen. I suddenly couldn't get enough.

Stop. This is Q. The man you would die for. Does it matter the thought of a belt or whip terrifies you? You're doing this for him—not you.

The pep-talk granted me enough sanity and peace to suck in a much needed breath.

Franco shut off the engine, then came to open my door. Sunshine bounced inside, taking with it the remaining dark awareness ebbing between Q and me.

I looked at Q briefly, suffering a full body jolt. His eyes were hooded, turbulent; his chest rising and falling with power. His entire soul reached across the car to touch me, warn me— threaten with just how much he needed me alone.

Franco took my hand, helping me from the car. Q's eyes dropped to where Franco held me; his jaw clenched. He didn't like anyone touching me—least of all strangers—but he smothered his temper, allowing Franco some leniency.

"Ready to go?" Franco asked, tugging my fingers. Breaking eye contact with Q, I allowed Franco to guide me from the vehicle. His large hand was warm and dry, effortlessly hoisting me upward.

"Thank you," I said, letting him go the moment I stood.

Franco stared, his bright green eyes probing mine. His lips parted as a thought flashed across his face. Leaning in, he said quickly, "I've never spoken about what Q did to find you, but you're stupid to let the fear keep you hostage. If you saw what he's capable of….You wouldn't be fearing anyone but the monster in your bed."

Q climbed out, slamming the door behind him. He came forward, glowering at Franco.

"*As-tu fini?*" Are you quite done? Q's anger lashed us, snarling the tropical air into a turbulent eddy. "Can I have her back now? Or are you planning on taking her out to dinner?"

"Q…he was only being—"

"I don't fucking care what he was being."

Franco shrugged. "She's my boss too, you know. Have to keep the employers happy." Two very strong and opinionated male egos clashed. Lowering his head, Franco glared under his brow. "Keep your anger for those who deserve it, Mercer."

Franco gave me a smile. "Like I said, you're safe with him and I'm always there as back-up."

Q coughed as if he couldn't believe Franco's nerve.

My emotions toward Q's head of security were mixed. At the beginning I'd hated him, then I grew to care for him, seeing him as a loyal employee, but now…now I sensed he'd been initiated into Q's world a bit too well. He seemed dangerous— wearing the same edginess and unpredictability that Q did. Whatever happened in their hunt to find me, Franco had adopted the darkness.

I doubted Suzette would be pleased. I always had a suspicion she had a little crush on Franco. I knew Suzette was madly in love with my husband to be, but it wasn't sexual love, more like a saviour complex, kind of love.

"That's comforting to know. Thank you." I pressed against Q, trying to unwind the tightness in his body.

I wanted to ask what Q had done in Brazil, but a grisly still-warm heart leapt into my mind and suddenly I didn't want to know—I had enough filth inside my brain.

Q bared his teeth. "Yes, very comforting. Now fuck off and flirt with someone else's woman. I won't need you for the rest of the night."

Franco splayed his hands, brushing away the angst between them. "Book me a room, and I'll stay out of your way.

You know my number if something happens." Giving me a small salute, he grinned. "Enjoy your evening. Don't say I didn't warn you about whom to fear."

"Franco! *As-tu perdu la tête, putain?*" Have you lost your fucking mind? Q was absolutely livid. His eyes narrowed to slits, muttering something incomprehensible under his breath.

I didn't get a chance to say goodbye as Q grabbed my elbow, charging me toward the entrance. I looked over my shoulder, relieved to see Franco laughing, fully enjoying getting a rise out of Q. At least he hadn't quit or aimed a gun at Q's back.

"Q, it's okay. He was only trying to—"

"I know what he was trying to do, and it damn well worked. Fucking idiot." He nodded tersely at a man in a green suit who opened the large glass doors for us. "I have no right to be pissed off, yet I can't stop it. Guess I'll have to apologise."

I shivered as we walked from island heat into freezing air-conditioning of a five star glitzy hotel. I wanted to say something—anything to have the Q who'd been so gentle and forthcoming come back.

There were many forms of pain, and right now my heart was suffering.

"Pain is your only option, puta. *Hit her."*

I closed my eyes for a second, slapping the voices away.

Q stalked through the hotel lobby, dragging me in his terrible wake. Needing to find normal again, I asked, "Do you own this hotel, too?" I blinked, focusing on the imposing pillars, the ginormous potted plants, and grand piano with expensive looking cocktail bar to the right. The lobby spoke of island tranquillity and exoticness.

All this—this wealth—came with the package of being with Q. I still struggled to get used to it.

Q slammed to a halt, yanking me against him.

Instantly my heart clawed up my throat. The burning, searing awareness of his erection dug against my belly. His eyes looked too ferocious to be gentle.

He's going to hit you. The minute you're behind closed doors he'll strike.

I wanted so much for the rush of wetness between my legs. The intoxication of lust in my blood.

"You wouldn't like that would you, *esclave?* Yet another property; yet another possession." He shook his head. *"Je ne comprends pas pourquoi tu détestes autant l'argent."* I don't understand why you hate money so much.

My heart pumped harder as a few guests glanced over, their faces freezing in judgement. To anyone who didn't know us, the way Q held me would look like a bad argument or worse, domestic violence.

"Q, don't be so rough. You'll have security asking questions."

He growled, "I'd like to see them probe into affairs that aren't any of their goddamn business."

I couldn't stop the knotting of my stomach or the slight queasiness of Q's temper. Something else must've upset him. Franco couldn't have riled him up this much. Could he?

Wishing I could force him to look *at* me instead of *through* me, I whispered, "Is everything alright?"

"Don't speak to me," Q muttered. His tone tightly controlled and ice cold.

I've done something wrong.

I was sure of it.

He's guessed.

No, that couldn't be possible. *Please, don't let that be possible.* Only moments ago he'd been sweet and kind and very much together. Would I always suffer whiplash where his mercurial emotions were concerned?

Looking around at the milling guests, I hissed, "Stop making a spectacle, Q. People are looking."

"They can look all they want. And to answer your question, no, I don't own this hotel. If I did, I would've kicked everyone out by now so I could teach you a lesson right here."

My eyes flared. "Teach *me* a lesson? What the hell did I do?" My lungs worked harder, saturating my blood with anger, ready to fight, ready to retaliate.

"You—you....Goddammit, I don't know." He sighed. The blazing fire in his gaze snuffed out, becoming human once again.

My own temper fizzled. Taking a risk, I rested a palm over his heart. "Take me to a room. Use me to forget whatever's upsetting you."

Use your chains. Use your scissors. Use whatever you want.

Before the image would've made me throb for a release. Now...now I vibrated to avoid it.

His shoulders tightened. "I've wanted you since you woke up screaming this morning." His hand imprisoned mine, pressing my fingers harder against his chest. "I won't hold back. I *can't* hold back. Tell me now if that's going to be an issue."

Tears rushed my spine. Sadness filled my heart.

Yes, it's an issue. But no, I won't tell you.

Stepping into the role of Old Tess, I murmured, "I want you. I need you to hurt me, Q. I need to remember."

Q's back snapped straight. With a fierce kiss, he dragged me the rest of the way to reception in a flurry of footsteps.

The woman behind the desk was gorgeous with long black hair, thick eyelashes, and moon-sized eyes. She radiated an aura of strength and independence—exactly the type of woman Q admitted he liked—someone who wasn't broken. Someone who would fight him.

A sharp band of jealousy struck from nowhere as the woman smiled at my master, batting those ridiculously thick eyelashes. I watched Q carefully, trying to read how affected he was by her.

He didn't even glance at her. Dropping my elbow, he snatched his wallet from his back pocket, yanking out a credit card. Handing it over, he ordered, "The best room you have available and a suite for a colleague."

The receptionist's mouth parted slightly as she took the credit card, eyeing Q with interest. Her smile encompassed coyness rather than professionalism. I welcomed the snarl in my stomach. I loved the ignition of rage. *Adored* my willingness to fight.

It was so different to hurting the women in Rio. This I would gladly start and end.

Something shifted in me. Something small but fundamental as I took back a piece of my life—acknowledging my urge to hurt another.

"Is there a problem?" I said, dragging the girl's eyes to mine. I had the sudden need to smooth my hair. I wished I wore a tailored dress or some exorbitantly expensive jewels. I felt so *ordinary* next to Q. But he was mine.

Hands off, bitch.

Her smile froze, turning to brittle efficiency. "No. No problem."

We both jumped as Q slapped the counter. "When I asked for a room, I want it now, not tomorrow."

The woman narrowed her eyes, bending to look at the computer screen. The cattiness and female challenge between us faded as her interest in Q died a quick death thanks to his rudeness.

After a second, she said, "We only have the Presidential suite available."

"Fine. Book it."

"How many nights will you be staying?" She fluttered those obnoxious lashes in Q's direction.

"Not sure. Keep it open-ended."

Her eyes popped wide; I swallowed back my smugness. Q was dangerous. He was dark. But he was also the most generous, sexy, powerful man I'd ever met.

Happiness ballooned as Q glanced my way. He didn't acknowledge me, but we were linked too deep. We belonged.

I'm the luckiest girl in the world.

"Um, well. We can't just *hold* it. It's four thousands euros a night. Should I book for the one night, or a week, or what?"

Q bristled, electrifying the air. "Charge me whatever you want but give me the keys." His eyes fell on me, melting the ice in my blood, turning me into a flickering candle ready to burn.

Holy crap. It wasn't often that I blushed. But damn, Q set my cheeks on fire.

The girl dropped her eyes, her fingers flying over the keyboard.

A moment later, Q fisted the old-fashioned key she held up, and dragged me like his hard-won prey toward the elevator.

"I'll keep the other key here for your colleague. Oh by the way, dinner is included in the room rate. I'll advise your butler to confirm your menu selections," the woman called after us.

Q slammed to halt, spinning back toward her. "If anyone interrupts us, I'll have this entire hotel bulldozed to the ground. No dinner. No reservation. No menus. Nothing." A smile decorated his face, struggling to project a businessman rather than a beast. *"Merci."*

I didn't say a word as we rushed to the elevators. He punched the 'up' button. His fingers tightened around mine until mini-heartbeats pounded in time with my fear.

The lift pinged. We entered.

One second.

Two seconds.

No one else entered.

Three seconds.

Four seconds.

The doors closed.

The lift hadn't moved before Q launched himself at me.

Grabbing my hips, he hoisted me upward, slamming my back against the mirrored panelling. Instinctively my legs wrapped around his body, joining us tightly together.

The second Q rested between my legs, he thrust upward, grinding himself violently against me. His glowing eyes captured mine, his mouth tightening into a grimace. "Fuck, I'm hard. Can you feel it? Fucking hell, Tess. *Qu'est-ce que t'es en train de me faire?"*

What are you doing to me?

The air no longer held oxygen, only need.

I bent my head to kiss him, but he denied me his lips. Tilting my face, I managed to find his cheek, then throat, then ear. Tracing my tongue around the shell and fleshy lobe, I murmured, "You need to be in me. *I* need you to be in me."

He growled, driving up harder. The beads of my spine throbbed against the unforgiving mirror.

"You have no fucking idea, *esclave*. Needing you frays my patience. Needing to come makes me insane. I'm running out of control." His voice dripped with black desire—stealing thoughts straight out of my head.

My ears roared with blood; I grew wet with every uncontrolled and savage thrust. I relished the melting, hoping against hope I remained turned on. Fear had no place here. Not while I had the man who'd saved my life between my legs.

Q's anger switched to feral desire. I latched onto his strength, keeping myself locked in delectable lust.

I moaned as Q fisted my hair, giving him access to my throat. His wet mouth covered the sore brand and the stinging pain of an unhealed wound sent a tangle of terror through me.

I wanted to be with him—more than anything. I wanted to feel him inside me. I wanted to hold him close and have his body blanket mine. I wanted to feel safe.

"Hit her, puta. *Kill her,* puta. *Obey us!"*

"Goddammit, *esclave*. I need you. I need—" Q's breathing was ragged, harsh. His hand dropped from my hair to my breast, cupping me with vicious fingers. Sensitivity erupted to agony; I bit my lip, scrambling to keep hold of desire.

I'm not strong enough.

My eyes squeezed. I willed my body not to expose me.

In some far away universe, the elevator doors opened.

An embarrassed cough.

It sounded out of place to the heavy breathing and absorbed world we lived in.

Q twisted his head. "Ah, fuck me," he grumbled. His hips withdrew from mine and the violence of his touch receded to let me slither down his body and land on my feet.

An elderly man in an immaculate tuxedo, bowed. His black eyes looked flustered, shining with wry amusement. "I believe you booked the Presidential suite. I'm the butler, Andre."

I gawked, unable to act normal while so much intensity bubbled in my blood.

Q however slipped into egotistical businessman, dragging me from the lift. "Yes, we're staying in the suite. No, we don't need anything. You're dismissed for the rest of the night. Thank you for your time."

The butler bowed again, his lips turning up ever so slightly. "I'll be on extension 232 if you require anything." Entering the lift we'd just vacated, he smiled. "Good day to you both."

The doors shut but it didn't cut off the small peel of laughter.

My heart hadn't had time to stop racing; my hands shook. Once I entered that room, I could no longer be weak. I could no longer indulge in the horror and memories drowning me.

Q believed I was the perfect masochist to his sadistic needs.

I am that girl.

I am.

"Nosy old bastard," Q muttered, fishing the key from his pocket. The entire floor housed the Presidential suite. There was only one door, and Q attacked it with the key. It swung open thanks to a well-placed kick.

I laughed softly. "He didn't exactly want to see two people groping each other. Hazards of the job I can imagine."

Q lassoed my wrist, yanking me into the room. With a dark smile, he slammed the door and spun me against the wall. The second my back hit resistance, Q froze. His eyes fixed me in place, adding more bubbles to my blood.

I forced myself to relax. *Give in.* I had to trust him and let go completely.

Don't tense.

I had to trust in my strength to survive whatever he would do.

He can't know.

Our breathing accelerated, filling the suite with overwhelming tension. Q raised his arm, slowly, so, so slowly, dragging out the anticipation until I quivered against the wall.

"Where were we before we were interrupted?" His eyes fell to my brand, his jaw locking. Something animalistic flickered over his face, transforming him into something far scarier than human. "Seeing my mark on your skin—it does things to me, Tess. It affects me here." He thwacked his chest with a fist. "It calms me here." He tapped his temple.

Q was so strong and invincible but beneath it all he was insecure—just like me. He needed daily affirmations that I wouldn't leave. That I wouldn't lock him out like before.

We were the same.

We need to talk.

Q reached forward, running his fingertips along my jaw. In their wake, he left me on fire. My heart scurried faster and faster, hurling itself to its doom.

"So many things I want. So many things I need to do." Q's fingers trailed down my throat, making their lazy way to hold my neck hostage.

My hands balled by my sides; my breathing turned fast and reedy. I didn't say a word. I couldn't.

He's going to hurt you. Spank you. Bite you.

The panic was worse than the pain and out of nowhere a familiar tug happened deep inside. A tug of promise—a shelter where I'd once hidden.

The tower.

Horror shoved away the first brick sliding into place. *No!*

Never again would I shut myself off. No matter what I went through I couldn't go back into that circular prison. I wouldn't find my way out again.

Q's fingers squeezed, reminding me of the day he'd strapped me to the cross and waited to see how far I'd let him go.

I couldn't stomach the stretching tautness. If I let Q draw out the connection, he'd taste my reluctance.

I did the only thing I could.

I threw myself at him.

Q's fingers broke away from my throat, falling to his side as I jumped on him. He grunted as my body weight knocked his balance, making him stagger backward.

I was the one taking. I was the one reclaiming our relationship and even though I knew pain would be forthcoming, I relished the power at the surprise in Q's eyes.

But then it was gone. Replaced with fierce lust and unfathomable possession.

"Fuck, Tess." That was all Q managed before I slammed my mouth against his, shutting him up. He groaned as I wrapped my legs around him just like in the lift.

His biceps rippled, holding my weight, only to spin me around and smash me against the opposite wall.

I clawed at his back, hoping to enrage him enough to use me fast and hard. Fast because as much as I wanted him, I wanted it over quickly. Fast was good—fast hid everything slow would reveal.

His tongue lashed out, taking complete possession of my mouth. I squirmed closer, pulling his hair, forcing him to hurtle toward violence.

He growled as I reached down and grasped his cock as hard as I could.

"Fuck." His hips pistoned, crunching my wrist between us. My mouth opened in a silent scream but Q used the advantage to kiss me harder, deeper, wider.

"What are you?" he grunted, rocking into me.

"You're worthless. You belong to us. Withdrawal will make you do anything, obey anyone. You're ours."

My body jolted; I pressed harder against Q wanting to run from the abysmal thoughts.

"Answer me, *esclave*." Q's touch bruised, but he didn't raise his palm or reach for his belt.

"*Je suis à toi.*" I panted. Revelling in the freedom of the phrase, I repeated, "*Je suis à toi*, Q." I'm yours.

"Just like I'm yours." His passion poured down my throat to my heart, heating me, protecting me. His lips crushed mine, and his arms bunched, pulling me away from the wall. Blindly, he carried me, but a second later we crashed into a sideboard.

The hard wood smacked into my thighs; Q swore under his breath. With glazed eyes and need glowing on his face, he swiped an angry arm behind me, knocking off expensive porcelain and a vase holding cascading lilies.

The flowers teetered then committed suicide on the marble floor below. The tinkling of splintering glass and china mixed with our heavy breathing. Cold water splashed my legs, soaking into my jeans.

Q didn't give me time to look at the mess. His lips found mine, drowning me in his hunger. Hoisting me higher, he placed me on the sideboard, scooting me to the edge for easy reach. His lips tore from mine, his eyes latching onto my chest.

Bending over, he took the delicate material of my singlet in his mouth and tore it with his teeth. Once torn, he grabbed the neckline and ripped.

The cotton didn't stand a chance, shredding like gossamer to follow the same path the flowers had. I moaned as his mouth latched onto my nipple through my bra. I fought the anxiety in my blood, waiting for the sharp nip of teeth— knowing the slight onset of pain would undo all my wetness, turning me from willing to pretending.

"You taste so good. So fucking good," he growled, his fingers fumbling at the clasp. The hook sprang free, and Q jerked it off my body to toss over his shoulder. His eyes darkened from pale to smouldering. His jaw clenched as every muscle in his body locked into place. "Goddammit, you're too fucking perfect."

Reaching for me again, he pushed me back to taste. He manhandled me exactly how he wanted—using me like the perfect toy—*his* toy.

Every pull and suck of his mouth sent fire whooshing through my veins and into my core. Every lick and tease of his teeth made me forget.

Forget the voices. The pain. The suffering.

He became my entire world.

His lips left my nipple, leaving me cold and wet. His eyes charred my every thought.

With ruthless fingers, he attacked my jeans button. His knuckles brushed my clit through the material, sending a bolt of pleasure clenching my body.

Yes!

So long since I felt such inhibition. He granted immunity from everything but the selfishness of sex.

The zip released with one yank, then Q's fingers looped around the waistline.

He pulled. Hard.

I almost fell off the sideboard. Bracing my hands on the smooth wood, I arched my hips, giving him room to tear them down.

My thighs were moon-white, marked only by remnants of kicks and torture. They were only faint shadows but Q's eyes narrowed. Tracing the fading bruises, his face filled with harrowing rage. *"Jamais. Ils ne prendront plus jamais ce qui est à moi."* Never again. Never will they take what's mine.

My heart sank further into my body, hiding from his temper; it came alive again as a burst of tenderness softened his features.

He leaned over, descending his mouth to the sensitive skin of my hip. With a slice of sharp canines, he decimated the scrap of lace.

My mind whirled as I sat fully naked before him. Q froze, drinking me in.

"Destroying my clothes again?" I breathed. Loving his lust—the ferocity and abandonment. He was loving me like I needed him to: full of passion and no pain.

"It's only fair seeing as you destroyed my fucking heart." He kissed me, making me swallow his words.

With strong hands he spread my knees, placing himself between my legs. I fumbled with his belt, cursing the rush of nostalgia and regret. I missed the lust at the thought of him using the leather. I missed the fuckedupness that made me his.

Q pushed my hands away, unbuckling in one fast pull. I swallowed hard as he tore the belt free.

A moment hovered between us.

A moment where his eyes asked questions, and I kept mine from answering.

A moment where he ran the leather through his fingers, deliberating whether to use the still-warm belt as foreplay.

I fought the tremble; tussled with the truth.

If he chose to use it, I would accept. If he wanted it, I would obey.

Then the moment ended and Q hurled it away—his body twisted with the effort. His chest heaved as if the action drained his self-control beyond endurance. The heavy buckle crashed into something breakable in the distance, sending more noises of breaking china.

"I don't have time for games. I need you on my cock. Now."

With a furious jerk, he pulled off his trousers, underwear, and shoes in one swipe. His cock sprang free, glistening with pre-cum, beckoning with silky steel and promise of oblivion.

My mouth fell open at how gorgeous he was. How perfectly made and achingly divine.

Every muscle twitched with longing, sending euphoria waltzing through my veins.

My pussy throbbed; my breathing accelerated. I welcomed back the joy of wanting to come.

I needed to take back this part of my life.

I was ready.

I swayed forward, biting his shoulder only to receive a mouthful of cotton. My eyes were endlessly heavy as I looked up. "I need to see all of you."

Q clenched his teeth but allowed me to grab the hem and draw his t-shirt up. Up, up, revealing clouds, barbwire, and sparrows.

Every feather, every swirl of ink imprinted itself onto my heart. His tattoo encapsulated him like nothing else ever could.

"Q—" My hand lashed out, tightening around his erection. Images of eroticism and passion filled my mind as his heat scorched my palm.

His head fell back as a groan wrenched from his lungs.

My teeth ached; my blood hummed for connection.

Fill me!

My other hand dropped between his legs, cupping his tight balls. His eyes flared wide as I rolled the delicate heaviness in my fingers, wanting to bring him to his knees and serve him.

He thrust his hips into my hand, forcing his length back and forth. Every ripple of hardness, every ridge of his perfectly made cock sent my cells exploding.

"Do you want me, Tess?"

I bit my lip, nodding, transfixed by the velvet iron in my fist.

"It's yours, *esclave*. What do you want me to do with it?"

His transfer of ownership sent a flush of untainted happiness. "I want you deep inside me, *maître*."

His eyes snapped closed. "Fuck, I love hearing you say that." He cupped my pussy, his grip hard and possessive. "*Never forget it.*"

My neck couldn't hold the sudden density of my head. I cried out as one long, loving finger slipped inside me. Just one. Only one.

But I wanted to fucking explode.

"How much I've missed this. Missed your taste. Your sweet, sweet cunt," Q murmured, his eyes luminous with lust.

"Q—take me. Please—I beg you."

"You beg me?"

"You'll beg for more. Withdrawal is a bitch, and you'll beg, pretty girl. You wait."

I shook my head, scattering the thoughts.

"Yes. Fill me. Take me. Please—"

His cock lurched in my hands as I ran a thumb over the slippery tip. The slickness of his arousal turned me on beyond belief.

His finger withdrew, lulling me into a haze, then he thrust two fingers deep—stretching me with ownership.

The brief moment of slowness shattered as Q wrapped an arm around my shoulders, bringing me closer. His cock rippled in my touch, demanding something...demanding more.

His fingers massaged me deep, drawing more wetness and pinwheels of passion to radiate in my blood.

"Put my cock in you, *esclave*. Do it."

The sideboard put me at the perfect height; Q was so close to entering me.

Q removed his fingers, smearing the glistening liquid over the head of his erection. Seeing him touch himself was the final push I needed.

I wasn't Tess.

I wasn't a survivor or murderer or slave.

I was a woman drunk on the need to come.

One entity. One goal. One destination.

"God, I need to be inside you. So deep, so fucking deep," Q groaned.

My hips rolled forward as I guided the tip of him to press against my entrance. We both shuddered at the first connection.

Lifting me up with one arm, he positioned himself closer, spreading my folds with the thickness of his cock. With eyes locked, we froze at the temptation of sex. The room dripped with anticipation.

I bit my lip as he pushed forward, stretching, taking.

He stopped halfway. His eyes glittered, looking at where we joined. The basest of human acts, the rawest form of love.

Then the slowness and time for words disappeared as Q pulled back and with his face tightly controlled thrust hard.

One savage thrust filled me to the brim and something unlocked inside. The bricks of my tower scattered further as confidence filtered through my previous dread.

Tears sprang to my eyes—not because of pain or weakness but because of pure paradisiac joy.

Joy of being taken. Joy of belonging.

Q reeled off oaths under his breath, jerking me closer, pressing deeper.

I went floppy in his arms, focused only on him. His pelvic bone pressed against mine, rubbing my clit so perfectly an orgasm sparked from nowhere.

No build-up. No warning.

"Oh, God." I grabbed his neck, needing something to hold onto while the cyclone of pleasure built in my core. Q groaned as he fucked me. Hard and strong and delicious.

My pussy squeezed, intent on one thing, leaving me floundering.

Q's hands latched onto my hips, holding me firm, allowing him to thrust harder.

My breasts bounced as my body rocked on the wood. I leaned backward, bracing myself against the wall as he pulled my legs to wrap around his body.

The moment my legs locked around him, he surged upward. His cock hit places that acted as a trigger to the fiercest cyclone in history.

Tightening, swirling, building, sparking.

My mouth parted as a ragged moan erupted from my lungs.

"Fuck, yes," Q yelled, his fingernails digging into flesh. He drove harder, stroking my pussy until every inch of me thrummed like an entire chorus of typhoons.

There was no pain.

Nothing but sweet, sweet pleasure.

I couldn't stop it. I didn't want to stop it.

I didn't ask permission or delay.

I gave myself over to the unravelling storm inside.

I came.

Every band of release made me shudder in his arms, and I was only vaguely aware of the world outside.

Q fucked harder, growling louder.

I didn't care about anything but the intense waves of pleasure wringing me dry.

"Goddammit, Tess. Fuck it. Take me." His voice was far away. I became nothing more than a vessel for him to come into. My soul was elsewhere, living in prolonged bliss. My thoughts were dust and ash.

Pain.

A flash of horrendous pain.

My eyes flew open. The wondrous storm switched to angry squalls—lashing me with darkness and hell.

I was ice cold.

I was terrified.

Q planted both hands on the sideboard, driving into me almost possessed. All I could focus on was the blooming red handprint on my thigh where he'd spanked me.

And then he came.

Rhythmic spurts, shuddering muscles, lust so violent it looked otherworldly on his anger-flushed face.

He'd hit me to come.

He'd needed to punish me to find release.

He took his pleasure from my pain.

The bricks I'd tried so hard to destroy lurched into formation. The foundation of the tower went from rubble to stacked in a blink.

My tower wanted to claim me again. It wanted to save me.

The pain made me want to hide.

With a war-cry, I smashed the cylindrical prison and prayed with everything I had left that I was strong enough.

Strong enough to survive.
Strong enough to survive Q.

Chapter Four

Stroke me, provoke me, adore me, I implore thee, take all of me, ensnare me, play me to your tune

The release wasn't enough.

It'd been too quick, too tame.

Even as I'd driven deep inside Tess, coming hard and fast, I knew it wouldn't sate me for long.

It wouldn't sate me because it'd been *normal*. Fucking vanilla. Sex wasn't what gave me pleasure and got me off. It was the dominance—the role-play, the mind games, the linking of masculine and feminine through bodily control.

The one strike I'd delivered had been enough to send me over the edge, but not enough to stop the churning in my gut for more. I needed worse. I needed dirty.

I sighed, throwing an arm over my eyes.

Tess was still in the bathroom. She'd been in there for at least forty minutes.

What the fuck was she doing?

My eyes travelled around the suite. From the bedroom, I could see most of the lounge and part of the drawing room where dinner and business meetings were concluded. Each room took up a colossal amount of space with huge windows bordering the view of the seaside, colourful umbrellas, and lobster-red sunbathers.

I threw myself back onto the covers, staring at the ceiling. The suite consisted of soothing shades of white: eggshell, alabaster, and chalk. I knew because the hotel stupidly provided a decoration guide complete with drapery design, carpet blends, and colour swatches.

As if I'd come here for fucking decorating advice.

I'd flicked through the magazine after rolling it up into a tube, testing it as a spanking device. I'd discarded it because the slick glossy pages were too heavy—it would bruise. And although I wanted Tess to pant and a few tears to be shed, I also hated the thought of marking her. Which twisted my gut with perplexity.

I missed the straight forwardness of before. The joy at knowing Tess could take it. Now, I had no fucking idea what she wanted or even what *I* wanted.

Did I want to hurt her?

Yes. Fuck, yes.

Did I want to make her cry?

Yes. I loved her tears.

Did I want to protect her and never lay another finger on her?

More than anything.

I would've castrated myself if it meant I could be free of the evil lurking in my blood. Tess didn't deserve any of that. Tess deserved to be made love to. Not fucked. Not used by a man who had issues deeper than the fucking ocean.

The door opened.

Tess came out of the bathroom. I sucked in a breath as she made her way toward the bed. Her naked body was flushed and scrubbed. Droplets from the shower sparkled in the late afternoon sunshine streaming through the window.

My eyes dropped to the red outline of my hand on her

thigh.

Ah, shit. Seeing the mark tangled my conscience into further chaos. My heart raced in bitter regret, while my cock leapt with fucking joy. The blush. The thrill. The knowledge I'd put it there sickened as well as bewitched me.

I wanted more.

No, you don't, you sick bastard.

My eyes fell to the ugly yellows and greens mottling her skin. Fading abuse from other bastards like me who got off on abusing women.

How can I be like them? How could I hurt the woman who owned my soul?

I struggled to suck in a breath as Tess climbed gracefully on the bed, carefully avoiding my eyes. Every movement was understated, carefully orchestrated as if she was invisible. Her hair was coiled upward while damp strands escaped, sticking to her neck. Her spine stood out, her collarbone a stark necklace. She looked so innocent and young.

But strong. So fucking strong.

I waited to see if she'd come to me. My arms throbbed to hold her. I wanted her to curl against me and let me guard her—I would be her protection so the nightmares would never find her.

But she didn't come closer.

With a soft sigh, she reclined against a pillow, staring upward. Her eyes were large and lost. Her face tense and timid.

My blood boiled. What had she been thinking about in the bathroom? Something had to have happened for her to become so withdrawn.

It didn't make sense. I hadn't hurt her. I knew she'd enjoyed me taking her. She'd come. She'd wanted what we'd shared. I knew that with utmost certainty. Her release had milked my cock, telling me blatantly how much she enjoyed it.

So why? Why the silence and sadness?

Confusion itched my muscles, making my temper flare.

"*Plus de secrets, esclave.*" No more secrets.

Tess looked over, her eyes filling with warmth. "No secrets. Just tired."

Damn fucking *lies.*

The large bed created a barrier between us. Lies filled the silence, secrets distanced us—pushing us further and further away.

I'm done.

Nothing would stop me from cracking open her mind and finding out the truth. I was done fucking waiting.

Throwing myself off the bed, I prowled around the mattress toward Tess. My cock hung heavy between my legs, reminding me I had plenty more to give. I'd use it to break her. I'd drive her mad with wanting and then I'd ask. I'd *demand* to know.

Tess's eyes closed, either blatantly ignoring me or hiding yet more secrets.

"*Esclave.* Get up," I ordered.

Her gaze flashed open; she sucked in a gasp. Her vision drifted down my chest, over sparrows and ink to latch onto my rapidly growing erection.

It jerked under her inspection, begging for her wet heat.

Tess froze; something flickered across her face but then was gone. For a split second clouds rolled over the sun, drenching her in shadow, painting her face with grief. But then the sun broke through, and she smiled.

Her body moved like water, slinking and rising from the pool of bedding to stand before me. Fuck, she was stunning. And mine. *All mine.*

I locked my muscles to stop myself from reaching for her as she came to stand before me. Every moment echoed with strength then shyness. Rebellion then obedience. Her entire demeanour played havoc with my head.

One moment I saw the woman I fell for, the next all I saw was prey. Prey I wanted to molest and break and bend to whatever sick fantasy I desired.

My jaw locked as she raised her chin, looking me in the

eye. I wanted her to bow to me. To serve. To let me do whatever I damn well pleased.

Everything inside—everything I'd been missing—sprang back to life. My soul that'd been scarred and tattered thanks to Tess's abduction slithered away, leaving me angry. So fucking angry.

The anger started as a burn in my heart—a spark with a flash of gasoline, erupting into a flame, igniting my blood until my entire body set alight with furious need.

I needed to take Tess ruthlessly and painfully. I needed to remember who I truly was at heart. She might have let me brand her and accept my callous ways, but I'd held back. All my life I'd held back.

And every time I did, it layered more darkness in my gut. Building into something manic. Tess had let me use her, but it was nothing, *nothing,* compared to what I wanted now.

"Je suis désolé." I'm sorry.

Her lips parted, her skin whitening.

My arms banded around her—picking her up in a vice. "I'm not done with you, *mon coeur.*" My heart.

My mouth stole hers; my legs almost buckled at the fresh taste of her shower, cloaking the muskiness of spent desire.

Her lips went slack, allowing my tongue to dip inside her mouth. I groaned as she kissed me back. Her hands left the ramrod position by her sides, coming to rest on my hips. Her fingernails scratched my skin, dragging me forward until my lips bruised hers in a searing kiss.

"Q—please—"

Her beg wobbled with passion…no, wait—

My heart squeezed in panic.

It can't be. It couldn't happen.

I pulled back, glaring. I searched for some sign—some hint she wasn't coping. Her blue-grey eyes stared back. For the first time since I'd met her, I couldn't sense what riotous emotions she kept hidden.

Did she mean what she said? Or was that a lie, too?

She was unreadable.

The panic morphed to rage; I dragged her against me. My lips latched onto hers, kissing her hard. I tried to break her perfect façade. I wanted to crawl down her fucking throat and steal her heart and soul forever, so I'd always know her innermost hellions.

The monster inside—the one who lay dormant for weeks—came roaring back to life.

Control.

Smash her. Test her. Force her to give you her fears.

The sickly entice slithered in my blood, whispering of blackness and violence.

She won't tell you unless you make her.

Wasn't it my right to know everything about her? I had blood on my hands for her—the least she could do was talk to me—let me inside her soul.

It is your right. Just like her screams and pain are yours.

I shook my head, dispelling the rapidly building darkness. I never listened to the monster—why was I granting it power now?

Because you can't help what you want. Take it. Stop fighting.

Shit, I was losing control.

I shouldn't have let myself get so wound up. I should've taken my time before, drawing out the moment, giving me the chance to keep the infernal beast wrapped in chains where it belonged.

Tess kept something hidden—I sensed it on a carnal level. I didn't know what'd changed but it called to me—twisting me inside out until I slipped further away from right and into wrong.

Something was different. Something I couldn't see or hear or touch, but it drove me insane.

My fingers crept up, latching around Tess's throat. Her muscles worked hard as she swallowed. Her eyes were empty orbs—empty of fear or lust or love.

I fucking hated it.

"What have you done?" I ran my nose down her cheek, inhaling the scent of expensive hotel soap. Maybe I could smell the truth. Maybe then I might find out what she was hiding.

She squeaked as I spun her around, backing her into the lounge. Every step she took, the urge to give myself over grew stronger. It'd never been this bad before. This *insistent.*

Her fingers locked around my wrist, holding on while her feet moved backward. "Q..."

"Tell me, Tess. Tell me what you did." *Tell me how I ruined you.* Because I had. There was no other reason for the way she shut me out. "Tell me why I'm feeding off something you're projecting? What is it? What did you do?" I shook her, hating and loving the spike of emotion in her eyes. It was neither fear nor lust.

It scrambled my thoughts, confusing the shit out of me.

The chaise lounge in the centre of the room halted our journey, pressing against Tess's legs. She jerked to a halt, still holding onto my wrist. "I don't know what you're talking about."

I glared into her eyes—dying to see what she hid, dreading it at the same time. "You're lying—but I don't know why." Shaking my head, I tried to grab hold of sanity.

The monster inside urged me to string her up and whip the words free from her mouth. She needed to be taught that keeping things from her master was not fucking allowed. Lying was the worst treason of all.

But then the voice of reason smashed my limbs.

You'll never forgive yourself for doing this against her will.

But that was the kicker. I couldn't tell if this was against her will or if she wanted it as much as I did.

Tess's pulse hammered beneath my grip; her skin turned cool as winter. For the first time in my sorry existence, I couldn't control the bastardly desires roaring in my blood.

Giving her one last chance to stop this, I whispered, "Tell me to stop. Tell me what you're not letting me see." My eyes dropped down her naked body, searching for clues of horror or lust. She was blank in both nuances and speech. "Do you want me to hurt you, *esclave*? Do you want me to fill you with my cock and grant you pain while you come?"

Something darted in her gaze, then was gone. A snake in the grasses of fucking temptation.

Tess dropped her hold on my wrist, stroking my cheek. Her gentle caress jolted me, granting me a lifeline in the sea of black.

I loved her.

I adored her.

I didn't want to hurt her.

"You never have to ask. I'm yours. I want what you want. I want whatever you give me." Her soothing voice twisted my brain.

See she wants this, too. You've nothing to worry about. Take her. Stop holding back.

Relief and excitement shoved away the hesitation and uncertainty. My fingers tightened, cutting off her air. Her eyes flared but displayed no other sign of alarm.

Don't. Pull away. Something isn't right.

That voice. The words of wisdom I always listened to.

Too bad it faded with every heartbeat.

Pressing my lips against hers, I never looked away from her blue-grey depths. She stood so regal, not slouching or trembling when I released my grip. "Are you telling me the truth?"

Tess never spoke to me in French, but she whispered, *"Je comprends. C'est bon."* Yes. It's okay.

Her touch threaded through my hair, cupping the back of my skull. Her nails sank into my scalp, causing me to break out in shivers. The sharp thrill reminded me all too well of being strapped to the bed and at her fucking mercy.

She'd torn me apart.

She'd flayed me alive.

She'd made me weak.

The beast inside growled; I trembled, trying to keep the

cage locked and secure.

"Take your hands off me, Tess," I said, low and curt. Gritting my teeth, I fought against the violent craving. The one screaming of retribution. I wanted payback. Strike for strike. Lash for lash.

Tess stiffened, dropping her arms.

The sane part of my brain—the part unshadowed by monsters—fought to understand what had changed. Something about her drew everything evil to the surface. She called to this awful part of me.

Squeezing my eyes, I hissed, "I need you to stop."

Stop so I don't hurt you. I don't want to fucking hurt you.

Yes, you do.

"There's nothing to stop," she murmured. "I want this. I want you."

"Stop!" I roared, shaking her. My fingers burned to choke. Unable to stand touching her, I shoved her away. She fell onto the chaise, her breasts bouncing with the force of her fall.

I spun away, clutching my head. *Get out. Get out!*

I had to get control. I had to find a way to protect her. None of this was right.

Then why does she give you permission?

I opened my eyes, hoping to see the strong unsullied woman I'd fallen so madly for. I needed to see her strength. But all I saw was a shell. A vacant shell.

Fuck!

I took a step back, cursing when something sharp poked my sole. I looked down and my stomach hollowed out.

My belt.

Hit her. Strike her. Turn her white skin red.

Breathing hard, I stared right into Tess's flushed face. Where was my *esclave*? The equal measure of fuckedupness I'd come to rely on was gone—twisted into something entirely different that I couldn't understand.

Her fire had been replaced by acceptance and resilience. Her eyes didn't taunt me to hurt her, or glimmer with lust. She stood, waiting like a perfect fucking slave.

Goddammit!

My anger went from simmering to explosive; I lost another part of my soul.

Her panting chest drew my attention; my eyes devoured her naked flesh. "I can't stop it. Whatever you're doing—it's making it worse. Ten times worse. A *thousand* times worse." The roaring grew louder, tearing my brain apart with the need to give in. "Tess—you're..." *You're not safe. Run!*

Her entire body flushed with fear before being hidden by submission. Her back straightened. Her eyes screamed some silent message while her mouth devastated my remaining self-control.

"Do it. Please, Q. You need to. I see how much you need to."

I wrenched my hair. *Tell the truth. Stand up to me.*

Only she could stop this. Only she could put me back on the leash I desperately needed.

"I'll hurt you. Do you understand that?" I could barely speak through clenched teeth.

Silence.

Tell me no. Be brave.

She bowed her head. "Yes."

I shook my head, disbelieving. "I'll draw blood. Do you want that?"

Her shoulders rolled. "I understand."

"I'll make you fucking scream. You can't mean it."

Her body hunched. "I do. I do mean it."

The beast roared, and I had nothing left. No sanity, no strength. She'd given me absolute control while presenting her fear and acceptance in front of a man who'd fought against his baser desires all his life.

This was why I ran from weak women.

This was why I *never* let myself go near a slave who'd been used to the point of graceful compliance.

Because I wasn't fucking strong enough to say no. I

wouldn't hold back—not now.

The leash snapped free. The cage flung wide.

I snatched the belt off the floor.

Breathing harder than I ever had before, I slammed down on the chaise beside Tess and yanked her over my lap.

The rapid pace of her chest rose and fell; her clammy skin stuck to my thighs as panic sprang from her pores. I'd crossed the threshold of no turning back.

Tess wiggled, but I held her down.

"Q...Q, wait." Her voice rose an octave, filling with terror.

Before, it would've been enough to cut through the dense black fog I existed in, reining me back.

But not now.

Now it fucking fed me.

Having her splayed, so vulnerable over my legs, set free every diabolical demon inside. I would hit her. I would fuck her. And I wouldn't stop until I tasted her blood.

Bending over, I hissed in her ear, "You're going to writhe for me. You're going to scream."

She swallowed a sob, dropping her head. Her entire body went boneless over my thighs. Yanking her hair free from the tie, I fanned out her blonde curls, stroking her back with trembling fingers.

My cock throbbed in time with my heart. I could've come just by rubbing against her prone body.

I flinched as Tess wrapped her arms around my calves, anchoring herself to me. Her body wracked with shudders, but she didn't make a sound.

Pressing her shoulder blades with one hand, keeping her in place, I folded the belt in half with the aid of the chaise. Grabbing the buckle, I ran my fingers from her shoulder blades, down her spine, to stroke her ass.

So white. So pristine.

My vision was all greys and blacks. Colour no longer existed in my world. I'd embraced everything I deplored—there was no leaving until I'd sated what needed to be sated.

Not only did I want to physically abuse her, I wanted to mentally ruin her, too.

If I were sane, I would've told myself I was a sick fuck and to end this madness before it was too late.

But how could a monster be sane? A monster did what he wanted. A monster took what was given.

"Do you love me, Tess?" My voice was black, heavily accented with a language that was meant for romance not bloodshed.

She nodded without hesitation.

I ran my finger down the centre of her ass, deliberately taunting her with softness. "Do you want this as much as me?"

Again another nod instantly.

"Do you want me to stop?"

She shook her head.

Such a perfect slave. Such a perfectly well-trained slave.

With a palm, I stroked her gently, loving the twitch of her hips. Her hair hung around her face, obscuring her features. Her mind might not be mine, but her body was.

Mine to paint with violence.

I slid two fingers between her legs. She stiffened as I found her folds. I angled my hand to penetrate her but her thighs snapped tight, blocking my right as her master to touch her.

A headache thundered into being—gathering tight and painful behind my eyes. *How dare she deny me!*

"Tu payeras pour ça." You'll fucking pay for that.

Raising my hand, the sun glinted off the buckle as the belt came down fast. The first slap of leather made my vision sputter and fade. The headache morphed into a mind-splitting migraine—my last defence against the beast inside.

Headaches were the bane of my life—but also my salvation.

Stop!

My eyes focused on the red lash across Tess's ass—there

was no chance of stopping.

I was too far gone.

Another strike and my cock jerked with delirium. This was what was missing in my life. This deliciousness. This supremacy. I'd never hit so hard. Only two strikes and already blood blisters formed.

Tess's fingernails dug into my calf, but she didn't make a sound. Her entire body locked into place, feeling like she'd transformed into a diamond rather than blood and bone.

I hit her again.

This time across the top of her ass. My mouth filled with eagerness to lick at the tiny crimson droplet welling from the strike. Her white skin turned into a criss-cross of pink and red.

With a fingertip, I rubbed the blood across her flesh in a smear of rust.

Tess whimpered.

Her whimper did two things to me—shattered my black-riddled heart and hurtled me faster into hell.

My headache latched onto my nervous system making me hot and jittery and sick. I wanted to throw up.

Stop!

The monster had grown from whisperer to commander. I had no way of halting. Hitting her wasn't enough. I needed to mark her everywhere. Her ass had been claimed. It was time for other places.

Tossing the belt away, I pushed her off my legs onto the carpet. She landed on all fours, her breathing ragged, face mottled with emotion. She refused to meet my eyes. Her lips were parted, panting hard, matching my out of breath breathing.

Stalking to the side table where a red candle rested, I scooped up the lighter beside it and lit the wick. The flame burned bright, hurting the backs of my eyes.

Carrying my prize back to the chaise, Tess's gaze locked onto the flickering fire. Tears gushed down her cheeks, tracking over her white skin in a river of grief.

I wanted sympathy, horror—some emotion that reminded me of my humanness. But I'd lost it the moment Tess gave me permission to cave. Nothing else mattered than doing what *I* wanted. And I wanted to burn her.

Grabbing her wrist, I plucked her upright, dragging her to the small table at the back of the couch.

"Q—please...don't."

I laughed, placing the candle on the edge of the wood. Picking her up, I laid her onto the piece of furniture. She winced as her flayed ass stuck to the varnish.

Pressing her sternum until she lay flat, I said, "You had the choice to say no." Taking the candle, I smiled at the small puddle of melted wax. "You no longer have that choice."

Holding her down with one hand, I poured a little of the wax directly onto the swell of her right breast.

She screamed, her fists clenching at the onslaught of heat. The liquid quickly hardened to solid. The slash of red looked like blood.

My cock fucking begged to climb inside her. I needed to come. Hard. I needed to sink down as far as I could until she knew just who owned her.

Stop!

My cock fucking wept. *It* was the monster. That piece of meat was the driving force of this whole nightmare.

Tipping the candle again, I let it splash over her left breast, licking my lips at her gasp of pain, the flash of terror in her eyes.

"God, I'm hard. So fucking hard hurting you."

Tess turned her face away, tears flowing in a steady, uninterrupted stream. I leaned over her, licking at the delicious salt. I poured another dollop of wax right between her breasts, a large seal of blood-red fire.

Tess bit her lip, moaning in agony. "Enough! Please enough."

What the hell was that? "Nice try, Tess. I know you're loving this, too. I'm used to your games. Your begs won't stop me. You gave me this power! I'll stop when I'm good and fucking ready."

Tess cried loudly as I tipped another spritz of wax over a nipple.

Her tears looked genuine but I knew my little minx. I knew she wanted this, just like me. She wouldn't have agreed if she didn't.

The instant the wax hardened, I latched my mouth around the greasy residue, biting it off. My cock lurched at the glowing burn mark left behind.

Not only did the wax look like blood but it branded her, too.

The pits of hell opened its gates at the morbid pleasure thrilling through me. Blowing out the candle, I put it down. With eager fingers, I picked at the hardened wax. Tess moaned as I peeled it from her irritated skin.

Depositing the pieces taken from her, I savoured the revealing of her burned flesh. Waves of blooming heat that *I'd* put there. *Me.* Her master.

The last piece, I dangled over Tess's mouth. "Open."

Her face blanched, her cheeks glistening with moisture. "You can't be serious."

Fuck, she was incredible. Her acting impeccable.

"Deadly. Eat it and I'll let you up."

Tess shook her head.

With cruel fingers, I twisted the nipple I'd burned. Her mouth opened in a silent scream. Placing the small piece of wax on her tongue, I glowered as she screwed up her face.

Raising an eyebrow, I let her make the decision of more punishment for disobeying or the end of torture by obeying.

It took a never-ending second before she grimaced and swallowed.

"Good girl." In a fast move, I pulled her upright, before pushing her down onto all fours on the carpet. She sniffed, a small sob escaping her wracking body.

Can't you see you're fucking ruining her?

The sane thought came from nowhere, bringing the power of a migraine, shoving ice-picks into my temples.

Oh, fuck, what am I doing?

Pain compounded on pain. I cried out, clutching my head against the agony in my skull. I fell forward, collapsing onto one knee.

Tess tried to crawl away, the curtain of curls hiding her face but not the red punishment on her ass.

"Where are you going?" Grabbing her ankle, I pulled her backward. "I haven't fucking finished." Her legs splayed; my mouth watered at the sight of her pussy.

I wanted to taste. I wanted to fuck.

Don't do this!

Climbing over her, I pushed her onto her stomach. Locking a leg around hers, I kept her thighs completely open. Exposed.

My fingers slid up her thigh, aching to touch her.

The monster licked his lips at the thought of finally having satisfaction. Of finally taking her like I'd always wanted—rough, against her will—ruthless.

Every inch I travelled, she didn't say a word. Not a peep or sound as she buried her face in the carpet.

The migraine made my mouth go dry; the sun became my worst fucking enemy. Too bright; digging into my eyes, ruining me further.

This is wrong!

I'm past caring.

It felt so good to finally let go. To drop my barriers. Tess *wanted* it. She'd encouraged me.

I couldn't wait any longer. My fingers latched around my cock, guiding it to her pussy.

"I'm going to take you. I'm going to come so deep inside you."

I thrust against her, wanting to lodge myself inside with one impale.

She cried out, her back bowing with agony.

I rocked forward, unable to understand why I couldn't

enter her. *Come on!* I needed to be inside.

Reaching between us, my forefinger stroked her clit, dropping to where the head of my cock pressed against her folds.

My world screeched to a fucking halt.

What—?

The beast froze, giving me one clear, untainted moment. She wasn't wet.

Not at all.

Fuck. This can't…no…

A surge of agony hit me like a baseball bat. My migraine shoved the monster back into its cage. Beating it with hatred, yelling, cursing, threatening to murder everything awful inside.

What have I done?

I scrambled backward, dry-retching with horror. "No. No. Fuck, no."

Tess was the driest I'd ever felt. *She isn't wet.* Everything I'd let my foggy fucked-up brain conclude had been a lie. She was drier than the Sahara.

Low moans sounded as Tess panted hard. She hadn't moved, lying unprotestingly and ready—ready for me to fucking rape her.

My heart broke into a bazillion fractured fragments. My ears filled with screeching from the horror in my soul. "What have I *done?*"

Fuck.

Fucking *fuck!*

I could barely function. My body crashed from its high of sadist animalistic needs, leaving a junky who'd never be fixed.

"Tess—oh, my God."

Blinking away the pain of my headache, I gathered her freezing body off the floor. Rocking back, I sat and leaned against the table leg, cocooning her on my lap.

Her body wracked with shivers, shuddering with every ragged breath.

Shit. What have I done? What have I *done!*

Silence echoed horribly loud. A minute ticked past. Then another. I didn't know what to say. I had no clue how to fix the atrocity of what I'd committed.

I wanted to carve out my sick, sick brain and beg for forgiveness. But this—this was unforgivable.

Then Tess hiccupped, turning her face into my chest. Her trembling arms slowly wrapped around my neck, spreading the slickness of her tears. They turned from seeping to raging, soaking into my worthless flesh, staining my soul forever.

My fractured heart oozed with corruption and terror. Everything she'd said was a lie. She'd made me hurt her against her consent.

I'd spun the worst kind of lies by listening to the darkness inside me.

I howled silently, slamming the cage into place, locking it forever. Never again would I let myself be swayed. Never again would I believe what Tess said.

Lies had the power to tear apart a relationship—it also had the power to kill.

How much further would I have gone?

I never wanted to know the answer.

My eyes smarted with rage—rage so hot and torrid I wanted to kill myself for being so fucked up. Then the rage dissolved under the colossal weight of guilt—rock after rock—burying me alive.

"Why?" I whispered. "Why did you let me do it?" My arms banded tighter, completely terrified she'd walk out the door.

How could she ever stand to look at me again? Nothing could fix what I'd done. No apology or heartfelt note could ever excuse almost raping the woman I would die for.

I couldn't stomach it. I couldn't breathe with the enormity of what I'd become.

Burying my face in her hair, I gave myself over to despair. "Tess, *je suis tellement désolé.*" I'm so unbelievably sorry.

She hunched in on herself, but her arms wrapped tighter

around my neck. My migraine pressed me further into the depths of hell. I suffocated on her hair. I'd never be able to look into her eyes again.

I was scum. Fucking awful *terrible* scum.

"Why? Why, Tess?" *How could you let me do this—after everything?*

She sniffed, raising her head. I gripped her harder, forcing her to stay, shaking until my teeth clacked together.

Pushing me a little, she sat upright, snuggling closer in my arms. "Because I love you, and I didn't want to let you down."

I couldn't. I couldn't do it.

I squeezed my eyes, unable to look at her. I was the worst kind of villain. Once a devil always a devil. I'd finally shown my true form. I'd shown Tess just how heinous I truly was. I'd lost my soul.

"Let me down? Fuck, Tess, you've just destroyed me. You let me do that against your will."

She shook her head. "It wasn't against my will. I let it happen. I gave myself to you because I love you."

A cavernous hole opened in my chest, sucking me down and down. I didn't deserve her love. I deserved nothing. *Nothing.*

"You can't love me. Not now."

Her face shone with tears but the strength I'd needed so badly shone in her gaze. "Yes. I do."

I couldn't bear to look at her anymore. Bowing my head, I concentrated on the sickness rampaging my body. I threw myself into the pit of pain knowing it was all I ever deserved.

"Q—" Her hand landed on my cheek. "Look at me."

I couldn't.

"Q—it's okay."

Rage.

She'd made me become this…this *monster* by being the perfect submissive. She'd drawn out the part of me I'd forever kept dormant. There was nothing okay about that.

"Don't. Just stop it. None of this is okay. Don't you get it?

I would've raped you. I would've been no better than those fuckers I've put down like dogs. Don't you *dare* tell me this is okay!"

Tess flinched but her touch never left my face. Her eyes locked onto mine, looking angelic and so forgiving.

The anger suddenly evaporated, leaving me a trembling wreck. Resting my forehead against hers, I whispered, "We're broken."

Tess froze. "No. Don't say that."

"We are. I've ruined us. Ruined you. Ruined everything."

"I'll get better. I'll find myself again. I know I will."

I didn't believe her.

"Did you even want me before—when we first arrived?" The need to know filled me with undeniable urgency. She'd come for me. She'd been wet. But what if I took advantage? What if she hadn't wanted me to go near her? I was already condemned.

"Yes. More than anything. I loved having you inside me."

My arms lassoed tighter, trying to calm the confusion inside. The migraine coated everything in gritty agony—lacing with tears I wished I could shed.

Then it hit me.

The truth.

The truth Tess had tried so hard to hide and by doing so fed the demons inside.

She no longer wanted pain.

The jitters stopped, leaving me freezing cold and numb.

She doesn't want what I do anymore.

Tess curled closer, her eyes swimming with tears. She knew I'd figured it out.

"I'm so sorry, Q. So sorry."

I couldn't stand her apologising—not when I'd be forever indebted and endlessly sorry for what I'd done.

"You've nothing to apologise for."

"But I can't give you what you need anymore. I'm the one who ruined everything."

Temper thawed my numbness. "It wasn't you. It was *them*." Capturing the back of her neck, I glared into her eyes. "Listen to me, Tess. Nothing and I mean *nothing* can stop me from loving you. I don't fucking care if you no longer need pain. I've sworn my life to you—if you'll still have me—don't you ever feel guilty for this."

"But it isn't enough." She used her hair as a cloak to hide her true despair, but I saw it. Fuck, I tasted it. "It isn't enough for you," she breathed.

She's right.

I hated that she was right.

No matter how much I wished it. No matter how hard I tried. I would never be able to control myself without a small outlet—a small avenue of granting what I so needed.

You almost broke her. That's enough to bury those urges forever.

A small curl of confidence strengthened me. I could use the debilitating fear of what I'd just done as a deterrent. Yes, I could bury them. Because I never wanted to hurt Tess again.

"*Esclave.* I don't give a fuck anymore. I refuse to lay one finger on you. After today, I'll keep my needs under control." I sighed, hugging her harder. "I want you. You and me. Together. That's all that matters."

All my life I never thought I'd find someone to match me. I'd carefully kept my heart locked away for that very reason. No woman should have to put up with a man like me.

But life decided to create a perfect other. A girl so strong and brave I was in total awe of her.

And I fell flat on my face in love with her.

I'd had the perfection of a life I never thought I could have for three fucking days. Then the devil stole her, hurt her, damaged her, and left me with a shattered dream.

Fucking bastards.

I howled for my loss. I snarled for the ghost of the girl I'd fallen for.

I'd lost her and any chance of complete happiness I stood to have.

Looking at her, I drank in her beauty. *I've lost you.*

Tess shifted in my arms. "You haven't. Don't ever think that."

My eyes flared. "I didn't say anything."

Her gaze turned liquid with sadness. "You didn't have to. I know you think you've lost me. But you haven't. You never will." Her chilled body scattered with goosebumps even in the warm room. The sunlight had faded to twilight, leaving us in shadows.

"This changes nothing. I still want you to love me in your way. I need you to still take me. Promise."

My lips pulled back. "You can't be serious. I'm not going to hit you for my own pleasure. That makes me no better than everything I've run away from." I swallowed, trying to keep my heart from threading with anger. "It was different before. You wanted it. I fed off you—I lived to please you. But now..." I sucked in a breath. "Don't ask me to hurt you again, *esclave*, because I won't. Ever."

She shook her head, curls cascading over her shoulders. "Don't say that. I want you to. You have to believe me."

My muscles locked in incredulous anger. Imprisoning her, I glowered. "Forgive me, Tess, but everything you just said is bullshit. Your lies piss me off. I know you don't want it."

Her face went from imploring to young—so fucking young. She looked lost and afraid and on the verge of tears. The truth she'd been trying to hide burst forth. "You're right. The thought of you hurting me terrifies me. I no longer need it to feel alive. I no longer crave that bond through pain." Her eyes glassed with unshed tears. "But it doesn't mean I don't want you or need you to take me however you want. *Je suis à toi,* Q."

I dropped my hold, my body seizing with understanding.

That's what set me off before. *That's* what conjured all the rottenness from my soul.

She'd given me power over her, all the while deploring it. The mixed signals had turned her into ultimate prey.

I shoved her off me, bolting upright. Yanking my hands through my hair, I stumbled backward. "You can't do this."

Tess scrambled to her feet, spreading her hands, looking as if she calmed a beast. "I already have."

"God, Tess. *Qu'est-ce qu'ils t'ont fait putain?*" What did they fucking do to you?

Somehow, I'd broken the one slave I thought would be forever strong enough to defy me. Her inner spirit was gone. Her will to fight me vanished.

My wonderful Slave Fifty-Eight had turned into the one thing every cruel master wanted.

She'd willingly given me every part of herself.

Her pain.

Her sanity.

Her free will.

She sacrificed her happiness all to keep me pleased.

Fuck.

I groaned as the gross realization of what I'd lost finally crashed into me.

She was perfect.

She was mine to control.

She would never argue or say no.

She wasn't just in love with me. She believed she fully belonged and would spend her life never displeasing me or fighting back.

She was the perfect slave.

My heart raced to a dying beat. "God, Tess. What have you done?"

She couldn't have decimated me more. She'd taken all my dreams, throwing me headfirst into the dark. She'd made me become *him*.

She'd turned me into my fucking father.

Standing on the precipice, I visualized my future. Two paths. Two choices. One, I could accept Tess's unselfish gift and take her—become her true master forever. Or I could reject her offer and fight to get my woman back.

Take her. Accept it.

I growled as a slow burn scorched through me.

Temptation. Sheer fucking temptation. It would be so easy to accept the blackness and take her as the ultimate submissive.

Too tempting. Far, far too tempting.

But by accepting, I would condemn myself to a life worse than death. I'd lose myself forever.

I'd be no better than the man I strove never to become.

I would kill her.

Tess stayed bowed at my feet; her gorgeous face glowing in the gloom. She looked like a goddess straight from another universe—sent there to see just how far I'd fall.

She was sublime. She was majestic. She annihilated me.

"Tess—" My lips wouldn't move. I wanted to tell her to snap out of whatever enactment she played. I wanted to shake her, slap her, hit her until the old fire and thrill of pleasure and pain came back into her eyes.

But I couldn't do it. I couldn't go near her—not while she stayed so open and willing at my feet. I could feel the beast inside reaching for her, snarling at the taste of fully owning her. If I let myself touch her, it would be over. She wouldn't be my wife. She would be my slave. I would never find balance again.

I was better than that. Tess deserved more than that.

I had to find a way to end all of this horror.

I had to rewind time.

"On your knees, esclave."

Tess slid to the floor, looking so fucking beautiful in a sheer silver dress and no underwear. Every bruise, every cut, every bite glowed beneath the fine material, stamping my ownership. Marking my claim.

"Please—not again," she whimpered, sliding to the carpet.

Her disobedience drove me mad—I'd teach her a lesson about her rights. Namely that she had none.

"Your only purpose is to please me. Open that pretty little mouth."

Her face blanched, but her lips parted like a good little slave. She wore no collar but the brand on her neck glittered silver with permanent scarring.

Mine.

My hands landed on her head as my cock slid into her mouth. Deeper, deeper, harder, harder.

She whimpered but accepted, spit trailing down her chin as I used her.

The need to come overpowered me, tingling my back, locking my quads. I threw Tess to the floor, and a whip appeared in my hand. I wanted to come all over her while making her skin glow red.

"I won't. Don't make me," Tess pleaded. She fell silent as I struck her.

And struck her.

"I'm not making you do anything you didn't want. You did this. You made me become this. You gave yourself to a monster."

I hit her again.

And again.

And again.

I jolted awake.

Launching upright, I glared around the opulent suite. My hand disappeared under the pillow for the HK P2000 hidden there. Franco wasn't the only one who carried concealed weapons.

Heart revving, eyes darting, I flicked the safety off ready to fucking eradicate any bastard who dared come near Tess again.

The room was dark as a tomb—no light peeked through the black-out curtains, no trickle of illumination anywhere.

The dream echoed behind my eyes.

Tess had been resplendent. Accepting my violence with the beauty of a slave who'd been to hell and back. She lived only to make a devil happy.

My mouth was dry, but my cock was rock hard. I couldn't shake the image of Tess's mouth wrapped around my length; I still felt her dream-lips sucking, her tongue licking…taking.

Fuck.

I wanted to tear out my black soul and burn it. I wanted to crucify everything disgusting inside. Maybe if I purged myself with fire, I might get rid of the nastiness.

Redemption.

I needed to find some way to redeem myself and halt this path—the road leading to becoming Quincy Mercer II—true born son of Quincy Mercer, the raping bastard.

Shaking my head, I forced myself to focus on the room and not my rapid descent into purgatory.

Something woke me.

Something caused my body to switch straight into killer and protector. I had to stay vigilant just in case one of the many assholes I'd dealt with had come for me—and they would. I knew the underworld they existed in; retribution would be on its way. In a way the waiting was worse. I wanted it over with—so I could kill.

My hands twitched, gripping the gun harder, training it on shadowy corners of the room.

"No. Please—"

My heart skipped as Tess seized beside me. Her eyes screwed up, a dew of sweat gleaming on her upper lip. Even in the darkness I made out every perfect sweep of her eyelashes, following the soft curves of her body.

Her.

She'd woken me.

I should've known—it was hardly a new occurrence. Her voice must've plaited with my dream, lacing fantasy with reality. Her pleas had been real, but not for me. Somehow I'd taken the past and Tess's amazing willingness to give me what I needed, and twisted it with how she was now. She would never say no to me. I learned that the hard way.

Her lies had confused the shit out of me, making me lose complete control. I could blame her for everything—but ultimately it was all on me.

Me, the cocksucker who didn't deserve her.

My back went rigid as she squirmed. Her obvious distress sickened me, yet in my dream I'd relished it—wanted more of her cries and begs.

I hadn't cared she didn't want me. I loved that she didn't. I *loved* the non-consent.

I'm heartless and fucking cruel.

Suddenly, my body weighed too much. The migraine had broken thanks to the brief sleep, but the dregs lived in my skull—puncturing my brain with tiny needles. At least my body punished me. I'd earned the pain.

Tess. Goddammit, I couldn't look at her without dying of guilt.

You burned her. You almost fucking raped her.

I dropped the gun onto the mattress, letting my body sag. My hands disappeared into my hair, holding a mind churning with so many black things.

Her body jolted but she stayed deep asleep—too trapped by her nightmare to wake.

My arms tensed, wishing there *was* a trespasser in the night—I would make him bleed. I would tear him fucking apart.

The migraine pulsed, gathering power now I was awake. A fresh wave of sickness spread its nausea-inducing fingers up my back, latching around my throat. I wanted to fall to my knees and spew my fucking guts out for what I'd done.

Guilt could kill a man—I'd never been free of the fester all my life but now it'd grown monumental.

I groaned as a lance of pain hit behind my eyes. I hadn't had headache this bad since Tess had been stolen. And I had no one to direct my rage onto but myself. This time the motherfucker who had to die for hurting her was me.

Fuck, I missed Frederick. I missed his cool-headedness, rational thinking, even his crazy ideas. He kept me sane. I hated to think how I would've coped without him in the wings. Keeping me focused, reminding me I *was* strong enough to ignore the needs and be a better man.

Picking up the gun, I ran my fingertips over the weighty metal, stroking the weapon that'd been used to take the lives of sadistic men. I'd fought against them. I'd ended their horror, giving the women back to their loved ones. All apart from one.

I looked over at Tess; her voice popped into my head.

"My name is Tess Snow. Not Sweetie, or Tessie, or Honey. I'm a woman only now realizing what she's capable of. I'm no one's daughter. I'm no one's girlfriend. I'm no one's possession. I belong to me, and for the first time, I know how powerful that is."

I relived the moment where Tess had returned, bowing to me in the foyer. She'd taken away all my power by giving me all of hers.

"I came back for the man I see inside the master. The man who thinks he's a monster because of his twisted desires. I came back for Q. I came back to be his esclave, *but also to be his equal. I came back to be your everything."*

I squinted at my palm where I'd sliced the flesh, making a blood-oath with Tess. I'd sworn to honour her, cherish her, protect her. I'd married her in my heart that very second in my office, sharing everything that I was while hiding everything I could. She'd come back to me knowing nothing of the real me. The monster.

She trusted you despite everything and look at how you repaid her!

My body stiffened. *I have to fix this.*

It was my duty to fix what I'd broken—not just today, but for everything I'd done and everything that'd happened.

Tess slept on, giving me space to untangle my thoughts. After the incident, I locked myself in the bathroom and spent an hour under scalding hot water, trying to expel the evil from my veins. When I'd finally had the balls to come out, she'd been asleep—curled up like a homeless kitten hugging a pillow.

I hadn't meant to fall beside her and close my eyes, but the migraine forced me into a spiral of unconsciousness, giving my imagination time to haunt me while my body healed.

"I won't! Kill me. I don't care. I won't!" Tess shuddered,

her voice shattering the silence.

My muscles tensed at her outburst; she fell silent.

Watching her, I drank in the slightness of her arms, the twitch of terror going through her limbs. Her body overheated, yet her teeth chattered with cold.

I couldn't stop fury bubbling in my chest. "Tess. *Je veux te sauver mais je n'ai pas la moindre idée de comment le faire. Si je pouvais briser chaque horloge pour remonter le temps je le ferais si seulement je pouvais te voir sourire et être heureuse à nouveau.*" I want to save you but have no fucking clue how. If I could smash every clock to rewind time, I would—if only to see you smile and be happy again.

A horrible thought barrelled into me. Maybe the only way to make her happy was to let her go? Maybe I needed to stop being so fucking selfish and let her walk away—from me, my life, from every bad thing that'd happened.

My heart twisted into a painful knot.

I'm not fucking strong enough to do that.

I was cold enough to admit I would rather keep Tess, even with her soul in tatters, than let her go. And that just made me hate myself even more.

Fuck!

She thrashed suddenly, throwing her arm out, catching my chest with her sharp nails.

I hissed in a breath. A keening moan escaped her.

Goddammit, I might never have the courage to set her free—but I wouldn't sit back and let her circle further into madness.

Tucking the gun under the pillow, I scooted closer, grabbing her clammy form. She fought, but her thin arms and floppy legs were no match. My body wrapped around hers, dragging her into me.

"No. Don't hurt me. Not again. I can't take it again."

Every implore caused the ache in my chest to pound with boulder-sized guilt. I no longer had a ribcage but a gaping, vast hole that I had no fucking clue how to fix.

Even though her words weren't meant for me, they were too apt—the perfect conclusion of our fucked-up relationship.

Locking my arms, I held her close. Sliding onto my side, I tucked her back to my front, wrapping a leg around hers. Spooned and cocooned—protected by my body.

"It's okay, *esclave*. I'm going to fix this. I don't know how yet...but I will."

Tess didn't respond. Even with the heat of the room and warmth from the sheets, her body was ice. Worse than ice: it was dead—sucked into a dream where the only thing she wished for was to die.

Another shudder passed through her. My palm twitched with the urge to slap her awake, but I knew from experience it didn't work. It only made me feel like shitless scum. Instead, I pressed my mouth against her soft curls, swallowing my anguish.

I wanted to fucking scream at how broken everything was. This was torture. Worst fucking crucifixion imaginable.

Don't accept it. Don't fucking put up with this.

I wanted to fight on her behalf. I wanted to tear her brain apart and delete what I'd done. Now she'd seen what I really wanted how could I hide? How could I ever convince her I would never raise my hand to her again—even though I would always dream of it?

Her body stiffened; I locked my arms tighter. I was ready for this part. It was the same night after night.

The nightmare came in threes: first the screams, then the pleas, and lastly the acceptance of absolute terror.

"Je suis là." I'm here. I didn't know if she heard—but at least she wasn't going through this alone.

Her body seized like an epileptic. My biceps ached from holding, anchoring her to me, adrift in the storm of nightmares.

"You win. I beg. I beg you to end my life."

The tears began. No sound, just a soft waterfall trailing her cheeks. Droplet after droplet of sadness. "Kill me!"

My stomach churned. I *hated* being so fucking helpless.

Hated lying there unable to *do* anything.

Pins and needles stabbed my fingertips as I held her too hard. The protectiveness in my blood drummed with need to desecrate her demons. Her vulnerability angered me; I struggled briefly to see her as the strong fighter and not a broken slave.

Tess walked such a fine line in my life—she had to be strong, but not too strong to tempt me to break her. She had to be submissive, but not too weak that it called to the monster inside. Such a fine line where one slip meant either being shoved away in repulsion or dragged closer in poisonous obsession.

Not for the first time, I worried I was completely psychotic and in desperate need of help.

At least she wasn't giving me mixed signals while she slept. And I no longer needed to find out the truth. I knew.

She hated pain.

Deplored pain.

The one thing that'd brought us together was the one thing driving us apart.

A flutter of her breath tickled my chest. I glanced down. The palm print from when I struck her in the hallway looked almost black in the gloom—outlined on her white thigh like a curse. The red burns from the wax on her breasts were beautifully horrific.

My heart banged with disgust and passion.

You're sick.

I bowed my head.

I know.

I'd wanted the truth, but Tess hid it too well. She had no idea my instincts would pick up on her tales, messing with my mind. The beast couldn't tell what was real and what was not—driving me further into the dark.

But now she knew who I truly was. Knew what I'd kept hidden. The starkness of her lies were nothing to how black I really ran.

"You should've told me, Tess," I murmured against her

hair. "You helped me find my humanness but you took it away with your lies."

My eyes flared. Was the unfixable fixable?

Maybe I had to let her hurt me again—pain for pain. Give her equal power. It worked previously, but not…completely. The research I'd done on Tess's emotional shutdown stated she suffered symptoms of Dissociative Disorder. It wasn't something curable overnight—if ever. Sure, I'd forced her to return to life, but it didn't mean she wouldn't try to hide again. I had to go deeper than that. I had to break every chain of the disorder, changing her impulses from shutting down to believing in me.

I wouldn't be able to repeat letting her emotionally and physically scar me—that had been a onetime deal. I'd never be able to give up control again.

Damn fucking Frederick and his ideas. It was his fault my mind was messed up. He'd made me become this…this *thing.*

I had to come up with something else—something chain-smashing, lie-killing, life-fixingly perfect.

My teeth ground as Tess stiffened, shaking her head against my arms. She mumbled something incomprehensible. The nightmare was coming to an end.

The bed suddenly felt too soft, too reminiscent of the mattress I lay upon while Tess coaxed me closer to death with the aid of floggers and cat o' nine tails.

Untangling myself from her, I swung my legs over the side and dragged hands through my hair. With heavy limbs and a heavier heart, I made my way to the other side of the bed.

She looked so innocent and delicate; a blonde wraith sent to tempt and destroy me. But beneath the façade was a fighter—the same fighter who'd turned my world upside down, made me fall in love, and collared my demons.

I needed to get that fighter back.

Tess curled inward, looking like an ethereal being about to fade from this world. She was the sparrow I'd freed but never caught. The one bird who'd put *me* in a cage instead.

My eyes fell to my chest. I traced the red healing 'T' over my heart, before following the inked feathers and beady eyes of my favourite bird.

The symbol never failed to make me feel better about myself. I didn't see a tattoo, I saw a promise; a message written on my skin, giving me faith to keep going—knowing I was better than my thoughts. Better than my fucking fantasies. I'd proven it by saving women I could so easily have broken.

My hands fell to bare skin on my right side where no clouds or barbwire existed. It wasn't fair to leave that part unwritten. That part belonged to Tess and my future.

Tess's body jolted as she slammed onto her back; her mouth opened in a silent scream. Sucking in greedy breaths, she cried, "No. Not again. I won't—"

Goddammit, I couldn't listen to this night after night. I couldn't torture myself lying beside her when I couldn't save her.

I *would* fucking save her, and in turn, I'd restore my self-worth.

Any second now she'd wake and hurl herself back to life. Any second now I would catch her and hold her while she sobbed from whatever filth she'd relived.

She would turn to me for help. And I would be there for her.

You almost raped her today. You're a fucking asshole.

The memory compounded my headache. How could I want to hurt someone who ruled me?

My stomach knotted, acknowledging the truth. Tess had so much power over me. More than anyone in my entire life.

She's my fucking queen.

The darkness gave way to light for a brief moment—the roles switched in my head. Abusive master to willing slave.

My eyes snapped wide. I snorted in the darkness. *I'm the* esclave.

Her messy hair snagged on the pillows, throwing herself onto her side. Her tiny hands fisted while her body turned in on itself.

Standing over her, I forced myself to pick up the splintered pieces of my heart from this afternoon. I was done suffering the gauntlet of right and wrong. No matter how much I wanted to accept her flawless gift of absolute ownership, I wanted more.

I *deserved* more.

I was fucking besotted. She would never just be a slave. And I would never just be her master. Our connection went past flesh and blood. It was soul-deep and ever-lasting and I refused to fuck it up with one mistake.

We'd reached a pinnacle in our relationship. The ugly truth was aired. It was time for decisions.

Fuck letting lies win. Fuck letting the past ruin our future.

Tess and I were stronger than words. And I refused to let them wedge us apart and destroy the only good thing in my life.

I would stop this—end all this decay before there was nothing left but rottenness and nothing to salvage.

I would start a new beginning. A clean slate.

I had to do something drastic.

My eyes widened. *You already know what to do.* Fuck, why hadn't I thought of it sooner?

My headache kept pace with my heart as I glared at Tess. I'd wasted so much time.

Lefebvre and the shower.

It worked last time.

Could it work again?

Energy exploded through my limbs. Looking at Tess one more time, I stormed into the bathroom.

Turning on the light, the glare stung my eyes as I hunted for my clothes. Collecting my trousers off the floor, I jerked them on, followed by a black shirt I'd unpacked before.

My reflection showed a man sleep-dishevelled and wired to his fucking eyeballs, but for once there was a glimmer of hope. Glorious fucking hope.

This is wrong. Wrong on so many levels.

Ignoring the seeping worry in my veins, I didn't give myself time to second guess. Fishing into my back pocket, I grabbed my cell-phone and punched in a number I'd known by heart since I was five years old.

It took a while to connect. The ringing sent spasms of pain through my head. I stabbed a finger at my reflection. "This has to fucking work, so don't screw it up." The mirror stole my threat, echoing back the image of a lunatic. Doubt reared its unwanted head. My eyes looked almost soulless; my five o' clock shadow unkempt. The tiny scars on my cheeks, brow, and nose glistened like tiny crescent moons.

Goddammit, pick up the fucking phone.

The number rang and rang.

"Bonjour?" a sleepy female voice came down the line. About time.

"Suzette. You're going to do something for me."

Shuffling, followed by a yawn. "You need something at two in the morning, and you're not even here?" Her tone mixed with annoyance and obedience. "Did you forget something?"

Before Tess came into my life Suzette was the only female I let get close. We'd never been more than saver and slave, then employee and employer, but our connection had grown to friendship. She pushed me even when it was dangerous to do so. She saw the real me—the one I never acknowledged—and encouraged me regardless.

When Tess arrived it was Suzette who gave me permission to be a bastard. What were her words? *Be like them for a while, because even on your worst days, you don't rival what they did to me.*

I'd never asked her what she'd lived through; I didn't need to. She told me in her own way—in the panic attacks and sudden terror of my temper. But beneath the small fractures, she was strong.

"I need you to arrange a wedding."

Suzette giggled. "I thought you eloped so you didn't have to do any of that?"

I imagined her rolling her eyes as if I was some stupid child who'd forgotten his lunch for the day. She'd taken the role of caring for me a bit too well.

"That was the original plan. *Oui.*"

Another laugh. "But now you've changed your mind and want an over-the-top, completely impractical wedding?" A pause. "Did Tess refuse your crazy idea of marrying in the middle of nowhere?"

I snorted. "No. She didn't refuse." Even after everything I'd done today she *still* wanted me. The knowledge would never fail to rip the breath right from my lungs.

"It's hardly a dream location for a girl. She deserves more than a pelican for a witness."

"Suzette," I growled. "Instead of undermining me, how about you agree to fucking help."

My mind raced, forming the crazy idea faster and faster. Tess would have every reason to kill me. She would probably try.

I ran a hand down my face, shaking my head. God—this was fucking dangerous.

"So—why do you need my help?" Suzette prompted.

My mind switched from what I was about to do to the wedding. I didn't want big—hell, I didn't want anything more than someone joining Tess's life to mine—but Tess had said she wanted Suzette there.

She wanted Brax, too.

No fucking way was that little cunt going to be at my wedding. There was only so much I would tolerate.

I paced over the tiles, gripping my chin in thought. The original plan was still my favourite—but I wanted to give Tess the world. And I would.

"You're going to arrange our wedding."

"What?" Something banged in the background; Suzette yelped.

My heart exploded. Intruders. Fucking traffickers.

"Suzette!"

Suzette made a sucking noise. "Sorry. It's dark. I ran into the door. Bashed my fingers."

"Goddammit…" I breathed out heavily. Franco left a decent team of security in Blois but who knew what the underworld morons would do to get to me. I didn't want any more blood from people I cared about.

My patience was wearing thin. I wanted them to make a move *now*, so I didn't have to sit in the shadows and wait.

Pushing the urge for a fight out of my head, I demanded, "Pay attention. Did you hear me? You're in charge of the wedding."

A postponement really pissed me off. I still suffered the overwhelming need to make Tess mine in every way possible— to both man and beast—but this new plan…this plan that could royally fucking backfire in my face…it might be everything we needed.

To pull it off I had to embrace a little of what I always ran from. To make it work I had to make Tess believe.

"Yes, I heard you. You're coming home while I arrange it, right? I need time."

"No, we're not coming home. I expect you do it quickly." How long did it take to arrange a simple ceremony?

"I can't do it quickly. If you want to give Tess the dream, I need at least a month."

"No, fucking way. You have five days, Suzette." My heart galloped, fixated on the idea growing rapidly out of control. Every second sent me hurtling into the unknown. "You have five days to arrange a suitable wedding. Invite who you think should be there. You're in charge."

A surprised squeak hurt my ear. "*Five* days? No, there's no way—"

"No arguing. Do it."

I made eye contact with myself in the mirror. *Do you seriously think you can pull this off?*

That was the kicker. I didn't know. If I was honest I was fucking terrified. But I had no choice. Tess couldn't go on like this. *I* couldn't go on like this.

The only way forward was to go back.

Back to restart time.

Suzette grumbled, "Why do I get the feeling you're up to something again."

Because I am. Something that could mentally screw us up completely.

Suzette sucked in a breath. "Please tell me you're not doing something crazy. Like releasing all your birds or letting Tess butcher you?"

My jaw locked. "You're not to mention either of those two things. Ever. Again. Am I understood?" I shuddered involuntarily. I hated that Franco and Suzette saw me so weak. For a while, I worried I'd have to fire them, so I never had to look into their eyes and remember.

But they didn't watch me with pity like I expected. If anything their loyalty and respect increased.

A soft sigh echoed down the line. "I'm sorry. Just—"

"I'm going. Five days, Suzette."

"But! But, I have so many questions. Where do you want it? How many guests? What sort of vows?"

"That's for you to figure out—"

"Wait! Whatever you're doing, Q…just remember a person can only take so much before it's all over."

What the fuck?

I reared back, glaring at the phone as if it had somehow transmitted my idea down the line and into Suzette's thoughts.

Suzette was intuitive. Just like Tess.

I looked over my shoulder to the bathroom door. Fuck, if I was so obvious, what if Tess sensed what I was about to do? What if she'd run again?

Urgency and fear hijacked my legs. I stalked to the door, wrenching it open to glare into the bedroom. Tess hadn't moved, bundled tightly in the sheets.

I'm coming for you.

My headache raged with the finality of my decision.

I was done with the phone call. Every passing second was a second I could never get back. "Get it done, Suzette." I hung up. Shoving the phone into my pocket, I sucked in a ragged breath.

This was it.

No turning back.

The moment I started this, I had to keep going. Regardless if Tess swore, cursed, or wanted me to die. She might absolutely despise me afterward—but that was a risk I would take. For her. I would willingly wear her hatred if it meant I cured her.

Turning on the tap, I splashed my face with cold water, glaring at my reflection. *Man the fuck up and do it.*

Pacing to the door, I tore it open. My hands opened and closed as adrenaline filtered through my limbs.

Tess didn't wake, comatose with the devils inside her. If I had my way it would be the last nightmare she ever had. Tonight I would enter her thoughts and slaughter every last fucking one.

Prowling through the darkness, I found the wardrobe and wrenched it open. A small light came on, highlighting a multitude of dressing gowns. Towel, fleece, silk, and cotton.

Ripping out a silk sash, I ran the material through my fingertips. It was soft, cool, and black. Perfect.

Grabbing another belt from a cotton dressing gown, I yanked it to see if it stretched. Just a little give. Good to know.

With the belts clutched in my hands, I faced the bed.

Tess whimpered, her hands bunching the sheets. From here, her face was flushed, not deathly white. She was close to waking.

I moved forward, glad of the dark. It was my friend, my ally. The accomplice in what I was about to do.

The bed hit my knees. I climbed onto the mattress, crawling forward till I positioned myself hovering over Tess. My fists indented the bed either side of her head as she slept.

I allowed myself a moment to drink her in. To trace the

almost disappeared bruises on her arms. To grow hard staring at her perfect figure. But it was the brand on her neck that enraptured me.

The angry burn settled the growling monster inside. She would never be able to remove the scar. She'd announced permanently she would never leave me. No matter what I did to her.

My heart lurched, willingly allowing a small flavour of anger and darkness to settle.

Tonight was the last night she would suffer. Tonight, I would kill the past and invoke a new future.

By doing to her what the other cocksuckers had done before.

I'd broken the hold of her rape by giving her a new memory. I took her in the shower—replacing Lefebvre with me—turning horror into something more liveable.

I didn't think it would work. It was a stupid, *stupid* thing to do.

But it did work. And I had to believe it would again.

I was about to make Tess relive everything.

I was about to stamp out the past and replace each incident with a new memory.

I was about to kidnap my fiancée.

Chapter Five

Bind our twisted perversions, love me dark, leave
your mark. love my faults and imperfections
My night and day, my moon and sun, your light
turns my black to glittering grey

"*D*o it, puta!"

I'd held off as long as I could. I'd fought and raged and been beaten
for my troubles. But I couldn't disobey any longer.

I pulled the trigger.

The bullet lodged inside Blonde Angel's forehead.

With a whoosh of black swirls and icy wind, the dream
unlatched its claws from my subconscious. Winds buffeted as
Leather Jacket and blood and dead women snuffed out. I sailed
up, up, up through the grotesque memories and back to reality.

Only this time. I didn't wake up to Q's arms around me
and his kisses in my hair.

I woke up to a fate worse than death.

My instincts understood before my mind, dousing me in
howling fear.

It's happening again.

It was dark. Quiet. Serene. A lie. The worst kind of lie.

I'm not safe!

Heavy masculine breathing brushed my face as two large hands exploded through the shadows—reaching for me, going for my eyes.

No!

In an awful second, time screeched to a halt and two things happened. Two major things that showed just how much I'd changed from when they'd taken me in Mexico.

The first was I shut down.

I switched off.

All the passion and rage and spirit when I fought Leather Jacket was replaced with cold calculating numbness. For a moment all I wanted to do was give up. To let my heart cease its ragged beat and let the inevitable happen. After all, fighting didn't work.

How many times must fate slap the same lesson in my face before I understood giving up was my only option?

Darkness even worse than night stole my eyesight. Something cool and slightly slimy was pressed over my face. The brush of strong hands on my ears made my skin crawl— the pressure of the blindfold sent my heart into a fulcrum, spinning faster than anything before.

Give in. Just give in.

I sent the message to my muscles: *relax. Time for evil to win.* But something stopped me from being a victim. Something deep, too deep to switch off.

And that was the second thing. Smashing away the weakness of prey, filling me with fire. Energy I no longer knew swirled from nowhere, seesawing my emotions between complete submission and rage so brittle and blizzard-cold, I no longer knew myself.

Fight. Kill. Or die trying.

My instincts catalogued everything. My attackers position, his breathing, the pressure of the blindfold on my eyes. His knees were on either side of my waist, the only weight came from his hands on my temples, holding the blindfold in place. The mattress dipped as he shifted.

I stayed prone and frozen, even while I sparked and conducted a battle inside. A battle of acceptance or murder.

My hands curled, calling forth the reckless survival I'd always tapped into. Half of me lamented—*give in!* Fate would never let me be free—I would never deserve Q. I couldn't afford to keep paying these unpayable tolls. But the other half couldn't give up. It wasn't in my genetic code to allow something so precious to be stolen.

A never ending second ticked past where my heart whizzed faster and faster until my chest bled with fear. Neither of us moved. No needle was shoved into my arm; no curse was sworn in my ear. It was as if he waited. Paused to see what I would do.

A test then?

A test to see if I'd finally become the perfect possession to be traded. Had White Man won after all? Had he broken me by letting me believe in the falsity of safety?

The epitome of brokenness was no longer caring. No longer functioning. No longer willing to exist.

Am I broken?

The blunt question sliced through my brain—taunting me with the weakness of the word.

The ultimate question was did I want to die?

I don't want to die.

Did I want to live?

I don't want to live like this anymore.

I grew hotter. Madder.

They'd taken everything. They'd taken too much. And yet they'd come back for more.

It isn't fair.

I filled with resentment. Furiousness.

What are you going to do about it?

The confusion inside grew hot, evaporating to steam,

billowing faster and faster with anger.

I won't. I won't be broken.

I was stronger. I was a fighter. I would die being true to myself.

I was livid. I was rabid. I went insane.

My mouth opened; I screamed, "Not this time, you fucking asshole." The tense moment shattered, raining around us in shards as I switched.

The frozen victim became a crazed warrior. I wanted his blood.

The man grunted in shock; his hands grabbed chunks of my hair—keeping my head locked against the mattress.

The pain in my scalp was nothing. Did he think I cared about a little agony after everything I'd been through?

Jerking manically, I screamed again, tearing the follicles free from my scalp. The pain reminded me of something I'd forgotten. Something I should never have taken for granted.

I'm Tess Snow.

And I would survive or die. I was done just existing.

The grip on my hair fell away. Fumbling hands tried to tie the blindfold behind my head, but I would no longer make it easy for him.

My hands flew up, connecting with a bristle-covered jaw. The facial growth shot an image of Q into my head. Where was he?

My heart ruptured and tore and shattered into useless pieces. *They've hurt him.* They'd stolen him—that was why he wasn't there to save me. The thought of never seeing Q again was the last of my undoing. I was free. Utterly free from everything but that moment.

"You hurt him!" My fingers curled, turning nails into weapons as I dragged them down his face. "I'll make you pay."

My assailant reared back but I moved with him, slicing, swiping, connecting with his face, neck, and throat. His arms came up, knocking my hands away, but he didn't pounce or pummel me into unconsciousness.

I didn't know why he hesitated, but it would cost him. Never again would I let them take me. I either won this or I died. Two options and I didn't really care which one.

The man's legs stayed pinned on either side of me, squeezing, trying to keep me from wiggling free, but he didn't have what I had: the clarity of destiny.

My mind turned blank. The fear of what had happened to Q disappeared. All I focused on was killing.

With curled hands, I struck anywhere I could. His chest, his thighs, his jaw. Each strike was met with an angry growl but no retaliation.

His hands tried to capture my wrists, but my anger made me a flailing mess to catch. The world spun and spun as I sucked in too much air.

White-noise crackled, roaring in my ears, deafening me to everything but my strumming heartbeat.

The sheets wrapped around my legs as I kicked and squirmed. His weight kept me trapped, so I did the only thing I could—I launched upright and head-butted him.

Stars.

Shooting stars. Comets. Fireworks.

Bright light replaced the darkness of my blindfold as our skulls clacked together.

The man groaned, cursing low. He rolled off me, dropping off the bed.

The instant I was free, I ripped the blindfold off. Not that it helped in the dark. Instead of running, I attacked.

Throwing myself onto the floor, I latched onto his back, punching everywhere I could. The pain in my knuckles was vengeance.

He reached behind, grabbing my naked flesh to toss me off him. The carpet cushioned my fall. I kicked hard as I could in his direction. My bare foot connected with something far more perfect than a knee or thigh. It hit his prized possession.

"Fuck!" he roared.

My body stuttered just for a moment. That voice. Then

white-noise stole me again, keeping me focused on my task. I shook my head. I refused to listen. I *wouldn't* listen. Not to lies or promises or even the voice of the man who I loved more than anything. It wasn't his voice. It couldn't be, and I refused to be side-tracked from murder.

"Fucking bastard. What did you do? Where is he?" The anger and sheer-minded confidence was like a long lost lover, cocooning me with belief—belief I could win. How had I been so weak? How did I forget this velvety power of self-reliance?

I laughed suddenly. I was *grateful*. Even though I would kill him. He'd returned to me what I thought was lost forever.

Not one tear leaked from my eyes. Not one plea or beg. I was free.

Then a body collided with mine, slamming me against the floor. His hard form stole the breath from my lungs. My strength and fire flickered, sucking me back into tameless horror.

I went berserk.

Legs, arms, fingers—my entire body became a weapon.

"Fuck me," he grunted, his voice hidden by the rage roaring in my ears.

Expect it. Any moment.

I tensed for pain. I knew it was coming. He hadn't hit me yet, but he would. I'd drawn blood—I tasted it in the air. I'd made him angry—I felt it in his fingers as he tried to stop my flailing fists. He would strike and soon.

Kill him!

"Let me fucking go!" In a twist and a huge surge of power, I knocked his hands away and slapped him. My throat burned I breathed so hard.

"Fucking hell, stop!"

Stop? And make his kidnapping easy? As if.

I kicked, grinning with delusion when something crunched beneath my foot. Suddenly, he let me go, his body climbing off mine. I yelped as a hand wrapped around my ankle, dragging me toward the table at the bottom of the bed.

"No!" Carpet burn scalded my back. I tried to jerk out of his grip, but his fingers bit harder.

Something skidded off the table, slamming to the floor. "Goddammit."

That voice again. My heart lost its violent rage, coughing with confusion.

Then his body was back on mine, slamming my head down, planting a palm over my mouth. This was it. He'd inject me with something and steal me away. My chance to either die or kill would be taken from me.

He spun me onto my stomach, pressing my face against the carpet. With a sharp knee wedged in my lower back, he wrenched my arms behind my back, wrapping something unyielding but soft around my wrists.

Our harsh breathing filled the room. I wriggled, kicked, did everything I could but my female form was no match for his brute muscle. Adrenaline had made me strong but not strong enough.

The moment my wrists were bound, he climbed off me, leaving me gulping back tears and rage.

Every last inch of energy swirled in my chest—ready to fight and fight and *fight,* but a switch clicked on, drenching us with light.

Light.

Beautiful, all-seeing light.

Black-clad legs stalked past my vision. I couldn't understand.

The legs folded to kneel beside me, flipping me onto my back. My eyes locked onto my kidnapper. Onto my lover, protector, husband to be.

The adrenaline disappeared with a bang, drenching my muscles in disbelief.

Q panted above me, his face an unreadable mask. His hot palm slammed over my lips as he dragged his other hand through his hair. His eyes were wild. "Fucking hell. I've lost my fucking mind."

And just like that the freedom from pain and past was gone. I snapped back to the Tess who no longer knew how to fight. I shivered as everything hot and true abandoned me.

My gaze flared wide. Had he finally snapped and embraced the darkness I always knew lived within him? Was he sleepwalking? *What the hell is happening?*

Fear overshadowed everything; another shiver went through me. I wanted to speak but he never released my mouth. I wiggled, trying to convey my wishes in my gaze.

Let me go! Talk to me!

Q's eyes blazed. "Don't move, Tess. For God's sake and all that's fucking holy. Do. Not. Move."

Forcing my breathing to slow, I obeyed.

Even though every molecule inside pinged and ricocheted, I lay like a corpse as Q menaced above like some son of the underworld. Dressed all in black he looked like a deliverer of death himself.

He shut his eyes, slowly removing his hand from my mouth. Dragging it over his face, he sucked in a gulp, then another. Blackness shimmered around him. "I didn't think you'd fight. I thought you'd be too broken to fight. Goddammit, if I knew you'd be so strong—that it would affect me like this—*shit*."

Suddenly, he hurled himself upright and slammed his fist into the wall. "Shit, shit, *shit*." He stumbled to the bed, sitting heavily. His splayed legs cradled his head as he rolled forward, grabbing his messy hair with white fingers. *"A quoi je pensais, putain?"* What the fuck was I thinking?

I didn't move. I didn't speak. I had no idea what was going on.

Q trembled with his head bowed, his large body locked with whatever issues he fought.

I didn't know how much time passed but the room returned to its peaceful silence. My shoulders and wrists ached from lying on them. Twisting my aching body, I managed to clamber to my knees. Shuffling forward, I whispered, "Q—"

Q held up his hand. "Don't come near me, Tess. Not yet. This was a big fucking mistake. How did I think I could do this to you when it's too close—scarily close to..." He didn't continue but I knew his thoughts as clearly as if he'd spoken them.

It was scarily close to all the badness inside him—the *true* fantasy. The ultimate wish to steal me away and use me. No consent. No love. Just pure dominance.

Inching my way across the carpet, I didn't care about my nakedness or even the goosebumps covering my skin. A metre separated us and all I wanted was to go to him. It was imperative we fix this. Otherwise, it had the power to destroy us.

"Q..."

A minute ticked past, then five, then ten. Finally, his back straightened. He smoothed his hair with shaky hands, looking up. His face was colourless, eyes wild and deadly. "I'm out of my mind." His lips curled in a cold smile. "I'm—God, I don't even know anymore."

I'd never seen him so lost—so threatening but unsure. His gaze begged me to forgive him while his body stiffened with self-hatred.

"You're not out of your mind."

Q snarled, "I am." He punched himself in the chest. "How else do you explain my reasoning to do what I just did? How *could* I? To you—my God, Tess, you've already been through so much without me putting you through more. Fuck!" He punched the mattress, his knuckles pounding the sheets.

I shifted closer, welcoming the heat of his anger. "Whatever you were trying to do, it was for the right reasons."

Q snorted, looking manic. "The right reasons? And what if I can't remember it? What if I got so caught up, I let you think they'd come back for you? What sort of fucked-up bastard does that?" He shook his head, breaking eye contact. "You don't know what it felt like. Having you fight me—truly, *truly* fight me. You were so fucking fierce, and I wanted nothing more than to take you hard."

His hand fell to grip between his legs. "I want you so fucking bad, *esclave*. It's tearing me up inside to even admit that—admit to wanting to take you by force, especially after what happened today."

His lips pursed; he shook his head with weighty sadness. "*Les bonnes raisons ...merde...*" The right reasons...shit...

My heart rabbited at the immense pain in his voice. Whatever he'd been trying to do, I hated to think of him so lost. He had blood on his hands for me. It was a debt I would never be able to repay. If he wanted to take me—to crave the lust inside—then I'd let him.

Cursing my bound hands—needing to hold him and offer forgiveness, I inched closer. "Tell me. What were you going to do?"

He laughed suddenly; it was laced with dark disbelief. "That's the screwed-up thing. I didn't have a complete plan. I was working on instinct—trying to help you." His eyes locked onto mine. "I want to fix you."

My heart softened, weeping at his confession. "You *are* fixing me. Every day you're helping by being you. You have to believe in yourself."

Q muttered something. I didn't push him to repeat, and the room fell into a hushed silence once again.

Another block of time passed while we sat in our own thoughts.

Q finally said, "No matter how many ideas I chase, they all lead back to one." Sitting taller, he straightened his shoulders. "If I said I might have a way to stop your nightmares, would you let me do it?" He stared hard, eyes probing deep. "Would you trust me, even though I can't promise I can control myself? Would you still let me try?"

I didn't need to contemplate. We both knew we were at the end. There would be no going forward unless we accepted our demons and began working together to abolish them. We'd been kidding ourselves up to this point—believing in a future that didn't exist.

My voice rang true. "Absolutely."

Q sighed heavily. "You give me too much, Tess."

"I've given you my soul." I shrugged to show how little it truly was. "It's yours, Q, because I've taken yours in return."

His mouth stayed silent, but his eyes let me glimpse just how tortured and savage he truly was. He had a personal vendetta against my nightmares. Whatever he had in mind wouldn't be conventional, approved, or even safe, but confidence slowly replaced my panic.

If I said yes, it would be exactly as if I'd been taken all over again. Two options: live or die. Survive or give-up.

Q took a deep breath. Unfolding himself from the bed, he stood on long muscular legs, dressed in tailored black. *"Tu me fais confiance, esclave?"* Do you trust me, *esclave?*

The question was loaded with so much unsaid. I *did* trust him. But there was still part of me that feared him.

"Yes," I whispered.

Q's hands curled. "Another lie. But if you let me, I'll turn it into a truth."

My heart picked up its beat. There would be no turning back. No admitting we'd made a mistake. Just like when Q let me whip him, this would either fix us for good or ruin us forever.

Please…let me survive. Please let Q survive.

"I believe you."

I wanted to be free of the past. To cut ourselves from the tethers of madness and horror. To start our marriage completely free.

Q's face tightened with barely concealed rage. "I want to take you back. I want to give you peace. I want us to find each other in our own perfect unsullied darkness." His eyes glowed with passion. Despite how hard this would be for him, he vowed to set aside his needs purely to fix me.

Regardless if he would be able to do it—I would let him try.

I nodded, ignoring the flash of panic in my heart. I was so fragile. Q had every power to break me for eternity. Break my soul, my mind, splinterize my entire existence.

I hope he does.

My eyes widened.

I hope he smashes everything away.

Maybe Q had the power to eradicate my cracks and fissures—demolishing everything I was in favour of a brand new me—making me blissfully complete.

Q moved, motioning for me to come closer. I used momentum to jump from my knees to feet; my legs cramped from kneeling. My wrists stayed locked together as I traversed the small distance.

The moment I got close, his strong hands landed on my waist. His touch was a threat. His touch was a promise.

His head bowed, lips coming within millimetres of mine. "I'm going to have to make you believe in order to make you free. Do you understand?"

Not really. But I nodded. The freedom of putting myself completely into his control was beautiful.

"Everything I do, even if I lose myself along the way, remember I love you so fucking much. I'm doing this for you. And afterward…I'm going to make you my wife."

My heart sprouted wings and for a moment I felt like a sparrow escaping a hunter's net. His promises made me shudder with longing. I wanted that. God, how I wanted that.

Q nuzzled my nose with his, such a sweet gesture—so tame and normal. My stomach twisted into untieable knots. "If there was another way, I'd do it, but I can't see one. This is our crescent-moon, Tess. It's more important than any honeymoon; it's about us fighting our demons, so they don't taint our future."

Pulling back, his pale eyes locked with mine, ensnaring me, sending my heart whirling. "You and me. We need this." His accented voice was hoarse and impassioned and swept up with promises. Q was right.

We needed this.

More than we knew.

"I'm yours for however long you need, *maître*."

He chuckled softly. "You're mine for eternity, *esclave*. But the next few days belong to putting our monsters to rest."

He pulled away, holding up his hand. Wrapped in his fingers was a black length of fabric. His eyebrow rose as he dangled the blindfold. "Ready?"

No.

Yes.

I don't know.

I sucked in a breath.

I nodded.

Permission granted.

Q attacked me.

I never knew how Q got me out of the hotel without rousing suspicion. I never knew if he wrapped me in a sheet or dressed me in clothes or carried me out naked. I would never find out how he orchestrated something so terrible all in the name of love.

All I knew was horror.

Cold, aching, howling horror.

He'd told the truth about making me believe. The moment he launched, I forgot everything we'd just agreed and drowned. Drowned in fear, memories, the horrible past.

I couldn't stop from fighting.

I was incapacitated from fighting.

Q gave himself over to his monsters, embracing the role of kidnapper. We stepped into our nightmares, letting them swallow us whole.

"Stop squirming and I won't hurt you," he hissed in my ear, sounding entirely swallowed by darkness.

I tried to reply but he stuffed a gag into my mouth, obliterating my cries.

My mind jumped into insanity. My lungs grasped for useless air.

Together we spiralled into a void.

The tower I'd knocked down so many times shot into formation, giving me no choice but to step aside and let the large, circular prison segment my mind. It crumbled upright, reversing its demise to rise from the dust of its foundations, soaring high.

Q's fingers wrapped around my throat, clutching my windpipe.

The tower beckoned, waving flags of safety, serenity. *No!*

Q squeezed, accelerating my hyperventilation.

The need to hide was an unbearable call. The single door in the tower swung wide, hinting at solitude and silence.

I took a step toward sanctuary. Toward temptation. I wanted to shut off completely.

Q was no longer my master. He was my nightmare.

His lips descended on my ear, delivering the final blow. "Welcome to my kingdom. I'm going to make you scream."

My mind raced for the tower, but it was too late.

Q's fingers cut off my air. Black spots danced, blending with the blindfold. My vision succumbed and I surrendered to the dark.

I woke in my kidnapper's arms.

Gagged, bound, and blindfolded, the only sense I had available was hearing. Wet slaps of an ocean in the distance, chirps of waking birds, the rustle of tussock, and crunch of gravel. Q's arms stayed locked around me, keeping me floating above the ground.

My tower loomed fully erect in my mind, waiting solemnly for me to return to its unfeeling hub. The temptation was strong, but Q's sleek muscles moved against my side, rocking me with every step. I made a promise to him. A promise that I would never shut him out again—no matter what happened. *I intend to keep that promise.*

My skin prickled with a chilly sea breeze, but only on my arms and ankles. I'd been bundled into something warm—fluffy. The blindfold hid any hope of seeing where we were and the gag halted my questions. Panic existed like liquid fear pumping thick in my blood.

"You're ours now, puta."

I cringed at the memory. No matter what Q did to make me whole again, I had to remember one thing. One fundamental crucial thing. This was Q. The man I loved with every fibre. He wouldn't sell me, rape me, or break my mind with drugs.

Are you sure?

My heart raced as the outside world suddenly changed to muffled and hushed. The heavy weight of a building I couldn't see wrapped around us, masking Q's footsteps with a thick carpet.

In my mind I tried to visualise a quaint home where only softness and healing existed but I couldn't avoid the more likely scenario of pain and fear. Room after room we travelled, Q's body heat both relaxing and scaring me. His arms and stomach tensed, carrying me down a flight of stairs. The air temperature was cooler as we descended. It felt heavier down here, as if the weight of the unseen building was a tomb.

More muffled footsteps. I lost touch with common-sense. I hovered as if by magic. Then Q's shoes echoed on tiles, coming to a stop in a room smelling faintly of juniper.

I gasped as Q released his hold, swinging my legs downward to connect with textured flooring. My feet were bare, toes digging into the rough tiles like an anchor. The fluffy warmth around me tickled my legs as it shifted with my body.

Not saying a word, Q grabbed my bound wrists, undoing the tight material holding them pinned. I ached for connection. I wanted a hug, a whisper, something to keep my fear at bay. I needed reminding of his love and the reasons why we were doing something so utterly dangerous.

But I got nothing.

He hoisted my arms upward, securing them onto some sort of apparatus from the ceiling. My lungs strained, breathing hard through my nose. The helplessness of hanging—gagged, blindfolded, and completely at his mercy—sent a flurry of bricks toward me, forming into a path, leading to my tower.

No. I'm strong enough.

Every muscle tensed, waiting for a whip or some horrible pain, but Q drifted away. No sound. No body heat. His presence fading into the ether.

The tower became my enemy rather than friend—beckoning too hard, filling my mind with the need to run.

Step inside and no longer care. Step inside and hide.

I squeezed my eyes, fighting the seduction. I had to be strong enough. I *was* strong enough. Q asked me to trust him—I wouldn't run. I was *done* running.

Seconds ticked on without me; I didn't know how long I stood there. Time played tricks with me, delivering false memories of Rio and Mexico. White Man had never been my capturer—it had been Q all along. Q drugged me. He beat me.

I clamped down on the gag, forcing myself to chase away the lies. I focused instead on the iciness of my hands from lack of blood and the unrelenting ache in my shoulders from being trussed. I wanted to sit. I wanted to roll my spine and stretch. But all I could do was hang and wait like an animal headed to slaughter.

Harsh fingers touched my cheek.

I jolted, cursing my heart cannonballing around my chest. Q undid the gag, pulling it free from my mouth. I groaned in relief, wiggling my jaw, lubricating my dry tongue with saliva.

His fingers clamped around my chin, pressing against my

lips. "Take this."

I stiffened, trying to move my face from his probing fingers. My eyes remained veiled by the blindfold; I yearned for sight. I needed to know where we were. I needed to latch onto Q and know I wasn't alone.

The pressure on my lips came again, demanding. "Take it," he snapped.

My stomach somersaulted. *He's trying to drug you. Just like them.*

My hands clenched and I repelled away. "No. What are you—"

"Don't speak. You're not allowed to speak." Two fingers entered my mouth by force. The taste of salt and citrus shot right to my heart. This was so wrong.

My teeth ached to bite. To sever the invasion before my mind could turn against Q. I was wrong when I said I was strong enough. I wasn't. I wanted nothing to taint my love for him—and this—this would murder everything I'd tried so hard to retain. "Stop. This is a mistak—"

Q's touch turned from harsh to brutal, placing something acidic and foreign on my tongue. "Swallow."

Tears stung my eyes; I fought in his grip, shaking my head violently.

Never again did I want the fog of hallucinogenics or mind-twisting chemicals. *What the hell is he thinking?* He knew how bad my withdrawals were. He'd seen how hard it was for me to crawl out of the smog.

Q breathed hard in my ear, muttering in French, cursing in a stream of anger. His arm wrapped around my thrashing body, tilting my head back. His hand came under my jaw, clamping it shut. "Swallow!"

I whimpered, soaking the blindfold in gushing tears.

"Do it or I'll hurt you."

My heart pounded; the tower no longer needed to beckon—I inched closer on my own. Fear drove me forward. The horror at being forced to take something that would remove all my mental power.

It would all disappear the moment I stepped inside.

Oh, God. What the hell were we doing? We were tempting fate—waving an invitation at everything we ran from—enticing horror into our lives.

I stood trembling, disobeying. The acidic pill slowly dissolved on my tongue, making me nauseous. I would let Q do anything but drug me. Anything else but that.

Q sighed. The anger in his voice faded to grief, shedding the theatrics, showing the actor beneath. He kissed my ear with incredible softness. "I need you to take it. It's nothing strong—it will last an hour or two, max." His tongue swirled around my lobe making my terror-laden body warm and begin to thaw. "Please, Tess."

I moaned, shaking my head, trying to free my chin free so I could talk. I didn't want to swallow. I had to make him see how terrified I was of drugs.

His fingers wouldn't let me go, letting the pill dissolve even further. "You have to *believe* in order for me to bring you back. Remember?" he murmured. "I won't be able to help you if you know it's me. It will ruin both of us. Please...you'll be safe. *Je promets*." I promise.

I shook my head for the fiftieth time, my eyes wild and damp beneath the blindfold. All method of communication had been stolen. I couldn't appeal or argue. Q held me firm, fully intending to shove me head first into a chasm of horror.

Swift panic shot through my body.

Q's right. No matter how much I loved him I would end up hating him for this. I wouldn't be able to stop the connection between him and my past.

I shuddered, acknowledging the truth. I had to go back. Completely. Truly. There was no faking this. No cutting corners. And I couldn't know it was him driving me deeper.

With a groan of sorrow, I swallowed.

"Good girl," Q whispered. He paced around me, his fingertips dragging around my neck. Stopping in front again, his hand slid into the material I wore, cupping my breast. "We probably have about fifteen minutes before that takes you away from me."

I jerked, testing the ceiling restraints. As much as I loved him, I didn't want pain. If he raised a whip or paddle, I wouldn't have the strength not to enter my tower. And once I stepped inside—I wasn't coming out. I wouldn't be able to.

Q spread the front of the gown open, his hot breath tickling my skin. "Fuck you look incredible, *esclave.*"

I sucked in a harsh breath as his mouth descended on my nipple. His arms came around, dragging me close. Every ripple of muscle and sweep of his tongue sent a jagged bolt of passion into my core. My body reacted instantaneously, knowing any moment everything I knew would be stolen from me.

After what happened, I wanted his touch. I needed to *feel*. To be soothed and assured that whatever stupidity we were about to do wouldn't hurt us. *We're doing it for the right reasons.*

Q's mouth was hot, wet, full of sinful fire. Everywhere he touched seemed amplified—my mind making it intense and visceral. I arched into him, pressing my flesh further into his mouth.

He groaned, licking, sucking. His arm clenched hard, possessing me completely.

When will it affect me?

I bit my lip as Q nibbled gently, his mouth trailing from my nipple up to my throat. His teeth grazed over my tingling skin. "You're all mine. Completely at my mercy." His voice layered with husky lust.

My eyes popped wide as a new fear rose. Was *he* strong enough? Would he be able to break my chains and not lose himself in the process?

Q hugged my tense body, sensing the reason for my panic. Planting a kiss on the 'Q' branded into my neck, he murmured, "I have it under control. When it takes you, don't fight. I'll keep you safe."

My breath caught. There'd been another time when he

said I was safe. At his office. With his birds on top of the world. He lied.

My heart skipped; a rush of sickness raced in my blood. *Is it affecting me?*

My mouth went dry. I smacked my lips, trying to lubricate my throat to speak. "Q—" I croaked.

I moaned as Q undid the cord around my waist, spreading the fluffy material wrapped around my body. He sucked in a harsh breath, ragged passion echoing in the sound. I stiffened as his fingers trickled from my cleavage and down my stomach. "Do you have any concept of how much I miss the woman I fell in love with?"

My heart squeezed at the sadness in his voice.

His fingers kissed my ribcage, stroking so soft it was almost a tickle. "I miss your fire." His touch dropped a little, flaring over my hips. "I miss your strength." His fingertips turned inward, tracing my lower belly, brushing through the trimmed hair between my legs. "I miss you taunting me."

His scent of sandalwood and citrus drugged me far more effective than anything he'd given. I willingly gave myself to the heady combination. Q owned all my senses now. Not just my sense of touch, taste, sound, and sight but also my instincts, obedience, and trust.

He owned everything.

His touch teased, stroking so close to where I wanted him most. His lips landed on my ear, burning me with whispered words. "I miss your fight, *esclave.*" His shirt brushed against my nipples as he leaned into me, putting pressure on my wrists bound to the ceiling. The friction sent a wave of pleasure clenching my core. "I miss your love of pain."

My stomach lurched. My voice came out as a wisp. "I'm still the woman you fell for. Please don't miss me when I'm standing in your arms."

He shook his head, brushing his five o'clock shadow against my sensitive throat. "You're not my Tess. You lied to me. You made me hurt you against your will."

I shook my head. I couldn't verbalize the depths of my love for him. I didn't want to admit I willingly put myself into his power. I would let him hurt me all over again if it gave him happiness. I wouldn't fight—and in a way that made me weak. Terribly weak.

Something skittered up my spine, entering my brain like a drop of black ink in water. A speck, hovering in crystal liquid before starting to spread.

It's happening.

"I told you I wouldn't hurt you again. And I mean it." His nose trailed along my collarbone; his finger dipped lower, feathering over my clit. "But if this works...I'll know. I'll turn your lies back into truths." Q cupped my pussy, his strong fingers the epitome of him and his masculinity.

I tensed then liquefied, completely in his thrall.

"You'll grow wet for me again. You'll pant for me again."

His voice tripped and warbled in my head, spreading the drop of ink, sending tentacles of black.

I blinked, trying to keep my thoughts clear. "I am wet for you, Q. See?"

His fingers spread my folds ever so gently—every touch a delicious tease.

Another droplet of ink appeared in my brain, spreading, staining, tainting.

I moaned as Q dipped a finger inside—just the tip, hovering as the ultimate tantalize. "You're damp, *esclave*...not wet...not yet." He dragged me closer, sliding his finger deeper.

My mouth popped open, consumed with his touch. I wanted to pant and moan but the rapidly spreading blackness dragged me further and further from his web. My body jerked as a rush of surreal coldness took me hostage.

Q sighed, the tinge of anger-sadness creeping back into his voice. "We're running out of time." He pressed his finger deeper, urging my body to melt and swell. "There's so much I want to say to you." His arm imprisoned my lower back, jerking me closer while his finger thrust upward. His heat undid me all while more black droplets stained my mind.

It's taking me.

Q kissed my cheek, flexing his finger in the perfect way. "Tell me why we're doing this." His tone wasn't a demand, more like a beg. He needed to be reminded himself. He sounded scared….lost. "Talk to me, or I'll stop."

I could barely remember how to speak; my mind spinning and dipping with every new droplet. "To turn my lies into truth," I moaned, bowing in his arms as his finger moved harder, turning dampness into wetness. "You're going to fix me…"

The blindfold stole my sight, amplifying my awareness of the drug-induced mania building inside.

"I trust you, Q. I—I want you."

He chuckled, hiding the lace of pain. "You want me? You want this?" He drove his finger deeper, his knuckles connecting with sensitive flesh.

My pussy rippled, sending a wave of sensation into my lower belly.

My head fell back even as a torrent of black liquid and fog filled my mind. I wanted to stay in his arms forever. I wanted to never let go of the tingling erotic pleasure.

I wanted more. More, more, *more.*

"Yes—"

Drip. Drip. Drip.

"You want more, pretty girl? Beg."

I gasped, fisting my hands, tugging on binds hanging me from the ceiling. *No!*

"Keep talking and I'll make you come. I'll give you a release," Q whispered, slowly penetrating me with another finger.

My mind had taken over, contaminated with whatever he'd given me. My body switched from hot and needy to fearful and cold.

White Man flickered in and out like a faulty hologram. *"You want it? Beg. You know you'll beg eventually."*

"Please—not again." Pincers weighed down my mind, dragging me deeper into the inky puddle residing in my brain. I wanted nothing more than to cling to his hard form. I didn't want to be lost again. I didn't want to spiral into fog. Squeezing my eyes, I tried to claw my way back to reality. Q held me tight. "Let go. Don't fight." His two fingers stroked my inner walls, stretching me, keeping me tethered to a hypersensitive body. The coax was dangerous—fooling me into thinking I wouldn't suffer if I surrendered. I *would* suffer.

I shuddered, flushing with a wave of desire even as I swam upstream in a river of blackness.

Leather Jacket appeared, hazy and unformed, his foul lips twisting into a grin. Waiting—waiting for me to be washed into his torture once again.

"Q—I don't want to. Please. Don't let them take me."

"It's okay. Trust me." His touch no longer had the power to keep me sane, every passing heartbeat dampened the desire in my blood, favouring brittle panic instead.

Ropes around my wrists. Blindfold on my eyes. I was helpless. *I can't do this.* Swaying forward, I found Q's neck, latching onto his slightly salty skin. I bit. Hard.

Q jerked, his fingers twitching inside me. "Tess..." he growled. "Stop fighting."

"You like it rough, don't you, pretty girl. We'll sell you to an owner who will look after you."

No. I would never stop fighting them. Not after what they made me do. Made me become.

But no matter how hard I clambered to stay coherent I slid down and down, deeper and deeper.

Q groaned, his fingers diving harder. Now there were no lust sparkles or pleasure, now all I felt were bullets of shame. My hips spasmed backward, dislodging Q's touch. I couldn't do it anymore. His fingers fell away, leaving me empty and all alone.

I can't fight it.

My heart went sluggish, a curtain of drugs falling over me.

"Tess..." Q's voice lost its perfect baritone, morphing into my enemy. "I need to know the truth—why did you sacrifice yourself? Why did you let me almost rape you?" French accent traded for Spanish, and Leather Jacket swirled into being.

No longer hazy or unformed—every inch of him was real. The blindfold didn't keep images out anymore. I saw him plain as truth. His yellow-stained teeth and creaking, reeking jacket. His greasy black hair and dirty fingernails.

"Did you like my fingers inside you, *puta*?" Leather Jacket sneered.

Q. God, please let me wakeup. This couldn't be real.

I licked my lips, invoking courage I no longer had. "Let me go."

He shook his head. "Not until you answer me."

Tell him. Tell him before he hurts them!

Honesty exploded up my throat, not answering Leather Jacket—but Q. The admission was for him even though he no longer existed. "I wanted to make you happy. I'd gladly give you my life to do that."

Q suddenly appeared, smashing through the putridity, standing tall. "What do you mean?"

Wanting to answer before I was stolen away again, I said, "I would die for you, Q. That's what that means. All this talk of belonging to each other—well, you truly do own me. I would gladly give up my life if it meant you'd be happy."

Q disappeared again, replaced by Leather Jacket. His hand came from nowhere, spanking my thigh with a wicked hot strike. Burning tears flocked to my eyes.

"You still haven't answered my question. Did you like my fingers inside you, *puta*?" he asked. His voice smooth and coaxing but beneath it lived a layer of deadly steel.

I hiccupped with building tears. *What's going on?*

Drip. Drip. Drip.

The ink completely stole my mind.

Then guilt crushed heavily. Blonde Hummingbird and

Angel.

Their silhouettes appeared, bloody and bullet-ridden.

"If you won't answer my other question, perhaps you'll answer this. Did you enjoy hurting them? Did you enjoy murder?" Leather Jacket threw his head back, laughing. The sound cut right through me, dredging up everything I wanted to forget.

My tower stood taller, knowing I would have no choice but to step inside its circular walls if I wanted to survive.

I couldn't live in this limbo anymore. I couldn't live with these lies, these fears—this *guilt*.

I wanted to be whole. I wanted to be happy.

Leather Jacket grabbed a handful of my hair, tugging hard. The burn in my scalp sent bugs and beetles, residual from the drugs, skittering over my skin. Their feelers and creepy-crawly legs welcomed me back into the muck I'd lived in.

It wasn't often I craved another hit. I hated drugs—but in that moment I would've willingly traded anything for the smoggy numbness.

Whatever Q gave me wasn't enough. He'd pushed me overboard, letting me sink into my twisted mind, but it was *too* twisted—I would never be able to untangle the mess.

Give in. Give up.

"Please! Just let me go." I hated my weak confusion.

Leather Jacket shoved me, making me spin and dangle from the rope. Catching me after a circulation, he dragged me against his foul stench. "You're mine again. All mine. I'm never letting you go." He kissed my cheek, evil black eyes glowing. "We're equals, you and I. And I'm about to fucking show you."

Suddenly the blindfold was torn off. Q shattered the vision of Leather Jacket.

I sobbed, seeing him so clearly, even while a waterfall of gunk contaminated my mind. I hated drugs. Hated them! Hated what I became when I took them.

Drip. Drip. Drip.

"Ah, Tess. You're leaving me. But only for a little while."

Leaning forward, Q captured my mouth in a gentle kiss. His lips were soft and sweet and perfectly Q. He didn't kiss deeply, or request access with his tongue. He just fed me strength— strength I sorely needed.

For one precious moment, I didn't need to fight. I knew who I was. I knew why I had to give in. We shared our love even while we acknowledged for the next few hours I would hate him.

There would be tears. There would be screams. There would be facing demons and a past that might ruin us. But if we survived, we would be unconquerable.

"*Je t'aime*," Q murmured, pulling away.

The curtain slammed down, shoving me face first into the cloying ink. It wasn't a matter of giving in—the drugs were the master now.

The transition from sweet lover to controlling diabolical trafficker happened in a blink. Q, with his gorgeous jade eyes, disappeared. Leather Jacket took centre stage, revelling in his ownership.

He grinned, shedding his jacket and cracking his fingers as if he had a monstrous task before him. His eyes were flat and cold. "Told you, you were mine, *puta*." Stalking forward, he dragged a finger down my exposed cleavage. "Our first exercise is to clean you. You're fucking filthy."

I swallowed my fear, heart hammering. *Please say shower. Please say shower.*

Leather Jacket's mouth twisted into a horrendous smile. "It's time for your bath."

The last drip snuffed out my light, transporting me back to Rio, to Mexico, to nightmares.

Chapter Six

Intertwined, tangled, knotted forever, our souls
will always be twisted together,
our demons, our monsters belong to the other,
Bow to me, I bow to thee, now we are free

What the fuck am I doing?

I had no fucking idea. This wasn't right. It *couldn't* be right. Nothing about drugging and mentally torturing a woman who'd been through so much was right.

It was a stupid idea—moronic to think I could walk her through the past and replace the memories. I ought to be fucking shot. *I'm an idiot.*

Tess's eyes were vacant, staring right into mine, but not seeing me. Not anymore. Her lips parted, breathing hard with whatever hallucinations whispered in her ear.

This was worse than the fucking nightmares. This was induced by *me*. For the next couple of hours I had to shed everything I'd fought so hard and become her worst fears. I had to become the man I'd sworn never to be.

I glared at Tess, hanging and bound. The dressing gown

gaped wide, showing her perfect body and luscious breasts. She was sent to make me sin. All my life I'd abstained from my true nature but then cruel fate gave me her.

My hands clenched, unable to deny the billowing blackness settling over me. Creeping from ignorable to fucking intolerable. Each moment I let myself continue this charade, the light inside blotted out until I no longer recognised myself.

The only thing protecting Tess from my snarling scream-thirsty beast was love.

Unconditional love—miraculously keeping me on a leash. She owned my heart and soul. That was the only safeguard preventing me from not giving a shit anymore and diving head first into debauchery.

*No one would know….*Something slithered in my brain, whispering sickness and want.

She dangled like a feast—surrounded in darkness, drugged out of her mind. *I could do anything….*

My stomach tensed as desire shot up my spine. It would be so easy to mount and fuck her while hanging from the ceiling. I could be cruel and heartless. I could hurt her the way I wanted with no repercussions. She would never know it was me.

You'd be him. You'd walk straight into fate.

My lips curled; I spat on the floor as a rush of bile filled my mouth. To ever think I was weak enough to become my father made me suicidal with rage.

I would *never* do that to Tess. No matter how my sick cock ached.

Locking my knees, I made an oath. A pact with my fucking soul.

Whatever I did here, I would never overstep two boundaries: rape or blood play. If Tess ever became strong enough to endure my needs, completely sane and willing, then I'd give myself some leniency. But not before and *definitely* not with an unhinged druggie I was trying to save.

Tess's dilated eyes trained on me, never looking away,

despite the haze. "Why—why are you doing this? He'll come for you again, you know." Her head dropped as if suddenly too heavy, the drugs sucking her deeper.

I shuddered at the thought of what she'd been through—what I was putting her through once again.

I knew she didn't see me. She saw *them*.

The drug did what Franco had said. I'd asked him to find something—a hallucinogenic that lasted a couple of hours. He'd disappeared, returning a little while later with a single yellow pill.

I didn't know the name of the chemical or even where he got it from. And I fed it to the woman I wanted to grow old with. How fucking irresponsible!

My jaw worked hard, grinding my teeth, flaring a rapidly building headache. I'd fed it to her because I made the choice. A choice I already fucking regretted. But it was done now. The only thing left to do was suffer the consequences.

I snapped my fingers in front of Tess's face, making sure she was completely consumed by visions. Time to begin.

"Fuck me, I'm going to hell," I muttered.

Tess sucked in a breath, but there was no flicker of love or comprehension. Rather, her eyes blazed with a hate so pure and piercing, my heart stuttered at the thought of her ever looking at me that way in reality.

I wished I could enter her mind and see which asshole haunted her.

My hands curled at the thought of the man, Smith. The cocksucker responsible. His heart now rested under a rose bush, his body torn to pieces and burned. Or did she see the man who'd raped the girl beside her, earning the wrath of Franco cutting off his cock. Either way—it didn't matter.

She was in hell—so the fuck was I.

This was my burden. *I* was the reason she was broken. *I* was the reason she'd lost so much. And I was the only one who could bring her back. And I had to do it before…

I don't know how long I have to fix her.

The thought slipped through my carefully fortified defences. I refused to think so morbidly—but I couldn't lie to myself. They were coming. And I had no intention of leaving Tess like this if they achieved what they wanted.

Are you ready to do this?

Never. But I moved forward anyway. Tess flinched; eyes hazy and unfocused. She hadn't looked around the room or asked where she was. None of that mattered because all she cared about was freedom. Freedom from a third kidnapping and pain.

I wanted to scream: *'whoever you see in your head—they're dead. I slaughtered them. Their blood stains my hands.'*

But I didn't. She had to believe this was true. She had to give in completely.

Now. Do it now. I didn't know how long the pill would last. I had a lot to accomplish before it ended.

With trembling hands, I reached above and undid the fastening. I'd strung her from a low hanging chandelier— deliberately drawing all the curtains and turning on no lights. I didn't want Tess to see the room until I was ready. Once she returned to me—then she'd understand.

I pulled the cord around her wrists; she stumbled forward. Her body landed on mine and I groaned as her breasts squished against my chest. So soft. So pure. So fucking perfect.

My heart bucked with need. I would've given anything to be able to tackle her to the floor and drive myself inside. To take and give and consume and adore.

I swallowed hard as my eyes landed on her pussy. My mouth watered to taste her—to dip my tongue inside. She'd been wet, soaking before.

I'd wanted to make her come. I'd wanted to give her one burst of pleasure before the drugs stole her, but I'd been too slow.

Now, it was up to me to be a bastard all in the name of curing her. I had one chance at breaking her nightmares, and I refused to fuck it up.

Yanking the rope, I dragged her forward. She moaned in pain as blood rushed back from having her arms up for so long. "Stop bitching." My cock ached. Fuck, it ached. Everything about what I did called to the monster. Tess's fear clogged my nostrils, making it so damn hard to remember I was doing this for her. Not for me.

"So you're the master who doesn't let himself play." Smith's voice slammed into my head. It didn't matter I'd stolen his heart—he'd come to destroy me.

My back locked straight as I growled under my breath, repeating what I'd said to him that night. "I'm the man who knows right from wrong."

"No, you live in denial. One day you'll see the truth. It will happen. You can't ignore who you truly are forever. One day the decision won't be yours anymore, and when that happens operations like ours will be your saving grace."

Fuck.

I couldn't live like this much longer. I couldn't live so torn.

I clutched my head, sucking in greedy breaths, forcing my mind to fill with images. Images I deliberately blocked from my past.

"Do you want a taste, Quincy? You keep sneaking into rooms you're forbidden to fucking go, all because you want a piece of pussy?" My father motioned me forward with his free hand, while his other thrust thick fingers into a screaming blonde.

My ten-year-old stomach threatened to evict the cherry pie Mrs. Sucre had made me, but if my father told me to do something, I had no choice but to do it.

Inching across the carpet, my eyes fell on a tangled mess of hair and limbs. A girl. Skin that should've been dusky and pink was now grey and lifeless. Even her blood had turned from bright red to brown.

My feet reeled backward, faster and faster. "No!" I screamed. "I'll never be like you. I'll never touch a girl like you!"

My father laughed. It started as a chuckle but grew and grew until it felt as if the entire room shook with corruption. "You're wrong, boy. You have my blood in your veins. You'll grow up needing exactly what I need.

And there's nothing you can do to fucking stop it."

Hitting the blonde so hard she fell onto her knees, he held out his hand again. "Now, come. Take your place as my son and heir. Come and play with your subjects like a good Mercer boy. I'll even let you fuck one of them."

I ran.

I ran away from my father. I ran away from any hope at having a mentor in my life. I ran to my mother, only to find she'd drunk herself into a stupor.

I found out later she drank to drown out the screams. She committed suicide by alcohol all to forget what her husband did down the hall. Leaving her son to fend for himself.

The memory shattered, and I stumbled to the side. I'd never had a flashback—such an intense recollection come to life. I fucking hated it.

But the glacial disgust and hatred I'd felt that day lodged itself in my chest, granting me a defence against the dark whispers in my head. I didn't need to make an oath not to hurt Tess. Sheer repugnance of what lineage I'd come from would do that.

Tess kept her chin down, either accepting her fate or acting like the docile prisoner. I didn't trust her one bit. Not after her strength in the hotel. Fuck she was wild. And beautiful, so mouth-wateringly beautiful.

She'd fought me like I'd always wished to be fought. With the abandonment of sheer survival. She would've gladly taken my life—or given up her own in order to win.

Was she strong enough to survive this? Was I strong enough to step into the role as trafficking asshole and come out on the other side intact?

The questions were irrelevant. I had to be.

I am.

"Come," I growled, tugging on the binds.

Tess's head snapped up, eyes blazing grey fire. "Just kill me. I'm done playing your games. You had your fun and now I refuse."

Hearing her strength mixed with equal terror made my heart shoot out of my chest and splat against her feet.

I wanted to caress her cheek and murmur, *'Don't be strong. Don't fight. It will be easier to hit rock bottom if you just let yourself slide.'*

But Tess would never just give up. She might want to. She might think she had. But she didn't know herself like I did.

She would never stop fighting. And I needed to teach her how, so I could build her up again.

Forgive me.

Gritting my teeth, I cuffed her around the side of the head. My cock thickened, throbbed.

She narrowed her eyes. "Don't touch me!"

It was pain she hated. Pain was the catalyst in this mess. I had to use pain against her.

Fuck! I struck her again, this time hard enough to knock her to her knees. She swayed but shook her head, snarling, "Back to your old tricks? Back to beating up women because that's the only way you get off? You're sick!" She spat on the floor, her saliva mixed with a small tinge of blood. "Just sell me already, at least a new master will know how to fuck."

Her tirade tore my chest open. How dark was her mind? How much blackness did she keep hidden in that angelic face?

Squatting on my haunches, I grabbed her chin, glaring into her eyes. "Do you want to be fucked? Is that it? You want a master who will abuse you and give no shit to your happiness or humanity?"

Tess tore her face out of my hold, hissing, "I *have* a master. And he's good and kind and the only man I would gladly give my body to for his pleasure. But you keep stealing me from him, so I'm done. Do you understand? I'm *done* being stolen and drugged and hurt. Sell me! I want to be sold. I never want to see you again!"

I couldn't swallow. I couldn't breathe.

I wanted to stop this terrible fucking idea.

"Tess..." I murmured.

Her eyes practically popped out of her head. "How do you

know my name? No!" Wracking sobs clawed up her throat; the crack in her ferocity gave me a spark of faith. It was working.

God, fucking forgive me for what I'm about to do.

Slapping her cheek, I growled, "That's right. We know your name. Tess Snow. Tess. Tess. Tess."

She shoved me, but her arms were weak. I shoved back. She sprawled onto her side, before cowering into a ball.

Standing upright, I said, "We know you let your master string you up and taste your blood. We know you let him suffocate you to the point of death. We also know you love giving fucking blowjobs—apparently you have quite the talent."

Fuck, I'm scum. Why was I doing this? It was so, so wrong.

Nudging her balled body with my foot, I added, "So, Tess....are you sure you want to be sold. Knowing you'll survive only on the cum from men forcing themselves on you? Do you want to spend your life strung up and at their mercy?"

Just like the poor women who served my father.

"Answer me, Tess Snow. You're not so fucking innocent now."

Every word I uttered whipped Tess worse than any cat o' nine tails. I broke down her defences, throwing back memories she no doubt thought as treasured and totally private. I ripped her mind open, flipping it back with scorn.

Grabbing her by the hair, I hauled her to her feet. She clutched my fingers, trying to control the burn in her scalp, but I shook her instead. "Tell me! Do you wish to be sold? Or do you wish to be free?"

She hiccupped, her face flushed with tears. "Free. I want to be *free.* Let me go. Please. I'll do anything. *Anything.*"

"Wrong answer."

"But you said—"

I couldn't suck in a decent breath—I felt lightheaded, high, and sick to my fucking stomach. My cock rippled with pre-cum. I had to close my eyes from the misplaced rush of pleasure.

"I know what I fucking said. I asked if you wanted to be

free or be sold. I didn't ask for anything in return. Did I ask you to suck my cock? Did I ask to fuck you in return for your freedom?"

I wobbled on my feet, too enraptured with the mental images of forcing her to do just that. I'd blow right down her throat with one lick of her tongue.

Her head hung, hiding her feverish face with tangled blonde curls. Between ragged pants she said, "I don't know what you want from me!"

"I don't want anything!" I roared. *I want you to take back your destiny. Take it. Admit you want your freedom. Don't offer anything in return. Just take it.*

Her sobs took over, dragging her into sorrow.

It was obvious I needed more time to get the message across. Shaking her again, I snapped, "You failed this lesson, Tess Snow. But we'll visit it again soon enough."

Her head flailed from side to side. "No…please. Just let me sleep. I'm done. I'm *done.*"

"Don't fucking talk back. And you're not done. Not by a long shot." Spinning on my heel, I yanked the rope, bracing myself against the conflicting hatred and lust oozing in my veins. Tess followed behind—her bare feet slapping softly against the expensive travertine.

I threw a look over my shoulder. My body suffered a sick roll. Tess shuffled, her eyes downcast in her own drugged-up world.

I wanted nothing more than to smash through the fog and apologise. I wanted to beg for forgiveness for putting her through this.

I had to believe I was helping, because right now it felt like I was making it worse.

Tess didn't make a sound as I dragged her through the dark-shrouded house. I ignored the rich decor of the twelve bedrooms, five bathroom home that'd been designed by myself and an architectural team. Sitting pride of place on a cliff overlooking the sea, it was part of the subdivision I'd participated in a few years ago. It was also the house that granted one sex slave in return for the bribery of Tenerife planning officials.

It was empty. Fully furnished and staged as a show home to encourage cashed-up rich fucks to buy into the twenty-plus complex.

It'd been a quick phone call to secure and ensure complete privacy. Franco would make sure we weren't disturbed. There wasn't a more perfect place for the first stage in the crescent moon with Tess. I had no desire to ever come here again—the bad memories would be left in its walls, and Tess would be free.

Stepping into a bathroom the size of a small lounge, I dragged Tess to a standstill. New sun tried to enter the room, but I'd drawn every blind, every shutter.

Tess and I were formed in the dark. The dark had moulded us, changed us, almost broken us, but in its black embrace we would find healing and peace.

"Look at me, Tess Snow."

Her eyes met mine, flinty and fierce. Tears decorated her cheeks like silver droplets, and I wanted so fucking bad to lick them off her skin. I wanted to consume her misery and fight it for her.

"It's time to wash it all away." With unforgiving hands, I untied the belt from around her wrists and shoved the dressing gown off her shoulders. She stood trembling and naked. I bit the inside of my cheek, forcing myself not to touch her. My fingers *screamed* to stroke her, to dip inside her again.

"Don't fucking move," I ordered.

Tess's lips tightened, but I didn't wait to see if she'd obey. I couldn't look at her another second. If I did, I'd break my first rule: no rape. God, I wanted her.

Going to the large freeform bath, I swung the ornate taps and pressed a chrome plug into the bottom. Water gushed, splashing wetly into a tub that'd never been used before. It wasn't as big as the Tuscan bath where Tess had been stolen, but it would have to do.

Glancing around the large bathroom, I made out the silhouette of the two person shower, the twin vanity, and glittering towel rails. Only I knew what the room looked like in the daylight. To Tess this would be nameless—faceless. A dungeon.

A small noise jerked my head up. My mouth fell open as a curse ripped its way up my throat. "Fucking fuck me."

She'd disobeyed me. She'd run. *I should've known!*

My dress shoes slipped on the tiles as I charged after her. "Tess! Goddammit, come back here."

My headache roared as a dose of dark eagerness splashed through my blood. *She's run.* When I caught her she'd be my prize—my conquest.

Why the hell didn't I keep her tied? Did I think she'd forget about our masquerade and stand obediently for me? Did I believe she was so afraid of whoever she saw in her delusion to obey? The burn for freedom was stronger than her fear of pain or retaliation.

The knowledge walloped me around the head.

It's stronger than her fear of pain.

If I could get her to accept freedom. Get her to think she *won* her freedom....

Hope. Glorious fucking hope. I knew what I had to do.

But first I had to catch the bloody woman.

A chase was not good for a man like me—a man walking the tightrope between civilization and animalistic needs. Running triggered one thing in my brain: prey.

My breathing increased as I charged through the house. Room after room—empty. She was tripping on substances I'd given her. Reacting to nightmares I fed to her.

And now I'd turned into a worse predator than I already was.

Every room I ran through, the more my headache grew. I lost control of the cage I'd locked the monster in; the beast hurled itself into being. Running after prey. Hunting for the weak. Searching for a woman I wanted to fuck so damn much. *Stalk her. Take her.*

All my righteous thoughts of saving her were deleted by the overpowering rage in my stomach. It fired hotter and hotter, craving her beneath me—surrendering to me.

The situation turned from terrible to downright dangerous. I salivated at the thought of catching her.

My mind ran riot with so many sinful things of non-consent, screams, and endless fucking orgasms. Slamming her to the ground, spreading her legs. Both of us gasping for breath while I took her in retribution.

Shit, Tess, you really shouldn't have run.

I slammed to a halt as a noise sounded from the back of the house. The beast inside howled while the man panted with black delight. I'd found her. The moment I caught her—

I'm going to taste her. I'm going to make her cry.

Then rationality knocked aside my monstrous thoughts. I had to get her before she found an exit. If anyone saw this. If anyone was witness to the CEO of *Moineau* Holdings chasing after a naked woman screaming about being kidnapped for the sex trade….Shit, my company would be ruined. *I'd* be ruined. I'd end up in jail.

I couldn't let that happen.

Sprinting faster, I grabbed onto walls, hurling myself around corners, slowly gaining ground on the running footsteps up ahead.

A glimpse of blonde as Tess sprinted, disappearing around a corner.

My body shuddered, cursing the tight balls between my legs, the lust thick in my veins. *You're almost mine, Tess.*

Power supercharged my legs as I hurled after her. She was headed for the back door.

No! My heart exploded as I careened around the bend just in time to see her beeline for the exit—the exit we'd entered through. She'd been unconscious. How did she know it was there?

Tess grappled with the handle while I stood gawking like an idiot. In a twist and leap, she barrelled through the door and into beaming sunshine.

Shit!

I charged, bowling after her, squinting in the new dawn. Tess was fast, but she was no match for me. I gained on my runaway slave and every black part of me yelled in triumph. My mouth watered with freedom.

I'm going to show you why you don't run from me.

I wouldn't be able to control myself when I caught her. I wouldn't have any hope at stopping what would happen. I would throw her down, rip off my trousers, and bury myself so fucking deep inside her I'd guarantee to make her scream.

Each whizzing heartbeat sang a different story. *Run. Stop. Run. Stop.*

There would be no stopping. Not until I'd wrung myself dry inside her.

Then, from my peripheral vision, a hurtling black suit and pumping arms appeared. Franco tore after Tess, effortlessly grabbing her, clamping his arms around her panting body.

I blinked, unable to believe what happened. Not only had Franco saved my reputation with the outside world, but he also saved me from raping and destroying her.

My entire body wanted to pounce, to drive deep inside. I needed to claim her. I needed to remind her she should *never* fucking run from me.

The beast inside howled. I wanted what Franco had stolen. I wanted the rage and freedom to hurt her. I'd been so close to taking her. So close to not caring about the aftermath.

Tess screamed, squirming in his arms. His green eyes flashed, managing to slap a hand over her mouth, locking her tight against him. Franco's arm wrapped around her middle, carefully avoiding any part I'd kill him for touching.

His eyebrow rose as I skidded to a halt.

Jealousy took three long seconds to hit.

But when it did—fuck it crippled me.

Green. Hot. Liquid jealousy.

Fuck, he was touching her. Double fuck he was touching her *naked!*

I stalked forward, clenching my fists. "Franco…" My voice wobbled with pent-up, spewing aggression. "Get your motherfucking hands off her." *I'll rip out your jugular.*

"If I let her go, she'll run. Before you kill me, give me your shirt." His eyes dropped to my chest. All I wanted was blood. Rivers of it. His. Hers. I didn't really fucking care.

With barely functioning limbs, I ripped it off, sending buttons flying.

My teeth chattered with the urge to destroy the fucking bastard. How dare he have his hands on *my* naked woman! Tess's eyes were wide, drinking in my rage. She moaned, trying to speak behind Franco's hand, but he kept her silent.

"Donne-la moi! Maintenant." Give her. Now, I snarled.

He nodded, opening his arms. With a shove, he forced Tess to stumble forward. I took one step, grabbed her elbow and spun her into my furious embrace. With one hand, I wrapped my shirt around her, breathing a little easier when it covered parts no other fucking male should see.

I still wanted to fuck her, but I was obsessed with protecting my territory. Another man had threatened what was mine and the urge to slam her to the ground and claim took second place.

My eyes locked on Franco. He glared right back.

"Don't touch me. Get off me!" Tess wiggled; I smacked a hand over her mouth.

"Shut up," I growled. "Seriously, now is not the time to fucking push me. You will *not* like what happens if you do."

I didn't give a rat's ass if that made no sense to her. Would a trafficker say that? I didn't know. But it was the goddamn truth and my blood infernoed with the need to take her. Every part of my body felt foreign and sharp and so on edge.

My gaze returned to Franco. Fuck me he'd held her. *Naked!*

His body tensed, falling into a supple position, ready for a fight. "Mercer—think about this." His eyes narrowed.

Think about it?

His hands on her naked skin. Her body pressed against him. *Naked.*

The beast howled with utmost possession. He'd touched my property. He'd seen what no one else was allowed to see. No one! It didn't matter that he'd been in the room when we'd found her. Naked and spread-eagled on the bed in Rio. It didn't matter he knew she was mine. It didn't fucking matter, because I needed a fight. I needed something. *Anything* to stop myself from spiralling into this dark pit of hell.

"It's okay, Mercer. She's yours." Franco held up his hands. "Seriously, I get it."

My nostrils flared as I struggled for control. My fists wanted nothing more than to connect with his jaw.

His head tilted; apprehension filled his eyes. "Is it going okay? You're not…um…not losing it are you?" He inched closer, eyeing me up.

I wished fire would sprout out of my gaze and burn him. I wished I had spare arms to punch him in the chest and kick him when he fell. I was violent. Bloodthirsty. Oversexed. "Do you think I'm not strong enough? That I'll give in?" My voice held a deadly undertone.

He shrugged. No judgement or fear existed in his face. "Just asking. Don't want you to fuck yourself up while trying to help her." He smirked. "Excuse me for saying, but you look completely manic."

I'd bottled so much up, I was ready to explode. I probably looked like a fucking psycho.

His eyes fell to Tess squirming in my arms. Her lithe body rubbed my cock in such delicious ways making me throb with an orgasm living permanently in my balls. "Having difficulties?"

A loud laugh exploded from my mouth. Difficulties? Try mountains of them. The laugh helped demolish the tension in my limbs. It turned dark, petering out.

The black clouds broke; I sucked in a ragged breath. Insanity gave way to sanity, soothing my feral heartbeat. I'd almost lost myself.

I'd been too caught up in the charade—I almost became him. I'd stepped over that line and would've broken Tess if Franco hadn't caught her.

Time played its cruel joke again, draining me as if it'd been days, not minutes.

I'm not strong enough. I'll snap before it's over.

Franco followed my breakdown. "You probably have another hour before that thing wears off. Don't take too long."

Urgency laced my heart. I only had to survive another hour, then Tess would be free and I could get as far away from her as possible. I could find an outlet for all this blackness inside and spare her from my rage.

Gathering my tattered energy, I collected Tess in a stronger grip. My eyes met Franco's as I dragged her backward to the door. I should thank him for helping, but I couldn't. Seeing her naked was all the fucking thanks he'd get.

Tess fought, wrenching her mouth free from my grip. She winced as something struck her foot. "Let me go. No! I don't want to go back in there." Her heels left indents in the grass as I stole her back to her nightmares.

"You don't have a choice. And if you ever recall what really happened today, try and remember never to run from me again. You were lucky this time. Next time—" My voice drifted off as another wave of need crippled me.

Her heat and wriggling body scrambled my self-control.

Reaching the door, I yelled at Franco, "Don't worry about what's going on in here. Just do your fucking job and keep watch."

Franco smiled, saluting me flippantly. "Keep watch for her running again or intruders?"

I bared my teeth, slamming the door in his face. I left him standing in the sunlight while I welcomed Tess back to the dark. The soundproofed dark where her screams didn't matter, her tears wouldn't be seen, and no one would find out how fucking dangerous all of this was.

Breathing hard, I stomped through the house with a fighting naked woman in my arms.

"I won't do it. I won't hurt them. You'll have to kill me this time," she rambled, her fingernails clawing at my arms. I clamped my fingers over her mouth again. I couldn't listen to how much damage I caused.

I hissed as she drew blood, but managed to keep the monster locked in its cage—I had no fucking clue how.

This house was too big—too far to drag a woman who I wanted so fucking bad. My jaw ached from clenching by the time I marched her into the bathroom. The minute I'd slammed and locked the door, I unglued my fingers from around her lips.

Tension suffocated the room, swamping the area with Tess's panic and my self-restraint. She backed up, seething, "You said I could be free. I took the initiative."

I dragged my hands over my face, scrubbing hard against the headache, grime, and severely tested discipline. There would be no breaking her. She was too damn strong. I had to hope my second idea would work better than my first. It would also test every inch of my self-control.

You're tempting fate. Don't do it.

Ignoring myself, I growled, "You didn't ask permission. You think you can get what you want without asking?"

Tess pressed her lips together, not saying a word.

Scowling, I stalked toward her, crowding her against the wall. Her eyes flared, dancing with panic and anger. I pressed my body against hers, shivering with how good she felt. Every inch of my erection throbbed, digging into her belly. I lost my thoughts, my decency, my fucking human spirit.

Her stomach rose and fell with uneven breaths; her delectable curves tempted me to hell.

Take her. No one would know. Just one thrust. Just one release.

My cock became possessed. Every rub of her, no matter

how gentle, was enough to send me into full-body convulsions.

I needed to come. Badly. It tainted my every thought, made it that much harder to stay sane.

Tess looked up, glaring deep into my soul. "You're a traitor. A liar. And a thief."

I backed away, unable to ignore the churning in my gut and overwhelming pressure in my balls. Why had she said that—what did she see?

Tess moved quickly, dashing to the door.

Goddammit.

In a quick strike, I planted myself in front of her, barricading the exit.

She glowered, then in a totally defiant move, ripped my shirt off her body, and threw it in my face.

I shoved it away, breathing hard, willing myself to keep control.

Christ, she was fucking amazing. Lean muscles, tight stomach, beautiful full tits. "What the hell are you doing to me?" I groaned.

Shit. *I shouldn't have said that.*

Tess didn't seem to notice; she planted her hands on her naked hips, hissing, "You were wrong to bring me back. You should've left me alone. You'd won. Don't you get it?" Taking a step closer, she accented every move, sashaying her hips, seducing me with every fucking twitch.

"I'd lost myself. I'd turned my master's life into a misery. You'd won!" Her head bowed, her gaze flickering down my chest. There was nothing weak or coy about her now, it was complete steel and rebellion.

She looked up through hooded eyes. "But now…" One step closer. Another. "Now, I'm beginning to remember."

My entire body froze; my cock grew ever harder. She stopped a breath away; the tip of her finger stabbed me in the solar plexus. "I'm remembering how to fight." The flash in her eyes unravelled me. My knees buckled, stealing control just for a moment before I forced myself to stand tall.

The headache I'd been fighting crashed over me with blades, daggers, and needles. "Don't touch me." I cleared my throat, hating how my voice cracked with heavy lust. *Touch me. Fuck me. Bend over and let me sink inside your sweet, sweet cunt.*

"Oh, poor you." She pouted, taunting me. "Big bad Leather Jacket doesn't want me to touch him." Her mouth twisted as she slapped a hand on my naked shoulder, sending a bonfire of want through my blood.

Fuck…this wouldn't end well.

I loved that she stood up to her nightmares and seemed to be winning. I loved that by standing up to me, I could change the theme of her dreams by backing down, eradicating the horror forever.

What I didn't love was the unforgiving need making my brain bleed and teeth turn to dust in my mouth. *Just a little longer.*

I curled my hands so hard my short nails punctured flesh, growing slippery with blood.

Not moving muscle, I ordered, "Get in the bath."

One thing.

Just *one* thing left to do to shatter what I believed to be the main issue. Then I'd be free. My job would be over, and I could run like the fucking animal I was.

When Tess didn't move, I towered to my full height, glowering into her eyes. "Get. In. the. Fucking. Bath."

Tess cowered, the strength spluttered and fizzed. She took a hesitant step toward it.

Then iron replaced her bones, slamming her to a halt. She stood regal and proud and entirely fucking naked making my throat close up with how much I wanted to hurt her.

"No. Fuck you." With a roar, she flew at me. Her palm slapped my face, sending my head snapping sideways.

And that was it.

I was done.

Control snapped.

Sanity slipped.

Needs roared to life.

My hand came up, wrapping around her throat. So, so breakable. "How about I fuck you? Then we'll see who walks away." I threw her against the wall, sliding her upward so her feet dangled off the ground. She weighed nothing. Absolutely nothing compared to the monster's fury.

Tess sliced at my hands with her nails, choking in my hold. "You always were pathetic. Making up for your lack of cock." Tess's hands suddenly stopped fighting me, dropping to squeeze my erection.

I swayed; my forehead crashed against the tiled wall.

No. No. Yes. Yes.

The monster tore at my brain.

Headache.

Lust.

Need.

I shoved my hips into her hand, making her cry out in pain. Her cries made me pant for more—made me fucking delirious.

Her eyes popped wide. "So you do have a cock. You must've had cosmetic surgery, you bastard, because when you raped Blonde Angel you were infested with spiders and the size of my little finger."

Confusion collared the beast and I blinked. Holy shit, I'd been so close. She didn't see me. She didn't know it was me. And I refused to take her when she was so far out of my reach—so removed from the truth.

Her hand squeezed my cock, deliberately hurting. But I was beyond pain now. I *wanted* pain. I wanted her to punish me, so I could come so fucking violently I'd pass out. My vision went black.

Not yet. You're so close. Get it together.

Somehow, I did the hardest thing in my life.

Dropping her, I kicked her away, almost doubling over with the need lacerating my blood.

"I told you. Don't fucking touch me." I had to finish this.

Now.

Even sprawled on cold tiles, lost in a sea of darkness, Tess glowed like a cosmos or brand new galaxy. She looked fresh and completely unbroken. She licked her lips, saying in the coldest, strongest voice I'd ever heard. "You know what I just realized? I'm not scared of you anymore. So fuck off and leave me alone."

She's close. So close.

Happiness and joy spread from my heart, battling back the monsters inside. Just a little more.

I cursed my shuddering body as I loomed over her. "Not fucking scared, huh? Then what are you still doing here? Give me what I want, and I'll let you go."

Ask what I want. Please fucking ask what I want. Then I wouldn't suffer guilt when I raped her. I'd be free to do whatever the hell I pleased.

Her eyes went from grey to star-bright.

Fierce awe shot into my heart.

"I want my freedom."

Yes. I'd done it. She'd demanded it. She'd claimed it. I backed away, fumbling for the door handle to run.

But then her fierceness fizzled; a small cry crawled from her mouth. "No wait! I'm sorry. You've always wanted to fuck me. Do it. A trade. Then I'll know I owe you nothing. Do it and leave me in peace." She sucked in a breath, eyes glassy with tears. "Please, swear if I give you what you want, you'll let me go. Promise you'll never come for me again. Promise you won't make me hurt any more women or sell me or ruin my life. Please!"

She crawled toward me, latching onto my trouser leg. "Please. You wanted me to beg? I'm begging. You told me I would one day. And it's come true. I'm begging you to end this once and for all. I'm giving you what you want in return for freedom."

She climbed my body. I knew I stood no fucking chance of saying no. I would ruin her all when she'd been so damn close.

Her tears rained, sobs taking over her voice. "Please. Promise me that this will be over. How many times do I have to pay?"

Her hands fumbled on my belt buckle. "Do it. Do it!" Tess cried, almost crazed with the thought of being free.

I groaned as she squeezed my length, dragging me forward by it like I was a plaything. Every place she touched scorched my willpower. I almost came on the spot at the thought of getting what I wanted so badly.

I wanted to fuck her like the criminal she thought I was. I wanted to hit her and bite her and use her with no remorse. I wanted blood and bruises and pleasure.

And I wanted Tess to scream. But I wanted her to scream *my* name. Not some fucking kidnapper's.

The ultimate ownership of her pain and screams belonged to me—not them. And I wouldn't, *wouldn't*, let her take that from me.

With a howl, I knocked her hands away from my cock and threw her over my shoulder.

Her softness and tiny fists pounding my back twinged the last remaining thread of my self-control. I had just enough to do what I had to. Just enough to end this. For good.

I dumped her into the overflowing bath.

Slamming to my knees, she had time to grab a breath before I grabbed her skull and shoved her underwater. The liquid crashed over her face, sucking her down like eager death.

Her scream broke the surface in forms of large frothy bubbles. Sound ricocheted as the noise left its bubble, escaping into the air.

Tess went wild. Her legs kicked, smashing into the soap dish and ornaments around the bath. Water sluiced everywhere, drenching my trousers and shoes. I held her down while my headache turned my vision to tunnel.

I held her down as my blood mixed with the water thanks to her sharp nails on my arms.

Every second I drowned her, I thrust my hips against the bath, bruising myself, deliberately bashing delicate flesh against hard fibreglass, trying to teach the beast in me a lesson.

This was the bastard I was. This asshole who drowned the woman he loved.

Ten seconds.

Tess was berserk, fighting with everything she had.

Fifteen seconds.

Her fight stuttered, succumbing to lack of oxygen.

My heart felt like it would explode and my brain disintegrate—I let her up.

I couldn't catch my breath.

This was it. This was the moment where everything I'd done better work. If it didn't, I had no other hope.

Such a short amount of time left. *Come on, Tess!* My hands clenched, hanging onto my last shred of discipline. The last defence against the beast from fucking her senseless.

Scrambling to my feet, I backed away. Grabbing the last item I needed from my pocket, I kicked off my drenched shoes and trousers. Standing in black boxer-briefs with my cock standing so fucking stiff, I braced myself for what was to come.

Tess exploded out of the tub like a mermaid queen. Her skin was white, blonde hair clinging to her breasts and shoulders in molten gold. Her chest rose and fell as she went from drowning to surviving. Everything about her said fighter.

But it was her eyes I latched onto.

They were otherworldly. So fucking manic.

"You bastard!" She flew at me.

I backed up, crashing against the wall. She slapped me, kicked me, pummelled every inch. Every strike made me want to grab her hair and force her to her knees. I needed to be inside her. I needed to release this overbearing burden inside but I locked my hands behind my back, holding tight to the final key. I shut down my thoughts, my needs—I let her do whatever she wanted.

I let her pour everything from her soul into mine. I would

bear it all for her. I would make her whole by sharing her pain.

"You deserve nothing! *Nothing*. You fucking bastard. You deserve to die."

Yes, Tess. Go on.

Take her. What about what you want? She owes you. Do it!

I shook my head, dispelling the thoughts before they could swallow me.

"I'm *taking* my freedom. I'm not asking. I'm not begging. I'll never beg again in my *life*."

My heart raced and soared.

Come on. More!

Everything I'd hoped would happen, came true. With every hit, Tess seemed to shed an outer layer. One tarnished with fear, uncertainty, and whatever foulness she'd lived with for so long. Everything she never let me see, all her lies, and secrets fell to the floor.

My cheek burned as she slapped me with all her strength. Standing before me was the woman I'd fallen madly fucking in love with.

I said goodbye to the slave I'd reclaimed in Rio and welcomed back the girl who claimed me when she returned from Australia.

The disease was gone—the festering over once and for all.

Everything disappeared. All the nightmares, the tears, the anger. All of it.

This woman was stronger than I could ever be. And I didn't know how I fucking deserved her.

My hands unlocked, begging to touch. But I couldn't. Not yet.

She had to say one more thing to be completely saved. I held my breath, waiting, waiting.

Finally, her face filled with unlimited courage; she smiled in disbelief. "I'm done with you. I'm done with all of this. I'm free."

And there it was.

She'd taken it.

She'd taken her freedom with no begging or trading or cajoling. She'd done what I'd hoped.

Simplicity and truth sliced through all the cages and nightmares she'd built for herself. Granting her truth, letting her see things in a totally different light.

Her body flushed, releasing the guilt of what she'd done to the other girls. She shed the horror of hurting them. She finally came to terms that it wasn't her fault. None of it. None of them had any choice.

Her sigh was full wonderment and joy.

Freedom.

It was done.

Thank fucking God.

Throwing the pill from my palm into my mouth, I grabbed the back of her neck. She shoved my chest, but she was no match for me. Slamming my lips against hers, I forced the second and final drug onto her tongue. The taste of her unlocked all the padlocks I'd surrounded the beast with, and I knew I had seconds left before I undid all the good I'd managed to do.

She growled, trying to bite me, but it was too late. She choked, swallowing the final stage in a rush of rage.

The moment it was done, I bolted.

Get out. Get out.

Charging out of the bathroom, I shot down the hall and ran. I ran until I had enough distance to talk myself out of going back if I snapped.

Out of breath, out of control, hanging onto sanity by a thread, I braced my back against the wall and yanked out my cock. My boxer-briefs tore with the violence of my touch.

The second my fingers latched around my length, the world ceased to exist.

I dropped the cage, unravelled the chains, and let the monster free.

Bashing my head against the wall, I fisted myself and jerked. I strangled my cock as if it was another demon deserving to die. I punished it. I fucking hurt it. I moaned and groaned and thrust like a beast possessed into fingers that only brought pain.

I couldn't breathe. I couldn't see. All I focused on was the arching, sparking, seething need in my balls.

With my other hand, I grabbed the tight aching things and with a roar, gave myself over to what I'd wanted since I kidnapped Tess from the hotel.

I came.

Thick white spurts, arching through the darkness, splattering against the floor. I growled as heat built and cramp stole my legs from under me. With each wave, I kept up my brutal torture on my body. I wrung its fucking neck, brutalizing it for making me so subservient to horrible desire.

As the last ripple erupted from the tip, I slid down the wall.

My heart was a frenzied lunatic.

Sweat covered my entire body and a chill turned my shivers of pleasure into shivers of cold.

But despite feeling guilty, sick, twisted, and completely fucked-up, a small smile graced my lips.

I'd done the unthinkable and won.

I'd had the opportunity to ravish a slave.

I'd had the chance to be the monster I'd always wanted.

But I hadn't.

I'd kept her safe.

And she was free.

Our monsters found solace in each other's perfect heart, the devil himself couldn't tear us apart, You belong, I belong, our twisted souls forever

It was like waking from a nightmare.

Clouds parted, mists dispersed, clarity took hold. But it wasn't a nightmare. I'd *lived* it. I'd breathed it. My heart raced, my body had bruises that weren't there before, and my mind…my mind was…empty.

I was weak and wobbly but beneath the rush and sickness of adrenaline lived a small incandescent ball, lodged in my heart, growing bigger and bigger. Every breath it grew brighter, swallowing the darkness and weakness inside. I no longer ached for the girls I'd hurt. I no longer felt crippled by guilt. I didn't seethe with rage at what they'd stolen from me. I didn't fight constant tears at the thought of disappointing Q.

All of that was overtaken by wondrous liberation.

The nucleus of the old me—who'd fought and won and returned to a master who turned out to be my soul-mate— sprang back into power. It was like spreading crumpled wings, learning how to fly again.

The moment Leather Jacket had run, I'd claimed my freedom. Everything seemed less oppressive. The guilt was still there...just liveable. The memories still haunted but they were ignorable.

Leather Jacket had razed my self-confidence to the ground, but by letting me win—he'd given it back.

My hands curled at the thought of running after him. I wished for a gun and a bullet etched with his name. I wanted to chase him. I wanted to kill, but the luminosity inside demanded no more blood. No more tarnish or slime or death.

Serenity. *I'm free.*

Nothing in the world could make me give it up.

I turned toward the bath, surveying the dark bathroom with the detachment of a dream. Liquid drenched every inch, creating a gloomy water-world. My naked body rivuleted with droplets as I practically paddled toward the huge bath.

Staring into the still rocking waves, I waited for terror. I waited for flashbacks of being held under and choking but...nothing.

No memory came to fill me with horror; all I remembered was Leather Jacket releasing me and running. If his intention had been to kill me and finish the job—he should've stayed away, because now—now I remembered the good as well as the bad. I'd been reminded of everything that I'd lost.

Crushing, joyous tears travelled up my spine, blurring everything. I'd never felt so emptily happy. Thoughts echoed with no rebound, my mind could focus on one thing and not be swallowed by the past.

The silence was ten times, no a hundred times better than my tower. This silence had no walls or cages. This silence came with no stigmata or consequences.

I'm free.

Q.

My heartbeats danced. I wanted to tell him. I wanted to test my conclusion that I was strong enough for him. Would pain still make me run? Somehow, I didn't think it would.

Where was Q? It seemed an age since I'd seen him—the longest we'd been apart since he rescued me.

Maybe this time it's your turn.

My eyes flared. Did Q need rescuing? Had I been so wrapped up in my sad little world that I'd put too much on him. The answer was too loud to ignore.

Yes.

It was my turn to give him what he wanted. My turn to give him the relief he needed through pain. But…not yet. I wanted to exist in this precious, perfect moment a little longer. I wanted to solidify the truth and realign every piece of me that'd been scattered by Leather Jacket. Puzzle pieces slotted together, building the complete picture. I was back. My self-worth and belief was miraculously returned.

Sweeping a leg over the tub, I sighed as every muscle unlocked and melted, sliding into the hot water.

The heat cushioned me, hissing against the minor burns on my breasts from the wax Q used and flaring the remaining spanks from before, but I didn't care. I let go of everything, drifting in happiness. I'd won. I'd done it. I'd survived.

Then something cloud-like crept over my mind.

Something warm.

Something soft.

Something sweet.

"Tess?"

That voice. All depth and gravel and sinfully French.

I stretched as the one syllable of my name echoed in my limbs. I'd never *felt* a word before, but I did now, and I wanted more. I wanted sonnets whispered in my ears. I wanted lullabies murmured in my mouth.

I opened my eyes.

The bathroom was still dark, but something seemed to be wrong with my brain. I no longer saw darkness; I saw fractures of light, sparkles, glitter in the grey.

"Wow," I whispered.

Something touched my cheek; I shivered instantaneously. It was too much. Too damn delicious. It was as if the sun trickled through my skin, sending rays directly into my heart.

My eyes travelled up and I blinked.

He was stunning.

He was dazzling.

He was poetically spectacular.

Q's gorgeous lips spread into a gentle smile; his eyes were pale perfection in the gloom. *"Tu vas bien?"* You okay?

My entire body rippled. I gasped as a rush of lust intoxicated me. All I could focus on was his mouth—his stupefying, scrumptious mouth.

I blinked again. *What's happening to me?*

All I wanted was his lips on mine—his tongue licking and desiring.

His jaw held tiny droplets, his naked chest spangling with grey and silver rainbows. I became hypnotised by a teardrop running down his abs.

Those abs!

His tattoo came to life as inked sparrows ruffled their feathers, darting free from the swirling clouds and barbwire.

I couldn't look away, completely enthralled by the magic Q performed. How did he do that?

Something firm and controlling pinched my chin, guiding my eyes up, up. I locked onto Q's gaze, sighing heavily. How could one person carry so much?

"Pain and need and love and confusion," I whispered. His soul reached through his jade eyes, drenching me with everything he lived with.

I bit my lip, jolting at the shock of how smooth my mouth was, how tasty the bathwater was on my tongue.

Desire unfurled faster and faster in my belly.

Q frowned, impossibly making him more roguish and handsome. "Tess...? How do you feel?"

How did I feel? Amazing. Lusty. Powerful. *Consumed.*

I stretched again, arching my back as water lapped around my body. I wanted to moan with how good I felt. I'd never been so warm or contended or *horny.*

My eyes snapped to Q's. Him. I had to have him.

"You're so beautiful," I murmured.

Q froze, his eyes searching mine. Slowly, his lips turned up into half a smile.

I pressed my thighs together. I couldn't stop my body from overheating and needing. I'd been cursed or charmed— some sort of potion lived inside. I had no other explanation for how much I needed him.

I laughed, throwing myself headfirst into whatever spell I was trapped in. My voice fell from my mouth, tinkling and chiming like a bell. Was that truly me? I sounded magical. I sounded like a princess straight from a storybook.

Who was I? Sleeping Beauty who'd been woken by her prince?

My eyes locked onto Q's. No. I was the one who'd fallen head over heels for a beast who spoke in foreign tongues.

Tongue.

A flush of heat and wetness built between my legs. I would give anything to have his tongue on me. I wanted his head between my thighs. I wanted his fingers clawing at my hips. I wanted to be used, bruised, adored.

Q cocked his head, chuckling under his breath. "I think Franco miscalculated the dose."

I shook my head. I didn't understand. All I understood was his voice had the power to make me come. The deep tenor vibrated through my heart, sending tiny orgasms exploding in my veins.

I needed to be touched. I needed to be kissed.

Kiss him. Let him know.

Launching upright, I splashed a wave over the tub. Q

jerked back, but wasn't fast enough. Wrapping my arms around his neck, I dragged him down toward me. His hand slipped on the rim, plunging his arms into the water, landing on either side of my body.

His mouth opened to curse, but I swallowed whatever he said. My lips stole his, and the moment I tasted him, I went a little mad.

My core squeezed with delirium, demanding to be filled. My eyes rolled back at the sheer bliss of kissing.

He tasted like freedom and violence and pain.

Pain…

A slight hiccup in my magical world before the cloud in my brain smothered it with need. Yes, I wanted pain. I wanted his roughness. I wanted his whips and chains and feral love. I wanted him inside me.

"*Esclave*…wait…" Q tried to speak, but he only gave me the opportunity to slink my tongue into his mouth. Joy bounced and fizzed in my heart, demanding more.

I moaned, dragging him closer. My hands dug into his hair, tugging with sharp-laced desire. His mouth opened, either in shock or passion—I didn't hesitate. I thrust my tongue deeper into his mouth, willingly drowning myself in all things Q.

I wanted to cry at the deliciousness of the kiss. His lips. His heat. The silky, satiny wetness. The scorching, sizzling heatness.

Oh, God. My core burned; my heart fireworked in my chest.

Q groaned as I bit his bottom lip. I wasn't gentle, bruising his lips with mine, dropping my hands from his hair to his face, holding his sculptured cheekbones, rasping my fingers on his stubble. I wanted to consume him.

His tongue lashed out, licking, teasing. His body leaned closer, pushing me further into the water. His hands on either side of me fisted, prodding my sensitive sides.

I moaned. My heart no longer existed in my chest. My

entire ribcage was full of nymphs and pixies all casting spells, spreading their lustful dust.

"Q..." I needed his touch. I needed his mark. I needed so, *so* much.

His lips pressed harder, bringing smoothness along with roughness from his five o' clock shadow. His head tilted to kiss me deeper; my lips burned with a glorious rash from his mouth on mine.

I never wanted the kiss to end.

But Q pulled away.

I wanted to cry. I never wanted to leave this enchantment.

His fingers cupped my jaw, holding me steady. Rockets and gunpowder detonated where he touched. My vision coated with a haze of amethyst and plum. Shades upon shades of purple. My favourite colour.

"You're high," he whispered.

If he meant feeling the best I'd ever felt, then I agreed. I was on a kite, soaring high, higher, embracing the sun and making the stars my home.

I shook my head. "High on you." I craned my neck, seeking his lips. Tears tickled my spine at being denied a kiss. "Kiss me. Q...I want you so much."

His eyes hooded, filling with lustful smoke. "You do?"

I laughed at the absurd notion that I wouldn't. I'd ride him for the rest of my life if I could. I'd glue my mouth to his so the only way to survive was to feed off each other.

I shivered in need so painful, even the water was a deadly tease. "So much." Unlatching his fingers from my jaw, I guided his hand to my breast. I arched, pressing every inch of me into his palm. "You're holding my heart as well as my flesh. Q— please. I want you inside me."

His fingers stiffened around my breast, pressing delicate tissue.

God, that felt good. Too good. My blood became a highway, speeding along with sparklers, setting powder-kegs ready to burst.

His teeth clenched; his grip released me, then tightened. He looked torn. Confused. At war.

He can't deny me. I wouldn't survive it.

Needing to share the magic, I murmured, "I want you so much I can't breathe. I hate this water because I wish it was you around me, in me. I'm wet for you. I'm drenched for your fingers and tongue. Love me. Q—please..."

Q squeezed his eyes. "Fuck." His forehead furrowed as his large body shuddered. He tugged his hand from my breast, fighting me when I tried to keep him close. With an angry twist, he tore his palm away, breathing hard.

His gaze opened. *"Vachement tentant."* So fucking tempting." He shook his head, his lips pursed with restraint. "I can't. Not when you're high. I didn't think it would be this bad. I just wanted something—I wanted you to enjoy it—to teach you how you used to love it."

His hand suddenly swished through the water, cupping my pussy. His face distorted as he pushed a finger unapologetically into me.

God, yes. I screamed with sublime joy. My muscles clamped around him.

"Goddammit, *esclave.* You're so damn wet. And now I won't know if it's because of your need for me, or what I've made you swallow."

My hips bucked as he removed his finger. "It's for you. All for you," I panted.

His face twisted; fear crept into his eyes. "You do remember what happened before...don't you?" His touch landed on my jaw again, wrenching my face to meet his. "Tell me—what do you remember?"

I nodded, distracted by the coils of damp hair whispering over my shoulders.

"Tess. Answer me. What happened?"

His voice was so amazing. Just like the rest of him. I sighed in perfect contentedness. "I told Leather Jacket to fuck off." I giggled. It sounded crude and whiplash sharp, but it filled me with fire. "He tried to drown me again—I know he would've taken me back to hurt more women." I frowned, vaguely remembering every fear and terror tripping over me the moment he shoved me under the water. I'd been so sure I would die.

My fingers curled. "But then I fought back. I fought like I'd forgotten. And—" I spaced out, thinking of the wondrous possibilities my future held, now I remembered who I was.

Q shifted beside me impatiently. "And....Shit, what else?"

I looked up, letting my hands float to the surface, dragging them through the water. "I won." I shrugged as if he knew already. "I won. I'm free. I'm happy."

His eyes dropped to my lips, darkening with need.

The urge to kiss him obsessed me, drumming my bloodstream with a war-beat. "Kiss me. Celebrate with me. I want you so, so much." In a rush, I scrambled upright, trying to grab him. My fingers scratched his neck as he jerked back, keeping just out of reach.

His eyes searched mine, crawling deep inside me until he hammered at my heart. He touched me—right there. He reached inside my chest, cracked open the beating organ, and ripped it right from my body. I was his to devour. I wanted to be bitten, eaten.

Tears welled in my eyes. "Please...kiss me. I need you to kiss me."

Q's hands landed on my shoulders. His features contorted as he battled with things I didn't understand. "If I kiss you, what then?"

"Then I give myself to you."

His eyes blazed. "If we do this, we do it my way. *Tu es à moi.*" You're mine.

"All yours."

He lost his battle. "Ah, fuck it."

He went from unyielding to slamming me backward into the water. His lips smashed against mine, forcing me to open wide for his invasive tongue.

My core melted, thrilling with every lick. His sharp teeth caught my bottom lip, pausing, as if to see what I would do.

In answer to his tentative bite, I tore my lip away, capturing his instead. Unsheathing my teeth, I bit down. His throaty growl undid the rest of my control.

I kissed him, fully intending to leap from the bath and force him to take me on the floor.

But Q shoved me away. He stood tall, towering over me.

The glitter from whatever Q gave me made him immortal in my eyes. Made him divine and god-like.

My heart seized as he ripped down his boxer-briefs. Not giving me time to drink in his impressive erection, or the way his muscles bunched and shadowed, he reached behind me and with a possessive shove, pushed me away from the side.

His long legs spread, climbing into the bath. He gripped the edges, lowering himself into the water.

His powerful thighs entrapped my body while strong arms wrapped around me, dragging me against his chest. The water level rose, licking at my shoulders.

I shuddered with how hard and hot he was against my back. It was like lying against living marble.

Q's voice rumbled in his chest, vibrating through mine. "You say you're free, *esclave*. Tell me…free from what?" His hands stroked my stomach, drawing ever widening circles.

He expected me to speak? I'd lost that ability the moment he slipped behind me.

When I didn't reply, Q raised one hand out of the water. Cupping his palm beneath a dispenser tiled into the wall, his pectoral bounced me as he pressed the plunger, filling his palm with coconut shampoo.

I squirmed, very aware of the hardness digging into my lower back. I didn't want to speak—I wanted to spin in his embrace and slide onto him.

Oh God, the mental image was too much.

Q brushed aside the wet curtain of my hair, sucking on my ear. *"Dis moi."* Tell me.

My breath came fast; I did my best to obey. "I'm free…from everything."

He tutted under his breath, dropping his mouth to press against the oversensitive brand on my neck. "I want details."

I suffered a full body convulsion as Q's hands landed on my head. His long, strong fingers slinked through my wet curls, spreading shampoo with slow, sweeping pressure.

I sank further against him, morphing into liquid. My vision danced with purple shooting stars, lighting up the bathroom.

How was I supposed to think when he touched me that way? Each stroke both relaxed and tensed me.

"Tess…I'll stop if you don't tell me."

My eyes flared wide. I never wanted him to stop. Ever. "I'm not afraid of baths anymore."

He laughed softly. "I'd hoped that would be the case." His soapy hands slipped down my neck, trailing over my clavicle, cascading to my breasts. "Not wanting to be in a bath with me would be terrible news." His teeth nibbled on the top of my ear forcing me to suck in a shaky breath.

Tracing back up, the pads of his fingers massaged my scalp, sending scents of coconut to envelope us in a tropical world. Bubbles and froth trickled down my chest, looking like expensive spun glass and jewels.

"I've never washed anyone before you, *esclave*, but this is the second time I've had the pleasure." His fingers drifted to the back of my neck, rubbing and coaxing with fierce ownership.

I moaned. Loudly.

"Do you remember the first? *La première fois que je t'ai lavée de ton passé?*" The first time I cleaned you of your past?

I let my eyes flutter. Memories of him holding me in his lap as hot water rained from above, filled my mind. I'd been naked while he wore a soaking cashmere suit. He'd replaced himself with memories of the rape. He'd taken all power of the memory, switching it into something I could survive.

Q grabbed me tighter, murmuring, "You're mine, esclave. *Mine to care for. Mine to fix. I'll allow you to cry while I wash you, but the moment you're clean, you're to stop. Do you understand?"*

I blinked through tears, shuddering so badly I couldn't answer.

"Everything about tonight will be forgotten, and you'll only remember what I do to you. Is that clear?" He shook me. "Answer me."

I nodded. There was relief in being ordered to forget and I would obey.

I'd never been able to *see* love. I knew what it felt like, how it hurt as well as healed, but until that moment, I didn't know what physical form it took. Now, I did. It was a swirling world inside me, interlocked with the swirling world inside Q. Our two dimensions superseded our bodies and existed not in us but *between* us.

It was knowledge.

The knowledge I'd be there for him, and he'd be there for me.

It was blissful comprehension of never being alone and always cared for.

"I love you, Q." I couldn't hold back the tears this time, completely overwhelmed with gratefulness. "You truly are my master. Not because of the power you have over me, but because of the power you give me."

Q's fingers twitched in my hair; his chest rose and fell, sticking to my back. His heartbeat thudded, and I knew I wouldn't have one lifetime with this man—I would have multiple. I refused to believe death would tear us apart. He was me as I was him. There would be no separating us.

Q dropped his hands from my hair, wrapping his arms around me. So much was promised in that embrace. So much exchanged and acknowledged.

I missed you.

I know.

I'm so sorry.

Don't be.

We're not broken anymore.

He hugged me as if I'd float away and only remained

locked to him by force.

"I missed your fight, *mon coeur.*" My heart, he murmured, pressing a delicate kiss on my temple.

"I'm not afraid of fighting back anymore," I said softly, immersed in his incredible warmth.

"I'm glad." With a fierce squeeze, he let me go, returning his hands to my head. We stayed silent as he massaged more bubbles through my curls, before pushing my slippery body down his.

Once upon a time, I would've fought at the thought of being pushed under water, but now…I didn't care.

"Do you trust me, *esclave?*"

"Forever."

I let him push me under, holding my breath while his worshipping fingers washed the suds from my hair. I was aware of every touch, every inch of him. I was nothing but a ball of oversensitive nerve endings.

Once the bubbles were gone, Q hoisted me up his body, dragging me along his very hot, very hard erection.

I want him. Completely. No holding back.

The thought whizzed around my body, spreading eagerness and courage. I wanted Q to take me like he'd always wanted. I was no longer afraid. He wouldn't go too far because I understood what lurked beneath all his darkness.

Ownership. He wanted to brand me, mark me—all in the name of claiming. But he already owned me completely—he no longer needed to compete for that right.

Shifting, I reached behind and wrapped my fingers around him. He jerked in my touch, blood throbbing beneath the velvety skin. He felt hotter than usual as if he'd bruised himself, aching with injury.

Q sucked in a breath, pressing my hips to collide harder with him. He drove up against my back, rubbing himself in my fist. "Fuck…" His teeth sank into my shoulder.

Pain.

My heart raced at the sharpness but there was nothing

else.

No fear.

No guilt.

No other thoughts than pleasure.

The past was dealt with. Finished. The lost parts of me were fixed and out of the wrapping new. The allure of painful excitement existed once again in my heart, and I wanted nothing more than for Q to deliver.

There was no guilt to wade through. No tears at the memory of Blonde Angel or Hummingbird. My grief for them was as it should be: respectful, mournful, but not life-consuming terrible.

I wanted the taboo.

I craved the forbidden.

I panted for the prohibited.

Q thrust up, dragging me from my thoughts. The purple haze was back along with the consuming need to connect.

I wanted him. No walls or cages or second thoughts. Him. All of him.

"I'm ready," I whispered. "Don't hold back."

Q shook his head, grinding his cock into my tight fingers. "Don't say things like that. Things you don't mean."

I wished he could see into my heart—hear the truth resonating off its walls. "I *do* mean it. I'm ready and willing and oh so terribly wanting."

He froze. Sucking in a breath, he didn't say a word, as if he couldn't understand what I offered.

Q had healed me. It was time for me to heal him.

Convince him.

While Q stayed immobile and silent, I murmured, "I want your belts and whips. I want your nails and teeth." Twisting in his arms, I lay on top of him, belly to belly, chest to chest. I locked eyes with his.

He seemed lost, bewildered, completely bewitched. "I mean it, Q. Everything. All of it."

His face slowly evolved from unreadable to suspicious to

hopeful. His eyes tightened, shadowed with apprehension. "Are you sure?" he croaked. Clearing his throat, he added, "I never want to hurt you again. I told you that. Why would you ask for it when I already said you don't have to give me something you don't want to give."

"Because that's not true."

He glared. "What's not true?"

"That I don't want to give it to you. I do. I need to say thank you—I need—" Bowing my head, I kissed him softly.

He never closed his eyes as if searching for a lie, disbelieving I could want everything he'd always hidden. "Will you take me?"

His Adams apple bobbed, swallowing hard. The scepticism swiftly changed to restlessness. His hips spasmed against mine, searching, seeking. "This is your last chance." His fingers gripped my ass, pressing me hard against him. "Last chance to back out."

"I don't need it."

Q's eyes fired with need. "Tess?"

My body melted under his stare. It was all I could do to keep eye contact and not kiss him senseless. "Yes?"

"You let me do this, and I'll take you so far into my world, you'll be lost forever—mine for eternity."

I smiled. The cloudy haze in my brain sent exquisite ripples through my muscles. I had no doubt I would be lost, but I would also be found. I would leave my world permanently. I would be initiated into Q's completely. Q suddenly tensed; his lips thinned. *"J'ai une demande."* I have one request.

"Name it."

He kissed me hard, melting my muscles, shattering my mind with purple stars. When he pulled back, his voice was flat and slightly cold. "You ask me to be myself. And I want to. How I fucking want to. But, Tess…I need you to promise. I'm not so fucking heartless to hurt you, make you cry and scream—because believe me I will—without a way out if you need it."

His eyes pierced mine. "Remember the word you used the night you told me it was over?" His voice sounded bitter, miserable.

I hated I'd hurt him so badly. I had a lot to make up for. "I remember." My hand left the water, dripping with droplets to cup his cheek. "I'll say it if it gets too much. I promise. I won't let you force me back into my tower."

He nodded, tiny lines appearing around his eyes as he concentrated. "You say the word and it's over. It ends. You say sparrow, and I stop. *Tu as compris?*" Understand? His gaze dropped to my lips, waiting to see my oath rather than just hear it.

Wanting to give him my vow in the language he'd been born with, I whispered, *"Moineau. Je sais que c'est le mot de sécurité, mais je ne vais pas en avoir besoin."* Sparrow. I know the safe-word, but I won't have need of it.

"Why not?" Q asked.

"Because I'm always safe with you."

Q guided me forward, leading me through the dark.

My damp hair clung to my back while my equally damp body stayed warm, wrapped in a towel. I couldn't stop looking at Q. Even in the gloom his muscles cast shadows, making him look not of this world. The perfect V, disappearing into the towel, made my mouth water for sinful things.

I didn't know what lived in my system but the incessant need and sparking excitement completely overshadowed it. I was no longer high on substances—I was high on Q and what he would do to me.

Q's fingers entwined with mine, leading me to parts unknown. He looked over his shoulder, checking to make sure I hadn't changed my mind. I hadn't. I wouldn't. I *wanted* this.

"It makes sense. The darkness," I whispered.

Q chuckled. "I doubt it."

I frowned. *What is his reason?* Mine was a guess—but it made sense—to me at least. It made sense because of what he said before kidnapping me. I studied Q's naked back, thrilling with the knowledge he was all mine. "You want to keep the dark as the first stage of the crescent moon. The eclipse before the dawn."

Q slammed to a halt looking as if the symbolism knocked him on his ass. "Huh. I hadn't thought of that. But you're right. That does make sense."

Curiosity filled me. "What was your reason?"

His lips twitched, but he shook his head. "We'll go with your idea. Come." Pulling me forward, he descended a set of stairs which appeared ominously from the gloom.

It led to nowhere—nothing but pitch black.

My heart rate picked up, spreading the haze of magic around my veins. Visions of sexual discipline and delicious reward swarmed me, instead of terror.

Wrists Bound. Mouth kissed. Q's tongue between my legs.

I wanted to run headlong into pleasure.

Not speaking, Q tugged me down the stairs, going slower as we both lost our vision to blackness. He moved effortlessly in the dark. Despite his slower footsteps, he seemed to become one with it—absorbing it.

Slowly, my eyes adjusted from black to shadows. Outlines of wall fixtures and large islands of furniture showed a chasmal room. My bare toes sank into thick carpet; I shivered as the silky strands tickled my soles.

Q guided me toward a large shape in the centre of the room. I couldn't make it out. Yanking his hand forward, the inertia made me trot, swinging like a pendulum on his arm. I gasped as he spun me to face away, crowding me against the hard object.

He pressed his hips against my ass, rolling himself, deliberately taunting me with everything I wanted. My heart exploded with desire; I rocked back into him with no restraint.

He groaned low in his throat, grabbing my hips with bruising fingertips, driving harder against me. Fighting my violence with his—gluing us together in a quick flash of passion.

"Recognise it, *esclave?*" His voice dropped several decibels, sounding more and more like a luciferian master. His hips never stopped pulsing, scrambling my brain and any hope at conversational skills.

With shaky hands, I reached forward, following the satin of polished wood, dipping my fingers along the ridge to…softness.

Felt?

"A pool table," I whispered.

Q fisted my hair, tilting my head to the side. His mouth descended on mine, a tongue opening the seam of my lips effortlessly, despite clamping shut. The moment his tongue entered my mouth, a finger plunged into me, hard and fast.

"Oh, God." My mouth opened wide; I trembled with the onslaught—the act of ownership. He wasn't gentle, he wasn't sweet.

"This is mine. Everything is…"

I knew what he wanted. The word balanced on my tongue but I swallowed. I would never say it.

"Mine," he growled.

The flashback ended as suddenly as it began. The wetness between my legs increased remembering the power, the need, the *desire* we both shared. It didn't matter I'd been sold to him. It didn't matter I hated him—my traitorous body loved him from the second I saw him at the top of his staircase.

Q followed my train of thought, leaning over me. His naked chest stuck to my shoulders, prickling with overheated need. "You were so wet for me. So eager, even while telling me to fuck off."

I bit my lip as the swear-word whispered across my neck.

His teeth caught the top of my ear. "You wanted me that night…just like you want me now."

I'd been so confused. Lusting for things I hadn't understood—loving his strength and cruelty despite despising it.

"I was so sure you'd take me."

I moaned as Q planted his hands on the table, trapping me completely. "You had no idea how much I wanted to. After letting you go, I pulled out my cock and came, all over myself." His hips rolled again, his mouth latching onto my neck. "Fuck, I wanted you. I wanted to string you up and make you beg. I wanted to drive so deep inside you you'd never forget me."

My knees wobbled; everything inside liquefied.

In a possessive move, Q placed a thigh between my legs. With a kick he opened my stance, driving his thigh to connect with swollen aching hotness. I jolted the second his naked skin touched my pussy, granting something to rub against—something to tame the burning in my core.

Unashamedly I rocked, letting my head fall back. "Q…"

One hand suddenly wrapped in my hair, yanking my head sideways, leaving my jugular exposed. Q breathed hot on my brand, itching it, scorching it. "Everything I did that night is nothing compared to what I'm going to do today." His thigh pressed harder, forcing me to grind.

My breathing stuttered loving the pressure, riding his leg like some wanton creature. Q placed both hands around my neck.

I froze, very aware of the power he had—the way he held my life in his fingers. An endless second ticked past where he didn't move, then his hands tightened, squeezing.

"I've just had an epiphany, *esclave*." His voice sounded far away.

I swallowed, struggling a little with his tight grip. My heart thrummed but it wasn't panicked. I trusted him—having him dominate only made me wetter.

"You're truly not scared of what I want to do—and in a way that strips me of the need to hurt you." His voice ebbed and flowed, quietly sorting through his thoughts. "But at the same time, it gives me the freedom I've been looking for all my life."

His hands slowly dropped, spreading from my neck to my shoulders.

I gasped as his fingertips became nails, marking me with shallow grazes. Every touch hurled me into a hotter fire than the one before.

"And with freedom comes both relief and annoyance." His hands suddenly dropped to the knot in my towel, tearing it free. The moment my breasts were exposed, he cupped me boldly. Weighing my sensitive flesh in his palms, he rolled my nipples with dexterous fingers.

I bucked in his hold, my eyelids growing heavy.

The cloud I existed in thickened, swirling with intense power. Q's touch turned from pleasuring to orgasmic. Every twist and tug flamed my sensitivity, sending shockwaves erupting from my chest directly to my core. Every roll of his thumbs echoed in my clit, linking both erogenous zones like I'd never experienced.

"Ah." I bit my lip, seeking more, chasing the promise of release. "Harder."

His fingertips pinched my nipples. I thrust backward, spreading moisture on his thigh, rubbing against his erection.

He hissed, squeezing my breasts. "I always thought when I got you like this, I wouldn't be able to hold on. But what happened in the hotel—it's strengthened my control. It's stolen some of the craziness deep inside."

He removed his thigh from between my legs, giving me nothing to rub against.

I growled under my breath, frustration hot in my blood. "What happened in the hotel was consensual, Q. Just like now—I *want* you to lose control." I arched my back, wedging his cock harder into my ass. "Lose it. Give it to me. The pill you gave me makes me crave everything about you. Sweet and safe isn't what I want."

He froze. "You're saying you only want this because I

drugged you?"

My eyes fluttered open, real life intruding on our sensual world. "No. I want this because I'm so horny. I want this because I miss you."

His hand fisted in my hair, holding me still. "Do you remember me saying that—before everything that just happened? I told you I missed your fight—your spirit. Do you forgive me for making you believe? Do you forgive me for giving you substances against your will?"

His voice changed my heartbeat from slow and heavy to fast and light. "What do you want me to say? That I wasn't terrified at swallowing something I didn't know? Fine. I was. Petrified. I don't know what you did to make me see Leather Jacket. I don't know what happened between us while I was in some other dimension. I have no idea where we are. I don't know why my entire body feels as if every touch is a tiny orgasm. I have no idea about anything."

I stayed frozen, still held by Q's fist. "But I don't *need* to know. All I need is to trust you. And I do. Isn't that enough?"

"No. It isn't," Q muttered, tugging on my hair. "You think you trust me—but I'm not so sure." He bit the sensitive skin behind my ear. "I know what happened between us—I know what I almost did, and I don't know if it's a good idea to step into the dark so soon."

My anger—that had been missing for so long—sprang into being. "Don't. You can't."

"Can't what, *esclave?*"

"You can't deny me. I'm finally giving you the opportunity to bring me into your world and now you're chickening out." I stomped my foot, the haze in my brain tinging everything with red. "Take me. I'm not asking; I'm demanding."

He chuckled. "Is that a threat, Tess?"

His tone shot right through my heart, granting equal measures of hot and cold. *Yes. Say yes. Push him. Force him.* My pussy clenched, hungry for sex. "Yes, it's a threat. It's about time you punished me. I've been bad—I deserve everything you can give."

His heat disappeared as he took a step away, spinning me to face him. My back slammed against the table as the towel fell from my body, puddling on the floor. "Punish you? Why the fuck do I need to punish you?"

My chest fluttered, sucking in shallow breaths. The word 'punish' echoed in my brain.

Punish.

Punish.

I blinked. Didn't he realize I knew he'd struggled with me hurting him? For weeks he'd shut down, dealing with whatever issues I'd put between us. I'd shut him out, made him doubt. I'd *damaged* him. "For that night," I said, not needing to elaborate.

Q snarled. "You think I'm still hung up on that?" He gripped my hips, digging his fingers painfully. "You let me bring you back to life. I couldn't be more fucking grateful. And if you knew what I'd done only an hour ago, you'd know it's not you who needs forgiveness."

His voice softened, something dark filling his eyes. "I told you never to lie to me, but I lied to you."

What? My heart lodged in my throat. I frantically searched his eyes. "Why? How?"

He shook his head slowly and with such finality all my pixie dust and lustful haze disappeared, leaving me a block of ice. "Q?"

Looking deep into his gaze, I shrank away at the bleak resolution reflecting there. "It wasn't what I said—it was what I thought. All this time, I've been annoyed at you for not trusting me. And now you *do* trust me…but I'm not sure *I* trust *you.*" Sighing, he pressed the tip of his nose against mine. "I accept everything you're giving me. I want to let go—not fully, as I don't have the power to come completely undone—but enough to show you what I need. I want to hurt you. I want to make you cry—I want to punish you, Tess, but I don't trust you're doing it for the right reasons. I think you're doing this entirely for me and not for *us*."

Was that true? *Am I giving him my pain, with no limitations, purely for his pleasure?*

No, I didn't believe that. I'd been so wary of everything Q had to offer up till now. I'd wanted it but skated around it at the same time. This time…I truly wanted to fling myself head first into his world. And his refusal frustrated the hell out of me.

With gentle fingers, I hooked them into his towel, fumbling to undo it. His eyes darkened as the damp fabric fell away from his hips, leaving him naked, crowding me against the table.

"No more thinking. Put our demons to rest right here, right now. Let me prove you *can* trust me. I'm done being scared, Q. I'm done being weak. I'm going to love everything you give me. I'm going to scream and come and cry. And then I'm going to fall in love with you even more and demand you marry me the moment the sun rises tomorrow."

Q shuddered, looking as if he wanted to strike and consume all at once.

I froze, waiting to see if he would kiss me.

He didn't.

"Do you know what hurt the most?" he muttered.

"No." I worried he'd slipped into insecurity, talking himself out of whatever was about to happen.

"It was your willingness to hand over your sanity and happiness. And now you're doing it again and it's fucking with my head—"

"I'm not doing it again. I really—"

He bared his teeth. "I haven't finished. Don't interrupt."

I dropped my eyes, flushing with heat.

"You're fucking with my head, but this time…I believe you. I believe you're doing this for you, too. I believe you *do* want me to make you scream, and I'm going to fucking love it." He gave me a half smile looking like the true devil in the darkness. "Does that scare you?"

There was no lie. No half-truth. "No."

His body shifted; the air filled with promise. In one swift move, Q spun me around, imprisoning me against his front and the table. The edge of the wood dug into my hips as he folded over me, pressing his chest on my back until my breasts squashed against the felt.

With nothing between us, his skin burned mine, intoxicatingly delicious.

"Good answer. This time—*Je te crois.*" I believe you.

My heart sprouted feathery wings, tickling my chest in hope. "You're going to give in?"

"I'm going to give in, but not let go."

Okay, that would have to do for now. "You're going to trust that I want this as much as you?"

His hands trailed over my sides. "I'm going to trust you, *esclave.*"

"You're going to punish me?"

"I'm going to punish you."

"How?" I whispered.

Q paused. "How?"

"*How* are you going to punish me? I want to hear you say it." Locking eyes with his over my shoulder, I squirmed against the table, dropping my hand to my front, touching the wet heat between my legs.

Q's nostrils flared, his gaze riveted on my disappeared hand. "Tess—fuck."

I'd missed this—taunting, provoking. He may be in control, but I had all the power. I moaned as I stroked downward, loving how slick he'd made me.

Harsh fingers latched around my wrist, yanking my hand away. Anger decorated his face, along with sharp-edged desire. "That's not yours to play with. That's mine. And I'll tell you how I'm going to fucking punish you. I'm going to taste every inch of you. I'm going to steal all your inhibitions. You're going to come on my fingers, tongue, and cock. You're going to unravel, Tess, and I'm going to lick up every drop."

His hand twisted my neck, tilting me sideways to kiss me. His mouth crashed against mine, swallowing my moan, locking his arms around me. I couldn't do anything but accept his brutal assault. I skipped from reality the moment he caught my tongue, sucking as if every inch of my mouth belonged to him.

I knew what I was letting myself in for. I knew Q wouldn't take it easy on me. I also knew I never wanted anything more in my life.

Kicking my ankle, Q spread my legs, positioning his cock right in the centre of my ass. Breaking the kiss, he growled, "Time for talking has ended, *esclave*. Now's the time for fucking."

He'd said something similar just before whipping me on the cross. A thrill shot through my blood; I melted.

A hand landed on my ass, bringing with it flames and thunder. I jolted in his arms, biting my lip against the pain. "I'm going to own every inch of you tonight. Including your mind."

I couldn't breathe. Even the purple clouds floating in my blood couldn't stop one question blaring in my head.

Do I still want this?

Did I still want pain or had that been false bravado—making me believe my own lies.

Q's hand came down again, striking me in the same place, igniting a bonfire. My eyes prickled with tears even as the fire from my skin slowly migrated into my blood, heating me, dissolving every inch of my past.

Yes. *Yes, I do.*

The knowledge sent my hips rolling, provoking Q as I wiggled.

He struck me again, lower this time, more thigh than ass, but it felt just as good. A stinging good—a pain I'd forgotten how to compute, but my body remembered. I gave myself over to it. I wanted to turn my mind off completely.

"Who fucking hurt you, *esclave*?" Q demanded, striking me again.

Huh? I blinked, clawing my way back to conscious

thought. Looking over my shoulder, I locked with his wild eyes. It took a moment for the question to sink in, but then I knew. I knew what he wanted.

For the first time, I let myself get angry. Terribly, ridiculously angry. At *them*. I snarled, "They did."

Q narrowed his eyes, breathing hard. "Who caused you agony?" His hand stroked my burning skin before slapping me again—the hardest one yet.

Uncomfortableness flared, along with a rush of pleasure. I filled with reckless, needy energy. "They did."

"Who stole you from me?"

"They did."

"Who taught you to run from pain?"

"*They* did."

His hand lit up my ass, followed by his fingers tracing my crack. He dipped his touch between my legs, moving tortuously slow.

I panted and writhed, caught in the sparkly web of anticipation. *Touch me. Stroke me.* A whisper of a caress then Q removed his hand, teasing me to the point of rage.

"Who will make you love pain again?"

I wanted to demand he touch me, but I gave him what he wanted. "You will."

"Who will grant you freedom with pleasure?" His fingers dipped again, feathering over the delicate skin. This time he granted me one stroke—one mind-blowing stroke across my clit.

His touch was a weapon. An aphrodisiac. I was wet. Slick. *Desperate.*

Q's voice thickened to a growl. "Who will make you come while hurting you?"

"You will," I gasped as his touch went lower, dipping between my folds, driving me insane.

"Who will make your body remember? Who will keep you safe?"

"You, Q. Just you."

His hand disappeared. I moaned at the lack of stimulation, then cried out as he fisted my hair, wrenching my head upright. His lips found mine, his dark taste invoking a primal urge inside.

He stole my thoughts, my sanity. My hands shot behind me, digging my nails into his firm ass, yanking him forward to thrust against me.

His kiss was a hammer, his fingers a wrecking ball—with each one he smashed the remaining glass prison in my mind, making me his equal, but also keeping me firmly in the position of submissive.

A wash of gratefulness filled my heart. I was unbelievably lucky. So blessed. Q not only gave all of himself, he also made all my black desires come true. We truly were born for each other.

He panted in my mouth, rolling his hips, taunting me with the one thing I wanted most of all. His teeth captured my bottom lip.

And bit.

I cried out as my skin broke. A trickle of metallic fed from my mouth to his. Q seethed, seeming to increase in size until all I knew was him. The moment my blood hit his tongue, it was over.

No going back.

Only going forward into sin.

"God, I want to bite you, drink you. I want to drain you, so you live in me always," he grunted, picking me up in one arm, hoisting me higher on the table. Only my tiptoes reached the floor while my breasts squashed against the felt.

His nose tickled my spine as he kissed his way down to my tailbone. "Put your hands on the table, and don't move."

I trembled but obeyed. I ran my hands along the fuzzy fabric, relishing in the desire sweeping in my blood.

Looking over my shoulder, he smiled. It transformed his face from brooding to boyish until it was gone, replaced with a cocky smirk and possessive glint in his eye.

"Stay exactly like that, with your glowing ass ready for my pleasure." With another spank, he disappeared into the darkness like a ghost.

I swayed a little, my tiptoes straining to keep still—exactly as Q demanded.

Not having his heady presence close by, the pixies and nymphs in my chest sent more dust through my body, tingling, warming until I shuddered with ideas of what would happen next.

Where is he?

I looked around the room.

I saw nothing.

Absolutely nothing.

Nothing else mattered but the pool table, the darkness, and Q—wherever he was.

I loved the anonymity. The unknowing.

A metal clink sounded a few paces away, followed by a footstep.

Then silence.

We could be married for years, and I would never get used to how silently Q moved.

Slowly, goosebumps spread over my arms. It wasn't nerves dancing on my skin but excitement. I wasn't cold or terrified. I was weightless and buoyant, waiting for my master to return.

A hand landed on my waist making me leap upright. My heart bucked in surprise.

"Jumpy, Tess? Afraid of what's coming next?" Q didn't wait for my answer. He pressed my shoulder blades down, stalking around the pool table to the other side.

His eyes were the only pinpoints of light until he flicked a switch, bathing the apple felt with a golden glow. The chandelier above painted us with golds and burnt oranges from the tinted crystals.

Q no longer looked devilish but royal.

My heart flew free, fluttering to the ceiling.

"Donne-moi tes mains." Give me your hands. The order

whispered through the golden light, quintessentially him. His raspy, melodic voice had a power over me he wasn't aware of. I instantly locked my wrists together, jutting them toward him.

Q didn't say a word as he accepted my gift, wrapping soft, black fabric around me. The silk looked like morbid blood, as if I'd slashed my wrists in a fit of insanity.

The moment he'd restrained me, Q tugged the cord, making me stretch even further across the table, securing it somehow. Once tied, he strolled back toward me, setting my heart jumping and body dissolving under his intense stare.

My back was icy cold while my front was toasty warm. The two sensations, coupled with my lack of mobility, made my lungs suck in air as if oxygen was about to go extinct. The closer Q came, the more lightheaded and woozy I was.

I flinched as he cupped my ass.

"What are you going to do?" I didn't bother testing the binds. I knew Q—he had a way with ropes—there would be no chance of escape.

"Sometimes, the only way to make your dreams come true is to shatter them," he said, circling me like a predator. "Sometimes, the only way to make your nightmares disappear is by facing them."

I didn't like the sound of that. "I won't have nightmares anymore. I faced those issues today."

Q stopped behind me. "That may be true, but I'm all for making sure." He ran a harsh hand down my spine. He stepped to the side; I tensed for a wallop. "But maybe I'm not talking about your nightmares anymore."

His hand darted to the side, reaching something I couldn't see. I sucked in a breath as the same hand slinked around my hips, moving toward my pussy. His touch caused me to press my head harder against the table, cursing my trembling legs.

Without a word, Q stroked my folds, smearing my wetness with forceful fingers. My eyes snapped shut as sparks erupted from his touch, then popped wide as something firm and unyielding clamped around my clit.

It throbs. Fuck, it throbs.

"Q?"

"You get one question. After that, I refuse." His voice thickened with his accent.

I squirmed, trying to figure out what he'd pinched on my clit. For the life of me I had no idea. "What did you use?"

Q rubbed my back and ass as if I were a prized horse he was about to mount. "It's a clothes peg. And before you ask, everything I use on you tonight is what I've found around here. I didn't come prepared—but I do know pain is pain—regardless of what causes it."

He dropped his head, dragging his teeth over my hip. "Now shut up, *esclave*, and let me savage you."

My eyes watered; my clit burned and thrummed with every heartbeat. The cinch of the peg kept me on edge, compounding the orgasm I desperately wanted.

Having Q touch me gave a small sense of relief. If he stroked me, he wasn't far enough away to whip or use any other item he may've found. But then he stepped away, leaving me cold and totally vulnerable.

Oh, God.

The first strike bit into my skin like a thousand insects.

Insects.

My legs gave out—the table supported all of my weight.

My mind split into two pieces. Flashbacks swarmed.

"We'll beat you bloody, pretty girl."

"I'm going to fuck you, puta. *You're next."*

"Hurt them, or we'll hurt you."

The horror of Rio sucked me backward, then other memories came thick and fast.

"How long have you wanted this, Tess? How long have you wanted to be fucked?"

"I'm in love with you. You've stolen everything but given me so much in return."

"Your pain is my pain. You honour me by letting me mark you."

My body wanted Q's dark medicine but my mind fought

off the lustful haze, running away from pleasure into grief.

No! I didn't want to. I wanted to stay strong.

"Tess." Q leaned over me, tapping my cheek. *"Reste avec moi."* Stay with me. "Only concentrate on now. Not then. Claim it back."

I moaned, cursing myself. I thought I was free. I felt as if I had too many layers. Layers upon layers of complications. I'd freed myself from one, only to find another.

The pool table creaked as Q leaned on it, brushing away a curl from my eyes. I looked up, locking onto his gaze. Brandishing whatever he'd used, he trailed it down my back, making me shiver. "I'm going to punish you every time you let your thoughts drift."

My nipples stiffened against the felt. Seeing Q destroyed all my thoughts, granting me strength to embrace what I needed. I nodded.

"Every time you shy away from pain, I'll punish you. It's for your own good. "

I nodded again, not trusting my voice.

Q gave me a look so full of adoration and togetherness, I knew I wouldn't have to fight to keep my thoughts in the present. He'd taken me utterly hostage.

"Good girl," he murmured, leaning off the table. His fingers found my pussy again and I arched my hips into his palm. A single finger pressed inside, conjuring liquid and need, while his knuckles knocked the peg on my clit. Intense stars bolted down my legs.

The next hit came as a total surprise, across the back of my thighs.

More insects filled my mind.

Spiders.

Termites.

Beetles.

Just like my hallucinations in Rio.

A headache built behind my eyes, trying to ignore the past and focus only on Q.

Q removed his touch, smearing my dampness over my lower back. "Tess...." he growled. "Don't make me warn you again." His voice resonated with anger. "Conquer your fear." He struck. "Rule your pain." He struck again. "Find pleasure in your terror." And again. "You're stronger than this."

His voice was a spotlight in the never ending void sucking me down. I latched onto it, holding tight.

He hit me again. Different spot. Different pain. The fear came thick and sickly sweet, but I managed to ignore the memories.

Q might hurt me. He might bruise, make me bleed, and completely consume me, but he would never destroy me. He'd protect me to the brink.

Moving away, he struck again, focusing on the left side of my ass where he hadn't spanked. His breathing grew heavy and hard. "Fuck, Tess." Q squeezed my ass cheek. "You're so fucking beautiful."

His voice was the key to completely freeing me—the reverence and wonderment in his tone. Something changed inside. Something swift and fleeting. The last remaining proverbial chains clanked away, smashing into the glass walls, leaving me finally, *finally* unencumbered.

I sighed as I managed to refocus completely on the present.

The peg between my legs went from torturing to tempting once again. I bucked my hips, wanting more of the throb.

Q dragged his punishment of choice over my burning flesh. "I'll give you one guess as to what I'm using on you." He rocked against me, bumping his hot cock on my hip. Another flick of his wrist delivered more intangible pleasure-pain.

My mind raced. What did he have? What caused multiple burning marks on my skin? The sharp sting hinted he probably broke my skin.

"Um, a ruler?" My voice barely made a sound.

Q chuckled. "Wrong guess."

The pain came again, and euphoria that I'd forgotten

blanketed over me. It turned everything gooey and slow and hushed. Only the crack of Q's strike and the scalding heat remained.

The peg became my best friend, building me higher and higher, pinching me closer to an unbelievable orgasm. Something uncoiled in my core, growing and growing, wetter and wetter.

He hit me again, lost in his world.

Time ceased to have meaning as Q turned me from submissive to slave. With each strike, I welcomed the fire, transmitting right into my belly.

The next hit me hard. The first wave of an orgasm slipped through my control. I didn't know if Q would let me come, and I was incapable of asking. I wasn't human anymore, just lust.

Q paused, reaching from behind to push one firm finger inside me.

I cried out, tears running from my eyes at the joy of being touched.

"Do you want to come, *mon coeur*? Do you want to explode for me?"

His voice sent me closer and closer to the edge of no return. I nodded, creating static electricity with my hair rubbing against the table.

"In that case, *viens pour moi.*" Come for me. Withdrawing his finger, he shifted closer, bringing his gorgeous hardness against the back of my thighs. It branded me hotter than anything else. I wanted it. I would cry if I didn't get it.

Fiery stinging spread on my ass, hurtling me down and down into myself where nothing else existed but senses. I couldn't think. I could barely breathe. My body turned inward, focused only on Q and the peak and pierce of what he did.

Another hit and Q's fingers crept up between my legs to my pussy. I moaned as the peg kept me wobbling on the very edge of release. With a vicious pull, he tugged it free, releasing the floodgates of blood and ecstasy. I screamed as his fingers slammed inside.

I lost it.

My hips bucked of their own accord, grinding onto Q's two amazing fingers. My swollen clit required no stimulation—skittering into waves upon waves of pleasure.

Q groaned, stroking my inner walls, forcing my body to shatter into infinity. "Fuck, you're tight. Keep going. Come, Tess."

The crest was a tsunami of bliss, crashing with power. Q thrust in perfect rhythm with my contractions, drawing out the orgasm until the last wave smashed into me like a wall of fire.

Once the last ebb rattled my body, Q placed the item he used beside my head, folding his body over mine. His heat made my raw and delicate skin simmer with pain but I loved his weight, his authority. "I told you, you'd come on my fingers. Guess what the next one is, *esclave.*"

I mumbled something, opening extremely heavy eyelids. The first thing I noticed was the whisk. A whisk?

My eyes shot to Q's. "You—" My voice was broken from his erotic torture. "You used that on me?" It made sense, the caustic threads of pain—multiple stripes. I hurt everywhere: my cheekbone and hips hurt from the unforgiving table and my shoulders burned from being tied while my ass felt like flames would combust at any moment.

He nodded—his eyes as pale as I'd ever seen. "Yes. You should see your skin. It's a crisscross of perfection." He pressed his erection right between my cheeks. "You didn't answer me. Tell me how I plan to make you come next." I knew what I wanted, but I had a feeling Q meant to drag this out. Having him inside would be the last thing I'd earn. I had to try, though. "Your cock. Please fill me, *maître.*"

He followed the contour of my shoulder, nibbling gently. "You haven't earned that yet. I'm having too much fun."

Climbing off me, taking his heat from my wounded ass, he circled the table and untied the rope holding me down. The instant I was free, he came back around, holding the leash like I would run at any moment. Even if I was terrified of what he had planned, I couldn't run. My legs weren't functioning; my pussy still shivered with fading echoes of my release.

Q helped me stand, rubbing my lower back as I hissed with discomfort. When I stood upright, he looped his fingers in the silk around my wrists. Jerking me close, I slammed against his naked body. His mouth brushed against my ear, whispering, "My tongue, *esclave*. That's what's next." He nuzzled my hair away, scraping his teeth on my brand. "You'll come so fucking hard. You'll beg me to lick while I hurt you. Because that's who you are, Tess."

I winced as his teeth led a threatening trail down my neck. Who was I? I didn't even remember my birthday or hair colour—Q's lips were venom poisoning all my thoughts. "Why? Why will I come while you hurt me?" I honestly wanted to know. Had he made me this way? Had circumstances evolved me? Or had I been born with all these black complexities?

Q kissed me. His lips sealed over mine with domination, spearing his tongue into my mouth. I opened to him, loving the vicious but worshipping affection.

Then I screamed as a harsh hand landed on the sore skin of my backside. Q tore his lips from mine, murmuring, "Because you're mine. My little monster. And I refuse to let you forget it."

My knees wobbled.

Pushing me away, he smirked. His fist wrapped the leash around his knuckles before striding forward into the dark.

I had no choice but to follow. Walking through such a gloomy unfamiliar room had my instincts screeching on high alert. I wanted to turn on the lights, but the bold way Q directed me kept me trusting—safe.

We stopped beside a wall, the light from the chandelier over the pool table wasn't able to spread its feathers of light this far. I squinted, vaguely making out a heavy hanging piece of art in the shape of something unrecognisable. Reaching out, I touched it. It was made from hollowed metal judging by the cool slick surface.

Q stretched upward, reaching for the mooring point. The ceiling slopped, making one end of the room high, while the other was touching height. Looking closer, I noticed the industrial looking hook holding the floating piece.

"What are you doing?" I asked, giving in to the temptation of gawking at Q. Fully stretched, completely naked, his muscles bunched as he unhooked the chain and lowered the sculpture to the ground. His biceps trembled as he dragged the piece away, leaning it against the wall.

Collecting a handful of what looked like fabric ropes, he strolled back.

Coming to stop in front of me, he stood proud and almost narcissistic in his perfection. He'd fully embraced being in control—doing what he wanted.

"Remember what I once told you? How I wanted to eat you for days and there would be nothing you could do to stop me?" His voice held a tone I couldn't decide if I loved or hated.

"Yes."

"Yes, what?" His eyes flashed.

"Yes, *maître*." My belly twisted with anticipation.

Q held up the intricate web of ropes. "Do you know what Shibari is, *esclave*?"

I couldn't take my eyes off his hands as he twisted and twirled the rope back and forth. He was a snake charmer, and I'd fallen completely into his conjury.

He took a step closer, ratcheting my heart rate. "It's the art of rope and bondage. An art I've fantasised about using on you for a fucking long time." His hand lashed out, grabbing my bound wrists. I struggled a little, knowing it was useless but wanting to spar with him anyway.

Denouncing him and toying with him made me wild in the past. I wanted all that he promised. Hell, I would tackle him to the ground to force his tongue to take me now, instead of making me tremble in wait. But I also wanted to make him hot. To give him *his* fantasy of taking me against my will.

"I won't let you."

His jaw twitched; head tilted slightly. "*What* did you say?"

"I don't want any more ropes. But I do want your tongue." Loving the flutter in my heart, I threw my arms around his head, jumping a little to get my bound wrists to clear his height. The moment I held him, I traced my tongue along his bottom lip, whispering, "You don't need ropes to make me come." *Even though I'm dying to see what you do to me.*

Q shuddered, kissing me hard. His tongue dived deep, conjuring a moan from my soul. His slick heat made me melt in his arms.

"Don't think I don't know what you're doing," he grunted, walking me backward to smash against the wall. "It's not going to fucking work." Ending the kiss with a painful nip, he unhooked my arms. "You're trying to get me to lose control, but for once in my life I'm enjoying straddling the line of right and wrong. I'm loving hurting you but also pleasuring you. And I know you're loving it, too."

The hand not tangled in ropes came up, wrapping around my throat. "God, I missed you, Tess."

My stomach flip-flopped at the ray of truth in the darkness of our games. "I love you," I murmured, accepting his gentle kiss.

The softness morphed to tension again as Q pulled away. His lips twisted into a grin. "You're going to look divine."

Unknotting the rope in his grip, he ordered, "Stand there and don't move."

I stood breathing shallowly as he draped one long piece over my shoulders. It tickled my skin, slinking around my waist. His face darkened with concentration and I tried to follow his quick hands.

More twists, more loops. Each rope sent my body thrilling.

Q dropped to his knees, nudging my legs apart. Looking up, he said, "I'm not a master at Shibari, so this isn't going to be perfect."

I inspected what he'd done so far—the thicker knots on some points, the looseness of others. Rows upon rows of ropes, leading from my shoulders and back to my hips. "It looks like you know enough."

He smiled. "I've practiced enough to know how to make a harness."

My heart stuttered at the thought of him doing this to another woman. Fierce hot jealousy filled me. My fingers curled by my sides.

Q noticed. Of course he fucking noticed.

"Something you want to say, Tess?"

I bit my cheek. There were plenty of things I wanted to say, but—oh, screw it. "I hate the thought of your past. You're mine."

He chuckled. "You're so cute when you're jealous." He followed the contours of my body, threading silk around my thighs, knotting them intricately.

The black colour made my white skin come alive, like a canvas covered with lashes of paint, or even handwriting—a contract of ropes.

I hated the churning in my stomach. I had no right to be possessive of his past. We all had them—it was pointless to torture myself with who he might've done this with.

Trying to distract myself, I glared at his tattoo, letting the birds fill my vision as Q tied the last knots around my knees.

Standing, he appraised his handiwork. Prodding a finger in one knot, and testing the tightness of another, he finally nodded.

His hand fell to his cock, stroking himself, his eyes drinking me in. "I wish I had a camera. You've never looked more beautiful." Pulling me forward, he whispered against my mouth, "And I said I practiced. Not that I practiced on someone. This is a first for me, too."

A smile tugged my lips. He let me go to gather the chain from the statue he'd removed.

Undoing the carabiner, he smirked. "Turn around."

Oh, God. *Am I ready for this?*

My heart thundered as I shuffled in place, facing away. I shivered as Q came close, hooking the carabiner and chain to the rope harness behind me. With strong arms, he suddenly picked me up, cradling me against his front.

"J'ai besoin que tu fasses quelque chose pour moi." I need you to do something for me, he said, nuzzling my neck.

Having his hot breath on my skin undid all my worries. "Anything."

"I'm going to flip you upside down. I'll keep hold of you as your grip will be compromised because your shoulders are fastened, but you need to stay as still as possible."

My eyes flew upward to the ceiling. He was going to secure me upside down, hanging? *What did you think was going to happen?* I seriously hadn't thought this through.

I swallowed my fears, nodding. Q manoeuvred my body first to face him, then sideways. I held my breath as vertigo stole me.

From vertical to horizontal, I clung to his hips as best I could. From horizontal to vertical, his cock brushed my breasts. With undeniable strength he forced me upside down, holding me steady.

I clamped my arms around his thighs, cursing the ropes around my shoulders not letting me hug him.

I jolted as a rush of hot breath brushed against my core. Oh, *God*.

My eyes squeezed, hyperaware of his mouth so close. I wanted it. I wanted another orgasm. His arms bunched, holding my weight. He jostled me, keeping me pinned with one arm while reaching for the hook with the other. His attention was wholly on stringing me up and not on the part of me screaming for attention.

"Hold on. I'm just securing—" His distraction allowed me time to revel in his hot form against mine.

I clutched him hard, cursing my jitteriness at the newness of what was to come. His body stretched and tightened, straining on his toes to secure the chain back onto its original hook.

The ropes tugged my back, curving around my body, cocooning me in a prison of silk.

"Let go, Tess," Q ordered. His hands fell to my waist, trying to push me off him.

I only gripped harder. I didn't trust it. Images of slamming onto my head gave me a phantom headache. Blood rushed to my skull, roaring in my ears.

"Let go, *esclave.*" Q pinched me, stepping away, forcing me to release. I swung, snapping into place, held by the chain. The ropes took my weight, tightening against my body, but not enough to strangle or cut off my blood supply. The knots Q had created kept it from slicing me.

Everything I knew was different. Up was now down. Down was now up. I felt awkward and uncomfortable and completely strange. My legs were bound loosely together, letting my knees fall downward like an upside down crouch, leaving me blatantly exposed and open.

My arms were tied to my body, giving no hope of escape.

Q disappeared and came back with a stool. With strength I'd always found such a turn on, he hoisted me higher, gradually shortening the chain until my mouth was at the perfect height.

Hip height.

Cock height.

I blinked, fighting a rush of nausea. It was surreal to be hanging upside down, so vulnerable.

Stepping off the stool, Q kicked it away. His hands whispered over my stomach, slowly changing my discomfort to eagerness.

Even upside down, Q painted an incredible sight. His legs were spread, powerful quads tight and covered in a splashing of hair. His cock hung heavy and hard, perfectly straight and begging to fill me. His tattoo only added to his mystique and erotic allure.

Planting himself in front of me, he stroked my dangling hair before caressing my cheek. "I never thought I'd get to see you like this, Tess. I'm ready to fucking blow just thinking about all the delicious things I can do." His touch turned dangerous as he cupped my breast. "Who's your master?"

My eyes refused to stay open as he squeezed my nipple. "You."

"Who do you belong to?"

"You."

His touch danced over my sides, pushing me, making me spin slowly. His fingers trailed around my rotating body, never stopping their exploration. I flinched when he touched my burning backside and thighs, the tender skin way too sensitive.

"You're my every fantasy come to life. I can't believe you're real." His mouth kissed my upper thigh, his five o'clock shadow rasping. "I'm going to worship you." His breath skated over my pussy.

I moaned; I'd never been so sensitive, so aware of the predicament I was in.

His lips moved to my hipbone, nipping tenderly. "Do you know what I'm going to do first?"

I whimpered, closing my eyes, focused entirely on his words whispering over my skin.

"I'd planned on punishing you. I'd planned on marking you, like I did with the wax on your breast. I'd planned on doing so many things but my self-control won't let me." He spun me around, slapping hands on my smarting ass. "Do you know why I can't?"

I shook my head, feeling heavy and slow with the rush of blood in my ears. "It's because I need to be inside you. I need to claim you. I've marked you enough, and I have plenty of time to mark you after—but right now—I *need* to fuck you."

I shivered. Lust replaced heaviness, flowing thick and fast.

Q brought me to face him. His cock filled my vision; my mouth watered.

"However, before I can fill you, I have to do one thing. I

promised. And I never break my promises." His mouth came achingly close to my pussy. His hands landed on very sensitive inner thighs, keeping me spread. I cringed in embarrassment, then cried out as he trailed his nose through my folds. "Goddammit, you smell divine."

I twisted in the ropes. *Lick me.* "Q—"

"What was my promise, *esclave?*" His breath tickled my clit, making me jerk in the ropes.

"You said..." I couldn't continue—his nose nuzzled me again.

"Go on..." He pulled away, leaving me throbbing for more.

"You said you would make me come on your fingers, tongue, and cock."

"Good girl. And do you think you deserve my tongue?"

Damn his mental torture. I wanted to scream. I wanted to grab his head and force him to lick. But I hung completely helpless. "Yes...I deserve it. Please—give it to me."

Q's fingers bit into my flesh. "Ask nicely, Tess. Do you want me to taste you?"

I bit my lip, humming in acknowledgement.

My mouth popped wide as his tongue licked once—thoroughly and languishingly—over my entrance.

"Say please if you want me to fuck you with my tongue, *esclave.*"

My core liquefied. "Please. *S'il vous plaît.* I want your tongue, *maître.*"

I groaned as his mouth latched over my pussy. So possessive. So sure. His tongue swirled my clit, using the flat muscle to drench me in saliva before thrusting the tip deep inside.

Oh, my fucking God.

Fire replaced my blood. Gasoline seared my veins. Every heartbeat was a match.

The orgasm from before heightened the sensations, my stomach muscles clenched, my entire body wanted to run from his relentless tongue.

I needed something. I wanted to hold something. I demanded something to distract myself from the incredible, overwhelming pleasure. I was completely at Q's mercy. The knowledge he could do whatever he damn well pleased turned me into a wobbling mess.

His hands held me firm. His tongue licked with power. Every sweep sent my head pounding with pressure. I wouldn't last long. Already my toes curled at the onslaught. His rough-smooth cheeks created their own fire against my thighs as I fought to bring my legs together.

"I'm going to make you come. Right now." His mouth smashed against me, bruising. My entire world detonated—blinked out like a cataclysmic explosion.

He sank inside—deep and strong, giving me nowhere to hide. His tongue did exactly as he said it would—fucked me.

"Oh, *God.*"

I'd never been so devoured, so taken. The firmness of his mouth and dexterity of his tongue unravelled me to the point of insanity. He was serious about making me come—his tongue thrust hard, building a nucleus inside wanting to release.

Needing to do something, *anything,* before drifting away on a sea of pleasure, I opened my eyes. His cock stood tall and hard, only centimetres away from my mouth.

Two can consume.

Licking my lips, I used my stomach muscles to swing forward. Capturing the tip of him, I wasted no time sucking him into my mouth. A centimetre, then an inch, until his hotness touched the back of my throat.

His tongue spasmed inside me. He sucked in a ragged breath, then surged his hips forward, gliding deeper into me. He gave me everything I wanted in one sure thrust.

I lost myself to his musky taste. The saltiness of his excitement, the silky steel of skin, the throbbing blood in his veins. I couldn't control anything and Q surged forward again, using my mouth, fucking my mouth just like his tongue fucked me. Every twitch of his hips rewarded me with a tongue sweep, plunging deeper.

My breathing caught and hitched.

My head was too heavy, too full of blood. My toes tingled from being upside down. All basic power had been taken. I couldn't talk. I couldn't move. I could barely breathe.

I was his.

His to use, lick, punish, fuck.

It was torture. It was heaven. I'd never done anything so untamed and sexual.

Q traced his fingers from my inner thigh to my core. He flicked my clit, driving his tongue deeper inside.

The first tingle of an orgasm had me frantically sucking, licking in return. He groaned—the vibration echoed through my pussy, sending me ever closer to coming.

I cried out, breaking the suction around his cock. It didn't stop him thrusting into me—treating me like a sex toy. For some reason the callous way he sought my mouth made me lose all inhibitions.

I no longer cared about him being so intimate with every pink part of me. I no longer cared about my freezing legs and pounding head. All I wanted was freedom.

I wanted to come.

Opening my jaw as wide as I could, I accepted his next thrust, swallowing his erection completely. I was so languid, so loose, filled with sparking desire, my gag reflex didn't engage as he slid down my throat. My nose pressed against his balls, inhaling his masculine scent.

"Fuuuck," Q growled, his focus on me interrupted.

Power filled me. Even though I couldn't be any more defenceless, I'd somehow taken charge—if only for a second.

Q's hips shot forward, filling my mouth with every eager inch he had. "Goddammit, Tess." A ripple shot from the base and a splash of hotness hit my tongue. Q pulled out, breathing hard. "Fuck. I'm not ready to come. When I do, it's going to be so far inside you, you'll know exactly who your master is."

His mouth collided with my pussy again. And this time—there was no mercy. His tongue drove deep, making me blind with need.

Then he bit me.

His teeth captured my clit in painful surrender. Sharp. Hard. Sweet, sweet pain.

I came.

Ribbons of pleasure unspooled in my belly; I stiffened in the ropes. His hands kept my legs apart, forcing his tongue into me.

I bucked and convulsed as my inner muscles rippled in his mouth.

Each wave squeezed around his tongue, milking him. I'd never been so wet, so turned on. My entire body danced with spangled light.

The moment my orgasm ended, Q detached a rope and undid a few knots. Then I was swinging.

Swinging with no warning until my feet hit the floor. I stumbled, utterly befuddled on how to stand. He'd shattered my mental abilities.

Not that it mattered.

Q grabbed my hips, splaying my shaky legs. Letting the chain hold most of my weight, he jerked me backward, and in one savage thrust, sank his beautiful cock deep, deep inside me.

I screamed at the fullness—the intrusion.

His fingernails broke my skin as he pounded into me, pushing me forward before pulling me back.

I was drenched.

Dripping.

My body offered no resistance, and I stretched with delicious welcome. My cheeks were wet from sucking Q, my limbs tingled with life. But nothing would ever compete with the amazing combination of my burning ass bruising against Q's hipbones as he drove deep, deep, deeper.

"God, you're so fucking tight. So tight." He sounded different—raw, animalistic.

One hand left my hip, making its way to where we joined. I jerked as he found my clit. It physically hurt after two mind-blowing orgasms.

Stealing my moisture, he travelled back up.

I froze as he touched the one place he hadn't before. The puckered hole that up till now I'd never thought of including in sex. I'd seen videos, read about it, but I hadn't been tempted.

If I was honest—it petrified me.

I clenched my cheeks, trying to wiggle from his finger. But he forced me still, thrusting his cock harder.

His digit pressed threateningly. His breath heated my ear. "I haven't gone here yet. I wanted to take my time. But I'm giving you fair warning, *esclave*. I want it. I want all of you. Nothing is safe from me."

I shuddered as his touch turned harder, probing. "And I'm going to take it with or without your consent."

My heart went from beating to screaming. No! I didn't want it.

Q rocked again, his cock hitting my g-spot in a perfect thrust.

I blanked out for a moment with pleasure, then stiffened as his finger swirled with lubrication, pressing hard. Coaxing, teasing, working my body against me.

"Q—don't." My heart flurried with panic not desire. My brain scrambled with the incredibleness of his cock and the terror of his probing finger.

"You said you'd let me do anything." With another press, he breached the seal of my body.

Pain.

Bitter pain.

Foreign pain.

Automatically I pushed back, horrified at the unwelcome entry.

I felt violated. Dirty.

I drew blood as my teeth clamped hard on my bottom lip, stopping myself from crying. I didn't want to give away my fear. I didn't want to excite Q any more than he was. His breathing rasped over me, drugged with desire.

With another thrust of his cock, he pressed his finger deeper. The overwhelming feeling of being too full—too stretched—made me feel...

I no longer knew.

I couldn't discern if I hated it or loved it. It wasn't known, and I wasn't ready to understand what it meant.

"I can't wait to fuck you here, Tess. Shit—" His finger hooked inside, stretching my body as his cock drove upward. The combined pressure sent an extra thrill down my spine—my back snapped straight.

"It's mine. Just like everything else about you." Withdrawing his digit, he fisted his cock, sliding wetly out of me to nudge against my hole.

I couldn't help it. My hips rolled forward. I wanted to run. I wasn't ready. *Not ready!*

Q slapped my ass, amplifying the punishment from earlier, dragging me backward and sinking inside my pussy.

I exhaled heavily, moaning in relief. I wanted him there. And only there.

His breathing was short and angry. "You won't get away when I'm ready to take that part of you, *esclave.*"

The threat hung between us. My fearful question fell from my lips. "But not today?" *Please say not today.*

It took a never ending minute for Q to reply, but finally he huffed. "I won't push you to do something you're not ready." Running his hands up my spine, he worked to my front, capturing my breasts. "Not today."

The relief melted the terror in my blood, filling me with quivering need. I thrust backward, causing his cock to strike the top of my womb.

I wanted to say thank you but my brain was jumbled. I wanted to tell him I would be open—maybe, but all I wanted to focus on was him in me—together.

He groaned, using my hips as anchors, driving upward.

"God, I want to come—"

I wished I could see him, understand his sudden hesitation. "Then come."

He thrust again before pulling out. He stepped back, leaving me hanging with my arms pinned to my sides, not knowing what the hell was going on.

Q fumbled with the carabiner behind, untethering me from the chain. My weight shifted from ceiling to being crushed against the earth on lust-laden limbs. The moment I was free, Q spun me around, backing me up against the wall.

My shoulders slammed against the surface. I didn't have time to breathe as he picked up a knife from a table close by.

My mouth went terribly dry.

His eyes were luminous, burning a path right to my soul. Hooking a fingertip under one of the knots, Q sliced it with a flick of his wrist.

We didn't say a word as he cut off every loop and fetter. My heart bounced. I was empty without him. My eyes kept drifting to his glistening hard cock, wishing he would enter me again.

When the final rope fell away, we locked gazes.

Time stood still as we stared and stared and made promises and told stories and weaved our souls ever tighter together.

Q broke the spell, dragging a rough thumb over my lips. "*Je t'aime.*" I love you.

My body went heavy. I knew what he wanted.

Desire. Thick craving desire.

My eyes widened. *Holy hell, I want it, too.* Badly.

My eyes fell to the faded scar where he'd nicked just below his nipple the night in the carousel room. He'd let me suckle. He'd let me taste everything that he was.

Q smiled softly, keeping eye contact as he positioned the sharp blade over the scar and re-opened it with a shallow slice. The black ooze of blood in the dark sent my soul ricocheting around my body. It wasn't right. It was so, so wrong.

But fuck, I wanted to taste.

My gaze glued to the trickle of blood. My mouth fell open as Q grabbed my waist, hoisted me up, and slid inside in one effortless move. His hands held me tight while I wrapped my legs around his hips, imprisoning him.

His eyes glazed, thrusting upward, filling me impossibly deep. "Take me," he whispered, leaning back.

I couldn't say a word as I curled into him, pressing my mouth against his chest. My tongue came out and ever so gently lapped his wound.

The instant the sharp metallicness of his blood hit my tastebuds, everything rewound, imploded, exploded, detonated—existed no more.

Everything was inconsequential compared to this man. I couldn't let the past steal my future. I couldn't let what I'd done fog my happiness. And I couldn't, under any circumstance, let Leather Jacket and White Man steal my joy of pain.

I would never run again. I would never hide again. I would never fear Q's delectable punishment.

I was home.

I'd been so caught up in his taste, I didn't feel Q's assault on my body. I returned to reality with a slam. Q's face was tight, his hips pounding into me with rhythmic pulses, driving himself closer and closer to the end.

His teeth were bared. He looked strong and real and entirely dangerous.

My back bowed as he thrust harder, harder. I loved his possession—found ultimate bliss in his arms.

"I have to…Tess. Forgive me." I cried out as his mouth latched onto my shoulder, the sharp puncture of teeth breaking my skin. He sucked deep, dragging my own essence into him.

It was the most basic of us. The life-force in our veins. The neural highway where our soul swam and gave animation to lifeless bodies. By drinking me, he not only took my body, but also my soul in liquid form.

An orgasm spiralled from nowhere. Spurred not from the

exquisite joy of having Q inside me—but from the joy at knowing I belonged.

It wasn't a body orgasm. It was more than that.

It was a soul orgasm.

Q braced himself, spreading his legs to thrust harder. My back bruised, my breasts jiggled, and I threw myself into the brightest, sharpest release yet. The orgasm started thorny and almost unwilling, but Q relentlessly pursued it.

Another thrust and I came.

It split me in two.

My legs squeezed my master until he grunted with pain. I relished in the power rippling down his back before he followed me into heaven.

The first spurt matched my release perfectly and with pristine synchronicity we found our breathless ending.

We transcended simple life.

We shared absolutely everything.

We slithered down the wall to land in a tangle of sweaty-sated limbs.

With our bodies wrapped together, we lay happily in the dark.

Chapter Eight

*Master and slave, owner and owned, you sate my
need and feed me
We are blood of blood, echoing heartbeat and
answering breath; nothing can break us, not even
death*

I wish people knew.

I wish more people realized this gift.

*You changed my world, Q. You sheltered, protected, and avenged
me—but even that wasn't enough to bring me back to life. My heart hurts
to think of others who've lived what I lived. Other survivors who had to
return home and pretend.*

*Pretend time healed them. Lie that they're better. Hide that the
nightmares haven't stolen their sanity.*

Everyone needs a Q.

Everyone needs to learn the lesson you taught me.

Pain is therapy. Pain is healing. Pain is the only thing that purges.

*I'm not doing a good job at writing this down, but after yesterday, I
have to try. I have to get my jumbled thoughts on paper—if only to show
you how much I love you. To let you witness how much you saved me by*

being you.

I don't think you'll ever understand how indebted I'll always be to you. Q—you own me, not because I love you, but because you...you're my—let me see if I can explain.

Sometimes, when life has taken bites out of your self-worth, when fate lands you in the path of horrible circumstance and your body is full of holes from carving out your heart for others, it's impossible to be whole again. Those holes just get bigger, the nightmares just get stronger.

Life becomes an enemy, whittling away at the remaining parts you have left.

But pain.

It strips you back—it tears off your withered, hole-riddled skin. It destroys the past and annihilates concern and worry. Pain does to a human spirit what acid does to paint. It strips away all the layers of filth and gunk until nothing but the basic material exist. The grime is gone, leaving a complete fresh start.

Q—you are my acid.

Through granting me pain, you gave me a fresh start.

I'll never be able to repay you.

Your Esclave forever,

Tess

I'd read Tess's letter over twenty times. Every word she'd written, in her cute feminine flourish, resonated deep inside.

She effectively took every hatred I had about my past— who I was, what I wanted—and chopped it into fucking pieces with a guillotine. How could I hate my need to hurt her when it was what saved her? All my life I'd suffered self-hatred, wishing I was different—kinder, wiser, gentler. Instead, she'd given me...truth.

She'd given me more than freedom—she'd allowed myself to stop hating my needs and...accept.

My mind conjured images of the women I'd saved. Slaves who'd been raped to near death; whores who'd been tortured until every drop of blood puddled on the floor. All women: daughters, wives, sisters. Each one I thought I'd helped by giving them a place to heal before sending them home to their loved ones. I gave them the best of care—bought top-of-the-line medical treatment, psychologists—and when they were less broken, I sent them home with a cheque for one hundred thousand euros. I placed them back with family and gave them a safety net, taking the stress of bill paying and jobs away while they focused on fixing their broken lives.

I thought I'd figured out a recipe to rehabilitation.

I believed family and love would be the ultimate saviour, but what if I was wrong? What if those women had been irrevocably changed? What if Tess was right?

Tess's hand fell on my forearm, wrenching me from my thoughts. "You okay? We're here."

Yesterday had been about breaking her. But it ended up breaking me. I'd been prepared to go dark—treat her fucking awful—just like I always thought I wanted.

But that was the funny thing.

I *had* everything I ever wanted. Once again she took the allure of darkness and brought her ever shining light to morph it from forbidden to cherished.

Even though I hit her ass until she bled, it wasn't her who was sore, but me. I felt stripped bare, revealed for what I was— a fucking fraud.

I'd lost the need to be savage. I'd lost the curse in my blood. I still hadn't come to terms with how I felt about it. I was angry but also fucking relieved.

I'm not him after all.

Franco appeared from the cockpit. "I'll go get the car. Stay here." He disappeared down the plane steps, leaving us alone once again. His surly tone reminded me I'd left him outside for twelve hours yesterday while I indulged my fill. And he was pissed. Not to mention his stress levels suspecting everyone now the official news had got out. I was an official target.

They're coming.

My hands curled involuntarily at the thought of what might happen…soon.

The flight from Tenerife had been uneventful. After the mind-blowing release and breathless conclusion, I'd bundled Tess from that place and returned to the hotel. Franco hadn't said a word about catching her naked. He'd avoided my narrowed look and behaved like a perfect *silent* bodyguard.

We'd had room service, before a very innocent shower, and then sleep. Wonderful sleep.

Why wonderful?

Because Tess hadn't had one single fucking nightmare.

And I was egotistically proud of that.

Shaking my thoughts away, I replied to Tess's question. *"Oui, allons-y."* Yes, let's go. Smiling, I stood and stretched. The cream leather was comfortable, but my entire body ached as if I'd fought a thousand traffickers. I suppose I had in a way—I'd become the men haunting Tess and shattered their power. Then I took her. Fuck, I took her.

The wintery sun burned my eyeballs as Tess and I descended the aircraft steps. Franco appeared driving a black Phantom with the logo of *Moineau* Holdings on the side etched in gold.

"Wait? We're back in France?" Tess squinted against the glare, noticing the large terminal across the way with the very obvious Charles de Gaulle signage giving away the location. Her face flushed as a riot of memories entered her eyes.

Franco squealed to a stop and flung himself out to open the door for Tess.

"Esclave—what are you thinking?" I hated when she got that faraway look. I wanted to chase—to enter her mind and not be left as an unpaying spectator.

"I know what she's thinking," Franco said, a huge grin spreading his face.

What the fuck? I glowered but Tess laughed. "I'm guessing you would."

I looked between the two of them getting angrier by the second. "Anyone care to tell me, or are you enjoying your inside joke?"

Franco shook his head, taking Tess's hand to help her into the car. My back bristled but I held my tongue, waiting for someone to talk.

"It was about here that I first met Tess." He squeezed her hand before letting go. "Sorry about that—throwing you to the tarmac and all. I felt bad that I rolled your ankle."

"What? You hurt her?" I stomped forward.

Tess smiled. "Good thing you didn't give me an opportunity to go for your gun. I would've shot you and never known what a nice guy you are—beneath the whole collecting slaves for a sadistic master of course."

Franco laughed; not giving away a thing that only twenty-four hours ago he'd caught her running from said sadistic master. Bet Tess wouldn't be so fucking happy if she knew he held her fully naked and totally compromised.

My teeth hurt I clenched so hard. I hated not knowing everything about her. "Tell—" I snapped my mouth closed. *No, you don't need to ask.*

I could guess. Franco completed all the slave handovers. Tess probably ran—as was her trademark by now—and they all had a very uncomfortable flight home.

I always sent Franco and two other guards to collect the bribes as they arrived. Not to make sure of the girl's protection but on the off chance the trafficker was a new player on the scene. Franco's unofficial order was to remove them from society before they got a foothold and became a threat. It wasn't possible to take out the henchmen of bigger organizations like Red Wolverine, but smaller outfits—they were killable.

Cursing under my breath, I stalked around the car and let myself in. Franco ducked, throwing me a look through the car window. I knew what he tried to convey: *I've had your back right from the start, so wind your fucking neck in.*

He was right.

So I did.

Tess smiled as Franco shut the door. Settling back into the

seat, her fingers entwined with mine. We stayed silent while the car started and pulled away from the airport.

"Don't be mad at him. Despite me wanting to kill him that night, he didn't go out of his way to hurt me."

I patted her hand, brushing away my temper. "I know. *Je suis juste un idiot.*" I'm just being an idiot.

Tess shook her head. "You're a lot of things—but never that."

My heart seized; I had to look out the window. I thought I loved her before. But that was before I had any fucking idea what love really was. It was nothing, *nothing*, compared to what I felt now. I was possessed by her. Totally consumed.

She was my home. Plain and simple—the biggest investment of my life.

"Are you going to tell me why we're back in Paris?" Tess asked, looking out the window at passing cars.

My mood lifted and a trickle of excitement filled me. Today was the day Tess really stepped into my world. Not just sexually or emotionally but materially.

Today was the day I gave Tess everything.

Bringing her hand to my mouth, I kissed her knuckles. "It's a surprise, *esclave.*"

And if you so much as argue, I'll put you over my knee and spank you—regardless of witnesses.

Tess thought I was rich. She didn't know quite how rich. But in thirty minutes, she would.

Moineau Holdings glittered with glass and sun-refracting metal as Franco pulled to the curb outside.

I opened the car door, pulling Tess out with me, leaving Franco to pull back into traffic and head to the parking garage next door. My eyes scanned the footpath, glowering at pretty women and well-dressed men—suspecting everyone.

I didn't like being in the open without back-up, especially with Tess as such a vulnerable target. And I definitely didn't like being back at work where people knew me—where buildings offered perfect coverage for anyone wanting to take out a man threatening their downfall.

My body balanced between being soft with Tess and ready to rip someone's chest open if they so much as looked at me wrong.

Get inside before you murder someone.

Wrapping an arm around Tess's waist, I propelled her through the sliding doors and into the lobby.

Tess froze, jerking my body to a stop with hers. "You've brought me back to your office? Why?" Tension tightened her voice. Just like her fear of a bath, she had to overcome her terror of this place. I thought she would've been safe here—but it only taught me never to trust anyone.

A headache appeared from the rapidly building stress in my body. I fucking hated headaches. Especially the one I'd had that day when she'd been taken. I'd been a useless invalid. If it hadn't have been for Frederick, I would probably have had a stroke trying to do everything myself.

The memory of losing her made my gut churn.

Stop thinking about it for fuck's sake.

I forced my thoughts to turn to why we were here. I wanted to surprise Roux—he was going to be the accessory to this next part of the crescent moon—he just didn't know it yet.

"We'll only be here for a bit—then I'm kidnapping you away again." Where—I hadn't quite figured out yet. Suzette still had three days before the wedding. *Shit, I better call her.* No telling what sort of craziness she'd planned by now. That woman was a fucking menace.

Keeping my arm firmly around Tess, we made our way to the elevators. The mosaic sparrow on the floor never failed to lift my heart. People thought this was just a property conglomerate. Goes to show how much they knew.

Then again.

I'd looked at the news on my phone this morning. Things were getting out of hand. Whatever Frederick was doing, I was about to tell him to fucking stop it.

Pressing the up button, Tess's breathing turned shallow. Her eyes darted around the huge, light-filled lobby. No one was around which was good—I didn't have to worry about spilling blood in my own building. The way my body tensed, I'd most likely strike first then ask questions.

Not exactly a good look for the CEO to tear off an employee's head just for saying hello.

Ducking to Tess's level, I murmured, "I'm not going to leave you alone for a second. You have nothing to fear." I would personally guarantee it.

She flashed me a grateful smile. "I know—just being back here—after feeling so amazing yesterday…it's hard to accept that yes the past isn't ruining my life anymore, but I still haven't put it all behind me."

The elevator pinged; I pushed her on. With every step Tess lagged. Her back was stiff, movements jerky.

I frowned, watching her as the doors closed, imprisoning us in the small space—alone. Pressing the floor I needed, I touched her cheek. "It's just a lift."

She flinched away.

Goddammit, I hadn't done everything I'd done to have it all be for fucking nothing. I pushed her shoulder, forcing her to face me. I had every intention of slamming her against the wall and demanding she focus on me and only me.

But she took me completely by surprise.

Leaping into my arms, I stumbled backward. The mirrored walls bruised my shoulder blades as Tess's mouth pressed against mine. Her breathing was still shallow but now for an entirely different reason.

Her fingers disappeared into my hair, jerking my lips harder onto hers. Ah, fucking hell. My cock reacted straight away.

My arms shot up, gathering her curvy form.

She dropped her fingers to my face, deliberately scratching me—driving me beyond interested into insane.

Pushing off from the wall, I spun around, crashing her against it instead. Her mouth opened wide, and my tongue plunged inside, taking, tasting, owning, *devouring*.

Our hands were separate entities as our mouths slipped and licked. I grabbed her breast through her grey jumper. Wanting my flesh on hers, needing my cock driving into her tasty warmth.

I wasn't sated. I needed more. I wanted her to bow to me and fight at the same time. I wanted so much from her—I wanted it all.

The doors opened.

A feminine cough wrenched my head up; I locked eyes with Helen. Red hair, vivid green eyes—attractive with freckles dotting her nose.

My receptionist of three years.

Releasing Tess, I grabbed her shoulders, and positioned her in front of me—trying to hide the raging hard-on in my trousers. Running hands through my hair, I made sure the white shirt I wore wasn't too crumbled and quickly inspected Tess.

Her jumper was mussed but her black jeans looked presentable. The disarray of curls made me want to drag her back into the lift and press the emergency button until I finished what she'd started.

"Mr. Mercer. *Bonjour.*" Helen smiled, eyeing Tess with a professional coolness. If I hadn't been around women—in all states of mental health—I would've missed the flash of competition in her gaze. And I would've definitely missed, and not enjoyed, Tess's answering glower full of possession.

She was fierce, my Slave Fifty-Eight. And I had no doubt she'd scratch out any female's eyes who made any move to encroach on what she considered hers.

And good. That made me fucking happy. And hot. So damn hot.

Hoping my depleting erection wasn't too obvious, I strode in front of Tess. *"Bonjour. Est-ce que M. Roux est là ? J'ai besoin de le voir."* Hello. Is Mr. Roux in, I need to see him.

Tess stayed glued to my side, a smile on her lips, but her eyes shrewd and assessing.

Helen smiled at Tess, acknowledging whatever woman code they shared, before finally giving me a look I recognised as defeat. *"Oui, il est dans son bureau."* Yes, he's in his office.

"Merci." I grabbed Tess's hand, dragging her away from the sterile first impression of the manager's level. The only things visible were Helen's desk, a large matching mosaic sparrow behind her, and some comfy chairs in the adjoining room for early appointments to wait.

Tess tugged on my hand as I strode through the floor, nodding at passing workers. I didn't have a fucking clue who they were. I only needed to know the top of commands; the rest of the workforce was their problem.

"We're not going to your office?" Tess asked, dodging a woman carrying an armful of files. Her eyes danced around the floor, taking in the large windows that let washes of natural light and the amazing view of Paris inside. Plants and paraphernalia gave the place a homely feel. No partitions separated workers—everyone had free reign on where they wanted their desk to be. Some were clumped together in a circle, others with lined up neatly. But all surrounded a large break area with a big TV, gourmet coffee and food, and a fulltime masseuse to work out any kinks.

"We can't," I said.

"Why not?"

"It's gone." I waved back at a man I distantly remembered, who'd helped with a local merger. Frederick's office was at the end, next to mine—or rather my temporary one.

"Gone?"

I looked into her blue-grey eyes—looking more grey thanks to the colour of her jumper. "You seriously didn't think

I'd be able to let it stay standing after what happened."

Tess shook her head. "You destroyed it?"

I nodded. Just like the room where I'd let her hit and scar me. It was demolished. Forever. Good fucking riddance.

The moment I saw her hair on the bathroom floor and the empty syringe, I knew I couldn't let the diabolical thing remain. It was empty rubble up there now. "I'll convert it to a helipad eventually, but right now, the birds can have it."

She pulled on my hand, yanking me to a stop. Her eyes locked onto mine. "Thank you."

My forehead furrowed. "For what?"

"For getting rid of it. I can handle a lot of things but I don't think I could've stepped foot in that space again."

I looked around to see if people were watching. People pretended to be busy, but I knew we were the entertainment. But—oh, fuck it. I dragged her close and kissed her. Her fingers squeezed my chest. Pulling back, I whispered, "Don't you think I know that?"

Stepping back, I added, "And I didn't do it just for you, Tess. I couldn't go back there either. I would rather my entire company came crashing down than ever go back into a room where I failed to protect you."

Tess's eyes swam; her cheeks pinked as she blushed. Blushed? What the hell was she blushing about? I'd had her hanging upside down with my tongue as far as it could go inside her while I drove my cock into her mouth. *That* was blush-worthy. Having me admit I tore down an office in her honour was not.

"You're far too good to me."

I shook my head, hating the twisting in my gut. I wasn't. I was the opposite. Complete fucking opposite.

She lowered her voice. "Q...I've been so wrapped up in me, I haven't asked what's going on with your business. Did everything that happen ruin your company's reputation?" Her shoulders stiffened. "I didn't cost you your livelihood, did I?"

Before worry could consume her, I grabbed her chin.

"Now is not the time to talk about it, but no. It didn't." I placed my hand on her lower back, pushing her the remaining distance to Frederick's office. If she started asking questions about my unspoken hobby, I didn't want it to be on the busy floor with overeager ears.

Little did she know that yes, what I'd done had gotten out. And no, it hadn't ruined my image. In fact—I couldn't quite believe what was happening. Another reason why I needed to talk to Roux.

Arriving at his door, I rapped my knuckles against the frosted glass. I kept telling him he needed a receptionist, but I suppose he'd taken my job while I focused on Tess, and Helen worked for him now.

Frederick opened the door with his back to us. His hair wasn't its usual perfectly slicked style, seeing as one hand was lodged in the strands. His attire of understated three-piece navy suit with elegant purple tie made me very aware I wasn't exactly dressed to impress.

I missed wearing a tailored wardrobe—but I didn't miss why I wasn't wearing them—I'd much rather be bone-fucking-naked if it meant I could ravage Tess twenty-four-seven.

His voice raised in a French curse as he removed the Bluetooth headset from his ear, spinning to confront us. His face, with its perfect skin and manicured eyebrows, looked about twenty years old not thirty.

His bright blue eyes landed on Tess, then shot back to me before his jaw fell in shock. "Mercer! Man, I thought you'd run off to get hitched."

Tess stood a little straighter, watching him with a fierceness I started to recognise as defence. She had history with Frederick—I still didn't know what they talked about the night he watched me almost rape her, then tuck and run after she used the safeword—but she knew Frederick was my closest friend. The only thing close to family I ever had.

Until her.

"Had a few loose ends before tying that particular knot," I

said, entering his office and slapping his shoulder. *"C'est bon de te voir."* It's good to see you.

He nodded, lips spreading into a smile. "You too. Missed your angry face. What's it been, three weeks?" It didn't sound like a long time, but in the scheme of things, seeing as we used to spend ten hours a day together—it was a long fucking time.

"Bet Angelique's happy you don't have to babysit me anymore." By babysitting he damn well knew I meant traipsing around the world murdering psychopaths and bribing twisted assholes.

He laughed. "Well, she got pissed that you left me in charge of this place, leaving me to work double hours, but she got over it."

I rolled my eyes. "How did you make it up to her?" Did I even want to know what they got up to behind closed doors? I genuinely liked Angelique with her straight black hair and intelligent pretty face, but I couldn't see any kink in her. I often wondered if Frederick was as completely straight laced as he liked to believe.

"Wouldn't you like to know." Roux laughed. "Well, seeing as you'll find out soon enough, I'll tell you now." He motioned us forward, spreading his arm to encompass the heavy oak desk and black leather couches facing each other. "I hired her."

"You what?" My head snapped up as I sat beside Tess on the supple leather.

"Hey, you couldn't expect me to work here every hour of the day and not get nagged when I got home, could you? I figured I'd put her on the payroll—that way we'd see each other all the time." He sat down, hoisting his navy trousers before sitting with his legs spread on the opposite couch. "Don't tell her this, but she's amazing. That stupid law degree she'd been practicing—hell she's doing wonders for *Moineau*. Not to mention, she's great at bringing me coffee—amongst other things."

I blinked. Did he just hint at office sex? In *my* building. Who was I fucking kidding? I was happy for him. I'd worried

I'd put too much responsibility on him and was glad he'd flourished.

Frederick turned to Tess, looking her up and down. "How are you?"

Tess's eyes flickered to mine, adrift with questions. I kept my face unreadable but it only took a second for her to slot the pieces together. Damn intelligent woman.

She nodded, keeping her back straight and face impassive. "I'm better. Thank you. Without you pushing Q—I don't know where I'd be."

To anyone who hadn't whipped her with a whisk last night, she looked poised and collected. Only I knew the stiffness really meant wariness, not aloofness.

Frederick shrugged. "No thanks necessary. I'm glad it worked out. I couldn't stomach the thought of you walking away from what you two obviously have."

I huffed, glaring daggers at him. Frederick got the message and shut up.

Tess said, "I never got a chance to thank you for helping Q find me, either. I know you were there. I vaguely remember parts of it—your voice. You holding me."

My muscles locked down. She fucking *remembered?* I thought she'd been so cracked out she hadn't recalled what I'd done on her behalf. Did she recollect the reeking, dripping heart as I placed it at her feet?

Frederick shot me a glance, raising his eyebrow as if to say: *I told you. You should've just killed him and not put more awful memories in her head.*

I glowered at him. *Fuck off.*

"I'm glad you're doing better. I knew Q would bring you back. Had every faith." Clearing his throat, he looked at me. "You know, I got a call from Suzette yesterday." Amusement shadowed his features. "Seems you've let her go a little wild."

Tess's eyes narrowed. "What did she say?"

I leaned forward, clasping my hands between my spread legs. "Yes, Roux. *Qu'est ce qu'elle a dit?*" What did she say?

His eyes twinkled. "Nothing much. You know she never tells me anything. Closed book."

I laughed. I couldn't help it. "Bullshit. I happen to know you're on her speed-dial. She spills everything to you." I glared harder, knowing full well he knew far too much about my ridiculous meltdowns—thanks to a meddling maid. "You know what I'm talking about."

Tess looked between us, trying to unravel what we left unsaid.

"She knows she can call me. She and Angelique are getting rather close, too. It's nice to see her making friends."

"Oh, fuck me. My maid and your wife talking?" I couldn't think of anything worse. I'd have to fire her.

Frederick laughed—a large timbre that drew a genuine smile from Tess. I wasn't surprised; Frederick was a smooth son of a bitch. "You know she's the most loyal staff member you'll ever have. And she knows we would never do anything to hurt you. Leave her alone when you see her next." He raised his eyebrow, hinting that he knew.

Knew about the wedding.

He'd been invited to a wedding that I had absolutely no idea about. Who else had she invited? Goddammit, I really better call her before she invited all of Paris.

Frederick clapped his hands together, reclining into the black couch. "So, as nice as it is to see you, Mercer, I'm taking this isn't just a pop in. You want something."

Tess looked to me, her eyes wide with curiosity.

I smiled loving the thrill of anticipation. I couldn't wait for her reaction when I told her what we were here for.

"There's a file in your cabinet under my personal record. Can you get it?" I asked, looking Frederick straight in the eye.

He frowned, trying to work it out. The funny thing was—he knew. He'd watched me write it.

Hauling himself upright, he traversed the office before unlocking one of the filing cabinets and pulling out my particular portfolio. It was empty but for one piece of paper.

Everything of importance I kept on encrypted hard-drives and in a safe hidden at my chateau. But this—I needed a witness to make this legitimate.

Cracking open the file, his eyes flew to mine. Clearing his throat, he asked, "You sure about this?"

I locked my fingers together, focusing on the rush of blood rather than snapping at him. Ridiculous question. I wouldn't deem it with an answer.

Frederick nodded slightly, grabbed a pen from his desk, and came to sit back down.

Tess scooted forward as Roux placed the file on the small table between us, spinning it around to face her. He smiled, holding out the pen. "You're up. Have a read, and if you're okay with it, sign away."

I rolled my shoulders, dispelling some of the rapidly building tension in my spine. Tess vibrated with questions mixed with apprehension.

Frederick never took his gaze off her as she reached for the file. Asking me, he muttered, "Do you think it's a good idea… after all, the current market is rather…volatile."

Tess froze. Her eyes snapped up. "Volatile?" Looking to me, she added, "What's going on? Do I even want to know what's in here?"

Yes, you damn well do because then you can get over my wealth because it won't just be mine *anymore.*

I glared at Roux, before glancing her way. "Yes. Frederick is only aware that if you sign it, you share equal risk. If the business crashed tomorrow you would be held accountable, same as me, for any debts payable. But I have no debts outweighing my assets, and it isn't going to crash tomorrow, so there's no fucking risk to worry about." Grabbing the edge of the folder, I opened it. "Stop delaying and read the damn thing."

Tess flat-out ignored me. Planting a hand over the writing on the page, she asked Roux, "Tell me. Did you mean that or something else? I think I have a right to know."

Goddammit, why was everything so hard with her when it came to money?

I leaned back, seething in the chair. My arms crossed; I wished I'd gone with my other idea of forging her signature and never showing her the damn will. I'd been so close to doing it, but Frederick talked me out of it. Bastard.

Roux placed his hands on his thighs, thinking through his answer carefully. As he should. Because he was a bastard.

"Q's right about the debt. But I'm not worried about *Moineau* Holdings going under. That won't happen. It just can't—not with the strength of the company. What I am—not so much concerned about but definitely interested in seeing future projections—is a new side of the company that is brand new last week."

I rolled my eyes. This was the part where Roux made me sound like some Mother fucking Theresa and for Tess to fawn all over me. I didn't mind the fawning, but it wasn't like the newspapers portrayed. It wasn't at all like they said.

I got my hands dirty. I put motherfuckers in the ground where they belonged not turned them into a law enforcement that was almost as corrupt as they were.

"What new part?"

Frederick grinned. "Well, ever since Q tore off his mask and flew out of his birdcage—get it?" He waved his hand, chuckling at his own joke. "People know what hobbies Mercer is into. They're aware of some, not all, of the details of what he did to get you back." His eyes flickered to mine. I wanted to clamp a hand over his mouth, but I looked away, effectively giving him permission to continue. "Q's contact at the local police force spoke to the press."

I growled at that. I'd sworn him to secrecy for over ten years, and now he'd fed me to the paparazzi.

Frederick pointed a finger in my direction. "You know you had no choice. He stood up for you when people were painting false accusations." Looking to Tess, he finished, "Anyway, the company has undergone some changes, and we're still not sure where those changes will lead us."

Tess breathed hard, tucking a riot of curls behind her ears with a rapid twitch. "What changes?"

Roux met my eyes. "Care to jump in and explain, Mercer? After all, it's your fledging."

I scowled. I didn't want to hear what I already knew, and I had no desire to talk about it either—even though I was secretly pleased and rather honoured how the news had gone down with the world.

You want her to inherit everything. It's only fair she knows exactly what she's accepting.

I sighed, unlocking my arms to sit forward. "You're doing such a good job. Finish it."

Frederick nodded. "Fine. Well, the bad news is, the company lost its backing from over forty-eight percent of its regular investors. Overnight they cut association with all subsidiaries of *Moineau* when they heard the news Q accepted sex slaves as bribes to finalize developments. There was an uproar when they heard he not only accepted them as bribes, but kept them in his home."

Tess gasped, a hand flying to cover her mouth. "Oh, my God."

Frederick sighed, enjoying the theatrics of telling a sordid tale. "I know. Terrible. Death threats were sent, a few properties were defaced, and we prepared for the end of Mercer's empire."

I rolled my eyes. He made it sound like the apocalypse. None of that mattered. It was superficial at worst. Even disgusting rumours couldn't hurt us in the long run.

Tess wrapped her arms around her waist, leaning forward. "This is awful. Can't someone explain?"

Roux held up his hand, his blue eyes grave and bleak. "Then the rumours started flying that Mercer used them for his pleasure. That he killed them once he'd finished—seeing as no one ever saw a harem of women running around his estate. And believe me. They searched.

"Local villagers spread filthy lies about Q inheriting more than just *Moineau* Holdings but also his father's side business as well."

At that my stomach knotted into a trillion pains. Fucking people saying I was like him. It didn't matter they were lies. It still tarred me with the same brush. Still made me seem like the monster I never wanted to be.

"But that's not true!" Tess cried.

Frederick pursed his lips. "International law enforcement got involved; they seized most of our files—not that they'll find any wrongdoings there. We're pristine in every area of the business."

I snorted. Yes, everywhere apart from my red binder full of sadistic sons of a bitches, bribes, dates, and names of the girls I'd taken as payment for buildings constructed on their behalf. I'd broken the law by dealing with criminals, but in a business point of view, we'd done nothing wrong. I delivered a service for a transaction rendered. It didn't matter I used a barter system of women rather than capital.

Tess twisted her fingers. "Someone has to sue them for slander, surely. How can they say such a thing?"

Frederick held up his hand, a smile tugging his mouth. "But then other villagers stepped forward claiming Q was nothing like his predecessor, and they had it all wrong. Local doctors broke their Hippocratic Oath to stand up for Q, explaining his outstanding care of the women who'd been broken by bastards. And that's when the local police chief came forward and spilled the truth.

"No names but an approximate tally of all the women Q saved along with a guestimate on dollar value of what he'd spent repairing what others had broken."

Tess swivelled to face me, her eyes glowing with unshed tears. She looked at me as if I were some celebrity or even worse…a god. I wasn't. She *knew* that. Shit, I'd fucked her like a beast possessed only a few hours ago. She knew me better than anyone at how close to home those first rumours were.

Frederick muttered low, purely for my ears. "Thanks to them they saved your business, but no thanks to them they've taken—"

"Enough, Roux." My eyes narrowed, warning. Tess didn't need to know the other rumours. The ones whispering in the dark alleys of misery. *They're coming.* And there was nothing I could do to stop it.

Tess went white. "So…what happened?"

Roux fell silent, waiting for me to answer. None of this was interesting. It was a waste of time. A waste of precious fucking time where I could be kidnapping her somewhere else.

Time.

The traitorous bitch was once again working against me. In more ways than one.

My heart hammered. "Nothing until *someone*"—and if I ever found out whom, I'd shoot them—"told a tale of how a woman I'd saved from traffickers in Mexico fell in love with me. They spun a ridiculous love story of a man berserk with terror when those same bastards came back for her to teach him a lesson."

The tears in Tess's eyes broke the confines of her lashes, trickling down her cheeks. My heart physically hurt at the love beaming from her—it was tangible, heating, hugging me.

"Online tabloids and international magazines spread the story like wildfire—embellishing, editing, but ultimately getting it surprisingly right. And when the news got out I'd found you but you were almost irreparable—well, that's when the phones started ringing for an entirely different reason."

Tess didn't say a word, blinking in shock. My headache grew as stress layered my system. I didn't want to talk about this. I'd deliberately kept it from her—I refused to let myself think about it as it made me feel…I didn't fucking know. Humbled. Honoured. *Amazed.* I felt loved by more people than I'd ever met, and after a lifetime of never being cared for, I had no idea how to deal with it.

"So what happened?" Tess prompted.

I laughed softly, unable to believe what the future of my company—my *father's* company—faced. "Being heralded as a saviour didn't exactly ruin my image. It didn't matter people were calling me sick and so entrenched in the underworld they couldn't believe a word of truth.

"There were more people who believed in the good than the bad, and it's been used to my advantage." Taking her hand, I pulled her toward me. My muscles shuddered as her warm weight rested along mine. Her hair tussled over her shoulders; smudges of sleeplessness marked under her eyes. "You're going to be the face of the new *Moineau*, Tess. Be prepared."

Her lips parted. "Wait...how?"

Frederick jumped in. "The forty-eight percent of investors we'd lost were rapidly replaced with smaller donations, lesser scale projects, and a *lot* of interest to join Q's crusade against trafficking."

Tess turned in my arms, annoyance shining on her face. "Why didn't you tell me any of this?"

"That's not all," Frederick continued. "His good deeds will be recognised by the prime minister himself. Q's business no longer deals with the filth of the world in order to save the innocent. Rather, he is now supported by organisations who will fight against that filth by pooling resources and authorities Q didn't have on his own."

My heart thudded, sending heated blood through my veins at the thought of all the extra women I'd be able to save but never see. All the sorrow I could fix; all the families I could reunite.

My company had branched out. Property and slaves. Who knew there would ever be a correlation.

Frederick beamed, his blue eyes practically blazing like daytime stars with happiness. "*Moineau* Holdings is no longer just a property empire. In fact, half of the company's equity has been channelled into a new venture under the *Moineau* umbrella."

Tess froze beside me, holding her breath.

"The latest enterprise is called Feathers of Hope, and we've donated exactly half of all *Moineau's* proceeds to fund the worthy cause."

Tess looked between the two of us, the file on her lap completely forgotten. "What does it do?"

Roux answered, "Feathers of Hope provides homes, rehabilitation, and therapy for all the women involved in the sex slave industry. It also backs private law enforcement along with larger firms in order to shut down slavery rings and prosecute men responsible."

Tess started to quake. I cinched her harder against me, hating the onset of shock. Fuck, it hadn't been my intention to make her panic. This was why I wanted to keep it simple and not drag her into everything. She'd probably have a heart attack to know how many people wanted to meet her. Interviews were turned down every day for her exclusive story of survival.

I smiled. It was her face people wanted on the Feathers of Hope logo—not the two feathers linked together with a red bow that we had now. She'd be immersed in my company—whether she wanted to be or not. It was just a matter of time.

Time I might not have.

Goddammit, I promised myself I wouldn't think about it. Roux had no right to remind me—especially in front of Tess.

Tess looked up, her face whiter than a ghost. "You're a hero. *My* hero. Their hero. My God, Q—"

I snarled, hating the word. "No, *esclave,* I'm not. I'm making up for the sins of my past. The sins of my father and all the fucking bastards I've had to deal with in order to free a small fraction of women. I've so many things to pay for, including my own sick perversions."

And nothing made up for those sins more than handing over the red folder with every sick fuck who'd raped and traded women.

Tess's fingers suddenly clutched my shirt. "Wait…are you safe?" Her eyes flew to Roux, her muscles locking with panic. "Please tell me he's not painting a bull's eye on his back by doing this?"

Shit. Why the hell did she have to ask that damn question? I'd deliberately kept her from TV broadcasts and webpages unfolding the latest allegations and threats on my life. Most of them were false—I was still alive after all.

But some…some were real.

Frederick laced his fingers together, placing them in his lap. "That's not for me to discuss." He gave me a pointed glare. "But rest assured he has a legion of supporters and an army of people willing to protect him."

An army could only do so much against determined murderers. It was all up to me in the end. And I had a plan.

Tess spasmed in my arms; her skin went frigid with fear.

"Before, when he operated on his own, he was in worse danger. Pretending to be a devil among devils would've always ended badly," Roux said, noticing Tess's anxiety.

I didn't have the heart to tell him I never had to pretend. I just shed my humanity and allowed myself to be free. I fell into the role of master looking to purchase a slave. I might never have touched one, but it hadn't stopped my mind from conjuring depraved acts I would never speak about.

As sick as it was—I would miss that part. Miss stepping into the dark. I would miss being dangerous and walking amongst the blackness of the world, rubbing shoulders with men who were so like me—men I belonged with but would never let myself be a part of.

Living in the light was fucking hard. But it was the sacrifice I paid to keep my sanity. I had no choice but to embrace the sun and leave my darkness behind.

Enough talking.

"Read the file, Tess. I won't ask again."

I was done talking about this. I wanted to leave, and we couldn't until the matter of signing in front of a witness was complete.

Roux cleared his throat. "Um, I know you're going to bite my head off, but it's my job as your business partner to ask."

Tess looked at the paper.

I ground my teeth. "I know what you're going to say, and no it's not your job as my business partner—or friend. So drop it."

Tess held up the pen, sitting straighter. "Wait—tell me."

Oh, for fuck's sake.

Frederick rolled his shoulders, chagrin loud and clear in his body language. "It's nothing against you, Tess. I'm just looking out for a friend. Don't take it personally." His eyes zeroed on me. "So—you're sure?"

I shoved Tess away, ready to stand up and show him just how sure I was. Tess tugged on my hand, keeping me seated. It took everything I had to stay in control. "Did you and Angelique sign a prenup?"

Tess relaxed. "Ah. I get it. I'll gladly sign one—it's no issue, really."

Frederick smiled at her.

I swore, "You're not fucking signing one. End of story." Shoving a finger in my supposed friend's face, I growled, "Answer me, Roux."

His cheeks flushed as he ran a hand through his hair. "Well no, but only because we met in high school around the same time I met you. I was penniless before you asked me to come work for you. I never had the wealth you do—even now when you've been totally generous."

Memories flickered of his friendship through those awful days with a drunkard for a mother and an asshole for a father. He'd been the only one who I let get close, and only once my mother died and I shot my father. I still remembered the afternoon he met Angelique. In a way—I was responsible for that, too.

Shaking my head, I scattered the memories. "You could've had one drawn up. What stopped you?"

Frederick stiffened, anger creeping up his neck. "My love and trust in my wife stopped me." He flung his hands up. "Fine. I get your point."

Smiling at Tess, he softened his voice. "Sorry. My mistake." Motioning to the unread paper, he said, "Read it. It won't bite."

Tess laughed nervously. "Are you sure about that?" Risking a look at me, she added, "If the paper doesn't—Q might."

Roux laughed, slapping his thigh as if it was the funniest fucking thing he'd ever heard. Bastard.

I growled, tearing the paper out of Tess's fingers and shoving it in her face. "Read. It. Now." Plucking the pen from her slack hand, I added, "Then you sign and we're gone. We've been here long enough as it is."

I want out of France. The temptation to return to *Volière* was strong—at least there we might be safe.

Tess threw me a look, her eyes glinting. Ripping the page from my grip, her gaze settled on the waxy seal at the top. Decorated with my logo of a sparrow flying over sky rises, she skated down to the small but extremely life-altering paragraph.

Quincy Mercer II hereby agrees that all his wealthy possessions, fortune, investments, and all goodwill are hence forth owned jointly by Ms. Tess Snow soon to become Tess Mercer. Upon his death, Tess will be the sole recipient of Mr. Mercer's fortune and any living heirs they might have.

The moment I knew she'd read it, I stole it again and slammed it on the table.

Tess said something incomprehensible, trying to steal it back, but it was too late. Uncapping the pen, I scrawled my autograph onto the parchment and held it out to her. My heart swelled with knowledge she would be forever protected, looked after, and kept healthy by all things money could afford.

Even if I wasn't around.

"Sign it, *esclave.*"

She shook her head, eyeing the paper as if it had herpes. "I can't...let me think for a moment."

Too bad. I wasn't a patient man.

Capturing her wrist, I shoved the pen into her right hand, and jerked her forward to place the nib against the paper. "I'm not letting go until you sign."

"Mercer," Frederick muttered.

I threw him a look; he wisely shut the fuck up.

Tess bit her lip but hesitantly obeyed. Her penmanship was compromised by my grip, but I didn't care.

The moment she finished the little flourish at the end of her name, a weight lifted off my shoulders. One more way she was joined to me for life. One more way she'd proven she was mine. One more way I could make sure she was always cared for regardless of my future.

I loved my wealth for one thing only: to save women. And now it had saved the most important woman of my fucking life.

Her.

Always her.

Eternally her.

I tossed the paper at Frederick. "File it with the lawyers. We're leaving." Reaching down to hoist Tess to her feet, she whispered, "Q…how much…how much did you just sign over to me?"

Ah, the moment she'd find out the truth and know she could no longer hate my fortune because it was hers.

A shot of jittery happiness erupted down my spine. *Get ready, Tess. I'm going to love watching this sink in.* No more running from it. No more pretending her life hadn't changed forever.

Not removing my eyes from hers, I demanded, "How much, Roux. The joint owner in *Moineau* Holdings wishes to know."

Tess shuddered as Frederick came close, patting her on the shoulder. His eyes were gentle, understanding—from one person who'd had no wealth to another. "You've just inherited nine billion, seven hundred thousand euros, as of this morning. But that figure is growing daily."

Tess promptly fainted.

Chapter Nine

**body of body, shared thoughts and lustful need,
we bow to this swirling new greed**

I must be dreaming. This can't be happening.
I pinched myself for the billionth time.
Hah, billion.
I'm a billionaire.
I put my head between my legs. I'd never felt so…surreal.
There were no words to describe the euphoric weakness or the
heart-numbing flabbergast.

Q's hand landed between my shoulder blades, rubbing
gently in circles. His loving touch belied his true feelings. I'd
never seen Q like this. I personally thought he'd gone insane;
he'd finally cracked, and I'd never find the sometimes sullen,
always temperamental man I fell in love with.

The plane's engines suddenly increased in decibel,
shooting us down the runway like a rocket. Looking up, I
steeled myself against Q's handsome face. The same face that
hadn't stopped smirking since I woke up from my stupid
fainting episode.

"It's not the end of the world, *esclave.*" His pale eyes danced, not showing me any mercy.

I glowered and looked out the window—pointedly ignoring him. It *was* the end of the world—my world. He'd had a lifetime to get used to the luxury and complications of money. It wasn't fair to force me to sign a piece of paper—under duress no less—and accept his entire fortune when I had no right to it at all.

Turning to him, I snapped, "I want to go back. I want Frederick to tear it up."

Q reclined; his long legs stretched in front of him, crossing at the ankles. His hair shone from the sun streaming in the circular window as the plane swooped into the sky. In his black trousers and white shirt, he was a splash of sophistication in the otherwise hushed cream world of the private jet.

"Now why would I do that?" He couldn't wipe the damn smile off his face. "Struggling to come to terms with something, Tess?" Chuckling, he leaned over and cupped my cheek. "Perhaps you're having second thoughts about falling in love with a man who just changed your perception on how you see the world."

My belly fluttered. He'd already *done* that. He'd made me a lover of pain. He'd made me an accomplice in a charity I hadn't known about until an hour ago. He'd turned my life completely inside out, back to front, bleached it, then cut it up and sewed it back together.

All while keeping something from me. The comment from Frederick, the tension echoing in Q's limbs. No wonder he'd been cagey whenever I tried to watch TV or go online. He'd hidden all the news from me. He also downplayed just how dangerous it was to have people know the truth.

Foreboding sat like a heavy smudge on my heart.

This is too much! All of it. I needed to know the truth. How much jeopardy was he truly in? *He needs to stop being so damn blasé.*

"Can you be serious for one second?" I hadn't been cross with him before but his smug grin really flipping annoyed me.

He laughed, throwing his head back, elongating his perfect neck. My mouth went drier than a desert.

Holy hell, how was I supposed to concentrate when everything about him exuded raw sex?

His gaze locked on mine. "What seems to be the problem?" Reeling off on his fingers, he said, "It can't be the fact you'll never go hungry, or cold, or homeless. It can't be the fact you'll always be safe and be able to afford the best protection and healthcare. And it certainly can't be the fact that you can use that money to help others." Rolling his eyes, he smirked again. "God, you're acting like I made you sign a death sentence and not a life *improving* sentence."

Swivelling in my chair, holding onto the cushioned arm rest as the plane banked suddenly, I said, "You don't get it. You're giving away half of the money that's rightfully yours, and you're treating it like it's nothing."

And hiding your safety from me.

His eyes flashed, losing his mirth, trading it for his well-known aggression. *"Ça y est tu peux passer au dessus."* It is. Get over it.

"No. Not until I've processed it. Don't you understand I'd won the lottery by finding you? That all my wishes were granted when you fell in love with me? How can I justify being a billionaire in monetary worth, when I'm already *beyond* wealthy by having you?" My eyes burned as tears puddled from nowhere. Damn, I didn't want to cry. I didn't want to appear weak. I didn't know how to formulate my real concerns because I didn't even understand them myself.

My real fear stemmed from Frederick's veiled comment.

"They've saved your business but taken—" Taken what? How soon? I couldn't stomach the thought of Q being hurt.

Q frowned; he lost the edge of anger, confusion filling his gaze. "Tess—it's because of those reasons why I gave you the money. I've never trusted anyone to use my wealth in the same way I do. I never had the urge to share that responsibility. It's *because* you love me that you're perfect to accept the weight of the Mercer fortune."

I looked out the window again, swallowing the lump that had the audacity to choke. *I'm afraid I'm not worthy of all of this. I'm afraid life will expect me to pay another toll, and I'm terrified I won't be able to afford it.*

Q pulled his legs toward him, stretching to wrap a fist in my hair.

My heart flurried as he gently but firmly tilted my head to face him. "What's this really about, *esclave?*" His eyes searched mine, and I knew he'd never understand. I'd agreed to marry him. By that alone, I would've spent my life surrounded by wealth because I would spend it surrounded by Q. It made no difference.

But my real terror was the prick of instincts honing in on things Q kept hidden.

Oxygen caught in my lungs. I'd been planning a lifetime together, so why did I suddenly have the horrible notion Q planned for much less?

Q's face was cast with shadows as the plane pierced clouds, blocking out the view of the disappearing French countryside. "*Peu importe ce qu'il y a tu peux me le dire.*" Whatever it is, you can tell me.

I shook my head, swallowing my tumultuous concerns. He didn't need to know I guessed something was amiss—not until I had concrete evidence and could demand an answer.

Resting my palm on his warm thigh, I said, "It's fine. *I'll* be fine. Thank you. Thank you for trusting me with everything that you are." *And stupidly planning for things I won't let come to pass.*

Q's jaw clenched and for a moment I worried he wouldn't let me hide the truth, but then his hand dropped from my hair, brushing against the 'Q' branded into my neck. The skin was no longer painfully sensitive; I shivered at the soft caress.

"You still don't get it." He shook his head, eyes alive with vitality and connection. Bowing his head, he brushed his lips against mine. "You may have become richer in bank balance— but Tess…you made me richer in my heart. And that's fucking priceless."

My body gave way from substance to molten, and I arched my chin to kiss him. I wanted to shed my skin and fly. I wanted to free my soul, so Q could see just how much I loved him. My note wasn't enough to describe how much he'd changed my life. He was more than healing acid—he was my blood. We shared the same heartbeat and if he died I had no doubt my life would cease, too.

Q's eyes drifted closed. His tongue licked my lips, changing the kiss from sweet to sultry. He gathered me in his arms, bruising my spine with his fierce embrace. His taste drugged me. All I wanted was to be naked and beneath him.

Safe. I wanted to be safe.

Breaking the kiss, I whispered, "Where are you taking me this time?"

Q laughed softly. "Always so inquisitive." Kissing the tip of my nose, he murmured, "I'm taking you on that date, *esclave*. Our very first one, and I expect to get to second base."

I moaned as his hand cupped my breast, rubbing his thumb over my nipple. "You're already at second base." My breath was as soft as the wispy clouds outside.

His mouth trailed along my jaw and down my neck, licking exquisitely softly. "So I am." His touched turned firm, massaging my breast, unfurling desire in my core. "Stop being so damn easy to seduce." Teeth replaced his tongue, turning soft to sharp.

"I can't help it. I'm completely helpless against the man I'm going to marry."

His arms banded tighter; a low growl bubbled from his chest. "Fuck, I love hearing you say that. Say it again."

I smiled, shivering in his arms. "The man I'm going to marry."

"And after we're married, how will you address me?" His lips trailed fire over my collarbone.

"You'll be my husband. My *maître* husband."

He bit me, his large body trembling. "I like the sound of that."

My insecurities broke my self-control. "And you'll be mine forever, Q. Won't you?"

He pulled back, scowling. "A marriage *is* forever, *esclave*."

I nodded, forcing my eyes not to show my true concern.

A marriage maybe forever, but a human body was not. And Q seemed to think he was immortal.

But I knew the difference. I'd hurt him. I'd scarred him. The invincible master bled...he could be killed.

Rome.

A honeymooner's dream. Or, in our case, a crescent moon.

My mouth fell open as Franco opened the car door, granting me his large hand to climb out of the vehicle. Someone needed to slap me. I'd left reality and stumbled straight into the pages of my own fairy-tale.

The hotel soared upward as well as outward. I couldn't see where it ended or begun—arched windows with Juliette balconies stood like perfect soldiers in a battalion of architecture. Pillars and porticos with dark brick, alabaster marble, and a red carpet leading to a lobby accepted me like royalty. And through the green-tinted glass of the entrance, the largest tiered chandelier I'd ever seen screamed fortune. The hanging crystals looked like an upside down wedding cake—if such a cake existed with fifty layers and thousands of jewels, all hanging from a colossal ceiling with Pegasus, Hercules, and Zeus immortalized by the finest painting imaginable.

Zeus's lightning bolts struck guests milling below, while cupid and his fellow cherubs shot heart-arrows like rain.

A party of three ladies entered the lobby, ignoring me on the curb gawking like an idiot. Each woman had a model-perfect Italian man trailing after her—their arms full of Louis Vuitton, Chanel, and Prada bags.

Franco's finger pressed beneath my chin, snapping my jaw into place. "Showing your tonsils to the clientele isn't the best first impression."

I shook myself, waking up from the stupor of obscene wealth. I pointed at the ceiling where the lights spilled onto the night-shrouded sidewalk making me feel like an imposter for ever thinking I could stay there. "Look at it. It's breath-stealingly beautiful."

"No, that's you. This is just a cleverly designed hotel meant to lure men like me to spend exorbitant amounts of money." Q brushed against my shoulder, glowering at Franco for touching me.

A look flashed between them, adding to the smudge on my heart, stealing some of my wonder-filled joy.

Franco's eyes were flat and distrustful of everyone in every direction.

Pretending to be oblivious of the building tension, I said, "That may be so, but…Q. This isn't even our honeymoon, and you're spoiling me rotten. How will you top this when we finally get married?" Another question formed on my tongue, but I swallowed it back. *Exactly how soon will that be?* After Q's rush to get me hitched, he'd gone ominously silent on the subject.

Q looked over my head at Franco. "Check us in. You know what to do. We'll head straight up." With a quick scan of the street, Q grabbed my hand, dragging me from night-time to glowing lobby and toward a private elevator at the rear.

A man in a tailored tuxedo bowed as we pushed the up button and waited beside a flower arrangement that looked like a living fountain of orchids, lilies, and ferns.

"*Ciao*, Mr. Mercer. Very pleasant to see you again, sir."

Q nodded, taking in the man's shiny black hair parted to the side, his white gloves clasped in front of him, and the spotless presentation of a body well-maintained for a man in his late fifties. "*Merci*." His tone was cool and clipped; his body vibrating with a new rigidity I grew to recognise as self-preservation.

The lift arrived. The man climbed inside and pressed the necessary floor. The doors closed, sliding upward to our floor. "Your room is available, as always. Would that be all you require, or should I have some canapés and champagne sent up?" The man smiled first at Q, then me. His eyes brightened as he took my hand, planting a dry kiss on the back of my knuckles. "*Mi scusi*. Sorry, madam. Excuse my rudeness. I am Alonzo, designated butler for all VIP guests."

Q tugged me away, planting himself between me and Alonzo. "Thank you for your service, but we won't be needing—" Q cut himself off, a calculating look entering his gaze. The lift came to a stop, its doors opening to reveal thick white carpet and matching ivory floral arrangements at regular intervals along the long corridor. "Tess, head down to the left. Give me a moment." He shoved me forward, giving me no choice but to stumble off the elevator.

The doors shut, leaving me stranded, gaping like a fool. *What the hell?*

Should I wait? Should I obey? I had no clue which room was ours and judging by the fancy keypads on each door it wasn't a key I needed but…a fingerprint?

Did Q chose this hotel for opulence or security?

Just as I took a few hesitant steps down the corridor, the elevator doors opened again and Q strode out, collecting my elbow as he prowled over the carpet.

I looked over my shoulder but didn't see Alonzo. "What are you up to?" I asked, letting Q propel me forward.

"I have no idea what you're talking about." He wrenched me to a halt, slammed his thumb against the small screen above the door handle, and opened it when a light flashed green. Pushing me inside, illumination automatically flashed on, drenching the huge open-plan space with warmth. Massive abstract artwork framed the walls while floor to ceiling glass brought the postcard perfect view of Rome into our bedroom.

Fountains and cobblestone streets looked magical in the

rising moonlight, while men and women held hands, making their way to dinner.

Q came up behind me, slinking his hands beneath my grey angora jumper. I tensed, expecting him to spin me around and pounce. The bed beckoned, raised on a two-step pedestal with the most incredible painting of pinks and oranges above. Rose petals were strewn across the snowy sheets.

My morbid thoughts turned the petals to blood. I quickly checked over my shoulder, making sure the door was closed.

Then the view disappeared as Q wrenched my jumper over my head, and unhooked my bra, all within a second of each other.

I slapped an arm over my exposed breasts, very aware of the lights being on and no curtains drawn, but Q spun me, grabbed my waist, and unceremoniously threw me over his shoulder.

"Q! What the hell are you—"

He spanked me, letting his fingers explore the seam of my jeans. Not saying a word, he stalked into the bathroom. The minute he carried me inside, he plopped me onto my feet, and unbuttoned my jeans. My eyes snapped shut as his knuckles grazed my clit, tugging on the thick denim until they rested at my ankles.

His eyes fired with lust as his fingers hooked my knickers, stripping those off me, too. In exactly ten seconds of arriving in one of the most gorgeous rooms I'd entered, I was stark naked in a bathroom full of expensive cosmetics, the fluffiest silver towels, and a shower big enough for a team of sumo wrestlers.

Q sucked in a breath, his face darkening as he rubbed the front of his trousers. "Goddammit, do you have to be so fucking tempting?"

The harsh want in his voice shoved away my annoyance, layering me with heavy attraction. His chest rose and fell; the top of the 'T' branded above his heart teased me with the three open buttons of his shirt. I needed him to touch me. *Now*.

I kicked my jeans and knickers away, loving the heat

building in my core. I loved the power he granted. The power of being naked in front of him with his body locked into position, calling to mine with a need past all realm of intellect.

"Why do you make me wet every time you look at me like that?" I countered his question, focusing inward on the trickle of dampness inside.

"It's only fair you're wet, Tess. Because I'm so fucking hard I could hammer a nail right through marble." His eyes feasted on my skin; his hand grasped his cock roughly, angrily.

We devoured each other, separated only by a metre. A stupid, silly little metre that I wanted eradicated.

I took a step toward him.

The motion snapped him back into whatever whirlwind idea he currently chased; he moved away. Holding up a hand, he ordered, *"Va dans la douche, esclave."* Get in the shower.

I shook my head, heat prickling my skin. My gaze fell to Q's trousers, licking my lips at the bulge of his desire. "Come in with me," I murmured, stepping toward him as he kept inching away.

He couldn't take his eyes off my naked skin. "No. If I do, we'll never get to dinner."

Running my hands up my waist, cupping my breasts, I taunted, "I'm not hungry for food, *maître.* Who needs dinner when I can suck on you?"

He groaned, his step faltering. His hand abandoned his cock, fumbling with his top button. "Fuck, you don't play fair."

I might not be playing fair, but I was winning.

Taking another step, I basked in how hyperaware my skin was. His intense stare stroked me, making me hum, *smoulder.* My tongue wanted to lick him, my mouth wanted to suck him, my body wanted to ride him, and my mind wanted to explode into a gazillion pieces of bliss.

Q dragged the zipper down, teasing me with black boxer-briefs, barely concealing his raging erection. My tummy clenched, and my hand fell between my legs. My head was suddenly too heavy as I tantalized myself, panting to taste him.

Q looked up, latching eyes with me. Anger ticked his jaw, or was it tightly restrained need. "Tess?"

"Yes…" I whispered, totally absorbed in fantasies of what I would do the moment Q got naked.

He stormed toward me, grabbed my wrist, and jerked my fingers away from the slickness of my core. His face contorted. "I told you that is *mine*. Not yours. You think you're winning. But I can deny you—I have enough self-control."

My hand lashed out, gripping him through his open fly. His cock leapt in my palm, intensely hot and eager. "Are you sure about that?"

He grunted, pushing his hips into my hand, before slapping my touch away. Wrapping his fingers around my throat, he murmured, "If you keep up your little game, I'll make you wish you hadn't. Obey me. Get in the fucking shower." His lips slammed against mine in a cruel, brutal kiss. I cried out as bruises became an addiction and pain became an obsession. I *needed* him. It wasn't fair—he started this by undressing me. He had to finish. I had to come.

Q tore his mouth from mine. "Wash, so I can take you out on a date."

I shivered, fascinated by his perfect lips, craving them between my thighs. I wanted what he'd given me last night. I wanted to be bitten, dined upon—his banquet of choice forever.

Words vexed me—they skipped and darted from my mind as lust clouded—making me mute and needy. "And…and if I don't?" I cupped his balls through his boxers.

Q shuddered, dragging me closer. His proximity sent fireworks detonating in my stomach. "If you don't, I'll fuck you against the window. Everyone on the street will see you writhe for me. Strangers will see you come." Imprisoning my jaw, he growled, "Do you want that? Are you a secret exhibitionist, Tess, because I'd gladly show off what I have in my bed. I'd happily sink deep into your heat and mark you in front of men who will never know the extreme fucking joy of being inside you. I'd love to thrust hard, smashing you against the glass, knowing husbands of other women got hard seeing how incredible you are—how responsive you are—how damn fucking sexy you are."

Oh. My. *God.*

My heart stopped beating. I lost complete control over my thoughts and senses. The mental images Q painted set my blood blazing with gasoline. His voice was so powerful I felt the bite of chill from the glass on my nipples. I could feel the slimy surface, scrambling for purchase as Q pounded into me.

I'd never thought of being watched before. I'd always been rather shy about my body, conscious of imperfections, but Q made it sound erotically delicious.

I bit my lip, deliberating. *How can you want people to see something so private, Tess?*

I didn't have an answer, but my body melted, liquefied, *burned* at the thought of Q delivering his threat.

A loud knock shattered the carnal awareness thrumming between us.

The freedom of thought shattered, sending my mind reeling with fear. Who was there? Were we safe here?

My instincts weren't on high alert for myself—but for Q.

"Fuck," Q muttered. With a harsh hand, he pushed me away. "Get showered, *esclave*. Your outfit for tonight is here, and I personally want to dress you in it."

I didn't remember the shower. I didn't remember much of anything apart from the replay of Q having his wicked way with me against the windows in full view of strolling couples. I didn't pay attention to the hot water licking over my sensitive skin, or the shakiness of my hand as I applied mascara or blow-dried my curls. And I certainly didn't give power to my over-active instincts. I wouldn't ruin tonight by being afraid of nothing.

But I did remember striding into the bedroom, wrapped in a fluffy towel, and stopping dead at the sight of Q.

Would he ever cease to amaze me? I'd never get used to

how darkly handsome he was, with his widow's peak, luminous pale eyes, and sculptured cheekbones.

He was a festival for my eyes: black leather loafers, perfectly ironed grey slacks, crisp silver shirt, open blazer, and no tie.

I couldn't latch onto the seamless thoughts in my head.

When is his birthday? I want to buy him a shirt that matches his eyes.

Where did he get those clothes?

It isn't fair he's so beautiful—I look like a homeless runway on his arm.

I must've done something right to deserve him.

The thought I decided to go with was: "Is there another bathroom in this suite?"

Q shook his head, smiling wryly, enjoying my tongue-tiedness. "Yes. His and Hers. Now come here. I have a surprise for you."

I glided forward, noticing he'd drawn the curtains. I sucked in a breath as he hooked a finger around the knot in my towel. "It's only fair I dress you, seeing as I stripped you before."

With a sharp tug, the towel unravelled, pooling at my feet. My blood scorched to have him, kiss him, but at the same time, I loved the tease—the knowledge he was taking me out on a date, and I wouldn't be able to ravish him until we got back.

Guiding me toward the bed where two packages existed, he positioned me at the foot of the ginormous mattress, and opened the smaller box.

I swallowed hard as he pulled out a matching set of purple lingerie.

Purple.

The same colour I'd bought in the hopes of seducing Brax. I swayed as every little change in my life sucker-punched me. It felt like a different universe where I'd laid my heart open and tried to be honest with Brax. It felt like a century ago I'd thrown away an innocent vibrator all because he'd been hurt and scared.

Q leaned closer, diving into my eyes. "Tess...?"

I forced the memories to fade, but there was one question refusing to disappear. I wanted to know the answer. I wanted to finally acknowledge how all my dreams came true in a way I'd never suspected. "If I said to you I used to have a vibrator and made myself come with the thought of some unknown master biting my shoulder and striking me with a whip—how would that make you feel?"

I knew Brax's response: *I don't have to fuck you to be a man, Tessie.*

I didn't know Q's and I wanted to. Desperately.

Q's forehead furrowed, holding out the lacy bra. "How would that make me feel?" His head cocked. "Is that a trick question?"

I laughed quietly, hiding my nervousness. "No. I honestly want to know."

Q tossed the bra on the bed, before planting his large hands on my hips. "I'll tell you how that makes me feel. It makes me fucking hard at the thought of you getting yourself off. I can picture your flushed cheeks, taste your wetness, hear your pants." His head dipped, kissing my neck. "I adore the thought of you fantasising about the exact things I've done to you—almost as if you were always meant to be mine."

Pushing me away, he held up the knickers and dropped to his knee. I obediently stepped into the lingerie as he held it, shivering as he pulled them up my legs. "I should've had Alonzo buy something else for us tonight," he murmured, positioning the lace between my legs.

"What?" I breathed.

"A vibrator. I can't get the damn image out of my head of watching you come and then using it on you all over again."

I didn't need wings. Q made me fly with words. He wasn't unsure, or jealous at me seeking pleasure on my own. He wasn't prudish or tame. He was perfect. He was *mine*.

And I never wanted to lose him.

"When will you marry me?" I blurted.

Cringing, I let Q thread my arms through the bra straps, then held up my hair for him to clasp it. The roles had changed—it wasn't Q pushing me anymore but me pushing him.

Q didn't answer. Instead, he opened the last box, lifting out the sexiest, demure dress I'd ever seen. A seamstress's work of perfection with silk and netting in every shade of grey possible.

Silently, Q helped me into it. The sleeveless gown kissed just below my knees, cocooning my body like air.

He stepped back, nodding. "I'll marry you when I'm damn well ready, *esclave*. But tonight, I'm taking you to dinner."

"Chose anything you want." Q smiled.

I looked at the menu again, frowning at Italian. Knowing French gave me a benefit—I was able to get the gist of the word, but I didn't have Q's aptitude for foreign dialects.

Carbonara with horse? *No, that can't be right.*

Parmesan shredded with rabbit? Could be, but I didn't want to risk it.

Placing the heavy menu onto the table, I said, "You order for me. I have no idea."

Q chuckled. "You know, letting me order for you is a turn on. Knowing you trust me enough to give me control over what you eat makes me hard."

I crossed my legs, trying unsuccessfully to ignore the sharp clench at his voice. "Behave. You're the one who wanted to do this. Not me. I would've happily dined on you all night." *In the safety of our hotel room.*

Hearing how prolific Q's business was on the news unsettled me. I didn't want to be in public anymore. I didn't feel incognito or unimportant. I felt *watched*.

His eyes narrowed, fingers gripping the menu harder. "You're the one who has to behave, *esclave*. I'm more than happy to have you as my entrée."

A waiter appeared from nowhere, interrupting the rapidly budding lust between Q and I. "You ready to order?"

I smiled, glancing around the fine-dining restaurant. It wasn't large and each booth ringed the perimeter of the room—a red velvet curtain draped on either side of each seating area, giving patrons the sense of dining alone. The hypnotic piano and violin serenade plaited effortlessly with the ebb and flow of diner's voices. Not to mention the amazing scents of garlic, herbs, and fresh pasta filling the space like a tastebud-tempting haze.

Q gave me a glance before reopening his menu and reeling off in perfect Italian.

My core tingled at the lyrical tone of the man I would marry. So accomplished. So distinguished. So very, very different behind closed doors.

The waiter nodded, jotting down what seemed like copious amounts of food. Once finished, he bowed, took our menus and left to relay the order.

Q surveyed the restaurant, his shoulders tense.

I leaned forward. "Exactly how much food did you order?"

He focused on me. "I ordered every starter available. I figured we can share and *taste* a bit of everything." His gaze flashed on the word 'taste'. I crossed my legs, trapping the ripple between them.

Something rubbed against my ankle; I jumped.

Q chuckled under his breath. "Subtle, Tess. Really subtle. How am I supposed to play footsies with you if you leap a fucking mile?"

I laughed—I couldn't help it. "Did you just say *footsies?*" I flung up the tablecloth, pretending to search. "Where's my sadistic master—what have you done with him? He would never utter such a word."

Q leaned forward, stealing my hand. His face darkened. "I'm right here, *esclave,* and you'd faint again if you knew the things running through my head."

"What sort of things?" I whispered, caught in his web like a stupid butterfly who stared death directly in the face and didn't do a thing to stop it.

"Things like laying you on this table, throwing up your dress, and eating you in front of everyone."

My throat snapped closed; heart went wild. I tugged my hand away. Q's fingers latched around my wrist, keeping me prisoner. "Tell me. I've seen every inch of you. I've been inside most of you—and soon to be *all* of you—and I've murdered men who dared steal you away." His thumb drew little circles on the underside of my wrist disrupting my ability to concentrate. "What exactly is conversation etiquette for a first date, if we already have…*history.*"

Our drinks arrived.

Q leaned back, letting me go reluctantly. We waited for the waiter to place a tumbler of whiskey for Q and a fancy cloudy martini for me. Q nodded in thanks as the man left.

Swallowing away the desire Q had conjured, I pretended to be heavily interested in my drink. Peering at the liquid, I asked, "What did you order?"

Q grabbed his glass, swirling the whiskey, sending fumes of malt and alcohol in my direction. He took a sip, visibly relaxing as the spirits hit his tongue. "I ordered you a lychee martini. Drink up, Tess. I plan on taking advantage of you tonight and you need to be sufficiently intoxicated—as first date rules tend to imply."

Once again his eyes cast around the restaurant, subtly, quickly, but now I'd noticed his awareness every nuance was obvious.

I took a sip, surprised at the sweet but very strong concoction. "You don't have to get me drunk to have me in your bed tonight." I fluttered my eyelashes, enjoying the game he'd started.

His gaze was deadly serious, boring into mine. "What if I want you drunk? So I can ease you into accepting another part of what I want to claim?"

Holy hell, I couldn't think when he looked at me like that. It didn't matter a thrill of fear darted into my stomach, spreading, shivering with apprehension.

Anal.

Q wanted to claim all of me and that was the last part unconquered. I took a gulp of the martini, not to obey, but to steady my nerves.

Q smirked. "Good girl. Knew you'd come around to giving me what I want eventually."

I couldn't make eye contact. I wasn't ready. And I both loved and hated the panic he'd instilled—which would remain the rest of the dinner—knowing what awaited the moment he got me back to the room.

Needing to change the subject, hoping he'd forget all about it, I muttered, "The hotel—you keep a long standing room there? Why?"

Q blinked, taking a sip of whiskey. "I had a lot of business dealings in Italy last year. We expanded rather heavily into the Italian market, and I needed to oversee a few...complications." His jaw ticked; he tried to hide it by swallowing another mouthful of alcohol.

"By complications...you mean girls?" I kept my voice low, looking around the restaurant. The beauty of the booths bordering the perimeter meant no one looked directly at us and were too far away to eavesdrop.

It didn't stop Q from never relaxing or glaring at the waiters as if they were assassins.

His face tightened, but he nodded.

"How many?"

"Four last year—before I met you." He took another swallow, before placing the heavy glass on the table. *"Je ne veux pas en parler."* I don't want to talk about it. Running a hand through his hair, he added, "We're on a date—not talking business. So, tell me. What have I been missing out on by not putting myself on the market."

I smiled, appreciating his attempt at humour. "Well, there's things like sweaty handholding, nervous laughs, endless awkward silences. The very first kiss where our noses bump and—" Brax popped into my head. Everything I'd listed, I'd done with him. The giggles, the forehead bashing as we went for our first kiss. *Why the hell am I thinking about him?*

That was in the past. I didn't want to do any of that with Q. However… "And of course the generic list of questions." *That* I wouldn't mind indulging. I wanted to know more about Q—I wanted to know everything.

"Generic list?"

"Yes, you know. The how old are you? What do you do for a living? Do you want kids? That sort of thing." I took a sip, cursing my thudding heart. Such innocent questions but rather large milestones we hadn't talked about. Especially the last one.

Q sat back, collecting his glass to nurse the amber liquid. His lips twitched. "Okay…I'm twenty-nine. My birthday is the eighteenth of December—which makes my star-sign—fuck, I don't know." He took a sip. "I run my own company, which you now part own, and yes eventually, I think I do."

My heart flopped out of my chest and into my martini glass. An image of a miniature version of Q came from nowhere. I'd never thought of having children. Never entertained the idea of being responsible for another human being—let alone one created by the man who I'd grow old with. But…wow…

Q's eyelids lowered to half-mast. "That's only a recent development. I swore I'd never have something so vulnerable in this sick and twisted world. But—since meeting you…I have this crazy need to make you immortal."

I couldn't breathe.

"But at the same time, I don't want a little girl—I would drive myself insane—I've seen too much shit happen, and I'd have a heart attack trying to keep her safe."

My heart wouldn't stop clanging. I never thought Q would want children. Never in a million years. Dammit, now I couldn't get the image of a little girl running after Q, with long dark hair, surrounded by sparrows and other winged creatures.

I swallowed hard, taking a gulp of the lychee alcohol. I flailed around, trying to think of a change of subject. "Um, I think that makes you a Sagittarius." Oh, God. I wanted to slap myself. What a ridiculous thing to say after the man I was in love with admitted to a commitment bigger than marriage, more life-changing than even nine billion dollars. Children!

Q narrowed his eyes. "I see two things make you nervous: what I'm going to do to you tonight, and talking about any offspring we may or may not have." He ran a finger over his bottom lip. "After all, we do need an heir to take over our company. Can't rely on Frederick to propagate—I think that man shoots blanks."

I wanted to laugh.

But all I could focus on was *ours*.

Our company.

Our children.

No longer mine, and his, and separation.

Together.

Ours.

The waiter appeared with a groaning tray of food. I leaned away, throwing back the rest of my drink, silently thanking the intrusion. I needed time to think. To pull myself together.

Plates of delicatessen hors d'oeuvres, salads, gourmet breads, dips, gnocchi, prawns in ravioli, lobster fettuccine, tiny lasagnes, and feta wrapped with aubergine decorated the table.

I'd never seen such incredible looking food. And I wouldn't be able to eat any of it. My stomach was a churning mess; my mind consumed with images of a future I never thought I wanted.

The waiter smiled once everything had been placed accordingly. "Another drink?"

Q nodded, passing him his empty tumbler. "Martini and single-malt whiskey. *Grazie.*"

The waiter nodded, then disappeared to fulfil the request.

Q eyed the food, before glancing at me. His face tensed as he froze. *"Quel est le problème maintenant, esclave?"* What's the matter now, *esclave?*

I fluffed my curls, airing my suddenly heat-prickled back. Nothing was wrong—in fact, everything was amazing. We were finally talking, learning, exploring one another. I wasn't hungry for food, but *knowledge*. I wanted in—to his secrets, his thoughts, his hopes and dream.

I was endlessly greedy for anything he would share.

"I want to do something." Did I just say that? *Shit, Tess.* I hadn't thought it through. The idea just sprang into my head. Q would say no. Of course, he would say no.

Q smiled as the waiter returned with fresh drinks then left again. Q raised the whiskey to his lips. "For you to flush as bad as you have, I'm guessing it's either sexual or something you think I'm not going to agree to."

I copied him, sipping my martini. "Forget it. It's a stupid idea. Let's eat." I looked longingly at the food, knowing I'd end up with horrendous indigestion if I ate while so worked up. I had to relax.

"Tess…don't make me spank you in public."

My eyes flew to his where a small smile graced his lips. I sucked in a breath, trying to find courage. "Okay…have you heard of Truth or Dare?"

Q's nostrils flared. "Of course I've heard of it and you were right to flush. I won't play it."

Grabbing my fork, I speared a gnocchi and placed it in my mouth. It tasted heavenly—rich, buttery, but it could've been ash for how much I wanted it. Swallowing hard, I took another sip of my drink.

A rush of queasiness rolled my world; I carefully placed the glass on the table. Q was succeeding in getting me tipsy. My nerves only rushed the intoxication.

Silence fell between us while Q sampled a piece of everything. The way his lips slid off the fork and his jaw worked so smoothly as he chewed, pushed aside my nerves in favour of desire. He couldn't do anything without making it erotically charged and—intentionally or not—making me wet.

I tried to eat, succeeding in devouring a few pieces of prawn ravioli, before Q put his fork down. He gulped a shot of whiskey. "Have you played before?"

I instantly thought of Brax and his straight-laced ways. I thought of my parents and their cool indifference. I thought of my brother and his bullying. I thought of my friends and their giggling, slutty knowledge. Not once had I played. Not once had I done anything so reckless as to give someone the right to ask me any question or submit to any dare.

It was dangerous. It was ludicrous. *I should stop this.*

"No."

His face remained unreadable. "Why do you want to play?"

I clutched my fork, turning my knuckles white, brandishing it as if it would save me from the awkward conversation. "Because it will force you to answer questions you might not want to otherwise."

His eyes narrowed. "What sort of questions do you have in mind?" His fingers twitched around his glass, giving the impression he didn't want to play, not because it was a stupid game, but rather because he had too much to hide. I wanted to know what he kept hidden.

I wanted to know why he hadn't stopped glowering around the restaurant. I wanted to know why we stayed in a hotel with thumbprints for keys.

"I don't know. Probably stupid things that you won't care telling me. It's just the structure of the game that'll make it easier."

"Easier?" His eyebrow raised.

I nodded. "You don't exactly come baggage free, Q. I'm not going to pry into things better left unsaid, but I would like to know more about you." He remained silent, swirling his whiskey.

"Plus, you can avoid a question if you really don't want to answer, by accepting the dare."

"And if I don't want to do the dare? Then what? You force me to answer the question?" He shook his head. "No—"

I didn't know if this was part of the rules or not but if it got him to play I'd allow it. "You can drink—if you don't want to answer or do the dare—you can drink and move on."

His eyes locked on mine. "And you wouldn't sulk or argue if I refused?"

I scowled. "You think I sulk?" Shit, did I sulk? I tucked an unruly curl behind my ear. "No. If that question is off bounds, I'll honour that."

We fell silent. Q picked at the food, thoughts racing in his gaze. A few bites later, he asked, "And what about you? Will you answer a question I might ask—even if you don't want to?" Putting his fork on his plate, he leaned forward, eyes deadly serious, almost frightening. "I want into your head more than you probably want into mine, Tess. You sure you can handle letting me have unguarded access?"

My palms went slick with nerves; my stomach churned even more. "But I can accept a dare—I have a way out."

Q's gaze dropped to my lips. "Drinking, or a dare— nothing would truly save you. The moment you refuse to answer a question, I'll pursue it until you tell me. I might not get the answer tonight, but I will eventually…you'd tell me, Tess…you know why?"

My heart whizzed around my chest like a faulty sparkler. "Why?"

"Because I own you. *Tu es à moi.*" You're mine. "And your thoughts belong to me, just as much as your heart, body, and soul."

He shattered the achingly thick awareness between us by reclining and taking another sip. "If you accept those terms, then fine. I'll play." His permission layered with promise and warning. If I said yes, Q would have a free pass to anything he wanted. But if I did, I would have that same pass to learn more about the man I'd bound my life to.

It was tempting. It was scary.

I already knew my answer.

"I accept."

Q nodded, looking elegant and professional, as if he'd struck a good business transaction. Raising his almost empty glass, he signalled for the waiter. "In that case. We need a few more of these."

Chapter Ten

We were nothing before, now we're completely sure. Each other's possession, obsession, we're free just you and me

What the fuck was I doing?

Agreeing to play a juvenile game? It wasn't just a game—it came with disastrous consequences. There was no way I would have any luck playing it. I didn't mean to keep Tess in the dark—but there was a lot of my past I would *never* talk about. Things I refused to even remember or contemplate. Things I'd forced so far inside, I could almost pretend they never happened. I didn't want to show vulnerability by drinking, even if I refused to answer.

And I definitely didn't want to let her know just how nervous I was. Something about tonight…it was…*off*. I couldn't be sure if it was lack of sleep and the strain from yesterday, or if I had a right to be concerned. Either way, I didn't need Tess panicking over nothing. It was my job to carry the burden of safety and I'd finally fixed her—I refused to believe my time was almost up.

Damn motherfucking time.

But you'll get into her head. Free access.

Even if she refused a question, I would know what topics to chase; I'd understand her better by her avoidance, as much as her acquiescence.

But that would work both ways. Tess would know—even when I refused to tell her.

Was I in denial? Possibly. But it made me a happier person not having to deal with the shit coating my soul. Or the evilness encroaching on our future.

A pair of green eyes filled my mind.

Fuck.

It'd been so long since I let myself think about her. Forcing her far away—pretending she never existed. It was easier that way. *Liveable* that way.

I dragged a hand through my hair, desperate for more whiskey. I wanted to be seriously drunk for this—but then my mouth would be loose—my reactions compromised. Tapping my ankle against the chair leg, I let the small scabbard and knife strapped to my calf comfort me.

I can't be drunk.

My tongue would forget to lie; the truth would spill free— Tess would know exactly what I wanted to keep hidden.

The only way to get through this was to stay stone-cold sober.

Looking at Tess, I forced my heart from tripping like I'd taken a vial full of cocaine. Tonight was all about tripping her up. She wanted to play? Fan-fucking-tastic. I'd use it to my advantage, then I'd fuck her like I'd been dying to do since I'd strapped her to the cross in my bedroom.

Tess took a hearty drink, hesitation clouding her face. She caught my eye, only to look away with a flicker of a smile. Great—she was nervous. As she should be, because I was about to rip into her past, learn all her secrets, and ruin any idea of privacy.

The waiter appeared with more drinks; I waved him away

once he'd delivered. I'd eyed him thoroughly when we first arrived—wondering, suspecting. But he seemed harmless enough.

Taking a deep breath, I glared at Tess, tasting all the questions I had for her—wondering which one to start with. I'd wanted so many times to get inside her head—now that opportunity was all mine.

What's your secret fantasy?

If you could change a part of me—what would it be?

How many men have kissed you?

I knew how many sexual partners she'd had. Goddammit, I did *not* want to go down that line of questioning. Already, anger scalded my veins at the memory of walking in on that rutting motherfucking bastard Lefebvre raping her.

My hands curled. Shooting him had been too kind—no sense of justice for what he'd done. He'd gone after Tess because of my fucking father and his empire of trading women. My own flesh and blood used them worse than possessions—carelessly killing them when they were no longer tradable, fuckable. *Goddammit, don't think about him either.*

Family.

I knew nothing about Tess's family. That might be a good line of questioning.

Why have you never mentioned your parents?

The pain in my heart made me physically wince.

Nope, couldn't go that way either. The moment I pried in that area of her life, she'd turn it around and ask me. Family was strictly out of bounds.

Christ, what else was there?

I'm exhausted, and we haven't even begun.

Would Tess really want to know I lost my virginity to a slave who I'd saved before sending her home to her father? Did she really want to know the sick and awful thoughts plaguing me on a daily basis?

Shit, I should stop this right now, before any harm could be done. It was ridiculous. Fucking ridiculous.

Tess took a large gulp of her drink.

I paused. The panic in my system faded a little; I narrowed my eyes. Tess's cheeks were flushed, her body not as effortlessly poised.

A smile spread over my lips. I had to stay sober, but this entire game would play right into my hands if I got *her* drunk. If she lost all inhibitions any question was answerable, and anything I wanted to do to her when we got back to the hotel would be welcome. If she wasn't sober my anxiety of being in public and the horrible feeling of dread would go unnoticed.

If I got her drunk—I was free.

I grabbed my tumbler of whiskey, saluting her. "Cheers. Here's to Truth or Dare."

She smiled, clinked glasses, then took a large sip. False courage already. I wanted to laugh. This would work. Then I frowned—why was she so nervous? What the hell was she so afraid to tell me?

A plate smashed in the kitchen, ratcheting my heartbeat as every muscle prepared to wrench my knife free and kill. Kill them before they could kill me.

Because that's what they wanted. That's what I refused to think about and never wanted Tess to guess.

Silence stretched between us; I threw a large mouthful of the fiery liquid down my throat. Curling my hand around my glass, I muttered, "I'll go first."

Tess looked up, her eyes popping wide. "Oh…okay." Her fingers played with the stem of the martini glass, trying to hide her apprehension. She couldn't hide it—not from me.

"I know you have an older brother. Why don't you ever mention him?"

Go hard or fucking go home. I wanted to know about her family—hopefully she'd be too drunk to remember to repay the question to me.

She gasped, leaning forward. "How do you know I have a brother? I never mentioned him."

Silly girl. I'd sent her back to Australia. But I never

stopped watching. How could I when I knew I'd fallen head over fucking heels that night she gave me everything? I'd taken her pain virginity—I'd welcomed her into my clutches, then released her—knowing I'd ruined her but unable to keep her against her will any longer.

I raised my eyebrow. "I've put a tracker in your wedding ring—did you honestly think I wouldn't check on you from time to time in Melbourne?" Time to time—meaning every fucking minute. I'd been an obsessed creep.

"You spied on me?" she whispered.

I shrugged. "Spied…kept you safe. Same difference."

She laughed. "Hardly. But okay—if that's your first question. I'll answer it." Taking a deep breath, she said, "Yes, I have an older brother. His name is Samuel, and he's twenty years older than me. He wanted a younger sister about as much as my parents wanted another child."

My heart pummelled against my chest at the thought of Tess growing up in a household with no love, company, or connection. Assholes. Maybe they deserved payback. My mind ran wild with ways to make them suffer.

Her family would never see a cent from me. Ever.

"Why get pregnant then? If they only made your life a misery—what was the point?"

My brutal question didn't faze Tess. Her fingers turned white around her glass, but she answered bravely. "I was a mistake. My father had a vasectomy but it failed. They never forgot to tell me that every year." She dropped her hand, playing with the tablecloth. "When I turned twelve, they pretty much stopped pretending to raise me. I was self-sufficient in their eyes. They embraced retirement. It worked well for them—having a younger daughter craving attention, I did almost everything they asked me to do. They had a live-in maid, and a terrible cook, for free."

My heart wanted to claw its way out of my chest. She'd been a slave to her own family. Fuck me.

Then she'd become mine. No wonder she took to

housework with Suzette so easily. It was normal for her—a regression to the past she'd tried to escape.

Shit, this game sucked. Even though it was me asking the questions—her answers were fucking me up. I vibrated with anger, frustration, and a need to deliver vengeance.

I wanted some asshole to come charging through the door intending to kill me, so I could stab him over and over and trade my anxiety for revenge.

"Why didn't they adopt you out? That would've been the right thing to do if they had no intention of raising you right."

Tess pursed her lips. "They're very old-fashioned. The same reason why they didn't get an abortion. They gave me life and made the 'sacrifice' to raise me." Clearing her throat, she waved her finger. "No more questions. You're breaking the rules. You only get one question and now it's my turn."

Oh, shit.

Straightening my back, I clutched my glass, ready to drink before she even asked her question. My lips were sealed. If I was going to ever admit parts of my life prior to Tess, I wouldn't do it in a restaurant. However, as far as privacy went, we had tons of the fucking stuff. No one paid attention to us. No one sent my hackles rising. And Franco sat behind us in a separate booth only metres away for protection.

Nibbling on her bottom lip, Tess took her sweet time formulating a question. "You never mention your childhood. Did you have a happy upbringing? Tell me about your mum."

Ah, fuck. Definitely not drunk enough for that question. Out of all my family, my mother was the least shrouded in lies and monstrosity. *So answer it.* I gritted my teeth, keeping an eye on the door as a man in a black suit strolled in.

Fine, I would answer that one.

"She died when I was young."

"Oh, that's awful. How?"

My mind drifted, bringing to life a woman who I vaguely remembered.

"Quincy?"

I popped my head into her boudoir. I wasn't allowed in there unless she summoned me. I'd just turned twelve and would be leaving for boarding school soon in London. I couldn't wait. "Oui, mère?" Yes, mother?

"Come here. It's like I haven't seen you in months." It wasn't quite months, but it was definitely a week or two. I tended to avoid her— avoided the lisping, tearful woman who I'd never been close to.

She gathered me in a hug, clogging my throat with peach schnapps and lavender oil. "You stay away from your father, you hear me? Just stay away." She burst into tears; I unwillingly hugged her back.

I knew why she wanted me to stay away from him.

I knew his darkest secret.

"Q? Are you going to drink, answer, or dare?"

I shook my head, dispelling the memory. This game successfully stirred old thoughts I wished would remain buried. I wouldn't put myself through it again. I wouldn't be able to stop her from entering my mind if I pursued that line of recollection.

I drank.

The easiest of my family members to talk about—yet, I couldn't. Fucking didn't have the strength.

The man in the suit moved to sit in a booth. On his own. My leg twitched, brushing my knife against the chair leg. *Why doesn't he have a date?* The beast inside broke its hibernation, sniffing for a threat.

Tess frowned but let it go. Silence fell between us. What question could I ask that wouldn't spin around and bite me on my ass?

Tess rushed, "You said you share your father's name. If you hate it so much, why didn't you legally change it?"

My fist curled around the glass as dark rage seethed in my gut. He was *definitely* not up for discussion—in any form.

"Let it go, Tess. Family is not permitted in this stupid game." I looked into my glass, swirling the amber alcohol. I was tempted to swig again, but…she already knew the answer. It wouldn't make a difference as I'd already admitted to it more than once.

Dragging a hand through my hair, I said, "I kept it because it's a daily punishment. A reminder that no matter the temptation, I will never become him. The man named Quincy was a fucking monster—those genes live in me. I can never forget that."

Tess reached across the table, grazing the back of my hand with cool fingertips. I recoiled from her touch, nursing my drink. I didn't like this fucking game, and I couldn't stop the anger swirling inside.

My eyes fell on the man again. He seemed innocent but the hair on the back of my neck stood up. The beast inside sharpened its claws, ready to attack.

Were we being stalked or were my senses overrun with suspicion?

"Q…you're many things but you will never be him."

You sure about that, Tess? I didn't have the urge to go dark yesterday because I'd been high on love—intoxicated on doing the right thing and healing her—but what about next time? Would I still be tamed, or would I eventually want more than she could give me?

I laughed coldly, brushing the subject away. She wanted to pry—fine…I had just the question. "My turn." Glaring, I asked, "You told me you fucked your old boyfriend when you went back to—"

Tess's cheeks flared with temper. "I didn't go back. *You* sent me away. Don't confuse the difference." Her annoyance shimmered around her like heat waves, matching my anger, feeding, weaving…thickening the air between us.

This is getting dangerous.

Alcohol, prying into each other's past—it was a recipe for a screaming match or worse, me losing control.

"Fine!" I glowered. "I sent you back. Not that that's the issue right now. What I want to know is, why the fuck did you tell me that? Hadn't I scared you enough? Why did you deliberately provoke me when you knew what I battled with?"

Tess lifted her glass. The alcohol brushed her lips. Her

eyes locked with mine, refusing to answer.

I balled my hands.

But then she lowered the glass without drinking. "Because I sensed you needed to be pushed. I sensed your unhappiness. I know you're only truly happy when you let go."

Goddammit, I'd been afraid of that. She was way too reckless—always giving me things she wasn't strong enough to give.

"So you tied a bow around your pretty fucking neck and threw yourself into a life where I could do anything I wanted?"

She glanced quickly around the restaurant, eyes burning with heat. "Yes. And you know why? Because I need pain like you need to inflict—you taught me—"

"Taught you or *made* you?"

She planted her hands on the table, trembling with temper. "You didn't *make* me anything, so get off your ego trip and listen for once. I learned about my dark desires way before you. I stayed with a boyfriend who I loved as a brother because I was too damn afraid of being alone again—but I always knew I wanted more. Needed certain things. If anyone used each other in this scenario, it was *me* using *you*."

She slouched back in her booth, taking a gulp of alcohol.

Franco pulled the curtain aside, revealing his table and his cocky smug-ass face. His eyes darted between us, mirth glowing in his green gaze. "Not that I mind listening to this, but keep your voices down." He winked at Tess. "For the record— you're doing a damn good job getting answers I've been wondering about, too. Keep it up."

Pointing a finger at me, he said, "Don't make me hit you for swearing at your fiancée."

I snarled, reaching to smash his face, but he jerked the curtain back into position, chuckling at my fucking expense. Bastard. Absolute bastard.

Needing to do something with my hands, so I didn't sucker-punch my head of security, I drank. The swallow was small—I'd finished my second whiskey.

Exchanging the empty for a full one, I nursed it. Looking at the man alone in his booth, I tried to calm myself, noticing he'd ordered and nibbled on a breadstick. *See? Nothing to worry about.*

I risked a glance at Tess.

Her eyes were down; her glass also empty. She looked up, catching my eye. Giving me a tentative smile, she whispered, "I don't think I want to play anymore."

But I didn't learn anything new. I hadn't got nearly enough out of her. She started this—I'd say when we finished.

Pushing the new martini toward her, I muttered, "It's not over until I say it is."

She shifted in her seat, picking at the grey netting on her dress. "I don't think this game is meant for people like us."

My eyes narrowed. *"Des gens comme nous ?"* People like us?

"People with too much darkness—too much to hide."

My skin bristled. My mind filled with images of every dark thing I wanted to do. How could I want to do such god-awful things to her, when I was madly fucking in love? How could I sit there and argue when every protective instinct was focused on threats I couldn't see but knew were coming?

I sighed. "You wanted to play, Tess. So play."

Her blue-grey eyes met mine. "Fine. I can't remember whose turn it is."

"Mine." Was it? Who cared—it was now. "Do you have a middle name?"

Tess paused, stunned at my seemingly innocent question. "Um, Olivia."

My heart thawed, letting go of the lacing anger. "Olivia. Tess Olivia Mercer."

Her eyelashes fluttered. "Not yet...but I hope—soon."

I let a tight smile spread my lips. "Sooner than you think, *esclave.*" Two days to be exact. Two days before I could relax, knowing she would be cared for for the rest of her life if anything happened to me.

For some reason, I liked her not knowing—creating the

surprise. Fuck, I still had to call Suzette. I'd shoot her and bury her in a shallow grave behind my garage if she so much as invited one person I didn't know. And Franco's entire team of bodyguards would have to restrain me if she'd invited camera crews. This was private, and I wouldn't share my life for no amount of money, company promotion, or sick human curiosity.

"Do you have a middle name?" Tess asked. Ah, so her ploy was to parrot all my questions. I'd have to stick to basic rapid fire, lulling her into a sense of normalcy before sneaking in what I really wanted to know.

"No. What was your favourite movie as a child?"

Her eyes filled with innocent happiness. She laughed. "It's a little ironic—but *Beauty and the Beast.*"

I had no idea why that was ironic, but I let it go. She asked, "Who's your favourite band? I know you like music—you played enough when I first arrived."

The question was more loaded than she thought. I had a favourite singer—who happened to be a good friend and Tess would meet her soon. "Yes. Most of the songs I played were originals by her." Taking a sip, I mulled over another question. "What are you most afraid of?"

Tess blushed. "You're going to think I'm an idiot." Twirling her glass, she admitted, "Crickets."

My eyebrow rose. "*Crickets.* Out of every single venomous, eight-legged, sharp-toothed ferocious carnivore, you've decided to be terrified of a bug that doesn't have fangs or a lust for human flesh?"

She squirmed, flushing redder. "Yes. Don't mock me." Her eyes flashed. "Do you have any siblings?"

My world screeched to a halt. The beast inside tucked its tail between its legs, howling at the crack in my carefully fortified cage.

The one question I would *never* answer—even on my death bed. No one knew. Not even Frederick, who knew most of it. This game was over. I was done.

I drank the entire glass. The whiskey hit the back of my throat with a hot knife, licking my stomach with sickening heat. The alcoholic fumes shot up my nose, making me a menace to anyone who came too close.

Tess's eyes shot wide, very aware what my answer meant. Denied a response but ultimately given one at the same time. "Oh, my God. You have a sister or brother?"

Had.

And I'd refused to think about her for so many fucking years. But the pain hadn't lessened—the nausea hadn't faded.

My voice dripped darkness and warning. "Don't, *esclave.* That one is completely off limits."

My sister's green eyes consumed my thoughts, begging me, streaming with tears.

I was five when I first saw her—she was my earliest memory. I didn't even know her name. But she was my sister. I would've known even if *he* hadn't told me. We looked the same—matching jade eyes, identical dark hair. I found out later she was fifteen when I was five.

Taken and demoted from daughter to whore by the man who'd given her life.

The memory took me by the balls, hurling me back into filth.

"You little shit, what are you doing in here again? I'll fucking chain you to your bed if I catch you lurking where you don't belong."

I turned to run, but he grabbed the cuff of my collar, hauling me backward. "Where do you think you're going?"

My eyes spilled with useless tears as he pulled me backward. Back toward the girl I was fascinated with, hanging from the ceiling. Something caught my attention; I whipped my neck around, horror making me freeze. A man slouched against the wall, a lewd sneer on his lips. He was huge, hulking, evil.

"I think you need to see what happens to members of this household who don't fucking obey their father." My tyrannical père *threw me to the floor, kicking me firmly in the ribs. Before I could scream, he caught my chin, angling my face toward the beautiful, crying girl.*

She shook her head, jangling the chains around her throat, sending saliva dribbling on either side of the ball-gag in her mouth.

She was an angel. So pretty. So gentle. So endlessly sad.

"This is your sister, Quincy. And it'll be the first and last time you'll see her."

I squeezed my eyes against the horror of what came next. I was young but not young enough. Her image haunted me for the rest of my life.

The nameless sister who died two months later by my father's hand. He was right. I never saw her again.

I growled under my breath, desperate to hurt, throbbing with the need to tear men like my father apart. I'd only found out her name when I inherited the Mercer estate. Birth records at the local hospital claimed she'd died when she was ten, due to pneumonia. Her name was Marquisa Mercer. And she no longer existed. Thanks to *him*. The fucker.

"Q—Q—" Tess leaned across the table, shattering my black-riddled world, slamming me back to the present. "Are you—"

I was done before. Now, I was completely and utterly ruined. Hurling myself to my feet, I grabbed her wrist, yanking her from the booth. "We're leaving."

Franco scrambled out from his table. Taking one look at me, he gritted his teeth and went to settle the bill.

The man in the suit didn't look up. My worries about him were unnecessary. It didn't mean I felt any safer. Especially now. I couldn't stay in public when I felt this way—this sick and twisted way.

"I'm sorry, Q. I'm truly sorry if I upset you."

Swallowing back the rage, I locked away the memories where they belonged. Acting my fucking ass off, I jerked her against me, murmuring, "You didn't upset me, *esclave*. I've just had enough of Truth. It's time to Dare."

303

Pushing Tess roughly into the bedroom, I slammed the door.

The security of a lock and walls did little to calm me. I couldn't deny the icy warning growing more and more prevalent in my blood. I wanted to ignore it but it lived on the edge of my brain—taunting me with...*when.*

Franco had dropped us off at the hotel, and I'd barely waited for him to pull to a stop before yanking Tess from the BMW and into the foyer. I needed to use her. I wanted to pour the darkness out of me and into her light. I needed *something* to get rid of the disease inside—the disease of wanting to hurt.

Balling my hands, I advanced on Tess. My cock, sensing prey, leapt to attention, punching against my belt with lust. "I need to take you fast, dirty, fucking hard, *esclave.* I'll hurt you— if that isn't okay— *tu dois fuir.*" You need to run. My voice thickened as my vision clouded. The beast stretched, sensing violence in its future.

Her spread over the bed.
One droplet of crimson on the white carpet.
Her with my belt around her neck.
Her screams as I drove relentlessly into her.
Her tears as I licked her cheeks.

Tess spun to face me, her body quivering in the grey dress. My teeth ground, hating the material for hiding what was mine. I wanted to tear it into pieces. I wanted to destroy it.

Tess's face paled, her feet propelling her backward. "Q— I." She held a hand to her chest, drawing my attention to the swell of her breasts, the soft fragility of the woman I wanted to ravage. "What—what are you going to do?"

I laughed darkly. "Don't ask me that. I won't fucking bullet-point it." *I need to give you pain—just like you gave me by reminding me of Marquisa.*

Her lips parted as a rush of terror painted her cheeks. "Wait—what happened to dare? Dare me, Q. Don't just take, give me an option to say no."

I shook my head, hunting her toward the bed. "Don't tell

me to wait. You don't tell me what to do. That game was utterly ridiculous. I don't want to play anymore." My neck ached from the overloading of tension; the back of my eyes sprang with a headache—all warning signs I was losing control of the monster living inside.

"Get on your knees." I sidestepped, blocking her dash for the bathroom. I gave her the option to run. But running would only make it worse. She pirouetted, heading toward the thick curtains hiding us from downtown Rome.

Her hair was wild while the skirts of her dress kicked up with her panicked steps. My heart changed from thundering nastiness to fracturing with a small smidgen of restraint. She was mine. I couldn't destroy what was mine.

Shaking my head, I pinched my brow, forcing the headache to simmer.

A gentle thud made me look up. Tess bowed forward on her knees, her curls mixing with the grey of her dress.

Ah, fuck me. Seeing her so submissive—ready for me— made the headache roar along with a howl from my soul.

The huge curtains behind her looked like a silver waterfall, constantly shimmering with the illusion of liquid thanks to the lamps around the room.

My earlier threat of taking her in full view pressed against the glass filled my mind. She'd be fucking perfect, splayed and on display. My cock twitched at the thought of driving into her while people watched. The knowledge they'd want what I had would twist my mind until I rode the fine boundary of sanity and monster.

Inching forward, the darkness oozing in my blood took full rein. I wouldn't deny myself tonight. I didn't think I could. The whiskey wasn't helping—blurring barriers that had no right to be blurred, erasing the cage inside my mind.

Stopping in front of Tess, I rested my hand on the top of her head. Fisting her hair, I forced her neck upward. "*Rapide et violent.*" Fast and hard.

Tess sucked in a breath; her eyes darkened. "I don't want

it. Let me go."

I froze as a delicious ripple of pleasure fed me from her non-consent. My head cocked, letting the blackness billow. But I paused.

I *knew* this woman. I loved this fucking woman and that one sentence shone a spotlight in the otherwise dimness of my soul.

"*Je t'aime*, Tess." I leaned forward, crashing my mouth on hers, dragging her upright. Her hands landed on my chest, shoving me with feeble strength.

Her tongue entered my mouth, sharp and sleek, completely at war with her earlier conviction of not wanting it. To prove my theory of her goading me—just like so many times before—I stopped kissing her.

A little kitten growl sounded in her throat as I let her go, waiting to see what she'd do. Pulling back, her eyes burned. Then she threw herself into my arms, knocking me backward, gluing her lips to mine.

Damn this woman. This insanely incredible woman.

I groaned as her tongue re-entered my mouth, tasting sweet, fruity, entirely Tess. Her hands went to my belt. Kissing and fumbling and tearing, she clawed her way past the beast, letting me choose this—letting me let go in a healthier way.

I wasn't the only one with the need for brutality.

Time to use my woman like a master. Time to let the inner monster free just a little, all while keeping him on a fucking leash—proving once again I was better than him. I could control it. I had the power.

I'm stronger than I think.

The clink of my belt coming undone and her violent little hand latching onto my length hurtled me into thick desire. Grabbing her throat in a possessive chokehold, I smiled coldly.

Time to play.

"Dare, Tess," I whispered, layering my voice with lust and smoke.

Her eyes flared wide; her fingers twitched against the bare

skin above my cock. The rustle of the netting over the silk of her dress sounded loud as we remained frozen together. Pinching the material, I knew what I would do first. It had to go. All of it. In the way I preferred.

Reaching to my back pocket, I pulled out the one item I always carried. Some people stored a lucky stone, a trinket, or nothing at all in their pockets—I carried a bit of the past in mine.

Tess frowned at the glint in my palm. "That's the dare?"

I chuckled. "Nope. That's the foreplay."

She bit her lip. Her hands fell into the fountain of grey around her body. "Not this, Q. It's too beautiful."

The room was kissed by gentle light, making shadows come alive, morphing into creatures of the night scurrying over the white carpet, darting behind the curtains. I tilted my head, purring, "It will look even more beautiful in pieces." I wanted the floor to emulate the gravesite of destroyed clothing just like the day I'd caught her cutting up the items I'd given when she first arrived.

Tess spread her legs a little, balancing in her sexy strappy heels. My eyes dropped to her delicate toes peeking, her calf muscles taut. "I want you in nothing else but those heels wrapped around my shoulders when I lick you."

Tess swallowed hard, her eyes glazing with need.

"I can do whatever I want to you, your dress….Why is that, Tess?"

"Parce que, je suis à toi." Because, I'm yours.

A rumble crept up my chest. "You have no idea how much I love you speaking French. It makes me so hard. So fucking hard."

My unbuttoned trousers didn't give any relief to the throbbing in my cock. I wanted to skip foreplay and sink deep inside her. I wanted her screaming as I raced to the orgasm coiling in my blood. But first…I wanted to torment.

Looping my fingers through the scissor handles, I asked softly, "Do you remember what I did with these?"

Tess's eyes locked onto the silver scissors, her cheeks flushing with memories.

"Do you remember me cutting you? Slicing off your clothes that night before I took you over the bed? I hit you hard but you came harder. That was the moment I knew. The moment I knew you craved pain like I needed to inflict it."

"Yes. I remember," she panted. Her chest pinked, casting her white skin with the tempting shade. Her gaze shot to mine, bright and feverish. Was it the fear of where I would fuck her tonight or the martinis?

I hoped it was the fear.

"Are you drunk, *esclave*?"

She shook her head, hypnotising me with her blonde tresses rippling over her shoulders. "No. I was tipsy before, but now...now I'm drunk on other things."

My cock thickened. Snipping the metal blades, I pressed the cool bite against Tess's neck where the dress tied at the back. Her breathing quickened. She swayed, but made no move to stop me.

Holding eye contact, I cut the halter. I shuddered with longing as the material freed, drooping down her front. The swell of her breasts made my mouth water. I wanted to bite her. I wanted to see my teeth marks in her pale tender flesh.

"Dare, Tess."

She wobbled on her feet as I trailed the tips of the scissors over the tops of her breasts, dipping possessively into her cleavage. She moaned, flinching from the prick of the blade.

"You dare me to let you cut off my clothes?" She shrugged, shivering as I did another cut. "You clearly don't need my permission, *maître*."

I smiled, deliberately dragging the sharp tips up from her cleavage, transfixed by the red welt I left behind—I didn't break the skin, but Tess was so sensitive, flushed with blood. "That's not the dare," I murmured.

Her gaze swirled with confusion. "What is then?"

"How many times you'll let me cut you." A full body

shiver rippled through my muscles at the sick sentence. I should be repulsed, embarrassed by my need to mark her—especially because she let me brand her—but I wasn't. I'd told her the 'Q' sigil stopped those urges.

I lied.

I still needed the power over her mortal body. I needed to see her bleed for me, cry for me.

Her eyelashes flared wide as her pupils dilated—half with panic, half with lust. "How many times?" Rocking back, trying to avoid the ever steady snip down the centre of her dress, she hesitated. "Cut my dress as much as you want—leave me skin alone."

I shook my head. "That's not the dare." Slicing again, the tightness of the bodice started to loosen, revealing the purple lace cupping Tess's beautiful fucking breasts.

Her hands opened and closed, trying unsuccessfully to hide her nerves. "You're not playing the game correctly."

I snipped hard, deliberately catching the soft sensitive skin just below her bra line. "Oh no...how terrible of me."

Snip.

It was my way of cutting into her shell, carving an entry into her heart. I pushed the sharp tip into her bra, circling her nipple.

Her stomach rose and fell with every millimetre.

My cock literally burned to be inside her. Every tiny movement made my balls tighten and snarl against the prison of my trousers. Was it the alcohol coaxing me to reckless sensitivity or the knowledge of where I'd be filling Tess tonight?

I didn't really care if it was the whiskey. Tonight she was mine. *All* of her.

"You don't *ask* me how many times. You *dare* me." Her eyes smouldered. "So, master...how many times do you dare me to bleed for you?"

Fuck. Me.

The beast instead howled at the delicious fucking question.

So brutal. So unpretentious. Grabbing the back of her neck, I kissed her like a savage animal intent on drinking her soul.

Her hands came up, pushing against my chest as I plunged my tongue past her lips, giving her no choice but to open wide and receive.

Her touch seared my skin beneath my shirt; her roaming fingertips crept up my chest, running hot along my collarbone.

Then she ripped the material, sending buttons pinging and air rushing against my tattooed torso.

Her teeth captured my bottom lip, somehow taking control of the kiss for a second before I lost my cool and slammed her backward, upward, and onto the bed.

The air flew from her lungs into mine. I pinned her down with my fingers around her throat. "Three. I dare you to do three."

Her lips were swollen and red and so, so wet from our kiss.

She arched up, forcing her vulnerable neck into my fingers. Her breathing turned ragged. "Four. I dare you to do four."

Oh, my fucking God, what was she doing? Now was not the night to fight back—now was definitely not the time to make me lose the rest of my fractured control.

Something skittered in her eyes before hiding in their grey depths. I reared onto my elbows, releasing her neck. "Why?" Suspicion chased hot through my veins.

She looked away, but I grabbed her chin. "What do you dare in return?"

Her body stiffened, but her gaze locked with mine. "I dare you not to take my anal virginity tonight. Give me more time."

My stomach gnashed with livid teeth. "*That's* your dare? You're so damn afraid of something I guarantee will bring you pleasure."

My imagination stole reality giving me a snuff movie of erotic torture.

Her crying as I slid into her for the first time.

Her thighs and cheeks glowing from my spanks.

Taking her ass with my cock, while filling her pussy with a quivering vibrator.

My hands curled at that vision. I ached to fill her with my cock and a vibrator all at once. I wanted her stretched and overly full. I wanted her to know *exactly* who she belonged to.

Flipping her onto her stomach, I hoisted up her skirts and snipped with silver scissors at her knickers. They fell away, leaving her ass perfectly bare, the glisten of arousal slick between her legs.

She jolted as I pressed a finger against her clit, dragging the tip through her wet folds and up to the one place she denied me.

My cock pulsed with the first wave of pre-cum as she rolled her hips, trying to dislodge my touch. She was so tight, so shy, so fucking amazing.

"*Maître*, please…I'm not saying no…just not now."

"What scares you so much, *esclave?*" I pressed against her hole, loving the tight muscle, the blatant refusal to allow entry—so different to her pussy which beckoned with its wet, dark heat.

I'd never stop loving her taste or tightness, but I wanted this, too. A lot.

Gathering more of her damp desire, I swirled it around the puckered muscle digging fingernails into her hip when she tried to squirm away. "Tell me. In detail. And maybe I'll accept your dare."

Her head hung down, a curtain of blonde hiding her eyes. "I don't know. It's just foreign. Something I never thought I wanted. It's not…sexy."

Not fucking sexy? She obviously didn't see what I did. Didn't she know her shyness was a heady aphrodisiac? Knowing it was the one place no one else had gone. It drove me to breaking point.

I laughed, never stopping my stroking, dying to use force to break the seal of her body and take her anyway. "It's not sexy? Fuck, *esclave*. Seeing you like this, wanting you that way…it's the sexiest fucking thing I've ever seen."

Lowering my head, I bit the feminine curve of her hip, sinking my teeth hard. Keeping her locked in my hold, I spread her cheeks and ran my tongue down her seam.

She jolted as I pressed harder with my finger, breaching her body with digit and tongue.

She reared upright, a moan echoing around the room. I slapped a hand between her shoulder blades pressing her back on the bed, keeping her ass high and open.

It was a good thing my cock was still in my pants because the ache between my eyes was excruciating. The need to fuck building. Foreplay was almost over. Hard and fast was quickly approaching, and I wanted it. I wanted to slam inside her and come like a volcano.

Tess's face thrashed on the bed as I wiggled my finger a little deeper. A trail of wetness shone on her cheeks.

My mouth watered to lick her tears; her delicious salty sadness.

"Tell me how that feels." I didn't want to admit the chase turned me the fuck on. Knowing she was genuinely scared only made it more of a prize.

She shook her head, breathing hard. A hitch of tears broke her pant. "I don't know. *I don't know.*"

Thrusting my finger, I toyed with her ass, drawing yet more wetness from both her pussy and her eyes. As much as she denied it—it turned her on.

"I'll help make up your mind." Curving my back, I licked her again, dropping my mouth to latch onto her pussy. My cock felt as if I broke it in two, crushing it between my fucking legs.

Her cunt clenched as I pushed my tongue inside her.

Her face pressed against the mattress, hiding her tiny scream. "Dammit, Q. Damn you." Her hips rocked back, surprising me as she forced my finger a fraction deeper.

I almost came.

Removing my finger, I slapped her ass.

She flinched. My eyes tightened at the red handprint painting her white cheek. I struck again, obsessed with turning her flawless skin into a riot of violence. I wanted to grant her pain. Endless pain. A dynasty of pain.

"How does that make you feel?" I growled, smacking her again. The whiskey took hold, speeding me toward a conclusion. I couldn't drag it out any longer.

"Like I'm on fire. I'm burning for you, Q."

I dropped my hand to slap her pussy.

Her legs tried to close, but I kept her on display. Her folds were swollen, wet, so fucking ready for me to fill. "And this. How does it make you feel?" I slapped her again, twisting her clit in punishment.

She arched, fighting my hold on her. "It makes me feel like a whore. Your whore. I want you so bad."

My eyes snapped closed. If this woman didn't own my soul already now she did. She was perfect. A miracle. *Mine.* Her body didn't recoil from my merciless love. She allowed me the freedom I craved.

She'd given me so much. I couldn't take from her what she still feared—no matter the turn on. "Four," I growled, breathing rough and ragged. "Four cuts in return for giving you another night of freedom."

She moaned loud as I hit her again—the hardest one yet. A five finger shape decorated her ass, stamping firm ownership on the woman I would marry in forty-eight hours. She may be my wife soon but she would always be my whore.

"Tell me where I can cut you, *esclave.*" I yanked her back, rubbing her pussy against my trouser-clad cock. "Tell me!" The scissors lay beside my knee, digging into me as I thrust against her.

"Anywhere!" Her face flushed, her lips baring her teeth. "Anywhere you want."

Anywhere?

A slow smile spread my lips. "*Où je veux…*" Anywhere I want…

Tess nodded. "My legs, my breasts, my throat—it's all yours to mark. Do it!"

She'd given me a smorgasbord of places to mark her. But I had a better idea.

Snatching the scissors from the bedspread, I scrambled off the mattress. Grabbing her ankle, I pulled her to the edge, loving how the material gathered upward, bunching around her waist.

Her eyes popped wide as I collected her in a bouquet of torn dress and netting. Arms around her waist, I carted her to the window.

Tess froze as I placed her on her feet in front of the curtain. "Q..." Understanding flashed across her face. "You wouldn't—"

I gave her a harsh smile. "I warned you." Tearing back the curtain, I welcomed in the night sky. Stars flickered then dulled as wisps of clouds drifted across the dark like graffiti spray. The clear night was a perfect backdrop to the twinkling lights of the street below. Passer-by's linked arms, strolling in the chilly but romantic evening.

Only three stories. High enough to possibly avoid people watching or the perfect height for an exclusive glimpse.

"I would and I am," I muttered. "I'm adding to my dare. You said I could cut you anywhere. I want to cut you right here, against the window, while I make you come and give the world a show."

Swivelling her in place, I pushed her forward until her chest met the glass. Her hands came up, splaying on the cold surface. With unforgiving fingers, I tore the remaining bodice from her, fully exposing her heavy breasts.

She jumped as I cut off her bra and slammed her torso against the glass, forcing her nipples to meet the icy reflection.

Tess hissed as I forced her harder against the barrier—the only thing stopping us from falling three stories. A shiver ran down her spine.

Fitting my body behind her, I nuzzled her ear. "I think you

want people to see. I think you want people to watch as I finger you, fuck you, make you scream."

I dragged my hands over her sides to her hips, forcing her to accept a thrust as I looked directly into my own eyes.

The reflection of the lights behind us showed Tess flushed and glowing like a fucking goddess while I lurked in the shadows. Only my pale gaze was visible.

Stroking her quivering back, I cupped the back of her neck. Unable to help myself, I unsheathed my teeth, sinking into her shoulder.

Tess cried out, wiggling against the imprisonment of my body and the window. "Q—"

Grabbing one of her hands, I guided it to my stiff cock. "Free me, Tess. Then I'm going to take you so fucking hard."

I groaned as her fingers immediately obeyed, ripping the zipper down, fumbling into the tight elastic of my boxer-briefs.

She had no fear. No terror. I'd cured her. I'd brought her back to life. I was making her live in that very moment.

The second her eager touch found my raging hardness, she shuddered, pressing her ass against me. "Take me. Give it to me," she moaned. She sounded drunk, loose, horny. I'd never seen her look so pliant or erotic.

I groaned as she fisted me, pumping my cock hard and harsh. "Goddammit. You're going to make me come before I've even climbed inside you."

Dropping my hand, I gathered the bushels of material, exposing her just to me. I'd show the world her tits, but her pussy was mine. Kicking her ankle to spread her legs, I shoved down my boxers and trousers to my quads, leaving me fully dressed in a torn gaping shirt, blazer, and trousers. My cock was free—that was all I needed.

I plunged my hand between Tess's legs, clamping hard on my bottom lip when I discovered how drenched she was. My little whore was an exhibitionist. I couldn't wait to fill her, to make her lose complete control in full view of the public.

Angling the tip of my cock, I found her entrance.

Tess stiffened. "No. Wait—"

I growled under my breath, rubbing the throbbing head of my cock through her folds. "If you're having second thoughts too fucking bad, *esclave. J'ai besoin de jouir en toi.*" I need to come in you.

"I'm not saying no. Just—just hide my face." She looked over her shoulder, locking eyes. "Please. That's all I ask."

I wanted to argue but rationality made its way into my sex-addled brain. She was soon to be the face of Feathers of Hope. What the fuck was I doing putting her in such a compromising position? I had to protect her identity.

"Shit, I'm an idiot."

The netting of her dress dug into my naked hips; an idea sprang to mind. With the scissors, I cut the detailing off the dress.

Holding it up, I murmured, "This will stop them from seeing your face, but you'll be able to see out."

She nodded, sucking in a breath as I gently placed the black netting over her face, gathering the excess in my fist behind her head.

"Can you see?"

She nodded again.

"Anonymity," I whispered. "Feel free to let go. Give them a show, Tess." With one hand, I spread her dress, making sure both breasts were squashed firmly against the glass. Positioning myself at the delicious epicentre of heat, I bit her ear. "Scream for me."

A cry tore from her lips as I drove up hard, fast, *savage.* She bumped hard against the window as her slick wetness welcomed me. I thrust upward, sheathing myself fully. Balls deep. Exactly where I belonged.

"Oh, God. Q. *Yes.*" Her fingers slipped on the glass, her hands growing sweaty with need.

My eyes fuzzed as her heat fisted around me, sending a ripple of pleasure down my legs.

The reflection bounced back to us—my eyes were dark

and wild, my jaw tight and angry. No one could see me behind Tess but there would be no mistaking what was happening to her if they happened to look up.

Look up. See me ravishing this stunning creature. Be jealous.

I pulled the netting tighter across her face, using it as leverage to drive up again. She moaned, thrusting backward, meeting my cock.

The knowledge anyone could look up and watch filled my blood with fire. My belt jangled as I fucked her—I grew hot still fully dressed but I'd never been so sexually angry—so needful for a release.

She panted, loose and receiving against the window, her mouth parting with every pound. Her gathered dress protected her hipbones from slamming into the glass as I ruthlessly took her.

There was no finesse. No rhythm. It was a straight claiming. Fast and hard.

Fast and fucking hard.

The first spiral of pleasure erupted from my balls. I threw my head back, driving deeper. Tess would have bruises on top of bruises tomorrow. Her face contorted with pleasure-pain as I used her. But every single thrust, she met me. Every grunt she echoed.

Then someone looked up.

A stranger's eyes locked onto Tess's naked breasts, flat against the glass. I growled, pounding so hard her heels left the floor. She cried out, her fingers scrabbling for purchase.

"Oh, God. There's someone. They're—"

Another spiral of bliss shot up my spine. The man frowned, trying to work out what he saw, then took a shocked step when realization hit.

That's right. I'm balls deep in this woman you can only fantasise about.

Something clicked in Tess and her need turned wild. Her pussy clenched around me, locking my teeth from the vicious orgasm building in my blood.

Fisting the scissors, I struggled to keep my eyes open from the overwhelming pleasure.

I made my first cut.

Right on her shoulder blade. A shallow, single line welled with black blood, infecting me with power and lust and need.

"Fuck, oh…" Tess cried. Her back arched but she didn't twist the wound away.

"That's it. Remember pain, *mon coeur*. Remember how fucking delicious it is."

Another man stopped, gawking at Tess pressed hard against the window. He leaned to speak to the other voyeur who hadn't taken his eyes off my wondrous woman.

I rode Tess like my orgasm rode me. Hard, brittle, existing in the taboo of intensity.

I didn't have much time.

Four.

I have to finish before I blow.

The second cut was directly beside the first. A long slightly irregular line where a bead of blood rose but didn't trickle. I didn't taste, just let the blood glow with sin, intoxicating me more than any whiskey.

A couple stopped below.

Tess moaned loudly as they pointed upward, mouths hanging open. Her pussy rippled as I planted my feet further apart, pounding upward, chasing my final goal.

Holding the netting harder around her face, I gulped in air, driving harder and harder. Sweat ran down my temples; my heart jackhammered against my ribs, smashing them into dust.

"Q…yes. God, yes. Fuck." The first band of Tess's orgasm wrenched a groan from my lips.

"Don't come. Wait," I hissed between my teeth. The moment she started coming, I wouldn't be able to hold back.

I cut her again, clenching my jaw against the unrelenting orgasm gripping my spine. Sparks and tingles and a pain so bright I could barely see held my body hostage.

Tess's hand suddenly disappeared between her front and

the glass. A rustle of silk as she dove into the fabric of her tattered dress, finding her clit. Her spine bowed as she stroked.

"Fuck me, Tess." I wanted to be down there. I wanted to project my soul to the audience below and watch Tess finger herself to heaven.

I pressed the scissors against her shoulder but Tess let out a scream. Her entire body seized as an orgasm ripped her in two.

I never made the final cut as I fell forward, burying my head in her throat as I let go—allowing the magic to explode out of me and into her, spurt after spurt, mixing our bodies as well as our fucking souls.

Then a soft *snick* sounded in my ear, cutting my release into pieces. The heat in my blood turned to ice and snow and sleet. A blizzard whistled in my chest, stabbing me with icicles and sub-zero temperatures.

I had to stop. Danger. *Stop!*

But Tess continued coming, dragging me along with her.

"Fuuuck!" I collapsed forward, slamming a hand against the glass to stop from suffocating her. I. Couldn't. Stop. My hips were demonic, delivering every drop of come I had to give. My fingers dug at the smooth reflection as the final wave drained my balls, stopping my heart with a horrible mixture of panic and relief.

A masculine chuckle entered the sex-hazed world Tess and I existed in, smashing it to smithereens, bringing death and destruction.

A slow clap sounded. "Well, that made me fucking hard, congratulations."

Double motherfucking shit.

I should've stayed on high alert. I should've known something was wrong. I should *never* have let my guard down.

Tess froze. Not breathing. Not living. Shutting down completely.

Terror filled my limbs at the thought of losing her again. But I didn't have time to worry. I had a murder to commit.

Unclamping my fist from holding the netting around her face, I threw it away. Not once looking behind me.

Who the fuck were they? The man from the restaurant? Some other cocksucker who I'd suspected following us back to the hotel?

I knew what they wanted. I wasn't naïve to know this wouldn't happen. Hell, I'd been tense for weeks, just waiting for their move. But planning for a future and facing it head on were two entirely different things.

Gritting my teeth, I pulled out from Tess. My body moved stiff, full of ferocious anger as I forced my still hard cock back into my trousers and buckled up. With infinite gentleness, I pulled Tess's dress down and reached in front of her, bringing the ruined bodice together as much as possible to keep her hidden.

"Q? What's going on?" Tess's voice wobbled.

I kissed her temple. Spinning her around, I looked deep into her eyes. *Is this the last time I'll see her?* I'd planned so much—just in case the worst happened. I'd signed my fortune to her—so I'd always know she had money. I'd wanted to marry her to give her the power of my name.

That might not be possible now.

Frederick was right—ever since I'd seen the first article on TV, I'd been fighting against time. Time needed to fix Tess. Time needed to fight her demons before I wasn't able to anymore. Everything that'd happened to Tess was my fault and I'd wanted to undo my wrongs before it was too late.

The news saved my business but marked me for death.

Fuck, stop those pessimistic thoughts. I would bathe in blood before I let them kill me.

Brushing damp curls from Tess's cheeks, I murmured, "Trust me. Everything will be okay." *It has to be.* I wanted to die as an old married man after living a lifetime with my perfect other. Not here. Not today.

I refused. I fucking refused.

"Mercer!" Franco's voice cut through my worry just

before a fist collided with my cheekbone.

Pain. Hot spreading, throbbing pain.

Tess screamed as I fell to my knee. I shook my head, scattering the stars from taking over my vision.

Blind rage released an injection of adrenaline and I tore upward. My time may be up but it didn't mean I would give in to the heinous bitch. I had a personal vendetta and fully intended to win.

Another punch landed on my jaw, sending me stumbling into Tess.

She yelled, "Don't you fucking touch him!"

The ringing in my ears amplified as another man grabbed Tess by the hair, dragging her away. Hurling her to the floor, he kicked her.

I saw red.

I saw blood.

I saw hell.

Launching myself at him, I swung low and hard. My knuckles bellowed as his head cracked backward, eyes rolling with the uppercut. As he fell, I brought his limp carcass forward, smashing my knee hard into his ribcage and dropped every barrier inside.

I lost all sensation of what I did. What parts I tore, what agony I inflicted.

His scream bounced off the walls as I shed all humanity and went rogue.

I'll kill him.

No one. Absolutely fucking *no one* would touch Tess again and survive. I would tear their motherfucking heads off.

"Q!"

I ignored Tess, delivering wrath like a devil-filled tornado. Punch. Wallop. Kick. I wanted to turn his body into a lake of blood.

A silenced gunshot went off.

Time stuttered.

Pain.

Lancing horrendous pain sliced into my thigh.

Sickness raced up my back, coating my tongue with bile.

Motherfucker shot me.

I roared with agony, feeding off the hot lick of fire radiating in my leg. Stumbling away from my unconscious victim, I bent over. Pushing a fingertip into the torn flap of my trousers, I found the bloody mess below.

My breath came hard and deep as another flash of pain consumed my system. My finger was torture but I found the exit hole. No broken bones. No severed arteries. A flesh wound.

A wound sending my anger ratcheting from uncontrollable to psychopathic.

"No! Oh, my God. You shot him!" Tess attacked the asshole who'd lodged a bullet in my limb, bringing a rain of tiny fists onto his torso.

Tess, don't!

The man batted her arms away, his face contorting with rage. Tess kicked him, screaming.

He slapped her hard, wrenching her neck sideways with force. She went instantly limp, falling into his arms.

No! Fuck no. Not again.

I hurtled toward him, intending to rip his throat out but another man captured Tess, dragging her disorientated body against him. She shook her head, trying to clear the dazed fog, fighting meekly as he grabbed her breast with horrible fingers.

Glowering at me, he yelled, "Stop! Everyone! Behave or we'll take turns with your little slave before cutting her throat. Got it?"

The threat worked.

I slammed to a halt, breathing hard. Rage siphoned around my body, making me tremble, but I embraced cold calculation.

Glancing around the room, I catalogued everything.

Five men.

A pentagon of doom caged me against the window with Franco in a bloody pile a few metres away. One of his eyes was swollen shut, blood covered his shirt, and he sat painfully, nursing his right side.

Five men.

Three with black hair and smooth blank faces, two with brownish hair and sick satisfaction wrinkling their eyes.

I didn't recognise any of them.

Red Wolverine?

No, I did enough damage to his operation to risk coming after me so soon.

Emerald Dragon?

No, they were based in Singapore, or was it Hong Kong—either way, I doubted they'd have the resources to come to Rome—not with the heat surrounding their names after I handed over my address book of fuckwit traffickers.

So who are they?

It didn't matter. Tonight would be the last night they'd be alive. I didn't need to know any more than that.

I looked at Tess. Her eyes were clear, blazing with anger. Her fierceness gave me strength. No matter what I'd done with my life—healing her and giving her back her fire was enough to land me, maybe not in heaven, but hopefully not in hell.

I'd fixed her in time. Barely.

I would've been happy about that—if it wasn't for the entirely unwinnable situation I faced. Five men against one. Franco was no use to me and I wouldn't do anything to put Tess's life in peril again.

"Give her to me and I'll obey," I growled.

The room shimmered with violence. A standoff. My knuckles hurt, needing to be lodged in his teeth. My thigh throbbed but shock worked wonders on deleting most of the distraction.

Ten seconds of waiting.

Finally the man nodded, shoving Tess toward me. Striding forward, I wrenched her behind my back. The second her form touched mine, huddling my back in a fierce embrace I sighed, gathering my wits for the next fight.

"Q, I'm sorry—I tried," Tess cried.

Ignoring her, I kept my body between her and the unwelcome bastards. I concentrated on the best plan available for keeping her unharmed.

You have to get them to leave.

That was my only option. And I didn't like what I'd have to do to make it come true.

"Who the fuck are you? What do you want?" I hissed.

Tess trembled, her rapid, shallow breaths hitting the back of my neck. Something snapped inside her, turning her silent tears into terror-filled gasps. Pressing hard against me, her teeth chattered. "They can't—Q...I can't do it again." The edge of lunacy in Tess's voice made my anger reach a whole new boiling point. "I'm bankrupt. I can't afford another toll! Please. I have nothing left."

Don't revert, Tess. Please don't undo all my fucking hard work.

"Get the fuck out!" I roared. "Get out before I fucking murder you!" Ignoring their guns and soulless eyes, I reached behind, crushing Tess's front against my spine. I hated how wobbly and cold she was. "I won't let them take you, *esclave*. I promise." *On my sister's grave, I promise.* "Stay with me."

The gunshot in my leg turned from a fire to a cataclysmic inferno.

A silenced semi-automatic was pointed in my face. The man wielding it, sneered; his teeth perfect pegs of white. "We're not here for her."

My heart bucked. Spanish accent.

Spain.

Everything clicked into place.

Lynx.

He had midway houses in Rome to traffic the overwhelming number of women he traded in Spain. The complications I'd told Tess about all revolved around that cocksucker. Young, ambitious, with no fucking remorse. Lynx had been a personal enemy ever since he killed a girl I'd agreed to trade for—just because he didn't like the shirt I wore to the meeting.

Asswipe. Fucking juvenile sadistic delinquent.

Tess stifled a sob, sucking back her downfall into crazy, latching once again onto reality. She twisted in my arms, trying to get free. Glaring at the men, she yelled, "Just leave. Go back to the hole you crawled out of. Don't do this!"

A man with black hair laughed. "Do what? This?" Closing the distance between us, he swung the gun at my temple.

I didn't think. Just reacted. Ducking, I launched. Lowering my shoulder, I plowed into his chest, crunching him to the floor in a heap of body parts.

I didn't care about my leg. All I cared about was ripping out his fucking heart. He gasped for breath punching anywhere he could. He managed to knock the air out of my lungs, bruise a rib, kick my knee.

He was strong, but he didn't have psychotic rage thrumming in my veins.

Tess.

Above all I had to keep her safe.

I landed a square punch, sending his fighting body into a loose pile of bones. My fingers latched around his gun, wrenching it from his hold. Limping to my feet, I aimed at the ringleader who'd royally fucked up my night.

"Ah, ah, ah, I wouldn't do that if I were you."

I swung around. My stomach splattered to my feet. One of the brown-haired men had Tess in a vice-like grip, his gun bruising her temple.

Fuck!

Instantly, I threw my newly acquired weapon away.

If it was just me, I could've taken them on. I might not have won—but I would've done some serious damage before they killed me.

But I was handcuffed by my love for Tess. I couldn't put her in any more harm than I'd already caused. How much more did that poor woman have to go through because of me?

I'd brought nothing but death and horror into her life. I'd

brought her back from the edge once. I'd paid my debts and I refused to layer her with more.

My eyes locked with Tess: *I'm so fucking sorry. So unbelievably sorry for everything that I've caused.*

Tess exploded into action. Shoving the guy off her, she sprinted the distance between us, colliding with my chest. "Don't you *dare* look at me like that Quincy Mercer. Don't you dare say goodbye." Her voice cracked as tears gushed from her eyes.

I wanted to hug her forever but another man punched me in the jaw, dragging Tess out of my embrace.

"No!" I spun in the assholes hold, ready to tear off his ears. My heartbeat relocated to my thigh, thundering a fucking gong of agony.

"Enough!" The man struck my temple, crashing me into Franco. I tripped over his body. He groaned in pain, but his eyes were fierce and ready to fight. *"Je couvre tes arrières, Mercer. Nous pouvons les prendre. Ensemble."* I've got your back, Mercer. We can take them. Together.

His shoulder looked dislocated, and he bled out of his ears—concussion. His left hand was hidden in his bloody blazer. He'd put up a good fight but no matter how good, the odds were against us.

My eyes flickered between the Spanish men, waiting to see if they understood.

One man stalked toward Tess, shoving a gun against her head. Looking at me, he ordered, "Get up, asshole." He didn't seem to know what Franco said—just working on precaution. Obviously the dumb fucks couldn't speak French.

"Tu es blessé. Ne leur donne pas une raison de nous tuer. Tu connais le plan. Il faut s'y tenir." You're hurt. Don't give them a reason to kill us. You know the plan. Stick to it. I glared at Franco, willing him to stay down and not be fucking stupid. I needed him for the next stage. And if the next stage failed, I needed him to look after Tess.

Franco's face blackened. *"Je vais la garder en sécurité."* I'll keep her safe.

My heart stuttered in relief. I trusted Franco as much as I trusted Frederick. As long as Tess was with them, I could keep my mind sharp and find a way to survive—away from her—away from the distraction of trying to keep her from being hurt.

I have to get them to leave.

"Stop speaking in French if you don't want your little girlfriend's brains splattered all over the glass you fucked her against."

Goddammit, I needed to kill these bastards. And I would, one way or another. In this life or the next. My teeth ached to tear into them. My hands already steamed with phantom blood—their blood. I fucking hated to think of Tess seeing this—especially after everything I'd done to save her.

Stumbling upright, I glowered at the man holding my woman. "Leave her alone."

There was no denying I deserved this. After all, I'd put more traffickers down while searching for Tess than the worldwide Interpol had in three years, but it didn't mean I was prepared to pay their price.

What did they expect?

Money? My life? Torture?

If I knew their end goal, I might be better prepared. I'd know which weapon to use. The only positive thing was they'd come for me. Not her.

The man planted a kiss against Tess's cheek. She jerked away, only to careen back into his arms as he yanked her back. My spine stiffened, every urge inside saying attack. Fucking *attack*.

The muzzle of another gun bruised the base of my skull. "You're no longer in the position of control, Mercer."

My heart cannonballed but I kept my face blank. "Let's sort this out here and now. You want cash—fine. Take it."

He laughed, dragging the gun through my hair till he held it in the middle of my forehead. "We don't want your fucking money. We want something more than that."

Tess sobbed, fighting her captor. "Leave him alone!"

Tearing my eyes from her, I steeled myself. "And what is that?"

"Your fucking life of course. You've been costly to a lot of associates. Your debts are being called. Time to meet the unemployment line."

Tess screamed, going nuts. She managed to get free, only to slam into another man's arms. Her face was white, fear taking her limbs hostage in a jittery dance.

Fucking hell. My heart clawed its way out of my chest to go to her. To tell her it would all be okay. At least they hadn't killed me in front of her. If they meant to take my life, I wanted it as far away from Tess as possible. I didn't want her to see that. I didn't want to haunt her for the rest of her days.

"Fine! Let's go." Shoving the asshole away, I strode toward the door—cursing the burn in my leg, doing my best not to limp like a dog about to be put down.

"Where the fuck are you going?" the man yelled.

Stopping, I crossed my arms. Hoping my cocky nonchalant attitude would piss them off. I was still in fucking control. As much as they thought otherwise. "You want me. Fine. I'll come with you. But not here. Not like this. You leave her alone, and I won't fight. You can have your fucking vengeance."

Tess screamed, "No! Q—don't. You can't! Don't leave me."

My heart hurt worse than the bullet in my leg. Walking away from her would be the hardest thing I've ever done. But I wouldn't put her through anymore. I wouldn't ruin her mind any more than I already had. I'd done what I needed. She would be okay. In time.

Franco shouted in a ream of French, but I tuned them out. I didn't need to hear their pleas—this was the only way. Three lives instead of one.

It was a good trade.

My eyes locked with hers. My lungs stopped working at

the horror pinching her face. *"Pardonne-moi,* Tess. *Sache que je t'aime jusqu'à la fin des temps et je te retrouverai si ce n'est pas dans cette vie ce sera dans la prochaine."* Forgive me, Tess. Know that I love you till the end of time, and I'll find you again, if not in this life, then in the next.

Tess's eyes dried from tears, burning with terrible anger. Her face flushed as she shoved the man away. *"Non! Je ne te laisse pas partir. Pas maintenant. Pas après tout!"* No! I won't let you go. Not now. Not after everything!

I wondered if she knew she spoke in French. She was so fierce, her tongue lilting over the language as if she was born to it.

The leader seemed lost for words but the moment I tore my eyes from Tess and opened the door, he leapt into action. Stalking toward me, he pointed at the unconscious man I'd attacked, ordering his troops, "Pick him up. We're leaving."

I paused for one last moment before I was shoved out the door—carted away from any happiness I might've found.

Please let me see her again.

Tess stood frozen on a sea of white carpet looking part-angel, part-goddess, totally lost and heartbroken.

She shook her head, disbelief bright. "Q—please!"

My heart stayed behind with her—I didn't need it where I was going.

Au revoir. Goodbye.

The door swung closed.

I might have given in to protect Tess, but I wouldn't die for nothing.

I would take as many down with me as possible.

I would die with their blood on my tongue.

Chapter Eleven

Intertwined, tangled, knotted forever, our souls
will always be twisted together,
our demons, our monsters belong to the other,
Bow to me, I bow to thee, now we are free

It couldn't be real.
It can't.
I didn't believe it.
I don't!
The instant the door clicked, blocking me from Q, I felt adrift. Broken. Missing the matching piece of my soul.

I couldn't handle the amputation of something so fundamental. I couldn't think straight—my mind kept me frozen, replaying the gunshot, the beating, the never ending sentence of horror: *Your fucking life of course.*

They meant to kill him. He left so I wouldn't see. He left to *protect* me. Always protecting me regardless of his own safety.

Rage.

I'd never felt such a complex mix of rage and absolute helplessness. *I should run after them! Go!*

I gripped my hair, tugging it hard. My heart thundered, shooting agony through my chest. All instincts said to find a weapon and *go*. But I had to think clearly.

They're going to kill him!

There was nothing clear about that.

Go! I couldn't *not* go after them. Even though I was utterly useless—an emotional wreck at the upheaval of my close-to-perfect life. Fate had once again took everything—reminding me I was penniless even though Q made me so wealthy.

I couldn't stand by and let the toll strip me bare. I wouldn't let Q sacrifice himself. I was going after them. Balling my hands, I ran toward the door.

"Tess. Wait!"

My head whipped around, eyes locking onto a bloody man struggling to his feet.

Franco! Holy hell, I'd completely forgotten about him. Slamming to a halt, I wavered between the door and helping the one man who might be able to save me. He'd been with Q when they hunted for me. He'd have resources, knowledge.

I refused to look away from the door—the horrible door blocking me from the love of my life as he was marched away with a bullet in his thigh.

Another lacerating pain flashed through my stomach at the thought of anything happening to him. It couldn't. Not to Q. I wouldn't let it.

He can't die! Not now.

Then help Franco. He's your only hope.

Anger heated my body at the realization of my own mortality. I could chase after the men, try to be heroic and leap on their backs and cry and scream…but ultimately all I'd achieve was Q being shot sooner and me joining him.

"Come help me up," Franco ordered. "Whatever's going through your head—stop it. It's not as bad as you think." His deep voice slapped me out of my disbelieving haze, dragging me back to earth.

Clutching my dress, I whirled around. "Not as bad as I

think? Not as bad!" I stalked toward him. "They *took* him, Franco. They stole him from my arms and *shot* him." My eyes burned but no tears fell. I wanted to scream until my throat bled. I wanted to kill every single last one of those bastards who'd taken what I couldn't live without.

I can't do this.

You must.

Everything Q had done for me—to make me whole again—teetered close to cracking. My tower that I'd smashed after Tenerife shivered with its broken bricks, trying to rise from its ashes to claim me.

But I wouldn't let it. Not this time. This time I wouldn't be a victim. This time I would win.

Franco manoeuvred his body, hobbling to a knee. A rush of guilt swarmed at not helping him, but I stood concreted to the carpet. So many things inside. So many conflicting, terrible responses as my body and mind battled with what to do.

I'd never felt this way. This lost, angry, terrified kind of way. As a victim, the choice to fight was stripped the moment I was captured. But as the one left behind I had choices, decisions—hope.

But then fear struck, crushing that hope. What if I made the wrong decision? What if I trusted Franco to help but the window of time to get Q back was already gone? I played roulette with Q's life depending on the decision I made.

Action.

I needed to do *something.*

But being a statue was all I seemed capable of as scenarios rushed through my head, all ending in horrific ways.

Chasing after Q to find a bullet lodged in his forehead in the lobby.

Not chasing after Q to find they'd sent a ransom note and it would be a simple matter of an exchange.

Chasing after Q only to watch him be tortured—all because of me.

They took him because of me.

"Oh, my God." Why hadn't I seen it? I was so stupid. *I'd* done this. I'd ruined his life. Destroyed it. Demolished it. A sob began, building in girth and volume until I knew I'd explode into pieces if I let it go.

Arms wrapped around me, jerking me close to a metallic smelling shirt and tense broken body. Franco pressed me hard against him, giving me a rock to cling to while my misery threatened to drown me.

"It's because of me. It's my fault!"

"Of course it's your fault."

My eyes popped wide. He agreed! I couldn't do it. I curled over, nursing the ball of agony in my heart, wishing to die.

Franco gathered me closer. "It's your fault he's happy. It's your fault he's finally accepting his past and looking forward to a future he no longer has to hide from." He winced as his body wobbled. "This would've happened with or without you, Tess. You've only seen a smidgen of men involved in this industry. But Q knows thousands. He's personally ate with them, done deals with them. He was welcomed into a world where admission is for life and any misbehaving means death. Yes, hunting for you so recklessly sped up the realization of who Q really was, but it would've happened. Eventually."

He pulled away, looking into my gritty eyes. "And when it happened, he wouldn't be where he is today. He wouldn't fight as hard as he will now because he has love giving him power." His emerald eyes softened. "If they'd come for him, and you weren't in his life he would've fought—of course, but ultimately, he would've given in. Because in some fucked-up way he believes he deserves it."

I shook my head. "He doesn't—"

"You know him—the parts he lets you see at least. But I've been with him for nine years. And believe me when I say, he's always gone through life knowing he would die young. He never came out and said it, but he wasn't planning for a long life, Tess. He just didn't have the strength to keep battling whatever is inside him."

My heart felt as if it'd been mined of all the goodness inside, leaving it riddled with holes. Only Q could patch those holes, and it didn't matter what decision I went with because the conclusion was all the same.

I *would* get him back. Just like he saved me. I didn't have the luxury of second guessing and denial. It was time to go.

Clutching my torn dress, I pulled away from Franco. He stumbled a little, drawing my eyes to his torn trousers and blood-stained shirt. "Shit, Franco. I'm so sorry." I reached out to touch a gash on his arm only for him to flinch back.

Then I saw it.

A crimson-soaked tie wrapped around his thumb. Or rather...lack of one.

My eyes darted to his, filling with liquid. "What—what did they do?"

He shrugged. "It's the only access to your room. Key-coded fingerprints. I refused when they asked. Guess they didn't like that." Reaching into his pocket, he pulled out the severed appendage.

Bile swashed up my gullet and into my mouth.

I ran.

Skidding into the bathroom, I threw the toilet seat up and purged my system of lychee martinis and Italian entrées in a wicked wave of vomit.

Cold sweat dotted my spine as my stomach convulsed.

Franco's thumb. They'd cut off his thumb.

I retched again.

If they did that to get to Q, what the hell would they do to him now he was in their clutches?

I moaned, convulsing harder; my soul tried to claw its way out of my mouth.

Gentle fingers whispered across my neck, tugging damp strands, twisting them into a messy bun.

I looked up, still hugging the porcelain. Franco gave me a sad smile. "It's probably a good thing it's all out of your system. But we need to go. Do you think you'll be okay?" I couldn't help looking at his left hand, saturated in blood, wrapped with his tie around the stump of where his thumb used to be.

My stomach rolled as an image of Q's fingers being cut off consumed me, but I swallowed hard.

Stop being a fucking girl.

I refused to waste another minute. Wiping my mouth, I stood up and made my way to the sink. Franco shuffled with me, holding my hair so I could wash my face. The broken dress gaped and flashed my breasts but I was beyond caring. Franco and I were well past a bit of flesh. He'd just become my lifeline in order to get Q back.

"Give me one minute," I croaked through my bile-scalded throat.

Franco nodded, releasing my hair.

Rushing to the wardrobe, I grabbed a thick black jumper and jeans. Shoving the dress down my hips, I quickly yanked the jeans on and threw the sweater over my head, before wedging my feet into some ballet flats.

Franco limped toward me, a slight smirk on his lips. "Have to say that brought back memories of watching you dress into that slinky gold number for Q's dinner party." Then his eyes darkened. "Has he told you why he did that yet?"

My mind flashed back to the past—the mermaid filigree dress that hid nothing and offered everything to the Russian in the white jump suit. Shaking my head, I muttered, "No. But whatever his reasoning, I accept it. I knew even then he wasn't as bad as he came across. I think I loved him the moment you forced me to bow."

Franco half-smiled. "I only forced you because I understood the look in his eyes. He'd never had that look before."

Going to him, I slung his arm over my shoulders, taking some of his weight. "What look?" We hobbled to the exit.

It was good to keep my mind on other things. It distracted me from what Q might be suffering—kept me levelheaded.

Franco sighed. "Lust…attraction…maybe even love. Who knows." Giving me a quick smile, he said, "Either way. I knew he wanted you, and I wanted to see him happy."

Franco opened the doorknob; we made our way slowly into the corridor.

This is going to take forever. He's too injured.

I didn't want to seem ungrateful for having Franco's help, but we needed to go. We needed to hunt. How could we do that if Franco could barely walk and needed urgent surgery?

Franco hissed as I propelled him faster. "There's a plan in motion. It's not just us. So you don't have to panic."

My heart raced. *Q—hold on.* "What plan?"

"We had a discussion after Q rescued you. We knew the likelihood of them coming for him was high, so we had a system put in place. It's already started." Franco looked at his watch. "I'd say about twenty-five minutes ago—the moment they barged into my room and beat the fuck out of me."

My body grew hot then cold, roasting then frigid. I wanted to split myself into an army of people and scour Italy for Q. I wanted to know what plan was in effect.

He can't die. I won't let him.

The elevator up ahead pinged, delivering its cargo like a tsunami of weapons and badges. Franco and I slammed to a stop.

"What the—" he muttered as a hoard of policemen all in smart black uniforms and silver brocade rushed toward us.

We stood like an island as a sea of police officers darted past, disappearing into the room we'd just vacated. I blinked. Was *this* part of the plan? Enlisting the local force to help us track Q?

The hair on the back of my neck stood up. If they were here to help then great…but if they weren't…

Franco tensed, pushing me away to stand on his own two feet. His jaw ticked as he shoved his bloody, thumb-missing hand into his pocket.

A detective with slicked black hair and greying temples climbed off the lift, coming toward us. He narrowed his eyes. "Are you okay, sir? Ma'am?"

My heart latched itself to my voice box; I squeaked some

stupid reply. My instincts were prickling, warning. I didn't like him. I didn't like this. Which was ridiculous as they were the law. We'd done nothing wrong—we were the victims. So why did I suddenly feel like a criminal?

The detective's gaze fell on Franco, taking in his bloody clothing and protective stance. "What happened here tonight?"

Franco glowered. "Nothing. What are you doing here?"

The officer scowled. "We don't have to explain our presence to you. Especially when it looks as if we've come to a scene of a serious crime." His eyes pierced mine, looking me up and down.

I was aware of how I must look: white face, smudged mascara, and a jitter that looked as if I was high and needing my next fix. How could I explain the adrenaline in my system was from watching my lover be shot and marched away?

"Ma'am. Did this man hurt you?" His hand fell to his holstered weapon.

"What? No!" I leapt in front of Franco. "Not at all. Look we—"

"Tess—shut up." Franco yanked me back by my jeans loop. Looking at the officer, he snapped, "You're interfering. This is a private undercover operation. Now, let us pass."

The officer's eyebrow rose; his chest puffed out, swelling with testosterone. "You're not going anywhere until I determine what occurred here tonight." Taking out a notepad from his breast pocket, he scanned his notes. "Do you know anything about an indecent exposure incident that happened about thirty minutes ago? A passer-by said they saw a disturbance in one of the suites on this floor." His eyes zeroed in on Franco. "According to witnesses, a woman whose face was covered was forced against the glass while an unseen male had intercourse with her. That wouldn't be you, would it?"

Franco threw me an incredulous look, his eyes yelling a message: *Q did what?*

I would've blushed if I had any blood left in my head—it'd all congealed in my feet leaving me ice cold. The *one* time I let go and it landed me in police custody.

Shit, what could I do? *Lie.*

My instincts said to run. I needed to run before they—

"You're under arrest," the officer announced. "I don't care if you had nothing to do with that charge. You're covered in blood and running from the location of a complaint. You're both coming with us until we can find the truth of this matter."

Oh no. *No!*

"Sir, it isn't what you think. Please—" I begged.

"Tess, shut—" Franco began, only to groan in agony as the officer grabbed his elbow, tearing his hand from his pocket to secure metal handcuffs.

"*Che cazzo?!*" The officer's mouth fell open, staring at Franco's butchered hand. The tie wrapped around the stump dripped crimson all over the pristine snowy carpet. The detective glared at us, confusion and a slight thread of fear entering his black gaze. "Someone better start talking about what happened here tonight."

I wanted to wake up from this nightmare. This was beyond the realms of comprehension. Q had been stolen by men who would kill him—and we were being detained by a foreign police force who would delay us until it was too late.

A bubble of insane tearful laughter threatened to break.

Franco snapped, "Get me to the hospital. I'm not in a position to answer questions, as you can clearly see."

Policemen returned from scouting our suite. "All clear, boss. No one's there. However, we found blood and believe there were a few men who have left the premises."

My heart lurched. Yes, they'd left. *With Q.* Hell, this was awful. My mind raced with thoughts of stealing a gun. I could hold one of them hostage to get out of the building.

But Franco couldn't run. *Shit.*

"Arrest the woman. Take her for questioning. Take the man to the hospital."

Franco and I yelled at the same time: "No! I have to go with him." "She has to come with me."

338

The detective pursed his lips, deliberating. Finally, he muttered, "Fine. Take them both to the hospital. I expect to be able to interview them in a few hours."

I bit my lip, fighting the horror that had become my life as my arms were wrenched behind my back and the cold lick of handcuffs settled around my wrists. Franco wasn't cuffed, only barred by two large policemen, caging him in with black uniforms and unclipped guns.

"Come on," a policeman grumbled. I trembled, fighting another wave of nausea. Once again—this was my fault. It was my breasts strangers had seen. My little exposé that ended with us being marched away like heathens.

Then livid anger filled me. If these men turned out to be the reason Q died, I would hunt down every last one and murder them in their sleep.

I wouldn't let them stop me from finding him. I'd become a wanted fugitive before I let that happen.

Franco looked over his shoulder. His emerald eyes looked like terrible glinting gems. *"Ne dis rien. Tout est sous contrôle."* Don't say a word. I have everything under control.

I wanted to trust him. I wanted to believe that whatever plan was in action it would save Q even while we rotted in some Italian cell. But pessimism was my new friend and the black void of grief tempted, called to me.

We were stuffed into the lift side by side. Franco bent his head to my ear. "He isn't lost, Tess. He put a tracker in your engagement ring—did you not think he'd do the same precaution for himself? Especially when he knew he'd stirred up the attention of fuckwits who would try to kill him?"

I froze, his hot breath on my ear giving me much needed information.

I kept my voice low, aware of the six other men in the lift with us. "He's got a tracker in a ring?" Q didn't wear jewellery. And we weren't married yet so he didn't have a wedding ring.

Franco shook his head. "Not a ring. Deeper than that." He tapped the underside of his wrist, raising an eyebrow. The puzzle slotted into place.

Oh, my God. Q wore a tracker.

Not in jewellery or clothing or something that could easily be removed. He'd gone further than that. He'd given himself the best chance at being found even if they stripped him naked and threw away all his possessions.

He'd tagged himself like a pet—micro-chipped his body so his army of guards could follow his trail and bring him home.

He wasn't lost.

It was just up to us to find him before it was too late.

Time had become my number one nemesis.

Four hours.

Four long, excruciating, teeth-clenching hours.

Every second drifted me further away from Q. Every minute built a wall I would have to clamber over to find him. Is this how he felt when searching for me? This crippling helplessness?

Tick...

Tock...

Franco had been rushed to surgery to reattach his thumb. He refused to allow them to put him under, settling instead with a local anaesthetic to endure the procedure.

His list of injuries curdled my stomach.

Mild concussion. Dislocated shoulder. Twisted kneecap. Missing thumb. Not including the multiple contusions, bruises, and scrapes from the assholes who'd almost killed him in order to get to Q.

I lived an entire lifetime in those four hours. More than one. Multiple.

I went insane—hemmed in a private room, barricaded by two police officers waiting for Franco. At least they'd removed the handcuffs, but I was no less a prisoner.

My mind was my enemy, constantly flinging horror and torture of Q's demise. I finally gritted my teeth, humming nonsense under my breath, just to keep my brain occupied and not conjuring such awfulness.

Three times the officers tried to question me. Three times I refused. I wouldn't talk—not until I knew what Franco wanted me to say. I wasn't privy to what was in motion outside our sad little group. I didn't want to ruin Q's chances any more than I already had by being so reckless in a foreign country and getting arrested.

I looked up as the white door swung open. Franco was wheeled into the room by an orderly. One arm was in a sling, leading to a thick bandage around his hand. Only the tips of his fingers showed.

His face was black and yellow as bruises painted him like a watercolour.

I shot off the bed where I'd been going mad with waiting. The door swung closed behind the man in scrubs. "Are you okay? Did it work?" I looked at the bandage, eyeing it for any sign of a thumb tip. My eyes widened. "But there's no…"

"They tried, but the way the cocksuckers smashed the joint means it's pretty much useless. Plus, this is a local hospital. They don't have too many specialists on call unless I'm flown elsewhere."

I was torn. Completely cleaved down the centre. I wanted to run after Q but I didn't want Franco to live a thumbless life. Hell, that was the most important finger. I would be on my own. "Well, go. Tell me what the plan is and leave. I'll do the rest."

He shook his head. "I signed the paperwork already. Even if they did manage to attach it, I'd have to stay in for observation for a week. This way, I only have to pop in for a check-up in twenty-four hours." His eyes flashed. "I refuse to sit on my broken ass. Not while he's out there. A thumb can wait—we don't know…" his voice trailed off, filling me with terror.

We don't know what they're doing to him.

The sentence was left unsaid but it might as well have been scrawled in permanent marker and left to drift around like a haunting banner. It was undeniable which made it all the more awful.

"As much as I'm grateful for your loyalty to him, you can't throw away your thumb."

He shrugged. "I'm a millionaire thanks to Q's generosity. Plus, he's fucking loaded. If I save his scrawny ass, I know he won't mind forking out for some crazy expensive, new-fangled robot thumb." Franco locked the wheelchair with his good arm, flipped up the footholds, and held out his hand. "Now help me up. We're leaving."

Going to the side, I grabbed his elbow. I did the best I could to hoist his bulk from the chair. The moment he stood, he limped to the wardrobe where the doctors had put his clothes and with no embarrassment whatsoever untied the backless hospital gown and let it fall.

I coughed, averting my eyes. But not before I got an eyeful. He was built bigger than Q. Stocky, hard-packed muscle that wasn't as elegant as Q's sleek sensual form. But what he lacked in sexual appeal he made up for in sheer power.

He hopped and cursed, wrangling his trousers up over the bandage around his knee to his hips. With his face scrunched in concentration, he zipped his fly one-handed. Once that part of him was covered, he turned, holding out his blood-stained shirt.

"Help me. I can't do it."

Keeping my eyes downcast, I took the clothing and moved to his side to carefully remove his arm from his sling. "Did they put your shoulder back into place?" I kept my voice low, distracting him as I pushed the cuff over his hand, drawing it upward.

He gritted his teeth. "Yes, it's workable, just sore. It'll swell soon, and it'll get worse before it gets better, but I'll live."

"You've done it before?"

He chuckled, wincing as I wrapped the shirt around his back. "I've been with Q for a while, Tess. I've been in worse condition. *He's* been in worse. And we've both walked away, while the ones who challenged us didn't."

His body vibrated with dangerous tension; I allowed his strength to wash over me. Being around him half-naked made me extremely uncomfortable, but also strangely calmed me. I trusted in his abilities to bring Q home.

Franco placed his arm back for me to slink up the other cuff, settling the shirt into place. Once it clung to his shoulders, he faced me with a quirked eyebrow. "Do it up, please. Missing a thumb over here."

I laughed which turned into a weird snort-sob thing.

Q, I'm missing you so damn much.

I wanted someone to reassure me. I wanted a crystal ball to know he would survive and stay in one piece until we found him. It felt so wrong doing such normal things when every instinct inside wanted to hunt and murder.

Franco dropped the quip in his voice. "We'll find him, Tess. You'll see. The only one losing any body parts is me. After all, I'm the bodyguard. I take the hard hits so he doesn't have to." His large knuckles brushed under my eye, catching a renegade tear. "Believe me. I'm not going to let him die."

Franco was strong; I had to trust him. It was just easier thought than done.

The door swung open just as I finished securing the last button. A doctor, with hair so black it looked like polished obsidian, blinked in surprise. "What do you think you are doing? You're not discharged. Get back into bed, sir."

Franco growled under his breath. "I'm done. I've allowed you to poke and prod me. But now I'm leaving. I thank you for your expertise, but you can't hold me against my will."

"He might not be able to. But I can." The detective with black hair and silver temples appeared behind the doctor. His smooth jaw was stiff with authority; his body pompous and full of power granted to him by the badge over his heart. "Seeing as you're well enough to check yourself out, you're well enough to come in for questioning."

Nodding to a few of the men standing outside, he ordered, "Please escort these two to the station. I'll interrogate them myself."

Two policemen entered the room, pushing aside the doctor who clutched a clipboard to his chest. He didn't protest as one man came for me and the other beelined for Franco.

Franco shoved the scrawny cop away and made a show of shrugging into his blazer unassisted. Once the black jacket was in place, he gingerly looped his sore arm back into the sling. "If you want to start questioning, I have one. You have something of mine. Two things actually, and I want them back. My guns. Where are they?"

I jerked away as a pudgy baby-faced cop took my elbow. "Take your hands off me." I glowered. I had no intention of being separated from Franco. I didn't care who they were and what law they were upholding. I would fight all of them.

The detective bared his teeth. "Yes, and it's another reason why we are going to talk. Bringing weapons into Italia is a serious offence. I hope you have the necessary international paperwork, otherwise it could be a long holiday for both of you behind bars."

My heart sped up as panic filled my stomach. "Please, this is a terrible misunderstanding. Let us go. We'll come back for questioning when we've done what we need to do."

When I've got my fiancé back. When he's in my arms and home. Then they could lock me up and torture me for all I cared. At least Q would be safe.

The detective laughed—obnoxiously loud. "You think you can just *pop* in whenever you feel like it? Who the hell do you think you are? Some uppity tourist thinking they can flaunt the rules. I'm sick of your kind coming to my country and not respecting our laws. You're coming with us. And there is nothing you can say to prevent that." He nodded at the man beside me.

I cried out as he shoved me forward.

Franco swore as he suffered the same treatment.

Corralling us through the door, we were pushed down a long white corridor reeking of bleach and medicine. Bright lights pained my eyes as my brain worked overtime.

Think! I had to get out of this.

A wash of hot anger stole my panic, leaving me clearheaded and completely in control.

Q gave me his company. I was his intended. He'd given me nine billion pieces of power.

Money was power.

Use it.

Straightening my back, I planted my feet onto the linoleum and swung around.

The detective jerked to a halt. His badge was at eyelevel and I latched onto his name. Sergio Ponzio.

"Listen here, Mr. Ponzio. We're not criminals. We don't have time to explain but you're making a big mistake."

Sergio's black eyes flashed with a mixture of annoyance and mirth. "Really? And why is that? To me it looks as if I'm doing my job." Rubbing his chin, he tapped his foot dramatically. "Please…by all means. Enlighten me."

"Tess…don't," Franco hissed.

I wasn't going to mention Q. I didn't want pompous asshats getting in the way of whatever plan Q had in motion to find him. But I wouldn't put up with being manhandled and kept from doing my part in saving him.

Standing as tall as I could in my scruffy ballet flats, I snapped, "You're to let us go this instant. This man is my personal protection, and we have urgent business to attend to back in France. You do *not* want to delay me."

I wished I oozed wealth like Q. I wished I knew how to wield something so ostentatious but powerful. I was a fraud in jeans and a jumper but conviction radiated in my eyes.

Sergio's face darkened. "Was that a *threat*, miss?"

Oh, shit.

I cried out as an officer grabbed my arms, twisting it behind my back. Handcuffs snapped around my wrists, bruising the bone beneath.

"Wait!"

No. Please no.

Franco yelled, "Get your hands off her. She's the owner of *Moineau* fucking Holdings. Do your homework and you'll find out she's about to marry Frances' most powerful CEO." Franco cursed as a cop grabbed his unslinged arm, handcuffing him to his belt.

Then the corridor erupted with rapid chiming.

A cell-phone.

Everyone froze. Franco lowered his head, his body rolling in on itself. "Fuck." His eyes latched onto mine.

My instincts soared out of control. Whoever was calling had something to do with Q.

I went crazy. Twisting, turning, trying to get free. I had to answer that phone. "Please. Let us answer it!"

Sergio planted a hand on my sternum, slamming me against the wall. The cuts on my shoulder blade from Q screamed. "Behave. Otherwise we'll be carrying you out of here in a straitjacket."

Chiming escalated to techno bells and squeals. The phone's ring sliced my brain; I thought I'd pass out if it wasn't answered.

Franco snapped, "You have to let me get that. You're messing with things you don't understand."

I froze, never taking my eyes from him. My heart hammered in hope. Franco would get us free.

Sergio laughed. "And what don't I understand? Feel free to inform me because I'm dying to know."

The phone ceased its awful chime.

My heart died with it. Q—something had happened, and we hadn't picked up the phone. Had we ruined his chance of survival? Had these bastards taken away our one shot at finding him alive?

"Franco," I whimpered. "What are we going to do?"

Sergio crossed his arms, watching us carefully.

Franco spoke only to me. "I didn't answer, so the next stage of the operation is in effect. They'll assume I'm dead and go straight to Blair as team leader."

My face drained of all feeling. Would this unknown Blair come through for us? Would he be as ruthless and focused as Franco? God, I hoped so.

Franco softened. "Don't worry. They'll find him."

"Find who?" Sergio jumped in.

Franco lost his peace, looking like a monster confined to a cage. A monster who would gladly kill to get free. "The man you're stopping us from saving, you fucking asshole. If he dies while you're acting out some egotistical power trip, you're going to be very fucking sorry."

Sergio's face glowed with righteous happiness. "Threat number two. You're now classified as high risk prisoners, and I have full right to detain you until I feel you aren't a risk to my fellow officers."

Grabbing my elbow, he forced me forward. "Let's go. A cell has your name on it."

I had nothing left to lose. Nothing left to hide because if they locked me up, I knew in my bones I would never see Q again. I would die alone. I would cease to exist the moment I felt Q's life snip from my own. "Please! It wasn't a threat. It's the truth." I swallowed tears. "They took him. Quincy Mercer. Five men came and took him. You have to believe us!"

Sergio didn't say another word as he stomped us through the hospital, past gawking patients and wide-eyed nurses.

With a punch to the large swinging doors of the exit, Sergio dragged me from bright hospital to dark evening.

A patrol car waited at the curb.

I struggled. "No! You don't have any reason to arrest us. No reason at all!"

Sergio nodded for one of his men to open the car door. "No reason? Care to explain why pedestrians reported a topless woman pressed against the glass." His eyes flew between Franco and me.

Franco raised his eyebrow in my direction. "Damn fucking Mercer. He always has to go one step too far." He caught my eye, a half-smile on his lips. "Always cleaning up his mess."

My tummy clenched, remembering Q inside me. The burn of him cutting my shoulder. I'd give anything to be curled up in bed with him talking, watching a movie.

I'd sell my soul to find him unharmed.

Bowing my head, I mumbled, "That was me. I take full responsibility. Can you write me a ticket and let me go?"

Sergio chuckled. "Public indecency is more than a ticket, miss. But it's above that now. I believe there's a conspiracy here. I believe some man—possibly not this man with you— but another, forced you to have intercourse. I also believe the sexual activity was interrupted by someone in a jealous rage and is now injured—by him." Sergio pointed at Franco. "And until I understand the full story, no-one is leaving, *capisci?*"

"It wasn't me. I didn't hurt the man—but they fucking hurt me." Franco pointed wryly to his bandaged hand and sling. "As you can see by evidence A."

Sergio's eyes narrowed. "Just how many men had a turn with you, miss? A threesome? A bloody orgy in my city? How many infractions do you want to add to this tally?"

Franco shook his head, breathing hard. "It's not like that. If you stopped and listened for one goddamn second you'd be saved a lot of paperwork and possibly a man's life!"

Sergio lost his smooth good-cop routine, launching himself at Franco. Shoving him against the side of the car, he grunted, "We found blood on the carpet. And a bullet casing by the window. If we find out the bullet matches the guns we took from you, you're in serious fucking trouble. So don't start waving your dick around here because it won't fucking work."

Spinning away, he dragged a hand through his hair. "Get them in the car. Let's go."

My heart infested with panic as someone pressed my shoulders, shoving me into the vehicle. The vinyl seats squeaked as I fell sideways. I couldn't push myself up with my wrists handcuffed behind my back.

Tears bubbled in my spine but I refused to let them drip.

Franco's body partially landed on mine. He grunted in pain but managed to sit upright and with a bit of effort drag me into a sitting position. "You okay?"

My mind swam. How could this have got completely out of control?

Tick...

Tock...

Every passing minute took Q further and further away. I didn't want to look at a clock. I didn't want to see just how much time was being wasted by idiots of the Italian police force.

Q. I'm so sorry. This is all my fault.

A sob clawed up my throat.

Franco patted my knee. "Don't worry, Tess. It will be okay."

Sergio climbed into the front seat, looking at us through the barred partition. "That's what you think."

The interview room was frozen-over hell.

All metal and mirror and steel. My hands and feet were blue with a mixture of fear and ice. I'd been uncuffed and thrown into the room about fifteen minutes ago.

Franco had been taken somewhere else.

I paced around the small space like a caged animal. My brain wouldn't stop whizzing. My heart wouldn't stop clanging. Claustrophobia clawed at my throat as the walls frosted over with icicles, crowding closer and closer and *closer*. Burying me alive in an icy tomb where Q would never find me.

I'm alone.

Curling my hands, I shoved the self-pity away. I refused to bow to such useless emotions. I would get out of this. I would find Q. I would find him alive, and I would marry him the second I fell into his arms.

The heavy door clanked open.

Sergio Ponzio entered looking like a stuck-up peacock with way too much power. I hated the uncaring glint in his eyes. The unforgiving jaded look that said he'd heard every story, listened to every lie. He was finished having people make a fool of him.

Which was fine. I understood that. But when he was so blind he couldn't see the truth—putting another's life in jeopardy, then I couldn't understand that. I couldn't control the lava of frustration and hatred flowing in my veins. I didn't know how long I'd be able to stop myself from ripping his heart out—because he obviously didn't have one.

"Please. Sit," he said, pointing at the metal chairs.

I moved stiffly, sitting with my hands balled tightly in my lap. I had enough infractions to battle through, without adding battery and assault to a police chief.

"Water?" His bushy eyebrow rose.

I shook my head, looking into the top right corner of the room.

Enemy. Saboteur. Betrayer.

The clock.

Tick...

Tock...

It was four a.m. Q had been taken almost five hours ago. Six life-altering, terror-filled hours.

The sob that built like a thunderstorm inside threatened to break free. It took all my strength to force it back down.

"Name?"

I glared from beneath my brow. I wanted to spit and tell him to shove his damn questions. But I had to cooperate. I had to be as polite and demure as possible if I had any chance of talking my way out of this.

Don't get angry. Stay calm.

"Tess Snow."

"Nationality."

"Australian."

He looked up, a smile tugging his lips. "Long way from home. It's not the first time I've had to get tough with a drunken countryman of yours, or slap a citation for disorderly conduct."

I ignored that. I didn't want to interact at all—let alone reminisce about his other trophies. He viewed me as a troublemaker. I meant to come across as the opposite.

I'm rich. I'm powerful. I'm Q's.

Besides, I no longer felt Australian. In fact, after spending so much time with Q, I'd even begun to think in French, trading English as my favoured language, blending the two.

I'm no longer Tess Snow.

My eyes flared. "I gave you the wrong name."

Sergio scowled. "You're lying again? You do realize every lie makes your case worse." He shook his head, tutting under his breath, "You seem to like breaking the rules." His eyes fell to my jumper-covered breasts. "I admit, I would've liked to see the show you put on and not just write the reports."

You fucking pervert.

My spine stiffened. "I'm not lying. I *am* Tess Snow. But I'm also about to become Tess Mercer. My fiancé has already given me ownership of his fortune and I wield the power of the Mercer name."

His dark eyes tightened; face twitched. "Mercer?"

I sensed a crack. *Please let it be a crack.* "Yes of *Moineau* Holdings. Franco told you that. If you know of the company and the CEO, you'd be wise to release me and my employee."

Sergio chuckled, scraping his chair back as he popped the buttons of his uniform jacket. "You sure about that, Miss Snow? You're not lying again, are you?"

I ground my teeth. "How do you explain me staying in one

of the most expensive hotels in Rome?" I rolled my eyes. "Did you even look at the check-in registry? Quincy Mercer—my fiancé—will be on the registration."

Sergio placed his wrists on the table, linking his fingers together in a threatening display. "See, that's where your little story falls apart. A man named Joseph Roy checked in with no extra guest into the suite earlier this evening."

The breath in my lungs clogged, but then cleared in a rush. Of course Q wouldn't travel under his real name. Not now. Not with men hunting him.

I winced as a spike to the heart caught me by surprise. It didn't matter what precautions he'd taken—he'd still be stolen. *Stay alive. Please stay alive.*

I placed my elbows on the table, pressing my forehead against my palms. The world had become too much. I never thought I would want to be in captivity again but at least being the one stolen lent a certain luxury to my fate. I either survived or died. I wasn't responsible for someone else. I didn't feel the weight of an entire galaxy pressing down upon me with every passing second of failure.

Tick...

Tock...

Sergio kicked back his chair, standing over me. "Do you wish to change any of the details you've given? Last chance to stop lying before I go run your records."

I looked up. I didn't have any effort to speak. I shook my head.

Without a word, he disappeared.

Tick...

Tock...

The clock taunted me with every passing second. One minute passed, then ten, then twenty.

My body vibrated with the need to run. I couldn't sit there for too much longer without going certifiably insane. I felt so *useless.*

Finally the door opened. Sergio returned with a stack of

paper and a blank face.

Grabbing the chair, he shuffled closer to the table, placing everything in front of him. He dragged out the suspense, spreading the papers, fanning them into some sort of order, driving me mad.

"Do you know what I found when I called up your file?" he asked, almost softly. He'd lost some of the arrogant tone. He still wasn't friendly, but he seemed...what? Open to listening. Less likely to laugh and throw me in a cell and swallow the key?

I sat straighter, feeding off his change of mood. Hope trilled through me, fast and sweet. "I don't know." Glancing at the upside down copies, I couldn't read them—all in Italian.

I'd never contemplated if I had a file. Briefly, when I returned home to Australia after Q sent me back, I wondered why the police hadn't come knocking. I'd been reported as missing after all—but no one came to question, no one asked a thing.

Sergio held up a piece of paper. "It says here you were listed as missing by the Australian Federal Police. Then a few weeks later, your parents, Stephen and Mary Snow, closed your file under pretence of death overseas and asked for a death certificate."

My chair legs squeaked against the floor as I jumped in dismay. A rush of grief mixed with disbelief. My own parents told the police to stop looking for me? They'd been so eager to close that messy chapter and become the grieving parents. All to garner the sympathy vote at their next bowling club rally.

I always knew they didn't love me. It wasn't news, but it still hurt like a bitch.

Sergio watched my reaction, but I kept my tormenting emotions free from my impassive face.

He continued, "Your file was closed, but then reopened when you magically reappeared, with no flight manifest or record of how you entered the country, and slotted right back into life with"—his eyes dropped to the paperwork—"Brax

Cliffingstone.

"You retuned to university, finished your degree, then a month later picked up and flew to France."

Shuffling the pages, he said, "Why wasn't there a wrap-up interview from your disappearance. Why was there no closure or interrogation on your supposed kidnapping, brought to the attention of the AFP by Brax Cliffingstone? Care to explain how you had the AFP close your file with no conclusion whatsoever?"

The all-consuming love I had for my monstrous master overflowed. It was like swallowing a bowl of colourless light, trickling through my body, giving me strength I sorely need.

I laughed.

Q.

He tampered with my file. Somehow, he had contacts to ensure his anonymity and unique charity remained a secret. There was no explaining how I came into his company, or talking away the length of my stay at his chateau. So he did what he had to. He swept it all away.

God, I loved him. I'd never met a man with more resources, intelligence, or a bigger heart than him. And he was mine. And I was failing him by allowing this stupid cop to detain me.

I was done.

"Quincy Mercer can explain. Let me go and I'll fetch him for you."

Sergio ran a finger along his bottom lip. "Yes, and that brings me to him. You say you're together? But I don't see any mention of a marriage announcement or any news related articles of your relationship."

Tick...

Tock...

I didn't care. It no longer mattered.

I was getting out of there.

Now.

Crossing my arms, I demanded, "I want my phone call."

He glowered, his black eyes battering me with law-keeping authority. But I wasn't ruffled. I glowered right back, not backing down.

Finally, he huffed. "Fine." He stalked to the door, holding it open. "This way."

The moment light from the corridor bounced into the interrogation room, my heart leapt from my chest and flew away. Flew to find Q. Flew to give him hope.

I'm coming.

We're coming.

I struggled to keep my feet slow and plodding as Sergio guided me through a typical police station with cubicle workstations, brown walls, and oscillating ceiling fans. The reek of burned coffee hung stagnant in the air.

He stopped beside a desk strewn with notes and empty cups. He pointed to a phone partially buried beneath manila files. "You have two minutes."

Not for the first time, I thanked my photographic memory. Ever since Q gave me the note hidden in the pocket of the dress I'd worn back to Australia, I'd memorized his office number. It'd been embossed in gold on the heavy parchment of his business card.

By knowing his number, I felt like I'd never be too far from him—even while I slept beside Brax at night and went to university by day.

I also knew he allowed the office line to link to his home after hours. I just hoped either Frederick picked up or Suzette. Either would do. Both had Q's power behind them. They would get Franco and me free.

Picking up the receiver, I curled over the handset, punching in the number. It connected.

And rang.

And rang.

And *rang.*

Please pick up. Terror squashed my hope like a bug. This was my only chance—who knew when I'd get another one.

Who knew how much more time would pass.

Sergio looked at his watch.

Finally the ringing stopped, clicking into connection.

"Bonjour?"

Masculine.

For a flicker of a second, I suffered a stab of grief. I'd wanted to talk to Suzette. To lean on the girl who was so strong and my friend.

"Frederick," I whispered.

"Tess?"

My heart bounced, whizzing into action. Frederick would get things done. He'd get us out.

"Yes, it's me. Look, something happened." The tears I'd been fighting all rushed in a quake, obstructing my throat. I forced through, cursing the wobble in my tone. "They took him."

"It's okay. I know. It's all under control."

His soothing voice robbed me of strength, knowing Q's network of people were on the hunt. It wasn't just me. I wasn't alone in fighting for his life. "Thank God."

At that point, I didn't care about myself. All I cared about was Frederick using the resources to find Q. I completely forgot about my predicament or why I'd called.

My mind shut down as I went into shock.

"Tess? You still there?"

I clutched the receiver, wishing I could stuff myself down the phone line and be with him. I wanted to be beside the man who Q called his best friend.

What about his other best friend?

Shit, Franco.

"Frederick. I need your help." I pulled myself together, running a hand through my hair. "Franco and I—we're in jail. We need you to get us out."

I tensed, waiting for a barrage of questions. But he just chuckled. "You're about ten minutes too late. Already done. You'll be out within the hour."

My mouth hung open. "Ho—how?"

"Money buys a lot of things, and contacts in high places is one of them." His voice dropped. I pressed the phone harder to my ear. "He's okay, Tess. The tracker stays active as long as there's a heartbeat. It's programed to emit a new signal if that changes."

My heart seized. "What do you mean?"

"Well, we'll know if they cut it out. The frequency would be interrupted. We'll also know if they..."

If they what...

My heart lurched. He didn't have to say anymore. I knew. "If he dies...." My eyes turned blind, filling with liquid.

Frederick murmured, "It's okay. That won't happen. But yes. As long as his heart is beating, the tracker will guide us to him."

I wanted to scream! I wanted to hunt every cocksucking motherfucking trafficker and drain them until they turned from human to withered corpse.

The sweetness inside rapidly faded in favour of ruthlessness. I grew harder—colder.

He's still alive. Focus on that.

"Do you know where? Where is he?"

"He's been moved. They've taken him to Spain."

"Spain?"

The voices of the men who'd barged into our suite echoed in my ears. I'd been too afraid of Q being hit and then shot to pay any attention to nationality.

Sergio waved a hand in front of my face, tapping his watch. I wanted to bite his finger for being so cocky and horrible and ruining everything.

"Why? Why did they take him at all?"

Frederick sighed. "Because he pissed off a man called Lynx. And now the bastard wants payback."

Half an hour later Franco and I zoomed in a taxi to the airport. Sergio had escorted us out of the building himself. Glaring as if we'd single-handedly robbed him of any accolades or good-doing by arresting us.

Franco looked as if he would hit him, so I was glad when a taxi coasted past the second the handcuffs were undone.

My fingers were wrapped around Franco's phone, glued to the app that'd turned Q—my amazing tattooed sadistic lover—into a red blip on the screen.

Frederick was right.

Q was in Spain.

And alive. He was still alive.

I jumped a foot as Franco placed a hand on my knee. "You okay?"

He asked that a lot. I hated that I acted as if I needed reassurance. The meek girl I'd been slowly changed, embracing vengeance.

I nodded. I was numb with shock, high on hope, and shaking with terror—but yes, I was okay. "I'm alright."

Franco nodded, leaning into the seat, adjusting his sling with a small groan.

Tearing my eyes from the red blip, I asked, "How about you. How are you holding up?"

His piercing green eyes were tight with pain; his forehead furrowed as whatever painkillers the doctors had given wore off.

He gave me a cold smile, his teeth glinting in the streetlights whizzing past the window. "I'll be a lot happier the minute I've shot some motherfucking rapists." He sighed. "Seriously, I just want to find Mercer and then crash—for a thousand years."

He winced as the taxi bounced over a pothole. Squeezing his eyes, he muttered, "You've always had strong instincts, Tess. Right from the beginning. What are they telling you now?" He kept his eyes closed but his body hummed with tension. "Would you say they're keeping him for ransom or torture?"

Torture.

I didn't need to think. Or guess.

The most morbid conclusion doused my system in horror. No matter how I tried to deny it. I couldn't stop the images.

Fingernails being pulled.

His beautiful strong body being mutilated.

His gorgeous tattoo being sliced from his chest.

My tummy rolled; I slapped a hand over my mouth. Swallowing hard, I forced away the toe-curling images and worked on blanking my mind.

Franco sucked in a breath. "That bad, huh. Shit."

I wouldn't speak my nightmares—I didn't want to give them power. But I did know as long as I was alive, I wouldn't let that happen. Curling my hands, I hissed, "I'm sick of evil intervening with my life. I'm sick of paying a toll for doing nothing more than falling in love. Whoever this bastard is who took Q—he's going to scream before I let him die."

Franco twisted in the seat, his aura thickening, darkening, filling the taxi cab with a threat so ferocious it scared even me. His eyes flashed green fire. "And if I could make that wish come true?"

"What wish?"

"That I'd help you make him scream. That I'd allow you to do the honours to avenge your man. Would you be able to pull the trigger, Tess? Have you fully faced your nightmares to do for Q what he did for you?"

My skin prickled with foreboding. Franco looked cold, calculating, already slipping into the persona of a killer.

My heart thumped harder, my soul churning with a complex mix of right and wrong. Was I bluffing? *Could* I take a life? For all my bravado, when it came down to it—could I make a grown man scream before stealing his life?

"*Shoot her, puta.*"

"*Do it or we'll snap her fingers until you do.*"

I swallowed hard against the bile searing my throat.

Could I once again become a murderer and welcome more grime into my soul?

My eyes closed.

Q sprang to mind. Covered in blood, his incredible beauty ravaged by horror. *They* did that to him.

Gruesome heat.

Blood-smeared men.

Screams.

A cold-hearted power filled me. I was protecting what was mine. *Je suis à lui.* I was his. Retribution superseded right or wrong.

It reverted me to nothing more than a mate fighting for her lover. Delivering justice like for like.

I would rip out the hearts of the men who hurt him. I would willingly butcher and torture and maim.

I didn't want to hurt anyone. I would never stop being haunted by Blonde Hummingbird or Angel. But this time, it was the right thing to do. I wanted to hunt.

Q wanted me to stand by his side and help women who didn't have someone fighting on their behalf. Someone had to clean up the garbage in the world. He trusted me to be strong enough.

I am.

"Yes." My voice sliced through the thick cloud between us, sounding vicious, merciless. "I'm ready to kill."

Franco nodded, his lips twisting into a grim smile. "Who are you, Tess?"

"I'm his. I'm Tess. I'm his *esclave.*"

The final piece that was missing—the final piece that made me *me*—slotted into place. My true identity.

I'm a survivor. I'm strong. I'm ready.

Franco's face darkened with fierce pride. "And what do you want?"

"I want them to die. I want the blood of the men who took him to grow cold and turn to rust."

Franco reached into his holster, pulling out one of the guns Sergio had returned.

Handing it to me, he muttered, "Good answer." His voice dropped to a guttural growl, "I'll be beside you every step."

Chapter Twelve

The sun warms my feathers, the updraft in my wings, linked souls for eternity, you'll now wear my ring

Five minutes after capture

Fucking bastards.

Low life scum. They thought they could come into my life and fucking march me away like some weak prick?

Every step traded my sadness and sense of duty to protect Tess and turned it into livid rage. I saw red. I tasted blood. My body burned for retribution.

I'd done all I needed. We were out of sight—away from Tess. I could strike. My hands balled by my sides as a man with brown hair and wrinkles prodded my ribcage, forcing me off the elevator. My thigh was sticky with blood, seeping into the fabric, but the pain was absent. I had too much else to focus on.

You'll be the first to die.

The lights of the lobby hurt my eyes—stabbing me with

the knowledge I was letting go of the good inside me. I didn't need to unlock the cage this time…the beast took complete control. I was surprised I still thought in words and sentences and not in blood and gore.

I wanted them all dead. Every single one.

I wanted their souls for scaring Tess after everything I'd done to fix her.

Leaving the brightness of the lobby, I slammed to a halt as two non-descript sedans pulled up to the curb. I wouldn't be getting in the car.

Spinning around, I punched the man behind me. My knuckles smashed against cartilage and I smiled. Payback.

"Ah, fuck!" He stumbled backward.

Blood spurted from his nose. The crunch of bone resonated sweetly in my snarling brain. He cursed in Spanish, waving for two men to grab my arms.

I ducked, swinging in their direction, but a third man grabbed me from behind. No doorman saw, no pedestrians passed. Our fight went unnoticed as the men wrenched my arms behind my back, deliberately tugging too far. My shoulders bellowed. The old gunshot wound in my bicep from Red Wolverine screamed. *"Je peux encore vous tuer avec mes mains liées derrière le dos, bâtards."* I can still kill you with my hands tied behind my back, you assholes.

I'd let myself be corralled from the hotel room to protect Tess. It didn't mean I'd go any further without a fight. It would be their blood drawn first. Not mine.

"Stop talking in French. How about we just kill you now—save the trouble?" The man I'd punched fisted me hard in the stomach. I doubled over, winded. Sucking in air, I swallowed the pain.

Shitless, gutless prick.

"You do and how do you explain that to Lynx?"

He froze. "How did you know it was—lucky guess, you bastard. But you're right. Lynx would be pissed."

My voice was breathless, raging with anger. "Let my arms

go and we'll have a fair fight. If I win you fuck off. Tell Lynx you had your ass handed to you by a bigger bastard than him."

The man shook his head, eyes cold and flat. "You know how this will go, Mercer. Stop fighting and get in the fucking car." He punched me again, right in the gut. "Call that incentive."

My stomach throbbed thanks to his knuckles but I refused to buckle. "My incentive is to see you split open and screaming." I stood taller, wishing my arms were free to deliver my threat. "You're right—I do know how this is going to go. And it won't end well for you."

The guy grabbed my hair, tugging hard as if I was a truant schoolboy and not the man who would sever him into pieces.

Kill him.

Wrath steamed my blood, coiling my muscles. I no longer felt any pain—just a cold-hearted need to end them.

He ducked his head, whispering in my ear, "You cause a scene out here, and I'll go back up to that room and put a bullet between the eyes of the slave you were fucking. Rumour has it you have feelings for her. And I bet it would hurt you a lot more watching her die than anything we could do to you." He pulled away. "You disobey and we'll take our frustration out on your woman. Do you want that?"

Love and hatred became the same debilitating emotion.

I loved Tess.

I hated her, too.

She'd bound my hands more effectively than the two bastards holding me.

I had no fucking power. None. All because I would give my life to make sure she was never hurt again. It didn't matter we were out of sight—she was still vulnerable and the perfect leash to make me obey.

My head grew heavy with defeat. I refused to put her in harm's way. Not for anything.

Looking up, I muttered, "Give me your word you won't go back for her. Give me an oath you'll leave her alone, and I'll go with you willingly."

I'll trade my life for hers.

I knew what my future held.

Lynx would live up to his predator name. He chose the feline hunter because of what he liked to do with his victims: play. He loved to drag out their torment. Tearing the tail off the mouse, ripping the ears off a rabbit, draining whatever fight his prey had before snapping their neck. Devouring with no remorse.

I'd witnessed it first-hand. I'd seen the damage he caused. And I would fucking kill him for it.

The man holding my hair glared into my eyes—there was no intelligence but plenty of greed. Suddenly, he let me go, nodding at his men to do the same.

The moment my arms were free, I brought them to my front, rolling my wrists, taunting them with my decision. They eyed me warily, expecting me to strike again. But I'd already played my cards. They knew I wouldn't fight—not here. Not with Tess so close.

The man muttered, "If you come to Spain with no disobedience. You'll have our word. Our orders were to bring you—not to hurt anyone more than necessary." He held out his hand, his lips twisting cruelly. "Shake on it, or I'll have a man go and collect her—she might be good collateral to keep you in line. Unless your honour will do that for you."

Fuck. He knew me better than I liked. If I shook his hand, I would honour the agreement. I wouldn't try and kill them until I'd slaughtered Lynx and dismantled his operation from the inside out.

Protect Tess.

Gritting my teeth, I shoved my hand into his. His dry fingers wrapped around mine, shaking once with a fierce squeeze.

"You don't touch her. I won't touch you. You have my word, and that is law." The phrase I used to say all the time echoed with my past. My law. It was different to the law of society. Mine gave me freedom to be the devil in disguise. It gave me the right for vengeance.

I would be kept alive for now—at least until I arrived in Spain. Lynx would drag this out—toying with me, trying to make me crack with his fucking mind games. I was his prized accomplishment. He'd become the reaper who destroyed Q Mercer.

All the goodness Tess instilled inside me slowly trickled out, leaving my conscience like a dry river bed with nothing but daggers for thoughts.

Ending the handshake, I turned and climbed into the back of the vehicle. I kept my temper hissing in the background of my mind. I would be prepared to strike—but not yet.

A gun pressed against my side as a man settled in the seat beside me. His tanned Spaniard skin melted into the darkness of the evening.

"Lynx will be honoured by your presence, Mercer. I believe he has a night full of festivities."

My gut churned, but that was the extent of my fear. I refused to let the useless emotion dictate me. Fear wouldn't stop the future. Fear would only ruin my chance at *saving* my future.

I embraced livid anger, nursing it, flaming it.

The cars pulled away from the curb; I didn't look back. I didn't glance up to our room or try to glimpse a tearful Tess. I didn't focus on what I was leaving behind. I focused on what I would become in order to survive.

No one said a word as we navigated the streets of Rome, heading toward the private terminal at the airport.

The journey didn't last long. Too fast.

We pulled up outside a private hangar and a gun prodded my side. I climbed out of the car.

A captor demanded, "Hold out your hands."

I expected restraints, so I didn't resist as a cable-tie wrapped around my wrists. Once disabled, they marched me toward a small jet. I glimpsed my plane a few metres away. The white fuselage rested under a cloak of stars and clouds. The gold Q and sparrows on the wingtips looked as if it waved goodbye—sending me off to a battle I probably wouldn't win.

The air crackled with testosterone. Guns pressed my lower back, shoving me up the plane's steps. I entered the dark brown interior of the aircraft.

Lowering my head, I narrowed my eyes at the two men standing in the aisle. More men crowded behind me, blocking any escape.

Shit, I was in for more than champagne and soft blankets.

Calm. I felt calm.

Furious. I felt furious.

"Take my warning seriously, you cunts. Every hit you deliver, I'll repay you a hundred times worse." Growling low and deep, I added, "Kill me, and I'll fucking haunt you for eternity."

Tess.

The love for her no longer had space anymore—it was swamped with lust for murder.

"Lynx told us to bring you in one piece. But he didn't say you couldn't have bruises." The two men in front cracked their knuckles, inching closer. The cramped space of the cabin was a treasonous whore, giving them the upper hand.

There wasn't much I could do. Hands bound. Honour bound. I would bide my time for vengeance.

The first punch came from behind, knocking me like a ping pong into the awaiting fists in front.

Cheekbone.

Spleen.

Ribcage.

Kneecap.

Fists kept swinging and I had no way to hide or reciprocate.

Grunts filled the cabin as they turned me from human to a piece of exercise equipment—pummelling from all angles.

Blackness stole my vision as a well-aimed fist struck my

temple. I collapsed into a chair, breathing hard, tasting blood, hearing the yips and snarls of my inner demons.

Seven men to beat up one who was tied and defenceless.

Seven men who would have no intestines by the time dawn crested.

This was a playground scuffle.

The instant I touched down in Spain the real fun would begin.

Two hours after capture

"We're here."

The car swung into a private estate hidden down a driveway. The high hedges circling the perimeter acted as a natural fence. The property was nowhere near as big as the Mercer chateau, but it nevertheless housed fifteen rooms, numerous lounges, and at least three dungeons to rent. I'd been offered the use of one with any girl I wanted more than once.

From here it looked quaint and picturesque, with lights glowing warmly from rounded sash windows, and trees swaying in the night-time breeze.

The vehicle came to a stop outside the entrance. Someone wrenched open my car door; leaning in, he cuffed me around the back of the head. Fuck me, I ached. My entire body was bruised, hurting even worse than the gunshot in my thigh.

"Get out, Mercer."

I hadn't been cuffed since I was a fucking six years old. I wasn't about to take it when I was almost thirty.

I couldn't stop the cold smile stretching my lips.

Grave mistake. *Huge* mistake.

We were in a completely different country to Tess. My

honour didn't cross borders—I'd kept my vow to go to Spain willingly. But we'd arrived and all promises were over.

Elegantly—or as much as I could with a beat up body—I stepped from the car. The guard moved away, grinning at my obedience. I grinned back. Another man grinned. Fuck, we all grinned at each other.

Fucking pricks.

I struck.

With my bound wrists, it didn't give me the leverage I wanted, but I managed to splay my hands on either side of his skull and tear. I jerked fast and hard as if I uprooted a tree from dirt. And in a way—that was precisely what I did.

The *snap* of his neck echoed in the night sky before his body fell like a useless piece of timber.

"What!" The man who was in charge stomped forward, hands raised. "You fucking—"

I propelled both arms forward, forming one giant fist. The strike caught his chin perfectly, propelling him upright, sending him slamming onto his back.

I stood over him, ignoring my bruises, cut lip, and swollen eye, and invoked more anger to flow. It was the best painkiller—it would keep me free from agony until I had the luxury of relaxing.

"Don't *ever* think you can touch me without paying. It comes with a price and you can't afford it, you fucking scum." I spat on him, kicking dirt over his groaning body. *And I want everyone to know.*

I knew I'd been stalked. I'd taken precautions but not enough. Deliberately. "Touch me again and I'll send you straight to hell."

A strike landed on the base of my skull. I stumbled forward, cursing the rush of sickness and pounding headache. At least I didn't have a migraine. A migraine only came when I tried to rein in the evilness inside.

Tonight I was free. I'd let my humanity go the moment I said goodbye to Tess.

My muscles seized as a gun bruised my spine. "Move, cocksucker." Someone shoved me forward, giving me no choice but to limp ahead with my vision sputtering in and out from the blow to my skull.

The house loomed. I knew without a doubt if I went in there I wouldn't be coming out. But there was no other option. *Trust them. Franco knows what to do.* Franco had a to-do list and he would get it done.

My wrists rubbed together, searching for the hard node beneath my skin. It'd hurt like a motherfucker having it inserted. A small tracking device fully equipped with GPS, different frequencies, and indefinite lifecycle. I'd had the same doctor who'd tended to Tess insert it the morning I got her home.

At the time, I thought I'd gone overboard with precaution, but now I thanked my foresight. This would've happened regardless—I'd pissed off too many people to think I wouldn't suffer. But I would use it to my advantage. I intended to make an example of them. Slaughter their entire business—send a message to the remaining cocksuckers out there that I wasn't weak. That I wouldn't be killed easily. Lynx would be my announcement to anyone stupid enough to come for me. They would know exactly what I would do to trespassers.

I just had to stay alive long enough for back-up to arrive.

The asshole wielding the gun in my spine pushed hard.

I snapped.

Splaying my legs for balance, I spun around, slapping the gun away. The heavy weapon clattered to the driveway.

The guy's nostrils flared as he bent to pick it up.

Kick. Kill.

My leg twitched, and I couldn't stop the urge. My muscles bunched; the tip of my black dress-shoe connected with the underside of his chin. His head snapped backward, sending him sprawling to the irregular stonework of the driveway.

Blood instantly flowed from his mouth, eyes flickering closed.

"For fuck's sake—get Mercer inside!" The leader stalked toward me.

Instead of standing still, waiting for punishment, I prowled forward, pushing my taller form against his in a blatant threat. "I'm capable of stepping into a house on my own accord. I don't trust you and your fucking imbeciles with guns."

Muttering under my breath, I said, *"Tu as environ six heures à vivre. Vis les pleinement."* You have about six hours to live. Enjoy them wisely.

Not waiting for a reply, I headed toward the entrance.

Once again, I pressed the hard node under my skin. A small smidgen of relief soothed my anger. I calculated how long it would take a rescue party to turn up. If Franco had put the plan into effect before they took me, it would be anywhere from six to eight hours before the team would be mobile and on Lynx's doorstep.

I'll go with six hours.

Six hours to keep Lynx talking and away from any particularly life threatening tools.

Raising my bound hands, I knocked on the old-fashioned stain-glass door. The glass depicted a bare forest—tree skeletons in burnt oranges, browns, and blacks.

A memory of coming here thirteen months ago to collect a slave filled my mind—the games I played. The role I embraced of sadistic master buying a woman as if it was a normal transaction.

My heart sped up as the door swung open. I kept my features blank. Disdain dripped from every pour, no longer hiding how much I fucking hated the retard in front of me.

Lynx smiled, his tanned skin gleaming against the dark red of his suit. A black mandarin shirt, coupled with bright crimson shoes, made him look fucking ridiculous. His hair was the usual black mohawk, gelled into submission, while the shorter sides mirrored the same dark red of his trousers and blazer.

"Going on a date, Dante?" I raised an eyebrow. "Dressed like that I'd say you're fishing for cock not pussy." He wasn't gay—just a fucking tosser trying way too hard.

Lynx pursed his lips. He hated that I knew his real name. Dante Emestro. When he'd contacted me five years ago, asking for help with planning permission for an illegal racetrack in a low density area, I'd done my usual background checks. I'd jangled every skeleton, knew every torrid secret. I also knew he'd sold his sister when he turned eighteen, all to gain access to the underbelly of trafficking.

Nasty piece of shit.

His black, soulless eyes glanced at my ruined dinner attire. A smile spread his lips, no doubt taking in the swelling of my face and the multitude of bruises sustained from the journey. "You better thank your fucking stars I'm not gay, Mercer. Or tonight might've ended in a completely different way for you." He licked his lips. "However, I could add something along those lines to the activities if you wish?" He had no facial hair apart from a ridiculous chin strap. I would happily carve it from his face and shove it in his mouth for such a comment.

"I'd be careful, Dante. Don't want another curse added to your reputation."

"What other curse?"

I shrugged. "The curse you've brought upon yourself by bringing me here against my will." I leaned closer, noticing he looked older than his thirty-one years—mainly thanks to cocaine abuse. "I plan on killing you tonight. You're my trophy to show other cunts like you that I'm not going to put up with turf wars or killings."

He laughed loudly. "*You* plan on killing *me*? I think you have it the wrong way around, Mercer." Losing his mirth, he snapped, "You're a fucking fake. And I don't play well with fakes." Looking over my shoulder, he ordered, "Help bring Mr. high and mighty Mercer inside."

A kick landed on my lower back, sending me careening forward. With my hands bound, I couldn't keep my balance and sprawled at his feet. My thigh screamed as the wound sent more blood seeping. A steel-capped boot crunched against the back of my leg, smashing my kneecap into the stone floor.

Fuck! I wanted to howl. But I didn't. I ate the pain. Devouring it just like I would him.

But I couldn't kill him—not yet. I had no way of winning against his crew. My only chance was to drag this out until support arrived. I wouldn't sacrifice myself—not now I had so much to live for.

Tess. Shit, her scent filled my nose. Her cries echoed in my ears. I would see her again. *I will.*

A foot kicked my jaw. "Payback, asswipe." A river of blood ran down my throat—I'd bitten my tongue. I kept my lips smashed together. The agony fed my anger, wreaking havoc on my nervous system.

"Alright, enough. I need him conscious for the rest. Pick him up," Lynx snapped.

Wrath built faster. I warmed my hands by its licking flames. Patience. Fucking patience.

Two men hoisted me under my arms, dragging me upright. My eyes latched onto the closing door. The moment it locked, I mentally began a countdown.

Six hours and counting.

Don't do anything reckless. Keep him talking. Stay alive.

I had a fucking wedding to go to tomorrow.

Shrugging off the men, I stood tall, taking in the foyer. The typical signs of drugs, weapons, and broken women were prevalent.

"Like my latest editions, Mercer?" Dante pointed at two girls crawling into the entrance hall wearing nothing but a collar and pair of crotchless knickers. Their eyes were down, their skin pale.

My hands curled. Purple bruises marked their ribcages, yellow stains of old abuse, and malnourishment glazed their eyes.

I doubted they'd been there for long but already they existed in a grave, waiting for their soul to give up so they could be free.

"They'll be mine by the end of the evening." I already pictured the tenderness of Mrs. Sucre feeding them and the friendship of Suzette putting them back together. And Tess. She would be there—my queen—the woman who glued every part of me into a better human being.

Dante smiled—it was cold, malicious, and if I hadn't dealt with bastards like him all my life, I would've shit myself. But I had. I no longer felt their evil. I absorbed it—waiting till I could boomerang it back, making them suffer.

I liked to think they'd invited the grim reaper into their home.

"So proud. You won't be walking away with any of my merchandise, Mercer." Dante laughed. "Your pride on the other hand will be a worthwhile acquisition." Striding past the two collared girls, he kicked one in the thigh. "This way. We'll have a chat before we begin business."

My hands almost broke I fisted so hard.

The girls never raised their eyes, instantly following, crawling into the room off the foyer. The walls were bare of any artwork or personality, painted in garish reds and golds with black carpeting.

It was all one level—a sprawled out estate ensuring rooms were far enough away from the business hub so prospective buyers weren't distracted by other women's screams or the growls of rutting animals.

Following, as if this wasn't the end of my life and just a normal business meeting, I passed through the familiar double doors and into a large lounge. A huge painting of a gun dripping red hung above a fake fireplace with melted candles. The room had three semi-circle couches, all with a small podium and pole bolted into the ceiling before them.

The perfect viewing for pricks and paedophiles.

Lynx sat down, patting the red leather beside him. I winced at the aches in my bones, taking a seat on the end of the couch. My thigh still bled, but I had nothing to wrap it with. I needed to put pressure on the wound—stop any more blood loss.

Hiding my pain, I linked my hands between my legs. "The welcome committee isn't needed. I don't want to watch any of your sick fetishes." He'd made me watch the first time, and I'd yet to burn the image from my retinas. The girl had been one I hadn't been able to save. She'd died that night from what he did.

Dante threw his head back, chuckling as if I were a world-renowned comedian. "Always such a fucking prude." Waggling his finger in my direction, he added, "I know you're not, Mercer. I've heard the rumours. Paying women to do tame things in relation to what you could do to a girl you own." He shook his head. "I think it's time you stopped lying to everyone—including yourself—and give in."

Snapping his fingers, the man who'd squeezed Tess's breast and put a gun to her head appeared. Grabbing one of the girls from the floor, he threw her onto the podium in front of us.

Her face contorted as the pole slammed against her hip. Her hands slinked around the silver structure, eyes downcast and lost.

A rush of bile threatened to fill my mouth—bile filled with blood and the need to butcher everyone here. No one deserved to live. They deserved to be chopped up, turned into worm food, and eventually reincarnated as bird shit.

Bird.

My eyes locked on the black-haired slave, stretching her atrophied muscles, bending around the pole. Her ribs stuck out, breasts were small with large prominent nipples, and she had no hair between her legs—showing bite marks on her inner thighs and a piercing through her clit with a small chain leading to a piece of jewellery wrapped around her waist.

Her eyes met mine briefly. There was nothing left but hatred and contempt.

Looking away, she gyrated on the pole, flowing like a broken girl rather than a sensual mistress.

Five hours and fifty-five minutes.

Lynx leaned back, eyes glued to the girl. He snapped his fingers again, summoning the other slave to go to him. She crawled over, keeping her head low, showing the beads of her spine. Her brown hair was cropped to her skull, highlighting shadows of fingers around her throat and multiple ear piercings. She was the curvier of the two but still looked unhealthy.

Fucking animals.

The girl positioned herself between Lynx's legs, reaching to his fly without a word. He arched his hips for the girl to unbuckle his trousers, sighing deeply as she pulled out his bent, foul erection.

It took all my willpower to stay sitting and not throw myself at him. Four guards loomed around me—two in front, two behind. I couldn't do a thing as the girl spat on her hand, smearing her saliva over his cock and stroking him.

"Suck it." He grabbed the back of her neck, bringing her face to crash against his crotch.

Her mouth opened, swallowing his putrid length with no complaint.

His eyes rolled back, groaning as her cheeks hollowed, sucking him hard. "Yes, that's it. Suck. *Suck*." He shuddered as her lips opened wide, swallowing his entire length. He forced her even further, suffocating her against his pubic hair, holding her until she struggled for breath.

"Stop. It," I growled, echoing with darkness.

"I'd let you do anything, Q. Because I love you." Tess's voice whispered in my mind. Images of burning her with red wax sickened and excited me.

The room smelled of sex, feeding my sick senses with increasing lust.

Something other than anger lived in my blood now. Something twisting and tempting and entirely wrong. I had to get out of there. I had to run. Or kill. Both preferably.

Lynx opened his eyes, piercing me with his black gaze.

"You don't tell me what to do." To prove his point, he hit the girl on her shoulder. She moaned, tears welling, mixing with the glistening saliva on his cock. "She's mine to do with as I wish. I'm fucking God to her. And you're a sad excuse of a prick who denies his own needs." His hips twitched, pushing himself further into the slave's mouth. "You want this—just admit it and tonight could go a completely different way."

Fuck. No moisture remained in my mouth. My heart turned into a wildebeest galloping to its death.

Locking my fingers together, I snarled, "Let's cut the bullshit, Dante. You know I never used. I bought from you and what I did with them is none of your fucking business. I gave you what you asked in return. How many buildings did I help you with? Four? Five? Stop being an asshole, and I won't kill you."

Lynx laughed, his hand on the bobbing head of the girl blowing him. "See—all stinking lies. You want this. You want the control. The power. Admit it."

My eyes fell on the girl.

I sank deep into Tess's mouth, fucking her lips while she hung upside down. I'd never felt anything as good as driving into her throat while she was completely unable to stop me. I groaned as the orgasm I denied forced one thick wave onto her tongue.

Shit.

My fucking body betrayed me. My cock thickened. *Don't think about Tess.* She'd loved taking me. She'd wanted it. Unlike the poor girl blowing Dante.

Don't confuse the two.

Forcing Tess out of my thoughts, I muttered, "Without me, you wouldn't have the wealth you do. Spare me the cock-swinging contest."

His eyes narrowed. "You're such a French idiot. You're in denial." Grabbing the girl's ears, he shoved himself deeper. Her back convulsed with a gag reflex.

He slapped her. "You don't gag, bitch."

She nodded, resuming her task as if the glowing handprint

on her cheek wasn't burning.

I stood, towering over him, cursing my semi, hating the betrayal of my body. "Do that again and I'll—"

"Shut the hell up." Two men pressed on my shoulders, shoving me back onto the couch. My leg gave out, thanks to the weakness of being fucking shot.

I balled my hands. "It's not denial. I don't have to partake—just like I don't use drugs or gamble. Stop trying to convert me. Let her go and let's get down to fucking business."

Whatever that was.

"Q, you're not a monster. I know the truth." I squeezed my eyes, trying so hard not to let Tess into my mind. Not here. I wouldn't taint her memories.

My eyes fell on the upside down girl on the pole. Her legs were spread, showing me every crease and fold of her abused pussy.

My cock throbbed. Fuck! Overwhelming pressure built behind my eyes. I wanted to leave before the sickness inside could grow stronger. I would gladly walk to my torture if it meant retaining my morals and decency.

A moment ago I didn't want to think about Tess. Now I did. *Think of her in their place—being so badly used. You'd hate it.*

My semi turned into a full-blown fucking erection.

I'd hate it but love it.

Tess spread-eagled on a pole. Her hair wrapped in my fingers as I forced myself inside her mouth. Her moans and pants and cries.

Shit. I couldn't think about anything without it lacerating everything good I tried to retain.

I scrubbed my face.

Lies.

I fucking judge you. I'm your executioner.

Five hours and forty minutes.

"I heard a rumour, Mercer. About the sparrows you seem to have on every logo and possession."

I struggled to keep my face impassive. How the fuck did that piece of information get out?

Reclining in the seat, I did my best to ignore my cock, focusing on buying time for Franco and his team. "Oh? And what do they say?"

Lynx thrust his hips, his body shuddering as the girl sucked harder.

I averted my eyes. His mind games were about to get worse. I was sure of it.

Dante's voice was lust-laden and scratchy. "That it symbolises women you've saved. That you think you're a fucking hero."

Shit. Damn news reporters and invasion of my privacy. The sparrow was a relic to me—now they'd tarnished it, brought it into the filth I lived in. "I'm not a hero."

Where the fuck is he going with this?

"I also heard you *did* use one of the slaves you bought." His eyebrow quirked. "A girl from Mexico—Red Wolverine gave her to you."

I tensed. This was where the conversation went from civil to littered with minefields. I refused to talk about Tess with him. Flatly fucking refused. I didn't care how much he knew or how much he didn't. None of it mattered because by the time dawn arrived I would either be dead—or he would be. Either way, my reputation and what I did with Tess was irrelevant.

My mind filled with blonde curls, pink lips, and a strong innocence that made me bow to the woman I missed so fucking much. I better be in one piece to marry her tomorrow.

I'd fixed her but hadn't done the one thing I wanted above all. I wanted to call her my wife.

Hurry up, Franco.

I nodded. Once. That was all he was getting.

"I also heard you murdered Wolverine. Hardly fair since he gave you a slave you finally enjoyed."

My skin tingled with rage, muscles locking with the need to pummel his face. A bodyguard moved closer, sensing the fraying hold I had on my emotions.

Narrowing my eyes, I said, "Yes, I murdered that cretin.

Sliced his throat like fucking caviar and I did the same to his son."

Lynx froze, his eyes fluttering as the skilled tongue of his slave worked him closer to release. "So cocky, Mercer."

I shrugged. "It was easy. About as easy as it will be to murder you." My temper swelled. I couldn't do his question and answer session anymore. "Why did you drag me here? I'm done watching you get a blowjob. Fucking do something or let me go."

I was aware the question might catapult me into the killing zone, but I couldn't sit there any longer.

I wanted to leave. I *couldn't* leave. The lack of freedom made me slip from sane to crazy.

"You came for me, Q. Je suis à toi." Tess's voice wouldn't stop cutting through my thoughts.

Lynx stiffened, his mouth fell open as he rhythmically thrust into the girl's mouth. She went slack as he came down her throat, shuddering with his orgasm. The second his hips stopped pulsing, she licked him clean.

The last sweep of her tongue, Dante shoved her away and tucked his cock into his pants. Snapping his fingers, a guard handed him a lit cigarette.

Taking a puff, he murmured to the girl, "Did you like the taste of my come, slave?"

She nodded.

"Do you think you deserve a reward?"

She froze.

"Answer me."

Slowly, she nodded again.

Lynx smiled, lashing out with the burning ember he stabbed the cigarette into her stomach, holding it until her lips turned white from holding in her scream. Pulling back, he ordered, "Your turn on the pole."

She gratefully spun around. Not touching the seeping wound, she took her place on the podium.

My mind churned with waves of ferocity. Images of

stabbing him in the heart, chopping him up, hanging him from the ceiling for his slaves to whip and abuse were the only reason why I didn't risk certain death by hurling myself across the couch and strangling him.

Smiling, Dante wiped his lips. Crooking a finger at the black-haired girl on the pole, he summoned her from the pole.

She let go, hopping off the platform.

But she didn't go to Lynx.

She came for me.

Oh, fuck.

I sat taller, hating the sickening panic almost as much as I hated the growing lust.

She fell to her knees, never making eye contact.

I swallowed hard.

Five hours and thirty minutes.

"I've also heard you've fallen for the slave Wolverine gave you. Bad form to murder him after he gave you love, isn't it?"

My concentration split between Lynx's taunts and the girl breathing softly on my knees. Her hot breath heated through my trousers.

"I didn't kill him for his gift. I killed him for taking it away. If he'd never interfered, I wouldn't have had to take his life." I looked up, hoping my anger painted every facet of my body. "I'm sure you can appreciate revenge. After all, isn't this yours? Revenge for me not being a sick fuck like you?"

Lynx laughed. "This is just a get together amongst old associates. However, I must admit I am a little pissed at what you did to me a few years ago." He leaned forward. "I had justifiable reasons to come after you then, but I never did. Shows I'm a better man than you. Don't you think?"

He still hadn't got over the incident? Idiot. "Just because I knocked you out when you tried to stop me taking fair payment for that monstrosity you built in Madrid, doesn't mean you had reason to kill my bodyguard." Franco had not been pleased. Needless to say others died and not him.

"You stole an extra girl—that wasn't the agreement."

"The agreement was you wouldn't torture the ones I left behind. I needed more collateral. You're a high risk client, Dante. I'm sure you can appreciate that."

"*Was* a client, Mercer. Don't forget this conversation focuses on the termination of our association. Ending with a few severe penalties than just parting of business." He chuckled. "Parting of a few other important things, too, I can assure you."

My gunshot twinged but I kept the flash of fear hidden.

"If you felt so unjustly dealt with, why didn't you come after me then?" I grinned. "That's right—because you know the truth. I have more power than you."

He chuckled, tilting his head. "That might've been the case, but my how the tables have turned."

You're scum. Worse than scum. You're the disease that grows on scum.

I muttered, "If you want the award of being the biggest, baddest asshole then sure. You win." I saluted him. "Now fucking stop with the mind-games. I'm done."

Lynx grinned. "Sure. By all means." Nodding at the girl between my legs, he ordered, "Do it."

She sat up on her knees, reaching for my hastily buttoned blazer. The only thing keeping my naked chest from being on display. My throat closed at the memory of Tess ripping my shirt, ruining the buttons in her need. It felt like centuries ago.

"I love you so much, Q. I trust you."

Fuck. Tess.

I was so glad she couldn't see me now. See a whore fumbling at my belt, her hands brushing a hard cock that I wanted to cut off for being so twisted.

Pain echoed, amplifying the punches and kicks, hacking at my willpower to keep going. Five hours was an eternity. It was life-changing—or ending. So much could happen in that time.

I shuddered with violence as the girl's hands undid my jacket, spreading it open. The moment my tattoo was visible Lynx clapped his hands. "It's a lot different than the rumour.

I'd heard it was bats not birds."

Who the fuck had spread my secrets? Only a select few knew. A few paid prostitutes at the beginning of my career—they were the only ones who would tell. I trusted my staff and confidants completely.

I couldn't speak through my tight jaw. I refused to utter a word.

"What do you think of her?" Lynx motioned to the girl now bowing at my feet. My fly hung open, revealing the waist band of my boxers.

A sickly spasm filled me. I hated where this was going.

"She's underfed, sad, and no doubt thinking of ways to murder us."

Dante glowered. His mohawk bristled with gel as he stood. "I suppose you prefer overfed women who don't obey, is that it?"

I thought of Tess. Her incredible curves. Her feisty strength. My lips twitched, allowing one ray of light into my soul. "Yes. One in particular."

Lynx's face darkened. "You might as well get her out of your thoughts. You won't be seeing her again."

I sat solid, unmovable. Not rising to the bait.

Five hours and twenty minutes.

"Tell you what…I'll let you survive—after I take payment for what you cost me—if you can do one thing." His eyes flickered to the slave, filling with smug pride.

My heart splattered into my feet.

Shit.

I looked at the girl; her eyes flickered to mine. Her plea for help pierced around the room—I heard it so clearly I was surprised the windows and mirrors didn't shatter with her high-pitched sorrow.

"Want to know what it is?" Dante prodded.

I didn't need to know. I already did.

"Blow down her throat. Use her like I know you want to. And I'll let you live."

My lungs stuck together.

And there it was.

The crux of my life. The one thing that would end up killing me. Not only my vow never to be my father but also my vow to a woman who held my fucking heart.

Either I had to hurt this woman and desecrate a body that now belonged to Tess or die.

The decision crippled me.

I would never be able to explain either situation. I wouldn't be able to soothe Tess's tears when she found me murdered for honouring my loyalty to her. And I wouldn't be able to fan her happiness when she found me alive, knowing what I'd done to stay that way.

Honour was a bitch but there was no other way. I would die with no regrets. I would die being loyal.

Cursing the forming headache, I said, "If you ask your men, they'll kindly inform you I came rather well a few hours ago. They saw the event. I'm wrung dry." My eyes sparked, hot anger trickled down my back in a droplet of sweat. Nothing hurt anymore—only my heart. "But thanks for the offer."

The girl's face paled. She curled her shoulders, expecting a beating for no longer having the task assigned to her.

I wanted to pick her up and drape my jacket over her nakedness. Shit, I wanted her away from this creep and safe.

Lynx's fingers cracked, forming into fists—the first sign of aggression. "This isn't a negotiation, Mercer."

"I thought that's exactly what it was. A negotiation for my life." Glaring, I added, "Let's cut the crap. Name a price. Wouldn't you rather a fat cheque rather than a messy corpse to clean?"

He laughed. "Who said I'd be the one cleaning afterward?"

The tension in the room thickened. Dante lost his joviality, pointing at the girl. "Do it. Otherwise this nice little conversation will end, and you'll wish you'd taken the offer."

The girl suddenly reached for my waistband, tugging it away from my tight, unwilling body. I stiffened as her small hand dove into my boxer-briefs, grabbing hold of a cock that had no fucking right to be hard.

Five hours and ten minutes.

I grabbed her wrists, shaking my head. "No, thank you. Stop."

A cold muzzle pushed against my temple. Angry breathing hit the side of my face. "You don't have a choice, asshole."

Two options: die here with my pants undone and my skull shattered, or give myself another five hours for a chance at living.

A howl resonated in my soul. The monster inside couldn't understand my hesitation but my love for Tess was stronger. It didn't help when voices whispered permission.

"I'd rather you live, Q. Do whatever's necessary to survive."

"Do it, Q. I understand."

Tess's voice cajoled and danced, stealing everything.

Goddammit.

Removing my hands, I shut my eyes, allowing the girl to pull my cock out with her cold fingers.

Her touch was so different. Weak, unsure, full of history of other men she'd held—other bastards who'd used her body against her will.

Tess, fuck I'm sorry.

"Suck him," Lynx demanded.

My stomach curled as the girl bowed over my hips—her breath hot on my length. My cock lurched at the subtle sensation. That piece of meat was the reason I'd been conflicted all my life—driven by genetics I wished I could delete.

I can't do this.

I couldn't use a slave. It would be the slippery slope hurtling my soul to hell.

My hand landed on her chin, holding her a millimetre from sucking me. *"Arrêt."* Stop.

Let her blow you. Buy some time.

No matter the voices inside my head making it okay, I

couldn't.

The gun on my temple pressed harder. Lynx demanded. "You would rather die than have some woman's spit on your cock?" He laughed. "You're fucking unbelievable."

A fist landed on my cheekbone, snapping my neck to the side. Two men grabbed my arms, jerking them behind my head.

"Do it." Lynx snapped his fingers again. The girl grabbed my cock, her mouth descending, sinking down my length.

"Fuck. Stop!" I thrashed in the chair, not caring how much I hurt. I couldn't let this woman suck me off. I couldn't do that to her, to me, to *Tess*. Fuck, Tess. *I'm sorry!*

I bit my split lip as the girl sucked. Her teeth stayed sheathed, her tongue shy. My hands twitched, trying to get free. "Let me go, Lynx!"

My eyes closed, fighting the beast in my blood. It couldn't be fucking happier to have a woman on her knees against her will. My cock grew harder, swelling under her licking tongue.

I want to die. I couldn't do this.

I turned manic, thrusting up, trying to dislodge her lips. The girl moaned as I smashed against the back of her throat. In that moment I didn't have any urge to save her. She was on *their* side. Fucking raping me of any choice or honour.

Lynx clapped his hands. "That's it. Use her, Mercer. Let yourself go. You know you want to. Look how much your cock wants to." He pressed on the girl's neck, forcing her to sink lower, swallowing all of me—right to the base.

Fuck. Me.

My eyes wanted to roll. My balls wanted to explode. My heart wanted to fucking die.

The beast inside bayed in rapture—finally it said—*finally I get a taste of the life I've always wanted.*

It didn't compute to the inner bastard inside that this was all against my will. I was the victim—just as much as she.

Her head bobbed up and down, her nose pressing against my belly.

"Stop. Just please—stop." My quads tensed as the monster

inside stole all decency. It wanted her. It wanted to abuse her. It wanted to come. So. Fucking. Bad.

I can't!

I'm better than that. I'm better than him.

My stomach clenched with nausea. I was sick, an adulterer, the worst kind of man.

Her mouth increased pressure, her fingers circling below, grabbing my balls.

Two urges ran like raging rapids in my blood. One was the master I always kept buried who wanted to thrust into this slave and take. The other screamed for retribution. I wouldn't stoop to *his* level—not even if it meant I might save my worthless fucking excuse for a life.

Tess deserved better. I would happily sign my death warrant if it meant I never had to cheat or lie or steal.

"Make him come, girl. Hurry up." Lynx dictated her speed, wrenching her up and down by her hair, faster and faster until the prickles and tingles of an orgasm grew unwillingly in my blood.

My eyes widened as the beast growled inside, salivating at the thought of painting this slave's throat in a way I'd never done.

I'd been so strong. Always saying no. Turning down offers. Refusing to destroy women.

You're breaking every code you live by.

A groan tore from my lips as the suction from her mouth grew. The intensity of the inner fight between me and demon radiated outward. I fought harder, tearing my arms.

It didn't do any good.

"Suck. Faster, girl!" Dante never took his eyes off my undoing as my hips surged upward involuntarily. Handing control over to the monster inside—the monster I wasn't strong enough to fight.

The girl's tongue swirled around the tip. So different to Tess. So unskilled and unloving compared to Tess.

My eyes burned with self-hatred. A ripple of pre-cum

worked up my shaft. The girl worked harder, tasting the end, working me closer to the finish line.

The two men holding me chuckled, relaxing their hold. For a moment I hung suspended in a horrible place of ignoring my inner righteousness and coming.

It would be so easy. One thrust. Possibly two. Into the hot, wet, slippery mouth of the girl using me.

But I wouldn't be able to live with the aftermath. I'd never forgive myself. I'd never be able to look Tess in the eye again and believe I had any goodness left for her.

The girl swivelled her head, a slice of teeth hurtling me closer to coming.

I let the monster free—but not to climax. To hunt.

Ripping my arms from the men, I kicked up at the same time. My knee connected with the girl's chest, sending her sprawling to the floor. My glistening hard cock stood like a traitor between my legs but I didn't give a fucking damn because all I wanted was Lynx to die. Horribly. Drastically. Excruciatingly.

I hurled myself at him, sending us both to the floor. The orgasm that lived in my body switched to lustful need for his death.

We rolled, punching, shouting. He fought hard but he didn't have a beast riding him—a beast that desperately wanted to come and now was fucking angry.

Lynx's bodyguards dragged me off him, slamming me onto my back. Dante scrambled to his feet, throwing a painful kick to my ribs. "You're a dead man. Fucking dead—you hear me?"

I shrugged. "I already was. Least this way I can die knowing I kept my morals." My eyes landed on the girl. She wiped her lips with the back of her hand, holding her stomach where I kneed her.

"Je suis désolée. Ce n'est pas toi." I'm sorry. It wasn't you. I did up my trousers, tucking away the piece of my body that'd almost ruined me.

Her hazel eyes widened. I doubted she understood, but at least I'd said what I needed to. It would haunt me that I wasn't able to save her.

Turns out, I couldn't even save myself. Playing along with Lynx's games should've been easy—if it wasn't for the sins in my soul just waiting to strike me down. I couldn't afford to enter the darkness. I couldn't afford to slip—regardless if it meant life or death.

I wouldn't save my life by doing the one thing that would destroy it. Not when I'd planned on getting married tomorrow. Not when I'd had some *small* chance at getting into heaven.

Shoving the two idiots away from me, I stood. Facing Dante, I ignored the pain in my thigh, thankful at least that soon I wouldn't have to suffer the slick heat from the wound. "Enough. Let's get this over with."

Lynx clenched his jaw, his eyes tight with rage. "Fine, you fucking pussy. Let's move this conversation downstairs."

Four hours fifty-nine minutes.

My time had officially run out.

My eyes refused to open.

Every sense honed in on one particular pain. An excruciating agony in the back of my skull. Pounding, clanging, *throbbing*.

I groaned, needing to investigate the wound, needing to touch it—to try and alleviate the pain.

But I couldn't move.

Nothing obeyed.

Panic opened my eyes.

My vision was hazy, unfocused, especially in my right pupil. What the fuck happened?

"Ah, you've finally decided to stop sleeping away your final minutes, Mercer." Lynx appeared, but all I saw were his crimson shoes.

I frowned, trying to figure out what the hell was going on. Blinking hard, I forced my eyesight to make sense of something that made no sense at all.

I'm upside down.

Clenching my stomach muscles, I arched upright, taking note of my bound and very naked body. Black ropes wrapped around my ankles, tethering me to the ceiling. The gunshot in my thigh looked awful and bloody. My arms were lassoed to my sides, coiled tightly with twine.

Hot lacing terror filled my heart. "Wh—what?" My swollen tongue couldn't form syllables. It felt as if I'd bitten it again. "Tell—"

Lynx laughed. "If you're trying to figure out how you came to be hanging in the same dungeon you were invited to enjoy an orgy in, then I can clarify." His hand struck out, stroking my chin almost tenderly. "I pushed you down the stairs. You hit your head pretty hard at the bottom. Smashed a tile." He tutted as if I'd ruined his entire decor. "However, passing out you gave us the great advantage of preparing you like this with no other issues or complications." He patted my cheek. "Thanks for that."

My chest rose and fell as adrenaline turned me from rational to drunk on the need to run or fight or both. I never took my eyes off Dante as he snapped his fingers, silently ordering two men to place a small table beside my head. On it rested a small towel and a row of buckets of water.

I gulped—not that it worked hanging upside down. The pressure of vertigo made the ache in my neck and residue unconsciousness scream for mercy.

In the distance hung a sex swing with ropes, pulleys, and a wall groaning with sexual torture equipment. The cold black tiles of the floor and the chains looping from the ceiling made it seem as if I'd stepped back in time. I'd woken in a nineteenth century torture chamber.

"You came for me, Q. You saved me from them."

My eyes snapped closed at the memory of finding Tess in Rio. Those conditions had been worse. If she survived that I could survive this.

"I offered a civilized way out of this, Mercer. You're an idiot for not taking it." Lynx came closer, running a fingertip down my chest, swirling around the upside down sparrows.

I stiffened. I wanted to tear his body to pieces. My blood was cold and ready for his death.

He held out his hand. One of his guards placed a baseball bat into his open grip.

Oh, fuck.

My stomach muscles clenched in preparation; my entire body locking down to protect vulnerable organs.

"I think we'll begin with a warm up—don't you?" The *thwack* of the bat wrenched a groan from my lips, echoing around the chamber.

I jerked in the chains, dangling like a punching bag. I tried to double over, but my weight kept me hanging, completely at his mercy.

"Tenderize you a bit. Be a good way to relieve tension." Lynx laughed. He hit me again on my lower belly, scarily close to my cock.

A cock that'd been sucked by a woman who wasn't Tess. It deserved to be punished.

Lynx twisted the handle, securing a better grip. He swung hard and fast, walloping me as if I were a homerun.

I cried out, groaning as something crunched inside. A rib. The sharp shooting pain compounded to all the rest—consuming my thoughts with agony. My ragged breathing turned short and shallow, working through the wash of darkness.

Another blow. This one right on my chest.

My vision went black. Pain ebbed away as my soul tried to run.

"I love you, Q. I love your ruthlessness and strength. I love knowing you'll always come for me." Shit. Tears pricked my eyes. I'd broken

a promise. I would no longer be there for Tess. I wouldn't be there to rescue her.

Be happy you fixed her mind. Before...before I was stupid enough to let this happen.

"You still with me, Mercer?" A white hot jolt seized my muscles. I turned into a plank of human flesh as Dante electrified me with extreme volts from a Taser.

My jaw locked, bones hummed. Every inch of me stood to fucking attention.

Lynx stopped the current passing through my body, trailing a fingertip around my waist to my back. "Don't pass out. You do and you won't wake up."

I wasn't weak but the sound of passing out was entirely too tempting.

The next strike came from behind. The baseball bat struck my lower back, lighting up a different sort of pain—a radiating sensation-stealing pain.

I screamed.

I wasn't proud I screamed. I hated that he'd hurt me enough to earn it but fuck—it devastated my willpower. All feeling to my freezing legs above suddenly disappeared. The heat from the gunshot was gone. The tingles from the electric shock existed no more. He'd either traumatised my spine or crippled me.

The thought of not being able to stand beside Tess to marry her, or walk beside her as we grew old tore my heart into pieces.

It doesn't matter. You're about to die anyway.

Incredibly, the thought granted peace. Dante could do whatever the hell he pleased because ultimately it didn't matter. I would still end up in the same place.

I lost the will to tense. What was the point? It would only prolong it.

The next swing slammed into my kidneys like a bulldozer. Agony blazed in my groin and lower belly. Lynx prowled around, dragging a hand along my quivering body. I tried to twist away, moaning at the spreading pain. I wanted to curse him—but again—what was the fucking point?

He chuckled, sounding evil in the cold black dungeon. "I'm thinking we need to get rid of this tattoo." His hand slapped over the ink, trailing down to the 'T' branded over my heart. He clucked his tongue. "What the hell is this?" He shoved me with the tip of the baseball bat. I swung backward, creaking in the chains.

That is the one good thing in my life. The one redemption. My one untarnished love. Tess. She would always be the key to whatever heaven I entered.

I swallowed back my sadness—I'd never see her again. See her smile. Hear her laugh. I'd done everything I could to protect her. I just hoped she wouldn't switch herself off again. She couldn't live a life removed from emotion. I'd tried to teach her that—but I wouldn't be there to enforce it.

Lynx shoved me again, spinning me around. I closed my eyes, suffering a rush of nausea. "Answer me, Mercer."

I kept my lips pursed. He'd torn a scream from me but he wouldn't get another.

He huffed. "Well, it doesn't matter. Whatever it is, soon it will be in pieces on the floor." He spun me again, stepping away and dropping the baseball bat. "Let's loosen him up. I want him screaming."

A man stopped my pendulum swing, slapping me to a halt. He smiled, his face hideous upside down. "Say goodbye, fuckwit."

I sucked in a breath as he placed a heavy towel over my face. Shit. It blocked out everything. My warm breathing was trapped in the material. My hands clenched, hating the iciness of fear spiking my heart.

"I'm never afraid when I'm with you. Because I trust you."

Tess filled my mind, giving me something to latch onto. I couldn't see past the black towel, but I didn't need to. I didn't want to look at anything but the woman I wanted to marry.

My stomach clenched at the thought of anyone else

making her happy. I couldn't bear the idea of her falling for another or marrying someone completely unworthy. My forehead furrowed, loving the memories of her and hating them, too. Knowing I'd never see her again hurt more than anything Lynx could do.

I'd never see my perfect *esclave* again.

Je t'aime, Tess.

Fuck, I wanted this over with. I wanted to stop thinking and just…go.

I made a vow not to scream. I wouldn't die a pussy. I wouldn't give them the satisfaction of tearing my life from an unwilling body. I'd brought this on myself—I'd been too proud—too cocky, and I would pay the worst kind of price.

"Do it," Lynx ordered.

Water poured onto my face, seeping through the towel. My heartbeat thundered in my ears as liquid saturated the material, suffocating me drop by drop.

Waterboarding.

I'd seen it done. I'd witnessed a few women die from such a simple but very effective method of torturing.

The towel went from dry to soaked instantly, clinging like a heavy film over my mouth and nose. The weight of the material increased, smothering my face, giving me nowhere to turn or hide.

My mouth gaped, sucking at non-existent oxygen, breathing in wet towel and nothing else.

Don't panic. Just let it happen.

It was fine to order myself to do something—entirely different when my body took over. Survival instincts kicked in. I thrashed, trying to dislodge the never ending stream of water.

My stomach clenched, overriding the numbness in my spine and bruises on every inch. I hurled upright, doing everything in my power to free my nose.

But it was no use.

Goddammit, let me breathe!

Time ceased to have meaning as the trickle became a

downpour, no longer stealing my breath but forcing a torrent of water down my throat—drowning me in more ways than one.

"More. Give him more," Dante demanded.

The water level increased until I gave up trying to breathe. It was pointless. Holding what little oxygen I had, I counted the seconds until I died.

One second.

Two seconds.

Another wash of liquid tickled my throat, running in rivulets over my hair.

Three seconds.

Four seconds.

There was no point being brave. I was about to die.

My heart chased the last breath around my lungs.

Five seconds.

Six seconds.

My body absorbed the final dregs of oxygen—nothing remained. My body was master now—not my mind. Death throes took me hostage. Muscles jerked, hurtling me toward death, desperately fighting the restraints.

I would've given every cent I owned to have one last breath. One inhale of sweet, sweet oxygen. Even Tess couldn't distract me from the all-consuming need for *air.*

"I held on for you to find me. You came even when I didn't think you would. Hold on, Q. I'm coming."

Tess's voice was angelic, cutting through my panic. I wanted to tell her I couldn't. There was no point in her coming to find me. I wouldn't be there when Franco's team arrived. I no longer knew the timeframe after being unconscious.

But I didn't need to know. I ran out of time the moment I refused to accept a blowjob from a slave.

Air. Please give me air.

My body danced in its chains, slowly growing weaker as blackness inched over my brain.

Then I got my wish.

The towel left my face, and I threw all dignity to the dogs. I gulped and gulped, sucking in air as if I was starving—which I was. Starved of the simplest thing a human required to live.

Then, I screamed.

The fucking cocksucker made me scream. I had no choice. I couldn't contain the pain.

The agony came from my shin bone. Using the rapidly depleting muscles in my stomach, I curled upward, fixing onto the blood dripping from my sliced flesh. It trickled down my skin, running toward my groin.

Lynx stood beside me with a knife. The blade smeared with crimson. "We're going to begin a game. Every breath must be paid by a cut." His face moulded into the true devil. He cut me again, just below the first. I bit my lip against the sharpness—refusing to scream again.

"Every breath has a price. And when we get to here—"

Everything in me froze to ice. The tip of his knife wedged beneath my flaccid cock, raising the heavy organ from my stomach. Shit, shit. *No, don't.*

The sharp blade exploded my heart with horror. *Fuck, let me die.*

"When we've used up your legs for payment…this comes next. I don't expect you'll survive much longer after that." He twisted the blade, letting my cock slap against my stomach. Lynx pressed the serrated edge against my balls, deliberately dragging the knife lower and lower, right to the base—right where he would eunuch me and let me bleed to fucking death.

My head pounded—the need to replace air to my oxygen-depraved body forgotten. The beast inside turned feral—wanting so damn much for freedom to mutilate him in the same way.

I wouldn't have the opportunity to pay him back. I wouldn't be able to take payment for what he would steal.

"You know why I'll take this as my final trophy, Mercer?"

I didn't say a word. I didn't need to—he was high on whatever sick power trip he existed on.

"I gave you the opportunity to use it. If you'd blown down that girl's throat I would've let you keep it. If you'd fucked her in front of me, I would've let you walk away without torture. And if you'd killed her—like I know your sadistic tendencies make you want to—I would've forgotten this whole thing. Shit, I would've stood by you and assured the rest of the men who want a piece of you that you're one of us. That the lies you told were for the media and not to the men you pretended to be like."

Leaning forward, he whispered in my ear, "If only you'd played along—see how you could've survived?" Swirling the knife around an inked sparrow, he muttered, "Now you've pissed me off and I won't be happy just taking your life. You think you'll be free when you're dead?" He shrugged." You will be I suppose, but know this. I'm not done with you yet. I'm going to chase your little slave. I'm going to take her. I'm going to fuck her. And then I'm going to kill her just like I killed you."

No!

"Don't you fucking touch her. You have me. Do whatever the hell you want but leave her the fuck alone!"

Rage. Blinding, suffocating rage. I couldn't do it. He'd stolen the luxury of slipping into death. He'd taken away my will to die, replacing it with the terror of knowing I could do nothing to stop him.

Tess!

"Do you hear me? You stay the fuck away from her."

I couldn't let them take her again. I didn't care that Franco would never let her out of his sight. He had his orders. If he didn't find me in time, his loyalty was to her. He would give his life to protect hers—just as he did for me.

Lynx laughed. "You aren't in the position to tell me what I can and can't do. You're going to die, Mercer, but at least you won't be alone in hell for long. She'll be joining you soon enough." The knife pricked my cock again. "Pity for you, you won't have a dick to use when you see her again."

"Ne pas la toucher. Vous ne pouvez pas la toucher." Don't touch her. You can't touch her.

"Speaking in French doesn't work on a Spaniard, idiot." He removed the blade. "Cover him."

I sucked in gulp of air as the wet towel descended over my face. My heart bucked with terror. I had to warn Franco, Frederick. I had to get Tess to safety. She wouldn't die because of me. She wouldn't!

"Begin," Dante ordered.

The cascade started anew, drowning me with the aid of a simple cloth.

My lungs turned to fire. Seconds flew toward minutes as more and more water cascaded. I forced myself not to suck in the towel, desperate for breath.

Unconsciousness tried to claim me but I fought it. I couldn't. Tess!

But no matter how hard I held on, my brain shut down, body jerked; I died with every pour.

My life didn't exist apart from the black water-world. My thoughts scrambled. Tess. Air. Tess. Air.

I wanted both in equal measure. I wanted to run. I wanted to be free.

Tess morphed into being. Her gorgeous blonde curls, her all seeing blue-grey eyes. A halo of light appeared behind her, fading her from view as my heart threw itself toward its last beat.

Tess, run. Please.

Her presence never left me as a wave of heavy water splashed over me. I toppled on the edge, gasping, choking. Lynx overestimated my lung capacity—hurtling me toward death.

The last torrent of liquid was my demise.

Don't give up. You can't. I owed it to Tess to stay alive. I had to protect her. I had to be there for her always.

"Come with me, Q. Let go. It's better this way." The illusion grabbed me by the hands, dragging me forward. I didn't want

to go, but I had no choice.

My body gave up. Suffocated of air it shut down— snipping my life-force free from pain.

The agony faded, inch by inch, ache by ache, until I felt nothing.

Nothing but weightlessness...nothingness.

Sounds faded. The strain in my lungs no longer mattered.

Life tiptoed away from me, taking with it any promise of happiness I might've found by marrying my soul-mate.

But my soul-mate wanted me to leave with her. Her golden hand outstretched, glowing with welcome light. She wanted me to leave this black cold place.

I could be with her forever.

I want to be with you forever, esclave.

"Then let go. I'm waiting."

I didn't think why she appeared when she was living not dead. I didn't stop to ponder how she found me. All I knew was what I wanted. And I wanted her.

I let go. I went to her. I obeyed my *esclave*.

Dying was such a simple thing.

I felt no guilt, no terror, no worries. Only acceptance for something I couldn't change.

Darkness came for me.

My golden girl stuttered out.

The light she'd teased me was gone.

The sun turned to an eclipse and...I fell. Like an unwanted star I fell from the promise of heaven and plummeted to where I belonged.

Falling, falling.

Falling.

I fell straight into hell.

Chapter Thirteen

Matching darkness, mirroring light, truth and love we took flight,
one esclave and one maître, no longer captive or thief, just perfect certainty and belief

Franco's phone rang.

I froze. Instincts screamed, slicing sharp fingernails of panic down the chalkboard of my spine.

The car turned from saviour, rushing us to Q's aid, to a decaying coffin.

"Don't—"

Franco glanced over, his vivid eyes dulling with horror. "I have no choice." Shoving his uninjured hand into his trouser pocket, he pulled out the chiming doom.

Don't let it be. Don't.

We were almost there. The plane ride had driven me crazy—I would've sold my heart to be teleported or *something* to get us there faster. *We're so close!*

It won't be. It can't be.

I couldn't breathe as Franco held the phone to his ear. His

face went deadly white. Not uttering a word, he passed the cell to me.

My fingers turned to ice-cubes; all I wanted to do was hurl the phone from the car window, smashing the bad news before it could be made real.

It's not true.

He's fine.

The phone was a vulture stealing my happiness as I placed it to my ear.

"Tess?" Frederick's voice echoed all the way from Paris.

My heart went from beating to nothing. His tone said all I needed to know. I couldn't move. Locked in my chair, I became a statue of grief.

Frederick sucked in a shaky breath. "You there? Tess?"

I knew.

I knew why he called. It didn't matter we were ten minutes away. It didn't matter we had an army behind us. It didn't fucking matter. None of it.

Because my *maître* was gone.

I'd felt it.

An empty hollowness inside—gaping wide, *cavernous.*

"Don't, Frederick."

A long pause. No one spoke, breathed, lived. The world shut down forever.

"I'm so sorry, Tess…the frequency. It stopped."

My heart replicated his words—turning from living to stone. The dawn on the horizon mocked me with a new beginning when I no longer had one.

My finger went to the reject button, cutting the call just as Frederick whispered, "He's dead."

He's dead.

He's gone.

He left without me.

Very slowly with infinite control, I passed the phone to Franco. He took it, brushing his fingers with mine. "Tess…"

I recoiled. I didn't want anyone touching me. No one.

Never again. Loving was a weakness. Touch was an annihilation. Q had destroyed me.

He's gone.

The words pierced my heart with a thousand needles, puncturing my soul. *He's gone.*

Everything inside—all the goodness, happiness, hopefulness…*everything* shrivelled up. My will to live turned to black ash, sifting from my pours like dirty rain. Everything I'd been through. It'd all been pointless.

He fucking left me.

Bastard.

Anger was better than grief. It filled the cavernous hole, giving me something to latch onto.

The toll had taken its final debt. In return for Q's fortune, I'd been taxed too high. I'd been turned into a destitute widow.

He's dead.

"Tess, it's—" Franco gathered me in his arms, tugging me into his muscular bulk. I wanted to attack him. I couldn't control the rapidly heating, freezing, churning, storm gathering inside.

I was sad. Then angry. Then weak. Then *furious.*

Shoving Franco away, I snarled, "Don't touch me."

The streetlights clicked off, giving way to the watery pink light of a new day. A new day without Q. A lifetime without Q.

Franco pulled something from his pocket. He smoothed the paper, holding it out. "He made me promise to give you this if…"

My body stiffened.

"If what? He thought he'd die? He *planned* for his death?"

Why did he make you sign the will? Everything—it's all yours.

He'd bequeathed everything to me. And he'd done it so fast…almost as if he operated against time.

I stole the letter. Tearing it open, I swallowed bubbles of rageful tears.

Tess,

If you're reading this, then I guess…well, I don't need to put it into words. You know what's happened. Please don't hate me. I didn't leave you willingly. I know I have no right to ask this of you—but you can't undo my hard work. Promise me you'll keep living, esclave. *Promise me you'll stay alive. Franco knows what to do. Frederick will walk you through the future plans when you're ready.*

There really isn't much else to say. I love you so fucking much. Never forget that. Never forget the connection we shared, or the knowledge I'm waiting for you. Somewhere.

Je suis à toi—

I scrunched the letter up, throwing it on the floor in a fit of temper. There was more. More promises. More requests. More declarations of undying devotions.

But I couldn't read anymore. Lies. All of it.

Q had *left* me. He had no rights to me anymore. He had no right to make me promise not to enter my tower. He had no fucking right to ask me to continue living without him. I couldn't. I wouldn't. *I can't.*

It's not over.

My eyes narrowed, staring dry and tearless at the passing view. Q was dead. I'd paid my unpayable debt and now I wanted interest. I wanted what they'd stolen from me. I wanted a life for a life.

My anger filled the car interior with swirling silver rage. "I want to make them pay. I want to give them everything they deserve."

I'm going to show them how it feels to die slowly. How it feels to be soulless.

Franco took a while to reply, picking up Q's letter and placing it on the seat beside us. The presence of Q's penmanship and final thoughts took up space—filling the vehicle with his merciless love. He'd taken *everything* from me. My heart. My mind. My soul.

I would never forgive him for that.

"We'll make them pay," he muttered. "You have my

word."

My mind stained red. All the fight inside to remain good and pure disappeared. I threw myself headfirst into blackness. I accepted my life had changed forever. I had no intention of staying alive without him.

I would follow Q. It was the only option. Die or live an eternity locked in a tower unfeeling. I couldn't survive this unsurmountable grief. I couldn't let it consume me because if I did I would be washed away forever.

I had work to do before I died.

I had vengeance to deliver.

Violence. Blood. Screams. I wanted it all. I would make Q proud. I would avenge him.

You stole him from me.

You stole any chance of a happy life.

I was beyond angry. I was catatonic with rage. Tears had no place in the black void I existed in. Only greed—greed for killing. I would steal more than their lives in return.

I would steal their murderous souls.

Our convoy of killers gathered ranks outside the high hedges ringing the hellhole where my *maître* had died.

It didn't matter the sun sparkled, turning the world into a better place. All I saw was darkness. All I lived was darkness. All I wanted was death.

He's gone. But I'm going to join him.

Franco shattered my single-mindedness, dragging me back to an existence I no longer wanted to live.

Grabbing my hand, he forcibly curled my fingers around a gun. Squeezing me hard, his face shone with ruthlessness and pain. His injuries drained him, but he survived on bloodlust— same as me.

"Promise me, whatever happens in there. You come out alive. Don't be reckless. He wouldn't want that."

I promise to be reckless. I promise to ignore everything Q wants because he left me.

Q was gone. There would be no wedding. There would be no happiness.

Why would I agree to survive in a Q-less world?

I was done fighting. I was ready to join my master in a place that wouldn't tear us apart. I was done living in fear and terror—expecting the worst. I was done *living*.

But first—I would paint the sprawling villa in blood.

"I promise." The obvious lie hung like a filthy cloud. Franco scowled.

I hefted the weight of the weapon, counting the victims I wished I'd killed. Q had stolen that right, too. He'd killed on my behalf. Now it was my turn.

Leather Jacket.

White Man.

Jagged Scar.

All of them dead at his hand. Lynx was mine. Lynx was dead already and I rejoiced knowing I'd taken his soul. I no longer had any aversion to killing. This was right. They deserved to die. And I would gladly buy a ticket to hell in order to grant closure to my pain.

He's gone.

But soon, I would join him.

Franco sighed. "Let Blair and his team go in first. I've assigned Vincent to go in with you, seeing as I'll be hobbling." Pinching my chin, forcing my vacant eyes to meet his, he added, "I'll protect your life with my own—just like I did him. But you have to stay alive in order for me to do that. He wouldn't want you to—"

My stomach churned. "Don't tell me what he wanted, Franco. He's lost that right because he's *dead*."

Franco blanched. "Tess—you can't let this—"

"Can't let it what? Kill me? Ruin me? You expect me to

roll into a ball and cry my heart out? I'm past being told what I can and can't do. Stay out of my way, Franco. Let me find peace my way. Otherwise I won't be held responsible for what I'll do." Clutching my gun, I snapped, "Leave me the hell alone!"

His face darkened but understanding crossed his features. "I know the rage you're feeling. I know it's swallowing you whole. But, Tess—don't run in the opposite direction of who you are."

I growled low and long. "Shut up. Just shut up!"

You know Q wouldn't want this.

I shut myself up. I didn't want any thoughts or doubts. I wanted to stay in the clean clarity of vengeance.

Franco patted my shoulder. "I get it. I do. And I won't say anymore. But if you do this, you will never run from fear again."

I stroked my gun, counting the seconds till I could fire it. "If I do this, I *become* fear." I locked eyes with him. "I'll no longer be afraid. They'll be afraid of *me*." I'd never be a victim again because I would no longer have anything precious to tear from me. I was empty. I would stay empty until I died.

In a way that gave me power. Unlimited power I intended to wield on them. They'd turned me into a monster. They'd turned me into Q.

"I agree." Placing a hand on mine, he murmured, "Just don't forget you're human, too."

I ignored the hidden messages. I didn't pay attention to the hint that I shouldn't throw myself completely into my murderous rage. I didn't care if I lost myself. There was no one waiting for me to return this time.

A man in black military wear broke away from the milling shadows of Q's entourage. Coming toward us, he moved with stealthy confidence. His hands were free but two guns rested on his hips; multiple knives hung across his chest in a scabbard. Pulling the black beanie further over his blond hair, he said, "Ready when you are, sir."

Another man, taller with a rifle slung over his shoulder, appeared with a stick. Passing it to Franco, he grinned wryly. "Never provided a walking cane to go into a rampage but I think you need some help getting about."

I wanted to throw up. Jokes! They were making *jokes?*

How can they? Tears sprang up my spine, clawing their way painfully through my coldheartedness. I didn't want them. I didn't want caustic healing in the form of tears. *Empty. Stay empty.*

Franco bared his teeth. "Get that piece of shit away from me. I'm doped up to my eyeballs with painkillers. I can run while I don't feel it."

The man tossed the stick to the verge. "Your funeral."

The image of Franco dead cleaved my wounded heart. No, I wouldn't let anyone else die. I was done losing people I cared for.

"You're not coming," I whispered. A whisper was the only decibel I dared converse at. Everything inside boiled like a pressure cooker, building and building, steaming and steaming until my anger frothed and overflowed. The next time I spoke loudly, I would explode.

And I would murder the man who'd killed Q. I would be cataclysmic.

Franco shook his head. "I'm coming. The moment we find Mercer, I'll crash, but until we have him, I'm not stopping." Pointing at the two men, he ordered, "Blair, you're to go in first with five men. Do the preliminary sweep, clear any threats. Peter, you're in charge of Beta squad, head in two minutes after Alpha. Round up any slaves, staff, non-immediate threats to be sorted later." His eyes fell on me. "I'll bring up the rear with Vincent and Tess."

"Roger." The two men, one black-haired, and one blond, nudged knuckles before fading back to their teams to relay the orders.

He's trying to protect me.

Too bad. I wanted to be on the frontline. I wanted risk

and danger. I wanted something to hurl this rage onto.

My heart fizzled with anger. "I'm not going in last."

Franco frowned. "You are. You'll still have your revenge, Tess. But this is the safest way. You're the owner of everything Q built. Don't ruin his legacy by killing yourself."

The way he ruined me by dying?

I gritted my teeth, cuddling my gun as if it was my only lifeline. "You can't stop the inevitable," I mumbled so only the wind heard me.

Franco froze. "What did you just say?"

The inevitable will happen—I'm going to find him—where he's waiting for me.

"Nothing."

The first team, all dressed in identical black gear, armed with every arsenal available, darted out behind the hedges, heading toward the large driveway.

No! Wait.

I wouldn't hang back like a helpless woman. I deserved to mow down the killers of my lover. It was my *right*.

Out of everything Q had done to smash my tower—it was his death that finally released me from the rubble. The bricks, always teasing with erecting, had magically disappeared. My mind was a wasteland—completely grey and barren. I was exposed to every emotion and I only felt one.

"Esclave, don't do this. Remember everything I did."

Q's beautiful face consumed me—his strength, his smile.

But then he morphed and changed.

His vibrant eyes covered with a filmy white.

His tattoo hung off him in tatters.

Oxygen turned to reeking dust. My hollow heart rapidly filled with grief. It oozed through me, stealing my anger every second I stood doing nothing.

Not yet.

I refused to break down.

Not yet.

The last man disappeared; I couldn't stand still any longer.

I took a step toward the driveway.

Franco imprisoned my elbow. "No. You're going in with me. Three, four minutes, Tess. Patience."

Three or four minutes. That was an eternity. Time had stolen Q from me. Only minutes from our arrival, and the heartless bitch decided it was too many minutes too long. In another few minutes I might be useless with sorrow.

I obeyed time no longer.

My legs itched. My lungs gulped air. I prepared for battle.

Run.

Run. *Run!*

I took off.

"Tess, no!" Franco tried to grab me, but his broken body was no match for my quick paced rage.

I careened around the hedge, flying toward the open door. The soft *puffs* of silenced guns broke the hushed virginity of the morning.

The massive granite pillars glittered in the sunlight. Pansies and merry flowers bordered the doorstep, looking innocent, harbouring evil inside. The disguise was good. But I knew the truth.

They would die. All of them.

My hands didn't shake. My heart didn't stutter. I leapt over the threshold, trading sun for shadows.

"Tess!" Franco yelled.

I didn't stop. This was the beginning of my anarchy.

The décor was all red and black and morbid. Q's team crawled through rooms, dispatching traitors with a scope and trigger. Their black attire made them look like spiders, casting a web of retaliation, taking over their prey.

"Clear!" someone yelled, followed by a gunshot to the right. I didn't know where to look. Men's shouts sounded—then cut short. Running footsteps stomped—then thudded to a halt.

All around me men died—dispatched with precise coordination.

They stole my right! They took away my destiny—ending the men's existence before I could.

The crackle of someone's walkie-talkie slammed me into motion. They may have killed a household of bastards, but they hadn't found Q. No alarm sounded—no raised voices.

Q was still missing—and I knew his killer would be with him.

Raising the gun, I hunted.

Time lost meaning as I sank deep inside myself—tapping into instincts and heightened senses I never knew I possessed. I embraced the animalistic part—switching off humanity, thirsting for blood.

I prowled room after room.

Stripper poles and couches in one. Cinema and media in another. Kitchen. Bathroom. Office.

Bodies. I stepped over countless corpses from the efficiency of Q's team. Clean shots to either forehead or heart. Their vacant open eyes didn't raise my heartbeat or garner any emotion but hatred; deep seated hatred kindling in my chest where my heart used to be.

"Tess, you're not listening to me. Stop this—before it's too late. I can't save you again." Q's voice threaded with my conscience.

You can't save me because you're dead.

Shaking my head, ridding the craziness brewing inside, I entered a bedroom. And slammed to a halt.

Dark, dingy, not a dungeon, but not far off. Bunk beds lined each of the four walls. The lack of windows, and dampness from the floor, settled fast into my bones.

I sat on a threadbare mattress, looking around my new home. Girls huddled on each bed. All of them wore an aura of tragedy, eyes bruised with loss, skin painted with injuries and shadows.

A man loomed over me, his beard black and gross. Reaching behind him, he bared a knife.

The flashback of Mexico interlinked with the image in front of me. Bars across the windows, mattresses on the floor, women bound and gagged.

Two members of Franco's team helped the six girls from a variety of horrible positions. Some were collared to the wall, others were tied to poles, slouching painfully.

Their naked bodies showed numerous evidence of abuse. Tortured. Raped.

Not anymore.

Now they were free.

My eyes stung. Q had saved yet more women—more birds—and he wouldn't have the satisfaction of returning them to loved ones.

It's your vocation now—embrace his love of birds and focus on nurturing rather than death.

My fist trembled around the gun. I couldn't.

Bastards.

Devils.

I had to finish this. Whirling from the room, I ran. I needed to be far away—it threatened to unravel my hatred, dissolving me with tears.

I circled back to the front of the house, searching for a victim—any victim to transfer this rage onto.

My eyes fell on a staircase going down.

He's close. My instincts sounded an alarm, purring with knowledge. *Down there. Go.*

I took a step, only to be wrenched to a stop. "Bloody hell, Tess. What were you thinking?" Franco swayed, breathing hard. "I've been limping all over the fucking house. It's not safe. There could be anyone hiding, waiting to kill you."

I don't care.

"Let me go, Franco." I pointed down the stairs. "He's down there. I know it."

Franco's face whitened. "Let Alpha team go down. You don't want to see if you're right."

"You're wrong. I *do* want to see. I want to know what they did, so I can do the same."

I need to see he's really dead. I need to see the truth.

Franco shook his head. "Tess—this isn't you. Stop it."

I tore my arm from his grip. "You don't know me! Stop pretending like you care. Your boss is dead, and I don't want you to interfere. Go away." I hated my cruelness, but nothing would stop me from finding Q.

Franco stood locked to the landing.

Not looking back, I darted down the stairs. I held the gun high, my finger teasing the trigger.

My first kill happened too fast to remember.

A shadow. A blur. A shout. A curse.

Bang.

I no longer teased the trigger but compressed it, letting loose a killing projectile.

The man dressed in a black suit crumbled to the floor, holding a gushing wound in his neck. "Fucking, bit—bitch." His eyes narrowed to slits even as his arteries dumped litres of blood down his lapels.

I waited for a rush of sickness. I waited to feel different for doing something so barbaric, but I felt nothing.

Standing over him, I hissed, "Where is he? Tell me where he is."

The man gurgled, holding the wound tightly. "Wh—who *are* you?"

Ice lived in my blood as I crouched over him. "I'm your worst nightmare." Placing the gun against his crotch, I whispered, "I think you used this on trafficked women. I think you deserve more pain before you die."

He let his neck go, drenching his body in blood. "No! Wait!" He pushed feebly at the gun. "Don't!"

A silenced *puff* and his head snapped back, falling into death.

What?

A strong hand plucked me from the floor. I swivelled in their hold, glowering at my captor. Franco held a silenced pistol awkwardly in his bandaged hand.

"How dare you. He was mine to kill!"

"And you did. He was seconds away from death."

"Why didn't you let me finish it?"

"Because you've taken his life. You might be able to live with that—but torturing, that fucks you up, Tess. And I won't let you do that to yourself."

"I'm not weak. Stop treating me like I am."

Franco glared into my eyes. "You're not weak. I agree. You're strong—strong enough for Q and everything he gave you—but I made a promise to him. He made me swear I wouldn't let you slip away, hurt yourself, or do anything to jeopardise your commitment to him and his company."

"You don't own me. You can't do that."

Don't stop me from doing what I need!.

He shook his head. "I don't own you but Q does. He may be gone, Tess, but you're still his. You still have to obey—same as me." Sighing he said softly, "I'll let you kill Lynx, but I'll do the rest. My soul can handle it—yours can't."

It can. Because this time my victims aren't innocent.

Yanking me behind him, granting a protective wall of his body, he advanced down the black-tiled corridor. "Believe me. When the shock hits—when you finally let yourself feel, you'll thank me." Motioning with his gun, he muttered, "No more talking. Let's go."

I shoved him. "Let me go first. Don't steal this from me, Franco. I *need* to do this."

I need to avenge him.

"Shut up. I won't let you go first, so stop." His body was unmovable, blocking me from danger.

Gritting my teeth, I had no choice but to obey. His pace was agonisingly slow. A shuffle, a limp, but he did things I wouldn't have done—scanned each doorway, tried every doorknob, making sure it was locked and no one would ambush us. "You'll have your wish. I won't take that from you. Just let me protect you while you do it."

I wanted action. I wanted carnage. But it was silent.

Ominously silent.

What did you hope—you'd hear him? That he would be alive, and you'd hear his voice?

My eyes swelled with tears—finally recognising my stupid hopes.

Yes.

I'd been hunting in denial. Beneath my rage and grief blazed a fine layer of hope. It cindered the rest of my emotions. The hollowness inside had been filled with some other feeling. I didn't have a name—disbelief perhaps. My soul taunted me with a lie that he was dead.

I feel him.

Some ludicrous part believed he was still alive. The connection we shared hadn't been severed completely—it was there—weak, hazy, pulsing with darkness. But there.

And it ruined me further because hope was the cruellest emotion imaginable.

He's dead. I couldn't argue with that. No matter how much I wanted to.

Footsteps behind us.

I wheeled around, double fisting my gun.

The blond man in his beanie held up his hands. "We're on your side, Mrs. Mercer."

The title I wanted more than anything sent a bullet into my heart. I would never be Mrs. Mercer legally, but I would be in spirit. I was Q's. Regardless of life or death.

Not saying a word, I spun around, following Franco.

The dark richness of the corridor ended up ahead. Lighting gave just enough visibility so as not to fumble, but it was hard to make out the last door. Heavy wood with bars on top. A dungeon door.

Franco looked over his shoulder, his forehead beaded with pain-induced sweat. "Voices up ahead." He did some fancy finger moves to the team behind me.

I moved forward, sandwiched between the men. I hated that they'd formed ranks around me, protecting me when I didn't want to be protected. *I don't want to be protected.* Unless it was by Q.

Then I ceased all motor-control.

A noise.

A masculine groan, laced with agony.

Hope.

Glorious, sunbursting hope.

Q. I knew it. He's alive. Not dead. Never dead.

Shoving Franco aside, I shot ahead. Franco cursed in pain as his missing thumb slammed against the wall in my haste. "Tess!" he bellowed. But I was already gone, racing toward the final door.

Be alive. Please be alive.

I had no knowledge of my safety as I collided with the wood, exploding into hell.

Chains. Water. Blackness.

My eyes took everything in at once—a panoramic shot of horror. Two men stood in front of a male carcass hanging from the ceiling. Naked, bleeding, cuts upon cuts. Empty buckets littered the floor while a full one rested on a small table.

The man I focused on wore a dark red suit, his hair styled into a black and red mohawk, brandishing a bloody knife in my direction.

"Who the fuck are you? How did you get down here?" His Spanish accent echoed in the tomb.

Him. Lynx. My nemesis. My target.

Then my eyes landed on the massacre behind him.

All the hope I'd nursed sputtered out. All my love and prayers siphoned away.

Sparrows. Clouds. Barbwire.

My heart died.

No! Q was gone. I couldn't deny it anymore. No one could survive and have so much blood paint their body. No one could hang completely limp and lifeless if they weren't dead.

Someone cut him down!

Franco careened into the room. His large arm wrapped around my waist, jerking me backward. Shoving me away, he raised his weapon and shot the second man wearing drenched black clothing.

The man's neck flung back before his body fell like its puppeteer cut his strings, collapsing to the floor. The muted *pop* sounded so innocent compared to the sudden firework of gristle and blood decorating the wall behind the man.

Lynx reached into his waistband, pulling out an old fashioned pistol. "Don't fucking move!"

The hairs on my arms stood up, feeding off the anger in the room—the fine edge of living and death.

I didn't care which happened—live or die—as long as I killed Lynx first.

Blair catapulted into the room. Men crowded behind us, filling the corridor, providing back-up but also ensuring we had no way out.

Not that I needed a way out.

Q.

Franco grabbed me. I squirmed against his hold losing my ceaseless rage, filling with hot horror. Q just hung there, arms tied to his sides, black ropes binding his ankles to the ceiling.

Please, move! Let me know you haven't left me.

My eyes hurt, searching for breath, a quiver of a feather on his chest.

Nothing.

I swallowed back a rush of sickness. He hung upside down, butchered. His legs and stomach rivered with copious amounts of blood. His tattoo barely visible beneath the deep rust. A black towel covered his face, dripping with loud droplets onto the floor below.

I needed him down. I needed him in my arms.

Lynx glared. "I wasn't expecting an audience. But feel free to watch." He tore the towel from Q's head, revealing the bruised, slack face of my master.

The rage inside billowed, gathering momentum, hurtling toward one outcome. Him or me. One of us would be dead within minutes.

"Don't touch him," I hissed. I tore from Franco's grip,

stepping forward. I stood in the centre, wedged between right and wrong.

Franco and Alpha team shifted but remained silent. Unspoken law put me in charge. Nothing would be done or finished without my say so. And no one would kill Lynx because I would.

Lynx smiled, ignoring the men behind me—dismissing them just as I had. His gaze locked with mine and it was just us—us in this arena of death. "Who are you?" He stepped back, placing himself beside Q's upside down body. Pressing the muzzle of his gun against Q's temple, he said, "Wait, I know who you are. You've come for him then. Come to watch him die."

I hated his mind games—holding a gun to an already deceased body. Teasing me with hope—damn fucking hope. I wouldn't play his games. I knew the truth. He couldn't hurt Q anymore because he was dead. The tracker in his arm spoke the truth—not this *liar*.

I glided forward, compelled to touch—to confirm the white pallor wasn't fake. I couldn't ignore the pull, a vortex sucking me stronger and stronger toward Q.

I wanted to scream at Franco to cut Q down, but Lynx protected his prize.

The link between us sputtered, weak…gone. "I've come to watch but you're wrong about what. I'm here to watch your blood coat the floor."

Lynx's lips twisted. "You're as delusional as he was. Do you want to know what he did only hours ago? What another slave did to the man you love?"

I slammed to a halt, bombarded by images of Q sleeping with another, loving another.

He wouldn't.

"You can lie all you want, but I don't believe you."

Franco shuffled behind me. "Put down your gun, Lynx. Now."

Blair fanned to the side, building a wall of men all bristling with weapons.

"Stand down. This is mine. Do not move." My voice echoed with authority. The men fell silent.

Lynx smiled. "A woman with power. I like it." He stroked the muzzle over Q's cheek, indenting his skin, making him sway in the bindings.

My stomach snarled.

No one had the right to touch him. No one! *He's mine!*

Another step. I raised my gun. *Give him to me.* There would be no reasoning with him. In order to get to Q, I had to win. I had to take not ask.

"You like power? You have none. Take a look. You're outnumbered. I have a gun trained on your heart and your threats mean nothing to me. Stop touching him and I might let you die cleanly."

"I told you I'd come for you, Tess. Never doubt how much I love you." Q's voice echoed in my head. He'd sacrificed so much for me. He'd brought me back to life. And I'd repaid him by sliding into the darkest part of me. The part I never wanted to know. *I have to. I'm doing this for you.*

A moment spread like an eternity. Finally Lynx removed his weapon from Q, training it on me. His crocodile gaze glinted, lips pulling back against crooked teeth. "What's your name?"

I took another step, my finger trembling over the trigger. "Why?"

He cricked his neck, the gun steady in his hands. "Because I'd like to know the name of the woman I'm about to slaughter. I'll murmur it in a curse every night while I rape a woman—all the while imagining she's you."

The vile sentence didn't affect me. I was beyond affecting. "My name is Tess Snow. And you won't be cursing it. You'll be whimpering it."

He laughed. "Come closer and we'll see." His red shoes inched toward me, closing the gap, bringing us closer to the final conclusion.

"Tess! Don't." Franco's voice rang around the space. I ignored him.

"Do you know what I am?" I whispered.

Lynx's nostrils flared. "What you are? You're nothing but a—" He shook his head. "Wait, no...I see it—you're..."

"I'm his. I married the night and became his monster. And you should fear me." Nothing else existed inside. No residual issues of kidnapping, death, or pain. Nothing but peace.

I controlled my fate. Right here. Right now. And my fate was to kill and be killed. We would die together. I would wear his blood as I descended into the underworld.

"You ask if I see what you are. I do." His demeanour changed from angry to smooth. "You're not worthy of death, Tess Snow. Your previous owner is dead. I claim you as my new property. Come to me and I'll let you live." His gaze slithered over my body. "I'll treat you right. I've searched all my life for a woman like you."

Another step. Only a metre left. Grabbing distance. Shooting distance.

"A woman like me?"

"A woman so broken she doesn't even know. A woman strong enough to survive anything because she no longer *feels* anything." His arm lowered a little, believing his fantasy—that he could win me. That he could *acquire* me.

I laughed.

Everyone froze—the dungeon pulsed as I slipped from sanity to insane. I lowered my gun.

I'd never felt more clear. More powerful. *He's already dead.* I knew how I'd do it. "You want to own me?" Softness entered my voice, ghosting over the tiles toward Lynx.

"Tess—come back here," Franco ordered. "Whatever you're doing—stop it."

The awareness between me and Q's killer grew stronger, blocking everyone out. I didn't look at Q or pay attention to Franco. I was single-minded. Locked on my prey. Mouth watering with the knowledge I'd won.

Lynx smiled, eye's glinting with interest. "Yes. Stand by my side. I would be proud to keep you. You'd have my word I would never sell you—as long as you stayed this cold." His accent danced with sensuality, dragging me closer toward him. *Idiot. Buffoon.*

"You want to own my body. But what about my mind?" One last step. Space meant nothing anymore. Such a short space. A killable space.

His pistol lowered, hypnotised by his own illusion. "I want to own all of you. Give it to me and I'll treat you better than he ever did."

He. Q. My heart launched out of my chest, winging to my dead master. My skin was sleet and snow, but it was almost over. *Soon, my* maître. *Soon, I'm coming for you.* I noticed everything as if I'd stepped outside my body. Every nuance, every threat was achingly clear.

One more step. Lynx's body heat buffeted me—his expensive cologne made me want to vomit. But I looked into his eyes, invoking the sweetest poison of my soul. I made him *believe.* "I doubt you can," I murmured, looking up through lowered lashes. The room was stagnant with tension—it was soup—unstrained syrup.

Lynx was bewitched. "Doubt I can what?" He leaned forward, eyes latching onto my lips.

"Treat me better than he ever did." His body curved, swaying toward me, drugged on the poison I fed. "I'll accept your terms, if you do one thing for me. One tiny thing."

His lips hovered a fraction above mine. "Do what?"

I tilted my head, hair falling over one eye. "Ask what I want in return. Then I'll give you all that I am."

His forehead furrowed, his temper growing. "You're too bold. But I'll do it—one request, then no more." He reached for my chin, holding me. I ignored the insects crawling beneath his touch. Soon. It would be over....soon. "What do you want?"

My eyes rested on Q. His wonderful body, his gorgeous

features. I fanned the love in my heart, cocooning myself with strength. On barely a whisper, I said, "You can't give me what I want."

Lynx pulled back, the fog retreating from his eyes, finally sensing my trap. But it was too late.

"You can't give it to me because I want your fucking soul." I pressed my weapon against his cock. I fired.

A second.

That's all it took.

The bullet tore through soft intimate flesh, making him scream. And scream. And *scream*. His pistol swung upward but I was ready. I shot his hand. Blood filled the wound, spilling with a steady trickle. The weapon skittered away like a scared animal, sliding into a corner of the room.

Lynx crashed to the floor, holding his bloody trousers, incomprehensible with pain.

Franco tried to grab me, but I didn't stop or care. Slapping him away, I knelt beside Lynx, letting his groaning agony wash over me. I pushed a fingertip into his blood, gathering the life-paint, smearing it across my cheek. The cooling ooze was a hard-won trophy. I swelled with retribution.

I did this for you, Q. I've avenged you.

"Help—someone!" Lynx spluttered between his screams. Slamming a hand over his mouth, I shut him up. His feeble fights were nothing to the rage making me inhumanly strong. I didn't care my knees got wet as I kneeled by his head. I didn't care his blood soaked through my clothes, baptising me in horror. All I cared about was the last words I wanted to say. To him. To the traffickers who'd taken me. To evil itself.

I bowed over him, whispering in his ear, "My name is Tess Mercer. I'm no longer weak or afraid or broken. I've taken control of my fate. I no longer need a tower or dark angels or help. *I am fear.* And I take your soul in penance for everything that was done to me. I take it for the women you've raped. I take it for the women you've sold. I take it for my master, soul-mate, and husband. I take you for me."

Pressing the gun against his forehead, I locked eyes with his chaotic gaze. He begged me silently. He pleaded wordlessly. And no compassion filled me.

I hope you burn forever.

Trigger. Sulphur. Bullet.

He was dead.

No one moved or spoke as I rose gracefully from the puddle of blood, standing over the soulless corpse. I was a phoenix glowing bright with power. I took back everything that'd been stolen.

I didn't find the old Tess. She was gone. But in her place stood a new Tess. A woman who no longer feared. I'd looked evil in the eye and won. I'd been reborn in blood.

Franco shuffled forward, gently prying my fingers from the gun. "Tess—are you okay?"

His voice cut through my silence inside, reminding me I'd taken one life, now it was time to mourn another.

Turning to Q, I wasn't strong enough to fight the swell of grief this time.

Q hung there—his stomach didn't rise with breath, his dark hair glistening with wetness. He was gone and it was time to smother my pointless hope and accept. "Cut him down."

The team of men did as I asked, obeying my every command. A pulley in the wall dropped Q's body to a height where a knife could be sliced through the rope around his ankles. Two men caught him. Franco collected his legs and in a sombre ceremony they carried him from the dungeon. They carried my reason for existing back into the sunlight.

I trailed behind, smearing Lynx's blood between my fingers like a talisman. The emptiness inside rapidly filled with churning waves of sadness. My heartbeats were heavy and loud—gonging with every step.

One beat.

Two beats.

I focused on staying strong. I had to. Q was gone.

Once upstairs, the men placed Q on a couch in a small

conservatory. It was the only room that looked peaceful with plants rather than stripper poles.

I allowed the men to untie him—unwrapping his ankles, freeing his arms. I kneeled on the floor by his head, never taking my gaze from his white face. His eyes remained closed, lips slightly parted.

The waves inside splashed against my crumbling self-control. The first tear escaped my control, sliding down my cheek.

Franco disappeared. He came back with a blue blanket draping it over Q's nakedness.

He's dead.

No matter how much I told myself, I couldn't believe it. I didn't *want* to believe it. If I did it meant my life was over. Forever. I would remain alone.

Hope—that bastardly emotion—wouldn't let me go.

He doesn't feel dead.

He's not gone. He can't *be gone.*

The cord linking our souls together wasn't completely sundered. Or was I believing my own lies? Numbing myself to the truth?

Q please. Don't leave.

The first wave broke my iron control, sending a torrent of tears up my spine.

I cupped Q's cheek. I froze.

He was clammy. Not cold.

Hope took over my waves of tears, building a wall of wishes.

"Franco…" I looked up, begging him to confirm.

Franco hovered over me, his body seizing with injury. He lowered his good hand beneath Q's nostrils. Ducking beneath his arm, I pressed my ear against Q's damp chest, *willing* a heartbeat to thud.

My ear grew warm as I pressed harder, throbbing with the need to hear the fundamental part of him thrum.

Moments ticked past while we listened and waited.

Then my hope was confirmed.

Franco and I jerked back together. Our eyes met, wide with awe. "He's breathing," Franco said. I blurted, "His heartbeat is faint but it's there."

The churning waves vanished, leaving me with frantic calm. "Someone get more blankets. Water. Call an ambulance." I pressed my ear to Q's chest again, needing to hear.

Thud...thud...

You're going to be okay.

Q's unconscious form became the hub of commotion. Men dashed around, delivering blankets, first aid kits, and water.

I didn't move from Q's side. With gentle fingertips, I traced his cheekbones, whispering over his lips. "You're safe. Wake up. Please wake up."

Tears breached my eyelashes, dripping over my cheeks. But these were hopeful tears rather than heavy with grief. My body remembered how to feel, thawing the ice in my blood, bringing me up from the darkness and back into the sunshine. "Q—please."

Kneeling higher, I pressed my lips to his. In my mind I tasted his agony—the torture he'd endured. I licked away his screams, letting him know we'd come for him.

We weren't too late.

I'm here.

My body began to quake, exceeding any Richter scale as I filled with shaking gratefulness.

I kissed him again. Hard and fierce.

He didn't move but something shifted in my heart. I knew he'd heard me—sensed me. An awareness gathered in the space as Q clawed his way from unconsciousness, fighting to return.

In increments, he came alive.

His chest raised higher, his lips tightening as pain registered.

Then his eyes went from closed to narrowed to open. Pale jade blazed while the whites of his eyes were bloodshot and raw.

What the hell did they do to him?

I shook my head. I didn't want to know. I never wanted to picture him in such pain. I couldn't handle it. I'd never forgive myself for not extracting a worse toll on Lynx if I knew.

Q's gaze focused on mine, pulling me inside him, sewing us together stronger, deeper than ever before. "Te—Tess?"

I burst into tears. Throwing my arms around his neck, I peppered his face with kisses. I wasn't gentle. I couldn't be gentle.

He half-laughed, half-groaned. *"Tout va bien."* It's okay. His voice was cracked and rough, breathless with pain.

"You're alive. Q—" I couldn't stop kissing him, layering him with all the love I had. "We thought you were dead. How is this possible?" I stroked his cheek, imprinting his glorious face onto my heart.

Q stiffened, wincing as a flush of agony paled his features. "He d—did kill me, a f—few times. Or at least, I think so—I remember leaving—falling..." His eyes clouded. "I followed you, *esclave*. I thought you'd come—"

"We did come."

He smiled. "Kiss me again. I need to know this is real." His voice was barely audible, cracking and wheezing but I understood every word.

My lips caressed his, drinking him, loving him. It was a chaste kiss. No tongue, only breath and heat and a promise of never leaving.

Pulling away, I asked, "If he killed you—how are you alive?"

Q looked away, hiding the torrent of memories. "He had ta—Taser. Amazing what a volt of el—electricity to the heart can do—to prolong things."

His grogginess evaporated as his hand suddenly shot between his legs. Relief slackened his face. "Thank God."

I pulled back. "What? What is it?"

Q shook his head, alertness battling back his weakness.

"Nothing. I'm still in one piece. That's all." He sighed heavily, looking worn-out and barely conscious. His eyes narrowed. "Why is there blood on your cheek?"

Because it was my blood to take.

Franco appeared in the doorway, using the dreaded walking stick he'd scorned before. "Ambulance is on its way." Smiling at Q, he added, "You should've seen her, Mercer. Fucking scary as hell. But she killed him for you." Franco glared in my direction. His eyes blatantly vowing that what happened downstairs would remain between us.

I nodded, accepting his promise. I'd done what I needed to do. Q didn't need to know the details.

Q's face darkened, overshadowed with the strain of talking. "What?" He growl-croaked, "You killed Lynx? That's *his* blood on your face?"

I made him believe my lies and stole his life.

I nodded, fierce pride resonating in my heart. "He stole you from me. He had to die. And I had to be the one to do it." Taking his hand, I squeezed. "I know you'll understand, and I know you'll accept when I say it's done and I don't want to talk about it."

Q flinched, untangling his arm from the blanket. With a shaky hold, he cupped the back of my neck. I bowed over him, never looking away from his eyes. "What did you do, Tess? Please tell me you didn't undo my hard work." He stopped, sucking in a breath. His eyes were tight with agony. "Tell me you didn't ruin yourself by killing him for me. You didn't have to do that. I never wanted—"

"It won't happen." I knew his fears. He worried I'd relapse for hurting another like killing Blonde Hummingbird. But I wouldn't because I'd done the right thing. I was happy. I accepted my brutality and would gladly live with the knowledge I wasn't pure anymore. I was never pure. And if I went to hell for saving the man I loved—then that was the final debt I would pay.

I kissed him softly. "Taking his life granted me power. I'm

not afraid anymore. I'm in control of my fate, and I give it to you wholeheartedly." My stomach clenched, remembering his letter. "But if you ever leave me a note again, after planning your death and telling me nothing of the dangers you're in, I'll kill you, too."

Q leaned back on the cushion, his energy rapidly fading. "I did that to protect you."

"Well—I want to protect you in return." My heart lurched realizing just how vulnerable we all were. How quickly life passed—how much I wanted to live it. "Marry me, Q. Now. I don't care where or how."

Q's fingers added pressure to the base of my skull, bringing me down to kiss him. His lips moved against mine in a dance belonging completely to us. His tongue entered sweetly, seductively. He didn't kiss with misery or happiness or lust.

He kissed me with reverence. Thankfulness.

When we broke apart, he murmured, "*Je t'ai déjà épousée dans mon cœur, Tess. Au moment où j'ai posé les yeux sur toi, tu étais à moi pour toujours, mon amour.*" I've already married you in my heart, Tess. The moment I set eyes on you, you were mine forever.

Looking over my head, he said to Franco, "Call Suzette. Find out where she organised the wedding."

"Wait—Suzette?"

Q smiled, reopening the small cut on his lower lip. "We're getting married tomorrow. Suzette's been arranging it." His last reservoir of strength petered out, leaving him pale and breathing hard.

Franco towered over us, two injured warriors together. "I'll call her, and I'll do anything else that needs to be done— but you—you're going to the hospital."

Q opened his lips to argue but winced as Franco deliberately patted his sliced up legs beneath the blanket. "Hospital, Mercer. Then wedding. Don't make me kick your ass."

A tense moment existed before Q nodded. "I think that

ass kicking can wait, don't you?" His gaze fell to Franco's missing thumb. A rosebud of blood decorated the bandage where his digit used to be. Q frowned, taking in the sling and Franco's cane. "Thank you for coming."

Franco shrugged. "Couldn't be late to this party. Look how much fun you were having."

I cringed at the morbid humour, but Q smiled. "The fun I could've done without—but I'm grateful to you, Franco." His eyes fell on me. "And forever in your debt, Tess. You should never have had to do that on my behalf. I'm sorry."

Sirens sliced the morning peace. A flashing ambulance pulled into the driveway, its lights visible through the windows. Kissing Q's cheek, I whispered, "No apologises. I did what I needed to do." I nuzzled his cheek. "Your chariot awaits, *maître*. And your bride will be with you every step until she becomes your wife."

Q's body stiffened, fighting off a wave of pain. "And once you're my wife—you intend to leave my side?"

My heart was no longer a heart—it became a beacon, beaming with brightness, lighting the way to my future. "When I'm your wife, our lives will become one. I won't be by your side. I'll be *inside* you. Forever."

Q sucked in a breath, his eyes glowing with love. "In that case—get me to the hospital."

Chapter Fourteen

You are my saviour
My forever

The hospital was a necessary evil.

As much as I wanted to leave Spain and never return, I had to endure needles, questions, and doctors.

Hours upon hours of tests, MRIs, and stitching up the slices on my legs frayed my patience, giving time the opportunity to turn my injuries into bone-deep aches. My head pounded from hanging upside down and everything inside was bruised—my kidneys, my stomach—even my spleen. My heart was also banged up, but surprisingly fine—despite the rigorous assault it'd endured. My spine was swollen from the baseball bat, but I had sensation in my legs. *Thank fucking God.* And the bullet hole was no longer a hole after surgery sewed me up.

The catalogue of injuries went on forever but after everything I'd endured the only broken part of me was a cracked rib. That and my heart. Tess had done something irreversible down there. I'd hung unconscious while she did something I would never be able to delete.

Twisting my head on the pillow, I looked at her.

She hadn't moved from my side. She'd been there while the doctors numbed my legs and practiced fucking cross-stitch with my flesh. She'd held my hand while we waited for the results of my heart and blood pressure readings. She screamed at any doctor who tried to remove her from a procedure.

I fucking loved her. I couldn't stop looking at her— knowing she'd killed for me. She'd willingly crossed that threshold where no human should have to go. She took a life in payment for mine. She truly was my perfect other.

Tess glowed, a smile spreading her lips. "Do you need anything? Something to eat? Water?"

I couldn't stop the involuntary shudder at the mention of fucking water. Vile liquid. Killing liquid. I never wanted another sip or to see a bucket or towel again. That had been the worst part. I didn't care about the baseball bat or even the cuts on my legs. It was the black wetness that turned my stomach.

It was the breathless horror whenever my mind relived the past. I'd died. I'd given up. And that made me fucking weak. While I'd given up, Tess had become my saviour.

It made me proud. It also made me furious. Hospital staff looked at me as if I were a fucking invalid—compounding the emotions I battled. How could I ever thank Tess for what she did? How could I ever live with myself for being so fucking stupid?

Police had arrived to take my statement and for once I could tell the truth—the whole truth and not fear any repercussions. They'd left us in peace after the main activities and needlepoint on my legs.

Finally, after what seemed like days, I'd finally been left alone in a private room. Finally able to breathe without disinfectant or antiseptic stinging my nostrils. The grogginess from the anaesthesia wore off, leaving me stiff and sore.

My nervous system had a hard time tabulating it all. One moment an ache flared in my chest, the next my lower back. But despite the flushes of agony, I felt fine. I felt whole. I felt *content.*

I survived.

Tess squeezed my hand, bringing my scattered thoughts back to her. "Q—would you like a drink?"

I smiled, soaking in her perfect face. "I would murder for a shot of whiskey." My voice cracked and failed. According to the doctor, my throat suffered multiple lacerations from either screaming or trying to breathe H$_2$O instead of oxygen.

The fucking bastard really hurt me. But I was alive, and he was not. All because I had people behind me. I had goodness on my side. I had my *esclave*. My fearless strong *esclave*.

"You're not drinking." Her forehead wrinkled. "Who knows what you'll get up to if you have alcohol on top of the painkillers they've administered."

I chuckled. "I can think of a few things." I wanted to try out my cock—make sure it hadn't died in sheer terror at the threat of being cut off. I didn't know how close Lynx came to delivering his final threat. All I remembered was endless water torture, more cuts, more electricity, and welcoming darkness.

I'd been tired. So fucking tired.

Still was, actually, but now it was a sated tired. Satisfied with the knowledge I could sleep with Tess beside me, and we'd both be safe.

Tess blushed, love filling her face with a gentle fire. She carried an inner flame—a torch she'd been missing for so long. After everything I'd done, she was the one to bring back her light. She'd claimed her own destiny once again and in the same breath handed it over to me.

Her gift humbled me, layering my guilt for what the slave did the night before. Another woman's lips had been around my cock. How could I ever tell her that? But how could I ever *not*? Would the secret fester until it turned me into a rotting cavity? Or would she understand I didn't do it willingly? My body and soul were hers. Through and through.

You can't tell her. Not yet.

Maybe one day I would—but not yet. Not until I'd sorted

through the memories and dealt with them in my own way. Not until I'd talked to the girl and apologised.

Blair came into the private room where Franco, Tess, and I were awaiting the final results. I'd suffered countless x-rays to find out if the baseball bat had punctured any organs or caused internal bleeding.

"The plane is fuelled and ready to go, sir. The flight plan has been lodged and Suzette has been informed of an ETA of twelve hours."

Blair smiled at Franco passed out on a bed. His snores sailed from the other side of the room. The doctors had reassessed him, given more painkillers, and changed his bandages. No sooner had they stopped prodding him, he'd passed out cold.

Sleep was a miracle cure, and I wanted some myself.

I need to sleep so I don't look like a fucking corpse on my wedding day. I honestly didn't know how I'd function after everything my body survived but I wasn't waiting another day. Tess would be mine tomorrow. It would come true even if I had to say my vows in a wheelchair and not consummate for days.

"I've also made arrangements for Franco's future care. It will all be arranged when you return home," Blair said.

"Merci." I nodded. "Appreciate everything you've done. I'll leave you in charge of disbanding the team and arranging safe transportation for any women ready to return home. Work with the police. Give them any information they need and advise them to contact Frederick if they need more details."

The blond man, who'd killed beside me in Brazil, grinned. "Will do. I've got it under control. See you in France, sir." With a small salute, he left the room, leaving Tess and me alone once again—minus Franco snoring in the corner.

Tess moved, perching higher on the edge of my bed. She smiled, linking her fingers with mine. "Are you sure you'll be okay to travel? The doctors said you should stay here. Wait a few days at least."

"They always say that. They've done what they can for me.

Now it's my body's job. I can heal in other places than just a hospital." Hiding my wince as a bolt of agony tore through my thigh, I added, "I wouldn't miss the biggest day of my life. I'm marrying you tomorrow whether you want to or not." I hoped I looked threatening and not a man very aware of his mortality. "Lynx would've had to kill me to prevent that."

I shuddered, remembering just how close he came— multiple times. I'd never been one to cry for help—but he'd made me scream. Fucking asshole.

"I've already cleared it with the hospital staff to bring along one of the head doctors and a triage nurse," Tess said. "You both need experts if you're stupid enough to leave before they say."

Looking over at snoring Franco, I grinned. "I'm not concerned about my own wellbeing, but I agree he's a bit of a mess. Best to have someone who can knock him out if he gets out of hand."

Tess clamped her lips together. "They really hurt him. Just like they hurt you." Her focus turned inward, no doubt remembering the rush to find me and the mess I'd been in when they did.

My heart squeezed as shadows cast over her face. "I'm sorry you had to see me like that, *esclave*."

Her eyes flickered to mine. "Sorry? What on earth do you have to be sorry about?"

I sucked in a breath. Not prepared to tell her just how much I had to apologise for. I'd been completely reckless. Idiotic. "I should've had more security. I knew they would come eventually."

She sucked in a breath. "I want to ask one question, then I'll never mention it again." Her face turned hard. "Will you answer it?"

My temper intertwined with the morphine in my blood, making me wary. *She knows.*

Goddammit, I wasn't ready for this. "What is it?"

"You knew something like this would happen. I know why

you went with them—to protect me. But, Q, you're a billionaire. You should *never* have been in harm's way. You were reckless. Travelling with only one guard. You made it *look* like you were protecting yourself with fake names and guns but really—you let them take you—didn't you?"

Shit. How did I ever think I would get away with it? The way she'd watched me at the restaurant—her hesitation when we first arrived in Rome. She'd fed off my awareness— searching for the men I knew were stalking me.

My eyes narrowed. "You want the truth?"

She nodded.

"Fine. Yes, I made it easy for them."

"Why?"

"To use them as an example."

Franco stirred before falling back into sleep. "I've done a lot of bad things in my life, Tess. Messed with a lot of men who are just as rich as me and have the means to hunt and kill without ever being seen. It was the choice I made in order to avoid dying one afternoon by a sniper rifle and never returning home to you."

"But you could've brought more security. You could've—"

"No, Tess. It wouldn't have worked. They would've found a way, and I refused to run that risk. What if they'd killed you by mistake? What if they came after you again? This was the logical way—even Franco agreed with me."

"Agreed with you on what?"

I sighed heavily. "I had to look weak to appear strong."

Tess frowned. "That doesn't make sense."

I shifted against the pillows, already feeling stronger. I was calm—for the first time since the press aired my dirty secrets. "Not only did I remove Red Wolverine's operation, but you and Franco took out Lynx. Two major players who others respect. What do you think other traffickers will do? Now, I've proven twice as hard to kill?"

Tess shook her head. "I know what you're going to say,

but how can you be sure?"

"I can't."

Tess fell silent before murmuring, "You think they'll keep their distance?"

That's what I fucking hope. "I aim to use Lynx as an example. He came for me. He hurt me. But he died for it. And not only did I exterminate his team, steal his women, and disband his business, but I have the law on my side. No one will put me in prison for killing them. No one will make me stand trial for saving women." My body heated with the knowledge I'd built a protection detail better than mere men. I'd bought word of mouth respect and a reputation for invincibility. I'd done everything in my power to ensure I lived a long fucking life. "They won't try again—not for a while."

Tess suddenly stood. Her eyes glittered as she tore off her jeans and sweater. The smear of blood still marked her cheek—her trophy from battle. Her stomach muscles danced, slinking from her clothes.

My mouth went dry, staring at her body. She only wore knickers—no bra—the blush from the candle wax faint on her breasts. "You're impossibly stunning, *esclave.*"

My cock swelled, filling with desire for the woman who'd saved my life. She truly owned me. It was undeniable now.

I wrenched back the covers, inching over for her slim body to fit against mine on the small hospital bed. The moment her delicate form pressed against me, I breathed heavily. "Don't hate me for accepting pain. It was an insurance policy."

"To protect me."

I kissed the top of her head, wincing a little at the ache in my chest. "To protect you."

"You don't have to protect me anymore," she murmured.

I smiled, relaxing against her warmth. "Tess, I will protect you till my last breath on this earth—and even longer if I can. You're mine. You should expect nothing less."

Tess's frame shivered as tears dampened my chest. "You almost left me, Q. I hated you for leaving."

I held her tighter, letting her release everything she'd lived through. "But I didn't leave. I found a way to be with you. You found me in time."

Her voice was watery with sadness. "I *never* want to feel that way again. Promise me."

Rocking her, I let her cry. "I promise, *esclave.* I promise to never leave or keep things from you again. *Je suis à toi.*"

Franco had told me briefly about the arrest. About what she'd gone through. I wanted to smash the cop's face in for detaining my woman, but that would have to wait. Right now I would be the sponge to soak up Tess's tears, and tomorrow I would stand by her side. We would speak the binding words of eternal vows.

Tomorrow all of this wouldn't matter.

Tomorrow the future was ours.

Stepping into the solid wall of heat deleted our sorrows, giving us happiness instead.

The air-conditioned flight had taken us away from Spain, the hospital—away from what Lynx had done.

Seychelles at midnight was almost mystical in its paradise. The airport twinkled with lights, creating a buzz of anticipation while a welcoming blanket of relaxation descended. All my angst and stress from the past few weeks melted away, leaving me weightless for once.

This was the place I would marry Tess. The place where true happiness began.

The ten hour flight had given us time to rest, but the trade-off for sleep was stiffness. No matter how I forced my body to move, it'd lost the smooth power, replacing it with jerky tiptoes. The stitches in my legs tugged uncomfortably, the tenderness in my thigh throbbed, but nothing would stop me from being here—or marrying Tess tomorrow.

"Bloody hell, it's hot," Franco muttered limping down the plane steps. The moment he hobbled away from the stairs, I turned to take Tess's hand as she stepped carefully onto the tarmac.

"Wow," she said, glancing around. "It's beautiful. I missed the heat."

"I agree—"

My phone rang, vibrating against my ass. Letting Tess go, I pressed the receive button, bracing myself for the torrent of exclamations I knew was coming. I'd avoided talking to her at the hospital but couldn't avoid it now.

"*Bonsoir*, Suzette."

"*Mon Dieu*! You're alive. Thank the heavens. I've been going crazy! Franco wouldn't let me talk to you. He banned me from upsetting you. Then Blair said you were in hospital. Hospital, Q! I tried to call the doctors and find out if you'd be okay for the wedding. I contacted everyone I knew for information. But no one told me anything. Do you know how frustrating that is! People said you died! Q—" Tears filled her voice. "You—are you—"

I jumped in. "I'm alive—as you can very well hear. We're at the airport. And you'll be able to see for yourself that I'm in one piece if you let me get off the damn phone and into the helicopter."

I'd been informed of the location when we checked out of the hospital. Suzette had done a great job arranging a chopper transfer, but I still didn't know the name of our final destination.

Tess smiled beside me, enjoying the one-sided conversation.

"By the way—which island are we flying to?" My mind flicked through the atolls and land masses making up Seychelles. I'd never been tempted to buy property on this side of the world but I'd visited once or twice. The diving was incredible thanks to the crystal clearness of the reefs.

"It's called *Cheval De Mer*." She cleared her throat. "And

I'm not saying any more until you get here. The other guests have arrived, but they're separate from where you and Tess are staying."

Anger sprung with rushing fire, bringing gushing pain to extremities. *"Guests?" Shit, who the hell did she invite?* "Suzette! You *knew* I didn't want anyone there."

Silence.

"Suzette," I growled.

"You put me in charge. So…I took charge."

I rubbed my temple, cursing the shooting pains in my heart. Tension heightened the aches in my body. Fuck. "If I find there are a bunch of people I don't want, or if there are news reporters bobbing in the fucking ocean trying to photograph us—I won't just fire you, Suzette—I'll—"

"Threats and more threats. Don't you know they don't work on me?"

Tess placed a hand on my arm, granting me some serenity. Ordinarily, I would've grinned at Suzette's comment, pride filling me for her snarky strength. I'd given that to her. I'd saved her. But this time, I was pissed.

I wanted to scream. But my energy level was too low. "Don't make me regret this wedding."

She sombered, answering softly, "You could never regret it. You're marrying her." She hung up, leaving me glowering at the phone.

"Everything okay?" Tess asked. Her blonde hair was coiled upward, loose strands dancing in the hot breeze.

I pinched my brow. I didn't know how intelligent I'd been putting Suzette in charge. Who knew the catastrophe she might've orchestrated. But it was done now. I had no way of controlling whatever she'd put into action. I just hoped I wouldn't have to kill her for disobeying.

"Probably not, but there's nothing I can do about it."

This was why I wanted to elope to *Volière.*

You're marrying her.

Suzette was right. Nothing could stop the knowledge that

Tess was mine completely. No matter if she'd arranged a circus or a fucking Mardi Gras, having Tess sign her name beside mine would make everything else fade into oblivion.

I wrapped an arm around Tess's waist. "Ignore me. Been a long day. Let's go." Nodding at Franco, I added, "Time to leave reality behind."

Franco grinned. "Damn right. Had enough reality for a lifetime. I'm ready to pass out on a lounger and drink cocktails until my body doesn't hurt anymore."

Sounds like a great fucking plan.

Together our trio made our way toward the helicopter glinting in the starlight. It wasn't a Bell Relentless but it was still a nice machine with clean lines and blue and silver paintjob.

"Good evening, Mr. Mercer. Ms. Snow." The pilot nodded, shaking my hand. "Please, come aboard and make yourself comfortable. The flight will be approximately twenty-five minutes."

Tess climbed in, turning to give me her hand which I flatly refused to take. I wasn't a fucking invalid. Sure my heart had stopped a few times under torture. Sure my legs held more stitches than I wanted to count, but I wasn't dead. I could climb into a goddamn helicopter unassisted.

That didn't stop a shove from Franco on my ass as I bent forward. I stumbled inside, swallowing my groan of pain. Everything heated, flaring with discomfort. Steadying myself, I muttered, "You obviously don't like having thumbs. Do that again and I'll make it an even missing pair for you."

Franco laughed. "Just helping an old man. Doing my civil duty."

Asshole.

Grabbing his arm, I yanked him unceremoniously into the cabin. He landed with a thud, cursing.

"Oops. Didn't know you were so delicate. Just repaying the favour."

Franco looked up, his emerald eyes sparking with laughter. "Not as delicate as you. You know, I'm getting over seeing you naked, Mercer. Hanging upside down like that. I have to say, I wasn't impressed."

The joke barbed, but I knew what he was doing. He'd been in charge of finding me alive—not just because it was his job, but because he genuinely cared for Tess. No one wanted a grieving wife on their watch.

The sparring was a way of unwinding—dispelling the anxiety of the past few days. With my lips twisted into a smile, I pulled my leg back—fully intending to kick him.

Tess looked at us in horror. "Are you trying to send yourself back to the hospital? Stop it!" Her blue-grey eyes flashed as she sat down in one of the eight chairs situated much like an airplane cabin. "Both of you."

Franco smirked, climbing to his feet. "Better listen to your woman, boss. She's got you on a tight leash. Don't want to disobey." He smacked me on the back. My eyes watered with residual agony from the baseball bat injuries.

Repaying the favour, I planted a heavy hand on his healing shoulder. "Least I have a woman. I feel sorry for your cock. Which hand did you use to jerk off? Left or right? Guess not having a thumb is going to be a bitch for that."

Franco swung, missing my jaw as I ducked. We were both breathing hard with pain, but broke into laughter.

Tess rolled her eyes, muttering under her breath, "I don't get it. Does everything have to be a competition between you two?"

We answered together, "Yes." Franco added, "Just giving him payback. He owes me a thumb and until he pays up, his ass is mine." His chest puffed, lowering himself carefully into a chair. "He's alive because of me—he owes me. Big time."

I chuckled. We'd survived a lot in the past few days. If we couldn't laugh about it what was the fucking point.

Tess held up her finger, pointing at us as if we were incompetent children. "You're forgetting *I* killed Lynx. If anyone owns Q's ass, it's me." Standing, she crossed the small distance between us and blatantly grabbed my left ass cheek with her fingernails.

I jolted under her hold; my cock—who'd been too much of a fucking pussy to twitch till now—thickened under her intense gaze. I'd wanted her in the hospital but this was different. My system wasn't layered with drugs. I didn't care about my pain—all I cared about was sinking inside her.

"You're mine. Are we clear?" Her lips parted, recognising the paralyzing cloud of lust between us. I wanted her. Naked. Screaming. Coming.

Dropping my hand, I grabbed her in the exact place she held me. Dragging her close, I whispered, "If we're still on the topic of whose ass belongs to whom, *esclave*, don't forget—this…" I trailed my fingers possessively to her crack. "This is mine. And I'm taking it the moment you're my wife."

She bit her lip, eyes sparking with grey fire.

The captain and co-pilot finished their pre-flight checks, turning to look down the small gangway. "Eh, are you ready to leave?"

I let Tess go, never taking my eyes off her. She wobbled a little, sitting back down. Turning to face the flight deck, I nodded. "Yes, we're ready."

The rotor blades kicked into gear. The turbines went from silent to screeching.

"Great. Please sit back, relax, and enjoy the journey."

There would be no relaxing, not after Tess's tease.

Wait till I get you alone, esclave.

I was ready to embrace my future.

Twenty-five minutes later, a small island in the shape of a horseshoe came into view. Even at night it looked like utopia. Subtle lighting illuminated one side of the island, while a few less brightened the other side.

An island. Away from world news, doctors, or traffickers. If Suzette hadn't already done so, I would demand a security crew to man the waters surrounding us—keeping all of us safe. I didn't plan on leaving this place until I'd healed. As far as I was concerned, our crescent moon was over—our honeymoon had just begun.

No one spoke as we soared toward land, skimming over the black ocean in a whirl of rotors. At least this time we flew. I would've had a fucking fit if we had to travel by boat.

Never again.

The helicopter landed gracefully on a helipad built into a large jetty. It seemed whoever owned this place valued high class amenities such as yacht moorings, seaplane dockings, and helicopter pads.

My kind of place. I might have to buy it if the rest was this perfect.

Tess made eye contact, her cheeks flushing in happiness. "It looks amazing."

I softened a little toward Suzette. So far, she'd done well.

The helicopter shuddered as the engines were cut, slowly silencing, allowing the gentle slaps of waves against the jetty and cicadas in the trees to welcome us with an island serenade.

The captain and co-pilot climbed out first. They opened the cabin door, positioning the steps for us to disembark. Moving after sitting hurt like a motherfucker. It seemed to get worse not better. I needed some relief. I needed Tess in my arms and painkillers in my veins.

Franco climbed down, turning to help Tess onto the platform. "Crap, it's even hotter out here," he grumbled. "Suzette better have packed some shorts for me otherwise count me out from your wedding. I'll be a fucking puddle."

Tess laughed quietly, patting his chest. There was a deeper closeness between them that hadn't gone unnoticed. They'd been through things I hadn't been privy to, but instead of jealousy, I was relieved. Relieved that the two facets of my life were knitting together seamlessly.

Tess was no longer an outsider. She'd been initiated into my world—earning her place by my side and no one could ever deny it.

A noise made my eyes travel upward, locking onto a sprinting figure wearing white trousers and a pink top, flying down the jetty. Suzette.

Joining Tess, I kissed her cheek, avoiding the dried blood on her skin. I wanted to clean it off her. I hated seeing something so barbaric smearing her innocence—but it was her right to wear the blood of the enemy she'd defeated. And she wasn't innocent. Without her, I wouldn't be alive. If she wanted to get married filthy and blood-covered—I wouldn't stop her.

I moved out of the way as Suzette bowled toward us, wrapping her arms tightly around Tess. "I can't tell you how amazing it is to see you."

Tess buried her face in Suzette's neck. I didn't catch what she said, but Suzette grinned. "You have to tell me everything. And I do mean *everything*."

Her hazel eyes landed on Franco. Shyly, she untangled herself from Tess, going to stand in front of the mangled body of my trusted staff and friend. "Are you okay?"

Franco shrugged. "Just a normal day at the office."

Suzette flinched, noticing the bandages, slings, and walking stick. "The doctor and nurse you sent arrived about an hour ago. Do you want me to get them? Do you need anything?" She looked at me. "And you! Oh, my God, don't ever do that again. I prefer you alive—as do a lot of people."

I chuckled. I'd never been good vocalizing my emotions—not like Suzette—but I hoped she knew how much I valued her.

She stepped closer. I opened my arms, smiling as she walked into my embrace. Her body was smaller than Tess, less curvy but no less strong.

Her eyes welled with tears. "I'm so glad you're okay. All of you." Her arms tightened. I gritted my teeth against the flare of bruises and cracked rib.

"We're here. All alive."

She pulled away. "Don't do that again. Ever."

"I've already told him that," Tess said, her eyes soft on mine.

My heart stuttered, filling with need. I dreamed of a soft bed and painkillers. I hankered for nakedness, gentleness, and maybe even a spa. I would give anything to lie beneath the stars and let hot water bubble out the kinks in my body. Tonight was the eve of our wedding and I wanted to spend it with Tess. *Only Tess.*

"Yes, well. You've been warned." Suzette planted a finger in my chest.

I couldn't stop the flinch giving away my soreness.

Tess came closer, pressing her shoulder against mine. "I'll tell you everything, Suzette. But be prepared for a long story. Q's idea of a crescent moon is something that shouldn't be repeated."

"You're not telling her everything I hope." I glared at Tess. She couldn't be serious? After everything I'd done? Almost raping her. Then drugging her to bring her back? That was strictly between us.

But Suzette no longer cared. Her shoulders straightened with decision, wrapping her arms around Franco.

His eyes met mine, perplexed.

Tess's face softened, looking as if she witnessed something she'd wanted to see happen for a while.

Franco hesitated, then his arms went around her, squeezing tight. After an awkward second, he released her.

Suzette wiped away a few tears. Clapping her hands, she said, "Come. I'll show you where to go."

Travelling the distance down the pier took longer than normal with two men not in their prime. By the time we arrived on the sandy path of the island, a few staff members dressed in cream shorts and t-shirts came forward with icy towels and welcome cocktails.

Towel. *Motherfucking towel.*

I flatly ignored it. I would burn every fucking towel that ever came near me. The irrational fear latched onto my throat and I grabbed the drink. My mouth thirsted for alcohol— anything to dull the intense reaction and my thundering heart. *I'm afraid of a goddamn towel. How fucking embarrassing.*

I turned to Tess, clinking my glass to hers. I couldn't just throw it back. I didn't want her to know I had other things to work through—not just external injuries but mental scarring as well.

Her gaze melted me. "To surviving," she whispered.

Franco clinked his glass to ours. "To you. To the best couple I've had the privilege of knowing."

The sincerity in his voice made me pause. The moment became serious and poignant. Franco and I had been linked after Rio, but we'd all become closer thanks to Lynx.

A family.

I may be alone in the world, with no flesh and blood relatives, but I had the best family anyone could wish for.

"To winning." I threw the fruity concoction down my throat. The sickly alcohol stung my raw mouth; I craved proper liquor.

Tess and Franco did the same, depositing the empty glasses with the staff. Together we followed Suzette into the hushed mangroves and palm trees of *Cheval De Mer*. Seahorse Island.

The bushy vegetation canopied a boardwalk which lay beneath a fine lashing of icing sugar sand. Lanterns swung in the trees, guiding our way. There was nothing but whispers of waves, a gentle breeze, and idyllic stars above. It was dreamlike. It was heaven.

"After everything we've been through, I can't believe we're here," Tess murmured, her eyes darting from the hanging lamps to the stencils of leaves above us.

I looped my fingers with hers, sharing a precious moment of perfect peace. "It's done. We earned this."

The boardwalk split into a fork. Suzette guided us to the

left, stopping in front of a sprawling building made from wood, thatched roof, and tinted glass. Stepping onto the wraparound veranda, the true beauty of the place was visible. A courtyard with a white plunge pool, daybeds, private bar, and huge granite slabs looked otherworldly in the silver-gleam of the moon.

Statues of huge seahorses circled the pool, a fountain trickling from each mouth.

"*Tu t'es surpassée,* Suzette." You've outdone yourself, Suzette.

Tess's mouth hung open, gliding forward in a trance. "This is beyond what I could've ever imagined."

I agreed. It was magical.

Suzette grinned. "I'm so glad you like it." Moving toward a large sliding glass door, she pulled it open. "Come, I'll show you to your rooms. Don't worry. You have this side of the island all to yourself. The guests aren't permitted to come over here, so it's completely private."

Stepping inside, I instantly knew I wanted to recreate a space like this at home. The area was airy with a full glass roof, welcoming the palm fronds to cast shadows on the white porcelain tiles. The furniture was all oversized, luxurious, looking like a cloud—waiting for someone to throw themselves onto the pale blues and beiges of the upholstery.

Suzette turned to Franco. "Can you take Q to his room? It's that way." She pointed to the right. "I'll take Tess to hers."

I slammed to a halt. "Excuse me?" Separate rooms? Who the fuck was she kidding?

Not going to fucking happen.

"We may not be married, but I've had Tess in my bed for months. That isn't about to change." My voice deepened with warning.

Suzette planted her fists on her hips. "It's the eve of your wedding. I'm not letting you see each other until tomorrow. Superstitious or not. I think it'll be good to relax and centre yourself with no distractions." Waving a finger in my face, she added, "And Tess is a distraction, so you're on your own tonight. Not to mention you need to heal."

I looked at Tess. Her eyes shot wide, then she laughed. "I guess there's no arguing." Her body swayed toward mine, unconsciously willing me to demand her to sleep in my bed. Together. As it should be.

"Don't ruin the perfection you've created so far, Suzette. Tess is sleeping with me."

Don't make me bury you under a palm tree.

Suzette scowled. "Who did you put in charge of the wedding?" She planted a finger in her chest. "Me. I'm the boss of this event, and I say you're not to see each other until tomorrow." Waving her hand, she finished, "So, shoo. Franco, escort your boss to his private room."

I held up my hand, temper bubbling. "I can find my own fucking room."

Franco laughed. "I'm off. I'm not going to break up another battle." Heading to the door, he called, "Night all."

Tess watched him leave. She jumped as Suzette captured her hand, tugging her away from me. "But—"

My cock hardened drinking Tess in. Her unwillingness to leave, the equal need in her eyes. She was so incredible. I didn't want to be away from her for a second. Shit, she'd *killed* for me. I would lay down my life for her every day for the rest of time to repay her.

"Go." I glared at Tess. *I'll come for you later.*

I couldn't stand there another second. I couldn't stomach the thought of being separated. I hoped she got my final message because without a word, I turned and stalked to my end of the suite. If I didn't, I would've lost my temper, made Suzette cry, and undone the magic of this place.

Half an hour. Then I'd go to her.

Suzette would leave. And I'd sneak like a fucking criminal into the bed of my wife to be.

And then I'd hold her and show her exactly whose ass belonged to whom.

There was no way I would spend the night apart. Last

night was the last time we ever did.

Entering the bedroom, I scoured every corner—glared into every shadow. We may be on an island, far away from trouble, but I wouldn't let my guard down again. I wouldn't believe I was strong enough to win another stupid battle.

My luck had been used up. I was alive. And that's how I wanted to keep it.

The room was the same exquisite openness. The huge bed groaned with mountains of pillows in blue and white, bringing the sea inside.

I didn't know how long Suzette would spend with Tess. They were women after all—gossip came naturally.

Damn women. I wanted *my* woman. Now.

Standing in the centre of the room, my aches and pains took hold. A surge of loneliness squeezed my heart. *I'm lonely.* How fucking ridiculous. I was lonely for Tess. *I just saw her.*

I rolled my eyes, but nothing could stop the deserted feeling. I turned in place, intending to stalk across the suite and demand Suzette give Tess back to me. I needed comforting. Ha! Me. I wanted her—to distract my thoughts from what I'd lived through.

You can't.

It would look fucking laughable. Limping to Tess like some child, begging for a hug. I wasn't that weak and I damn well wouldn't show Tess how screwed up I was.

Shit.

Lynx had done more than made me scream—he'd made me weak.

My body creaked as I moved. Considering a spa wasn't an option, a shower would have to do. I needed to wash away the past. Least it gave me something to do—gave Suzette time to clear the fuck off.

The bathroom was simple but modern with a frameless glass shower and beige tiling. I eyed the shower, hankering for heat on my aching muscles. But getting undressed proved to be a bitch.

Twisting my torso, the borrowed t-shirt made my life a living hell trying to tug it over my head. Every angle felt like another baseball bat to my chest. Panting hard, I finally untangled myself only to have the same battle with my jeans.

"Goddammit." I gritted my teeth as the denim slid down, revealing my legs covered in bruises and bandages.

It seemed the longer I was apart from Tess the more I hurt.

Another reason why I wouldn't let her sleep without me.

I needed her more than any drug.

Turning on the water, I stood like a fucking pussy. Water splashed into the drain, steaming and inviting but all I saw was death. Every droplet, so innocent, was a silent killer just waiting for me to step under the torrent.

Get in there, asshole.

Balling my hands, I stepped under the spray. Every muscle locked; my heart exploded in fear. My eyes stayed wide, terrified my vision would be traded for a black towel. I'd never had an issue getting over things I'd done or caused. I'd never had a second thought of being shot or torturing others.

But this.

That bastard had stolen the simple pleasure of a shower. He'd taught me how to fear and I fucking hated it.

I threw my head back, drenching my hair and face. My heart went ballistic, my lips locked together, and my nostrils flared for breath.

You can breathe.

No one is trying to murder you.

I forced myself to stay under the spray. I locked my legs from running and endured.

My heartbeat thundered in my ears, but I kept my breathing slow and deep. Gradually getting control on my runaway emotions.

By the time I'd washed, rinsed, and soaped away the past few days, my heart rate was calmer and I wouldn't make a fool of myself next time I needed a shower. It was just water.

Stepping from the steaming facilities, I looked down at the bandages on my legs. Drenched. Probably not a good thing to get them wet but I was past caring.

I was clean. And now I was bone-weary and ready to drop into a coma.

But not in an empty bed.

Not bothering to dry myself—that would require the use of a towel—*not going to fucking happen*—I padded barefoot and naked through the house to the other wing. I hoped to God Suzette had left otherwise she would get an eyeful. Not that it seemed to matter. Most of my staff had seen me naked—hazards of the job.

A few bedrooms branched off the wide corridor; I peered into each one before I found my *esclave*.

Her room was shrouded in shadow, making the passed out figure in the centre of the bed look fragile, lonely—so fucking vulnerable.

She'd had a shower too, smelling of fruit and whatever shit was in the shampoo.

Inching into the room, I moved as silently as I could with a mangled body. My heart physically hurt looking at her. Her features were smudged by the night but her blonde hair glowed like a lighthouse, guiding me toward her.

Gently, I pulled the covers back, hissing between my teeth as I lowered my body from vertical to horizontal. The pressure of the mattress against my back was like a fucking bat all over again. The fronts of my legs stung as the sheets stuck to cuts not covered with bandages. Every inch of me groaned in agony.

But I didn't care.

I didn't care because I was in bed. Safe. Beside her.

Tess's breathing changed as I shifted closer. Her form tensed into a tighter ball. "Q?"

"C'est moi." It's me.

Her body relaxed, radiating heat and welcome. Her hand came up, stroking my damp hair as I settled painfully onto my side. Her eyes met mine. "Are you okay?"

"Turn around, let me hug you. *Ensuite, j'irai bien.*" Then I will be.

Tess didn't utter another word. Obediently, she turned over, pressing her bed-warmed body into mine.

The moment her form slotted against me in perfect synergy, the aches and bruises and cuts all faded into non-existence.

Nothing else mattered anymore. I was exactly where I wanted to be. For life.

I sighed heavily, breathing in the fruitiness of her hair. "God, I needed that. Needed you."

She moaned as I wrapped an arm around her waist, trapping her against me. Already it was too hot beneath the covers but an atomic bomb would have to go off to tear me away.

My legs twitched as sleepiness attacked me fast and strong. So much for reminding her who owned who. My libido was in a coma already—tugging me down fast with it.

I yawned. "This. This is what I want for the rest of my life."

Tess linked her fingers with mine, resting them over her breast. Her ass pressed harder into my cock. My belly fluttered—my cock struggled to rise. But after everything I'd been through, it just wasn't going to happen.

Tonight wasn't about sex or domination. Tonight was about giving and taking. Feeding and sowing. Reconnection with gentleness rather than pain.

We'd both had enough.

The only thing I was capable of was holding Tess while I healed. I'd hit my final limit.

"You have me for the rest of your life, *maître.*" Tess snuggled closer, her body melting into mine.

Her words were the last things I heard before succumbing to the deep chasm of sleep.

I let go.

I fell into the light.

And this time, darkness didn't claim me. This time, I soared into the clouds because I held an angel in my arms and she made me deserving.

As long as I had Tess, I wouldn't go to hell. She made me worthy. She made me better.

I'd won.

We'd won.

We'd fought for our happily ever after. Lies had become truths. Tears had become smiles.

Everything was as it should be.

We deserved our triumphs.

Chapter Fifteen

My salvation
My together

Q left me when dawn arrived.

Kissing my temple, he clambered sorely out of bed. "See you in a few hours, *esclave.*"

I held onto his wrist, not wanting him to go. I couldn't understand why one moment I was giddy with joy thinking of what today meant for us, then I wanted to throw up. I was nervous, excited, happy, freaking out.

"You promise you'll be waiting for me?" I didn't understand my sudden insecurities. It just seemed like everything I'd ever wanted existed in a future I daren't grasp. I didn't want to think how close to perfection we were just in case it turned out to be fate's cruel joke.

Q bent over, his eyes tightening with pain thanks to his blue and black body. He stood naked, wearing his wounds with pride. The bandages on his legs stained with pinpricks of blood. "I'll be the one sweating at the top of the aisle hoping to hell you haven't changed your mind. *Je vais t'épouser aujourd'hui,* Tess.

Pas de fuite." I'm marrying you today, Tess. No running.

My heart strummed. Before I could reply, he left, walking his fine butt out of my room. My eyes trailed after him, landing on his bruises. My stomach heaved with anger.

Killing Lynx wasn't enough for what Q endured. I loved Q more than life itself and I'd finally proven I deserved him. I'd accepted the feral part of myself and survived. I suffered no remorse, *none*. And I would do it all again if I had to.

Q disappeared down the corridor. *The next time I see him he'll be mine for eternity.*

He'd be my husband.

The nerves in my stomach switched to sublime happiness. Unstifled joy sprang me upward, hurling me out of bed to meet my future.

I spent thirty minutes in the shower, giving myself no time restrictions to shave, primp, and prepare. The luxury of enjoying my own company with no dark thoughts ruining my happiness was priceless. I'd forgotten how it felt to be weightless—joyous.

Suzette arrived at eight a.m. giving me just enough time to order room service of fresh fruit and an omelette, and douse myself on coffee. The closer we came to the ceremony the more my tummy churned. Nerves fluttered unhindered, slicking my palms, racing my heart.

I wanted to be Q's so badly—I couldn't relax until it came true.

Suzette came bearing gifts.

Make up. Shoebox. Covered dress. And a bag that looked suspiciously like lingerie.

"Morning. Hope you slept well." She dumped the items on the bed, looking like the complete master of whatever she'd planned. Looking me up and down, she nodded. "Good to see you're showered and fed. Two things I can scratch off my to-do list."

Two women with plaited black hair and sun-darkened skin appeared, looking to Suzette for guidance.

Suzette grinned, waving them into the room and toward the dresser with its white lacquered wood and large ornate mirror.

"We'll set up everything over there."

I didn't say a word—I didn't think I was expected to as Suzette assembled order at the dressing table, plopping bottles, lining up mascaras and eye-shadow.

Coming toward me, she grabbed my hand, marching me toward the chair. "Sit."

I descended on the soft periwinkle stool and looked at myself for the first time in forever.

Oh, my God. *Is that my reflection?*

I looked haggard. My hair hung damp around my shoulders, lifeless. My skin looked ashen and the shadows under my eyes showed just how much I'd been through in the past few days.

But it was my gaze that scared me—that made my mouth hang open. I no longer recognised myself.

The crescent moon had completely changed me.

Gone was the softness—the innocence. I no longer looked like the insecure Australian girl I'd been. I'd stared death in the face; I'd stepped into the cloak of the grim reaper and stolen two lives willingly.

The grey was tempered with hardness, the blue glittering with strength. I didn't look weak or lost or afraid. I looked ruthless. My eyes were no longer one dimensional but hid strength of character, trials overcome, sorrow defeated, and horror tamed.

I look like him.

I clutched my heart, realizing what'd changed. I'd adopted the same chilly sharpness that both Q and Franco lived with. I'd embraced something that would never be changeable. I'd evolved into a woman who no one would deny belonged beside Q completely.

Tears welled, turning my vision into a watery dream.

"Aw, Tess. It's okay." Suzette's arms wrapped around my

neck from behind, her soft cheek pressing against mine.

More tears fell but I wasn't crying because of what I'd done. I cried because of what I'd *become*. I never thought I could be so strong, so self-assured—so...dangerous.

I'm worthy.

Finally—I was worthy. Not for Q or the abundant future he promised, but for myself. I felt worthy enough to be proud.

Suzette's eyes met mine in the mirror. "I know you killed to get him back. Franco told me a little about what happened." She pecked my cheek before pulling away, gathering my hair with her feminine touch. "You saved him—just as much as he saved you. Maybe even more."

My life would never be the same. The chrysalis of the Tess I never thought I'd find finally cracked its final layer. I emerged into my new world wondrously happy, courageously strong, and deeply in love.

"You're different, Tess," Suzette murmured. "Is that what you're seeing, too?"

I nodded, unable to believe the immense transformation.

I shivered as Suzette's fingernails dragged over my scalp. Her touch was soothing. "I'm happy for you, *mon ami*. I won't lie and say I've been waiting for that closure to come to me."

Closure.

That's what it was.

I didn't have towers or gates barring bad memories because the memories were dealt with. I no longer segmented off my mind. Because everything was in its rightful place, and I just *knew*.

Knew that this was my absolute home. My happy place. The epicentre of my soul.

"You're still struggling, Suzette?" I whispered, letting her busy herself with untangling my hair. Grabbing a brush from one of the drawers, Suzette proceeded to tame my curls, building the golden glow that'd been lost thanks to stress and lack of sleep.

"I'm not struggling, exactly. I've put it all behind me. But I haven't got to the point where I'm okay with it—you know?"

I captured her hand, holding her still. Her knobbly fingers were brittle and arthritic from so many unnatural breaks at the sadistic whims of masters. So many trafficked women lived nightmarish existences. I'd survived and I would use my newfound strength to work beside Q. I would dedicate my life to the Feathers of Hope charity and try to give every broken woman a happy ending like mine.

I placed my hands in my lap. "I understand completely. I was at that place when Q brought me back by giving me his pain. He'd fixed me, but there was still so much unresolved."

Suzette smiled. "Maybe, I'll find someone to save me, too."

I shook my head. "Q didn't save me—well, he did—but ultimately, he just showed me the way. He showed me I had the power to save myself. You have that power inside you, too. You just have to acknowledge it."

Tears wobbled in my eyes, overwhelmed with all that'd happened. "Thank you, Suzette. For everything." Our gaze connected; I poured forth every gratitude. "You helped me when I first arrived. You gave me clues about who Q really was. You're so much stronger than me in so many ways. I know you'll get there—because you helped me do the same."

She continued to work on my curls. "You didn't need me. You're the strong one, Tess. But I'm so happy to have you in my life—happy to have a friend." Her lips flitted into a sad smile. "And I do know what you mean. I sense it—inside. I'm getting there."

One of the island staff came closer. She had a pretty face with thick eyelashes and a diamond pierced through her nose. "Shall I begin, ma'am?"

Suzette cleared her throat, dispelling our conversation. Her smile broadened, hiding the vulnerability in her eyes. "Yes. We don't have much time." Suzette pulled me backward, screeching the stool legs over the tiles, giving the girl room to kneel at my feet and place numerous tools, varnishes, and a foot spa beside me.

The other staff member came forward with a small trolley, setting up her station by my left side to tend to my fingernails.

"Wow, I've never been so pampered." I sank my feet into the warm bath for my toes.

The women worked in soft silence, transforming me from a girl who'd killed yesterday into a pure princess today.

Never in my life had I bonded with girlfriends this way. I never owned nail varnishes or pretty things—my parents thought they were the devil's tools. I'd never had a sleepover or done something drastic with my hair.

My smile fell for what I'd missed out on, but I stopped the thought.

It makes this all the more special. I was glad it was Suzette helping me get ready. It was fitting because she was my closest friend—living with us, looking after Q and me—family. She was family.

I drifted in girly bliss. "You do know you're going to spoil me. I'll never want to do my own hair or nails again."

Suzette and the women giggled. "You're supposed to be spoiled on your wedding day." Suzette's face scrunched in concentration, taking sections of my hair, pinning it in a haphazard way. "Besides, I've seen your capabilities with hairdressing and your version of tying it up is a boring ponytail."

Only because I'd never had anyone show me how to style. I had a feeling my days of jumpers and jeans were behind me.

Slowly my tresses morphed from draping down my back to neatly secured in a loose chignon. I looked in the mirror, mesmerized as Suzette somehow preformed a miracle by making my hair stay up with no ties or over use of clips.

My fingernails were wet with *Love's First Kiss* pink nail varnish and I reached carefully to pat the thick French-inspired up do.

Suzette swatted my hand away. "No touching. It's up but a bit precarious, so be careful."

I frowned, tilting my head to admire it. I looked sophisticated and demure. Not exactly how I would've done it, but I was eternally grateful for Suzette's help. "I'll be dancing and spending the day in high humidity. Doesn't it need to stay up without ruining your masterpiece?"

Her lips curled into a smile. My heart stuttered at the flash of calculation in her eyes. *What is she up to?*

"It doesn't have to be up for long. Besides, let me worry about all of that." With that cryptic comment, she turned to grab the packages from the bed. "Thank you, ladies. I can take it from here."

I stood, carefully stepping over the tiles, trying not to smudge my toenails. Suzette upended a bag onto the mattress.

My stomach flipped. Littered on the white bedspread, looking sinful and entirely too kinky, was black, lacy lingerie. But it didn't stop there. Black stockings with a garter belt, a delicate bow stitched into the sheer material, along with a black leather corset with blood-red velvet ties.

My eyes flew to Suzette. "What is this?"

She glowed. "I figure you're going to be the virgin bride, dressed all in white, but the moment Q takes it off—he'll find his *esclave* again. Don't you want to wear it for him?"

I picked up the boned corset, inspecting the intricate sparrows stitched into the leather. Tears pricked my eyes again at the direct symbolism that I was one of Q's birds. The only one who stayed for him.

My heart winged thinking of tonight. I couldn't wait to have him in bed again.

"It's beyond beautiful. But won't it show under the dress?"

Suzette shook her head. "No. Leave all the worrying to me. It's time to get you ready. We don't have much time." Shoving the gown from my shoulders, she demanded, "Strip. I need to add concealer to any bruises you still have and dress you in an outfit that'll make any master hard."

"Your body is mine. Your pain is mine." Q's voice cut through my thoughts. What would he do when he saw the lingerie?

Would he cut it off or leave it?

Apprehension filled me. What if the sight triggered Q's darkness? *What if he won't wait any longer?* My back tensed, very aware of his innuendoes and veiled promises. Q would expect more from me tonight. It was our wedding night—he wanted to claim something he hadn't claimed before.

I swallowed hard. It was irrational to be so afraid, but I was. Nerves tripled my heartbeat.

Suzette didn't notice my silence. "I see the way he looks at you, Tess. He won't be able to contain himself."

I laughed. Q containing himself? Never. He operated with passion and rage and dark energy. There would be no containing him—or denying what he wanted.

But he's hurt.

My eyes widened. I didn't need to be afraid of tonight. There was no way Q would be up for our usual sex. He was injured. I breathed a sigh of relief. "I doubt he'll be reacting all that much, Suzette. He's not exactly in a condition to attack me."

Suzette unthreaded the corset. Her eyes glinted with the same deviousness as before. "Whatever you say."

What the hell is that? My spine stiffened, sensing a hidden agenda. "What are you up to, Suzette?"

Her lips spread into a wicked smile. "You'll see. It's a surprise—for both of you." Twirling me around, she pressed the warm leather corset against my middle. "The first part is my gift to you. The second..." her voice trailed off. Her fingers tugged on the velvet stays, lacing me inside.

"The second..." I prompted.

Her voice was far away, seeing things I didn't know. "The second part is for him. Purely for him."

Goosebumps spread over my skin. The thoughts I'd had of a traditional wedding, complete with rose petals and ring bearers, suddenly seemed like a fantastical illusion. Q had put Suzette in charge. He'd put a woman who'd lived with him for years, who'd lived through horror, in charge of a romantic event.

Did she even know the meaning of romance? Had the word been beaten and raped out of her leaving her tainted toward fairy-tales?

Trust her. Let her do this.

Expelling a shaky breath, I whispered, "If it's for him then I'm sure it will be amazing and he'll love it."

A minute ticked past, silence heavy between us. She finished securing my corset, then hugged me fiercely. "Thank you for trusting me and not asking questions."

"Thank you for organising my wedding."

We shared a smile. I didn't care what she'd planned. In a few short hours, I would be Mrs. Mercer and nothing could ruin my happiness.

"Come on. Let's finish. Can't have Q waiting." Suzette passed me the stockings.

"You know him better than that, Suzette. He'd be down here dragging me over his shoulder if I'm a minute late."

Suzette laughed. "In that case—we better hurry."

The rest of the time flew—beautifying me for my nuptials.

My stomach rolled. *I'm going to be sick.*

My lungs stuck together. *I can't breathe.*

My heart galloped. *I'm getting married.*

Music drifted across the island, dipping and lilting with the Seychelles breeze. I strained to hear more—to count how many guests would witness my union to Q—to envision the type of ceremony Suzette had put together.

Heading to a wedding that I hadn't planned or had any idea of what would happen twisted my stomach, but excitement existed, too.

I'm really doing this. I'm about to get married.

Sparrows, finches, and doves lived in my ribcage, trapped tightly beneath a corset etched with their fellow kin. Their wings made me float across the patio next to the seahorse pool all the while tickling me with nervous feathers.

I looked down at the white dress cocooning my body. Suzette had been elevated to goddess in my mind. She'd transformed me from lacklustre girl to flawless mannequin.

The dress was a mixture of lace and silk and taffeta—all in different shades of white. My right shoulder was bare. My left shoulder was adorned with a white rosette draping down the front of the bodice with exquisite lace.

My hips flared with a see-through organza train, the fabric whispering over the heaviness of silk. The elegance was perfect, the craftsmanship superb. And Suzette was right. Not one sign of the leather corset or lingerie I wore was visible.

The only thing ruining the virgin image was the black sprig of feathers in my hair, glittering with onyx gems.

Suzette beamed, holding my face in her hands. "You look incredible."

A staff member held a mirror for me to check any last minute issues. I took one last disbelieving glimpse. My eyes were globes of grey serenity, highlighted with silver eyeshadow. My lips were a blood-red, glistening as if I'd turned vampire and favoured the remnants of my last meal.

I'd never looked so pretty and for a moment sadness fell over me. My parents would never see me marry the man of my dreams—my friends would never witness my transformation from girl to woman.

It doesn't matter. None of this is for them. It's for him. For me.

Patting my hair one last time, I said, "Thank you so much, Suzette. I would never have been able to pull this together." Even the red lipstick, which I thought clashed to begin with, worked. Instead of cheapening the pureness of my attire it added a pop of dramatic—a flare of danger.

She stepped to my side, looping an arm through mine. "I'm so glad you're happy. That's all I wanted." Her body tensed. "Um…I haven't asked this yet—and feel free to say no—but…I want to walk you down the aisle." Her eyes flickered with reckless hope, tangled with already felt rejection. "If you'd prefer a man, Frederick is here, and he said he'd gladly give you away to his best friend." She looked away, hiding the pain in her face, fully expecting me to choose Fred over her.

My heart hurt to see such uncertainty in a friend who'd been nothing but a rock to me. It was time I took the role of supporter, guiding her to the emotion she wanted most of all— freedom from her past.

Grabbing her in a hug, I squeezed hard, cursing the boning of the corset. "I want you to do it. You'd be doing me an incredible honour, giving me away to the man we both love."

Her heart-shaped face shattered with happy moisture. She pulled away, dabbing at her makeup, practically pushing her tears back inside. She wore a powder grey dress, matching my style with one shoulder and organza train. Her beautiful brown hair was coiled into four thick curls down her back.

She was so pretty. *Franco will notice. He has to notice.*

I rolled my eyes, thinking of the clueless man. He needed a push in the right direction if he didn't get the memo today— but I had a feeling Suzette would tell him loud and clear. Weddings had a way of bringing people together—cutting through the unsaid mess, letting the truth blare.

Suzette once again looped her arm through mine. "Ready to get married?"

Lungs. Stomach. Heart.

I swallowed hard.

"Tu es à moi, esclave." You're mine. Q's voice whispered through my mind, granting me serenity.

Yes, I'm ready. Ready to change my world forever.

My nerves disappeared, leaving me with utmost confidence and love. "Yes."

Leaving the gorgeous chalet, we made our way around the

seahorse pool, heading inland, following the musical map coming from the venue.

The white sand had been swept from the boardwalk and scattered frangipani petals led the way. Staff members stood like sentries in equal distance, smiling as we passed. We had no others in our procession. Just me and Suzette.

I held no posies or veil over my face. The dress was all the embellishing I needed—that and the 'Q' branded into my neck.

I focused inward, thinking about the crescent moon. I'd known Q was in danger. I'd known and stupidly believed he was strong enough, protected enough, to stay safe. I hadn't planned on him playing roulette with his life. Or sacrificing himself for me.

He would've died protecting me. And although it was romantic to have that sort of power, it was a *huge* responsibility.

"You okay?" Suzette squeezed my arm.

Her touch wrenched me from my thoughts. "Yes, sorry."

I held my hand out, admiring my wing-inspired ring. After everything we'd been through, I hadn't had time to buy Q a ring. "I've failed in the only job I had for this wedding."

Suzette glanced at my ring.

"I didn't get him one. What can I put on his finger after our vows?"

Nothing. You'll have to wait till you're home.

We turned a corner, leaving the density of the palm trees to find a large white marquee, resting on the sands edge. The waves looked like turquoise glass, smacking gently onto sand— a silky ripple.

"Stop worrying. I have everything under control." Suzette grinned. "All you need to worry about is not tripping up the aisle."

We stopped outside the marquee. Two men in white uniforms smiled, pulling back the flaps of the venue.

"Ready to go to him?" Suzette whispered as we drifted forward, trading island sun for cool shadows. The tented world welcomed, hushing our footsteps. Tears glossed my eyes, imprinting the rapturous beauty.

"Suzette—" My red glitter high-heels wedged into the softness of the carpet, jerking us to a stop. "You did all this? It's incredible."

"You deserved a bit of paradise. I'm glad you like it."

I couldn't take it in. Too picturesque. Too perfect. The space was large, housing a row of five or six black chairs. Most were unoccupied, waiting for their owners who were part of the ceremony. It was small, intimate. Not that I'd expected crowds—or that Q would permit it.

The walls were covered with white satin drapery, making it seem like we'd stepped into a cloud. The ceiling held bolts of ivory fabric, swooping low, creating intimacy.

I'll never forget this.

Then my eyes landed on *him*.

And the room paled entirely. I no longer cared about drapery or flowers. All I cared about was him. The man I was destined for.

My master. Husband. Lover. Protector.

My heart was never mine. It was his along. I'd been the guardian. Now he'd claimed it.

Him.

Q stood at the top of the aisle flanked by Franco and Frederick; the two groomsman wore matching grey suits, mirroring Suzette's dress.

Q on the other hand wore white. His dark hair had been styled into the same pelt-like cut I remembered. His body stood proud and majestic, sheathed in a white blazer, waistcoat, and trousers. The only splash of darkness was a black tie. He looked incredible. He looked too much—too *priceless* to be real.

The moment our eyes met I felt faint, delirious.

He's mine. I'm his.

I wanted to fly up the aisle and imprison him in my arms. From here he didn't look hurt. From here he looked strong and savage—ready to kill or conduct a quiet business affair. He bordered the line of aggression so effortlessly.

His gaze stayed transfixed on me, his face locked into an unreadable mask.

Then the music changed.

It echoed with haunting bass notes, sorrowful flutes, and empowering chords.

A woman I didn't know stood off to the side. Her polished ebony hair fell in heavy sheets over her shoulders, threaded with silver feathers. Her dark eyes assessed me, an appraising—almost haughty look—on her face. Her dress was grey too, shorter, fuller around her calves and detailed with pearl buttons on the bodice.

A smile transformed her coolness with warmth. Bowing her head, she raised a microphone to her lips and began to sing.

It was as if her voice carried every weapon imaginable—destroying me all at once. I *knew* her voice. Her passion, the rasp, the melancholy hope.

I shivered as the lyrics drilled their way into my heart.

> *I have no more need to hide—not now that I have you*
> *I once had a loveless life—but now I'm falling true*
> *You waltzed into my world—making me turn tame*
> *You turned my wickedness into trust even without your name*

The verse was about us—sang by the woman who'd recorded Q's other songs—the same songs he'd played when I first arrived—the haunting melodies encouraging me to find the true Q—to hunt for the monster within.

The full circle on finally understanding his favourite artist stole strength from my legs.

Ever since I'd met Q, I'd been pulled deeper into darkness. I'd willingly embraced everything he'd given and would never be free.

I never want *to be free.*

"Let's go," Suzette whispered, tugging me forward, guiding me one step at a time. The humid island air glimmered with awareness. I never unlocked gazes with Q.

The sand beneath the carpet unsettled my footing, but my heart knew where to go. Every step was scary and foreign and unknown but at the same time joyous and perfect and right.

Q held out his hand, summoning me to him. His intense pale gaze sliced through my dress, leaving me completely exposed. My nipples stiffened as my belly quickened.

Images of him hanging beaten and bloody snatched me from white perfection. I squeezed my eyes against the horribleness.

He almost died.

I almost lost him.

My chest rose, sucking in a calming breath. But I *hadn't* lost him. He was here, waiting for me. Wanting to marry me.

My heart jangled. *Will I hate myself for what I did to Lynx?*

I waited for comeuppance.

I waited for guilt.

But all I felt was justified.

Shot, cut, electrocuted, and drowned, Q loved me so much he'd cheated death. He'd dressed a body that should be resting and stood atop an aisle where I would give him my heart.

Go to him. Be his medicine.

My pace increased. Suzette had no choice but to glide with me, quicker, quicker.

Q's eyes warmed the closer I came. His face held shadows of bruises, his lips thinned against aches and stitches.

You can be vulnerable with me.

He stood taller, understanding my message.

I can relax with you in my arms. His eyes transmitted the thought powerfully.

The woman kept singing.

Everything horrible is now locked with gates
All our demons are exorcized
You are my sinner; my undisclosed master of my fate
Please me, and I'll treat you fine

I never deviated or looked at the small number of guests. Every step they judged me—searching for any flaw that was undeserving of Q.

But they wouldn't find me wanting. I'd earned my place by his side. I'd grown up. I'd embraced myself completely. And I had nothing left to fear—everything I'd done and endured lived in my eyes for the world to see—telling my story.

But only Q had the decryption.

Only he knew what I'd done. Only he knew who I'd become. And only he knew my sins. Just like I knew his.

Acceptance. Love. Commitment.

They were the perfect sins. Sins I would commit for the rest of my life.

You are the one for me, my monster in the dark
You are the perfect mate for me, wicked and unmarked
Together we cannot be denied, our undeniable spark
Together we will find our perfect evolving never ending arc

My breathing turned from low and deep to shallow and bird-quick. The aisle came to an end. Suzette squeezed my elbow. "Go marry your monster." Letting go, she pushed me gently.

She sent me winging to Q. I left my past behind; I left earth behind—embracing my new home in the night sky.

The music drifted to a lasting note, fading away.

Q stole all my senses—just like he always did. I breathed in his citrus and sandalwood. I drank in his bruised face. I heard his heartbeat because it was the same as mine.

One beat. One thrum.

He stood steadfast; his eyes luminous with a mixture of love and trepidation. We stood stiff before each other. My hands wanted to touch. My lips wanted to kiss. And my heart wanted to erupt from my chest and land in his palms in gratitude. Gratitude for choosing me.

I was born for you.

His eyes tightened. His throat worked hard as he swallowed. The feathered wings in my stomach lived in him, too—mirroring our nervousness.

My breathing was shallow. *I want you in bed. I want to whisper the vows to you alone. I want to give myself to you in every possible way a woman can.*

Q's lips twitched, his head lowered, but he never looked away. The intensity of his gaze sent a ripple of pleasure right to my core.

I stood before him and shamelessly grew wet.

My eyes dropped to his linked hands, hiding the swelling bulge in his trousers. My pussy clenched, craving his touch. He was so damn handsome. So dignified and closed off. Only I saw the passion, the aggression.

My lips parted. I wanted his stern lips to kiss me sweetly. I wanted his harsh fingers to touch me gently. I wanted the privilege of hugging him while he took me slowly. Ever so slowly. Sinking together, drifting together, getting lost together.

I wanted love in physical expression.

Q broke his unreadable façade by taking my hand. His touch was a comet shooting from every finger, supercharging my body. His fingers tightened, cutting off my blood, transmitting his highly controlled need through one caress.

He stepped closer, tugging me into him.

The marquee ceased to exist. The guests were gone. The world was nothing. He was everything, and I needed him. *Now.*

A masculine cough right by my ear made me leap in my heels.

I tore my attention from Q, focusing on the man standing before us dressed in a well-cut linen suit.

Q chuckled quietly, rubbing his thumb over my knuckles. "We're not alone, *esclave*. Not yet." His lips moved but his words were lower than a whisper, understood purely by my soul rather than ears.

The celebrant, the man who had the power to turn our two lives into one, grinned. His soft sable eyes, dark brown hair, and weather-worn face made him friendly and approachable.

"Welcome," he said in a deep attention-grabbing voice. "I'm honoured to precede over your vows today. Are you ready to begin?"

Begin? So fast. No prelude or...

"You ready, *mon amour*?" Q raised my hand, kissing my ring. His dry warm lips teased a moan from my soul.

Looking into his eyes settled everything. Yes. I was ready.

I nodded, holding his fingers as my heart shook off its lust-induced slow beat, favouring a fast hopscotch instead. This was it. *I'm getting married.*

Q murmured, "I'm holding the woman I'm about to marry, so yes, you may begin."

Q's eyes never left mine. Our spirits reached out, interlinking, forming a private bubble where the world could be seen but nothing could touch us. He spun the wing circlet around my wedding finger. "You'll never walk again without me by your side, *esclave*."

My heart stole all the blood in my body, swelling with aching love.

The celebrant clasped his hands in front of him. "Fantastic. Let's start." Looking past us, he grinned at the groomsmen and bridesmaids. I ignored them in my peripheral vision, giving my full attention to my master.

It was just him and me.

As it had always been and always would be.

"Welcome, everyone, to the joining of Tess Olivia Snow and Quincy Mercer II. I will say thank you on behalf of the bride and groom for travelling to this sun-blessed country and gracing your good fortune to ensure this marriage is full of richness, happiness, and love."

The celebrant lowered his voice. "I can either give you vows to repeat after me—or if you prefer, you can dedicate your own vows to each other. Either will be binding and sanctified by me."

My stomach leapt into my mouth. *Vows!* What with the whirlwind crescent moon and Q's torture, I hadn't had time to write heartfelt promises or pledges. My eyes flared wide. *I've ruined it before it's begun.* I should've known. I should've planned.

"I'd like to say our own," Q murmured. "However, I want you to go first, Tess." Authority rang in his voice; the room swam with panic.

I clutched his fingers. "Q, I can't. I don't know what to say. I have so much—so much that I want to get right. I'm..." My eyes searched his. "I'm unprepared. I don't want to say something wron—"

"You're overthinking it. Just—"

"But what if I say something terrible? I've never been to a wedding or know what needs to be sworn. I'll screw up. Our marriage will be a sham." My spine tickled with tears, the damn corset squeezed my ribs like a vice.

Q cupped my cheek, bringing me closer in a rustle of silk. His mouth rested on my ear, granting me strength. "I'm just as nervous as you are." Guiding my hand, he placed it over his heart. The rapidly thudding muscle, that'd been through so much, thrummed beneath my fingers in a rugged tattoo. "See. I'm terrified. But I want to know what's in your heart. Dare, Tess. I dare you to tell me everything."

Having his life-force beat beneath my fingertips tempered my panic. I laughed quietly. "You're daring me to say things I have no idea how to articulate." I had no idea what the correct etiquette was. What was forbidden to discuss—what was permitted. "I don't know what to say, Q."

He pressed a whisper-soft kiss on my ear. "Just say what's in your soul. That's all I'm going to do. Nothing you feel can be wrong, *esclave*. Trust it."

I sucked in a gulp of air, dragging his incredible aftershave into my lungs. Thoughts raced through my head. The truth— that's where the horror lay.

Memoires swarmed thick and fast.

"I'd kill for you, Tess. I have killed for you." The day in Q's office—the morning I was stolen.

"Ah, esclave, *this wasn't supposed to happen."* The evening he'd found me raped by Lefebvre.

"There is pain in intimacy. Let me make your pain my pleasure." The shower where he replaced himself with the horrible incident.

"You'll do this or I'll kill you—do you understand?" The day he forced me to hurt him—all in the name of bringing me back.

I thought about his temper. His violence. His ruthlessness.

I thought about his compassion. His love for birds. His selfless acts of saving women.

So many things to say. So many things that would be forever treasured.

Speak from your heart.

I wouldn't bow to censorship. I would share our unconventional history. Q made me into the woman I was but I'd also turned him into the man he'd become. Our past formed us and it would be forever a part of us.

My courage was faint, but I straightened my shoulders. "I love you."

Q smiled, holding my hand. I took a deep breath, throwing myself into the truth, spilling my heart—painting our life with promises. "All my life, I never truly existed. I struggled to know what I was meant for. I followed a path I didn't understand." I swallowed. "I was lonely. I never felt the pinprick of heartache, or the warmth of a hug. But then I was captured and sold."

Q turned to stone, his fingers latching hard around mine.

"The day I was taken, my life ended. I thought I would die. I *wanted* to die. But then I was sold to a master who changed my world completely."

Q stopped breathing.

"This new master confused me, hurt me, but ultimately taught me what I was missing all along. I was missing *him*. He was the hole in my heart—he was my other half. I was no longer lonely, or searching for something I didn't understand. My grey world became prismatic, and I valued every lesson he taught."

My heart stuttered. No matter the happiness of being sold to Q, my trials hadn't ended there.

"But life decided I wasn't worthy—not yet." I closed my eyes, fighting back the ghosts of Rio. "I endured a price I didn't know I could pay, but once again I learned something. The right love—soul-mate love—is priceless.

"My master came for me—proving once again I never had to be afraid or alone but in return I shut him out, hurting him worse than anyone." My heart cracked for how heartless I'd been. "I shut myself off, unable to trust anymore—trust a life that gave so much but took away more in return. But now I know why. I learned my final lesson.

"Life taught me an eternal love will demand the worst sacrifices. A transcendent love will split your soul, cleaving you into pieces. A love this strong doesn't grant you sweetness—it grants you pain. And in that pain is the greatest pleasure of all."

I met Q's eyes. His lips were pressed into a fine line, containing the smouldering emotion in is gaze. He burned with everything he felt, barely containing it. The connection between us was thick and heavy and I wanted to be alone. I wanted to kiss him. Love him. Worship him.

"Q, I'm not just yours for this lifetime. I'm yours *forever.* I will follow you through unhappiness, confusion, and hardship. I will bask beside you in success, fortune, and laughter. I will obey you because I trust you. I will push you because I believe in you. I will fight with you because that is where our passion lives. And I will make love to you the way our demons demand.

"My blood is yours.

"My breath is yours.

"And I swear to you when this life is over, I will wait for you to join me. I will travel with you through galaxies and solar-systems to be yours once again. Because a love like this isn't replicable. You've ruined me. Devastated me. Destroyed me by choosing me as your wife."

A single tear rolled down my cheek. I said my final vow, *"Je suis à toi. Je suis ton monstre dans le noir pour toujours."* I'm yours. I'm your monster in the dark forever.

Silence was a heavy shroud, hushing even the tweets of birds outside.

Q hadn't moved. His body locked down, face hard and dark.

Perhaps I had no right to tell our story aloud. Maybe he thought I'd failed by being so honest. But I wanted Q to know that everything I lived through—every hardship was necessary—because it made me *deserving*. It taught me Q was worth every sacrifice. It made me strong enough to keep him.

The future was ours. Evolving together. Twisting our souls into one. Knitting our lives into inseparable tapestries. I could never love another like him. Fate designed us from the same darkness, the same fabric of wrongness.

Q cleared his throat. The celebrant didn't move, waiting for the thick silence to disperse.

Say something! I couldn't read him. He'd shut down, trembling with colossal energy, glowing with everything he trapped inside. "Tess—" Finally a crack, a small doorway into his feelings. *"Je suis—"*

Then he folded to his knees.

My stomach lodged in the tight boning of my corset. I'd never seen a man so proud, so strong and fierce, be so shattered and humbled.

Q's ferocious eyes ensnared me.

"Tess, je ne serai jamais capable d'exprimer à quel point je tiens à toi. Je n'aurais jamais les mots pour exprimer combien Je t'aime." Tess, I'll never be able to express how much I care for you. I'll never know the words to say how much I love you.

He looked away, gathering his thoughts. His back rippled with a deep breath. *"Je ne savais pas que j'étais seul. Je ne savais pas que j'étouffais ma douleur et mon besoin d'affection sous le travail. Je hais mon héritage, d'où je viens et je ne me suis jamais senti digne du bonheur. Mais ensuite, toi, esclave Cinquante-huit ans, est entrée dans mon monde. Tu m'as fait tout remettre en question."* I never knew I was lonely. I never knew I smothered my pain and the need for connection beneath my work. I hate my heritage—where I've come from—and never felt worthy of happiness. But then you, Slave Fifty-eight, entered my world. You made me question everything.

"Je voulais te briser. T'adorer. Te faire crier. Je voulais tant de choses mais par-dessus tout, je voulais ce que j'ai vu dans tes yeux brillants pour moi, que tu me fasses confiance. Je voulais ton âme." I wanted to break you. Adore you. Make you scream. I wanted so many things but beneath it all, I wanted what I saw in your eyes glowing for me, trusting me. I wanted your soul.

I reached down, begging him to take my hand. He did, pressing a sharp kiss to my knuckles. *"Tu m'acceptes pour ce que je suis. Mes ténèbres et le reste. Mes péchés et le reste. Tu es mon égal. Mon professeur. Je suis ton disciple. Je suis ton propriétaire. Je ne pourrais pas être plus amoureux de toi même si j'avais deux cœurs au lieu d'un. Ma vie est à toi. Mon âme est à toi. Je fais le voeu de toujours te consoler. De toujours te protéger. Je vais pleurer avec toi. Je vais rire avec toi. Je t'enlacerai tous les soirs de notre vie."* You accept me for me. Darkness and all. Sin and everything. You are my equal. My teacher. I am your disciple. I am your owner. I couldn't be more in love with you if I had two hearts instead of one. My life is yours. My soul is yours. I vow to always comfort you. Always protect you. I will cry with you. I will laugh with you. I will hold you every night of our lives."

Q's voice deepened, filling with heartache and overwhelming love. *"Je ne déteste plus mes démons, car tu les combats pour moi. Je ne me sens plus seul parce que tu es mon refuge. Je ne me fais plus peur parce que tu contrôles ma bête. Je suis ton monstre, Tess. Je tuerai ceux qui t'ont fait du mal. Je nourrirais ceux qui s'occuperont de toi . Je ne cesserai jamais de chasser tes cauchemars et de t'offrir une vie parfaite."* I no longer hate my demons because you fight them on my behalf. I no longer feel alone because you are my home.

I no longer fear myself because you control my beast. I'm your monster, Tess. I'll kill those who hurt you. I'll nurture those who tend you. I'll never stop hunting your nightmares or providing a perfect life."

My legs wobbled. The conviction in his tone, the edge of violence in his eyes—he shot barbs right into my heart. The echoes of his vows would live in me for an eternity. He'd made me immortal with his words.

I believed every vow. I cherished every promise. I never needed to be afraid or lost. Ever again. Because he would protect me and I would protect him. Always.

His eyes latched onto the 'Q' branding my neck. His face tightened with passion. *"Tu portes mon nom, donc je sais que tu seras toujours à moi. Permets moi de passer l'éternité à te protéger et à t'aimer, esclave. Je suis à toi. Je suis ton monstre dans le noir pour toujours."* You wear my mark, so I know you'll always be mine. Let me spend my forevers protecting and loving you, *esclave*. I'm yours. I'm your monster in the dark forever."

Silence fell as Q climbed to his feet, wincing. He looked drained but content as if he'd poured everything from him to me and had nothing left. His broken body needed to rest.

With a look full of black passion, he pulled me into a tight embrace. The celebrant didn't say a word as Q's lips pressed against mine. He kissed me with the fine edge of control and anger I was so used to.

His tongue slipped past my lips. I met his with mine, dancing together, making love together. I went limp in his arms. All the tension and love turned me from mannequin to puddle. I wanted the honour of pampering him, healing him. I wanted him naked in bed.

The kiss could've been a century or only a moment but it was the seal on our promises. A non-verbal agreement we were each other's for eternity.

Pulling back, Q stiffened. His eyes narrowed on something behind me. I tried to shift in his arms, but Suzette appeared, eagerness vibrating around her. "Please let her go, master."

Q's lips pulled back into a snarl. "What are you doing, Suzette. It's not over. Go away."

She ducked her head, cheeks pinking at his temper. "I know. But allow me to do something before the final vow."

My blood was replaced with molasses. Thanks to Q's mind-twisting kiss nothing made sense. All I wanted was to be alone with him. I needed to bask in this sweet vulnerability between us.

Feminine hands landed on my shoulders from behind, tugging me from Q's embrace.

Hey! Stop.

"Trust us, Tess." Her—the woman who'd been singing. She smiled softly. "I'm Angelique—Frederick's wife. Hi."

My brain skipped, trying to figure out what the hell was going on. "Um—hi." I stumbled in her hold, struggling to stay attached to Q. "Please, let me go."

"Yes, let her go, Angelique. You don't want me angry and you're doing a damn good job," Q snapped.

Angelique shook her head. "Not yet. Trust us." She pulled harder.

My arms went from holding Q to holding air. The only part locked together was our fingertips. Q stood there, breathing hard, his face twisted with pain. He looked livid but too banged up to move. "Will someone please tell me what the fuck is going on?"

"I will. Come with me, Mercer." Frederick jerked him, breaking the last remaining contact of our fingers. Q spun around, groaning in pain. "Roux—what the—" Frederick led him away, lending a hand as Q's stitched up legs seized from standing too long.

Let me go! I wanted to be the one who Q used as support. I wanted to hold him while his body healed.

Suzette cut off my vision, standing directly in front of me. "Remember when I said to trust me. That the second part was for him?" Her hazel eyes shimmered with nervousness. "Please...trust me."

I looked over her head to a fighting Q. Both Frederick and Franco whispered in his ear, holding his shoulders to prevent him causing more injury.

"You're ruining it, Suzette." I swallowed my anxiety, battling with trusting whatever she planned to do. "Please—"

She smiled. "It will make sense. Just let it happen." Her eyes flew to Angelique behind me. "Ready?"

"Yes." Angelique whispered in my ear, "It will be okay. I promise." Her hands fell to my sides just as Suzette gripped the front of my dress.

What the hell are they doing?

My eyes searched for Q but he was surrounded by his entourage. No doubt hurting himself trying to fight. *Let them do it. Get it over with.*

I relaxed a little and Suzette took my silence as permission.

With a sharp nod, Suzette ruined my life. The wondrous gown, so brilliantly made and oh so beautiful, ripped with the echoing sound of a lightning bolt.

The fabric ripped from the sides as if the weakness had been deliberately sewn into the dress, splitting like a well sliced cake.

It only took one tug to turn the white masterpiece into a disaster on the floor. It pooled, dead and forgotten by my feet.

What has she done?!

My heart exploded at being stripped of the only wedding dress I'd ever wear. All the preparation this morning for nothing—it ended up in pieces on the floor.

I blushed, bringing my arms up to hide my corset-clad breasts. The swell of flesh teetered provocatively on top of the tightly cinched lingerie. The black sexy pantyhose were on display, complete with saucy bow, and glittering red sequin shoes. My knickers were black lace, hiding my decency with nothing more than darker detailing between the legs. The garter belts clipped to the corset, imprisoning my legs with frilly black stays.

I'd been transformed from bride to whore.

I gasped as someone undid my hair with a sharp tug, spilling the careful up-do to waterfall down my back in lazy waves. The black feathers stayed, quivering in my strands.

Q shoved Frederick off him, his mouth gaping. "How dare you fucking touch her!" He stomped forward, undeterred by agony, zeroing in on me. But Franco wrapped an arm around his shoulders, holding him steadfast. Frederick recaptured him, mumbling in his ear.

"I don't care. I want none of this. What the hell are you doing!" Q wrenched his arm free from Franco's hold. "This wasn't your decision!"

Don't hurt yourself! My heart hurt for him. We were so private about our world. So sure no one would accept what we needed—so used to keeping it hidden.

To have his trusted friends expose us.

It hurt. A lot.

Standing in kinky lingerie sent embarrassment twisting my stomach, but it would be worse for Q. He hated others seeing me undressed. Especially dolled up like the slave he'd always wanted.

Wait…

My heart leapt. *Is that what Suzette's doing?*

I had to go to him—to give him comfort. I might understand what all of this meant.

"Tess. Stay." Suzette planted a firm hand on my sternum. "It's not over yet."

"But—"

"Let her go!" someone yelled. "Crikey, what the hell is going *on* here?"

That voice. Oh, my God, I knew that voice.

My eyes zeroed in on Brax.

Brax!

Q followed my moon-wide gaze, bristling with rage. He didn't look as if he'd survived a torturing session, more like ready to jump in the ring with anyone *stupid* enough to get in his way.

Shit. I feared for Brax's safety.

My ex-boyfriend jumped up from his chair, pointing a shaking finger. "Stop!" He wore a pastel blue blazer and jeans, his floppy brown hair slicked with gel. He looked older than the last time I'd seen him, more of a man than a boy.

Brax pushed a girl—our old neighbour Bianca—out of his way, stomping into the aisle. "What is the meaning of this? You don't strip the bride—it's awful. Stop the ceremony. Right now!"

Q shoved Franco off him, taking a calculated step toward the reckless boy from my past. His hands curled beside his hips. He spoke softly but it rippled down the aisle, skewering Brax in the chest. "You have no fucking authority here, boy. I suggest you sit down. Shut the fuck up. And don't give me a reason to escort you off this island with my fists."

My heart catapulted from frantic to chaotic. What had Suzette done? She'd ruined an amazing wedding…she'd upset everything.

I bent down, scooping up my discarded dress. "Suzette, let's fix this. Help."

Q reached for me, flinching as his body was dragged backward by Frederick. "Calm down, Q. Jesus, let us do what we're doing okay?"

Q threw his arms up, livid anger mixing with the painful sheen on his cheeks. "Whatever you're doing, I demand it to be over. Someone cover Tess, goddammit."

Suzette ignored my plea to fix my dress. She winged down the aisle, shoving Brax back into his chair. "Don't interfere. You're the only outsider here, so sit down and hush up." Turning, she headed to Q. Terror glowed in her eyes, but determination lent strength to her features. "Please. Stop fighting. Let us do this. Trust me, Q. Please! Give me one minute, then you can kill me, smite me, whatever you want. Just let us do this."

Q snarled, "How about you stop. Right now. I'm fucking done with whatever is going on here!"

I huddled, waiting for an explosion. The atmosphere in the room sparked with ignition—ready to blow up at any second. The celebrant's voice was the persona of calm in the horrendous storm. "Excuse me, everyone, but I have been made privy to this new arrangement, and I suggest you take the lady's advice and let her proceed."

Everyone froze.

Q breathed hard, his energy levels depleting. He stood panting, his face contorted with agony. "This is ridiculous."

"I agree. You fighting is ridiculous. Stand still for one damn moment." Frederick took his hands carefully off Q. When Q didn't sprint out of the marquee or punch him, Frederick took the opportunity to rip the white blazer from his shoulders.

At the same time Franco tore at Q's trousers. The material fell away, revealing shiny black slacks. In a blink, Q was disarmed of the illusion of pureness and re-dressed in darkness. His tie came undone, waistcoat, and shirt all ripped from his bruised torso.

What are they doing?

Q stood half-naked and I couldn't control the desire spooling in my blood. The dampness between my legs multiplied staring at the man who owned my heart. The damaged man who needed to lie down and let me lavish him with love.

My eyes fell to the scarring 'T' above his heart, barely visible amongst fresh bruises. My heart flurried. My self-consciousness and doubt faded away, drinking in his perfection.

Frederick turned to a hidden pedestal, returning with a black blazer beautifully tailored with embroidered crimson sparrows.

"What the fuck are you doing?" Q demanded as the new blazer was shoved up his arms and positioned over his shoulders. His naked chest and tattoo stayed visible through the gaping of the fabric.

Frederick growled, "Giving you a memory you will never

forget, you bastard."

Q's face darkened. "I had everything I wanted before you fucked it up."

Franco shook his head. "You had the white wedding, but you and Tess are more than that. You come alive in the dark. And that's what we're giving you. Believe me, you'll want this."

Q gritted his teeth, shrugging the new clothing into position. He transformed from angel to monster. *My* monster.

Q's eyes landed on me, striking the match, blazing gunpowder to my core. My stomach fluttered as his gaze devoured me. I wanted to run my tongue down his chest. I wanted to tear off his trousers and worship him with my mouth.

My damp knickers became soaking with how deliciously dangerous he was. How bruised and damaged and sore.

Dropping my hands, I let my corset and lingerie shine. I was no longer self-conscious. *I* was what Q wanted most.

I was the ultimate prize. I was his. And he…he was my master.

My flesh tingled. *I know what Suzette is doing.*

Suzette clapped her hands and the marquee suddenly left the day, welcoming the night instead. The transformation was seamless—choreographed to perfection. White silk fell as if slaughtered by angels. Velvet black drapery replaced it, covering the ceiling, turning sunshine to stars.

White heaven fell into a devil's lair. Black. Everything turned to black. Even the white roses around the room somehow changed to black dahlias.

It was magical. It was surreal. Suzette completely outdid herself.

She turned to face me. "*Now* do you understand?"

I shook away my stupor. Taking her hand, I whispered in her ear, "I'm his ultimate possession. He's shared his heart. Now it's time for me to share his ultimate wish."

Suzette's shoulders slumped in relief. "I'm so glad it makes sense." She moved away—very aware of Q bearing down upon me.

He yanked my elbow, demanding my attention. "Are you okay?" His eyes burned with undiluted need. He bit his bottom lip, consuming my ensemble. "Fuck, Tess, you look *incroyable*." His accented voice stroked my nipples, drawing more wetness to gather. His touch turned to a vice; power and lust and love glowed on my skin.

My eyes fell to his trousers, my heart skipping a beat as I followed the outline of his erection. He wanted me. I wanted him.

"I'm fine. Q—you're..." Stepping into his body, I whispered, "I'm so wet for you, *maître*. Seeing you like this. Knowing you're as hot for me as I am for you...it jumbles my thoughts. All I can think about is kissing you."

His arm wrapped around my waist, slamming my hips against his. "I'm thinking of more than just kissing, *esclave*. I'm going to bruise you with how much I need you."

I pulled away, gathering my scattered decency, trying to ignore the lava in my veins. "You're forgetting you're hurt. I'm not letting you touch me tonight. You need to rest."

"Rest?" He chuckled, pressing a kiss on my cheek. "*You'll* need to rest after I'm done with you. Your throat will need to rest from your screams."

I couldn't breathe; the corset squeezed tighter. I couldn't take my eyes from Q's brilliant tattoo, teasing me through the richness of his blazer. It looked incredible on him. Out of the two spectrums, Q belonged in black. He wasn't an imposter in black.

Lust heat-waved around us, granting sensual power. I stood in front of people in lingerie. I stood blatantly showing my desire for this man and I didn't care. I didn't care because this was *our* world.

It was no longer hidden.

By making us dress this way, Suzette had brought us from the shadows and into the light.

"Goddammit, you're a stunning creature, Tess." Q

couldn't tear his eyes from my raised cleavage.

I'm only stunning because of the way you love me.

I dropped my gaze. "I couldn't wait for you to see me in this—I just thought it would be for after—"

"It was never meant for after the wedding," Frederick said, sandwiching himself between us, taking my hand and placing his other on Q's shoulder. "It was always meant to be this way." He guided us back to the altar and the smiling celebrant.

Q smiled curtly at the celebrant, shrugging himself free from Frederick's hold. "I wish someone would explain what exactly all of this means. And I would've preferred a heads up rather than being stripped like a fucking prisoner."

Frederick smiled. "This is to wed both sides of you—the good and the bad, the light and the dark. We're giving you exactly what you need."

Giving my hand a squeeze, he said, "And we couldn't tell you before, because you wouldn't have done it. You're both shy. But we're your friends—your family. And we don't judge. We just wanted you to know that."

Letting me go, he looked at the celebrant. "Please, we're ready to continue." Giving Q another smile, he moved away, taking his place by Franco. Suzette and Angelique returned to their positions behind me and the chaos settled back into love-swelled beauty.

I wasn't nervous. I'd guessed what would come next. *I'm ready. I'm ready to stitch my life permanently to his.*

The celebrant looked at Q. "Are you ready for the final part?"

Q's face twisted and for the longest moment I feared he'd walk out the door. He looked uncomfortable—very aware his dark persuasions were bold and brash and there for everyone to see.

We couldn't hide any longer—not that we had anything to hide. *This isn't for me. It's for him.*

Reaching for Q, I froze as he stepped away.

He moved to the side where a small chest rested. Plucking

it from the floor, he brought it back, placing it at my feet. Taking my hand for balance, he ordered, "Climb up."

I wanted to ask so many things but obeyed, climbing onto the small pedestal placing me above Q's height.

"Q, what…"

His eyes met mine, full of endless love The corset once again ceased my breathing.

"You're mine to worship now and for always, Tess. I've put you above me, so everyone knows I value your life above all else. You are the reason why I exist. The reason for my happiness."

I swallowed hard.

His eyes tightened, battling so much inside. His fingers trembled in mine. "I'm ready," he murmured. "I'm ready to proceed."

We never looked away. Locked together. Padlocked by souls.

The celebrant said, "I believe your best man has the next requirement."

Frederick stepped forward, his hands clasped around something. Passing it to Q, he spoke in his ear, slapping him gently on the shoulder. I couldn't make out what transferred but Q stiffened, shaking his head.

Masculine whispers snapped in the silence followed by a curse. Q finally snatched the gift with a sharp nod.

Q raised his arm, showing me what he'd been given. My heart leapt into my throat.

A collar. A black diamond-studded collar with a gold ring at the front.

Of course. My heart thundered.

His eyes implored me. *Please…I've never asked you to be less than human.*

And he wasn't now. He was asking me to announce to everyone present—to him, to me, to the sanctity of marriage, that he was my master.

He is. In every way.

In an effortless move, I swayed forward. "Collar me, *maître*. Keep me forever," I murmured, scooping my hair off my shoulders, waiting for him to fasten it.

Q leaned forward, his fingers shaking against my skin. His eyes swam with adoration, body trembling with love and need. "You're given me the ultimate fantasy, *esclave*. You're giving me the right to collar you. You're giving me something I've always wanted but have always been too afraid to take." His lips pressed against my temple. "Thank you, Tess. *Du fond du cœur.*" From the bottom of my heart.

He wrapped the soft leather around my neck and over my brand. It irritated, but the discomfort was nothing to the surging possession in my heart. Q might collar me but I collared him in return. My ownership was invisible—wrapping him in unseen chains—chains unlocked only by my soul.

I shivered as his knuckles brushed the back of my skull. He carefully cinched the buckle, marking me as his. Marking me as *belonging*.

Tears dripped down my cheeks as he pulled away. His eyes were liquid too, matching my love ounce for ounce. With immense tenderness, he licked my tears away, washing my face clean of happiness. "God, I love you." His voice was barely there, but I bloomed bright and radiant.

The celebrant cleared his throat. "Do you, Quincy Mercer, take this woman Tess Snow as your lawfully wedded wife, now and forever, from this day forth?"

Q clenched his jaw. *"Je le veux."* I do.

My lips spread into an awed smile.

I do. I do. I do.

"I believe your maid of honour has the next requirement," the celebrant said softly.

Suzette gently tapped my hip, bringing my attention to her. In her hands rested a looped leash and something hidden. Pressing the small unknown item into my palm, she whispered, "You'll know what to do with the leash, *mon ami.*"

I nodded, thanking her silently. I knew. Of course I knew.

Turning back to Q, I held both items in shaking hands.

The celebrant asked, "Do you, Tess Snow, take this man Quincy Mercer as your lawfully wedded husband, now and forever, from this day forth?"

I swallowed the lump in my throat. If I spoke or moved my body would explode into a gazillion dazzling sparks. This must be how it felt to have dreams come true. This homecoming.

I revealed the gold and titanium steel band for the first time. I held my hand out.

With a small smile, Q placed his palm in mine, spreading his fingers, giving himself to me. His touch was just as unsteady.

Nerves made everything intense. Nerves made everything real.

This is real.

My eyes glassed, softening lines, blurring edges. Carefully and solemnly, I slid the ring Suzette had sourced over Q's wedding finger. My heart increased its beat. The ring slipped into position—a golden symbol forever marking him as taken.

Mine.

The symbol of our unity sent tears swelling behind my collar. I couldn't swallow the salt, too overwhelmed. I managed a whisper. Just a whisper. "I do."

Letting Q go, I unravelled the leash, clipping the end onto the ring of my collar. Threading the soft leather through my fingers, I ceremoniously handed the end to Q. "*Toujours.*" Forever.

He fisted the leash. His fingers turned white, his body shaking with amazement. "*Toujours.*"

We'd exchanged our vows in numerous ways. We'd proven our words weren't empty against sickness or health. We'd solidified every promise. Brought truth to every claim.

We wore each other's brand and mark.

We were no longer separate people. We were one.

One of the same.

My heart thrilled faster as Q tugged me downward, a hard smile on his lips. His mouth landed on mine and the marquee, guests, and everything else shot from comprehension. His tongue entered, dancing in a ceaseless waltz.

His dark taste unlocked the final piece of the true Tess. My journey was over. I'd gone from weak to strong to tamed. I'd gone from lost to scared to found.

The sun rose inside, spreading golden tendrils through my body, coaxed deeper by every lick. My core rippled, desperate for physical connection. I was no longer cold and confused. I was no longer alone and unloved.

I was home.

For always.

Q deepened the kiss, combusting the sun into a raging ball of fire. Heated lust stole my limbs, pebbling my nipples, drawing wetness between my legs.

Breathing hard, he let me go. "I need you alone. Now."

The moment Q pulled away, the celebrant raised his voice. "It is my greatest honour to present to you for the first time. Mr. and Mrs. Mercer."

Mr. and Mrs.

My heart tripled its wingbeats.

Our friends clapped and rice rained from above, full of black glitter. The little pricks of confetti stung but I wasn't contained by my flesh anymore. I'd expanded to something so much more.

Q wrapped his arms around me. Plucking me from the pedestal, he slowly lowered my body down his. Every slip was delicious torture. The heat of him. The hardness of him.

My feet touched the ground; Q smiled. "Hello, Mrs Mercer."

I moaned as his hand slinked up my side, deliberately catching the side of my breast. "Hello, Mr. Mercer."

"I'm so glad fate gave me you," he whispered.

"I'm so glad I deserve you."

His eyes darkened. "You deserve so much more than me,

esclave. But it's too late. You're mine, and I'm never letting you go." Time stood still as we stared into each other's eyes.

His hand cupped my cheek, hot, claiming. "We did it." I accepted his feathery kiss. "We're married."

Q kissed me. *"Nous ne faisons qu'un."* We are one.

Chapter Sixteen

My absolution
My treasure

It was done.

Tess was mine.

Legally.

Spiritually.

Every fucking way she was mine.

My fingers tightened on the leash, dragging her closer. I loved having control. Having her restrained in such a debasing but incredibly powerful way. The anxiety I'd carried finally faded. I had what I needed. I had her oath. I owned her soul.

My lips captured hers again, tangling with two emotions. I wanted to strip her right there and take her—injuries be damned, witnesses be fucked. But at the same time, I wanted to beat Frederick and Franco for forcing my truth to light.

They had no right to dress Tess that way, or provoke me into accepting there was nothing wrong with our relationship. Suzette had been out of bounds.

I was going insane having Tess half-naked. She was my *wife*. I wanted her covered.

But then you won't be able stare.

And I wanted to stare. So damn much. Tess was a fucking masterpiece. Full and feminine and so fucking tempting.

Pulling away, I readjusted my rock-hard cock. It hadn't calmed down since I'd set eyes on her when she entered the marquee. Her white dress had been stunning. *She'd* been stunning.

She still is.

I groaned, drinking in her garter belts and lace. Goddammit, I had no willpower. No control. She may wear the collar but she dragged me around by my cock. I panted for her. I would sit at her feet and fucking beg just for a taste. One glorious taste.

"Shit, Tess…I need you. I need to sink inside you and come. I'm going to explode."

My cock hurt jammed in my trousers. My balls throbbed with the need to come. It didn't matter my body was drained. My shakes weren't just from nerves but agony slicing through the painkillers. Nothing would stop me from taking her. I didn't care if I was slightly lightheaded and queasy. Sex. Sex would make it all better. Sex with Tess.

Happiness danced down my spine.

Sex with my *wife.*

Tess laughed, patting my naked chest. I hissed between my teeth as her gentle touch caught a bruise. The pain and pleasure shot to my cock, rippling with need.

This isn't a laughing matter, esclave. *I'll turn your smiles into moans of ecstasy.*

"I need you, too. But you need to rest, Q. Don't expect me to bow to you tonight."

"Bow to me? I want you so fucking much I'd ignore the safe-word with how much I need you."

Tess looped her arms around my back, following my tattoo. "Sparrow, Q. Sparrow until I get you into bed."

I groaned, anger giving me energy to get through the next few minutes. "You can say sparrow all you like, but it won't stop me from taking you."

Taking the final piece of you.

Her lips parted, understanding my unsaid threat. "You can't—you need to heal."

Grabbing her close, I muttered, "I'll heal when my cock is inside your beautiful ass. Now say your goodbyes. We're leaving."

Reluctantly, I let her go.

With wide eyes, she moved away to hug Suzette. The leash on her collar tugged my fist. I opened my fingers, letting it slip free.

She was swallowed by the small crowd, all wishing congratulations. Every guest stole time with my wife. Time. That bitch was yet again getting in the way of me and my goal.

Tess disappeared under well-wishes—the only part of her visible was her loose curls and black feather headdress. Shit, I needed to cover her. I cursed everyone staring at her beauty. I wanted to gorge their eyes out for seeing what was mine, but smug male pride tempered my rage. She was mine. Not theirs. They would never be allowed to touch. Only me.

Didn't fucking matter though. My cock was too hard. My instincts too feral.

I stormed forward, tugging at my jacket to throw over Tess's body.

Then darkness smothered my world as the little cocksucker who spoke out during the wedding, wriggled through the crowd and intercepted Tess. He tapped her on the shoulder.

She turned to him.

She turned to him, *smiling,* wearing the fucking sexiest corset and black lingerie. Her breasts tantalized, spilling over the supple leather. Her long legs closed the distance in a hug.

She motherfucking *hugged* him. Dressed like that.

I want his blood.

My heart shot painful adrenaline through my body. No amount of stitches, gunshots, or broken ribs could stop me from beating the little cunt into a pulp. Tearing my blazer off, I closed the distance. "Tess, get away from him." Ripping her from Twerp's arms, I slammed my jacket around Tess's front.

She gasped, pushing at my blazer imprisoning her. "Q—what on earth?"

I breathed hard, never taking my eyes from the little fucker who'd had his hands on my wife.

What in the flying fuck was *he* doing at my wedding?

"Q, calm down. You're not thinking straight." Tess's voice only pissed me off.

The boy curled his arm around a pretty brunette dressed in yellow. He brought her forward, distracting me for a second—intentionally showing he had his own girl and respected that Tess was mine. "That's a rad tattoo you've got, mate. Never been a fan of needles myself but I can appreciate the art."

Tess jumped in. "Q, this is Brax Cliffingstone and his girlfriend, Bianca. They travelled all the way from Australia to see us marry, so a thank you for coming would be nice."

A thank-you? They flew on *my* fucking money. Suzette would no doubt present me with a bill a mile long once we got home.

"Brax, Bianca, this is my husband, Quincy Mercer. I could go on and on about how amazing he is but that's irrelevant—you can guess how special he is because I married him."

Husband.

She called me her husband.

Special.

She called me special.

The words starved some of my anger, relaxing my screeching muscles.

Twerp's blue eyes met mine, apprehension tangling with false bravado. "Hey, mate. Nice to meet you finally." He stuck out his hand. "Congratulations. I'm super glad you guys were able to work out whatever issues you had. I'm stoked for you."

What the hell had Tess told this delinquent? *Her emails.* My teeth gritted. The emails she sent when she blocked me out.

She'd talked to *him* when she couldn't talk to me.

The frustration and anger rose, reminding me of the intense pain Tess had caused.

Fuckwit's eyes fell on Tess's cleavage. It was fleeting. But it was there.

My neck rolled. Fists clenched.

Yep, couldn't do it. I'd kill him.

I yelled, "Suzette. *Donne moi quelque chose pour couvrir Tess ou je vais* — " Give me something to cover Tess or I'll—

A black embroidered dress appeared from nowhere, matching the crimson sparrows of my velvet blazer. "Here you go. I've come prepared." Suzette gave me a wary look, holding up the wraparound dress for Tess. I dropped my blazer, shoving Tess toward Suzette.

I had to admit Suzette had done an amazing fucking job— I wanted to murder her, but she deserved a substantial raise for putting this venue together in five days.

My heart hammered while Tess slipped into the dress. Suzette secured it with a large bow at the back. The second Tess was encased in something suitable, I relaxed a little. Just a little.

Tess smiled. "Thank you. I feel better not being so exposed."

Me, too. I'd been ready to murder everyone.

Suzette grinned. "Not that you have any cause for being shy, but I understand."

Goddammit, my nerves. The overbearing monster inside prowled, snapping its jaws. The beast wanted to go suicidal. I felt threatened. Threatened by a boy from Tess's past.

There was no reason to be. But try telling that to a beast that didn't listen.

He's just a stupid boy who will never deserve Tess. Me, on the other hand—I still didn't deserve her but too fucking bad—she'd married me.

A headache overshadowed the rest of my injuries. I managed to unlock my jaw enough to say, "*Merci.* And I'm sorry for my temper."

I scanned the room out of habit, searching for anyone out of place. The guests smiled, milling around now that the service was over. Not that they were guests. Mrs. Sucre didn't count, nor did Frederick, Angelique, or Franco. There wasn't one unfamiliar face. Apart from the dickshit in front of me.

"It's okay, mate. Totally understand." Brax nodded, opening his mouth to say something equally annoying in his Australian twang.

I couldn't do it.

Growling under my breath, I said to Suzette, "You're in deep shit for inviting him."

Tess scowled, whacking my shoulder. "Q. That isn't fair. She did it for me." Smiling gently at Fuckwit, she added, "Sorry, Brax. Q's been through a lot the past couple of days. We really ought to be leaving. He needs to rest."

A geyser of temper exploded from my mouth. "Did you just call me *weak*, Tess? I'm perfectly capable thank you very much. I'm not going to pass out from a simple conversation."

Twerp jumped in. "Hey, don't be mad at her. Look, maybe it was the wrong thing coming here, but I wanted to see Tess and make sure she was happy. I love her. I wanted to wish her all the best. And you too—if you stopped being such a jerk."

Fuck, that's it.

Thank god I wasn't wearing a shirt because it would've ended up splattered with his blood.

Tess leapt in the middle of us. "Brax, stop it. Q, don't judge him until you know him. He's a good friend and you need—"

"I don't need to do anything, *esclave*. He's seen you naked. I'll never be his friend. So don't expect it to be all rugby games and fucking unicorns."

Tess blew curls out of her eyes, exasperation rather than fear on her face. That just irritated me further. Did I look so banged up I was incapable of inflicting pain?

I can rectify that.

The girl dressed in yellow giggled. "I doubt you'll see us again after today, but if it makes you feel any better, your wife has seen my fiancé naked, too, and I don't want to beat her up."

My eyes stretched wide. I couldn't come up with a response. I hated the thought of Tess being anywhere near this boy. I hated to think of anyone owning her heart. I was beyond jealous. I was fucking possessive and the beast inside only made it worse.

I wanted to piss a circle around Tess, blatantly claiming she was off bounds to everyone but me.

Calm down, idiot.

My heart raced but Tess laughed. "I'm glad you don't want to hurt me, Bianca. I'm just happy you and Brax are together. And please accept mine and Q's congratulations."

She had no right to offer anything of mine. I wanted them off this island, not to exchange pleasantries.

My rib twinged, letting a hug of pain fill my chest. *God, I'm tired.*

Fuckwit grinned. "I asked Bianca to marry me two weeks ago. I know it's really fast—but sometimes you just know, yeah?"

Tess softened, glancing at me. My anger petered out, replaced with vengeful lust. My cock sprang to attention dragging me under her control again. Damn woman and her magic. "I totally agree. Time means nothing when you know."

I swallowed, trying so fucking hard to keep the sexual need from my eyes. Forgetting about Fuckwit—he was nothing to me—I murmured to Tess, "Sometimes all it takes is a look."

Tess's lips parted and the strain of the past few minutes didn't mean a thing. The desire between us was all-consuming and I was done with this place.

Narrowing my gaze, I murmured, "Time to stop playing with the guests. You're coming with me."

Tess blushed. "That would be rude. We can't just—"

"Yes. We. Can. Now, Tess. *S'il vous plaît.*" She wasn't being fair. *I* was the injured one. I was the one in need of TLC. These guests could fucking wait until I'd had my wife beneath me, on top of me, tied up, and ravished. "You don't want me to ask again. You won't like what I'll do."

Suzette broke the thick tension. "You can't go. Not yet. I've got a small reception planned next door."

I couldn't think of anything worse.

I was married. I wanted all these people gone. I wanted to be alone with the one person who truly understood me. I wanted my wife.

"No. Suzette. Rearrange it. Tomorrow, I don't care."

"I'm sorry, Suzette." Tess shrugged. "Q really should get some rest."

I grumbled in my chest. I hated she thought I was hurt. I wanted a bed, yes, but I wasn't planning on fucking moaning about my injuries and going to sleep.

Did she not sense everything I was transmitting to her? Did she not understand that I could suffer two broken legs and *still* need to be inside her?

Fine. If it made our escape faster I would play the poor patient angle. "You know. I am feeling a little tired—I need to be in *bed* with my *wife.*"

Tess threw me a look while Fuckwit sucked in a gasp.

My eyes tightened, taking in his innocence—his pompous timidness. This boy had nothing on me. I could blow him fucking over and defeat him. What did Tess ever see in him?

Frederick suddenly threw an arm around my shoulders, eyeing up Brax. Shoving his traitorous hand out, he smiled. "Hi. Nice to meet you. I'm Frederick Roux. Business partner to this sour groom."

Fuckwit half-smiled, taking the offered handshake. "Nice to meet you. I've researched your company. Congrats on all your success."

Frederick laughed, letting go to nudge me. My teeth clamped together at being manhandled, especially because it highlighted just how much I *did* need to lie down. Fuck, I hurt.

"Nope, not my company. All this guy's. He's the mastermind." Slapping me on the back—making me groan—he added, "Congrats, Mercer, Tess. So happy for you both."

Tess beamed, running fingers through her hair. "Thank you for everything you did for us, Frederick. Rome, and Lynx…well you know—"

My stomach lurched, thinking how close I'd come to losing her. My fingers found the tracker under my skin. It would have to be removed. The Taser Lynx used had short-circuited it, but at least it'd done what I needed.

I'd held on and proved the point I set out to make. It cost a lot more than money but it brought shitloads of protection.

Fuckwit watched us, his forehead furrowed. "Did something happen?" His eyes narrowed. "Is that what happened the past few days? You look like you've been in a pretty serious fight." His gaze flickered to Tess. "You're not in any danger again—are you, Tessie?"

I coughed.

A swirling tornado of anger ripped me apart.

"Tessie?" My voice was whip-thin and blade-sharp. My body was still sore, the pain eroding no end of painkillers, but all I wanted was a fight. I wanted to hurtle this asshole away from Seychelles. Away from my wife. Away from any claim he thought he had on *my* woman.

"*Never* call her that."

Tess pressed her warm form against mine. "Q—don't. Brax calls me Tessie. It's a nickname that's completely innocent." Turning to Brax, she finished, "And no, I'm not in any danger. Not anymore. Thanks to Q."

"But you will be if you call her that again," I snapped.

My fists ached to ram into his jaw.

The celebrant arrived, smiling—completely oblivious to the standoff between us. "I have the paperwork that requires signing. Please choose your two witnesses and come with me."

"Perfect timing," Roux mumbled, throwing me a look. "Come on, Mercer. I'll witness another one of your documents." He followed the celebrant.

Tess let me go, grabbing onto Suzette. "Would you do the honour? Please."

Suzette's eyes watered. She looked from me to Tess, holding her heart. "I'd love to."

Great. Fucking fantastic. Yet more time stopping me from getting my wife naked. The second this was over. I was gone. With or without Tess. Who was I kidding? I would never leave her—especially with Fuckwit here.

The three of us trailed after Frederick, leaving Twerp and his little girlfriend. The celebrant had set up a station with a small table, leather binder, and pens. A crisp piece of paper rested on top.

I sighed.

This whole mingling after the wedding bullshit was fraying my nerves. I didn't know if it was the pain making me cranky or the fact Tess's past was trespassing on my future. I just wanted to leave.

Soon. Sign then I was free.

The top of the paper held an intricate flourish with the words:

This is to certify Quincy Mercer II descended from Quincy Mercer I and Veronica Fable married Tess Olivia Snow descended from Stephen Snow and Mary Carlton, both sound of mind and able body, in holy matrimony before the witnesses of...

"You sign here, Mr. Mercer." The celebrant pointed to a column stated 'groom'.

Taking the pen, I printed my name, then signed. The simple act of holding the pen aggravated the muscles in my arm from Lynx's bad batting skills.

I needed more drugs—especially if I planned on delivering my threats to Tess.

Beneath my signature, it changed from groom to husband. Shit.

Husband.

It hit me for the second time.

I'm Tess's husband.

This time it was a battering ram compared to the tiny realization. I was *hers*. Forever.

Tess's body heat seared into mine, reaching over to steal the pen. Planting a chaste kiss on my cheek, she printed her name...then paused.

My heart stuttered as the pen hovered over the signature of 'wife'.

"Do I sign with my old name or..." Her voice trailed off, her eyes meeting the celebrant.

The man smiled. "Your new one, of course. If you're taking your husband's name, sign it as Tess Mercer.

She froze.

Every instinct and bestial sense sprang to high alert. I tried to see past her outer shell, searching for the real reason why she didn't want to sign the fucking form.

Swallowing back my temper, I said as soft as I could manage, "*Tu vas bien?*" You okay?

She looked into my eyes, tears making the blue shine like the sea. I almost crashed to my knees with the sheer unconditional love in her depths. "I'm no longer Tess Snow."

My stomach twisted thinking about the girl who I'd watched transform into a woman. Ever since I woke up to her whispering in my ear at Lynx's house, I'd known she'd turned an irrevocable corner. She left Tess Snow behind the moment she smeared her cheek with the blood of her victim. She spread her wings and soared, putting her past where it belonged and embracing everything I'd always hoped she would.

Every time I looked at her I sensed it, sensed the depth and sweet depravity of my woman. I'd never meant to change her—but she'd changed herself. She'd become more—just more in every way.

I cupped her cheek, bringing her nose to mine. Tracing her throat, I caressed the top of the brand—the only part visible above her collar. She shivered, biting her lip.

"You walked away from that name, *esclave*. It no longer defines you."

"What does define me?" she whispered.

"Your invincibility. Your conviction. Me."

"You?"

My fingers drifted over her collar, tugging on the leash. "Yes. You wear my name now. You wear my fortune."

"I'm Tess Mercer." Her soft voice turned to a pant, flushing my body with want. My cock twitched in my trousers, ready to take her. Ready to finish this.

"You're so much more than that."

"What?"

"Tu es à moi." You're mine.

"Yours," she breathed, swaying she pressed her lips against mine. The instant her soft mouth touched me, my vision shattered into colourless light. The countdown to taking her increased its incessant tick.

I wouldn't last much longer. I *couldn't* last much longer.

Her lips kissed along my cheekbone, ending on the shell of my ear. "I was going to deny you, husband. I didn't think you were strong enough to take me. But you haven't stopped making love to me since the moment I entered this marquee. I believe you're strong enough. And I want you to take me away. Take me completely."

She pulled back, permission blazing in her eyes. "I'm *all* yours. Every inch." Gone was the fear about letting me inside the final part of her. Gone was the hesitation at exploring the unexplored.

My muscles locked into place, fighting a full body shudder. My cock punched the buckle of my belt, demanding to have her *now*.

Tess left me standing like a fool, sealing the marriage contract with a flick of her wrist. Tess Mercer.

My Tess.

My *esclave*.

Frederick grabbed the pen with a wink. "You're looking at her like you're about to eat her. You guys better leave before you end up saying screw the guests and giving us a show."

I let him finish signing before punching him in the shoulder. "We're only here because we're Suzette's prisoners."

Suzette giggled, taking the pen. "Fine, I know a man in pain when I see one. Go. I'll rearrange the reception for tomorrow."

A thick arm wedged between us, scrawling illegibly on the paper beneath all four signatures.

What the—

I looked over my shoulder. Franco.

He shrugged. "Hey, couldn't let you get hitched without the top quality authority of your favourite bodyguard. I just made that thing legit."

I rolled my eyes. "Trust you to ruin everything."

Franco chuckled, giving Tess a one armed hug. He'd discarded his grey blazer, revealing the white shirt beneath. His sling matched the fabric, hiding the fact he was injured. Sort of. The bandage around his hand had been changed, and the minute I could breathe without needing to sink into Tess, I would source a world class doctor to replace his thumb.

He would also receive a huge bonus.

Pulling away from Tess, Franco said, "You look incredible. I'm very happy for you both. I'll always have your back, Tess. You've earned my deepest respect." Tess dropped her eyes, unconsciously tugging the collar around her throat. Her cleavage was deep and fucking enticing.

"I'll forever be in your debt for helping me get him back. I think you deserve a long holiday and someone to pamper you." Her eyes darted to Suzette—not at all subtle and way too insinuating.

Ah, for fuck's sake what was with weddings and hook-ups?

She added, "Don't be an idiot, Franco."

His mouth fell open; eyes just as wide.

I grabbed the leash from her collar, wrapping it around my fist. "Enough, *esclave*. He'll figure it out. And if he doesn't, there are plenty of other body parts that can be sliced off to make him understand."

Franco spluttered. "Hey, what?" His green eyes landed on Suzette who turned bright red. She coughed, backing away, the tips of her ears flaming.

I didn't have any time for other people's lives. Mine was all I wanted and I was done being the centre of attention.

Tugging the leash, the collar slipped a little, glinting with an inscription: *property of Q Mercer*.

My eyes slammed closed. I was ruined. High on the need to claim.

My cock twitched, clawing its way through my trousers to my wife.

Yep, I would never be removing that collar.

Screw the reception. Screw the guests. I was done.

"We're leaving," I snapped.

Tess's eyes popped wide but slowly she nodded, tasting my need, echoing it back.

I'm married! I survived. And now I would claim my wife.

"Spoilsport," Frederick muttered good-naturedly. He clasped my shoulder, crunching me into a painful hug. "Fair enough. We can have the reception tomorrow on the beach. I'm sure Suzette has a few days' worth of events for us to enjoy."

Franco rolled his eyes. "That woman is a nuisance. She's too damn organised and when the hell did she become so freaking gorgeous?" His eyes trailed to Suzette who'd broken apart from our group, returning to Angelique.

"Since always," Tess stated, crossing her arms.

Franco frowned. "You're forgetting that I was the one who carried her into Q's house. She weighed nothing more than a bag of feathers, her hair shorn, her skin covered in burns, and her fingers completely mangled." His eyes tightened, looking at Suzette laughing with Angelique. "I've seen her at her worst. All I see is a broken girl who needed so much help."

I agreed completely. That was my issue, too. "That's how I see her as well. But maybe it's time we looked at her with new eyes. She's no longer that girl."

I glanced at Suzette, truly seeing the strong woman she'd become. Pride filled me. Compared to the broken slave she'd been—it was incomparable.

Franco's eyes widened as if truly seeing Suzette for the first time. He cleared his throat.

"You should talk to her, Franco, get to know her," Tess pushed.

I threw Tess a look. That was enough. I hated tampering in people's life, and Franco's was his own. Tough shit if he couldn't see past the past.

The celebrant placed the signed wedding agreement into a black folder, passing it to me. "Congratulations. I wish you a lifetime of happiness."

Clutching the document I would treasure forever, I muttered, "More than just one lifetime. Thank you."

Keeping Tess's leash tight in my fist, I marched forward, fully expecting her to heel. What, like a fucking dog?

Goddammit, my thoughts were all over the place. I needed silence. Just us. Swiping a hand over my face, I tugged on the leather. "Tess—come on."

She came forward, her lips playing with a scowl and a smile. "You've really got to rein in your temper."

I bared my teeth. "Too late to try and change me, *esclave*. You married me—knowing full well who I was."

And that made me the luckiest son of a bitch alive.

She laughed. "I would never want to change you." Her eyes flittered over to Angelique and Suzette who stood talking to Fuckwit and Bianca. "I should go and say goodbye, though—I don't want to be rude and abandon everyone."

I shook my head. "No. You're coming with me. This instant."

I wouldn't go back into the Bermuda fucking triangle of

after wedding politics. We'd barely found freedom as it was, and it'd taken far too long.

Frederick brushed past, heading for his wife. "I'll tell everyone, Tess. They'll understand."

Her cheeks pinked. "Okay, thank you. Guess we'll see you tomorrow."

No chance. I wasn't leaving that bedroom for weeks.

"Only if you're still able to walk," I breathed in her ear.

Her body jolted, and I took the opportunity to wrap my arm around her, guiding her toward the exit. "If you so much as speak to another person leaving this fucking tent, I'll put you over my knee in front of everyone."

And I'll love it. My stomach lurched at the thought of *finally* getting her alone.

Tess breathed hard, her breasts rising and falling. "You shouldn't get so wound up. Your heart needs a rest."

I laughed darkly. "Let me worry about my heart—you worry about yours." Slamming to a halt by the doorway, I whispered, "Because I'll make it fly out of your chest with what I'm going to do to you."

Tess wiggled in my grip, brushing against things that needed no other stimulation.

Surveying the black shrouded tent, I sighed with satisfaction. Everything had come true. Tess was no longer broken. I'd fought against the underworld and won. And now, now I intended to spend a few weeks on this island recuperating and making delicious sinful love to my wife.

Pressing Tess against my rock hard erection, I murmured, "I want to see you naked. I want you wearing only the collar and your high heels." Pushing her out of the shadows and into the light, I growled, "Come on, *esclave.* Time to consummate."

Tess stood before me, breathing hard.

I locked the sliding door, proceeding to draw every curtain so no one could see in. However, it didn't go dark, thanks to the sun streaming in from the glass roof.

I couldn't stop looking at the collar around her throat. *I want you naked. I want to drive into you holding that leash.*

My heart raced, burning off the remaining painkillers in my system. Every inch of me ached, but all I wanted was Tess. I didn't care about the burning in my legs or the slight twinge whenever my heart beat too fast. The bullet wound in my leg didn't stand a chance against the desire in my blood.

I could recoup later. Right now. I had husbandly duties to perform.

"Get in the bedroom, *esclave*."

I planned one more game to end our crescent moon.

Tess was mine in every conceivable way. She was back to the strong and amazing woman I fell in love with and today, I would finish my claiming.

She'd given me permission.

She was ready.

I would finish what I started in Tenerife.

The stress of the wedding left my system, leaving me levelheaded and able to focus on nothing but her. The world was inconsequential now we were alone. I trusted the team of bodyguards bobbing around the atoll to keep us safe. I trusted my friends to stay far away from our villa until I was drained dry and Tess could barely walk.

And I trusted that tomorrow, I might be able to be nicer to Fuckwit, after reminding Tess just who she would spend the rest of her life with.

Tess hadn't moved.

"I won't ask again. Get in the bedroom."

Tess bowed her head, watching me with lowered eyes. "Q?"

I inched toward her, suffering a rapidly building itch to chase—to hunt.

I'm going to consume you, wife.

"Yes, *esclave?*" I dropped my eyes down her front; my mouth watered to slice the dress from her. I wanted to drink in her gorgeous body—to drool at the tempting fucking corset.

I wanted to stare—now that no one else was watching.

Tess inched backward, activating the beast inside by submitting to me. "I'm giving you the last part of me—but I have one request."

My legs locked to the floor. What request? *She doesn't want pain? She doesn't want rough?* My eyes searched hers, but her secrets were hidden.

I cocked my head. "One request…"

Her gaze glowed with love. "I ask that you look after yourself. Let me do the work if you need to. I don't want you bursting your stitches or having a heart attack. Let me be the one to take you."

I threw my head back, a loud laugh escaping. "*Vous pensez que je suis fragile putain?*" You think I'm that fucking frail? Humour danced in my voice. "I'll show you who's frail, Tess. You should know me by now pain turns me on. I don't care I'm beaten black and blue. I don't care that I have holes and cuts for fucking miles. All I care about is your pussy."

Her cheeks pinked. Never taking her eyes from mine, she inched toward the corridor, walking backward, swaying her delicious tempting hips, her red heels clicking on the tiles.

"I'm fixated on touching you, tasting you, fucking you. Nothing else matters but that. Do you understand?"

I moved forward with her, hiding my limp, cursing the pain in my thigh.

Her breath was shallow, pinpricks of colour smudging her chest. "I understand. You're suffering the same illness as me." She kept backing up. Every step made my cock harder.

"What illness is that?" I whispered, my fists opening and closing in anticipation. Her skin was flawless again. No wax burns or bite marks. I needed to rectify that. After all, this was the consummation of our marriage.

"I can't stop thinking about your fingers inside me, or

your tongue licking. And, *maître*…"

Tess dragged delicate fingers along the wall, following the curve to the bedroom.

My ears burned for the rest of her sentence. I entered the space, crowding her to stand in the centre. "Go on…what were you going to say?"

Tell me. Fucking tell me before I explode.

The moment she stood still, her breathing quickened, sending the innocent room swimming with heady need and want. Her chest rose. "I love your cock, husband. Your fine, long, scrumptious, thick cock. I want to suck it. I want to bite it. And when you're soaking wet from my mouth I want…"

Fucking hell. My stomach tore itself to pieces.

I stormed toward her, grabbing a fistful of hair. "What, *esclave*. What. Tell me." My cock throbbed. It fucking whimpered for the blowjob she'd so eloquently described.

Her eyes locked onto mine. "When you're wet, I want you to take me. Take my virginity. Fill me. Claim me. Because everything about me is yours."

I couldn't do it.

I smashed my lips on hers, groaning deep into her mouth. Her tongue battled mine as if she'd waited for one hint at violence to unravel. Her moan echoed in my heart as we devoured each other in a fierce fast kiss.

Breaking apart, our eyes locked. The life I lived ceased to exist. I stood on the edge as my past was sucked away, leaving my soul humming with finality. It was as if a new chapter began. A fresh page, unsullied with badness or sickness or pain. Completely new, completely pure, utterly ready for our new life together.

I couldn't describe the freedom whistling inside me. The knowledge I could hurt this woman and she would love it, but I didn't *have* to hurt her. The drive, the incessant beast and monster, finally learned how to be…soft. My temper faded, leaving me *gentle*—truly gentle for the first time in my life.

"Tess—" I cupped her cheek, so madly fucking in love

with her. My eyes fell to her collar, then to her dress. The beast clawed a little, teasing me with the overwhelming urge to shred the clothing and throw her on the bed.

But the softer, gentler side was stronger for once. I would take Tess—the last piece of her, but I would do it in a way I'd never done before. A way I never thought I would be able to do.

A way I never thought possible.

Sweet. Loving. *Tame.*

There would be no need for bondage, spanking, or blood play. For that one wondrous moment, I wanted soft. I wanted to feel her breath on my skin and not her nails. I wanted to shudder beneath her lips and not her teeth. I wanted lovemaking not fucking.

I didn't want to fight.

"You're beautiful," I murmured, drugging myself on her. My aches and pains faded, losing power over me the longer I stood in her arms.

Her face turned up, a smile on her lips. "*You're* beautiful. Beyond beautiful." Her hands landed on my chest, her fingertips pressing ever so lightly on my tattoo. "May I, *maître?*"

My eyes grew heavy but not with domination. With love. She completely bewitched me, leaving me scattered in this new playground where caresses and kisses were more welcome than bites and screams.

I nodded, sucking in a breath as her fingers crept down my chest, heading around my waist. Taking a delicate step, she fitted her body against mine in the sweetest embrace.

I couldn't breathe. I could barely keep the emotion from bubbling through my twisted soul and spewing out of my pussy fucking eyes.

My chin rested on her head, gathering her to me, squeezing her in an endless hug.

"We're each other's, Q." Tess pressed a kiss on the healing brand over my heart. "I never want to be apart. I know we'll fight and argue and force each other to distraction but I will never stop loving you."

My arms banded tighter. My cock grew impossibly harder. My chest felt too small to contain the triple-quadruple sized love growing inside.

Pulling away, I said, "We will never be apart. Even when I'm angry you'll still be able to melt me with one word. Even if I'm being an augmentative jackass, I'll still bow to you and only you." Dropping my head, I whispered against her mouth, "You own me, Tess."

The second her lips touched mine the unsullied page of our future splashed with life. A future I had the privilege to live unfolded before my eyes: images of Tess barefoot and laughing. Colours of birds and wings and happiness. Each ideal came and went in a wash of ink, dispersing with unknown memories.

Tess moaned as my tongue entered her mouth, licking her, tasting her. Her lips opened, welcoming me deeper.

Our heads tilted, following each other in perfect synchronicity as the kiss evolved from tender to passionate. Her breath filled my lungs; my fingers burned to touch.

Never breaking the kiss, I found the bow at her lower back, undoing the restraint. Following the billowing material, I released the dress.

Tess shimmied from the silk, letting it fall from her shoulders. Her hands slid up my back to my arms, removing my blazer in the same slow intoxication.

Our kiss continued, lips locked, hearts linked as my jacket fell to the floor. Her hands went to my waistband, quickly undoing the zipper and button, allowing the trousers to cascade down my legs, leaving me completely naked. My hard cock sprang upward, freed from its prison, thudding against my stomach. The head prodded a bruise—a small undercurrent of pain in this dream of lust. But everything was bruised—so the pain didn't matter. All pain became great pain. And Tess was the greatest pain of all.

She affected me right where it mattered.

I was immortal holding my paramour.

Tess tried to pull away, but I kept her mouth glued to mine. She moaned again as I kissed deeper, tasting every morsel, demanding her utmost attention. With questing fingers, I found the garter belt clips and undid them. Reaching around, I unthreaded the first corset lace, working my way slowly, teasingly up her back.

You're mine to unwrap. The ultimate gift.

What the hell did I do to deserve her?

With every loosened lace Tess shivered, her mouth working harder on mine until her fingers landed in my hair, tugging me ruthlessly.

I stumbled, unwilling to use stomach muscles that'd been beaten with a baseball bat. We tripped together, never letting go or breaking the kiss. Our lips were hot and wet. Our thoughts connected—our bodies linked.

Regaining our footing, I undid the final lace. Unwrapping the corset from her body, I dropped it to the floor. Tess breathed a sigh of relief. Her breasts went from squished and high to natural and heavy.

Her nipples called to me—wondrously beckoning to my cock. I wanted to thrust between her breasts. I wanted to grace her perfect throat with a necklace made from come. So much I wanted to do. *And I can. She's my wife.*

A bolt of ultimate happiness chased away everything I'd lived through. Lynx and his fucking mind-games were over. I would get over my issues with towels and never look back.

Tess had defeated me in more ways than one. In so many ways that mattered.

My balls twitched in anticipation. A shooting pain radiated in my stomach. I couldn't tell if it was the overbearing need to fill her or if my body suffered under pressure. Either way—I ignored it, focusing on her heat and liquidity.

Tugging on the leash trailing between her breasts, I jerked her close. She gasped against my lips, her tongue dancing with mine in a tango full of need.

I wanted to make love to her forever.

I will *make love to her forever.*

Nothing would stop me from spending the rest of my days worshipping this woman.

My eyes opened, diving into hers. Our lips never stopped taking but messages were sent and understood.

I love you.

I adore you.

You're mine.

I'm yours.

Her hands dove into my hair, pulling me ever closer. Her touch claimed every part of me—she lived in my skin, my heart, my mind.

I drowned in her taste. I wanted her crying as she came. I wanted her unravelling on my tongue.

With strong arms, I plucked her from the floor, walking her to the bed. We never stopped kissing, licking. Time had finally obeyed me—stopping in this wonderful moment. The world ceased to spin—letting us indulge.

When my knees hit the mattress, I lowered her gently. Her weight transferred to the crisp white bedspread; her blonde hair fanned out in lazy waves.

I broke the kiss, leaning over her. "Fuck, you're so damn *magnifique.*"

Tess rolled upright, not caring her hair fell around her shoulders, hiding her breasts. With sharp determination, she pushed my lower belly, placing me where she wanted.

Her fingers wrapped around my hips and she gave me exactly what she promised. Her mouth swallowed my length in one long delicious pull.

"Holy shit, *esclave.*"

My brain stuttered out, blanking every sense, every thought. All I could focus on was the slippery heaven of her lips. Every nerve ending went straight to my cock.

Her head bobbed, sucking hard—almost violent in her speed and possession. I was her hostage, governed by a body desperate for a release. She was my witch. My whore. My wife.

"Tess—fuck." My hands landed in her hair, fisting her thick curls. My ass clenched, rocking into her wet talented mouth. Her hand grasped the base, stroking me in time with her sucks.

My eyes rolled back, giving every inch of control to Tess. For once, I didn't care she'd taken away my power. For once, I had no issues with her being in charge.

She owns me anyway. There was no difference if she took what she wanted or accepted.

"My mouth is yours, master. Always," she murmured, kissing the tip, sliding back down—down and down—her teeth whispering over delicate flesh.

Her fingers found my balls, rolling them, squeezing. They tightened, drawing close to my body, so hot, so fucking ready to blow.

"Q...I want to drink you," Tess said, wrenching my head back as she deep-throated me.

I groaned, losing my eyesight completely. "God, Tess. Your mouth is fucking magic." My body stiffened, bliss blasting down my legs. My stomach clenched, working through the pain, wobbling in her hold.

I want to come.

So come.

I can't.

All enjoyment faded.

I crashed from my blowjob high to a crevice of lows. My mind filled with images of the slave sucking me. Her tentative lips—her juvenile touch compared to Tess's mastery.

Shit.

Pushing Tess away, I swiped a hand over my face. *I don't want to tell her.*

Did I have the strength to tell her what Lynx did? That another woman had been forced to lick the same cock forever belonging to Tess?

Secrets will ruin you.

Tess had accepted me despite knowing nothing of my

past. She loved me in spite of knowing my present. She promised to never leave, regardless of what happened in the future, and I couldn't dishonour her by not being honest.

"Is everything okay?" Tess's lips were swollen, waiting for me to slide back inside and forget—forget about everything.

But I couldn't.

Falling to my knees, I took her hands. I didn't know where to start. She had to understand my reasoning before I blurted out the horror. Taking a deep breath, trying to find my runaway courage, I said, "I was so fucking frightened when I couldn't find you, Tess. When you were taken, I lost a part of myself. I willingly gave that part up to hunt for you—mainly because in some dark recess—I thought I'd never see you again.

"You own me completely, so when you were missing, I had nothing."

Her fingers twitched, linking around mine with encouragement.

"I did things, *esclave*. I butchered men and feel no regrets. I tortured traffickers and feel no remorse. I do things society wouldn't approve but I don't care because *I* do. It fits within my law—do you see?"

Tess shook her head softly. "Your law? Q...what are you talking about?"

It was surreal holding her dressed only in a collar, pantyhose, and knickers. I kneeled before her naked, spilling my heart. *Way to pick a fucking time.* But I couldn't go any further until I'd purged myself. She needed to know how fucking sorry I was.

"Q, you're scaring me. Why are you telling me this?"

Swallowing hard, I replied, "Because it's time you know the truth about me." *I'm doing this. I'm truly going to spill everything in one messed up conversation.* "I don't talk about my family because my father was a heinous fucking bastard who raped and murdered women. I hated what he did. And I shot him. I brought a gun and premeditated murder all because I couldn't listen to the screams anymore. But the moment I pressed the trigger, his tendencies shot into me. His evilness found a new host—in a boy who was his father's true heir."

I wanted to cut out my tongue. I never wanted to tell her. I always believed my past would remain hidden, yet I'd just spewed it on our wedding night.

Tess captured my chin, stroking my bristles. "There's nothing evil about you, Q. You aren't—"

"Let me finish." Her acceptance granted false hope. I was nowhere near done.

I had to rip off the bandages—exposing myself sharp and quick. If I didn't, I wouldn't finish and the secret would fester for the rest of my life.

I needed Tess to forgive me. *Please, forgive me.*

"You guessed right at dinner. I had a sister. Her name was Marquisa. She died at my father's hand, and I was too young to kill him. I lived with the man who raped and killed my sister because I was weak." I glossed over the grotesqueness, not willing to flay that particular memory.

Tess sucked in a gasp, her naked breasts rising with horror. "Q—no. That's awful."

"I wasn't going to tell you—I didn't want you to know, but I have to tell you something else—and I hope to God you don't fucking hate me." My eyes latched onto hers, filling with fear. "Don't despise me. I don't know what I'll do if you do."

Tess stiffened. Her lips popped wider, alarm flushing her skin. But she didn't untangle her fingers from mine. I took strength from that. "Why would I despise you, Q? I've accepted everything about you. Nothing you say can change that." She was so beautiful, so pure.

I hung my head. God, I hoped so. "I haven't been faithful to you, *esclave.*"

Her face turned white; her fingers turned to icicles. "Excuse me?"

Fuck. "Lynx made a slave girl suck me. I didn't want it. I fought it and chose to die rather than be unfaithful, but I had to tell you. I can't live with the knowledge I let it happen. It wasn't for long and I never broke my honour to you in my heart. But I had to apologise, so it never comes between us."

Tess didn't move.

My heart charged like a monstrous thing, wheezing for forgiveness.

When she didn't say anything, I squeezed her fingers. "Please. Say something."

Slowly, she tugged her hand from mine. My stomach hollowed out.

Then she laced her fingers in my hair, holding me still, peering deep into my eyes. "You chose death over some woman giving you oral sex?" She blinked. "Why?"

"Why?"

"Q—you almost died…all because—"

"I almost died to protect my integrity. That's the only part of me I have left. Don't you understand? I've killed my father. I've seen my sister be raped and murdered. I've watched and done nothing as my mother drank herself into the grave. I've built my life on nothing. I've run from a past I want nothing to do with. I have no control over that. *None*.

"But I do have my honour. It's the only thing I *can* control." I gritted my teeth. "I survived with the darkness in my blood by one means only. I thought you'd figured that out by now, *esclave*."

Her blue-grey eyes glossed with sadness, radiating kindness. "No, Q. I haven't figured you out at all, but this is helping."

I rushed ahead, hoping to make her understand. "Honour is my driving force. The only thing I can rely on when the monster gets too strong or the beast takes control. Honour is the only law I obey.

"I broke my unbreakable law when that woman sucked me. It ruined everything I stood for because I broke your trust in me."

Tess's lips clamped together. I captured her tears with a fingertip. "Don't you see, *mon amour*? I would rather die than have that honour taken away from me. It's my only guideline on right and wrong. And I love you too much to besmirch it. Please, I need you to understand and forgive me."

Tess cried softly, her cheeks flushing with emotion. "Forgive you? Q—there's nothing to forgive."

I trembled. My back hurt, my body screamed with pain, but I couldn't move. Not until I believed her. Not until I'd been granted absolution from this angel who was my wife. "Please...just say you understand."

Her hands captured my cheeks, kissing me hard. "If you need to hear it, then yes I forgive you." Her lips landed on my jaw, my cheekbones, my eyelids. "I would've forgiven you for anything because *he* made you do it. Q—you have nothing to feel guilty about because it was outside of your control."

She stopped kissing me, temper blazing bright. "What I can't forgive, is you willingly sacrificing your life because you let your morals sign your death sentence. We were almost too late, Q. Do you think I would've cared if I found you in bed with another woman—against your will—compared to hanging dead in a dungeon? Yes, it would've killed me to know you'd been with another girl but at least you'd be alive."

She sucked in a breath, gathering courage like a cape. "You've told me more today than you ever have, so I'll share the same courtesy with you. When you helped break me of Leather Jacket's hold, I went through things I never want to discuss. I don't know how much you saw or heard, but I would've willingly slept with him. In fact, I begged him to. I'm not proud of it. I hate myself for it—but I would do it again if it was the only way to live. Because my life isn't my own anymore."

My stomach rolled at the residual panic in her voice. Even now, after everything I'd done, they still had power over her. But I would make it disappear. I had a lifetime to make the past vanish. For both of us.

Tess kissed me, tasting of salt from her tears. "Do *you* understand? Your life isn't yours to gamble anymore, Q. It's mine. I don't care about your honour—if you're in a life and death situation you do whatever you can to stay alive. I order you to do whatever's necessary. Because your soul is mine and I refuse to let you go."

I couldn't speak. My heart galloped at the simplicity of the fucked-up situation. "If you own my life, who owns yours?"

Tess smiled. "You, of course. No matter what happens, it's always yours. I will never stop loving you, Q. It scares me how much I need you. But from now on, your honour comes second best to me—do you hear?"

I desperately wanted to kiss her and stop this spilling of fragile truths, but the confessions lightened my heart. "So you...forgive me?"

Tess nodded. "I forgive you."

I slouched, crushed by pain, weak with relief. Running my fingers up her stockings, I voiced one more truth. "I want to be normal. I want to love you without needing to hurt you. I'm sorry for what I am."

Tess grabbed my face, her fingernails digging into my cheeks. Her eyes glowed with anger. "Don't. I don't want you ever to say that again. You *are* normal. My normal. We're each other's normal. And there is no right or wrong. It's time we accepted it. I love you. So much. Take me, Q. No more talking. Make me your wife completely."

She lay back, looking down her body at me kneeling at the foot of the bed. Her swollen lips made me hard, her tear-stained cheeks made me grateful. The knowledge she'd forgiven me shed the guilt I'd carried, removing a layer of pain at the thought of losing her.

My lips twisted into a smile. "You're my wife already, but I have no issues pounding the message home."

She laughed, shattering the angst, replacing it with desire. Everything we'd discussed disappeared, leaving us empty and healing and ready to move forward. Who knew airing dirty laundry was a good idea? But it was. I'd never felt lighter—minus my beaten and bruised body.

I ran my hands up her inner thigh; Tess shivered. "I'm going to undress you till you're only wearing that incredible collar."

"Um, I can help you if you like…" Her arm flew upward, hitting something hard. She twisted, looking above her. "Oh—"

Above her head rested a basket overflowing with purple crepe paper. Pressed into the wrapping were gifts. Tess pulled it toward her, her eyes widening. "She really does think of everything."

I stole the basket from her, raiding the small container. Inside rested a blindfold, cheap handcuffs, small flogger, chocolate body paint, glittery purple vibrator, and lube.

Body paint? *Yuck.* Blindfold? *Don't need.* Handcuffs? *They'd last all of two seconds.* I tested the sting of the fake flogger. It lacked a perfect snap, but could work.

My eyes landed on the vibrator. And I knew exactly what I wanted to do.

Tess plucked the note from the side. "Enjoy, newlyweds. We look forward to seeing you at breakfast tomorrow. Love, Frederick, Angelique, Franco, and Suzette. She looked at the toys, her eyebrow raising. "That's a lot of people to chip in for some vanilla playthings."

"They have no imagination. The best things to use are the most mundane." I dragged a fingernail up her thigh, loving her shiver.

She breathed shallow, hypnotising me. Her breasts were soft globes with tiny erect nipples, her skin slightly indented from the boning of the corset.

She lay back slowly, never looking away.

My cock swelled. I thought for a second of using the blindfold, flogger, and cuffs, but the need for gentleness hadn't left. It cushioned my thoughts, keeping my beast distracted—tamed.

The toys didn't excite me. I didn't want to tie Tess up—I wanted to feel her fingers in my hair. I didn't want to hurt her—I wanted her moans of ecstasy.

Connection. Sex. No pain.

Just her. And me.

On me, over me, on my tongue, on my cock. I wanted to fucking worship her with every inch.

Never breaking eye contact, I pulled the vibrator and lube free, before tossing the basket over my shoulder. It landed loudly, scattering items beneath the dressing table.

Tess's mouth parted. "You don't want—"

I grabbed my cock, stroking once, twice. Loving the anticipation...desperate to tease. "Not today, *esclave.* Today I'm taking your moans as payment rather than your tears."

Her face scrunched, battling a wash of love. "How do you read me so well? How did you know I needed just one time where it was gentle?"

I rose upright on my knees, crooking a finger for her to come closer. Her toned stomach flexed, arching, closing the distance so her lips were millimetres away. Gazing into her eyes, I murmured, "I know because what you feel, *I* feel." Resting my hand over her heart, I whispered, "I need you like we haven't shared before. I need to take you this way. I can't explain it."

She sighed. "I can—it's because we're in tune. We shared parts of ourselves we thought the other would never accept. The knowledge that this is *truly* forever...it's given us freedom to be soft." Her lips captured mine, pulling me deeper into her drug, cancelling out my aches, flaring liquid heat in my veins. "I'm the luckiest woman in the world."

Returning to my position between her legs, I placed the vibrator and lube on the floor. Pushing her downward, I smiled. "You have that wrong. I'm the luckiest master in the world." With the pads of my fingers, I caught the top of her stockings. She bit her lip as I rolled them down her silky skin. I removed her shoe, tugging the sheer material clear.

My cock throbbed to be inside her, loving the tension, the quivering delight in the knowledge we weren't going to fight—

not today. Today we would share something entirely different.

Repeating the process, I removed her other stocking, placing them with her shoes on the floor. The only things remaining were her knickers and collar.

A small slice of who I truly was rose. I bent over her hips, biting through the lace with one sharp cut. The material broke, falling away easily when I tugged the ruined lingerie down her legs.

The moment I glimpsed what I'd wanted since Suzette tore off her dress, my mouth went dry. *"Mon Dieu, Tess, tu es si belle putain."* Goddammit, Tess, you're so fucking beautiful.

I stared between her parted legs. Her golden hair was maintained and soft, her folds glistening with desire.

"Q—please..." she moaned. The leash from the collar fell between her breasts, a splash of blackness on her perfection. I looked for the permanent scar branding her neck forever. The beast inside purred, knowing it was undeniable now—this woman was mine. I no longer needed to carve my autograph into her every night, making sure my imprint lived in her skin—it was done. Officially. Unofficially. In every way humanly possible.

My symbol of commitment existed on every facet of her.

I pressed the wedding band around my finger with my thumb. I was hers, and I couldn't be fucking happier.

Licking my lips, I pressed a gentle kiss right over her clit.

Her reaction was explosive, bowing upward, her fingers clutched the bed. Her sensitivity was insane compared to the control she maintained when I hurt her.

She'd truly let go. Not caring about anything but my hot breath on her core and the deliciousness of what was to come.

I kissed her again, licking once with a pointed tongue. She moaned—loudly.

Her pleasure sent a ripple of pre-cum spurting from my cock. My quads clenched as the sublime reaction made me crave more. *More.*

I pounced on her, covering her pussy with my mouth,

sucking in her delectable taste, willingly turning my world topsey turvey with how drugged and intoxicated I was.

Her body rippled every time I licked her. Her mouth fell wide as I pushed my tongue deep, deep inside. Her muscles contracted, dragging my tongue even further. The first ripple of an orgasm warned me to pull back. I didn't want her coming— not yet.

There was something else I wanted. Something I would take. But first...

Groping for the vibrator, I silently positioned the glittery phallus at her entrance. I nibbled her clit, distracting her with my tongue.

Her fingers groped the bed as I sucked harder, flicking her folds faster, driving her higher.

The gentleness and sweetness inside felt so different to a lifetime of needing pain. I got off on her mewls of pleasure just as much as her moans of agony. Born of a sadistic monster, I couldn't fight what he'd poured into my blood. But tonight, all I needed was Tess.

Nothing more. Nothing less.

With another lave of my tongue, Tess left sanity, becoming a ball of lust. I loved that I'd driven her to the place where nothing else registers but sex. I needed her there—to enjoy what was to come.

Still sucking on her clit, I pressed the power button. The vibrator came to life, humming, sending shockwaves through her folds, echoing on my tongue.

She screamed. "God—Q. More. It feels—fuck, it feels—"

I didn't let her finish.

Sliding the vibrator deep, I licked harder, overloading her system with pleasure.

Her hips rocked, forcing my mouth to crash against her pussy. Her hands disappeared into my hair, shamelessly pulling me into her. My neck ached, my back bellowed, but I wouldn't stop until she came.

"Q—yes...shit, yes."

I chuckled at Tess's language, gawking at her wriggling body above. Her breasts jutted out, her nipples hard as fucking rocks. God, she tasted divine. I wanted to eat her forever.

My tongue ached to give way to teeth—I wanted to bite her. Just one tiny nip. But I kept up the relentless pressure, driving the vibrator deeper inside.

Her pants and whimpers were fucking erotic, twisting my belly. My cock throbbed with her every moan, demanding to replace the vibrator and come.

But as much as I wanted to come, I wanted to be somewhere else when I did. This was for her. Just for her.

My tongue picked up speed, urging her upward. *Go on, esclave. Come. I want to hear you scream.*

Pressing the power button, I cranked the speed. Her body jerked; her fingers yanking the sheets beneath her in a savage pull. "Oh, *God!*"

I smiled, flicking my tongue, ignoring the sweat running down my temples. My wrist hurt from thrusting the vibrator. I was insanely jealous of the innate object penetrating my woman. I could orgasm just by Tess coming apart.

"I'm going to—Q—stop if you don't want me to—" Her head arched, hair flying in every direction as her body bunched.

Humming against her clit, I murmured, "You have my permission. Come, *esclave*. Fucking come on my tongue." I pressed the button one last time. The vibrator turned from teasing to torturous but Tess writhed in sensual surrender.

Her hips pulsed in time to the thrusts I delivered, my head bobbing with her, keeping my tongue busy on her core.

"Q—shit, I'm coming. Q!"

Her entire body convulsed, her fingers became fingernails, clutching my head, rocking her hips into my mouth. Her cries demanded, searched, *seethed* for something.

I know what she needs.

I loved that she was right. This was normal. For us. Pain was our happy place.

She wanted it.

So I gave it to her.

I bit her clit with a feral growl. My heart collided painfully with my ribs, but I didn't care.

She came.

And came.

And *came.*

Her cries echoed around the room, turning her limbs from quivering with tension to melting with satisfaction into the bed.

I breathed hard, aching and stiff, but very fucking smug. She'd come and it was all because of me.

Her eyes opened, looking almost black from her release. "Q…" Her head lolled, fingers falling from my hair. Her voice was heavy, slurred, completely sated. "That felt incr— incredible."

I loved her sleepiness. Her vulnerability. I adored what it meant for me. My reward.

Removing the vibrator, I kissed her pussy. I grinned as her oversensitive clit shivered beneath my lips.

Turning off the toy, I left it on the floor. Tess kept her eyes closed, not moving from her open-legged position. I went to stand, but my body was mutinous, bellowing with pain. A simple movement of standing took five times as long as normal. I gritted my teeth, straightening out the kinks in my spine, gathering the lube, and climbing into the bed.

Every movement clashed like agonising cymbals. My body needed rest. I needed sleep, but I didn't want to miss out on the best opportunity of my life.

I wouldn't let any headaches, or battle wounds stop me from finishing what I'd started.

Tess was mine.

The second I lay down, Tess snuggled her back against my front, sighing deeply. I relaxed into the pillows, cupping her breast. The heaviness of her flesh activated every protective, possessive part inside. A guttural growl sounded in my throat. "You have the most incredible body. Made just for me. So accepting of anything I do."

She snuggled closer, tugging a pillow to cradle her head.

I twisted her nipple, my mouth watering to give her tits the same attention as her pussy. Tess didn't move or make a sound.

I laughed gently. "Are you sleeping, *mon cœur?*" Nuzzling her neck, I breathed hard. Her soft form in my arms was too much. I couldn't stop my hips rocking, pressing my cock against her ass, seeking a release.

Tess moaned, wriggling closer. Her heartbeat fluttered under my touch. A minute ticked by while I held her. Slowly, energy entered her sex-sated limbs. She stroked my forearm wrapped around her. "I'm not sleeping, *maître*. I know what you want from me."

My heart leapt. I clenched my jaw, forcing my hips to stop. "I won't force you, Tess. If you're still afraid…"

She pressed a gentle kiss on my bicep. "You're not forcing me. I want you. Just…take me gently. I'll do whatever you want—but you have to tell me what to do." Her voice wavered, but I didn't focus on her nerves, only on her permission.

My eyes snapped closed, loving her more in that moment than ever before. She'd put herself completely into my control. Trusting me to do this right. Loving me enough not to fear me. I didn't need whips and chains to earn her complete submission—she'd given it to me—right here, right now.

My cock wept as I stroked her shoulder. *"Allonge toi sur le ventre, mon cœur."* Lie on your stomach, my heart.

Tess obeyed. I helped her roll over, scooting her body to the centre of the bed. I braced myself with an elbow, looking down the sweeping lines of her back to the perfect pillows of her ass. *Fuck, I want to mark her.*

The violent thought disappeared as fast as it came. My palm itched to strike—to paint the white with red, but the urge faded, leaving me with heavy sweetness.

Placing my fingertips on the base of her neck, I pushed the tangled strands away, leaving her back completely clear. Pressing a kiss to her shoulder blades, I murmured, "Don't tense. Trust me."

She nodded, breathing shallow as I very carefully, very slowly, dragged my fingers down her spine, over every bead, along every hollow, tracing the hills and valleys to the fullness of her ass.

Every touch sent my heart pounding; my cock jerked. Her face was unreadable but she flinched as my finger trailed her crack. *This. This is mine.*

Her face scrunched, eyes squeezing shut as I dropped lower. She looked so damn shy—so provoking.

My voice dropped to a deep command. "Tess—don't fight me. Obey me and you'll unravel."

She forced out a heavy breath. "I trust you." Her face smoothed once again, her body becoming boneless.

My breathing turned heavier. Sitting upright, I positioned myself, straddling the back of her thighs. I fisted my cock, pumping once, twice, fucking adoring the view of her untouched ass below.

So timid, so pure. But I knew the real Tess. She wasn't timid or pure. She screamed for pain. She would scream for this. And the combination of the two made me the luckiest, happiest son of a bitch in the history of fucked-up individuals.

Spreading her cheeks, I pressed firmly but gently against the puckered muscle. Her eyes squeezed tight, fingers whitening around the sheets. "Q…"

"*Se détendre.*" Relax. I ran a palm over her lower spine, fighting the quick urge to strike. Shit, I wanted to mark her— just once.

Her tension melted away again, turning her body limp.

With my other hand, I reached between her legs, pressing two fingers inside her soaking pussy. "Remember how hard you came, *esclave?*" My fingers twitched, coaxing the pleasure to rekindle—linking her synapsis of release while probing her ass, getting her used to my request—knowing she would let me in…eventually. "You screamed when you came. Remember my tongue on your clit?"

Her mouth twisted. "Yes, I remember. I loved you using the vibrator—but I craved your cock."

"And you'll get it, *esclave*. So fucking soon."

I was ready to blow just talking.

She moaned, rocking her hips into my hand. I pressed harder against her hole, letting her get used to the invasion. Her back trembled, but she didn't pull away. My fingers gathered some of her wetness, gliding over the puckered muscle.

She bit her lip, her body radiating heat. "Don't tease me, Q. Get on with it."

I chuckled, leaning over her to bite her waist. "I'm enjoying you too much to rush this, Tess." Diving two fingers into her pussy, she groaned, pushing her face into the pillow.

Withdrawing, I ordered, "Open your legs wider."

I let her go, grabbing the lube and uncapping the strawberry scented gel. Tess kept her eyes closed as I smeared a generous amount on my fingers. Her legs inched open, revealing how wet and swollen she was.

"Goddammit, Tess. You have no idea how much you turn me on."

Her eyes locked onto mine, drifting to my cock. "I think I do. I want your cock. You're making me wait and it's making me wetter, hotter…if you don't take me soon, I might have to do something drastic."

I grinned, draping my broken body half on hers, half on the bed. "You want this?" I thrust against her thigh, gritting my teeth at the wave of desire locking my quads.

"Yes. I want you." Her breathy voice hitched as I spread her cheeks again. With unforgiving fingers, I turned her dry skin slippery with strawberry gel, never taking my eyes from her face.

She bit her lip, forehead furrowing as I ringed and teased.

"Tell me—what does it feel like?" I whispered. Her back clenched as I pressed harder. Her body responded to the pressure by trying to escape. Her hips tilted downward, dislodging me. "Ah, ah, no running from me. You know I don't like it when you deny me."

I swirled the lube, clenching my jaw. Fuck, I needed to breach her. "Tell me...."

"It feels—" Her teeth snapped together as I surged forward, flexing my hips against her thigh, branding her with my aching, burning cock. "It feels strange. I don't know if I like it or not."

I'll make you like it. I would make her love it.

Kissing her shoulder, I couldn't help sinking my teeth into her flesh. Giving her pain to latch onto, I thrust forward, breaking the seal, entering her with my fingertip. The collar kept her throat prisoner and my hands itched to tug the leash. To hold the reins and ride her.

Her body quivered, hiding her moan against the mattress.

She was so tight—so unwilling to let me intrude. It drove me mad. The beast inside panted to just take and fuck. But the softer side knew I had to prepare her. I would hurt her in other ways—but not this.

Thrusting in and out, I eased her body to accept my intrusion. Strawberry surrounded us, smelling sickly sweet.

"Now how does it feel?" I rocked my hips. "See what you're doing to me, Tess. I'm so fucking hard. No other pain in my body compares to the ache in my balls from needing you." My voice rasped over her, scattering goosebumps on her skin.

She panted. Little pulses of energy hijacked her spine, tipping upward to meet my touch. "It still feels strange. And wrong."

I chuckled, pressing deeper. "There's nothing wrong about this, *esclave*." I bit her shoulder again. Every passing second drained me of sweetness, giving me the darkness I knew so well. My thigh twinged, the muscles in my torso were sore and stiff, but I couldn't stop.

I rubbed against her hip, gritting my teeth as a sharp wave of release threatened to explode. "Goddammit," I growled. *I'm so fucking turned on.*

Tess breathed, "More...don't let me overthink it. Give me

more."

I groaned; my frayed self-control snapped a little. "You want, and I'll give. Your wishes are the reason I'm alive."

Withdrawing my finger, I unfolded another, probing at her entry. I gave her no warning or time to adjust. Two fingers breached her body.

She bit the sheets, a groan erupting from her lips. Her heart slammed against my chest.

Tugging the leash, reminding her I owned her life, I whispered, "Are you afraid, *esclave?*" I pressed a row of kisses along her neck. I needed to be closer—which was fucking ridiculous 'cause I half lay on her already. I wanted to blanket her. I wanted to lie on top of my wife and let her know there would be no escape from me. Ever. I wanted her to know my body would protect hers, all while taking payment in the most delicious ways.

Holding my weight on one arm, I fucked her with my fingers.

She nodded. "Will it hurt?"

For a second, I considered pulling away and sliding into her pussy instead. Her wet heat was so fucking close. It would be so easy to enter and come. The monster in me agreed, growling at the thought of spanking her, punishing her for not being strong enough to give me what I wanted.

But tonight was special.

Tonight was the first night of the rest of our lives. I wanted to celebrate with something we would never forget. I fucking needed her. So damn much. I wouldn't deny myself.

"It won't if you don't fight. Do you trust me?"

Removing my fingers, I leaned back to spurt a generous amount of gel onto my cock. The instant the cold liquid hit my overheated tip, I groaned. Sparking pleasure erupted in a small cloudy bead, mixing with the lube. *Fuck me, I almost came.*

How the hell was I supposed to touch myself and enter her without blowing?

My heartbeat crashed against my ribs. Angling Tess below,

I arched my hips.

Tess sucked in a breath. I shuddered with lust, hovering over her like a demon possessed. My cock dripped with strawberries, wedged between her ass cheeks.

"Yes. I trust you."

I drew blood, biting my lip to stop myself from driving into her. My eyes turned gritty and sore—need thickened my blood.

Tess looked behind, her eyes tracing my chest to where we joined in a sticky mess of pink gel. "Do it, Q. Don't make me wait." Her voice wobbled but a small tinge of passion hid within her fear. Her hips rocked, gluing us together.

"Goddammit, Tess. You're seriously overestimating my self-control not to hurt you. I want you. So. Fucking. Bad." My hips thrust of their own accord. "Having you like this, it's driving me insane."

She smiled softly, feeding off my need, relaxing into the power I gave her. "I told you. I trust you." Her hand came up, wrapping around the base of my cock.

Goddammit to fucking hell. My elbows gave out; I crashed against her body. A throaty growl erupted from my chest sounding exactly like the beast inside. "*Esclave—*"

Her tight little fingers stroked my girth—stealing every thought, every pain—taking me completely prisoner. "Yes, *maître?*"

I couldn't remember my name, let alone speak. Her fingers spread the gel from tip to base, squeezing the throbbing erection until my head pounded. My teeth were dust from clenching so hard. I couldn't do it anymore.

"Arch your back. I can't wait any longer." I tore a pillow from the top of the bed, wedging it beneath her hips. Her mouth popped wide as her ass presented at the perfect height.

I fisted my cock, rearing back to sit over her. My legs screamed at the sheet against my stitches but I was past fucking caring.

Tess looked over her shoulder. Her eyes wide, face white,

but her breathing wasn't panicked. Slowly she reached to her ass, spreading her cheeks.

The simple offering blew my fucking mind; I throttled my cock. I wouldn't last. I *couldn't* last. Not when I was so close.

Keeping her ass spread with one hand, she reached with her other to grab my length. She didn't say a word, guiding me downward. Her fingers didn't stroke or tease, they just delivered me to my ultimate goal.

Our eyes locked and I fell forward, planting my palms on the mattress on either side of her. I let Tess take me. I gave her all control—hoping to hell I could hold on long enough to push inside. I'd wanted to play with the leash. I'd wanted to tease and play. But this—this incessant need to be inside—it couldn't be denied.

"Take me, Q. *Je suis à toi.*" The instant the head of my cock pressed against her puckered muscle, I lost control of my mouth. "Fucking fuck, Tess. I'm about to fucking come all over your back."

She laughed softly. "Don't. Wait till you're in me. I want you to come inside me." Her fingers tightened, pulling me forward while forcing herself back.

There was resistance, heat, pressure—a barrier that wanted nothing to do with my cock.

Then release.

A giving, a softening.

"Ah!" Her eyes squeezed with a pain; her fingers fell from my erection, clutching the sheets. Every muscle in my body locked down as I forced my way forward, millimetre by millimetre, stealing her virginity.

She breathed hard, her body shivering with uncomfortableness. I thrust a little, easing my size into her body.

Fuck, she's even tighter than I thought.

"Oh…ah…" she groaned, jerking with agony. I knew I should stop. I knew I should retreat. But I couldn't. My cock had taken control and I pulled back only to rock forward, invading deeper, stretching wider.

My entire body trembled. My eyes snapped shut; all I could focus on was the incredible tightness around the rim of my shaft.

Her hand latched around me again, squeezing hard. "Stop—let me get used to you."

Shit. Stop? That was asking for a fucking miracle. Growling through a tight jaw, I said, "You take me. Control the speed." I locked my elbows, afraid to move an inch incase I slammed into her. "Take. Your. Time."

A second ticked past where her body hummed with tension. Finally, she nodded. We didn't say a word as her fingers shook around my length, holding me still while her back tensed, arching upward.

Fuck. Fuck. Me.

Her hesitation was the worst kind of aphrodisiac. It fed me. Fuck, it fed me. I lost all softness, wanting to bite and spank and own.

She pushed again. I groaned as my tip travelled deeper, growing hot with her body, throbbing in time with my heartbeat. Her ass resented my claiming but she never stopped working, never stopped inching me further.

Tess gritted her teeth. A tear trickled down her cheek.

I froze. "Stop. If you're in pain. Stop."

She shook her head. "Do it. You take me. I'll work through the pain. Please, just do it."

Two sides of me. Husband and master. The husband hated the idea of his wife in pain. I wanted to cut off my cock for causing her such discomfort. But the master loved his slave's agony, drinking on it—getting high on it.

I struggled to stay coherent.

Tess's hand fell away, placing both palms on either side of her face. Her eyes squeezed tight, giving me complete control.

"I'll try not to hurt you, *esclave*," I grunted, grabbing her hips to anchor myself. With my jaw clenched, sweat trickling down my temples, I rocked into her. Time lost all meaning as I worked her, teaching her body I could fit—giving her no choice but to accept.

Centimetre by centimetre, I took her. Fucking worshipping this woman who trusted me so damn much.

Tess's back glistened with moisture as my last thrust hit resistance.

I'd claimed her. My cock was as far as it could go—balls resting against her cheeks.

"Damn, you feel amazing," I whispered, bowing over her, kissing her salty shoulder.

She trembled. "You're so big."

I chuckled. "Thanks for the ego stroke, *esclave*."

Her lips quirked. "I meant you feel huge. I'm throbbing and aching and sore and…"

My arms bunched. *Go on—fuck her.* The incessant demand thundered in time with my heart. But I couldn't. She needed time to adjust—to grow used to the tightness. Wrapping the leash around my fist, I tugged gently. Her spine curved, moving with the collar around her throat.

"What else…you stopped yourself. Tell me. I want to know." I dragged my teeth along her shoulder, lapping up her fear.

"I'm not going to lie and say it doesn't hurt. That first thrust was worse than awful. But now…it's fading. I can feel every inch of you. Every nerve ending is assaulted by overwhelming fullness, but the pain is changing…" A look flittered across her face, then she clenched.

I lost my fucking sanity.

Her tight strong muscles clutched my cock, milking me with fire. My stomach seized, my back bowed, my eyes rolled.

My hand came up, landing with a loud smack on her ass. *Shit. I didn't mean to do that.*

"Je suis désolé." I'm sorry. "It just—fuck it feels good."

She did it again, dragging a stream of curses from my throat.

She laughed, creating even more pressure and sensation

around my cock. I slammed a hand on her lower back, forcing her into the mattress. "God—you keep doing that and I'll blow. I'm holding on barely, Tess."

"What do you want, Q? Tell me…I want to know."

I groaned. My vision filled with flushed skin, blood, and tears, but I swallowed those tendencies. I didn't need them. Not today.

"I want to come in your sweet ass. I want to bruise you, so you'll know this belongs to me—just like every inch of you does. I want to show you how much I fucking love you."

Her inner muscles squeezed, hurtling me closer to the edge.

"Do it. I want all of it. Lose yourself in me."

Lose yourself in me.

Lose yourself.

Damn, how I wanted to. But I couldn't. Not completely.

With shaking arms, legs, fucking shaking everything, I thrust forward.

Her lips went slack; her eyes popped wide. "Oh." The surprise echoed around the room. My stomach squeezed tight.

"Does. It. Hurt?" I growled, clutching her hips. I thrust again, rocking more than fucking—making love.

Once.

Twice.

Stop! I had to stop.

Sweat beaded; I battled waves after waves of a very determined orgasm. My balls were marble hard. My quads burned from tensing.

Tess rocked back. "More. Give me more."

"Tess—" I couldn't fight anymore. She wanted more. I'd give her more. I fell over her back, imprisoning her to the mattress. My forehead pressed against her shoulder blades and I thrust. Man, I fucking thrust.

She cried out. My heart lurched to a halt but her cries turned to moans. It wasn't pain lacing her voice—it was pleasure.

"Describe it—what do you feel, *esclave?*" I whispered hoarsely. My eyes landed on her collar and the inscription: *property of Q Mercer.* I swallowed a groan of happiness.

"Like…pressure…you're rubbing and bruising and it feels so strange, but it also feels…."

I drove inside. "Feels?"

Her lips parted in a moan. "It feels good. So good."

My heart winged. I rocked again, biting the inside of my cheek, staving off another wave of pleasure. "I told you it would feel good."

Her hips arched, pressing into mine, crushing my balls against our bodies. "*So* good," she panted. "More, Q. Take me."

And that was the extent of my self-control. I'd run out of strength.

Seeking her ear, I bit her lobe. "I'm going to take you now, Tess."

She hummed in her throat.

My fingers looped around the leash, holding her firm. I would ride this woman. This insanely incredible woman. "I'm going to claim you as your husband, master, and owner. I'm going to fill you so deep, you'll scream."

"Please," she whimpered, her body writhing beneath mine.

And that was all I needed.

My forehead resumed its position between her shoulder blades. I let go. My mouth fell wide as pleasure I'd never felt before rocked down my spine. Insanely sharp, spurring me on, slicing my soul into pieces.

I gave myself over to ecstasy. Tess cried out as I made love to her.

Harder.

Harder.

Long and invasive strokes.

Claiming.

Taking.

Loving.

Fucking.

Tess's fingers opened and closed on the sheets, her pants meeting mine, her body rising to meet my every thrust.

Every second I came undone, losing my sense of self, giving my past, my darkness, my hopes and dreams to my wife. The master of my heart.

I lasted another ten seconds.

Ten mind-splintering seconds of bliss.

The desire in my blood lit a match, annihilating everything in my blood.

This was just the beginning.

The beginning of my eternal happiness.

The beginning of a future I never thought I would have.

I'm married. My sins aren't awful. My desires aren't frightful.

Tess was my complete circle. She was my home. My refuge. My best friend and partner. We'd found each other not just for this lifetime but forever.

My beast purred. My monster stretched.

I've been tamed.

And I fucking loved it.

I came.

Fucking came in rhythmic pulses. Splashing Tess with everything I had to give.

Wave after wave of thick, painful release shot from my balls. It ricocheted down my legs to my toes, building intensity before crashing from my body into my wife.

My wife.

I came hard and deep into the woman I'd married.

The woman I'd claimed.

The woman who would always be mine.

The crown to my throne.
YOU ARE MY HOME

I'd never been prouder.

Q. My master, husband, protector, and friend strode across the stage to shake hands with the prime minster of France. With a cool, professional smile, Q accepted the scroll, concentrating on whatever the prime minster said in his ear.

Holy hell, he's handsome.

Suzette squeezed my hand. "I always hoped he'd be recognised for everything he's done. Everything he's kept hidden."

I bowed my head toward hers, mixing my blonde with her mahogany. "I doubt he wants this much spotlight, though."

Every time we went out in public, my instincts were on high alert. I'd learned to trust them—speaking my mind if I wanted more security, or asking Franco to do an extra background check on an association.

I would never let anyone take Q away from me again. I'd meant my vows and spent every day upholding them.

Suzette laughed. Franco poked her side, pointing at the stage where Q disengaged from the prime minister, heading toward the podium and microphone. "Pay attention." His voice was harsh, but he winked. "That's our boss up there."

Your boss. My master.

I shifted in my seat, happily remembering just who my master was thanks to the ache between my legs.

Suzette sighed, her lips playing with a grin. I didn't know what was going on with them—if anything—but whatever it was, they kept it a well-hidden secret.

Frederick and Angelique caught my eye across the aisle, giving me a warm smile. I returned the greeting, mentally reminding myself to check on the menu with Mrs. Sucre for their bi-weekly visit.

My eyes returned to the stage where Q stood tall and proud. No bruises marked his face anymore. His legs were a crisscross of silver scars from Lynx, the bullet-hole in his thigh healed to match the one in his bicep, and all check-ups on his heart were clear.

He'd been lucky.

I'd been lucky.

The honeymoon in Seychelles came back. The sun. The moonlight swims. The sex. God, the sex. Tame, soft, and slow. Angry, abusive, and fast. Q had evolved into a lover who read me so well. Giving me pain when I wanted it. Giving me pleasure when I needed it.

Q cleared his throat, scanning the crowd. His pale eyes latched onto mine. His lips curled into an affectionate smile before disappearing into aloof businessman.

My heart beat heavily with love. He looked distinguished and delectable in a graphite suit and sea-green shirt. He'd forgone a tie in favour of revealing a small piece of tanned skin—the exact place I kissed last night while he slid inside me.

The click of camera lenses sounded like a lightning storm behind me, illumination flashing like tiny fireflies. The hive of reporter's voices itched across my skin. I still hadn't warmed to being in the public eye—but they came with the package now.

Everyone wanted a piece of Q…and me. And he'd finally agreed to let them in.

I'd taken my place completely beside him—becoming the face of Feathers of Hope officially three months ago. The invitations to events, fundraisers, and interviews never ceased. I feared we'd drown in an avalanche of attention.

This ceremony was a small gathering—only twenty or so members of parliament, and people who'd had direct contact with Q in his endeavours—such as the doctors who'd been with him from the start, therapists, and police chiefs.

The next part was for the world.

That part scared me. Our private existence was about to be gossip and tabloids. We would lose all anonymity. Q would be thrust into more fame than he already had from *Moineau* Holdings, and the unauthorized stories written about him coming to find me.

The cameras flashed harder as Q held out his hand, beckoning to me.

"What is he doing?" I murmured, slinking further into my chair. Today was about him, not me. I would never get used to being in the spotlight. I'd gone from a small town Australian girl to a married billionairess, who stood beside her husband by day and submitted to her monstrous master by night.

My brand had been on magazines around the world—*the woman who scarred herself for love.* I was proud to show Q's mark— it was the other intimate ones I didn't want them to see. The bite marks on my inner thighs. The wax burns on my breasts. Even though life swept us swiftly with its current, Q still found time to tie me in Shibari and broaden my horizons on what my body could feel.

Franco laughed. "You didn't expect him to open up his life to complete strangers without having back-up did you?" He grabbed my elbow, forcing me to stand. "Go on. Be his back-up. He doesn't need me this time."

Franco's injuries had healed well. His thumb was in the

process of undergoing regular surgery to equip his brain receptors to accept the trial robotic. He'd be one of the first in the world to have one—top of the line—a thousand times better than a real digit.

I fought his hold. "Wait. He doesn't want me. I can't wave a gun at anyone and tell them to back off. You go do it."

Franco chuckled. "Words are needed here, Tess. Not bullets. Now go." He shoved me, stumbling into the aisle.

Damn egotistical ass. I'd have him fired.

Suzette giggled. "I don't think the prime minster would appreciate bullets." Her eyes flickered to Q, whose face had darkened with growing annoyance. "You better get up there before he loses it."

Holy hell. I wasn't ready for this.

Tucking a curl behind my ear, I second guessed my outfit—worrying I'd come across as a young idiotic woman who had no right to be on Q's arm. My hair was a messy tangle of curls—Q hadn't exactly left them sleek and blow-dried fresh after getting carried away in the limo.

We'd been married for six months and our need for each other grew more insane rather than depleting. Who knew how many household items could be used in play? Who knew how much love my heart could contain when he adored me so sweetly? Who knew how many different tears I could shed when he let himself free?

Happy tears.

Fearful tears.

Lustful tears.

Vengeful tears.

Franco moved his legs out of the way, so I wouldn't trip. He patted my butt. "Get up there, Mrs. Mercer. Your husband needs you." Shoving me again, I had no choice but to lurch toward the stage. I glowered over my shoulder.

Suzette slapped Franco's arm. I couldn't hear what she said but Franco smirked, grabbed her hand, bit her palm, and placed it on his thigh.

I smiled. *I knew it.*

Q's voice cut through my nerves. "Sorry for the delay, ladies and gentlemen. The minute *my wife* decides to join me up here, I'll begin." My attention flashed to the stage, goosebumps spreading with a mixture of fear and need. I loved when he called me his wife. Especially in that tone.

He wouldn't hold back when we got home.

I better hide the collar. He'd scared me last time he used it— letting himself get a bit carried away. But he'd made it up to me by loving me sweetly and importing a pair of beautiful parrots—slowly filling his aviary once again.

Hundreds of lenses zeroed in on me as I smoothed down my grey dress. A frill of lace decorated my chest, running diagonally down my torso to flare out at the hem. The matching jacket lay over the back of my chair. Winter had well and truly thawed—the heat in the room was stifling.

Striding forward, I climbed the three steps onto the small stage—thanking heaven I didn't trip. The moment I was in grabbing distance, Q snaked his arm around my waist, holding me tight. "Took your fucking time, *esclave,*" he murmured in my ear. "You'll pay for that later."

My heart kicked harder, thrumming from his proximity, heat, and gorgeous scent of citrus and sandalwood. He tugged me behind the podium with him.

"What are you doing?" I whispered, trying to keep my lips from giving away my nerves to the press.

"I'm using you, obviously."

I frowned. "Using me?"

He shook his head. "You still don't get it do you, Tess? I wouldn't be here without you. I wouldn't have found happiness. All of this is yours, not mine. I'm not going to take the limelight when it's falsely given."

A reporter grew impatient. "Mrs. Mercer—how does it feel to be married to a man who has personally saved over one hundred girls from trafficking?"

I lost the power to breathe, stunned stupid by the

question. The microphones, the cameras—they all loomed closer, hemming me in.

Oh, God. I'd be on TV. Friends from school would know everything. Family who I hadn't called would know what happened to the daughter they ignored. My life would be known by *everyone*.

Q tightened his hold, giving me strength.

But it doesn't matter. It didn't matter because Q was my life and no one else existed in our realm of togetherness.

I nodded, sucking up courage. "I'm privileged to share his life. He's beyond incredible." I cringed from my overly bright voice. *I sound like a freaking five-year-old.*

The reporter tilted his head. "Give me a real answer. You married the guy—why?"

My forehead furrowed. "Why?" What sort of ridiculous question was that?

Q stiffened, his muscles locking into place.

Hoping Q wouldn't say anything reckless on a live broadcast, I said, "The truth? It's simple. Marrying him was like coming home."

A small murmur of satisfaction bled around the room. Cameras clicked faster, hands shot up with notepads and recording devices.

Questions rained.

"Tell us what happened."

"What does fifty-eight mean to you?"

"Have you met any of the women your husband has saved?"

"Do you believe the cheating allegations that he uses the women he rescues?"

"Tell us about your wedding—is it true you released a thousand birds?"

Q held up his hand, silencing everyone with one savage downward sweep. "Enough! We've agreed to one interview, and those questions will be answered at the appropriate time." Looking as if he wanted to shoot everyone in the room, he said,

"I wish to thank everyone who donated to Feathers of Hope, for their continued support of *Moineau* Holdings, and for everyone who has been a true friend right from the beginning." Holding up the scroll, he growled, "But this has been given incorrectly. I'm not deserving of this accolade. I'm nothing but a man with a past looking for a way to deserve everything I've been given."

His eyes fell on mine, burning with desire; I flushed. Cameras clicked and I had no doubt the image would be splattered on newspapers around the world. Q had become a hot commodity, and he'd married me—an ex-slave…a kidnapped woman.

I'd caught my own prince. My own dark *wonderful* prince.

Q tore up the scroll.

I blinked. "Q—what are you—?"

The room rippled with concern. The prime minster stepped forward, his forehead furrowed. "Um, Mr. Mercer, I don't think…"

Q cut him off. "Please give me a moment. It's not what it looks like." He continued to rip up the thick parchment. I hadn't even read what he'd been graced with and now never would—he'd turned it into confetti.

Shit, what is he doing?

My heart raced, not wanting to interfere, but terrified he was making things worse.

Keeping the shards in his hand, he stalked off the stage, heading to the first row where doctors, therapists, and police—all who'd been with Q from the beginning—stood.

With a hard smile, he gave them a piece of the scroll.

Once everyone had a scrap, Q returned to the stage. Dragging a hand through his hair, he simply said, "Now the award has been rightfully given. To the men and women who fought on a daily basis—before any recognition or benefit. They fought against evil—just as all the supporters and workers of Feathers of Hope do. Thank you. And now, I'm leaving. We have another engagement."

Cameras flashed as Q grabbed my hand, yanking me off the stage.

We didn't go back to our seats, instead, Q slammed through the double doors, leading me into the huge entrance of the town hall.

"Q—we should wait—" I didn't like going anywhere without security. Ever since committing murder to avenge my master, I'd been ruthless inside. I pretended to maintain my innocence, but beneath it, I was vicious. I wouldn't have any qualms of killing or hurting if our life's were threatened. It didn't mean I wouldn't let others get their hands dirty, however.

Where's Franco?

Cameramen and reporters swelled behind us like an unstoppable wave. They clicked and queried, staying at a respectful distance.

"Franco's behind us. I just want to get to the interview and get it over with." Q's jaw ticked, guiding me fast toward the exit. He didn't say a word as he smashed open the doors, striding into the street.

A roar.

A cresting of voices, cheers, *gratefulness.*

My eyes widened, unable to comprehend. Q's fingers tightened around mine. He cursed, eyes looking frantically for freedom. "Goddammit."

Women.

So many women—some with friends, others with families, but all linked by the same look of reverence in their eyes for Q.

Q.

My husband was beloved.

Franco appeared, flanking Q while Frederick and Angelique appeared by my side. "Wow," Angelique murmured. "How is this possible?" Her long black hair was coiled into a bun; her white dress setting off her dusky skin.

A policeman in full mob gear climbed the steps. "I'm sorry, Mr. Mercer. We didn't anticipate this."

"What the hell happened here?" Q demanded.

The prime minster tapped Q's shoulder. "The state invited some of the women you've had a hand in saving. I'm afraid we underestimated the response we would receive." His wrinkled face and salt and pepper hair looked regal if not a little pompous. "It looks like you're in for a long afternoon."

Oh, my God. My heart went from thudding to whizzing. "Are these…"

Q's face was stoic, but his pale eyes burned. "You did this without consulting me?"

So many women! *So many risks.* My instincts fanned out, seeking a threat. Q's sacrifice to let Lynx hurt him had worked. No other death notes were delivered, no attempts on his life initiated.

But all it takes is one.

The prime minster looked at his shoes, abashed. "We wanted to show you just how honoured France is to have such an exemplary citizen. I'm sorry if it was the wrong thing to do."

Q pursed his lips, scanning the crowd of women. His fingers twitched in mine, and I knew he recognised them— running through the catalogued condition they'd been in when they arrived—the environment in which he'd brought them from.

My stomach twisted with awe. Awe for how many lives he'd touched. I wished I could see his thoughts—follow his memories and understand.

"Q—this…it's amazing. They came to thank you personally." I clutched his arm, willing love through my fingertips. My chest cracked open with adoration for the man I called mine.

He looked at me, his face hard and unreadable. "This is extremely dangerous. Not just for me but for you. Don't you think traffickers will be watching this? Waiting to see if they can pick off women who have already been prey?"

Panic shot through my system. I searched the crowd, relaxing a little, noticing the familiar bodyguards dotted in the swarm. We were protected. We had a team behind us now. A network of people we didn't have before. No more attacks would be made.

I must stay confident.

"You have to say something…they need closure. Something, Q."

Q's face whitened. "What on earth can I say? Yes, I saved them, but I had no contact. I left them to Suzette to fix—I wasn't there in their healing."

I shook my head. "To them you're the hero. The one who came for them when no one else did. You have to listen. You have to do something."

The prime minster nodded. "Just a small speech, sir. Nothing big, then we can ask them to leave you in peace."

Q dragged a hand over his face. His shoulders tightened, hiding his nerves. Letting his hand fall, his annoyance was veiled behind the stern, forcible nature I knew so well.

My core clenched. I wanted to tell him he may be my husband, and I was beside him every hour of every day, but he still made me wet—just by being *him*.

"Fine. Give me a damn microphone."

A policeman appeared with a wireless one almost instantly. Q snatched it off him, never letting go of my hand. "If I'm doing this—so are you, Tess."

He marched forward, giving me no choice but to follow in his footsteps. We stood at the top of the stairs, staring into the souls of victims who'd been saved. Clearing his throat, he said, "*Bonjour.*"

The crowd hushed, all eyes—blue, green, brown, grey—all landed on Q. Fixated by the man who gave them back their lives.

"I want to thank you for coming to see me today. The gesture is both gratifying and humbling. But I assure you, it wasn't necessary. You gave me all the thanks I needed when you returned to your loved ones. The only payment I required was making you strong again."

Murmurs rose from the crowd. A blonde woman darted between spectators, slowly making her way to the steps of town hall.

My heart whizzed, prickling with awareness. My eyes narrowed at the darting form.

Q continued, "Despite the evilness of the world, good has prevailed, and I hope each of you has been able to move on and not let them win."

The blonde girl fought the crush of bodies. Her hand went to her pocket. Time slowed, moving in heartbeats, dying in increments.

"Franco!" I yelled, pointing at the girl. Petrified she had a gun—some weapon to kill Q.

Q yanked me behind his body, protecting me. Franco leapt down the stairs, imprisoning the girl's arm. It all happened in a blink—swift, efficient, trapping the would be threat.

But then her blue eyes locked onto mine.

"Please, no more. You've done enough! You're like them. You're a monster!"

I stumbled backward; my palm went slick with glacial sweat. Q's hand slipped from around my arm. I reeled away.

No. It can't be.

My hands clutched my hair as a cloud of torrid memories sucked me under.

"Hurt her, puta."

"I'm going to rape this one—then you'll know what it will feel like when I start on you."

My ears roared. My heart died.

Blonde Angel.

It can't be!

But it was. I'd stared into her eyes while hitting her. I'd listened to her screams while Leather Jacket tortured her. I would recognise her anywhere. She was a tattoo upon my soul.

She raised her arm, pointing at me. Painting me like the witch who deserved to be burned. The blissfully happy six months evaporated under the weight of what I'd done. How could I forget? How could I pretend I'd paid the toll when I'd *killed* a woman? When I'd brutally tortured another?

"Tess—Tess?" Q's voice cut through my horror, dragging me back to the sunny warm day in France. Innocent. Safe. But it wasn't innocent or safe.

My past had found me.

And now I must pay.

"Her," I croaked. "It's her."

Blonde Angel fought Franco, trying to climb the steps. Her eyes never left mine, locked together in purgatory. She wore such innocuous clothing—a pair of loose fitting jeans and huge yellow jumper. Her hair was up in a ponytail—she looked so young. So young!

My eyes fell to her walking stick, splintering my heart more surely than any bat I'd swung or any terror I'd rained.

"Please—I just want to talk," she called.

Her voice sent me straight back to Rio—to my dreams. There she'd been reincarnated to die night after night. Here she was real—a figment of my nightmares come to haunt me for my crimes.

Q wrapped an arm around me. I didn't register his warmth or comfort. I didn't register anything but bugs and beetles and pain.

"Please—let me pass. I promise I mean no harm," Blonde Angel pleaded.

Franco looked to me. His chiselled face was dark. "Tess— what do you want me to do?"

Blonde Angel fanned her hands. "I only need a minute."

I couldn't say no to her. Regardless if she was there to kill me. I couldn't say no to the woman I'd hurt so badly.

"Let her go, Franco." My voice was reedy, lost.

"Tess?" Q shook me, but I sank into memories.

That's it. Do it. Hit her. Harder.

Blonde Angel hurled herself up the steps, beelining for me. Her mouth opened, but I heard nothing. Only Leather Jacket lived in my ears.

"You're so weak, puta. *Beg for your life. Beg for it—maybe then we won't make you kill her."*

Tears.

They sprouted up my throat, trickling from my eyes. My entire body wept for what I'd done to this girl. She halted a foot away; both of us breathing hard, both staring silently. Her tears matched mine—a torrent of emotions on her heart-shaped face.

A story screamed in her gaze.

Confusion.

Hatred.

Sadness.

Forgiveness.

She cried out, deleting the space between us. I cowered, bringing my arms up to protect myself, but her body smashed against mine, clutching me hard.

I froze. Not breathing, hardly existing under the horror I'd caused.

Q grabbed the girl's shoulder, wrenching her back. *"Qu'est-ce que tu penses faire?"* What the hell do you think you're doing? His voice was livid, his body trembling with rage.

I opened my mouth to explain. *How to explain?* I'd told him what I'd done—what they made me do. But having the evidence standing as judgement was too much.

"I had to see her. I had to tell her," Blonde Angel sniffed, uncaring tears tracked down her face.

I sucked in a fearful breath. My limbs quaked. "I'm— I'm—" *I'm so damn sorry. So eternally, endlessly sorry. I'll never ever forgive myself.*

She shook her head, a smile breaking through her sorrow. "I had to tell you—I..." A fresh spillage of tears ruined her strength. Swallowing hard, she managed, "It wasn't your fault. All that time, I knew you cared. You accepted more pain to stop us from receiving, but in the end nothing you did could've stopped it."

She reached for me again, burying her face in my shoulder.

Something snapped inside. The grief I thought I'd dealt with gushed forth, purging the remaining darkness in my soul.

"I'm so sorry," I sobbed, clutching her, drowning in tears.

Q stiffened but never let go of my waist. I stood hugged by two people. My past and future. Anchored by my love, drifting on a sea of pain.

The world ceased to exist as I found closure in the arms of my victim. The arms of the woman who I'd watched be raped and traumatised.

Q's hand shifted to my lower back, linking me to the present where I was *good*. Where I'd repaid my sins by saving others. He gave me silent support while I came undone on the steps of the Paris town hall.

Slowly, my grief ebbed. Blonde Angel smiled, her face blotchy and red. I knew my reflection would match completely.

A smile graced her lips, a weight lifting off her shoulders, evaporating into the sunny sky. "Thank you."

I shook my head. "Thank *you*. For being strong enough to forgive me."

She pressed a kiss to my cheek. "We were both their victims. We knew that. It wasn't your fault."

"Tess—is everything okay?" Q murmured, rubbing my spine. His eyes never stopped glaring at Blonde Angel. He stood as my guard, soothing my soul.

I smiled softly. "I'm better. Now." Turning to Blonde Angel, I asked, "What's your name?"

She tucked a loose strand of hair behind her ear. "It's Sophie. And I'm guessing yours is Tess?" Her eyes flickered to Q, growing wide with awe. "I remember you. I remember you coming into our cell and some guards taking us away. I remember your home."

My eyes snapped to Q. "She stayed at our house and I never knew?"

He clenched his jaw. "I didn't want you to see any girls from Rio, Tess. For this exact fucking reason." His gaze softened. "I'm very glad you're happy now, Sophie, but can you please let go of my wife?"

Sophie laughed, rubbing the saltiness from her cheeks. "Sorry." Letting go, she added, "Sorry for jumping on you. I just—when I saw you—I had to—"

I captured her hand. "I'm so glad you did. I'll never be able to thank you."

I would never be able to articulate the freedom inside— the freedom I didn't even know I needed.

The prime minster cleared his throat. His eyes bounced from me to the woman hemmed in between Q and Franco. "Um, miss. Are you saying you had direct contact with Mrs. Mercer when she was taken in the reported second incident?"

Oh, no. My heart picked up. I couldn't have my crimes told. I wouldn't be able to advocate Feathers of Hope if people knew what I'd done in that awful place. "No—she—"

Q growled low and threatening. "Leave her out of this. She came to see my wife. Nothing more."

Sophie flashed me a smile, before facing the prime minster. "I respect Mr. Mercer, but yes. I knew this woman before I was rescued by him. I know what she went through, and I know how intrinsically good she is."

My heart fell out of my chest. I was full of deceit. I hadn't been good then. I'd been drugged out of my mind—their little puppet.

"Shoot her, puta. *Or we'll cut off her fingers."*

Why didn't I shoot Leather Jacket? Why did I have to obey?

Prime minster nodded, his eyes glinting. "Would you be so kind to say a few words to the crowd, on behalf of the charities Mr. and Mrs. Mercer run?"

"Quoi!" What? "No. Definitely not," Q snapped. "Leave her—"

"I'd love to," Sophie said, almost giving Q a heart attack.

Sophie gave me another smile and I knew I had to trust her. Whatever she said would be the truth—I couldn't control how people perceived it. There was no arguing with what I'd done.

Laying a hand on Q's trembling forearm, I swallowed my fear. "Let her, Q. Let her speak."

Q's jaw clenched, his nostrils flaring with anger.

"Very good." The prime minster handed Sophie a wireless microphone, guiding her to stand in front of us. "You may begin when you're ready."

The crowd hushed from bedlam to whispers. Their energy was infectious. My legs itched to run. I didn't want to be here—not when people learned the truth.

Sophie looked behind, holding out her hand.

What? *No. I can't!*

I squirmed backward, pressing against Q, seeking his protection like a wimp.

Q cursed under his breath. "I wish I could carry you away from this, Tess. But you can't run—not now." Pushing me forward, he murmured, "Stand beside her. Be strong."

My heart confounded with terror, horror, and everything in-between. I inched close to Sophie, avoiding the eyes of the crowd.

All women. Women saved by Q.

The only woman I'd had contact with, I'd beaten until she screamed for mercy. *I'm an imposter—a fraud!*

I couldn't breathe. The sun was too bright.

Please, fly me away from here.

Sophie linked her fingers with mine. Holding the mic to her lips, she said softly, "My name is Sophie White, and I owe my life to Mr. Mercer."

The crowd went deathly silent. The quiet click of cameras and whir of video recorders were the only noise. I stood terrified and judged beside the woman I'd done such atrocious things to.

I couldn't move.

"My story began with the death of my grandmother. We used to go to the regular flower show. I collect berry seeds—I make my own tea, you see…" Her voice trailed off before growing louder. "I was sitting on a bench, nursing my sadness, when a nice man sat beside me. He asked why I was crying. I told him about my grandmother—about how much I missed her. It felt so good to talk to someone, so when he asked me out for dinner, I didn't hesitate."

Her voice turned inward, filling with memories. "People think you'll get taken from dark alleys or seedy nightclubs. The truth is...nowhere is safe."

She swallowed. "They stole me three days before my grandmother's funeral. I never got to say goodbye. I woke up cold and bruised in the dark. I was there for ages—or maybe it wasn't that long at all—time plays tricks on you when you're no longer a girl but property."

Her hands tightened around the microphone.

My barcode tattoo with the sparrow inked into the cage, itched. *I'd* been property. I'd been merchandise for sale. I knew how it felt to be traded. And I also knew how it felt to be saved.

My heart lost its terrified rhythm. I stood taller. These women were my allies. These women were the reason why Q found me.

"I won't go into my captivity—but I will say that when Mr. Mercer arrived, I didn't want to live anymore. I was ready for death. I *craved* death. But he wouldn't let me."

My lungs stuck together. My own ordeal swamped me. Not only had Q fought to get me home, he'd sacrificed so much to bring me back to a life I no longer wanted. I'd been so busy wrapping myself up like Rapunzel in my tower—I'd forgotten how much I had to live for.

I hurt him so much.

He forced me to embrace pleasure as well as pain. He gave me a fuller life—a life I never deserved.

He loves me so much.

I turned to stare at my husband, suffering a flush of all-encompassing love. He smiled, the sun catching the tiny scars I'd marred him with.

Sophie continued, "Mr. Mercer opened his home to those of us rescued in Rio. He paid for our doctors, provided psychiatric help, and gave us time to heal away from our families. Families who we didn't want to let down by being broken.

"By the time I returned home, I was strong enough to be supportive of my boyfriend, Ryan. We forget, as the ones taken, that the ones left behind have it bad too—if not worse. They can't do anything to save us. If I'd returned to him before I was strong enough, our relationship would've failed—I wouldn't have been able to love him the way he needed.

"I won't lie and say it was easy. But life *does* go on." Her voice changed from storyteller to fierce advocator. "The key I found in surviving LAT... Life After Them...is...allowing yourself to acknowledge you will *never* be the same. Don't try and return to who you once were. It won't work. Give yourself the right to say you're stronger, better, wiser, harder. Don't let them win."

She twisted, looking over her shoulder at Q. "Thank you from the bottom of my heart. Thank you on behalf of so many other women. I'll never forget you and will treasure my life because of what you did to give it back."

A squall of tears charged up my back, blurring my vision. *Thank you, Q. For being you.*

Q rolled his neck. His eyes blazed with feeling but his posture was graceful as he moved to my side. Slinking his arm around me, he subtlety took possession, separating me from Sophie. He nodded, granting power and gracefulness in one movement. *"De rien."* You're welcome.

An orb of light filled me, growing brighter, bolder with every second.

This was the man who I loved and would always be proud of. I wanted to rain kisses over his face for all that he'd done.

The crowd grew loud, one voice rising with praise.

Q eclipsed my entire heart—giving me comfort in his dark embrace.

He waved. "Thank you, everyone. And thank you Sophie for having the strength to tell us of your ordeal." His forehead furrowed as an idea came to mind. "If anyone else would like to share their stories, and continue to gain support from one another, I will personally visit you over the next week as we tour with Feathers of Hope. As for now, you are my guests. Please speak to Mr. Roux for details on your accommodation."

Q smiled. "Now, you'll have to excuse me and my wife. We have an important interview to attend, and we're already late."

The crowd roared with applause, humming with happy energy as Q handed the microphone to the prime minster.

The prime minister took it. "Thank you for your time and generosity. The city of France will gladly contribute to your tour."

Q shook his head. "No, need. The financing is taken care of." Looking at Frederick, he said, "Find out how many rooms you need and book out the finest hotel. Franco will assist you if needed."

Frederick nodded, slapping Q on the shoulder. "Consider it done, my friend. Now, you really better go."

Untangling myself from Q, I gathered Sophie in another hug. "Visit me any time."

She grinned. "Maybe we can have coffee one day—just us."

I didn't know if the topic would be our past or future but I would spend time with her regardless. I needed to stop feeling guilty. I needed to move forward. "That would be nice."

We parted, drifting toward our respective places. Q gathered me in his strong arms, welcoming me back into the world I loved while Sophie disappeared into the crowd. The women offered hugs and high fives, swallowing her up in their collective embrace.

My body was drained. I had nothing left. I felt carved like a pumpkin with no seeds. But it was a good carving—a cleansing leaving me eerily weightless and completely vulnerable to the new existence before me.

I've forgiven myself. I would never curse my fate again.

Q had successfully given me every stage of healing.

I was whole.

Frederick grinned, planting a soft kiss on my cheek. "You guys really better go. They're waiting. We'll see you later in the week."

With one last glace at the crowd, Q stole my hand and guided me into the sunshine.

We entered the hotel suite on the tenth floor, frazzled, humbled, and completely drained.

Q hadn't let go of my hand as we traversed the crowd to the hotel across the street. Franco had kept us safe, his team of bodyguards ghosting around the swarm.

The moment we stepped into the room, a blanket of peace descended, hushing my racing heart, letting me relax for the first time since this morning.

My feet throbbed in my heels as we crossed the richly decorated suite. Q released me, dropping onto the English rose-print couch. "That was exhausting."

I smiled, slouching next to him. "Yes, but so incredible— to see those women worship you, Q. To know she's okay—it's amazing."

He scowled. "Not worshipping, *esclave*. Never that. They only have themselves to thank for taking their lives back. I was only the beginning, not the solution."

I wanted to kiss him senseless for being so proud—unable to accept the good he did.

His lips quirked into a gentle smile. "And who knew you had fans already. I'm going to get jealous if people start hugging my wife."

I laughed. "No fans—just a part of my past giving me freedom to let go." My eyes faded, thinking of Sophie. I was so glad she survived. So happy she'd been invited by the prime minister, giving me absolution.

"Come here, Tess," Q murmured.

My tummy flip-flopped at the quiet authority in his tone. I scooted closer, falling into his open arms. "What do you need, *maître?*"

He smirked. "Oh, I can think of many things I need." His lips landed on my ear, making me shiver. "I need you naked. I need you strung up, so I can show you how damn proud I am. And I need you screaming because my nerves are shot and being in public isn't getting any easier with you so vulnerable by my side."

I'm not vulnerable. I have you.

"If you promise to do that thing with your tongue again— I'll scream for you."

I gasped as his lips descended on mine, kissing me stupid. His tongue speared my mouth, dragging moans and pleas and promises from my soul.

The hotel door opened.

Q growled, his arms tensing around me. For a moment, I feared he wouldn't let me go—to hell with the reporter.

But then he released me, moving away. My lips twitched, noticing the way he crossed his legs, hiding his impressive, delicious erection.

The reporter, with her plaited black hair and vibrant hazel eyes, entered. We'd agreed to one interview. Only one. And then it was back to work.

A hotel staff member followed, wheeling in a trolley full of pastries, éclairs, and coffee.

The woman smiled, sitting down, brushing her navy skirt around her legs. She pulled free a pair of silver-rimmed glasses from her bag, placing them on her nose. Her smile was cupid-sweet and bright pink.

We waited in comfortable silence as the coffee was

poured. Once the waiter had left, Q grabbed a steaming cup, holding it to his lips. His sharp attention fell on the reporter, sizing her up with one glance. *"Bonjour."*

She snagged a cup of caffeine, mimicking Q in a sip. "Hello, Mr. Mercer. Mrs. Mercer." Her warm gaze landed on me; I smiled. "Hello, nice to meet you." Collecting the last cup from the table, I held it, letting the hot liquid soothe my fluttering nerves.

I'd never been interviewed. I had no idea what to say. What not to say.

I needed a rule book so as not to embarrass myself or Q.

Taking another sip, she said, "My name's Fiona, and I'll be conducting the interview today." She placed a recording device on the low coffee table between us, opening her notepad. Reclining into the Louis Vuitton styled chair, she grinned. "I wish to extend my gratitude for your time and expect us to be here for a few hours—but it all depends on how deeply you wish to tell me your story—and if you'd like to break during questioning."

I'll need a break. If only to gather my thoughts from the very distracting male seething with energy beside me.

Q nodded. "That's fine."

Fiona looked to me, a bond of femininity shot between us. She turned off the recording button. "Just before we start, I wanted to say on a personal level, your story has inspired me to help with Feathers of Hope. I've signed up to report on the women who want to tell their stories. I didn't think anyone would be interested in speaking, but I've been overwhelmed with their tales already."

Her eyes flickered to Q. "I feel out of bounds saying this, but I think I'm a little bit in love with you—mainly because of how much you love your wife."

Q choked on a sip of coffee, before rearranging his face into something resembling coolness. "I think the only answer to give is thanks?" He glanced at me. His eyes yelled a message: *what sort of interview is this?*

The sort of interview where you finally understand how much people adore you.

I laughed. "I think a few women are in love with my husband for what he's done—and I can share in that respect—but I do get rather possessive."

Q's lips tugged into half a smile. "Are you talking about the threatened restraining order last month, Tess? Surely not. Not you, my sweet blonde wife who would never put any claim on me."

My heart raced remembering my threat and the consequences that came with it. Q had thoroughly proven why I had no need for jealousy—granting me another mark right above my belly button, so I would always remember.

I grinned, placing an owning palm on his thigh. "I'd fight for you, Q. I *did* fight for you. And every day I'll never let you forget who you married and why."

Fiona giggled. "Is it just me or did it rise a few degrees in here?" Pinching an éclair, she took a bite, and turned on the recording device again. "It's so nice to see true love these days. I can tell I'm really going to enjoy this interview."

The atmosphere changed from friendly to business. Crossing her legs, Fiona asked, "Okay, my first question is for Mrs Mercer. In fact, I don't have any questions." She waved her pen in the air. "Basically, I want to hear everything. Call me greedy, but I don't want you to leave anything out."

Q tensed, his leg muscles locking under my hand.

Fiona didn't notice. "Tell you what—start from the day you got on the plane to Mexico."

Q moved. Uncrossing his legs, he sat forward, steepling his hands between spread legs. Dominating. Governing. Stealing all my concentration and making me shamelessly wet.

My heart bolted, filling with words and memories and everything I would share.

This was it.

My story. My legacy. The one thing that would be immortalized onto pages and told forever. It wasn't sweet. It wasn't easy. But I would spare no emotion or detail. I would be honest to the very last word.

I opened my mouth to start. To tell my tale of heartache, love, and loss.

I'd waded through blackness and survived.

I'd fallen in love with a monster and thrived.

I'd danced into riches in every conceivable way.

But through it all, Q had been there. My monster in the dark.

Q grabbed my hand, bringing it to his lips. *"L'histoire n'a pas commencé au Mexique."* The story didn't start in Mexico.

Fiona frowned, "Oh? Where did it start?"

My brand seared, resonating with heat from Q's intensity.

He glanced at me, sending fire into my soul. "Not where, but *what.*"

I melted. Utterly melted for my incredible husband. He understood me. He'd *always* understood me.

Fiona leaned forward, hanging on Q's every word. "What?"

"A number. It all began with a number. For me anyway."

My heart soared from my chest on sparrow wings. Birds filled my body—blackbirds, robins, and fantails.

I smiled. "That's true. That was the beginning. The rest doesn't matter."

Fiona's cheeks pinked as Q never looked away from me, sending the room swirling with desire. The moment the interview was over, Q would take me.

And I would be ready to accept whatever he wanted to give.

"What number?" she breathed.

Q tore his gaze from mine, locking her in his fierce pale stare. He riveted us with his power, trapping us in his net. "Fifty-eight. It all began with fifty-eight. And that's where my wife will start."

I looked at my wrist, tracing the numbers beneath the barcode and sparrow. I'd once been merchandise for sale. But then the winds of fate changed and blew me straight to Q. His cage became my home. His love became my wings. I became his bird through and through.

Tears pricked my eyes. I was so utterly happy, so faultlessly content, so completely *complete*.

Fifty-eight.

I'm Esclave Fifty-Eight. The girl who broke her owner.

My master had spoken.

I began.

About the Author

Pepper Winters is a NYT and USA Today International Bestseller. She wears many roles. Some of them include writer, reader, sometimes wife. She loves dark, taboo stories that twist with your head. The more tortured the hero, the better, and she constantly thinks up ways to break and fix her characters. Oh, and sex... her books have sex.

She loves to travel and has an amazing, fabulous hubby who puts up with her love affair with her book boyfriends.

Her Dark Erotica books include:
Tears of Tess (Monsters in the Dark #1)
Quintessentially Q (Monsters in the Dark #2)
Twisted Together (Monsters in the Dark #3)

Her Grey Romance books include:
Destroyed

Upcoming releases are
Debt Inheritance (Indebted Series #1)
Last Shadow

To be the first to know of upcoming releases, please join Pepper's Newsletter (she promises never to spam or annoy you.)

Pepper's Newsletter

You can stalk her here:

Pinterest
Facebook Pepper Winters
Twitter
Website
Facebook Group
Goodreads

She loves mail of any kind: pepperwinters@gmail.com

Other Books by Pepper

Je suis à toi *(A Monsters in the Dark Novella)*

"Life taught me an eternal love will demand the worst sacrifices. A transcendent love will split your soul, cleaving you into pieces. A love this strong doesn't grant you sweetness— it grants you pain. And in that pain is the greatest pleasure of all."

Q made me the happiest *esclave* in the world. He gave me his heart, his empire, his ruthless unforgiving love. And life finally left us in peace.

A man like my *maître* has special needs though, growing stronger as our lives intertwine. The only way to survive his monster is to agree to all his desires.

Including his latest wish.

I'm his.

And I won't refuse.

Coming Soon...

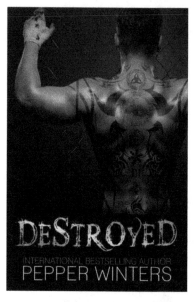

DESTROYED by Pepper Winters

<u>Reviews</u>

This book enticed & enthralled me completely. Pepper's stories are like a fine piece of art. They are profound, unique, raw and beautiful. --Kristina, Amazon Review

Pepper Winters has a ridiculous level of talent, and I'm in awe of how deeply she delves into her characters. There are not enough stars, seriously.--K Dawn, Amazon Reviewer

If you like a bit of grey in your romance then you need to get this book because it's one of the best books I've read this year.—Bookfreak

USA Today & Top 20 Amazon Bestseller.

She has a secret.

I'm complicated. Not broken or ruined or running from a past I can't face. Just complicated.
I thought my life couldn't get any more tangled in deceit and confusion. But I hadn't met him. I hadn't realized how far I could fall or what I'd have to do to get free.

He has a secret.

I've never pretended to be good or deserving. I chase who I want, do what I want, act how I want.

I didn't have time to lust after a woman I had no right to lust after. I told myself to shut up and stay hidden. But then she tried to run. I'd tasted what she could offer me and damned if I would let her go.
Secrets destroy them.

Buy on Amazon, Barnes & Noble, Kobo, iTunes

DEBT INHERITANCE
(Indebted #1)

"I own you. I have the piece of paper to prove it. It's undeniable and unbreakable. You belong to me until you've paid off your debts."

Nila Weaver's family is indebted. Being the first born daughter, her life is forfeit to the first born son of the Hawks to pay for sins of ancestors past. The dark ages might have come and gone, but debts never leave. She has no choice in the matter.

She is no longer free.

Jethro Hawk receives Nila as an inheritance present on his twenty-seventh birthday. Her life is his until she's paid off a debt that's centuries old. He can do what he likes with her—nothing is out of bounds—she has to obey.

There are no rules. Only payments.

Coming June / July 2014

Playlist

Songs for Twisted Together
Complied by the amazing Kiki Amit

Undisclosed Desires by Muse
Monster by Imagine Dragons
Demons by Imagine Dragons
Coldplay by Magic
Never Tear Us Apart by INXS
Adore by Miley Cyrus
Broken by Lifehouse
Between the Raindrops by Lifehouse
Everything by Lifehouse
No Light. No Light by Florence & the Machine
Breath of Life by Florence & the Machine
She is by The Fray
Love Don't Die by The Fray
Trust by Neon Trees
End of Time by Lacuna Coil
Closer by Nine Inch Nails
The Lonely by Christina Perri

My Heart is Broke by Evanescence
Addicted to you by Avici
Marry the Night by Lady Gaga
Something I need by One Republic
Darkside by Kelly Clarkson
Hunter by 30STM

Full Poem from Chapter Headers
By Pepper Winters & Ker Dukey

The blackness tried to swallow us whole, kill us, ruin us,
capture our soul,
but our demons didn't play well with others, the beast broke
free to make them suffer
we're altered, we're abnormal, our souls stained with each
other's mark. Our souls are that of monsters born in the dark.

Intertwined, tangled, knotted forever, our souls will always be twisted
together,
our demons, our monsters belong to the other,
Bow to me, I bow to thee, now we are free

Stroke me, provoke me, adore me, I implore thee, take all of
me, ensnare me, play me to your tune
Bind our twisted perversions, love me dark, leave your mark.
love my faults and imperfections
My night and day, my moon and sun, your light turns my black
to glittering grey

Intertwined, tangled, knotted forever, our souls will always be twisted
together,
our demons, our monsters belong to the other,
Bow to me, I bow to thee, now we are free

Our monsters found solace in each other's perfect heart, the
devil himself couldn't tear us apart,
You belong, I belong, our twisted souls forever,
master and slave, owner and owned, you sate my need and feed
me
We are blood of blood, echoing heartbeat and answering
breath; nothing can break us, not even death
body of body, shared thoughts and lustful need, we bow to this
swirling new greed,

We were nothing before, now we're completely sure Each
other's possession, obsession, we're free just you and me

Intertwined, tangled, knotted forever, our souls will always be twisted
together,
our demons, our monsters belong to the other,
Bow to me, I bow to thee, now we are free

The sun warms my feathers, the updraft in my wings, linked
souls for eternity, you'll now wear my ring
Matching darkness, mirroring light, truth and love we took
flight,
One esclave and one maître, no longer captive or thief, just
perfect certainty and belief,
You are my saviour
My forever
My salvation
My together
My absolution
My treasure
The crown to my throne
YOU ARE MY HOME